SPOOKHEAD
Press

Soundtrack

The songs for each chapter can be played on Spotify under the account *Ratmeister*.

7 Cures - All Songs

For Jenny,
Who let the boy play
with her typewriter.

"

Very well. He'd lighten up.
... for he'd grown convinced that play—
more than piety, more than charity or vigilance
—was what allowed human beings to transcend
evil.

"

Tom Robbins, *Jitterbug Perfume*

PRIDE

Blue

'Are You Well?' — Sombra

Maddox Price ...

JESÚS JAMES ASUNCIÓN is a recreational thief. Y'all taste him now? Rummaging through cupboards and drawers in the common room of Ben's housing hill? There he is, a bower bird hunting for spangles and gimcracks, for shiny colourful things. How they enchant him. How they tickle his innocent avarice, his guilty desire for possessing things.

Y'all disapprove of his klepto-hobby? Might you enjoy indulging in a little anger for it? Perhaps you pine for the days of laws and legalities—and property police—which would've brought punishment down on his thieving head. There's something truly tasty about those old, primeval, eye-for-eye urges, yes? But—like so many human drives—the thrill of vengeance is as perishable as a twentage boy's nocturnal schmacta. So put aside any Lust for retribution, any condescending Pride. In our enlightening days—this twenty-somethingth century—Jesús is no candidate for a Cure.

At most, he's a minor nuisance—there's no harm in his thievery. What could he purloin which deprives anyone? Y'all can always fab another one of anything, so where's the victim? There's no victim, because: fabbies! There's no loss, therefore no crime, no punishable deed. No need for police. No arrest, no jail. Ah, the wonders of the post-scarcity world we enjoy.

These days, even Nature itself tastes neither stitch nor nail out of place in fabbied goods. Such copy-perfect stuff. Imagine: y'all could fab a perfect narwhal in a bathtub, or a unicorn for a coat stand. Try it. Hours of fun for the whole family. Your princess daughter could fabby the pony she always dreams of. When she tires of brushing Treasure and cleaning up his unceasing road apples, hoik him in a council sucky bin. Watch with relief as hoof and hock vanish in a violet flash.

If Jesús steals your granny's heirlooms, fab new ones. If Jesús drinks your 500-year-old sacramental bourbon, any sympathetic Infinite has the right hi-fi fabby for making spirit y'all'd swear has years in a char-oak barrel. Any of us could festoon the bottle with a label as authentic as the original.

If Jesús steals your holy bicycle, where's the harm in it? Fab another! Even if an enthusiast for antique collectibles (as is our own dear Ben) has an Elvis Concho jumpsuit or a gold Graceland piano in their swimming pool, well, let Jesús have them! Fab another! Why care, when y'all could fill your fridges with so much gold the floorboards will crack?

Oh, here's one: maybe Jesús pilfers your daughter's favourite toy. That old plush bunny she loves so much, the one with the raggedy ear? I imagine a fresh Bunny is no replacement. So, maybe an old toy, ragged from loving wear and tear, is truly an irreplaceable thing. But look: setting aside sentimentality, there are precious few such things in our world.

Just as well there's no fabbing more of us, yes? It's beyond a weary Mind why anyone would need more husbands or accountants. Trust me, one husband per family is more than sufficient.

Jesús rummages shoulder-deep in a large drawer. There he goes. Watch him. His eyes wide and glassy, his smile a pair of fat sausage lips wrapping around the plate of his face. He finds something. Is it James Naismith's 1891 *Rules of Basketball*? Ancient samurai clogs? A tube of vintage lube? Who knows what Ben collects? Let's join Jesús as he discovers …

Jesús James Asunción …

The drawer is stuck. I yank harder. Its vacuum seal cracks, and it glides out. A misty lilac glow in there. *Pakshet!* There's a spooky field generator in the cabinet? I stop pulling the drawer for fear it will eat my arm off.

Doubt it's a booby trap. Would Ben risk one in his home? A strong spooky field will erase flesh and bone. It takes days for growing back a partial limb, they say. The phantom pain lasts for weeks after.

Ben would install no traps; he's far from a bitter old Infi who would use such tricks. His son Mal is always poking around in everything; he'd trip a trap in no time. I pray the field is a weak one—strong enough only for removing dust, microbes, and moisture from the cabinet. For keeping the contents (things centuries old) in best condition.

In the drawer, y'all see? Shininess. A rainbow of light. Reach deep in, pull out the thing—a flat palm-size box; blue, in ancient shrink-wrap; a diamond pattern on its top and bottom. Branding reads CONRAD INTERNATIONAL AND JUPITERS CASINO. Playing cards for games of gambling—52 in a deck if my memory is good. These might be fun for a day or two. I turn the deck over and wonder over the designs of the kings, queens, and knaves. The ace of spades.

Upstairs, in the Evoli quarters, the front door slams. Mal coming home from school. Early. There's no fun in him catching me. I pocket the cards and slip out.

My urges for filching things pass for now. I'll open the pack of cards this evening. Perhaps I'll learn some games they once played with them.

I have no taste of why y'all flutherbomb me (everyone in Europa and Indo-Malaysia says *flutherbomb* now. It means, join a person's fluther without first asking permission). As a sifar, my life is a humble one.

Are you familiar with Gentle Dragon? She recently joins the mission at the local clinic. She still takes my breath away, and I am forever grateful I live in an age when there is no aspect of her life or her person that she can keep from me. Stay in my fluther, if y'all like. We will watch together, yes? You taste the bright rainbow colours of her nursing uniform? The polish of her boots and utility belt? The crispness of her collar? Kementerian Kesahatan insignias, on her left breast and each shoulder, shine like … oh, so bright and beautiful and fresh—I want them! No souvenirs or sacred things yet hang from the chatelaine swinging from her hip. She's pretty—no—beautiful. I want her also. Unusual, a nurse with such long hair swinging free in a ponytail from under her mission cap.

She skips fast along a street at the northern end of the village. *Desa.* I should use Anglo-Malay here. The locals frown if anyone uses Regal English, or the supercalifragil English of North America.

Gentle Dragon turns off the street, up a short path for an apartment hill. Opens the Bodagh's apartment front door and enters. Poor Sigurd Bodagh.

'Thank you for coming, nurse,' says Sigurd's one partner Nessy, meeting Gentle Dragon in the hall and ushering her through. Gentle Dragon invents a friendly smile—always an unsettling expression on the face of a nurse.

What's the Anglo-Malay word for invent? *Mencipta*? Kay, kay, no shouting all at once! Y'all know the official language of Singapore is still Regal English? Please, go easy on a humble sifar from Cagayan de Oro.

'I am glad you memb the clinic, Nessy,' Gentle Dragon says with professional sympathy. 'We have concern for him.'

Nessy nods. Hunching, she wipes her eye with the back of a hand. 'He's in the living room.'

Nessy ushers Gentle Dragon down a narrow hall; passes bed and bath doorways until she enters the single living room. Gentle Dragon crinkles her nose, sniffing scents of frying duckweed burgers and boiling cabbage—tell-tale signs of a low-rep kitchen fabby in need of maintenance.

Frail. Weak. Sigurd Bodagh sits at the dining table pushing clumps of food around a plate while he watches a program on a large two-dimensional monitor on the wall opposite.

'A documentary about sap computers,' Sigurd explains.

Saps. Trust me, no nurse will ever Consign you for a Cure if you call the extinct Homo sapiens *saps.*

Nessy rolls her eyes while Sigurd goes on. 'So many boxes. Screens, devices, handheld things, fabby-sized things—all requiring desks and side boards and cupboards and closets ...' Sigurd trails off. He draws a shallow breath and shakes his head. 'Every year, they made new gadgets and threw the old ones onto garbage heaps. Heaps which, over the centuries, compress and wheeze and fart gases ...'

Nessy swallows her embarrassment; looks through the living room solarglass doors. A view of a communal yard and park. Wearing a kini bottom and the laty-latest in stain-eating Varikain apron, a woman fires up a BBQ. A young girl, with hair like iridescent anahaw fronds, sets a picnic table while two lithesome men primp their hair and supervise. Under a tree, a domestic tiger twitches her tail and flattens her ears while a giggling toddler pulls her whiskers.

Testing how long Nessy might hold her breath, Gentle Dragon tours the living room studying furniture and bric-a-brac. So much expialidocious clutter in there—in the fashion of decades back. Fake antique sap stuff: vases and 2-dimensional pictures in physical frames; monitors on the wall bleeding electric light everywhere; real house plants, hydroponics.

Sigurd blathers on in his own world. '... the same garbage deposits mining missionaries reclaim for fabby feedstock.'

'Sigurd, enough!' A sad and fretful Nessy lets her chin drop into the emotional cavity of her chest. She folds her hands. Her cheeks flush.

'Look. I'm eating something.' Sigurd holds up a single cracker. *Ahah!* his face is saying. A magician performing a trick. Deliberate and awkward, he mounts three peas on the cracker. There his magic act stalls. The sparkle in his eyes fades. The arch of his lips slackens. Flicking two peas off, he halves the cracker, and without appetite, closes his mouth around it. Chews. No swallowing. A weak smile.

'His weight still be good,' Nessy offers. There is yet hope in her.

'Is he taking the nutes we prescribe?' Gentle Dragon asks.

'I am.'

'Sometimes,' Nessy corrects.

Gentle Dragon haunches down beside Sigurd's dining chair so her eye level is below his. Takes one of his hands with a practice of gentleness. Examines the fingers. 'His nails are bluish,' she says.

Nessy feigns interest. She knows already how blue his fingernails are.

Gentle Dragon strokes Sigurd's hair; comes away with several strands. 'Are you having trouble sleeping? Any fatigue during the day? Dizziness or fainting?'

'Yeer,' Nessy answers. 'All of it.'

Sigurd draws his cardigan tight around and hugs hiself (the neo word for himself) against a shiver. Outside, BBQ smoke ribbons up and vanishes in a surrounder net flashing violet in the hot March sun. The domestic tiger rolls over for the toddler climbing on her.

'How are your teeth?' Gentle Dragon asks.

'Fine,' Sigurd says through clenching jaw. Nessy grimaces and shakes her head.

Gentle Dragon stands and sighs. Assumes a droopy face of convincing empathy. 'Tuan Bodagh, we must ask you come with. Just a short visit in the clinic for making sure you take your nutes and put some weight back on.'

'You're gonna take me?'

'It's for the best,' Gentle Dragon says in the same way you might break solemn news to a child.

'You're gonna force-feed me. I know what goes on in those minsters.'

'I assure you there will be no force-feeding. We'll just monitor you for a day or two. Make sure you get the best care.'

Sigurd misses Gentle Dragon chewing her lip. Nessy sees it, her face turning steel.

'No catting me like a deviant resisting a health Warrant.'

'Sigurd,' Nessy pleads. 'The nurse be trying for helping you.'

'I promise, no catatonia,' Gentle Dragon says, but who would believe a nurse? 'There's no need for pacifying you. You're in no shape for putting up much of a fight.'

'Will you allow Nessy visits while I'm there?'

'We'll place you in a public ward. Nessy can visit any time, night or day.'

'Thank you, Nurse Gentle Dragon,' Nessy says and regrets it the instant the nurse masks a scowl.

'My name is Nurse Lành Hiền Rồng,' Gentle Dragon says, almost scolding.

'I am most sorry,' Nessy blusters. 'I hear almost everyone calling you …' Nessy looks down for her toes.

'There is a tukky arriving soon.'

Nessy pulls Sigurd's chair back from the dining table. She and Gentle Dragon assist him on his feet.

'Just a short stay?' Sigurd asks.

'Just a short stay,' Gentle Dragon confirms. 'We'll give you good care.'

Sigurd nods. They assist him down the hall.

Gentle Dragon's reputation rises by a few razoos. Rising away from zero, from sifar; away from the pure existence of truly owning nothing. The Reckoning curses you, my beautiful Gentle Dragon.

Lành Hiền Rồng (Gentle Dragon) …

If ever a nurse's personality is a perfect match for the rainbow uniform, it's Field Nurse Skye Merewether's. For her, *Field Nurse* is a mis-title; she ventures from behind our clinic's reception-desk only for shoppers looking for insomnia treatments or a little more pep in their bedroom performance. Hearing her, y'all might believe nutes are magic potions full of mystery and arcane properties.

'She's harmless,' other nurses say. 'Leave her alone, unless you covet her position as receptionist for the rest of your mission.'

Skye is the last of the everything-happens-for-a-reason brigade. Anyone would think, in this world—where science concurs with spooky action at a distance—there'd be no need for reiki, or meridians, or astrology. Yet, if anyone flutherbombs Skye in her home, they'd see dolphin mobiles and unicorn figurines, frilled-neck lizard totems, dreamcatchers hanging in every room and—lining up on a sunny window-sill—a collection of antique bongs.

Hai, Skye is a believer in almost anything—anything except serious attempts at Curing anyone.

'It all evens out in the next cycle,' she often says, with a blank smile for cryptic emphasis. A smile blanker than her eyes.

This morning I make the mistake of approaching the clinic by way of the arcade connecting the mall's courtyard with the esplanade where our reception fronts. Skye, as usual, is in the arcade café, her yellow hair a scatter of hay around her strangely ruddy face, gulping down tall glasses of chamomile tea while telling fortunes from coffee cups. If I have my way, I would Consign her for this alone.

'Everyone knows it's just playing,' she'll defend, but she never reads the remains of your aya tea because, 'Ayahuasca is serious business.'

She sits at her favourite table facing the arcade in the front of the café, her unusually beady pale ice-blue eyes shooting acupuncture needles at all who pass.

'Giving up on your Infi quest?' she mocks, sounding brighter than sunbeams, while revealing slightly buck teeth. Maybe I could push past and ignore her. No luck. 'Ben Evoli is a waste of time, you know. Especially for a noviciate. Many others these passing years play at catching him.'

Despite wishing I could ignore her, I stop by her table and say, 'There's no *catching* patients. We're health care professionals, no police force.'

Skye snorts and says, 'She do the police in different voices,' probably quoting one of those ancient scriptures she loves so much. 'So what heinous acts are you *catching* him at this morning?' She fixes me with her creepy eyes. 'Coughing up a secret garbage mine? Torturing kittens? Stealing gelato from babies? Roasting babies over a slow fire?'

I quip, 'Only till their hair catches fire.'

Skye guzzles the last of her tea like throwing down a lager at closing time. I shake my head and set off. She skips after me, catches my shoulder and pivots me around. Her eyes are bulging balloons full of horror. Her finger snaps over her mouth. *Shhhhhh!* 'No invoking the White Witch around here. Ever.' Her fingers scrabble. From her chatelaine, she unhinges a gewgaw and hastily kisses it.

'What?' I'm playing dumb, of course. I know all about Detective Nurse Eir Frijberg, who they call the White Witch.

'Just … please. You want her mad Valkyries poking around here?'

I make my best *calm down* gesture, and resume skipping. The arcade splays into glaring sunlight on the esplanade. Skye taps me on the shoulder. 'He's meditating again, no?' she asks, as if sharing in a conspiracy. 'Talking with wasps, perhaps?'

I look at her like she's wearing a coat of flying-fox droppings. Feeling a chill. I ask, 'You are among his fluther before?' Is she spying on me spying on Ben?

She shrugs. 'You are careless of other nurses in *your* fluther. It's how they'll have enough for Consigning you for a Cure one day.'

At the reception entrance, the doors slide open. 'Before he's meditating, he has 4 million in his fluther.' I answer. 'Millions. Why should I notice you among them—all the desa locals, traders, professional and creative colleagues, reputation consultants and proxies …?'

She grins with victory. I stop and bleat after her. '… lovers; ex-lovers; would-be lovers; detractors and antagonists; potential blackmailers … all more interesting than you.'

She's already inside. I feel stupid for calling after her from the footpath. With a huff, I stomp after her.

'A nurse should always notice other nurses in her fluther, Little Dragon,' she instructs, taking her place behind the reception desk. She squares her shoulders and lifts her chin, playing judge at a judicial bench. She pats and strokes the desktop like an object of veneration.

The waiting area is empty. For when patients arrive, I should help her replenish the biscuits and tea by the fabby. Instead, I skip down the corridor for the day-care rooms. Ahead, the corridor walls brighten. From a dull grey, they glow in swirling designs of pastel rainbow colours.

'Put the big stuff aside, Little Dragon,' she calls out before I'm safely down the corridor.

'*Gentle*…. It's *Gentle* Dragon,' I correct, for at least the 14th time. 'But you should call me by my proper name, Lành Hiền. Field Nurse Lành Hiền Rồng.'

Skye waves me off. 'Field Nurse, no Detective Nurse. Forget Ben, the dull Infi. We'll never Consign him.'

I retrace the corridor for, and rehearse a little before saying, 'Eir Frijberg—the one you say we should never speak of? She is convening a conference of all the great health camerati. It's happening right now in Copenhagen. Our own KK sends delegates from Singapore.'

'High politics rarely affects a day in the life here,' Skye dismisses. 'You're a long way from Singapore or Osaka. Or Copenhagen.'

'Know you what they are discussing?'

'No?' She's lying. I doubt there's a minster or clinic anywhere immunised against the gossip.

'Eir has a task group investigating Infinites, they say.'

'Is this what they say? Then join it,' Skye says. 'I'm sure there's a little dragon-shape hole in their skill set they're wetting themelves about filling.'

I harrumph the proud air out. I should taste better than believe I could shift her on anything. 'Should I pull up another stool behind the reception desk then? Tell me. Which nutes are best for curing acne?'

'Sorry for dissolving your delusions, Little Dragon—you're misestimating the grandeur of our mission. Most of it is dispensing nutepaks. With occasional Warrants for petty jealousies, random acts of Gluttony … Maybe you catch some Fred Nerks lording their insignificant social status over a neighbour … it's all nothing but personal Mind hygiene. That's all. We clean the toilets of Minds. We get in early and regular before it all makes you vomit. That's how we do it. One little Cure at a time.'

Encountering Skye leaves me pacing the clinic. Normally at this time of morning, with the detective's lounge empty, I'd steal in, brew a pot of aya, then settle into the couch in the corner behind the door, recline it back, and go flutherbombing. I might get 30 mins before the shift's desk nurse finds me and assigns me some mind-numbing field patrol. Sending nurses out on the beat is all window-dressing—placing mannequins in rainbow uniform where they're most visible. We could patrol from a couch in the clinic, of course. Or, while perching on toilets in our homes. But *field work is a tradition.*

Gah! As I think those words, I hear them in Skye's voice. *Sorry for dissolving your delusions, Little Dragon.* Outside the detective lounge, I stop as if Skye's words stretch an impenetrable film across the doorway, trapping me in a solidifying resin of indecision. 7 Hells, Skye. Who are you? Just some disillusioned cynic, envious of my untainted dedication. You wish me a failure. How poor a mission is yours, cleaning toilets of the Mind. There are far more pressing needs in front of our noses, in this village, this desa. We have our own Infi—Ben Evoli—and his family, who deserve our fearless care. He's ill. I know he's ill.

With a clenching jaw, I will away Skye's undermining, and flop in a couch. Take a deep breath and search for Ben's fluther …

'I'm going up for the station for collecting a package,' Ben calls as he opens his front door.

'They no deliver, is it?' Ben's partner Aisha calls from the kitchen. 'Fine,' she adds.

'I fancy a walk.'

'You go without breakfast you think?'

'No appetite.'

'I'll eat Bapa's one!' his son says tongue and lung—so loud his words resound off every wall in the house. Outside, cockatoos screech.

'Walao eh! Mal, it's early,' Aisha scolds him. 'Always with the noise like that lah,' she says in her mash-up Singlish.

Aisha is, as Ben always introduces her, his one *istri* (his *one wife*). She missions as a Field Procomplement of Misi Pemulihan Seletar (Seletar Recovery Mission), one of Singapore's oldest disaster recovery missions. Is Aisha beautiful? Plain? There she is, pressing coffee, wearing an oversize taupe tee and cream tracky daks. Barefoot. Glittering fingernails and toenails, the polish must contain her own DNA if she plans for travelling outstation today, or she has no care a station's spooky field will erase it. Her streaky dark hair falls about her scalp in a short shag style. Deep round eyes and snubby nose dominate her flat face. A triangular jaw frames thin lips around a small dash of a mouth.

Ben skips out for the sunlight. Hot and humid already, the atmosphere is a wet sponge cake. Fragrances of grapefruit and lime on the terrace blend with frangipani and eucalyptus from the avenue. The last wisps of evaporating morning fog are spiralling dervishes dancing over dewy grass. A sea breeze whispers up the harbour, bringing scents of salt and oyster shells, sand, and seaweed. The heat is rising like a giant kite.

Ben flops on the slippy dip a few paces from his front door, gives a push and slides the four levels down. He sets out at a dour skip, crosses the avenue where hammocks hang between trees, like huge creamy calico clams swallowing sleepy heads whole. Farther around, waking villagers yawn and stretch in front of the longhouse. Hawker cooks are steaming dim-sum and stir-frying noodles. Roti canai are puffing up on griddles. The air is moist with the smell of Milo.

In the park, Kaboobie—the desa's wandering-zoo camel—sniffs at a bed of solar flowers which frazzle his thick grabby lips with an electric jolt. In a nearby tree, a kookaburra *chat-kaks* as if it's coughing up a lamb bone. Galahs and corellas squawk. Cicadas sing.

Motor whirring, a tukky follows Ben like his pet. Its maker is a new mobil-fabbing mission eager for customers. It will follow Ben up the hill until the station, its simple machine mind ever-hopeful he will climb aboard. It accelerates a little, then brakes. Repeating this over without approaching too near, its wheels quiver; its motor whirs up and down, whimpering. It sounds cute and pitiable, which is a deliberate part of its mindwriting.

'Aiyo!' Ben curses at the tukky. 'I just want a skip.'

The tukky cries.

Ahead, Field Nurse Kwon Chang patrols her beat, her uniform of rainbow fatigues standing out among even the more flamboyant costumes of the locals. She watches the tukky, raises her eyebrows, deciding whether she should shoo it away.

A cricket ball smashes a front-yard window. Scampering boys flee giggling with guilty glee. A household drone wheezes as it vacuums up shards of glass. If the house has no window-squirter, one will roll down from the council chambers in quick time.

Between Ben and the corner, Detective Nurse Dayang Seri from Regional Investigations skips towards a young man in his mid 40's. Berahim Pelawi. Others on the avenue make space. Berahim sees Dayang and fears what's coming. He stops and spreads his arms either side, his palms forward. Gulps his heart down, rises on the balls of his feet preparing for escape. Panic floods his eyes.

Ben gawks. His pet tukky hangs back a few metres, ever hopeful.

Field Nurse Caleb Jensen from our local clinic is tailing Berahim from Ben's direction. 'Berahim Pelawi!' she calls out with tongue and lung. This is always exciting. 'Are you well?' she asks, invoking the procedure for Consigning a patient.

'Yeer, perawat.' Berahim's voice cracks. 'Terima kasih for asking.'

My colleagues close within an arm's distance of Berahim. Both stand in aikido *hanmi*. Caleb places her hand on Berahim's upper arm, as a caring friend or relative might. She looks down into his eyes with softness. I must work on this look. My reviews say I'm either too stern or too sensual.

'You require care,' Caleb says.

'No ... no, please. I am well ... I just ... please.'

'Yeer,' Dayang soothes, calm and hypnotic. Both nurses embrace him. 'We know.'

'No ...'

'You have Lust.'

'No.' Tears trickle from Berahim's eyes.

His case is one of those love-going-wrong-going-obsessive stories: boy meets girl, boy expects girl, girl declines. Boy gets angry, confirms girl's suspicions. So far, no case for health intervention. However, when Berahim develops a habit of recording hollies of her—intimate hollies ... well, we're no bashful society, but those spark interest from the clinic. Our detectives discover he plays those hollies, over and over, in his Mind's eye, no matter who he has sex with. We have a pattern of downward-spiralling obsessive behaviour right there.

'Let us assist you.'

'No, please …' Berahim's lips thin; his mouth toughens; his eyes turn hard. He's about—yes. He coils, throws off the nurse's embrace—which only invites my colleagues take him down. His face meets the press-soil pavers of the avenue pathway. There is no blood, no splintering teeth. There will be no bruises. Our nurses are skilful.

Witnesses replay hollies of Berahim's brief dash: there's his break from the nurses' embraces; Caleb draws Berahim's arm behind his back, the deft tap of toe against ankle throwing Berahim off balance. There's Dayang cradling the falling Berahim, so he meets the path like a feather landing on a bed.

Dayang and Caleb lift him on his feet. 'Please, we are here for your care,' Caleb explains, with soothing compassion.

'Open your mouth,' Dayang says. Berahim, crestfallen and sweating, complies. Caleb reaches for her utility belt, produces a foil package. She tears it, removes a swab which she rubs on the inside of Berahim's cheek. Kinder than a spray in the face.

The swab works quick. Berahim is expressionless, a gently swaying tree, feet almost uprooting from the ground. Kwon joins the other two nurses with a folding stretcher for bearing Berahim. For a simple case like this, I doubt they'll move him to a minster—Medlow Bath, Darwin, Singapore. He'll stay in our local clinic for his Cure.

Ben retreats for the fringe of the spectators, radiating dread. A stony stare of guilt. Changing his mind about the tukky, he waves it over; takes a seat in the back. It whistles a happy tune. All over the world, Ben's millions of fluther-bombers will want for riding tukkies from the same manufacturers.

Ben Evoli …

Are you well?

A nurse's concern for our welfare is so professionally authentic, it's acerbic.

Are you well?

Why have I such dread for Berahim? He needs care and he'll receive it. Like millions before him, and the millions who will follow, he'll spend just a little time in therapy—in his case, no more than a couple of months, by my guess. After, he'll be renewed, refreshed, liberated. So, why would Berahim so dread the prospect of a Cure? Y'all know the answer. We neos live such healthy, peaceful lives, we *must* conjure some imaginary bogey woman. It's our evolutionary hard wiring: in the absence of cancer, war, crocodile attack and daytime soap operas, we cast nurses as our monsters under the bed.

For sure, having those antiseptically caring rainbow paratroopers taking even an hour of one's liberty is an icky prospect—with their matronly soothing croons and their religiously enraptured smiles. We fear them stripping our fluther away, truly separating us from our family, friends and flutherbombers. We dread the vacuum the secrecy leaves. Ask a Cured neo about their experience, and the clearest accounts are of weird dreams, good food, comfortable beds, and whiling away hours playing holly sports and games. No one recalls any therapy as such—other than a regular nute regimen. There are no electrodes; no lobotomies; no holes in heads; no exorcisms; no human centrifuges; no ice baths; no orgone energy accumulators; no greasy brass steampunk contraptions; no straightjackets; no fever inducements; no teeth pulling. And—most relieving of all—no accounts of talk therapy.

Now y'all are thinking, any of those cruel sap atrocities *could* be part of the nurses' regimen. How would we know? But look at the fabbies they install in clinics: nothing gothically horrible—certainly nothing they could fab nasty machines with; only nutes, food, clothes, and fresh linen. Perhaps the secret step in a Cure is torture by thick blankets and fluffy pillows.

Or perhaps it's all sex'n'drugs and rock'n'roll in there.

Are you well?

It tastes almost religious. Neos fear religiosity with the same shivering whispers they reserve for corporations. What were those ancient, organised religions good for? Graveyards of orphans; sex abuse; hijacked planes; crusades; manifest destinies; human sacrifice; burning at the stake; corrupt presidents; and cheesy sing-alongs with tambourines and cheap untunable guitars. Any wonder we regard nurses with the same queasiness we might a bottom-patting priest.

For how long will Berahim remain a patient? A few weeks? A month or two? He'll emerge emotionally fitter, happier, and more productive. Yet his friends and family—in the absence of an explicit narrative of his treatment—will wonder if the old Berahim emerges from the clinic at all. Or worse, his Cure renders him less than he is once before.

Green

'Stand' — R.E.M.

Nilajani Karunanithi ...

YET AGAIN, THE INCOMPLETE summons me, and so I stand here. Harsha, you warn me, and I never listen. Again again again.

The chalky grey light cold smoking me. Trepidatious, I admit. I'm sure y'all taste the signs, from wherever you are flutherbombing me. If y'all are using kinaesthetic empathy enhancement, you should dial it down a touch. I may be piddling before this is over, and you'll wish for avoiding the full Nila experience. Or maybe it's your thing. How should I know?

Picking at my fingernails. In the cave-light, the oppressive yet cavernous tunnel of an anteroom feels as airless as the moon. The coffee skin of my fingers and hands are as bluish grey as a ghoul's.

Presently, the two chaperones with gameshow smiles and crystal-sharp eyes promising the big reveal of a first prize, will open the doors before me. But there's no prize; I'm only in the shit again.

Shifting nervous weight between feet. Left. Right left. Right.

A chaperone trims her minimal smirk.

Aching for smoothing my hair down. Itching itching itching for it. And would but for the mission cap tamping close around my skull. Instead, my fingers fondle the chatelaine at my waist. Picking the seam of a thigh pocket. Going back for the chatelaine. Stop fidgeting, Nila! Always fidgeting fidgeting. I'm so woozy so light-heady.

The chaperones crack the doors open. A blade of heaven-intense light slashes out and widens, casting the chaperones as pale silhouettes.

'You may enter,' membs one.

Thank you muchy-much. Inside, the atmosphere is cathedral-still and silently absent of ambience. Still blinded, I fumble for the nearest chair. I should know its exact place by now. I sit and stretch the kinks out. Feel for the table. Sight returns.

Everything in here is a soft white. White are the walls, rough with, dimply orange-skin textures minimising reflecting glare. White are the evenly spaced pairs of doors. White are the consoles standing against the walls between 7 pairs of doorways. On each console is a white vase containing a generous stuffing of fresh white hydrangeas scenting the air with … no, these hydrangeas have no scent. There are oil vaporisers somewhere out of sight. Curious I never notice those before.

An enormous circular skylight summons an illusion of Judgment Day intensity. It draws my eyes in wonder, as with every time before. Somewhere in the skylight's machinery, a secretive lens focuses and casts a faint rainbow cylinder of unwavering size, always in the precise centre of the room around which is an annulus of 7 jigsaw-tight, curving table segments. The tables are white, as are the chairs attending them. No seating position directly in front of another. None of the pairs of doors opposing another. From where I'm sitting, everything is at angles and tangents. A deliberate design for downplaying confrontation.

Such a relaxing room. Anyone entering might taste all its trickery yet still be overcome with a sense of peace for the spirit. I could almost expect a field of rainbow-colour grass for a floor. Baby unicorns frolicking through it. Relax. Relax.

On the tables, pitchers of chill aya tea drip condensation. A sudden thirst. Thirsty. Pouring and drinking. Sipping. Gulping. Strong. The Incomplete will wait till the aya works it effects.

Time stretching out. I hate this part, hate this part. There is nothing but waiting squirming drinking and looking aimlessly about the room.

The Incomplete—whoever they may be—will specialise in the different disciplines of health missionary: fieldwork; detection; admissions; recovery; facilities; research and academia. Places around the table convey participant roles. The 2 on the circle's other side will play the most motherly. The 2 on the flanks—the *knives*—will be confrontational. The middle seats on either side are for the ones playing roles of objectivity.

Despite the chill aya, I feel flush. I have an urge for pacing the room but wish for no displays of nerves. No pacing. Will you just start already?

Finally. The left set of farthest doors swinging back. A bad sign? Last time it is the doors on the right. The Incomplete file in, skipping solemnly in with static expressions of beatific peace.

Breathe Nila breathe. Here they come. Out front are Zalim Nancy and Yashasri Prayaga (the knives). Following are the objectives, Kaniksha Karthickraja and Jangabba Mundine. One of the motherly players is my favourite mentor, Elsbeth Putney-Wells. She'll be on my side. Elsbeth warms my heart; the other—Imashini Jinavamsa—could shatter it like shale.

Their auras are small insipid translucent rinds around their fruity heads. Colours shifting peacefully slow, hardly a flash or flare arcing outwards.

Oh, sparkly! Studying the Incomplete's chatelaines and what hangs from the chains and loops. The ornate rings. The symbolic keys of humble metals. The career souvenirs. So many keepsakes looking like strangled jungle fowl stuffed with bling.

Let it be over. Throw me out of the mission; Consign me; treat me. Ha! You may even Cure me. Go on I dare you.

Cure me. Of what? Gluttony? These days, any compulsive or addictive behaviour is Gluttony; think past a medieval friar or baron tearing into a fat hock of pork or galugging on a wineskin. Any uncontrollable need for more is Gluttony. Call me compulsive? Claim I have an addiction? All I have is an exceptional dedication for my mission.

I will stop the personal investigations truly if I must. (What's wrong with a field nurse aspiring for being a detective?) Let me stay; I swear I will stop the off-duty investigations.

'We are The Incomplete.' Jangabba, barely above a whisper yet so clear. Unsure whether she utters from her mouth or she membs Mind-with-Mind. A trick of the room's acoustics, her words have the quality of a memb, lacking resonance or reverberation, the taste exactly as hearing with the Mind's Ear.

Looking at me expecting. Expecting …?

'I am your Complement.' I complete the formula, voice sounding squeaky. Face flushing.

'Welcome.' Kaniksha. Her voice also too dry for arriving through the air. But her mouth and throat move, pushing out breath, speaking with tongue and lung. The effect disorienting.

'*Diyaniya*, are you well?' Elsbeth from across the ring.

A sharp pain thin as paper, slices between my ribs. This is it then? Straight for a Cure? This could be good. Could be good. Hoping it's short. Could mean I'm yet in the mission, still a nurse. The eyes of the other five arc around at Elsbeth. Jaws hang slack. Eyebrows fly away from eyes seeking shelter in hairlines.

Elsbeth looks down with a muzzy shake of her head. In appearance and posture, she appears as if pressing her back against a solid tree trunk. Her ruddy cheeks have the impression of bark. Her flat nose and her watery eyes are so familiar, as is the indistinct forehead and jawline. Her hair sprawls blow-away tufts shooting everywhere except forward. Her neck cranes from slender shoulders, pushing her perpendicular face well forward. The lips of her small, dried apricot of a mouth seldom part. These features I know so well and have inestimable fondness for.

'I only mean for saying, are you comfortable?' Elsbeth revising. 'You are squirming about in your seat, *diyaniya*.'

Shrugging. 'I am here, *mava.*'

'We love you dearly.' Elsbeth.

'And hold you in the highest esteem.' An indifferent Jangabba.

'We recognise your passion and dedication for our mission.' An unconvincing Zalim, the only full male here.

'Yet again, you are indulging in pet projects.' Yashasri.

'In my own time.'

'All your time is your own time. Mission is a choice—a dedication but never an obligation. However, you're using your mission for elf-medicating.'

There it is. An accusation of illness. Prescriptions for addiction await. For Gluttony, perhaps Pride. Imashini composes a disconcerting expression of sympathy. 'You are unready for the mission of detective. Without the training. You know you must first complete the prerequisite service as a field nurse.'

'A life always flutherbombing others is no healthy life.' Kaniksha from her seat two places away. 'Much less a nurse of this camerata.'

How far are our nursing missions from the original meaning of the word, *camerata*? What would the original Renaissance intellectuals make of us? More than guilds, less than bureaucracies, we espouse egalitarianism; but where's our commitment for open enquiry over defending dogma? Long dead, that's where. As for our own mission, we're so super-superior, so muchy-much better than all the others. Hypocrites.

'And the neos you flutherbomb.' Jangabba. 'The times and the contexts ...'

'You're investigating Infinites,' Zalim states simply. 'You want for catching them.'

My bones stiffen, brittle poppadums. A yawning gap of time opens while everyone freezes. Unicorns would flee the room. The grass would wither. All the stark white makes me squint.

I say, 'There's no *catching* Infis.'

Elsbeth leans forward as if she mis-hears me. Imashini sits with back upright, chin out. A queen on a throne. 'Then? What?'

'I just ... I just want—' No words seem adequate. Throat drying up. All the pitchers in front of The Incomplete are full of aya. I want water, no more ayahuasca.

Imashini stares intense enough for wilting the hydrangeas. 'Speak up. Are you so timid?'

'I just crave for ... learning, *mava.*' Learning is the wrong word. So what? If they're throwing the book at me, it can hardly be a thesaurus. Go on throw a book at me.

'Learning? Learn what?'

'Learning the Why of things, *mava.*' Look up for the skylight, the flowers, the doors—anywhere but at The Incomplete. All silent. Six pair of eyes—prison lights searching out, peeling my ribs back with their intensity, cooking my heart with their fire.

My chin trembles. What's the point? If I withhold cooperation, they'll deploy a detachment of detectives for monitoring me night and day. I scratch the back of my ear. 'Why are we so afraid of Consigning Infinites?'

'What a preposterous question.' Jangabba.

My words shock them so profoundly they forget their breath. The atmosphere sharpens icy. Even Elsbeth in shock. The hairs on my arms stand up. A bitter metallic taste on the tongue. Skin feels as dry as paperbark.

'We all understand, *diyaniya*,' Elsbeth says. 'It's a common temptation, lurking among other fluthers, for flutherbombing one's life away.' As if I'm obsessing over some fleeting celebrity or influencer. I'm conducting legitimate investigations. I'm showing initiative. Dedication for my mission.

'Such habits become obsessive and addictive.' Elsbeth nods weighing the meaning of her words.

'You have an addiction,' Yashasri stabs, taking her cue from Elsbeth.

'Which is it? Am I a hopeless fan or am I playing detective where you are afraid?'

Imashini locks her hands together on the table and shakes her head on a stiff neck.

Elsbeth weighs her words. Or perhaps holds the tension. 'Have you been taking your nutes, *diyaniya*?' she asks, mothering me. What next? She'll run me a bath? Tuck me into bed?

Clearing my throat. I repeat, '*Am I taking my nutes?*' indignant. Hastily add, '*mava.*' I risk asking the hard question about Infinites, and now we talk about my nute regimen? 'That cocktail of nanites, gene editors, drugs, and herbal hoaxes you prescribe me? So many, they spill out of my hands. Yes, I'm taking them every morning with my glass of Arrack.'

Elsbeth scratches her cheek and frowns.

'You're provoking us,' Zalim pronounces in a pitch so falsetto it could set dogs barking.

'That's me,' I sneer. 'A provoker. The whole nursing mission needs a good provoking up their moribund arses.'

Howzat, Harsha? So much relief saying those words sticking in my larynx for months. The Incomplete may digest or choke on them. I'm screwed. Rogered. Harsha, I miss you. I would never lose it so, if we are still together. Miss you. Miss you.

Unable for looking even Elsbeth in the eye—the friendliest face. Zalim and Yashasri, with heads level and eyes fluttering wild, regard some far horizon lying at the edge of inner space. Kaniksha and Jangabba also with heads tilting back, eye muscles spasming. Imashini and Elsbeth also. They're fiercely membing among themelves, perhaps reviewing hollies of evidence.

It's beyond my control. Inside my skull, panic is an eclipse of moths in the frenzy of a hot light.

The Incomplete retrieve their attention, resolve back in the room. 'Stay away from Infinites,' Elsbeth says as she might warn a child against evil faeries in the garden. 'You'll bring nothing other than disrepute and misfortune upon yourelf.'

'And us.' Yashasri, with no small measure of petulance.

'There is too much at stake when a promising young nurse overreaches concerning Infinites.' Imashini.

The knives (Zalim and Yashasri) and the observers (Jangabba and Kanishka) stare into their fingers as into a fire, as if looking elsewhere would unleash something wild and untamed. Together they push chairs back, rise and turn for the door.

'You're letting me go?' I ask, tongue and lung.

'Yes,' Imashini answers without turning back.

'For now,' Zalim says, unhappy with the outcome. 'We are in disagreement, without confidence for any clear remedy for your condition.' She smiles with chill taunting malevolence. 'Please continue about your careless ways. Give us something which might tip our hands.'

Thank you Elsbeth. *Mava.* I know you save me. As always.

Yellow

'Corpse Flower' — Jorge Elbrecht

 *Ben Evoli …*

THE TUKKY TACKLES the steepest slope of the esplanade. Above treetops and surrounding buildings ahead, the translucent chitin-paste membranes of the spooky station's climate sails are cicada wings refracting autumn-morning light into glints of violets and pinks, blues, and greens.

'Ben.' A memb passes through my hancy filters.

'Dil, *machan*,' I memb my friend. 'What time is it there?' It must be four in the morning in Kolombo.

Membing: *Telinga jiwa* as we say in Indo-Malaysia. The Ears of the Soul. *Onespace telepathy*, Europans call it with no sense of romance. Who knows what Wastelanders call it? *TV in the brain?* Wastelanders are more like saps than any other culture. Whatever y'all call it, we take for granted our wetware capability for communicating between Minds without a need for cybernetic implants. Hancies, yeer, yeer, but they're just shallow implants for enhancing the capabilities we already have. Neos will never become cybernetic.

'No, no, we are in Brisbane,' Dil membs. 'Little Shya is playing in a cricket tournament this weekend.' Dil's Sri Lankan accent clips his Regal English words just so.

'That's action, *machan*.' Feigning excitement. I hate cricket. From memory, Dil's daughter Shyamali is a seam bowler, which sounds more like embroidery than sport.

'Her bouncer is lethal, Ben,' says the proud bapa. 'I swear, a ball in her hand is a weapon. She almost takes my head off.'

'Careful, Dil. You'll need a suit of armour.'

He chuckles out his pride. Then a pause for arriving at the point of his call.

'It's days since we're talking. Are you avoiding me?'

If y'all could offer a way I might break the silence, I'd drop my filters so you could tell me.

'No. Why?'

'You know why. The Inductee Gala.'

The tukky is making less than half speed as it weaves around pedestrians on the esplanade. A caper of kids wearing tiger projections jumps out, baring claws and roaring. The tukky rocks to a halt.

'Say again?' I stall. 'You're sounding flat, kinda mushy. You using a new hoot? Something wrong with your hancy?'

'No. And stop with always changing the subject,' Dil membs. 'You're attending this year, correct?' Dil's Regal English is perfect. All his c's and t's receive proper emphasis.

'Still deciding.'

'You already accept.'

Without joy I memb, 'Yeer.'

'Come on, Ben. We have the same conversation last year. And the year before. And the two years before.'

'I am hoping you might give it up.' My Tanah Selatan Anglo-Malay accent never sounds so nasal.

'Come on, think of Aisha. She'll love the party,' Dil wheedles, extracting a laugh from me.

'Aisha versus a few hundred Infinites? I know who I'm backing.'

'They will invite you every year till you give in. After five years still you refuse joining their camerata.'

'I am no Infinite.'

'*Hisab* says otherwise,' Dil membs. *Hisab* is the Sri Lankan term for the Reckoning. 'It practically stamps INFINITE on your forehead. If you jel your reputasi, will it answer with count of razoos? No. It simply says, *Infinite*.'

'You taste what I mean—I feel like no Infi. Perhaps there's a bug in the Reckoning's mindwriting.'

'If there is, no one will ever find it.'

The Reckoning is sequestered from AgniSpace (the infrastructure which exploits multi-dimensional onespace and underpins spooky tech, yielding applications for spooky stations, fabbies, sucky bins, holly storage and communication enhancement), with only the strictest of interfaces between. The Reck must be so: unreachable, unimpeachable, and incorruptible.

'Look,' Dil continues. 'Come have lunch with me if you are still tossing it round.'

'In Brisbane?'

In my Mind's Eye, Dil makes the uniquely subcontinental twist of his shoulders which means *you figure it out*: that is, *no* without being so rude as saying it. 'Let me spend the weekend with the family. We'll meet Monday. I am hearing there's a new Vegemite café in Veghel. All the gastronomic comforts of home.' He's kidding. I doubt there's a jar of Vegemite anywhere in The Netherlands.

'If I know you, you're missing home already. Let's make it Kolombo.'

'Sure. Anywhere other than your village. You must get out more. All the local Infi-worship is rotting your head.'

'If, by *rotting my head*, you mean it makes me consider living alone in a glacial crevasse, you're right.'

'I pity the locals ... with a genuine sultan living among them.'

'An Infi is no royalty.'

'Tell your millions of bent-brain flutherbombers. There are insufficient nurses in the whole world for Curing them all.'

'For what? Sloth?'

'They're nothing but couch samosas, Ben, living life vicariously through your fluther. They need Cures.'

Notice y'all, how those who already undergo a Cure are the ones most enthusiastically advocating them for everyone else? Dilan receives more than one, many years back. Of course, I quiz him about it, as any friend would, but he's as vague as the next patient about what goes on inside a minster. Unlike other patients, Dil is neither better nor less than he is before. Apart from the spinal injury.

I say, 'They may as well book a clinic couch for me as well, *machan*,' surprising myelf (neo for *myself*) with the melancholy of it.

'You're never Slothful, Ben.'

'Aisha sees it differently.'

'Attend the Infi Gala, Ben. She'll perk up after such a party.'

'I swear, *machan*, if I ever become as indulgent and elf-entitled as the common Infi, I have no taste as how I'd live with myelf.'

The tukky rocks on its suspension as it pulls up by the kerb at the station concourse. I curse tongue and lung: 'Must you stop right here? In front of ... this?' Passers-by awkwardly shrink away from the volume of my rant.

A 'sculpture' is taking pride of place in the centre of the concourse, half complete and already portending the full monstrosity it will become. Its doting creator and subservient engineers buzz around it like apish bees, touching up ever fussier details.

The artist spies me stepping out of the tukky. Her jaw swings down and almost slaps her chest; her hand covers her gaping maw. She jumps as if shot through with electricity, and comes scurrying crab-like, her pincer-hands up and waving about.

'Infi, no!' she implores with an Archaic French accent. 'Let us finish before you inspect it.'

I shade my eyes with a hand. 'I am here on another matter. No looking.

Pinky swear.'

My eyes already burn from the travesty of it. Two- or three-times head-height is a tangle of vines sprouting multicoloured phallic corpse flowers and giant vulvic orchids. If the artist is striving for some expression of sensuality, she fails. Instead, the incessant throbbing of its fruit and flowers suggests a carnivorous menace of a thing beastly alive, of a multi-limbed vegetable yeti with a hunger for sucking anyone's arms off if they stray too close.

'What is its title? *Pohon alat kelamin*?' *Genital tree*, for those of y'all who have only Regal English.

'We trust it pleases,' the artist membs with unbearable hopefulness. 'Perhaps, the inscription on the plaque, you comment, *oui*?'

'I must pick up a package, and I'm quite—'

'It will read, *In dedication to the first Infinite of Bandar Melambai, Ben Evoli dari Saffron dari* … etcetera etcetera.'

It will please Mal on hearing he's become an etcetera.

The artist pauses for breath, as if there is more of the dedication.

'Yeer, yeer,' I memb, dismissive. Jank reputasi. My advice is, never create anything too successful. It will haunt you the rest of your life. From the garden walls down the esplanade, the scent of Thai basil and rich wet nutes calm; I inhale deeply. 'Sorry, I'm expecting a courier. With an important package.'

The artist's disappointment spills out like a dropped bucket of custard. By fortune, one of her engineers calls with some issue about the installation.

A courier emerges from the shade of the station hall bearing my package. Picks his way across the concourse through the crowd, around hawker stands with their aromas of breakfast noodles and aya tea. His feet fall heavy with the weight of the carton he carries. He's a funny sight. The package appears as his torso with his legs growing out from under. His head sprouts from the top.

Wave him this way. As he approaches, a tukky rushes over, gleeful with victory. Others hesitate, their front wheels aiming left then right as they think on where their next customers may be. Two track west down the esplanade towards the bay. Another prowls up the hill. The rest sulk for their allotted parking bay opposite the station.

'Your delivery, Infi,' the courier calls with more than obsequious deference.

'Terima kasih. Just sit it down on the floor in back.'

'Allow me. I'll remove the wrapper.' He plumps the carton on the back flatbed, takes a blade to the DNA package wrap like he is skinning a fish. With a smile (no doubt anticipating his reputasi will improve) he rolls the webbing into a small fist-size ball, works it into a large thigh-pocket on his overalls. I wedge the package into the narrow footwell between the front and back seats of the tukky, wave thanks, and watch him all the way until he skips into the violet mist of the station's departure pool and evaporates.

Saf Evoli …

Mal's eyes are the size of his gaping mouth when Bapa arrives bearing a large box.

'What is it?' He drops his dirty breakfast plate on the table and rushes over. With grubby hands he grabs the box like he would snatch it. Bodoh Mal. Stupid. The thing is as big as you are. Bapa holds onto it, so Mal puts his ear on it like he might detect what's inside.

Ibu waves his mug at him. 'Mal, come finish your tea, dun look at me.'

'I need no ayahuasca.' Mal spits out syllables like swear words. Paws at the package. 'Is it mine?' Before Bapa sets it down, Mal tears at the squirty-foam packaging.

Whatever's in it will be for Mal. I never get gifts in big packages. Knowing Bapa, it's some ancient sap gadget. A membosankan (boring), broken gadget. Bapa's new junk always requires some fixing. Already they'll spend the morning, forgetting the rest of the world, while they figure out tedious things, like how it takes power.

'It's an Apple iMac, from early 21st century,' Bapa tells Mal, and receives a scolding stare from Ibu.

I wish I could be gracious, truly. Who cares if Mal gets all the broken toys? 'Drink your aya, Mal or you'll get Entanglement Syndrome.'

'Saffron!' Ibu scolds.

Mal snorts. 'Then I'll blow my nose and spatter brains all over you.' He's a devil laughing.

'Yeer, all onespace will pour into your Mind, your skull will crack open, and your brains will melt and puff out like cookie dough rising in an oven. Just like a sap.'

'Saf!' Ibu yells. 'Walao eh. How old are you?'

'24.'

'Then why fight with Mal, ah? You almost a woman this time.'

Thirty-one is years away, when Ibu will still treat me like a child. 'Well, at least make him help us clean up breakfast before he goes playing with his new toy.'

'You finish up here, little fella,' Bapa tells Mal. He's always too soft with him. 'Drink your tea. It's good for you. Help Ibu and your saudara. I'll set up in your swasta.'

'Why must he always get stuff?' Toss dirty cups in the sucky bin with enough force they shatter. The pieces clatter and disappear in the flashing purple of the spooky field. Even the house ignores my temper.

Ben Evoli …

As soon as we gog for sap cartoons, 14's of camerati with 21st-century entertainment content are pitching their TV magazines. With too many choices, I memb a local broker who, grateful for the assignment, has recommendations within a few mins.

With some coaching, Mal is barking search queries at the puter's screen which displays tables of lurid-bright text. Mal quickly learns how scrolling works. 'Hey, there's one they call *Ben 10*.' He giggles. 'It's you, Bapa!'

'I guess it is.'

'Play,' Mal commands with all the gravitas a boy can summon. A window expands and fills the screen. The cartoon begins. Mal pulls a face of disappointment. He taps on the screen. 'Why is the holly staying inside?'

'It's no holly. The images stay on the screen.'

'Oh.' Mal has the curious look of a puppy. 'Were there people like us back then?'

'No.'

'No? Look at the saps in the cartoon. They're us! Ben and Gwen have big eyes and little noses. You say sap eyes are squinty and their noses are big and ugly.'

'That's just the way they draw Ben and Gwen. They're still saps.'

'How could saps know how we look?'

'They had good imaginations.' Aisha would snort at me for dumbing it down for him (that's an ibu's role).

'Saps always needed screens to taste stuff, right, Bapa? TV's? Puters?'

Nod.

'They needed *gadgets*,' he stresses the word and giggles at his cleverness, 'because they could see no hollies in their own Mind, or see other people, or memb with them through onespace.'

'Right.'

'This would be great,' he says.

'Why you say so?'

'Well, then you'd have no one following you around in your head, seeing everything around you and knowing everything about you.'

I say, 'It might be lonely,' and feel immediate guilt for my disingenuousness.

Mal scrunches his face. 'I hate people seeing me all the time. It's scary.'

'It is sometimes.' With Mal, it's better keeping it simple. Truthful.

'It's how nurses know when we are sakit.'

I say, 'Yeer,' sounding gloomy.

'If the nurses say I am sakit, will you let them take me away?'

'You're too young for worrying about nurses. Anak-anak are never sakit you know? Only orang (adults).'

'There's no Consigning anak anak for Cures?'

Kiss the top of his head. 'No. Never. And we would never let them take you.'

Mal grabs me in a bear hug, nuzzles his head against my cheek, the puter and *Ben-10* out of his mind for a tik. 'Why is it we need hancies?'

This again. I'd prefer thinking of Mal as innocent and guileless, but his questions about nurses are for softening me up for what's always on his mind: wearing a hancy. I stroke my neck, feeling the thin neuromorphic coin-size disk of the hancy there, supple and scaly like snakeskin. 'Hancies help us taste better.'

Mal licks his paws like a cat. 'I taste fine.' Giggling.

'You know what I mean. Tasting as in ...' Wave my hands in the air. 'What we sense in onespace. Hancies help us taste it all better.'

'I hate hancies.'

Feel my shoulders slump. Whisper, 'We know.' Hope I sound soothing. 'We know.'

'I taste you and Ibu and Saf in my Mind already. Without a hancy. I taste everyone spying on me.'

'It's no spying, Mal; and never let a nurse taste you saying this.'

'I know. It's good. We're never lonely.'

I swallow a grunt with a grimace. Mal will discover soon enough he might still be lonely; even with a fluther of millions tasting his existence tik-by-tik, producing a rainbow thundercloud of an aura around him as big as a residential block.

'They look scary,' Mal whinges.

I bite my lip and choke an outburst against this silliness. 'Look.' With the gentle pressure of my thumb, I click my hancy out, and wince against the size of my fluther bearing down on me. I swallow nausea; being without my filters grates my nerves raw.

When I offer him the hancy, Mal shrinks away with chin down and shoulders huddled.

'Take it.'

'Nah.'

'You see how easy removing it is?' I could throw up without it. 'Just feel it for a tik,' I memb while holding it out.

'You taste a bit fuzzy now,' Mal says.

I grunt a yeer.

Mal searches my eyes, and finds something worth trusting in them, reaches out as if accepting bad-tasting medicine. He turns the hancy over in his fingers, scratches at the texture. 'It's like Lucy's skin,' he says. Lucy is the name he gives the blue-tongue lizard who suns itself in the back yard.

'Kinda soft,' he says as he flexes it between thumb and finger, noticing how it springs flat when he releases pressure. He applies more force, bending the disc into a thumb-size taco shell.

'Careful,' I order, despite knowing there's no cracking it.

The next thing, my hancy is ricocheting off the wall: Mal frisbees it at the sucky bin.

'Hey!' I shout, tongue and lung. I lunge for the hancy; fumble and grab it. I hold my breath while I click it into its seat above my collarbone. A lapping of calm washes my fluther back as the filters kick in.

'I should …' With all my powers of parental containment, I lean out of escalating this.

Mal scrunches his nose and stares.

A long breath. I wheedle, 'Once you get a hancy, you'll wonder how you could live without all the hoots you load on it.'

'Are hoots a hoot?' he asks with a dose of defiant nastiness. I doubt he knows what *a hoot* meant centuries ago. He must learn it from Saf.

I say, 'Hoots: hancy utilities,' which earns a look from Mal, accusing me of dadsplaining.

'I know what they are, Bapa.'

'Well, why would you go without them? All the multiplayer games …?'

Mal shrugs. 'I already play those.'

'How?'

'I flutherbomb my friends.'

'So, you hate hancies, but you're okelah with piggybacking on your friends who have hancies?'

'I guess,' he says. 'They let me.'

I deflate. Why expect a boy of Mal's age would taste the ethical inconsistency?

A montage of fast scenes plays out on the iMac's screen. 'With the right hoot, you could watch all those cartoons in your own head—anywhere, any time. You could store as many cartoons as you want in your hancy.'

Mal laughs as a cartoon fox is struck by lightning. Twice. 'I like the puter screen, Bapa. It's shiny.' Now I worry he'll want for lugging it everywhere he goes. 'I know you like it too,' he says with as much gravity as a little boy might summon.

He has me there.

'You ever wish you never have a hancy?' he asks with wicked innocence.

Strike 2.

'Okelah, I'll talk with Ibu.'

'For ghost?'

'From where you got this word?' Recall Dil using *ghost* word earlier.

'Saf.'

'Figures.' There's no keeping up with twentager slang.

'Bapa?'

'Yeer?'

'We should need no *enhancement*,' he says, his words weighty with immature emphasis. 'I'll never wear a hancy.'

Aisha Evoli ...

Enough! 'Stop, Mal.' Crave go for him but his swasta tastes ever more a bromance den. From outside in the hall, I look in at them both huddling around that la-la sap toy. I linger at the doorway. 'Never is a long-time ah?'

Why Ben undermine me? This is important lah. Mal plays with the stupid light box. I make a stern face. Ben stands awkwardly; rest a hand on Mal's shoulder. The metres between me and Mal feel as wide as a canyon. I hover in the doorway, peer into the boys' club. Maybe it's Ben's aura pressing me back. It spills out of the room and floods the hallway. Tastes prickly lah. Millions of followers hanging on every tik. Emotional vultures. They wait for these family conflicts like that. Nurses should take them for Cures, fine. But what good are nurses? They should throw them in a minster for a long time. But no. I am more the nurses' target for want followers gone. This is how inside-out health camerati are. I will get a Cure for want followers gone, and Ben will get a Cure for hoard sap junk lah.

'Let's talk about it later,' Bens membs. It annoy me, he wear that stiff old self-clean baju and seluar. Why he must wear the old clothes like that lah? He has overflow wardrobe. Fashion designers always give a sample, hope for razoos. I pick some lints off his baju. It must be months old. Very out of fashion lah. What for say? It's his favourite. Throw it away is more trouble than I like. Just look at it ah. A dirty red sail billow around the mast of his skinny torso.

'Later never arrives, Bat Ears.' Look at them. So pointy, poke through his thick black wavy angular hair—hair I want run my fingers through already. 'Mal is the anak in the desa only without a hancy.'

'No, there are others. Some wait until they're twentagers before taking one. He'll come around. Let's be better parents than impose our will this way.'

'People talk. You taste what they say. They say he a freak lor.'

'Ha! We're all freaks. The whole desa tiptoes around us.'

'He talk so loud all the time and never memb. You should see the stares in the street like that lah. Who would blame them one? The way Mal disturb peace?'

'Peace? Who has any peace?' Ben waves his hand though the aura above his head like he shoos flies away. 'Know you how many people living in the housing hill are flutherbombing me right now? How many within 50 metres just out there in the street? 100 metres? A kim? 100? From the opposite side of the world? Who can blame Mal for shunning it all?' Ben's hand is an eagle's claw at my elbow. There—pleading in his large eyes; his face set; his sharp handsome nose, that one like a keel in the tension between us.

I say, 'There is hancy filters, he can use like that. No one know better than you only.'

'We should let him make his own decision when he's ready.'

'Where got?' I should leave him be but, holala, need for say, 'And what that sap rubbish one? You hoarding—'

'It's collecting. And sharing.'

'You must say sharing; keep nurses happy.' Wave at Mal's door; think of the stupid puter on the desk in there.

'Anyone can use it.' He thinks he win an argument. Lelaki (man) are so dungu (dumb) ah? No one win an argument with logic.

'No one will, because you're Infi and everyone is too much awe of you, and too afraid for use your stuff lah. Even our housing hill residents stay out of the common areas in case you want. And already you rope Mal into this … obsession.'

Ben sets his jaw for cover fear. Obsession. If his istri believe it, next time a nurse take actions, is it? 'It's no obsession,' he says. Force hiself for stay calm. 'Besides, there's no denying Mal's interest in Homo sapiens stuff. It's all he ever talks about.'

'Yeer. It's scary. Saps wiped themvelves out, near killed the planet, leave us for clean-up. We still live in their junkyard, and you keep bring their junk home.'

'Istri, have trust. I am no obsessive hoarder.'

'I worry for Mal, Bat Ears. He's my little anak ah. Carry him in my womb for 14 months.' Yeer, two months premature. We all fear something might go wrong for him. 'I carry him and when my waters break, I choose natural birth. More than eight hours, that time.'

Ben reaches out, strokes my cheek. 'Istri, I never mean—'

'I worry for him. These are no days for reject the normal ways of growing up ah. You hear the news. Health camerati get bolder lah. They will come for Infinites. Come for you like that. I lose both of you. It would be so easy for them twist all the things you collect, take you for Greed. Or Sloth. You have no mission anymore ah. Where is your passion all those years since the Reckoning makes you Infinite? I worry lah. I worry neither of you are well.'

Skye Merewether …

Pagan titties! There are some inconsiderate people in the world. Who would be so careless? Ten minutes I'm rubbing at a stain from a teacup sitting overnight on my reception desk. Must I always be the one who cleans up at end of shift? Here I am, the only one in the clinic at this time of morning, while even the novice field nurses are out sitting in a park or taking in a view of the harbour, playing detective, jumping between one fluther and the next. While I must replenish the reception shelves with herbal nutes.

This dark ring is never coming out. I'll have no option but have removalists take the desk away and throw it in a council sucky bin. If I order a new one fabbied now, there's a chance it'll arrive today. Gah! I hate days starting like this.

A muffled cry of terror seeps through the ceiling from the whorehouse on the floor above. Some drama with a customer, no doubt. I suppose there may be a Warrant in it; I should peek, since detectives rarely have the patience for flutherbombing sex missionaries or their punters.

I join Dorothy Biggins, the local madam, and see calves and feet scrambling up a staircase. She is close on the heels of one of her missionaries. Another terrifying squeal. On complaining legs, Dorothy puffs down a narrow corridor. Doors slam open as more missionaries spill out of rooms, adrenaline pumping as they prepare for defending one of their own against a rogue customer. More gasps and blood-churning screams. Dorothy careens into a fast-filling suite and delivers me the sights and smells of a visceral scene.

I choke back the urge for spewing (my reception desk suffers enough indignity already). A pure reflex, I squeeze my eyes shut; but of course, my head is full of multi-sensory multidimensional assaults. It takes all my training for staying in Dorothy's fluther.

Like paint spray from several hoses, there's blood on the ceiling. The king-size bed is a glistening soak of bright red turning burgundy. As for the incomprehensible gore on the sheets, hands and feet twitch in unnatural arrangement—torn exposed muscle; snapped and splintered bones; a mutilated mouth serrated by cracked teeth; dead eyes frozen in a final tik of agony and anguish; limbs and torso all broken, reset at right-angles—everything slumping on the bed like a macabre cubist sculpture.

Another pair of eyes, terror-wide, glistening white in a sheen of whimpering blood: a missionary huddles tight in the corner as if his sole purpose is wedging there until the end of time.

No one makes sense of the sight. No one has a coherent question.

'What is—who?' I blather at Dorothy.

Dorothy blinks herelf back into her fruit. She points at the quivering bloody missionary. 'Two of you take him and clean him up. Stay with him until he sleeps. Someone memb the passing mission; have them lay this poor soul in a passing suite. You: memb the cleaners; tell them we have a level 5. No, tell them it's worse.' She huffs into her heavy lungs and reclaims some composure. 'Passing in public. Who would be so disgusting?'

'It must be murder,' says one of the missionaries, out of flat shock.

'Neos never kill,' says another, indignant at such a notion. 'Besides, how is this possible?' she says, gesturing at the carnage. 'Firecracker up the arse?'

I make the mistake of jumping for her fluther. Her sense of smell is so keen; the reek of piss, shit and gastric chemicals is overwhelming. I retreat for Dorothy's fluther.

'What illness is it?' Dorothy membs me.

I shake my head.

'I have no understanding of this,' she says. 'He is always such a good customer. Never any trouble.'

'You mean he never turns hiself inside out before?'

In normal circumstances, Dorothy would have harsh words for my sarcasm, but now she only looks at her feet as if chastised.

'He's a regular?' I ask.

Dorothy nods. 'Twyford Hendriks. Our only regular Infi. Oh, our reputasi!' she wails.

Why would an Infi grace our backwater brothel? 'Are you sure he's Infi?'

'Of course. Look him up if you doubt.'

I will; brothel missions ask too few questions. Impersonating an Infi might be possible, especially if the mission would rather avoid learning the truth.

'Mind you, I often wonder about the small size of his fluther.' Dorothy's suspicion is rising too. 'No, look.' She blinks me some hollies she finds. 'This's definitely the Twyford we know.'

'Hmm.' Hoping for some luck, I lash the hollies and run a query through various nursing camerati's archives. An Infi will always have nurses in their fluther. The question is whether I might find one of them.

Blessings! There he is. Twyford Hendriks, alive and well, attending a meeting in a hotel conference room in Marrakesh. I memb Dorothy with the news—he lives.

Would the real Infi go so far as murdering an impostor? And how would he hide it from the battalions of detectives stalking him every tik of the day?

Orange

'Watching the Detectives' — Elvis Costello

 *Vör Hoyur ...*

WE MAKE ARRANGEMENTS: every delegation must spook via Valby Station. With much handwringing we deliver our apologies, offering the excuse of the spooky field at Carlsberg Station being most regrettably down for maintenance. Rather than a short skip, they must ride tukkies down Valby Langgade, passing Park Søndermarken which promises so much renewal this week before spring. At the top of New Carlsberg Road, they will turn right for the entrance of Carlsberg Minster grounds, where they will confront our great granite elephants bearing, upon their great stony backs, a lintel on which rests a brick tower as heavy as an avalanche. Between the elephants and under the intimidating tower, the delegates must pass. No doubt they will read the golden words carved into the lintel: LABOREMUS PRO PATRIA *(let us work for the fatherland)*. They wear jhools emblazoned with swastikas, surveil the procession of delegates in stoic, intimidating silence, their heads tilting and ears flaring. Whether they mean for attack or play, let the arriving delegates may imagine. Once through, 2 more elephants behind the first will study our guests, who, if they feel the weight of the history of this place with apprehension or humility, then much the better.

The Elephant Gate marks one entrance for the minster grounds and the extent of our scatter nets. As they pass under the tower, the delegates' halos fizzle and shrink. No one outside the grounds can join fluthers of anyone inside.

And so, these delegates come from the other great health camerati, for conferring with us.

Nilajani Karunanithi ...

Ignoramus pro patria, indeed.

While the compliant delegations obey instructions, and travel nearly 2 kims after they arrive in Copenhagen via Valby Station, we uninvited nurses learn that Carlsberg Station, which is across the street from the minster campus, is indeed functional. We spook there and slip onto campus grounds unannounced and unobserved. By *we*, I mean *me*, the only health missionary with the nerve for sneaking into North Europa's hallowed headquarters.

Impatience is a virtue, and I want for tasting these Vikings' plots. If they're ramping up investigations of Infinites, how could I stand being left out?

Once on the grounds, it should be easy. No one questions a nurse wandering about aimlessly, with their eyes fluttering chaotically. Deep flutherbombing is a sign of an industrious mission ethic.

As soon as I'm under the scatter nets, I taste about for interesting fluthers. I jump between administrators, catering staff, the occasional detective (never stay too long with them), and groundskeepers. More than once, I stumble across sweaty huddles of the naked cavorting in dormitories. I find a kitchen hand preparing lunch. With all the excitement, I've eaten nothing today. My tummy is a grumbling troll under a bridge.

Vör Hoyur ...

Eir strokes the knife-edge creases in her dress uniform; gives a nervous, shampoo-testimonial flick of her head, setting a wave through the length of her hair all the way for her tailbone. Never a split-end nor a tangle—would y'all believe? Even as she wakes in the morning. She nods for the ushers who throw the double doors of the conference room open. Outside, queueing delegates take steps back, and regard us with flitting eyes. Who am I deceiving? They regard Eir.

They could view 7000 hollies of Eir, or watch from the fluthers of people around her, but nothing prepares them for Eir in 4-dimensional flesh. It's more than her height; at 2 metres, she's a head and a half taller than the tallest man and the average woman. It's more than her preternatural white skin. It's more than her hair, which sheens and dazzles and reflects the rainbow colours of the delegates' dress uniforms. It's more than the way the violets of their outfits flash in Eir's albino pink-violet eyes. Eir stands out even among the delegates' gene-mod skins. Eir's powder-white complexion compels others stare and muffle gasps.

Delegation by delegation, they file through in pairs; wearing saris, cheongsams, ao dais, thaubs, tunics, headdresses, and robes; wearing faces of awe, anticipation, or ill-concealed animosity. They exchange barbed greetings and wan pleasantries with us. First are the delegates from the Camerata *de Bem-Estar da Bacia Amazônica*, notable for bioluminescent ocelot stripes on their faces and hands. The delegates the of The Pacific Islands Church of Health wear grey business suits which accentuate their gene-mod facial tattoos, ever-changing in colour and bioluminescent intensity.

'Pleasing meeting you,' says a delegate from the United States of Texas Health Corporations. She tilts her head back and gazes up at Eir from under her rainbow 10-gallon hat.

Eir nods, covers her mouth with a hand, her eyes drift for a far corner of the room.

'I understand you are giving the keynote address for your camerata's next graduating class,' the Texan says.

Eir has no expecting this. She nods, her hand still covering her mouth.

'You must have much pride,' the delegate says.

I start: '*Ja*, we—'

'It's an honour sharing my experience with our new generation of nurses.' Eir wants the pleasantries over.

Only a remnant of the queue remains. The pair of *Nihon No Kenkō Misshon* are next. The 2nd delegate's cheeks are a cover of monochromatic paisley tears that clash with the floral motifs of her kimono. Both emissaries bear an elaborate crystal bottle of sake in the shape of a 3-legged crow. With a shot of fear, Eir realises they are gifts. The pair bow and formally extend bottles in both hands. One says, 'With thanking for host us.'

Eir freezes, knowing they expect she accepts a bottle; but her shakiness is coming and going all day, and she fears she may drop the gift. In a tik of panic, I clutch both glass crows by their necks. Having Eir's shatter on the floor is much worse than a little diplomatic indignity, so what option is there? The delegates are aghast.

'I'm most sorry,' Eir says. 'I ...' She peters out while swivelling her hands uselessly. The Japanese delegates realise their error and appear stricken in their shame.

Replacing the Japanese at the head of the queue are the delegates from the Kementerian Kesahatan of Indo-Malaysia. Shorter than average, heads craning back as if searching for a star in the heavens, they look Eir in the eye. Jaws dropping in mechanical unison, hinging on clockwork gears.

'They're all afraid of me,' Eir membs, which is unusual for her. When we are within Face, she prefers tongue and lung over membing.

I say, 'No more than usual,' which is true. For them, Eir's an albino praying mantis, with the divining detective skills they talk about in hush-tones, in whispers one might reserve for discussing terminal illness, irretrievable sexual experimentation, or demon-possession.

Nilajani Karunanithi ...

Eir Frijberg's meeting will soon commence. There's a flurry of activity as everyone on campus flutherbombs one or other of the delegates who will be in the room with the legendary White Witch. We all taste it will be a significant day for nursing missions; and no one attending Eir's meeting in the flesh will begrudge a fluther full of onlookers. No one will notice me lurking.

Activity around the minster is slowing as nurses and support staff find a comfy chair, a favourite window box or a tatty dorm bunk, while their Minds cast for the proceedings in the conference room.

A few mins back, a trio of field nurses—after sending some flirty glances my way—invite I follow them. Now we're on the floor under a table in the library. With uniforms in increasing disarray, it's obvious these 3 have little interest in the official activities of the day. It takes all my concentration, staying present in Vör's fluther ...

Vör Hoyur ...

Thirty-four delegates surround an oval conference table, their halos burgeoning with other delegates lurking in their fluthers, all lickerish for witnessing the proceedings.

Eir is more at ease now she is at table and no longer towers overall. 'We are too timid,' Eir announces, after the fidgeting stops. 'Evidence is everywhere if we have a desire for searching it out. But we are afraid of what we might find, because we are afraid of conflict with Infinites.'

They suck in breath. Eir will be direct, eschewing preliminary niceties. Her violet eyes narrow. 'We must recommit for our mission with compassion and love for our fellows. We must seek out sickness and Cure it.'

'Easy saying, but we name them Infinite with good reason; they have immeasurable influence and resources.'

'These are no demons,' Eir counters. 'Their power and reach should discourage none of us from caring for them.'

'They denigrate our mission,' one delegate objects. 'When was the last time an Infi volunteers for health care?'

'All the greater proof they need it,' Eir says.

'Campaigning against Infinites will destroy us,' another says. 'They will have 14's of ways for eroding our reputasi beyond anything we could counter. Before long, there will be no health missions.'

'You're assuming Infinites can influence the Reckoning against us,' Eir says.

'Hah! Of course they can. Everyone knows it.'

'Yet no one has proof. Such beliefs are all timid conspiracy theories,' Eir says.

'No, no. My colleague misspeaks. We only mean for saying many Infis are very popular. If we move against them, we move against popular sentiment. It might … affect … *our* reputasi.'

'In any case,' Eir says, 'if we are afraid for our reputasi, then our missions are already failing.'

'Well, our mission is far from the most popular. We'll never see a nurse of Infinite designation. Even you, Eir—with all the reverence you conjure; with your razoos at orders of magnitude greater than anyone else here—you would lose the most if we attract the Infis' ire.'

This is the opening we plan for, the moment where we might shift the debate. Eir lets the silence hang for some long tiks. I am in sweet anticipation.

'You are right,' she says. Everyone around the table relaxes and exhales. 'I should heed my own convictions.' The tension around the table rises again. 'I should fear nothing for my reputasi. I should be an example. If it pleases the delegates, I volunteer for a world-wide investigation into the health of Infinites, with conviction and compassion for the sickness I find.'

'This's all very inspiring, and more than a little Prideful,' another higgles. 'There's no guarantee other nurses will be safe from retaliatory actions.'

'Then,' Eir says firmly. 'I will make myelf and my team the public faces of the campaign, which will allow y'all the option for disavowing me if it turns as bad as some fear. Offer me up as a sacrifice if you must. In one way or another, someone must take a chance.'

'It'll all fizzle out. You'll never find enough evidence for Consigning a single Infi for anything more than Pride,' one says.

'Envy would be hard,' says another.

'Gluttony. You can get almost any Infi for Gluttony,' adds another.

'Only the foolish ones.'

Eir's fingernails scratch at the tablecloth. She has no appetite for the old classifications of Greed, Gluttony … gargling, glittering, whatever. In this she agrees with most Infinites.

'We already have evidence,' I issue, surprising myelf. Eir rests the weight of her hand on mine, pressing it down on the table linen. I bite a lip. All eyes search me.

'We know it!' a delegate from *Gesondheidsgenote van Suid-Afrika* objects. 'You start investigations years ago, and only now ask for a rubber stamp.'

'These passing 3 years, my team investigates a number of Infis,' Eir placates. 'Some minor, some major. For serious health issues. It seems wise we test our capabilities before wasting your time.' She slips her hand under the table and squeezes my thigh. A pulse of excitement reaches all the way for my eyebrows.

'Then you have evidence you will make stick?' the South African delegate pursues.

'Greed? Can you get them for Greed?'

Eir exhales the last of her patience. 'There will be no *getting* anyone, no *catching* anyone. We're no police force, and Infis are no criminals. Health is at stake. We must be compassionate and true in our mission. If you wish, you'll all have opportunities for taking part in the Consignments—and there will be Cures.'

If you wish. A poison chalice staining the mood of the room with a mix of covetousness and horror.

'If you already have the evidence, what need you of us?'

'All I seek is your blessing for progressing plans. When the time comes, I need your admissions teams ready. For the most part, I need you postpone any proceedings you may be planning against Infis.' More than half the room laughs, finding the idea of moving against Infis preposterous. 'Let no Infi suspect what's coming. And let there be no territorial squabbles among us.'

'That's all well and good, so how might you propose making your responsibility public? It must be immediate and unambiguous, or else any of us could be collateral damage in it.'

'Oh, simple,' an ebullient voice gushes. I have embarrassment it's mine again. Eir's hand on my thigh squeezes tighter, as if my blather is flowing up from my toes and she might cut it off. 'We're drawing up Warrants for Consigning the important ones all at once.'

'And which are those, if we may ask?'

Before Eir frames an answer, I bluster, 'The ones wearing watches.'

Eir Frijberg ...

March is often too early for picnics in cemeteries. But the day blooms bright and warm, and the residents of København are impatient for the outdoors.

Teo is still in town after the conference, so I invite her along. Vör will be unhappy. For the sake of the team, this pair must stop jostling one another.

Teo and I spook for Emdrup Station, then bike for the Bispebjerg health district where we'll meet Vör. When we arrive, she has the look of a sick chicken. Awkwardly holding 2 bikes—one she clearly reserves for me—she regards Teo with more resentment than I anticipate and lets one bike clatter on the kerb. Ignoring us, she mounts the other and races off.

'Let her go,' I tell Teo. 'We'll catch up with her.'

Taking the route at leisure, the gates of Bispebjerg Cemetery appear before we see Vör again. As we approach, she makes a pretence of admiring the façade of Grundvigs Church. If y'all gog for hollies, my loving fluther, you will see how much it appears a giant set of organ pipes. In silence, Vör remounts her bike and follows us down the avenue of tall poplars.

Vör's mood improves with food. Teo volunteers for cleaning up the plates and scraps; I straighten the blanket on the grass, lie back and let the sky pour in. Framing the intimate field of grass where we lay, an avenue of sakura trees is only just budding in the soft pinks of Spring renewal. With hope, the cherry blossoms will bloom soony-soon.

Vör dusts her hands and lies alongside, rests her head in the v between my thighs and groin. Teo watches with awkward uncertainty. 'Come on.' I tap the blanket near my head. Reluctantly she plops her bottom down; slinks her hips under my head; lays back.

I say, 'Come on, you 2.'

Teo shuffles. Giving in, Vör groans then swings her hips around until Teo can place her head in Vör's lap. The way they hold breath, y'all would believe both are enduring some form of torture.

'I bring little gifts for both of you,' I say tongue and lung, while I fossick in my kangaroo pocket. Vör lifts her head for giving me better access.

'Oh, what is it?' Teo asks, wide-eye and expectant, as she wrangles her blushing smile back between her ears.

I jangle the trinkets in the air above us. 'For your chatelaines.'

Both knit intense expressions as they process the meaning of the gifts: silver chains suspending a stylised diamond-encrusted eye with an emerald pupil.

'Evil eyes?' Teo says with some disdain. She understands the Envy reference. I feel her weight shifting away from me.

'They're lovely,' Vör says, her cheeks flush with pleasure. She takes one of the trinkets in gentle fingers.

'Please tell me the emeralds are fabbied,' Teo says with semi-quavers of scepticism.

I roll my eyes, *of course*, and gesture the thing insistently at Teo.

Vör already loops the chain through the ring of her chatelaine as Teo reluctantly concedes the gift. I pat the cluster of souvenirs clustering on my own chatelaine. 'I have one also. Now we are all safe.'

They exchange glances and relax their tight, thin lips.

Teo rolls on her back and looks through budding cherry blossoms at a greying sky. I rest my hand on her thigh.

'Are we going in early or late?' Vör asks. 'The Inductee Gala: are we going in early or late?'

Teo throws her hands up, raises her chin and makes a drama of turning her head away from Vör. 'We are yet deciding,' she says, grimaces and rolls her eyes.

I frown. The sky answers with tightening clouds huddling above roofs and treetops.

'If we wait until after the ceremony, if Ben Evoli accepts the watch,' Vör says of the trinket the Infis award new members of their inner sanctum, 'then he makes his choice.'

'A ceremony and a shiny toy are no condemnations.' Teo summons patience. As always, she'll be seeking harmony, seeking for putting herelf above her feelings. 'Is it sickness, owning—I mean stewarding—a piece of jewellery?'

'We are all aware of what the watch means,' Vör says.

'Which is?' Teo asks, her jaw setting.

'It means he joins a club is all,' I interject, despite my desire for staying out of it.

Vör grimaces as if she smells a bad thing. 'Then we are writing him no Warrant?' Vör asks, rising on her elbows. 'Water runs downhill. Ben chooses his place.'

'We are still investigating.' Which is all I want for saying.

'What are we investigating?' Vör asks, pretending mere curiosity. 'He's a mindwriter. He could hide almost anything. And he's an Infi, so we *know* he will hide things.'

'And what insight have our mindwriters, about what he could be hiding?' I quiz as patiently and gently as able, wary Teo is gloating. 'Almost nothing.'

Vör answers: 'He uses filters he keeps for hiself.'

'Then where's the evidence? Besides, every Infi uses filters,' Teo says, reminding Vör of the obvious. 'Which no one would begrudge. How would you cope with millions flutherbombing you every tik of every day?'

Vör snorts, which Teo, propping up on an elbow, exploits as an opening. 'Anyone with the razoos would use filtering hoots. Health missionaries would install them—'

'Lazy ones,' Vör stabs in.

'So, you'd Consign them for a Cure for Sloth?' Teo quizzes. I wish she'd cease testing Vör. 'For their reliance on hancy assistance?'

They both know I put no stock in the 7 classifications, the 7 ills and their 7 Cures. It's been nearly a century since we base Cures on those classifications. We should stop naming them on Warrants. We should stop pretending for the outside world these matter anymore.

'Teo,' Vör says as if addressing a naughty schoolchild. 'The sickness here is—as Eir reiterates on so many occasions—one of separateness, of exclusion, of pushing the other outside one's awareness.'

'The point is, would you declare all of those sick for wanting a little peace?' Teo almost sneers. Bringing this pair together, I realise, is doe-eye folly.

'Would you Consign them for it?' I ask Vör.

'A desire for filtering flutherbombers' incessant chatter is understandable,' Vör concedes.

'Many thousands of nurses flutherbomb Ben. None ever report gaps in access,' Teo baits, suspecting Vör has it in for Ben for some reason.

'His hancy hoots are custom,' Vör says, 'unavailable for anyone other than his family. This is suspicious.'

I say for a reminder, 'We have no complaints from a single flutherbomber about shut-out or loss of sensory quality.'

'Flutherbombers almost always say the opposite,' Teo adds and giggles. 'They say Ben's fluther is so high-fidelity, you can smell his son farting in the next room.'

'Ben is sick,' Vör says. Teo makes a face for me meaning, *See!* 'He's indolent and withdrawn,' Vör goes on. 'He's hoarding sap relics. 7 hells. He loses his enjoyment of sex, which is ironic considering what he's famous for.'

'So, he's a little unhappy,' Teo says. 'Meanwhile, Consigning him would ruin our reputasi in the process.'

'You have concern for your reputasi?' Vör interrogates, on her elbows and staring Teo down. 'Besides, one never tastes how the Reckoning calculates.'

Teo laughs. 'That's rich, Vör. Perhaps an Infi's daughter is more likely covetous for razoos.' A low blow from Teo, reminding Vör about her mother. Teo rolls away and sits up. 'Vör, we all want Infinites well,' she says. 'But this Ben ... there's something personal in it for you.'

Red

‘The Pushbike Song’ — The Mixtures

Lành Hiền Rồng (Gentle Dragon) ...

NO PEEKING!’ Aisha says as she leads Ben. With hand steadying on the rail, keeping head level for balance, other hand in hers, he takes measured gingerly steps down for the housing hill’s common room. There’s a cooler, less family smell down there. Less love seeps into the paint and throw cushions.

Ben makes like a sap, blind with eyes firmly closed, in accordance with the will of his *one istri*.

‘Never let me go, Aisha. Bones break easy.’

‘I got you lah,’ she membs. ‘I never want you in the clinic ha. Even for hour only while they mend your bones like that lah.’

The last step. Then around the couch; around the kopi table facing the fireplace.

‘Open eyes already,’ Aisha says.

Ben Evoli ...

Blink. A rectangle of turquoise over the mantel piece covers a large section of the fabby-stone chimney. An abstract painting. A visual play of petals and pornography.

‘You like, is it?’ Aisha prods, barely containing her excitement.

‘I, ah ...’

‘It’s *Series I White and Blue Flower Shapes*, by Georgia O’Keefe. A sap artist from 1919.’

'The original?' I ask lamely.

'You *siao ar* (crazy),' she scolds. 'You want nurses all over me? I am no collector, like you. It's fabby, but still …'

'I see what you're trying here.' The parallel with the abominable sculpture on the spooky station forecourt is undeniable.

'I just want you see even saps put secret body parts in art long time ah. When they are true secret like that.'

'I know all this, Aisha.' Placating. 'Much earlier than the 20th century, they put genital symbolism in their cathedrals. Spires like erect kopek. Cathedral doors and internal arches like puki mak.'

'This lovely work of art one. You agree, is it? You like ah.'

'It is lovely. I appreciate you want me feeling better. But the sculpture by the station is a travesty. It's no—'

'The desa honours you,' Aisha says.

'Everywhere I look, this thing is caging me in,' I say, sour. Far sourer than I intend.

'Your soul get old, Bat Ears.' Aisha rests into the couch, somehow takes me with her. Brushes the fringe of my hair back. Futile, because it springs forward immediately. Still, her familiar touch is soothing.

'This again.' I sigh. She thinks I should child again. Regressing into an innocent, playful, curious state, depending as a child on a foster family while they nurture my renewal.

'It's 5 year ah. Precious time away from me and Saf and Mal, true. But, Bat Ears, where your spark? Creativity burn in you like a fever, but you suppress it ah.'

'Jank creativity. The last thing I need is a plague of ideas from nurturing my inner child again. Look where it gets me.'

'Ah, poor Bat Ears. He writes hoots, and billions of people enjoy them,' Aisha mocks.

'They're a golden cage in a zoo where everyone visits and pokes at me.' Why is it I get so morose when Aisha presses me?

'If you keep choke your creativity down, you will douse the flames until there's nothing left lah. Nothing of you left. Just a smouldering, damp inner core and a dull outer husk.' I wonder where Aisha is getting this. The language of my pragmatic istri is never as purple. 'Then where this leave me? And Saf? And Mal?'

'Aisha, maybe I have no spark left.'

'Walao eh! You want throw everything away. Throw me away. Your anak anak. Take a nutepak.' … sounds more like the practical Aisha I love.

My intercontinental trip today is no more complex than travelling for the next desa. The same journey for Kolombo in sap times would require 30 mins by train for the airport (including a change at Central Station); then a tedious process of document and identity verification, registration, and security checks. Then you'd wait while they assemble hundreds for boarding a single plane which leaves only at certain times in accordance with a rigid pre-set timetable. Never miss the plane or it might be days before the next one. The flight for Kolombo took 9 hours assuming it's a direct flight with no stopovers. After landing and disembarking (which itself takes more than 30 mins), there's a reciprocal steeple chase of security checks. Then waiting for your luggage from the hold of the plane. Then waiting in line for transport for your final destination.

Which trip requires the greater madness, the greater ignorance of dangers? Hurtling for hours, many 1000's of metres in the air in a metal tube with 1000's of tonnes of high-combustion fuel? Or walking into an energy field of multi-dimensional geometry and somehow emerging out another field; any limitless distance away; by the grace of onespace, AgniSpace and the collaboration of a service team of missionaries. Instantaneous but frightening if y'all contemplate it. Mess up the destination vectors—even a little—and incomprehensible disaster awaits.

Y'all neos enjoy a liberty none of our ancestors ever had. In an instant I will meet a friend 8000 kims away.

For lunch.

Although our desa's spooky station is small—being only a short tukky ride from the bustling hub under the bridge at Luna Park—it is one of the prettiest and most modern. By the architect's cunning, environment sails, walls, structural components, and windows all present as integrated features in 7 shards. Arranged at regular angles around the central bowl for a single spooky field, they are delicate, multi-storey, scintillating, light-refracting and cicada-wing-like, reaching high above as if, with a few beats, they might lift the whole station for the sky.

Inside is much lighter than y'all might expect; there are more windows high in the structure than apparent from outside. Yet even in strong sunlight, the interior bathes in the violet glow emanating from the steamy field dwelling in a shallow 20-metre bowl-shape depression in the floor. Towards the bowl, the floor slopes gently down like a wide beach for the sea. As I step calf-deep in the bowl, the station's tepee roof appears as if opening out, admitting a supernatural white plasma light.

The field's effects intensify; as I drift deeper, they reach my heart. A weightless spin follows a heavy numbness. Time is the first of the fourspace illusions that disappears (3 dimensions of space + time = fourspace); beginning and end joins with a universal Möbius strip of infinite, instantly present still-frames. Swiftly they fade. Intense rays of omni-chromatic light curl and arc around the infinite dimensions of onespace. I desiccate into fine fractal sugar and dissolve into the black tea of the universe, egoless and conjoining. Down here—beneath the mental reinforcements of our neural meat—rests nude reality: one magnificent cradle-valley of relationship where otherness and there-ness are thin, smoky ghosts dancing over a primordial lake. There is no breath here, yet it takes mine away. Every nerve ending feels like it has a feather tickling it. I am almost at orgasm.

According to onespace physics, nothing moves—at least not in any way our fourspace-constructing senses might comprehend. Yet there I am in Bandar Melambai on ancient Cammeraygal Country in Sydney, Australia, and here I am in Kolombo, Sri Lanka.

I memb Dilan, 'I just arrive at Kollupitiya Station.' I taste him farther inland in Kafe Heladiv, perching on a stool, leaning against a wall, sipping dirty liquid from a tall glass.

'Why spook for Kollupitiya?' Dil membs. 'Baseline Road would be quicker.'

'You know me: any excuse for smelling the ocean and feeling a sea breeze.'

'And avoiding the humidity.'

In the station's atrium, grey-gold sunlight thick as custard, globs in through soaring solarglass windows. I skip out outside. After the neutral cool of the station, the steaming, sticky atmosphere is more palm sugar and chicken fat than air. It adheres on the skin, even so near the ocean. Dil is 2 kims inland.

Around the station forecourt, tukkies are jostling like waltzing toasters for winning customers among the arrivals. In the mêlée, one wails as something in it breaks and it must call for a tow-away.

'Aiyo! Is every tukky in Sri Lanka here?'

'Suppose they are for you since you are the only Infinite around. There's no beat nurse on the look-out?' Dil membs.

'No one visible. Wait. There are 2.' Among the melange of colours, the nurse's rainbow uniforms glow dull in the thick light. Old for beat nurses, they wear worn fatigues. Utility belts scuffed and limp. Missing kit. Even for nurses they are low reputasi. One's sporting an unshaven chin, caring nothing for a health missionary's regulation androgynous look. Her jaw slackens, her eyelids flutter. She's deep in onespace, I expect contacting tukky missions for clearing the traffic jam.

A local girl rolls up on an old pushbike, dismounts and shyly offers it. The bike appears functional. Chrome work is tarnishing. Rust and flaky paint everywhere. The girl takes a risk approaching an Infinite; some will interpret it as a play for reputasi and judge against her.

Accepting the rickety old thing, I say, 'I promise I'll pass it on for a good home when I finish with it.' Plant a foot on the pedal, swing a leg over the frame, get rolling. The girl claps her hands with happiness. Jumps around like a kangaroo on a pogo stick on a trampoline, reckoning on getting a new bike on the back of higher reputasi. Maybe I should send her a new one but for the message it sends about sucking up to Infis.

Memb Dil: 'I'm biking it up.'

'Really? Must be a real jam there.'

'Take a look, if you like.'

'What? Join your fluther? Never in your life. It's a weirdo zoo in there.'

'I keep offering you filters for turning the taste down.'

'Bah, my flutherbombers are enough.'

'Be there in about 7 or eight mins.'

The route for the café snakes through the health district busy with rainbow uniforms. Nurses muse at the Infi on an old bike.

Clinics, teaching faculties, and nurses' lodges abut the streets. They would crowd over them but for the modern aesthetic for curving higher stories back from the vertical. The buildings appear ever new, with the nano-level spikiness of their construction materials that repel moisture, dirt, fungus, and bacteria. Atop every roof and visible from the street, environment sails the shape of cicada wings reach for the sky and refract light as colourful as opals. Pylons reach down from rooftops like spindly legs, framing polygonal solarglass windows and veinous translucent walls. Behind the windows, rooms appear as stacks of glowing larvae sacs.

Up ahead, blocking the street, a tall paraboloid weather net contains a bacterial demolition site. One of the last concrete buildings in the district.

Scatter nets, weather nets, sucky bins, fabbies, spooky stations: all applications of the spooky physics model of onespace. Scatter nets disrupt sensory perceptions; weather nets capture particulates in the air; sucky bins take care of our waste and provide recycled materials for fabbies; fabbies produce much of our food, clothing, and shelter. And spooky stations, well … they're the ultimate drug high. One tik, a place surrounds you; the next tik, a different place—as if the universe, in the blink of an eye, tears down one movie set and replaces it with another. Movie sets? Oh, gog *movie*. It's a sap thing.

Neo technology begins and ends with spooky technology. Look what it dispenses with: planes, trains, automobiles, mobile phones, mobile homes, home theatres, pens, paper, books, frozen chooks, bitumen, fake plastic trees, aluminium smelters, palm oil plantations, satellites, warning lights, microwaves, Mexican waves, crime waves …

… and most laundries.

Every so often you must stop and marvel at it. Each time you throw waste in a sucky bin, an equivalent number of molecules turn up in any number of feedstock bins. A mechanical description, which says the waste passes through a chain of spooky fields that separate and distribute raw materials for feedstock is, at best, a magic-trick misunderstanding of a metaphorical dream. Nothing in the spooky model describes movement of material. It merely describes applying energy for making things disappear and reappear in controlled ways. Strong spooky theory says, nothing moves, ever. Metaphysics says there is nothing there in the first place, meh. Saps—with their linear fourspace mindset—would explain spooky fields as teleporters, or something of the same kind. Nothing is farther from the truth, though it's hard finding an accurate description when even modern language bakes in fourspace as a presupposition. Fourspace is a perceptual product of the evolution of brains, not a raw material. Those chains of spooky fields? A slightly better explanation may be, the spooky fields fold over each another in onespace, but *fold* is a fourspace construct as well. The Hindus were right; life is an illusion.

For skirting the demolition site, I take the next side street and emerge on a wider avenue bordering Viharamahadevi Park. Pump the bike peddles, glad for the nano structures in my sweat-eating clothes. Approach a huge intersection. The café is in a row of one- and two-storey squat buildings like blocks of honeycomb under the wings of bees.

Crowding at the kerb, an attitude of twentagers waits, all hoping for the bike. I dismount, choose one of the few girls hanging back, and give over the old thing. Her excitement rivals the girl at the station. I disappoint 14's of others.

Green-walls of ferns. Edible leaves and herbs fence the perimeter of the café's outdoor seating. Hydroponic irrigation hisses as it sprays fine jets of nute-rich water. Nestling behind, umbrella trees shade outdoor tables where a handful of customers take cold drinks and light snacks. Beyond those, an ageing sign naming the café swings from the last screw attaching it on the front window. When is the last time I see signage? Every desa at home bans street signs, building labels and advertising hoarding. With good reason: it's ugly and unnecessary. If y'all are curious for the name of anything, just jel it.

Through the door, a long bar stretches toward the back. Opposite is a single row of tables for four. In between is a passage just wide enough for a single waiter with a tray.

Dil will be out back in the larger squarish area hooking behind the jewellery mission next door. An array of tables, three and four deep, surrounds a bar in the middle. In the near corner is a stage—nothing more than a tiny platform, a single step up from the floor—over which a holly of a muso from who-knows-where is taking requests. At her feet is a holly of an open guitar case. Floating over it is an old poker-machine-style rolling counter displaying her reputasi, and a faux neon sign in blues and pinks of the performer's name: Dusty Perkins. Dusty's mouth is moving, and her fingers are caressing strings, but I hear nothing of her; there is a sound field enclosing a space around the stage.

Navigate around the bar; skip towards Dusty's corner. Feel a pin-wheel tickle on face and hands; push through the thin gelatinous sound field. Dusty finishes a song, adjusts the tuning of her top strings, and launches into a new tune. From the drawl of the lyric and the guitar-playing style, I'd guess she's from Texas. No one here pays her much Mind, but her razoos keep climbing. The counter is more for stage effect: movements in her reputasi will never track her immediate performance—unless the rumours are true, and there's something amiss with the Reckoning.

In the opposite corner, a cloud of hollies report news, current affairs, and sporting events. Up near the ceiling, a ticker scrolls headlines.

MORE QUAKE ACTIVITY IN CALIFORNIA.
MISSIONS SAY BRACE FOR THE WORST.

Dil typically is near the news hollies. About a third of the way over I push through another electric tickle. Miss Dusty and her guitar fade away.

Dil pops off his barstool. Greets me. 'Benjamin! The Infi arrives. Look at your damn aura.' His tongue and lung is at least twice the joy of hearing him memb. His sing-song voice, the lilt and cadence of his words, the even clip of his consonants. No memb carries the subtle fidelity of sound waves in physical fourspace.

'*Machan!*'

Hugs and back slaps. Deep laughing. He is small but when he laughs, he laughs so deep y'all would believe it comes from underground. His lungs are limestone caves tunnelling through his feet into the bones of the earth.

More back slaps. Over his shoulder on the table, two glasses glisten in the low light. One is half full of a thick, milky-charcoal liquid.

Step back from our embrace. 'Are you still drinking those cricket shakes?'

'Are you still grazing cattle for slaughter in your desert provinces? Are you so rich you can avoid insects in your diet? No, wait; you eat only tofu and salad down there. Duckweed in everything.' He appears he might spit.

'Insects and soybeans. We would starve without them. Or else eat fabby food every day.'

'Ah, your fabbies are so good, there's no telling the difference.'

'Real food is still better.' I memb the bartender for saké. She blinks me a menu. I flick out a holly of it and tip it flat on the table.

'Drinking at lunch?'

Shrug. 'It's passing beer o'clock at home.'

Memb the bar with an order of saké and a pot of aya tea. 'Hey, favour me?' I ask.

'Sure,' Dil says.

'Blink the singer a razoo? I would but, you know, it could trigger an avalanche of attention.'

Dil blinks the razoo. Dusty abruptly stops playing, squeals and stomps her feet. Her reputasi spinner is a blur of ascending numbers. She's like an ecstatic beauty pageant winner, crying. Picks up her things and flicks her holly off. Her guitar case flashes out of existence too.

'Hey, we are listening!' some Uncle Kiah from a table near the stage membs.

The bartender flicks up a holly browser, scrolls through a bunch of options and selects one. A new singer/guitar-player, in mid song, appears on stage.

'Celaka!' I swear. 'Are you noticing any strange behaviour from the Reck of late?'

'It's all strange with me.'

'It should retard updates and smooth out any sudden spikes.'

Dil shrugs. 'My reputation is a flatline, as ever.'

'Jank. Some will believe I cause this.'

Dil sips on his bug juice. 'We are here about your coronation, royal sir.'

'Will you stop it?'

'Well. Just tell me you are going,' Dil says.

I hesitate and Dil paints exasperation all over his face.

I say, 'You think after 4 years' of postponing, I might be ready.'

'The more you postpone, the less you are ready.' Dil sips water from his second glass, washing his shake down.

'I am going this time. For Aisha.'

'Good for you. And a relief for me. You know she tries recruiting me for it many times.'

We sit in silence for a min, eyes staring without focus over the shoulder of the other. The ticker scrolls:

WORLD POPULATION RISES FOR FIRST TIME THIS CENTURY.
HITS 5 BILLION.

Dil sucks in a breath. 'There must be thousands of nurses assessing your health. What would they make of you always delaying your induction?'

'There's little point in me worrying about avoiding nurses.'

'For avoiding nurses, we must be the Goldilocks of everything. Neither too compliant, nor too individual.'

'Too rich nor poor.'

'Too dead nor alive.'

'Too male nor female.'

'Shhhh!'

Stern looks of stony gargoyles from the customers at the next table, disapprove of our talking tongue and lung. They must be over 200 years old and wear a presumption of authority only the elderly without any real power can wear.

SPORT: GUNAWAN OUT OF FOOTBALL FINAL ON PRIDE WARNING.

'It's what the health missionaries wish for,' Dilan supposes. 'Everyone in the Goldilocks Zone.'

'All Goldilocks and no bears.'

'No bulls either.' Dil's mood sours. 'Who knows with nurses? Warrants come out of nowhere.'

Awkward silence breaks when the tea arrives. I say, hoping without making it an accusation, 'They Consign you with reason, Dil. You join a Chan.'

'I am better now. *Everyone should join all sorts of organisations, no matter how ridiculous, to get more people in their life, even if all the other members are morons*—Kurt Vonnegut.'

Grab the teapot handle; pause. Pour the aya, taking care against letting the rising surface ripple. 'Well, you took him for literal about the morons. Only morons try hacking nurses' hancies. If you wish for disrupting them, you should see me. I'm a mindwriter.'

Dil's eyes pop. 'You're serious? You, of all people, Ben … you could swing the balance of power—'

'Alamak! No.'

'We need someone clipping their wings. Tell me the health missionaries are no de facto government.' A grating topic between us. Dil always brings it up. 'They control *Hisab*, Ben. It's no mad conspiracy theory. It's truth. Neos still send Infis razoos. Infis! Their razoos are infinite, before and after, and nothing can change that. So where go the razoos neos still send them, Ben? Where go the razoos?'

'Are nurses controlling Dusty Perkins's sudden reputasi rise?' I wonder if Dusty will ever again mission as a musician.

Like most of y'all, Dil assumes some mechanistic arithmetic accounting exists for the razoos we award each other. The idea of unaccounted razoos going anywhere is completely false, because it all is unaccountable. That's the point. The Reck—or *Hisab* as they call it in Sri Lanka—remaining a mystery is paramount for defeating anyone gaming it. Which is why, if I am honest, the sudden rise in Dusty's reputasi after Dil votes her a razoo is unsettling. It helps little in convincing Dil (and too many of y'all) there are no shenanigans. Y'all so love conspiracy theories. There's no preventing Dil's inevitable conclusion: 'Into nurses' pockets,' he concludes. 'That's where the razoos go.'

Dilan Chandrasiri …

Ben's right: jamming nurse's hancies is moronic. But they ask for it. Their hancies are so primitive. Inevitable they would come with their Warrant. Why would I even run? Stupid, running. Tripping; falling three storeys; landing on a guard rail. Vertebrae C7-T2 cracking; spinal cord crushing. Health missionaries repair it, of course. However, a statistically insignificant number of spinal cord injuries leave debilitating pain. One of the few things about physical health which is still a mystery. So this's me: statistically insignificant.

He's giving me that look—assessing how bad it is with me. I wish he'd ask. I wish he'd gog it. Gawd knows he has the power. I can't tell him anymore. I feel like I'm yesterday's rescue mission.

I have no regrets for my Chan days, or the Cures in various minsters around the globe. No regrets either for the injury. Only, the pain …

I still want the truth: who really calculates reputasi? Who really decides who needs a Cure? The health missionaries fill the governmental gap in our society, in league with the AgniSpace camerati. Look at the control they have, operating all the bioelectronics connecting hancies. Without them, there's no gogging last year's *Duruthu Perahera* or jelling anyone's cousin's boyfriends' names. Tell me there is no temptation for exploiting it. Of course there is. And they're manipulating the whole reputation culture; skimming razoos, especially from Infinites. It's all too easy. Nothing is accountable because *Hisab* is inscrutable. Ask; who are the last ones altering it? The nursing missionaries! When they impose Infinite status on the hyper-influential. Saying it's for thwarting their ever-escalating obsessions with league tables. They all want to be at the top. But where are all the razoos going?

LATEST CELEBRITY WARRANT FOR GREED OVER SECRET GOLF COURSE

A golf course? It's just a big back yard. They say it's a symbol of exclusion, of Pride, Greed even, but hey! Folks could go swimming there, could build sandcastles. There's no security keeping anyone out. The local council are already reclaiming the land. Why still it Warrants a Cure? Tell me there's nothing else going on. With the right connections I would investigate. With the right connections …

'One tik,' Ben says. His jaw slackens; eyes roll back; lids flutter—busying with his gigantic fluther (his aura is tastable from blocks away). I could be plotting poison for him, and he would fail the noticing. Ben is a hostage of his own popularity. And he's going spare about the Gala. Better get it over with or we'll be grating about it again next year.

WARRANTS ON THE RISE.
HEALTH CAMERATI JUSTIFY CRACK-DOWNS.

Ben's eyes cease flickering as he comes back into the room. 'Running with a Chan; the whole passage in your life … it's sad,' he says.

'There's no need for feeling sad.'

'Well, you know … look, I support you. Sometimes, I lose pemahaman—'

'Speak English, Ben. We still speak Regal English here in Sri Lanka.'

Ben's saké arrives. He pours from the *tokkuri*. 'Why should we speak Regal English? Where were the English when the Oceania economies failed?'

I say, 'Being annexed by Scandinavia,' basting the words in mockery.

'Fortunate for them.'

I muse, 'The subcontinent is the last bastion of English culture.'

'I think the English would disagree,' Ben says.

'Ah, they were always Vikings. Ask them when you arrive at Kensington Palace.' No bite from Ben. 'You are going, yes?'

'I need no target on my head, *machan*.'

'There's already a huge target on your head. Refusing your induction 4 years in a row is what makes you a target. You're an Infi and you'll never be other again. Standing separate from them makes you truly alone, *machan*.'

Nilajani Karunanithi ...

When I first come in, there are vacant tables all around. The café's lunchtime rush builds. Only a few seats left: the usual mix of customers, mainly nurses wearing civvies. The café's just far enough out of the nursing district so some lay folks venture in also.

Sip aya tea. It's my free day, but mission is mission. It gives life meaning. Besides, I'm good at it. With the easy eye of training, scan the auras of the patrons. Some vivid, some pale; a few almost transparent; some revolving like gentle clouds; others are roiling surf crashing on a beach. There are no faces in there, of course. Any time y'all think you're seeing a face in an aura, your brain's pattern-matching overtime, seeing objects in rainclouds.

An aura over by the wall sparks and flashes like thunderstorm activity. Flutherbombing him: Dilan Chandrasiri, a Sri Lankan journalist, activist, and addicted conspiracy theorist. Unsurprising, he has quite a health record, a history of Cures. A physical injury too; spinal cord damage, which he suffers while resisting a Consignment. Why would he resist nurses assuming custody for him? We have his best health at heart.

Trauma injuries are repairable; a few kinds of spinal damage, as in Dilan's case, never fully heal. Interesting: minor scleroses of brain tissue too. Nutes might heal some of the damage by culturing doublecortin-positive cells at the lesion sites, if he takes them regular—which I doubt, tasting his current brain chemistry. Picking up elevations of cortisol and noradrenaline. He would tend towards paranoid thinking. I'd recommend taking more omega-3 fatty acids; vitamin D; valerian root; L-theanine; maybe 5-HTP—all easy-access in custom nutepaks from a clinic. Longer term, he will require another Cure. He should take more exercise, perhaps learn a musical instrument. Play more.

His fluther activity increases; his aura blooms into a canopy over his table.

A huge aura: tendrils writhe throughout the café. Readjusting my focus. Every other aura fading in the sunlight the aura projects.

For a tik everyone stops as if taking root in the floor or in chairs. Elf-consciousness simmers among all the customers. *What to do? What to do? Join the fluther? Leave? Can we stay? Act natural. Just act natural. Watch out for nurses! There must be 1000's in that storm-cloud of an aura. And more than a few lurking among the physical crowd. Oh, 7 hells. If we are careless, we could earn a Cure.*

Why is Ben Evoli—one of the most famous Infis of Indo-Malaysia—in our local health-district café?

Ben meets Dilan, the neo I am just now observing. A curious pair: the Infi and the one-time anti-nursing activist. Ben asks Dilan, tip the on-stage musician. 7 hells; the musician's reputasi skyrockets. What's wrong with the janking Reckoning?

Violet

'Separation Anxiety' — yeule

Teodora Mrowka ...

I derive no pleasure pouring scorn on Vör, but she lacks the inner harmony for appreciating the heart of our camerata. She thinks in chains of command, whereas a camerata, by its very definition, is an egalitarian bonding of peers, devoted for open enquiry and individual agency. She's emotional, unpredictable, and sees everything in us-versus-them, black and white. Y'all might wonder if she believes in old-fashion good and evil.

And she dreads spooking. A nurse, no less. As if she's some sap whose brains might ooze out her ears on her next spook. She side-eyes every sucky bin as if its field might break containment and swallow her up. I wonder how she remains calm under minster scatter nets. She's obsessive; sailing close for a Cure. Yet Eir coddles her.

There she is on the concourse of Reykjalundur Station in Mosfellsbær on the outskirts of Reykjavík, Eir's hometown. Due within the hour at the graduation ceremony for this year's class, Eir fusses over calming Vör. Y'all see them hugging? Vör soft and yielding, her ear planting against Eir's bony chest. Eir brushes Vör's hair in an awkward display of affection. Pats her rump.

Eir breaks the embrace. Vör stands there in an awkward orbit, a skinny little sprite with shaggy light brown mouse-fur. Eyes resting their focus somewhere just ahead of her nose. Under Eir's gaze she habitually adopts a slight round-back stoop which gives the impression her head and shoulders are for sheltering her heart from rain.

Eir takes her hand. They skip for the departure hall while commuters all around make way for the famous towering albino nurse and her companion.

All except for an overdose of spookheads—half staggering, half dancing—who almost collide with Eir and Vör. The group splinters, some striking for the café. Hungry, I suspect, from the effects of an all-night spooky crawl. Celebrating a birthday perhaps. Vör—never hiding her disgust of spookheads—wrinkles her rodent nose.

In the departure hall, violet light bathes over the 2 detectives and 14's of others wading into the spooky field basin. The field is a misty witch's brew in a shallow cauldron. Before Eir and Vör reach the thick of it, those spookheads are at the edge of the basin, making so much more noise than is polite in public. Probably hallucinating. While the spookheads push past, Vör steps back until the violet gas is below her knees. She looks whiter than Eir, a frozen popsicle in the rainbow wrapper of her uniform, resenting the prospect of sharing the field with the spookheads. One of them turns and laughs; spirals a finger out from her temple. 'Grow no horns,' she taunts. Purple mist puffs around her and sucks her in.

Vör Hoyur …

I need no spookheads knowing my vectors or, worse, loitering in my fluther. I need no sticky transpersonal connection with any. I will need a hot shower before the graduation ceremony. My skin is crawling.

'Little Mermaid,' Eir says, her hand on my elbow. 'Just pat the horse. Remember your training.'

Deep breath, turn inward after the last of spookheads vanish through the spooky field. Every step I take towards the field is like walking on sharp knives. My hand goes for my uniform's kangaroo pocket, reaches for a nutepak.

'Vör,' Eir warns, a mother about to count to 3. She tries covering her disappointment. Sighs.

Pick the nutepak; tear open the foil; and suck down the gel. Calming. Sorry, Eir. 'Kay, I'm ready.'

'You're almost chicken drunk with those nutes,' Eir scolds.

Skip down near the edge of the violet haze. The floor is a beach sloping for the ocean of the spooky field. Mist turns foggy; the concave walls of the hall twist back all around like collapsing headlands of a mysterious coastline. Another 28 metres, the event horizon of the field thickens. Toss the empty nutepak. Without personal DNA marking, the spooky field will suck the unconscious material into local feedstock bins.

Prepare for the moment. I hate this. Always have. Irrational. Fearing the field will tangle me in a wall, the ground, another person at the other end.

Clutching Eir's hand, I take another step and meet infinity.

Eir Frijberg ...

Careful where the ocean currents take y'all, my fluther, my jellyfish. You may wash up on a hot beach where uncaring midsummer partiers may throw you on a bonfire. If you persist on stinging Vör's heel, I will crush your head. Then what good your tentacles?

Fluther is such a funny word. Just the sound of it suggests a kind of ungainly flight, aimlessness, helplessness at the will of forces greater than your own. *Fluther*: it might reduce me for tittering; one of the silliest of the collective nouns; as silly as a *cavvy* of cowboys or an *asylum* of drummers (leave your drummer jokes at the stage door, I beg).

Fluther (noun): a congregation of people visiting the Mind of another for the purposes of witnessing actions and environment. Sight and sound; and for some degree—with enhancement technology—touch, taste, and smell. Also, biometrics—again with the right hoots in your hancy. Thoughts sometimes too if the person is loud enough with their internal dialogue. One might add:

Flutherbombing (noun): a pastime of unsolicited fluther-joining for entertainment, spying, voyeurism, or harassment.

I make no judgments. Take too dim a view of flutherbombing and we'd need an aid couch for everyone alive. Besides, it remains a detective nurse's prime method for gathering evidence.

Fluther. You lurking witnesses of my life share your collective noun with jellyfish. There y'all are, drifting on the tides of onespace; leading with your umbrella-shape bells which pulsate for locomotion. Tentacles trailing. Tentacles sometimes poisonous. As a congregation y'all resemble sap social networks, which I'm sure consisted entirely of semi-toxic jellyfish. Perhaps tentacles are necessary for forming those networks. Our fluthers are the most intricate social networks in human history.

So, my attentive smack of jellyfish; about Vör: keep your tentacles, toxic or otherwise, away from her. I taste who among y'all judge her harsh. Review your own motivations. Cleanse yourelves of Envy, and trust I choose well in choosing her.

Vör develops. True, she is yet for trusting her place in her mission, and it sometimes overwhelms her. But trust me; her moon is rising over the onespace ocean.

Teodora Mrowka ...

In the dim glow of the circular auditorium, no one finds *Detektiv Sygeplejerske* Eir Frijberg. It's an old trick she plays over and again, demonstrating how ably she empties herelf of Mind. She is untastable—for all the 343 graduating nurses of our *Sundhed* Camerata, their 700 or so guests and the many 1000's of others flutherbombing in. While in the deepest of meditative states, she could be within the hall or without. Anticipation of her appearance rises.

No one present enjoys reputasi within a 7ᵗʰ of a 7ᵗʰ of hers. All are whispering the *I* word, speculating Eir's razoos will continue accumulating, faster and faster, until the Reckoning must designate her as the first health mission Infinite. An Infinite nurse? Many nurses hope for it. Many more fret over the threats it forebodes.

'Why care?' Vör membs, sounding like an out-of-tune fabby violin. 'Your reputasi rises on her mission cap badge.'

I shudder. 'As if you have no interest in Eir's fortunes.'

'My interest lies only in bringing the sick the care they deserve,' she says. *Bre!* In the landscape of Vör's care, there's a moat around her and Eir. Everyone else is on the other side.

Frida Kjaergaard ...

For our graduation day, Skaði dusts snow from the heavens, commanding one more day of winter. With eager chattering teeth we scurry under the weather nets from Trelleborg Museum Station. Ahead, the Jørd Processpil Hal looms like a flat pumpkin with a huge tagine sitting on it for a roof. The solid timber building (a material deserving controversy, I agree) glows with warmth under the cold silver coin of the afternoon sun. I shiver and skip faster for the nearest doors rather than circle round to the correct entrance for our floor allocations.

Inside, the air is grainy with incense. The wide mezzanine level circling the bowl of the theatre is swarming with fresh dress-uniforms. Graduates buzzing amid friends and family. The alert sounds. Lights flash.

We take our places 4 tiers down on the green ring. Down one tier on the blue ring, graduates and guests step over and around each other, and settle on floor cushions. Closer around the circular stage, the lower indigo and violet rings are almost empty, being for dignitaries and special guests. They will fill at the last possible tik.

'Is she here?' Anders says leaning in, craning left and right, surveying the concentric galleries and the circular stage.

'Expect you'll spot her?'

'No. Because she is nowhere,' he says. *She* says. After 5 years, Anders is a nurse; I should remember my friend earns the female pronoun.

Anders slaps her thighs, her excitement and impatience getting the better of her. 'Where is she?'

'Who knows with the White Witch?'

Anders hisses. 'Never call her this.' He's always the one fearing for his—*her*—reputasi. Her razoos.

Who knows where Eir is? She could be 2 shoulders away, reclining head-for-toe with our classmates, hiding in the camouflage of the upholstery and scatter cushions. She could be strolling the mezzanine above. She could be hovering high under the roof on a White Witch's broomstick for all I taste. Swooping above the congregation.

Change the subject. 'Will she call we surrender our shells?' I ask, using the ritual term for removing our clothes, in recognition of the futility of hiding our fruits.

'Why bother? We already see each other 100's of times before.'

'You no longer flutherbomb me in the shower.'

'My point exact. I already see all there is for seeing.'

Anders and I never have sex. I'm unsure who puts who in the friend zone first, but it's mutual. Which is a relief. In a class of over 300, it's good having someone you never sleep with.

'It's a long day,' Anders says. 'And she'll be late.'

'Well, after the keynote, it's all over. You can go home and have a good night's rest on your family's bat farm—'

'Quail farm.'

'As you wish.' So, I call his family mission a bat farm … joking is the best way for venting about raising animals for meat and avoiding a potential Cure. A 3rd of the class has at least one Cure during the years of studying here.

Why must anyone farm animals for food? I mean, what are meat vats for? At a pinch, most kitchen fabbies can produce reasonable substitutes—without all the gizzards, sinews, bones, and fatty bits. You can fab a chicken tasting of whale, or a block of wood tasting of lobster bisque, monkey brains with the perfect texture of … well so I hear. So, what purpose a farm? Raising animals for slaughter is so … it's sap is what it is.

'It's our mission,' Anders says, divining my train of thought and thus shutting down any criticism of his family's meaning for their lives.

Change the subject: 'Tomorrow we'll be on mission! Fully qualified nurses!'

The lights dim and drain the colour out of everything. The audience hushes waiting.

'Hello. This is Eir.' Her voice! Speaking tongue and lung instead of membing, she chooses using the legendary acoustics of the hall. We hear her clearly from here. Her voice carries up for the mezzanine and out the exit doors. Maybe beyond. Peradventure, for the sake of her vocal cords, she plans a short address.

'There she is!' Anders points.

She appears centre stage as if straight out of onespace. Wild and deafening applause erupts by the clapping of hands. Breaking with tradition, she wears a simple colourless robe which, in the chiaroscuro of the space, reflects the rainbow colours of the surrounding uniforms and furniture.

About 100 officials kneel and sit around her, close enough for touching. She reaches out, stroking fingers and palms. She is wiry, impossibly tall. Her iconic white hair hangs free almost to the backs of her knees. Her piercing pink eyes are bright embers in her pale angular face. She raises her arms, half in wave, half from pride. Justifiable pride.

Young again in Eir's presence, the hall gives up a scent of fresh-hewn timber. Bashful, Eir puts her hand before her face and giggles. Playful.

'Oh *ja!*' she projects with the sound of her voice. '*Make a joyful noise. Let seas roar and everything in them; the world and those that dwell! Let the rivers clap their hands; let the hills sing for joy ... together.*' She pauses. 'Please, greet your neighbours, your fellow graduates. Greet them now, *ja*. Use your voice! Use your tongue and lungs, use your whole fruit. Vibrate!'

A cacophony of movement—a dance of voices erupts in the space under the tent-shape ceiling. We lean, swirl round, stand. Greeting each other. Eir lifts her hands, clicks her fingers—louder than if the ceiling timbers crack. Palms up, she acknowledges the vibrating air. 'Use your breath; your lips; your face; your arms and legs; hands; fingers and toes. Use all your physical space. It is good, *ja*? Revel in it ... but never too much. Risk no Cures so soon after your graduation.'

Quick laughter like chittering birds. Eir giggles, falls silent. Unsteady for a tik with wobbly knees, she staggers, and almost trips over nurses sitting around her. For support, she rests her hand on the head of one sitting cross-legs nearby—her fawning adjutant Vör Hoyur. We hold our collective breaths while tasting the same word: *dyspraxia*. Please, let Eir finish her address in dignity. She crouches, sits on a cushion on the stage floor, back-for-back with Vör. The audience hushes.

'The 4 dimensions of space and time are direct and intense,' she says, quiet and deep. A trick of acoustics makes the hall sound as the one speaking. 'No vicarious flutherbombing experience is sweeter or sharper or heavier or brighter or more orgasmic than physical fourspace. And no fluther is lonelier or colder; or more bitter or more remote; or more painful than a 4-dimensional cage—of tall versus short; broad versus narrow; fat versus skinny—trying to survive down the passage of time.

'And so, it is. As real as the 4 dimensions are, they are the great hallucination. Yet nonetheless, it is. Our fruit—our bodies—occupy it, tune for it as for the finest of instruments. There remains a fundamental truth of our being: no amount of mental presence; of knowing the ethereal bedrock of onespace; of losing ourelves in Mind; of attending or lurking in fluthers can ever separate us from our fruit and the physical ecstasy of fourspace. It is both blessing and damnation which is perhaps the source of all sickness. In joining with others in fluthers, ours are voyeuristic lives separate from our physical incarnations.

'I sit among you, the graduating students of our camerata, *det Fødererede*

Sundhedskamerata i Nordeuropa: the first health mission in neo culture, the first nurses who wear the rainbow fatigues. We explore a simple question: what if we treat Greed as a mental health condition?' Feel the energy rise. We are blooming with pride. 'As is then, those who join us today come from no sense of duty, but for a love of mission. And of course, none come for the reputasi.'

Laugh again. Her reputasi is astronomical and climbing.

Eir pauses as if marking a change. 'Two nurses skip into a bar ...'

Laughter.

'They drink 5 pints of ale each then spend the rest of the night writing Warrants for each other.'

Less laughter.

'*Ja*, it's a lame joke, but you know the statistic. Even with our best efforts of training and protecting ourelves, the numbers of Cures we prescribe for our missionaries are proportionally more than any other demographic. It's easy finding fault in each other, the colleagues you know better than perhaps your own families.

'Some generations ago, tribes of Homo sapiens persecuted people with my genetic condition. Witch doctors of those tribes believed certain body parts of albinos contained magic properties which would bring good fortune. These witch doctors hacked our limbs off; scalped us; used our organs in concoctions and potions ... Without limit, their savagery most desired the parts of children—arms, legs, ears and genitals—for fashioning amulets. Amulets made for easy sale. The witch doctors even exhumed the bodies of dead albinos. Imagine being an albino growing up among these tribes. Imagine, living in constant fear of kidnap, of someone hacking off parts of you, and surviving for next time. You would feel watched every tik of your life, and the next atrocity against you might be only tiks away. You might live for many years before successions of amputations took your life.

'We all taste illness in such abhorrent behaviour. Yet also taste something else. Something which is at the core of all sickness. *Separateness*. In neo culture, we would no more separate ourelves from onespace—the one ocean of transpersonal identity—than we would hack limbs and ears from our own fruit. Yet here we are in fourspace where we manifest as separate physical beings, separate elves. We are one and many—all those things and more—always drifting along the spectrum between complete separateness and complete unity. We who are healthy, move easy along this spectrum. Being stuck too much in fourspace or onespace—resisting easy movement—is being separate.

'We are stuck in our understanding of the ills too, with the traditional 7 kinds. Why must we categorise sickness by the traditional 7 before we might Cure it? Some even debate a hierarchy of the ills, claiming some worse than others. Some say Greed is the most heinous. Others say Envy—the most agency-sapping of all ills—is the source of all the others. But our mission is never about categories. Our mission is alleviating suffering, alleviating pain, whether the pain is Wrath or Lust or Pride.

'So let us let us examine the ills in all multitudes of forms. Outside of categories, ills conform in one significant way. They are all about separation, a need for excessively strong or excessively weak boundaries for the *self.*'

Eir's audience yields a collective gasp at her use of the old sap word.

'*Ja*, we use no such ugly word in polite company, huh? We neos enjoy mocking our sense of ego when we say *myelf* and *yourelf* and *themelves*. So please permit I reclaim the word *self* for meaning this state of separation I am illuminating.'

'Let me say, the 7 ills are an illusion! There are, at once, many, many more than 7, if we dare yield them identity; and also, there are many fewer. Multitudes of identity yields powerlessness; they are too many for healing. The agency of our mission, in our service as healers, relies on seeing the common thread. If we heal the underlying root cause, we heal all the ills in their multitude of identities.

'The ills are simply the assertion or denial of *self* in relation to another, with respect to worthiness, fairness, possessiveness, sustenance, time, passion, and disorder.

'The insight I leave with you on your graduation day is—at the core of all illness, is a compulsive or obsessive need of separateness against connectingness. Another word for this is *dismemberment.*'

 *Vör Hoyur ...*

'Vör, we have word.' It's Teo, from the far edge of the stage. What could be so important in the middle of Eir's keynote?

I memb, 'May it wait?' hissing. 'Just wait. Eir is near the end.'

I sit with my back supporting Eir's, feeling the vibrations of her words through my bones.

'... on the nature of your relationship with your patients. It is, of course, part of your mission you look for illness so you might alleviate it. However, I caution you against defining your mission by a count of Warrants you execute, or by the count of Cures you participate in. Cures have a way of slipping away from you. Clinical history tells of many Prescriptions resulting in adverse health outcomes for patients.

'And so, I give counsel: you must join with your patients in compassion and love rather than performing your techniques and therapies from the distance of judgment. Your patients are more than targets for your craft. A target is an *other*, from which a nurse might stand at a distance and operate on. Regarding a patient as *other* separates nurse from patient. Identifying *otherness* is a kind of sickness. You see how unsafe the 7 Cures are? They give legitimacy to treating *patient* as *other*.'

There are grumbles and squirms among the audience—discomfort from Eir's use of the abominable transactional preposition, *to*. Eir smiles; she knows she's accusing the health mission as transactional.

'The 7 Cures give legitimacy to treating patient as other,' she doubles down. 'Others have sickness while we have none. No! Sickness is in the whole, never the just the part. Sickness is in relationship, never in reducing to us and them. Sickness is a spectrum, never a reduction to simple classifications.

'So, Consign and Cure with compassion. You must first have love for those you would Cure. Compassion and love are the Cures of rending self from other.

'And finally, when you take up your missions for the first time tomorrow, allow yourelf some fun. Play, experiment, engage your glee and curiosity about all things. Experience everything for the first time. Having compassion, fun, care: these are what will save you from making the novice's error of finding illness everywhere you look. A wise nurse never goes looking for illness. Go and be wise nurses.'

The house goes black. A deluge of applause clatters. As the lights brighten again Eir stands, with frail carefulness and my guiding hands. Takes shallow, humble bows with her palms pressing together.

I memb, 'Kay, Teo, what is it?'

'The Infinite Ben Evoli is attending his Inductee Gala,' she says.

Attempt the best for masking my glee. I reply, 'We hear the same last year,' with deliberate sourness.

'We have hollies of him and a friend discussing it a few hours ago. He's reluctant, but his friend persuades him.'

I ask, 'Oh?' innocently, as if such events are beyond my tasting.

Teo hopes I might spill information about whether Eir will write a Warrant for Ben. Careful. Seem less eager. Eir will tell me before her. She has nothing. 'Eir is still considering all the Warrants.' Chew over that. I know more of Eir's Mind than Teo. So let her choke on it.

Indigo

'WANNABE' — ITZY

*Saf Evoli ...*

HOLALA! YOUR AURA!' Amara says. 'A zeppelin is smaller.'
'What's a zeppelin?' Lula membs.

'A balloon about the size of your pantat (bum), *amoi*,' I blink her some zeppelin hollies from a school assignment (Mal sometimes drags me with him for history classes. There is no counting the bodoh stupid ways Mal loves saps).

Lula looks over her shoulder. Pokes her tongue out me. Loses her sense of balance and wobbles her front wheel almost into Amara's pushbike. Amara jags away, her criminally beautiful long hair blowing across her face. Lula's face is chubbier and plainer in the framing of her regent ducktail hairstyle.

'Ha. Your aura is gonna crash into the overpass,' Amara membs. She straightens on her seat and coasts down the road taking us under the derelict railway. When we rehabilitate the area, a ride for the harbour will be easier. In the shadow of the arch, look up. Filthy brickwork chops over the top of my aura until I'm out from under. A swirl of water colours billows free, a balloon on a tether.

'I bet Joselito is flutherbombing you lor,' Amara teases. She rides forward, pumping her pedals.

While keeping eyes on the path kinking and rising ahead, I poke around among my fluther. My friends are speeding away while I'm in my head. Lula is rocking on her pedals, the cheeks of her pantat overhanging her bike seat. She has curves unlike any other *amoi*.

'Yeer, he's there. Ha. Nope, he leaves.'

'He's in mine already lah,' Lula says. Among her smaller fluther, she tastes him easy. 'Watching you from here.'

'Creepy,' Amara membs. 'It's the price of being popular lor.'

I memb, 'It's the price of my Bapa's popularity ha.'

'No spitting on your own polish, Saffron,' Lula membs. 'You have plenty of your own flutherbombers.'

'Followers I never ask for. What to do ah?'

Joselito is the birthday boy. It's his 31st; he's an adult now. Big joke. Shudder for thinking what birthday privileges he might claim tonight.

'Hugs and kisses at the leasty-least.' Lula membs. She reaches the crown of the hill first where a row of restaurants marks the border between our desa and the next. 'He'll ask you for a fire dance tonight.'

For blowing off energy, overtake the others and ride hard. 'Only if he keeps his clothes on.'

'Around the fire, there's no chance any boy will wear clothes like that lah,' Amara membs.

Please understand me: I'm healthy about bodies and nudiness and genders. I am 24, FJS. Wanna guess how many followers watch me nudy? Thankfully, nurses are quick in rounding up any *siao* gropers who need Cures. This's fluthers for you. Followers huddling around, watching, listening. Even getting kinaesthetic, enhancing touch (my tummy-rumbles too, I learn). Almost as sharp as being in my skin. I accept it. I am no prudish sap with stuffy ideas of privacy. My Bapa invents the greatest sex hoot in the history of the world, and that's ghost with me. So, yeer, bodies are ghost with me. *Damn shiok.* 'I just wish boys are more …'

'Modest?' Lula membs.

'Demure,' Amara membs, mocking. 'Less proud of their …'

Three girls on bikes giggling. Pumping the pedals faster, muscles and faces burning.

Down the hill. The Bridge looming, still spanning the harbour after centuries. Well, it's a replica, y'all taste—a faithful copy, except for the modern materials. The original was steel. Steel! Would y'all believe it? Always rusting and needing repair.

At water's edge, you can see under the bridge for the other side. The sails of the Opera House almost look neo, sparkling pink orange under the setting sun.

We swing round and follow an avenue of palm trees for the clown-face gate of Luna Park, where is Joselito's 31st party. I hate passing through its gaping mouth. Eating me. I ride fast under. Ahead, large slippy-slides and other play equipment rim a flat, green spread of an open park. Fires are pouring up from hearths for the sky. Orange waterfalls in upside-down gravity disappearing into invisible overhead weather nets.

'Joselito's is at Hearth 9,' Lula membs.

'It's around left, halfway back,' Amara adds as we pass a wide sandpit surrounding the largest slippy slide on the Lower North Shore.

We wind around fires and parties. Music and chatter. Smells of hawker food. Lula flutherbombs one of her friends for spotting the right hearth.

In an unlit fire pit, bush turkeys scratch in the cold ash. Nearby, a domestic tiger frolics with a tireless blue cattle dog. An amused pair of wallabies watch on. Kangaroos and wallabies always look like they're smiling and sad all at once, like a granny who worries she's hugging her grandkids for the last time. One of the wallabies scratches her belly and nods at us as if to say, *good night for it*. Farther back, another tiger is on her hind legs hugging a bluegum tree. A lyre bird, scratching in the dirt, mimics the tiger purring, and displays a full span of tail feathers. (Bapa calls the way lyrebirds fan their feathers over their heads a trumpian combover. I dunno … something about old sap men growing arse hair so long so they comb it over their bald heads.) Bird and tiger seem a happy couple. It makes me believe anyone can get along. Maybe one day Bapa and Ibu will be as domesticated as tigers.

Beyond the Playground, three pyramid-shape shadows lurk with pretty eyes and lashes. Camels. Suspect Kaboobie will sneak down here during the night.

A beat nurse smiles at us passing. All the while, her eyes flutter in that creepy way when nurses make deep onespace dives. It's blocks alien.

Another nurse approaches and waves. 'Backpack inspection,' she says.

I drop the bike and run for a hug. 'Nurse Intan!' The story is Nurse Intan Sidabutar missions in our local clinic for more than 100 years. Since before my conception, she never wears regulation fatigues, and no other nurse remonstrates her for it. A long time ago when I am only a kid, her sallow old cowhide-wrinkly skin, and glassy eyes, like cages of fireflies, would frighten me. Nurse Intan hugs. I look up at her face. Her leopard markings are fading. The spring coils of her greying hair looser than once they are. She kisses with lips like 2 squashed rubber tubes. In her arms, she feels soft and solid, like a mountain covered in pillows. She is who y'all would get if you cross a nanny with a contract killer.

'*Leng lui*. You carry no nasty nutepaks or drinks ha.' Nurse Intan's voice is deep with authority and care.

Sling my bag off for her. 'No, perawat.' Use my respectful voice.

Nurse Intan works her gentle and thorough way through the contents of our bags. 'Some older anak anak bring cannabinoids and MDMAX. You will take care consuming any of those, yeer?'

Yeer, sure: there's Mad Max at the party and I'll be taking none of it. Nurse Intan pulls 3 nutepaks with long tubes from a thigh pocket of her uniform. She pops one in each of our bags. 'Just in case.'

'Terima kasih.'

'You'll make a wonderful nurse one day, Saf,' Nurse Intan says, beaming with pride. No Pride, y'all understand. Just pride.

We skip our bikes over where others lie with handlebars digging in the grass.

'You'll make a wonderful nurse one day, Saf,' Lula mimics.

I feel warm and loved.

'If you live so long,' Amara says, ruining it.

'You arrive,' Ibu membs from wherever she is on assignment outstation. There's always a disaster somewhere in the world.

'Yeer, Ibu.'

'Where is Mal?'

'Staying at home, for some reason.'

'Okelah. And Bapa?'

'He is out all afternoon. I taste nowhere.'

'Hmm, okelah.'

'Ibu, I think Bapa is sad.'

Ibu memb-sighs. 'Your Bapa is always sad, Saf. It's where he feel most comfortable, fine.'

'I want him happy.'

'Me also lah.'

'Is it me? Do I do anything wrong?'

'You are his sun and moon and planets and stars, sayang.' Smile with my heart. 'I'm sure he will check in with you later,' Ibu membs.

I want for him already.

Grow ups still wear silly full-length hollies. Around the fire are Norse gods and goddesses, tigers on two legs, even some Homo sapiens projections: big ugly muscly hairy monsters. Koalas look okelah, I guess. BirdMe is the most popular. More than half of the lelaki (men) are wearing raptors with heavy beaks for mouths and oversize talons for feet. White-belly eagles, wedge-tails, buzzards. Wanita dress in daintier and prettier feathers. Maybe we are less gender-liquid than we believe. But why the silly costumes? You grow-ups around the satay braziers and eskies think you are so ghost wearing kotoran.

One ibu has a toddler in the pouch of her kangaroo projection. Other babies are in a single enormous crib, sucking thumbs and snuggling together. Their collective aura revolves above them in sweet pastel clouds.

Dancers around the fire are devilish black figures in front of the bright-hot fire. Could be roasting in the heat, judging by the *siao* (crazy) bent-brain way they throw arms around, lift feet and jump. Is the ground on fire? Hard telling girls from boys. Many girls are yet shorter than the boys. Hairstyles are muzzier than ever. Only clothing tells. Girls wear kini bottoms and jewellery. Boys wear nothing at all lah. Flapper-doodles on dancing boys are just giggle-shit.

Amara skips for some girls standing back from the group. Into Bonehead's open arms. Bonehead's my best leng lui too. In the flicky orange light,

Bonehead looks more other-worldly than normal. In normal light she is so pale as if fading away. Already her skin glows like she's the bonfire's source and fuel. Gravity's arms have no comfort for her. At almost 1.8 metres tall, she floats more than rests on the earth. With average payudara (breasts) and narrow hips, her movements are lissom and fluid. Snake-like. Her wispy fashionless hair orbits around her face, eclipsing her flat forehead and the perpendicular cliff of her face: an impression which her enormous eyes accentuate. Fleshy cheeks smooth and serene. A kind round chin of sorrowful beauty. Her mouth always sensually open. Large, bunny teeth resting on the luxurious pillow of her bottom lip. I still daydream of kissing those plump lips, a silliness more romantic than erotic. Around Bonehead I am a little girl clutching at a precious balloon floating away on a spring breeze. My heart aches with it.

I hang back from Amara and Bonehead for some tiks. Lula catches my eye, shrugs and smiles a banana-wide smile.

Younger boys are launching empty beer tumblers up at the weather net trying for tricking it into cutting them in half. They must toss things just right, so an object hovers for a tik and the field has enough time to work. Or so they say. Doubt it is true. There are hollies but anyone can fake anything with mindware. Just ask my bapa.

Skip around the fire with Lula. On the other side, kids are singing while one plays a fabby guitar (mine is better but the player makes up for it) and another runs MusiKai for a backing track. It makes me happy they're using Bapa's hoot. Their auras puff and swirl as their fluthers grow. They're good; their reputasi will rise, though the Reck will notoriously take its time.

Arm-in-arm, Lula, Bonehead and Amara meet me around the fire where there are few dancers. Lula hands me a spare drink. Take it and guzzle thirsty. Low-arak beer. Bonehead hands me a small nutepak.

'What's this?' Turn the pink-and-green metal-foil pack over in my hands. The brand is Chinta & Kelembutan. *Love & Tenderness.* I memb, 'I'll be hugging everyone inside 21 mins.'

'Sure,' Bonehead membs while covering her mouth. 'We'll take care of you.' She wraps her arm around my shoulder and sisterly kisses the top of my head. 'Keep it for later if you like.'

'We take ours already. *Damn shiok.*' Lula giggles and squeezes her thighs together, swings her knees.

'You'll take three before the night is out,' Amara membs, 'and you need it least, *amoi.*'

Lula giggles again, continuing her funny little dance.

The bonfire works its ancient magic, casting spells in crackling and popping whispered words. After a few drinks and a couple of hours, we're hot and sweaty. Lula dances with two boys, Suripto and Mike. Those tennis-ball buah dada of hers bounce and sway. Her nips trance the boys who, powerless for looking anywhere else, are getting thirsty on her. Amara and Bonehead have a boy *bánh mì* between them, his face pressing awkwardly sideways against Bonehead's chest while Amara reaches round him for hugging her. Drink my drink. Swing with the music. Near the fire, I almost cook. Nurses are dancing also, chatelaines clanking. Three are alone; two others mingle with party guests. With the weight of their utility belts, it must be steaming in those fatigues, even with the best sweat-eating cloth. Whatever. I love those rainbow uniforms. I'd almost trade one for my kini bottom but I doubt I have the nurses' stamina. My bare chest is shiny with sweat. Have the Chinta & Kelembutan pack under the elastic of my kini bottom. Save it for later. Sip my beer.

A shadow dances near—a boy with a *nampa* boy haircut, in a goldifilous metal-foil reflecting-coat and cooling-glasses. Only *nampa* boys wear cooling-glasses at night. Jel him. His name is Wono Simalango. A younger boy, Zebedee Dingbang, skips up alongside wearing a leery crapodactile grin. Expecting a girl would swoon in his presence. He's so yaya papaya.

'Hey, it's Saffron. How is Daddy SnakiDik?' Zebedee says tongue and lung.

Frown at Wono. Ignore Zebedee. Sip my beer. Dance.

'Bet you got in your hancy, right? SnakiDik? Your Bapa gives you all the great stuff?'

'Yeer-nah.' Stare into the fire.

'Come on, maybe you load it when he's looking away. I bet you got the latest version. A beta? Experimental? You wanna show me all the new features?'

I smile sweet. 'Oh, there is one.'

'Yeer?' Zebedee suddenly hopey-hopeful.

'It will make you wank yourelf until you're dryer than a coconut husk. I'll let you borrow it if you promise you use it already.'

Zebedee's grin flattens at the corners of his mouth. His eyes dull. Watching boys grapple with emotional computation is ghost. They are so blur lah. He leans in. Coils and stiffens. Points a finger.

'Jalang,' he spits.

'Hey, Zeb. *Sau*,' Wono says, putting his hand on the boy's shoulder, holding him away. 'There's always another girl.'

'Coz your bapa is Infi, you show me disrespect?' Zebedee ignores my aura roiling and swelling over us. Nurses are on alert, grow-ups watchful. Nurse Intan hovers at the edge of the fire.

'Hey, *machan*. Nurses,' Wono says, waving at a rainbow uniform.

Zebedee in my face. 'Nurses stay out of squabbles between kids while parents are around.'

'Come on,' Wono pleads. 'Everyone's watching, *machan*.'

Zebedee drops his accusing finger. Still in my face. I square my shoulders at him. He backs away. Wono has an apology blushing his cheeks. He's trying for hooking eyes with me. I find a log on the fire for staring at. Wono lights off after his friend. The colours drain from Zebedee's aura. Never bright or big anyway, it collapses around his head like a deflating balloon.

Less than 10 mins later, Zebedee is acting bodoh thirsty with Lula already. In her face dancing like he's trying to shake cockroaches out of his underwear. Lula shakes her head and pushes him away.

Zebedee digs his heels into the grass, pushes back, points aggressive at Lula. 'Cow! Lembu!' he shouts out tongue and lung. 'What lelaki would have you with those huge udders? Disgusting lah.'

Aiyo. The perfect way for upsetting Lula, sensitive of her rounder face, curvier fruit and, most of all, her handful-size payudara. Shaming Lula for her curvy figure is the worst nightmare for her. She wishes she is sleek and slim like a normal neo. Sure, she has a figure more like a sap wanita (woman) … if y'all ask me, she's beautiful in a way no one else I know is.

After a brief tik of shock, Lula starts blubbering. Bonehead and Amara cradle and comfort her. Nurse Intan scans for parents who might intervene.

Suripto and Mike, the two boys dancing with Lula before, shove Wono and Zebedee in the chest, pushing them away from my friends. Zebedee slinks away again, and Wono hunts off after him.

'Hey. *Paiseh*,' Mike membs, using the Singlish word for embarrassment. 'He's a monumental cock.'

Lula sputters a laugh.

'Yeer, he should stop ruining our night, then he know,' Suripto membs. He and Mike try cuddling Lula. Bonehead and Amara wrap around either side of her. The boys swallow their disappointment, draw us into a loose huddle. Mike puts an arm around my waist. Accept it already.

Lula takes a deep breath for damming the sobbing. Nurse Intan is there with a nutepak which Lula accepts, tears it open and sucks its contents in deep loud draws while sniffing her runny nose dry.

'I'll be okelah,' Lula membs, standing straighter.

'Come on, let's dance,' Amara membs.

'No!' The sound of a girl's scream from around the fire. Lula. What now?

A holly shared round. Partygoers lashing it and blinking it on. It's short and surgical. Watch in horror before I have the Mind for closing it. Please delete it if y'all receive it. A girl's worst nightmare. Imagine your most embarrassing moments; your most intimate moments; the times you look stupid. Already imagine a holly all those stringing together, images from countless times in ordinary daily life running together in a single holly. Producing something grotesque. 7 Hells! It even has Lula's first bleed in there. Then add flashes of cow udders between flashes of her buah dada, swinging, bouncing. A leer of idiot boys, including Mike, are chanting, 'Cow. Lembu. Cow.'

Please delete it. Delete this holly. Respect Lula. She's my beautiful friend, undeserving of such an ugly joke. For jank's sake, no laughing at her tits.

The party is over. Grow-ups are arguing. Nurses are handing out nutepaks and incant at least one Warrant. The KK (what we local call the Indo-Malaysian Kementerian Kesahatan, our Ministry of Health) broadcasts a deny-list notice for the holly. View it at your own risk. If your intent is bad, trouble will follow y'all.

Lula is inconsolable. Amara gulps back a wail as Bonehead, grinding grim fury into her molars, holds them in her tree-branch arms.

'Please, everyone, stop fighting,' Lula cries as if she is the cause of it all: nurses with their Warrants and villagers casting accusations and razoos against each other. It must be serious, because the Reck is moving in real-time, pushing reputasi in all directions.

I have little care for the idiot boys and their family's ruin, but Lula will always believe it's her fault. Her anguish is making me cry like a bayi also.

'Bapa!' I memb. 'Where are you?'

'Away, cahaya. What is it? Is something wrong?'

'I'm sorry, Bapa, it's important.' Cry. Just cry and wail, you bayi. Be a bayi in front of your bapa. Dungu!

'Breathe, cahaya. Tell me the matter,' Bapa membs, his voice soothing.

Sputter, 'A boy is nasty to Lula here before, calls her cow coz she rejects him.' Bapa is waiting; he knows there must be more. 'Makes her cry. He is nasty to me earlier too. I sent him away.'

'I'm sure it is no fault of yours, cahaya.'

'Dunno, I can take boys saying bad things … you know how Lula gets sad. He only picks on her coz I reject him.'

'How?'

'He makes an awful holly of all her, Bapa. It's awful.'

'I'm gogging for it, cahaya.'

'No! It's on KK's deny-list already.'

'I find it, here it is … oh.'

'It gets worse, Bapa. Grow-ups here start fighting over it.'

'For a huge argument, just start with a birthday or a wedding.' Bapa is funny, y'all think?

Sniffles. 'Nurses are arresting villagers, Bapa.'

'There's no such thing as arrests, cahaya. The nurses are Consigning them for care.'

'They're catting our neighbours and taking them away. The worst is—'

'What is it?' he asks, unable for guessing.

'The Reckoning, Bapa.'

'What about the Reck?' he asks sharp and serious.

'It's … punishing people.'

'That's impossible,' Bapa says in shock.

'It's true. The boy, Zebedee, his parents take the worst hit.'

Bapa says nothing.

'Bapa?'

'Lemme check,' he answers. 'Yeer, it's bad. Their razoos are dropping heavily. This should never happen.' Bapa sounds in panic. 'Zebedee's ibu loses her camerata endorsement. Other camerati are refusing services for the family. Their laundry privileges are cancelled—laundry services? Ha. That's funny, Jesús …' But Bapa sounds grim. 'Some restaurants are banning them … some other stuff … oh … they must cancel a holiday they are planning.'

'People say they deserve it for bringing up such a child. Others say the Reck is crashing over it.'

'People are always saying the Reck is broken,' Bapa says. 'Where is Lula?'

'She is here. There is a big cuddle huddle around her in the grass. She is safe, Bapa. And okelah now.'

'Okelah, this is the main thing.'

'Bapa.' Swallow before asking. 'Can you fix it?'

Bapa sighs. 'It's the Reck. There's nothing—'

'Please, Bapa. Lula is sorry for the family.'

'We'll never know if all the razoo changes are because of tonight's squabbles. The Reck never just reacts as things happen.'

'Please try, Bapa. We should avoid laughing at Zebedee before.'

'He asks for it, cahaya.'

'Even so, Bapa. Can you fix it?'

'What?'

'Please make everyone's reputasi like before. Like none of it happens.'

'Saf, you know it never works like this. The Reck bends for no one's will, even an Infi, no matter how many razoos we cast.'

'Then how will it matter if you try? Please, Bapa, just try.'

He membs nothing.

'Bapa? Bapa?'

'Okelah.'

As news of my conversation with Bapa spreads, the park falls silent with expectation. I hear waves lapping the harbour shores 100's of metres away.

Waiting, patient. All of us. Tiks feel so long. Heartbeats.

Bapa blinks one razoo for Zebedee's bapa and one for his ibu.

'Is this it?' murmur my friends and neighbours around me. 'This is all our Infi has?'

Bapa's followers, and their followers' followers, blink razoos also, this way and that, for and against Zebedee's family. Hearing rumours, and hungry for gossip of the Reck's malfunctioning, millions of them seek out and flutherbomb partygoers, spinning 14's of auras in a frenzy brighter than fireworks, and swallowing all the fires in the other hearths like stars in the dawn. Auras erupt like gas explosions. Everywhere are clouds heavy with luminous colour. Like huge ladles, they might pour molten rainbows on our heads.

There are no immediate effects on anyone's reputasi. The Reck always takes its time; covers it tracks; makes it impossible for knowing how it all works. At least that's how Bapa explains it. So it seems like the Reck swallows all the razoos and forgets they exist.

Then it starts to move. Everyone gasps. It appears Zebedee's family will be even worse off for all the activity. Already too much is happening; reputations are soaring and trashing. Auras around me are like slot machines and spinning wheels of a casino in one of Mal's hollies of sap days.

Fearful, I join the cuddle huddle around Lula. The pile of bodies rolls open for me. I nuzzle in closer with Lula and Amara. Above us, the light show continues.

The changes in reputations continue, slower and less erratic. The razoos of Zebedee's ibu seem to be spiralling every nearer what they are before. She has her camerata back, restaurants are open again for them. Their holiday is back on too. Jesús will launder their clothes again, if they ever need such a service.

As near in the telling, their reputasi settles where it is before. Everyone else's too.

'You did it, Bapa!'

'I can't have,' he membs from wherever he is in the world. 'This is far from the end of it.'

It is the end of it. All it takes is two razoos from my bapa.

Maddox Price ...

Auras around the fire make a colourful Kandinsky. Night air rolls off the harbour, bringing fresh scents as tantalising as chilled oysters, pungent even for my nostrils from the other side of the globe. After the melodrama, Ben's daughter Saf, her friends and neighbours, resume dancing with heavier feet and hearts. Even the boys lose their swagger. Less fluffing in their stuffing, y'all might say. Such a shame. In truth, there is little left for savouring.

Oh, Ben, what a spectacle. What a display. Such an awe-inspiring naked impolitic display. And all for the love of a daughter. Oh, you'll have the nurses on your tail. And every avaricious Infi slavering at the possibilities.

Any Infi has 14's of reputation brokers, whose plays and hedges may attract the health detectives. Infis have pet mindwriters who smooth out wrinkles the brokers might cause, with fractal algorithms, predictive declaratives, and so forth. All this techno-voodoo (the more credulous mindwriters admit) is surprisingly simple. Where things go spectacularly wrong is in the timing of recursions and iterations.

But our Ben. Somehow, the razoos of everyone in this little village drama are as before. Before the tears and shame, before the recriminations and the crowd-sourced vigilantism. Who would think it possible? His skill so fine, so surgical (if y'all could permit me such a barbarous word) it inflames only wonder. Are his brokers better than everyone else's? Are his incantations superior? Is Ben a modern-day Perceval? Dare he ask the unasked question? Has he in his possession the Infinite's Holy Grail: a way for controlling the Reckoning itself?

ENVY

Arithmetic

'Money' — Lime Cordial

 *Ben Evoli ...*

CENTIMETRES ABOVE THE STILL WATER, a wasp glides—a yellow and black angel with a stinger. She hovers then settles over the pond embankment for mining her mud. I watch at water's edge, sitting on the short salty grass a shin's length away.

Evaporating mist halos the pond, glowing white and gold in the waking sun's gaze. Garden oils spice the air as plants and trees exhale. Among swampy oak branches, 2 wagtails chatter in proud black suits of feathers. Hunting yellow butterflies among the flowering shrubs. A butterfly darts out over the pond. A bird swoops. There is breakfast.

The wasp gathers mud for building a nest. She tracks for somewhere on the opposite side of the pond. Before long she returns and hovers. In a fan-dance of membranous wings, she lands gracefully for digging again at her excavation site. With a new payload she sets off for her building site, her wings beating a blur, her tiny muscles contracting and ligatures tensing, burning energy. Missioning hard she appears at ease. Returning, so near my feet in open sandals. Before I flinch, she flies away again laden with building materials.

Why is the nest all the way over there? Why is the mud so special on this side of the pond? You, little tebuan, make many trips over the pond. I could follow you and see your mission on the other side. Where would be the mystery in this? Enjoy your privacy, little tebuan. A precious thing it is.

I relax on the grass and breathe the cool sweet salty spicy air. Enjoy the shade of the bamboo stand, the whistling and chattering of the birds.

The wasp returns. An unmistakable glow of a little aura around her, radiant in the morning light. My attention imbues the little creature, finds the stitch of its life in the universe's infinite creative fabric, and raises it a little above its neighbours. If y'all look close (with enhancement) y'all will see her sparkling little aura, wispy solar flares erupting and arcing in the gravity of her insect Mind.

Y'all hear her? I imagine she membs over and over, '*Happy happy happy happy …*'

Aisha Evoli …

I tell Ketut, 'Ben will tell you about those lah.' Ketut is Harjanti Budiman's little banana, her youngest before one. Harjanti and her family (3 same, one istri and 5 anak anak) live in the ground floor suite of our housing hill. Ketut's up here again in the common room with eyes wide, tugging his ibu's sarong till they are in front of the solarglass case.

Jesús stands behind Ketut, with hands resting on the boy's shoulders. Three seasons ago, one cold morning before dawn in July, Harjanti find Jesús sleeping on the local spooky station concourse. 'His moustache is like a thin, droopy Christmas tree,' she tell me later, take pity for him. In no time, love blossoms. Jesús moves in with Harjanti and her partners. After only a few weeks Jesús moves out, for some reason. Settle into the basement studio among the utility rooms. In one room he set up his *siao* (crazy) laundry. Sifar, aiyo!

'Look, Jesús Uncle! So colourful.' Ketut is bug-eye; almost scratch through the glass for got his hands on the contents of the display case: a small portion, ah, of sap money Ben collect. I see no attract lah. Better throw the lot in a sucky bin, then he know. They are colourful. Images of long-dead sap stare up out of the display case. Eerie portraits and busts float amid numbers and official text. Images of sombre stone building. Also, bird, animal, and fruit.

'Why are there only boys' pictures?' Ketut asks.

'Here's one with a woman on it,' Ben says, arrive just in time for hear the boy's question, points over one of the notes. 'It's from Central African States.'

Ketut looks closer. 'It's worth only 2000 razoos.'

'Two thousand *francs*,' Ben corrects. 'Close enough on today's exchange rate.' A playful twinkle in Ben's eye.

Ketut puzzles until Ben laughs and he realises it's a joke. But why Ben mess with the boy like that ah? Razoos are no currency; they a measure of reputasi. Everybody knows that one. Neos have no money, need no money. You offer a service, the Reck calculates your reputasi.

On one note a young wanita has a strange oval face ah. Above round eyes, her high forehead sweep up for short-crop hair. A flat, wide button-nose, generous lips. Girlish by sap standards. With larger eyes ah, she might pass for 100 years' age.

'Is that a pineapple there?'

"It is," Ben says.

Ketut laughs.

'Stupid saps,' Jesús snorts. 'Money was always corrupt. A tool for the Greed of strong nation states feeding on weak ones.' Harjanti looks stern. She might stomp on his foot. 'It starts wars with numbers rather than swords, another way of stealing treasure from under thrones.'

'What's on this coin?' Ketut asks, pay Jesús no attention.

I say, 'I know this one. A Namibian 50-cent piece ah. A quiver tree on it, which is no tree at all, just a big aloe plant.'

'Wow.' Ketut already moving on. 'Look. This one is worth 100 trillion razoos.'

Ben lifts Ketut's grubby finger off the glass. 'Ah, it's from Zimbabwe. It could buy maybe a day's calories for a small family.'

'Then why is there such a big number on it?'

Ben makes for explain inflation, which will go straight over the boy's head, so I fix a stare against him. Harjanti too, ah. Ben swallows whatever he would say.

While Ketut traces his finger along the glass case, Jesús starts up again. 'Money: more addictive for saps than cocaine,' Jesús says in his raspy voice. Despite his disgust with the meaning of money, he's a budgie in front of a shiny mirror. His eyes jerk from one colourful note for the other ah. Perhaps those rumours about him once being Infi are true. Everyone tastes how content with life he is, a sure sign he has a long Cure some time in his life. But an Infi become sifar? It's all siao gossip lor. 'Symbols of riches and power, possession and privilege,' Jesús says, 'amplifiers of Greed and Gluttony. The fancy designs—they are security features against counterfeiting. People in authority staring out, reminding everyone how precious these scraps are, how scarce. Reinforcing the lie of the scarcity of resources. Everyone must work hard for getting their piddling share. *How lucky*, the notes say, *for anyone glimpsing the inaccessible riches we imply. How lucky anyone is, holding some of us for a brief time before some rich Juan dela Cruz snatches us back.*'

Harjanti stares through Jesús's throat lah.

'See this one here?' Ben says for filling the awkward gap. 'It's a Jepang Military Yen, used only in the Second Great War.'

'A symbol of occupation and subjugation,' Jesús snaps and Harjanti widens her intense eyes.

'Or here: a 5-pound-note from Northern Ireland,' Ben says. 'It has a picture of a football player on it. George Best. Saps could buy nothing with it, exchange it at a bank only for other money they could then spend.'

'What's a bank?' Ketut asks.

'Never another word, Jesús,' Harjanti warns. Jesús shoves his hands in his pockets.

'Look at this one,' I offer. 'It's made out of leather.'

'What's a leather?'

Jesús looks *Kan Cheong* Spider at Harjanti, says nothing.

'It's a German notgeld,' Ben says. 'Would you believe they also made money out of pottery and wood?'

'Hard for carrying around in my pocket.' Ketut laughs; Harjanti relaxes. 'Stupid saps,' the boy says.

Ben, always uncomfortable with deriding our closest ancestors, moves on. 'You see there, the old man with the big brush moustache? He's Albert Einstein, who first talked about spooky action at a distance.'

'He invented spooky fields?'

'Well, no, although he tasted many things we require for making spooky fields.'

'Was he an Infi too?'

'In a way, he was more than any Infi, Ketut.'

These silly bits of paper are old news lah. Already Ben collect so many, he responsible for make it all accessible. Few come look ah, but when anyone show interest, he spend hours.

Among all the stuffy-looking old men with serious beards, balding heads and severe mouths, there's my favourite: a *leng lui* with breasts bare, surf on the back of a shark. The note was worth 3 dollars and it came from Cook Islands. No other country in the world would accept it.

I like the woman's headgear on the Icelandic 5000 króna note. Her name was Ragnheiður Jónsdóttir (gog her). On the 50 kanveeks note is a cute squirrel ah. The one I wonder about the most is the old man with an impressive beard on the Vietnamese 500,000 dong note. His eyes sparkle; his stern mouth smile only at the corners. I'm unsure whether I want for hug him or flee in terror.

'You have so much stuff, Ben Uncle,' Ketut says, too loud for indoor space. 'You should put it all in a museum.'

Harjanti coughs and Jesús shuffles his feet. 'I doubt Ben Infi is so prideful he needs a big museum,' he says.

'Well, I think your money is ghost, Ben Uncle. It would be fun carrying money in my pocket.' Ketut's eyes sparkle with boyish mischief.

Harjanti, *kan cheong* (means, *nervous* ah) blushes and wilts, draws Ketut against her with protective arms over his shoulders. 'Apologies. He's just a child,' she says, using the Regal English word for anak.

'We need no money anymore, Ketut.'

'I know,' he says, puff out his chest and squirm out of Harjanti's embrace. 'We have no money at all. We have the Reck for measuring our reputasi, and no one worries about being rich or poor anymore. That's right, isn't it, Jesús Uncle?'

Geometry

'Infinity' — Ocean Alley

Maddox Price ...

ENQUIRE OF THE RECK for my reputation or Ben's. The answer: *Infinite*. Ask about Jesús and it answers, *Sifar*. (Know y'all *sifar* comes from Anglo-Malay, meaning *zero*? What a galling example of cultural pollution.) Together, Jesús and me truly represent the extreme poles of reputation. (Please refrain from calling it *reputasi*. Save our precious English!) An Infinite's razoo count is so high and a sifar's count so low, the Reck obscures both.

This is where the similarity ends. Whereas we Infinites despise our designation, a sifar welcomes it, seeks it out.

A sifar devotes life and mission, concocting disproportionately elaborate schemes for driving their razoos so low the Reck gives up on them. The great many saps who lived in poverty would resent the luxury of it.

As for we Infinites, our designation infuriates us. With good reason. We love the rush of a new acquisition, the sublime delight of outmanoeuvring our competitors, the savouring of their losses. Let's make face of it, a win is never as complete as when some other Joe Soap is the loser. Another sap garbage deposit is never as satisfying as the one you appropriate away from a fellow mining missionary. And if as a result, the fellow should forsake the mining mission entire, then so much the better. The conquest is complete. Pop the champagne corks.

But alas! Another conquest is never a sweet as your virgin first, is it? My first, the sweetest of all: a lode of indigestible plastics, mother boards and rare-earth metals. A modest lode, true. Nevertheless, you imagine all those fabbies, buzzing and producing from feedstock bins you replenish. Your cockles and muscles swell with pride. And hunger for more.

You harness the hunger which drives you on for ever grandiose things. Your reputation grows, extending your reach. Your reach becomes so extensive you have time for savouring only a fraction of what you gather. Your joy and delight dims and sublimates. You have too much for appreciating direct, so you become obsessed with abstractions—charts, tables, numbers. Your love of quality becomes a craving for quantity, for vicarious abstract indicators rather than a moment's real and ruddy success. Subsequent mining acquisitions inexorably lose their individual exquisiteness, so you must satisfy yourelf with the sum of your successes, which at once both distances you from each individual success while it embraids you in grey shadows where you must settle for promenading in the garments of accumulated residue, while still longing for retasting your first win.

This's who you become: an abstraction, wearing garments which you mistake for identity. The measurement and cut of these is your reputation, as expressed by your razoos, which the Reckoning meticulously and impartially counts, accounts, massages, redistributes, normalises, and seasonally adjusts. Your pleasure is no longer the new mine or the more efficient mining process, but the ever-swelling tumescence of your reputation.

Until the day when the Reck designates you Infinite and calls full-time on your game. Then society requires you accept the final score: you win. And win equally. What the jank? My success is on par with the Infinite gelati missionary who produces a better taste of mango? With the saver of baobab trees? With the producer of holographic projection suits of budgerigars or titmice?

I want my razoos back. You might never believe you'd miss the keeping up with the Jones's—or the Torks, the Nesmiths or even the Micky Dolenz's (if ever there's evidence, I'm spying too much on Ben these days, it's the number of sap pop culture references infecting my speech). But without a reputational ranking on success's league table, the taste of success is an insipid and tepid brew.

At least a sifar's reputational duck is never forever. An Infi is Infi until … until what? Until the Reck achieves elf-awareness and decides accounting for everyone's missionary score is a dull life? What then: it motors off for an extended summer holiday, from which it never returns?

A sifar enjoys the latent power of regaining a reputation, if only they give up their hair-brain missions of squashing water; or painting art with fast-bleaching paint; or baking super-crumbly cookies; or, in Jesús' case, laundering self-cleaning clothes.

Speaking of whom, I realise I keep you too long. Run along and join Ben's fluther as he parries with his local launderer …

Ben Evoli ...

'Please, Infi, this is no trouble. This is a mission,' Jesús says, his voice rasping like he gargles sand.

He is at it for weeks already. From sock to songkok, whether self-cleaning or disposable, every morning Jesús saves our shirts and chuddies, dresses and lingerie. He washes, dries, presses, and replaces every item in our closets, drawers and wardrobes.

As much as I wish he'd stop, I have no options for making him. He chooses his mission, which deserves respect no matter what. Mission defines a life, and Jesús' life is his for the defining.

I'd rather he'd mission elsewhere, but others living in the housing hill wish no taste of it.

I say, 'You know, it's better for the environment if we wear disposables. You know, right?'

Jesús says nothing. Follow him for Mal's swasta. Mal bursts through the doorway as if a gawd squeezes him from a celestial pimple. He thuds down the stairs for breakfast without so much as a glance at us.

'Cleaning self-cleaning clothes is even sillier. It makes ultraviolet light less effective on stains and bacteria.' His face is implacable. I say, 'You're cleaning the self-cleaning out of everything,' in an intemperate tone which really says, *are you janking crazy?*

Jesús ignores my insult. 'It is a mission.' If Jesús' mission is performing a pointless unnecessary routine, no one may say it should be otherwise.

In Mal's swasta, early morning light casts a corona blue and fresh around the silhouette of Jesús, and sparkles through his little close-fitting helmet-size aura. Watch it revolve, calm and orderly. Within, blurry forms and hues coalesce. A trick of the light, it projects the rainbow colours of a nursing uniform. Never mind what some hack mystics claim; individuals are indistinguishable in an aura. You must join the fluther for tasting who might be peering out.

Jesús kneels and fossicks for pieces of clothing under Mal's bed—a nightmare quilt monster gulping the front half of Jesús into its maw. It coughs him up as he backs out holding day-old socks and chuddies fermenting in a young boy's sweat. It may be many more years before Mal learns the ease of throwing old clothes in a sucky bin.

I lean against the door jamb, cross arms, and chew back exasperation. Laundry is Jesús' mission; he even joins a camerata. It could be a ruse, but what? A sifar seeks no reputasi, so how can he benefit? He could be a flutherbombing junkie. If there's some angle he's playing, nurses would know. He could be heading for a Cure.

Jesús scuttles on hands and knees collecting the rest of Mal's discards off the floor. Lobs items with an easy arc for a hamper by the sucky bin hatch.

'You should tire of this,' I try.

Jesús looks up at me with eyes white in his thin dark face. 'Chop wood, carry laundry,' he says with more sand-gargling.

Roll my eyes. 'No one requires you so. The house welcomes you here without condition or expectation.'

'You have obligations.' He means for community. Providing Jesús with living quarters demonstrates I share the fortune of my reputasi.

'The same useless chore every day?'

Jesús stands cradling the basket. 'In Go—the board game? There are 10 to the power of 170 possible board positions. In the whole universe there are far fewer atoms, only 10 to the 80th.'

I look at him, quizzical, feeling stupid.

'Which tells you what about the universe?' Jesús rasps.

'There's more Consciousness than visible physics? The universe's imagination is magnitudes larger than her meat?'

'Atoms are wave projections from a singular universal point.' Jesús' eyes widen and his eyebrows arch. 'All of fourspace is just atoms projecting out of multi-dimensional vectors from a singularity. Onespace!'

Every anak knows it. Mal knows it. The saps learned it bitterly when Entanglement Syndrome struck them down while developing instant point-to-point transport, the precursor of spooky technology. We'd have no spooking without the mysterious underlying onespace. We'd have no fluthers.

The sound of a MusiKai composition—Aisha's—wafts up, the higher end of its tonal balance soaking into the walls and carpet which muffle the bass and lower mids. Cutlery clinks, bowls clang, and a pan sizzles across the rhythm of the music. MusiKai incorporates the random rhythms into her tune. The genre is typical Aisha: somewhere between dance metal and show tunes. She is happy this morning.

Jesús mistakes my lack of argument as encouragement. He's a monk padding down the hall for Saf's swasta, calls back, 'If a singularity ...'

The ineffable singularity: not one, not two, nor even a thing in the sense of thingness. The deeper the universe allows us under her skirts—the more we want for prising between her infinitely folding crinkly fractal labia—the more mysterious she becomes. We should stop looking. We will never taste her pure truth, only her side effects.

Onespace: being anywhere any time because we are everywhere every time in Mind. How was it in sap times, when travel around the globe took hours? How was it, experiencing only the physical hallucination of four-dimensional space-time, always feeling the distances between places and from each other, always alone with one's thoughts in abject privacy?

'Infi?'

'Huh?'

'I am saying, if a singularity projects the illusion of all those whirring atoms and, among all things, conjures the game of Go with all its possibilities, is there no room for finding life purpose from washing clothes?'

'But … it's pointless.' It's no place of mine reflecting on his mission …

'All the better.' He surveys Saf's swasta and finds nothing out of place. 'Meditating on the act of unnecessary laundering has no boundaries.'

'So?'

'So, since the board in the game of laundry has no edges, it has even more positions than Go.'

Okelah, Jesús. Launder our clothes if you must. In truth, your mission could taste no less sweet than mine.

Maddox Price …

Look and you'll see Ben has the expression of a sow feeding 14 piglets: boredom, resignation, patient suffering. Poor Puffin.

Local councils are the bane of Infinites. While councillors lust for the status of having you in their meetings, they frown on you having opinions. They crave only your stamp of approval. They sit in terror of offending you too, in fright of you rolling over in your piggy boredom and squashing their reputations piglet dead. They'll canvas your opinions about every minute detail, while all the time hoping you'll offer none.

Rather than attend, Ben could flutherbomb a councillor at the table or flit between fluthers, much as I am.

What a dump, these council chambers of Bandar Melambai. A mere annexe in the clinic mall of the local chapter of the Ministry of Health (Kementerian Kesahatan in Anglo-Malay). With even lower reputation than nurses, they have no alternative than the space in the southern corner of the KK's triangular mall complex. On the same floor is a bordeli, a hair salon, and a passing suite—sex, hair styling, and dying. What a combination! The bordeli is one of Piloto Iscariot's franchise missions, though duller than most if y'all ask me. The range of gender liquidity is less than I would demand.

Look at Ben. He'd rather be at home enjoying a gin and tonic.

Council meetings are a mixed blessing for a captive Infi. Ben's fluther shrinks dramatically, his followers strangely find no joy playing voyeur during council proceedings. Nurses are another story, packing his fluther, all hoping he might try influencing the council for his own elf-interest. Boom! Payday for any nurses catching him.

Ben pours a glass of water, looks around the board table. The table is a silly conceit—so ostentatious; so large, it requires fabbing right there in the room. Though its material is fabby timber, it smells of an infusion of natural hardwood oils, some local eucalyptus—y'all could guess by the scent, if your hancy is good enough. But—being within range of hair frying, neos dying, and nurses spying—the artificial scents of fake timber among the veritable olfactory tourbillion of unguents, incenses, and putrid gases (enough for watering eyes, scouring sinuses, embalming brains, and petrifying pancreases) are as noticeable as farts in an abattoir.

There's always a nurse present in the room at these things, usually a novice. Experienced nurses prefer lurking in fluthers than attending in person. The novice today is young, very young. Field Nurse Lành Hiền Rồng, or *Gentle Dragon* as her colleagues call her. A rare and dangerous creature: a pretty nurse (if y'all like triangular chins and girlish button noses). Most nurses baffle the Mind as for where they identify on the gender spectrum—squat and blocky, with shaven heads or short-crop hair, the most androgynous of all missions. Their gene-mod skin designs are incongruous mashups of warrior tattoos, rainbows, and ecology motifs. Quite different is Gentle Dragon, who has no gene-mod skin and wears long hair. One suspects she's using her youth and looks for seduction. Over time, her colleagues will chip it out of her. For now, it's working on Ben; he's taking no eyes off her. Dear Puffin, how delicious. If it's anyone other than Ben, it'd be fun theatre: an Infi falling tits over testicles for a nurse.

'You have a Kyōka 10g? Latest Jikken-Teki?' Mashe Nathovy—the youngest of the councillors, and quite the tech lover—asks as he sits down at Ben's right. Other councillors stifle gasps at Mashe's presumption.

'Yeer. Still getting familiar with it,' Ben says, a little embarrassed. He's looking everywhere but at Mashe, for an excuse for shifting seats. His discomfort is delicious.

'You have the top model? The one with 64 trilabytes of memory?' the tiresome Mashe blathers. With a juvenile grin like he's eating so many peanut butter sandwiches. White bread, of course. Fluffy and doughy. Check the back pocket of his shorts for a slingshot.

'Have,' Ben answers flatly. 'DNA-Quanta memory.'

'DNA-Quanta! This's available already?' Mashe contains his excitement about as well as a masturbating twentager.

Y'all can see Ben regrets mentioning it. 'Still in beta. I get early access.'

'Of course,' Mashe nods with over-eager sobriety. 'Hooters have privileges with the hancy makers.'

Ben scowls, pushes back, his chair rolling away from the table. 'Most sorry, Infi!' Mashe fawns. 'I misspeak. You are no mere hooter. The enhancement utility products you develop are extraordinary. You are a most exceptional mindwriter.'

Ben smiles weakly.

'Hancies are dangerous.' Sarah Pursglove leans in, one chair around from Mashe. Every fibre of Sarah's ancient crochet cardigan—and every hair on her head—is on end. She tilts her head and exposes her collar bone where you'd expect a hancy seat would be. Sarah's old enough for recalling when hancies are the great social fear, the tech harbinger of the end of times.

Ben looks in genuine pain. Gin is only a short tukky ride home, Puffin.

'You hear about the guys playing pool?'

'Oh, this old myth?' Mashe mocks. If Ben has any luck, Sarah will hook Mashe in conversation and leave him alone.

'It's no myth: two friends playing 9-ball; a little too much drinking. One accuses the other of cheating. The other gets angry, says some awful things which his hancy, well, enhances. The first implodes in an unstable spooky field, leaving his glass and cue stick clattering on the ground with a few items from his pockets—those without DNA tagging.'

'It's just a story,' Mashe answers, fully baited.

'But there are hollies. There's evidence.' Sarah is little more than a quivering spindle of amber hair and wool, a tortured amigurumi in an electrostatic field.

'Fakes,' Mashe says with his peanut-butter smile.

'Fakes? A bloody shank of the poor sod lands on a 12-year-old's birthday cake on the other side of the world!' What next, Sarah? Fabbies make you autistic? See, this is the kind of mental illness nurses should be healing. She even looks crazy. In the shade of Sarah's scatter of hair, a stiff top lip overhangs a sharp, triangular chin.

'It's rubbish.' Good on you, boy. If Mashe has a slingshot, he might yank it from his pocket at any tik.

Sarah looks aghast. 'Bits of him spook all around the globe. Broken bones, organ chunks, liquids …'

Mashe shakes his head. 'Nah. Impossible.'

'Gobs of his guts lodge in a bride's dress.' From deep within the fairy floss of Sarah's hair, her watery eyes remain on Mashe as she tilts her head back at creeping speed, levelling her chin at him like a weapon. It's an oyster knife, bright and sharp among the craze of dizzy hair and frizzy wool, aiming at Mashe like she might shuck him.

Ben bows his head, wishing for being elsewhere. I wonder again if poor Puffin's resting morose state will neutralise his usefulness for what's in store for him.

Mashe waves a dismissive hand. Sarah drops the bluff of her chin. 'You forget the holly of his cock landing in a cat feed bowl?' he challenges. 'Or the one of his finger appearing up the nose of some hapless person? His hair landing on a bald head like a toupee? Chunks of him in a meat pie? Blood in a glass of white wine? Or the one about his butt cheeks landing smack on a boardroom table just after the chair says, *I'll have your arse for this*? They're all just a bit of fun.'

'Well, the leaders of the manufacturer are now eating sifar tofu and sleeping in public long houses,' Sarah counters.

'Because idiots believe the camel crap stories, and ruin their reputasi,' Mashe says out of his smug, peanut-butter face. 'Where is the Reck when you need it? It should be smoothing out all such kind of stuff.'

Sarah shakes her head. I imagine a possum is foraging in her hair. 'What I think is wrong is how he gets away with it. No so much as a nutepak.'

Mashe: 'Gets away with what?'

'Murder.' Sarah's an accusing Grim Reaper pointing a bony, stabbing finger. 'It's a crime, it is. He should get punishment. Lock him in a jail, I say. We're too soft on his ilk. Sometimes I think we need an old-fashion police force. Bring back police, I say.'

Gentle Dragon slides a nutepak across the table for Sarah. 'Perhaps Councillor Pursglove might benefit from these?'

'Order, please,' says Mayor Joanna Gultom, whose chinless features are in the service of giving her the appearance of a honeysucker. Her cheeks, lips, and nose pinch together, and suck out towards other dimensions as if she may once surf on a black hole's event horizon. She raps her bony knuckles on the table: a weak gesture, lacking vigour. 'Secretary Cambo, may we have the agenda?'

Astronomy

'Rasa Sayang' — Hanie Soraya

 *Ben Evoli ...*

BRISK BUSINESS at the hawker stands. Woks sizzle over charcoal braziers. Oily smoke rises above the vertical gardens and vanishes into weather nets.

The esplanade overflows with visitors coming for the music recital in the desa's amphitheatre. Auras dance above teahouse tables. In the jewellery stores and salons, around the greenwalls of herbs and salad vegetables, under the umbrella trees with opening fronds sensing the promise of afternoon rain, auras spin like colliding dervishes, merging tadpoles, splintering bamboo. Viscous colourful globs spurt between auras—the sign of neos meeting and greeting at speed. I turn my filters up and the saturation of colour rinses away.

Around the bandstand crowds are a battalion of permuizik muda (young musicians) with doting parents and family members. Nearby, my usual teahouse is overflowing with ibu fussing over hopeful protégés, indulging them with brownies and hot chocolate.

I skip passing a pair of nurses patrolling the beat, looking for an outdoor table for taking tea. Down the bay end of the esplanade the higher-reputasi places will be quieter. Today I prefer staying nearer the bandstand. The teahouses nearer the station will serve almost anyone, including all these helicopter parents and crash-pilot kids.

'Salamat datan, Ben Face Infi,' membs Sugiarto Lesmono from Waviti Teahouse. Among his outdoor tables, he waves so vigorous he appears in possession of 5 arms. 'Here's a seat for you,' he says, gesturing at a free table. Please honour my house ah?' His smile is 8 octaves of piano keys.

Taking the seat he proffers, I look about for his putri, Jaya. She ambushes me from behind, assaulting the table with chopsticks; napkins; a pitcher of water; and a glass.

'Salamat datan,' she membs. 'How are you?'

'Well, terima kasih,' I say tongue and lung.

Jaya scrunches her nose, blinks me a holly of the menu and the daily specials.

'Just cold aya, sia (please).'

'Yeer, Tuan.' Jaya's posture slumps as she spins on her heels.

'She is very attractive, Infi. Perhaps I would enjoy her,' a wanita at the next table says, while caressing an aya cup in one hand. Beside her, a young lelaki kneels wearing only a choker, cooling glasses, a leather thong, and high-quality skipping shoes. Their auras entwine and pulse. She surveys the greying sky, ruffles her submissive's hair while his glasses never stray from watching her.

Apart from the families of the musically indeterminate, the teahouse patrons are wearing blank flutherbomber faces—loose jaws; passive lips; eyes out of focus. I watch for micro muscle twitches which might reveal their vicarious remote activity. The customer in front is for certain flutherbombing a snow-skier. Another quakes in a chair and clutches at a table for stability. In Mind, he's playing a holly of volcanic activity in the Pacific Northwest of California. They say a huge earthquake there is imminent.

Jaya brings aya tea and lingers, seeking my attention.

I taste Saf searching about. She knows I'm here. Memb a wave and a smile for her.

At the end of her patience, Jaya leaves in a fluster.

'Love you, Bapa,' Saf membs. Down the esplanade her band assembles preparing for their performance later in the afternoon. There she is, guitar in hand, her aura vibrant and pulsing. The brightest aura conceivable.

'Love you too, putri. Are you nervous?'

'Nervous? No.' She mocks offence. 'I practice for hours and hours.'

'Yeer, my cahaya. I hear every note night and day these passing weeks.'

Saf giggles. I feel complete.

Lành Hiền Rồng (Gentle Dragon) ...

Doctor Wazini Mvovo, who is at least 200 years old, runs a pop-up school from her house on the highest hill in the village. When the weather is good, in her front yard, locals help her pitch a gazebo tent, in which they arrange a classroom, lending their backs for moving desks and equipment out from storage.

Today is sunny and still dry. Children gather and sit in a semicircle round Wazini, who perches stiff on a stool. Artful and entertaining, she reminds me of the best at the KK Akademi in Singapore, teaching in layers of story and metaphor, blending magazine hollies with live experiments.

On desks are arrays of equipment: micro-centrifuges; smoke bellows; jars half full of something dark and pulsing; racks of tubes; micro-pipettes; pipette tips; and petri dishes. They are learning gene programming with ants.

'We only want 6 legs,' Wazini membs. 'How many?'

'Six,' the kids respond.

'Correct. Never 5 or 7. Eight is entirely too many. Because then we'd be engineering spiders. We'll make spiders next time. Who likes spiders?'

Kids erupt with *ews* and *yucks*. Shake their heads. 'I like spiders,' one says out loud from a desk at the back of the tent. And no sooner, other kids are changing minds. Liking spiders after all.

'Mal,' Wazini membs. 'What is our agreement about talking tongue and lung in class?'

'Sorry, guru Wazini,' membs Mal, son of Ben. 'It's rude.'

Wazini nods accepting Mal's contrition. 'Well, I'm unsure about spiders,' Wazini says. 'They taste awful, like crunchy Vegemite.'

There are more *yucks* from the class. Mal giggles. 'Spiders are—' Mal says out loud. '—much smarter than ants,' he finishes by membing.

Wazini smiles at Mal correcting hiself. 'Now the ant's head,' she continues. 'Make sure it resembles no brother or sister, just a normal ant head … with compound eyes, antennae, and mandibles … who knows what mandibles are? … Yeer, correct … now careful how you play with their genes, or you might bang a giant ant into existence. You will break my jars … and then there will be trouble, okelah? Let's have no pet ants eating your families … or you … yeer, yeer, mandibles chomping, chomping your soft little bellies. Who would clean you up afterwards? Say again? Yeer, you can make your ants any colours you like. Here's where the sequence is …'

At some point—it passes me by at first—her reputasi trends up. There it is, still gently climbing. Wazini seems either unaware, or ambivalent.

Ben Evoli …

A pile of packages obstructs our front door. Fourteen or so today. Complimentary deliveries of goods and gadgets we never need, from camerati we never hear of, hoping we—and my millions of followers—might favour their stuff.

'Khoosasi,' I curse for the trees. A wagtail chit-chatters its territorial anger.

Khoosasi is the council boy whose mission is collect all this guff and redistribute it among desa residents. Preferably before Mal has a chance of rummaging through it. Today, Khoosasi fails in disastrous fashion. The scene is like a cyclone rips through. Cyclone Mal. Tops of boxes are torn away,

THIS WAY UP signs point everywhere but up, packages bear dark stains of leakage. There's no avoiding it. A search party (by which I mean me unless I persuade Saffron) must venture into the boy-funk swasta of Mal's and retrieve any contraband.

'Eee-yer. It's gross in there,' Saf will say, negotiating for reward. Best keep it from Saf. At least then there's a tiny chance of keeping it from Aisha also.

'Khoosasi.' A pointless call for the wild. The boy will neither be within earshot nor among my fluther—one of the few in the desa who never flutherbombs me. There will be councillors watching and quaking. I give Khoosasi maybe 8 mins before he arrives. He must arrive before Aisha.

Sometimes I envy saps for their short lives. At my age they'd already be exploiting the joys of senility, clumping together in aged care facilities, planning campaigns of spite and resentment against their ungrateful progeny. Yet here I am at 88, years aplenty before the spare tyre of middle age rolls my way and rubbers up my bowels.

What 88-year-old sap would relish still raising children? Saf is 23 … no wait, 24? … it's March already so … Look, the point is, a sap her age was an adult, whereas Saf is a busted thermometer of a twentager bouncing between emotional heat waves and cold snaps. At her age, sap parents could shovel her out the door with a bottle of Bundy, a box of condoms, and stern warnings about People & Culture consultants. They could send her off for college, or gig-economy labour in a fast food mine. Yet I have the best part of another decade until Saf turns 31. Even at Mal's age (17), saps were already janking and voting in some capitalist gulag.

Sure, we live longer lives—and longer maximum-security sentences of child-rearing too. In Mal's case—well of course he's still a boy, the developmental equivalent of a 9-or-10-year-old sap. His brooding twentage years as an anti-hygiene terrorist are ahead of him.

'Khoosasi!' Come and shift this stuff before Mal tears into it.

In the kitchen, I make a hasty gin dan tonik, the old-fashion way. Mixing in a glass. No fabbing it.

Dusk. The temperature drops as a southerly squeezes the air like a wet sponge. Predictable rain starts falling. On the harbour-facing balcony, I set the gin on a side-table by the hammock. The hammock padding is askew in the netting: more signs of Cyclone Mal. Among the cushions is Gruff, no doubt shedding enough fur for knitting a beanie.

'Get out of there you mangy cat.' Gruff flashes lime-green and hisses. All wide-eyes, legs, and tail, he hastily forsakes his throne. Leaps for the chair in the corner as if it's his choice all the long. Reassembles his sense of imperious dignity. Settles and curls up.

I tidy the hammock padding; flop in; stretch out with my head resting on the spreader bar at one end; let it rock. Reach for the gin. Gaze out over the bay towards the harbour. Somewhere out there is an invisible line separating Sungai Parramatta from Port Jackson. I presume fish and dolphins all have the right visas.

Saf's guitar-playing filters down from her swasta. She is riffing over the tunes from her recital—5 or 6 times already. Mal lurks somewhere deeper in the house. The silence will be short. There it is: a spoon clanging in the kitchen sink.

Memb Mal, 'Are you eating? It's supper time soon.'

Rapid slap-stomp sounds of boyish feet on the hardwood floor as Mal charges towards the balcony. There he stands in the doorway, smears of food on his face and fingers.

'Can we have ducky cubes?' He's so loud he's putting more bubbles in my gin.

Saf's guitar stops. 'No, Mal,' she membs. 'You know duckweed grows in the pee ponds.'

Mal groans. 'Of course, I know. I take the bio-waste excursion, same as you.' Mal has a way of pronouncing big words: slower than his normal tempo, and with greater precision. He wants me knowing he understands them.

Saf appears at the door, pads barefoot around Mal. She jumps and rolls over me without rocking the hammock much, hugs my chest as she looks at her younger saudara. 'And already you pee in the pond all the time,' she accuses. Rests her head on my chest, claiming me. Gruff looks up and sniggers.

'When you use a tandas in the house, it only goes down there anyway.' He comes closer, intending he'll claim a subdivision of the hammock.

'Eee-yer! Stay away with those dirty hands,' Saf squeals.

I palm his chest, keeping him an arm's length away. 'Go clean up, fella. Then you 2 can go up for the lodge and tabao supper.'

Mal scampers away on heavy feet.

There's no real need for going up the esplanade. By supper time, there'll be hawker carts in the park across the avenue. Which Mal will ignore. He prefers the sifar food across from the lodge.

'Let him order as he wishes, Saf. You choose for the rest of us. Ibu will be home soon.'

'Yeer, Bapa.' Saf bestows the kiss of goddesses on my cheek.

Mal returns a little cleaner. He's got a hand in his pants, jiggling parts private.

'Oh, eee-yer,' Saf cries.

'Bapa?' Mal asks, his hand movement less vigorous. 'Think you Ben 10 has pubic hair?'

'Ewww,' from Saf.

'I doubt saps would ever depict such a thing in a cartoon, Mal.'

'Saps were prudes,' Mal says.

'If *Ben 10* has hair down there,' Saf taunts, 'it'll be sap hair. Way more than you'll ever grow.'

'I never want pubic hair,' Mal says.

'Walao eh,' Saf spits. 'You will grow. Very little, but you will.'

'When?'

'How old are you?' I ask, teasing.

Mal scrunches his face at me. '17.'

'Then maybe in the next year or so.'

'No,' he whinges.

Saf crinkles her nose. Unfolds herelf out of the hammock. 'Come on, you old bald turkey. Let's get dinner.' Saf skips ahead. Mal scurries for catching up. Hold my breath waiting for the front door slam. Aiyo, Mal! A tribal song of arguing voices, feet scampering for the slippy slide.

The tide of gin ebbs halfway. Hold the glass up; the sky's coral-orange glow filters through. Enjoy the peace until the front door opens and closes again, with a great deal more peace this time. Aisha.

'Khoosasi eat snake again.' Aisha already knows about Khoosasi's laziness today. Alamak.

'Yeer.' No point denying.

'I got time, take a shower is it,' she calls.

Flutherbomb her up the stairs for our swasta. She passes the bed and the frost-glass partition dividing dry and wet spaces of our suite. Gestures exploding fingers (such slender delicate fingers, perfect nails) at the shower which conjures a holly console. She swirls a few small circles in it. The familiar hiss of water surges in the shower pasteuriser. Nothing is quite like home as much as anticipating the water warming for Aisha.

It might be 25 years of marriage—

'26,' Aisha corrects.

We laugh. Aisha makes a seductive if day-weary show of removing her clothes, hangs her outer garments in the UV closet. Slides her utilitarian chuddies off. Tosses them with a loopy arc for the sucky bin. As she squats over the dry tandas, I'll leave her in relative privacy.

Rock out of the hammock; pad for the kitchen. Mix Aisha a drink and freshen my own.

'Bring it up already,' Aisha membs.

A watery hiss issues from the organs of the building—Aisha under the shower. Rivulets course over her. Imagine being one of those water drops. Savour its pleasure tumbling over the contours of her fruit. Its every effort for clinging on her fails, and it falls into the grate under her feet. Then down into darkness merging with a cascade passing through the hell of the diagnostic filter sampling her sweat, hair and skin flakes for pathologies. Under pressure, water passes into the pasteurising reservoir. With new heat, the water begins another ecstatic journey over Aisha's skin.

I bound up the stairs by 2's, taking care keeping the glasses level. Aisha reaches out while soaping herelf.

I ask, 'How is your day?'

Aisha exhales deep and sinks a little deeper into the shower, eyes close. 'Another day refreshing inventory.' Aisha, as a Field Procomplement, must oversee her mission's readiness in times of disaster—flood; bushfire; sap building collapse; spooky station accident. In quiet times, this often means re-evaluating their response capacity. While no one wishes for tragedy, Aisha is listless in the down times.

I ask, 'So a quiet one?' mischievously.

'Walao eh, you want curses on us, is it? Siah, bad luck complain this time is quiet. You be careful or you make a flood like that and then, many weeks on mission I must be away, then you know.' Aisha throws a soapy face cloth at me. A corner of it lands in my gin.

'Hey!'

Aisha laughs and folds most of the cloth in my glass, surging a sudsy tide of gin over the rim. I grab her and throw my arms over her shoulders. She kisses deep.

'Saf's recital is good lah,' she says. 'Terima kasih for blink a holly.'

The sound of a building collapse: the front door slamming behind Mal.

'Go save the house,' Aisha says. My erection softens with disappointment. 'I'll be a few mins. Fab me a nightgown? Maybe a light kimono.'

'What colour?'

'My favourite, sia,' she answers.

Adoi! What colour is her favourite? Some shade of aqua? At the wardrobe fabby, pinch and wiggle the control holly.

'Chuddies too?'

Before the garments materialise, I go find Saf fabbing plates and chopsticks while Mal rips into bags of food with exuberant violence. Cracks open his dinner package and digs in with fingers like earth-moving equipment. Mines a cube of greenish deep-fry duckweed tofu dripping sticky sauce. Stuffs the smelter of his mouth with it. Gobbles with minimum chewing.

Saf rescues the remaining packages from Mal's reach. Arranges the table. Places food plates and chopsticks. Fetches drinks. Aisha joins as we park butts on the benches. Gruff takes his usual station by Mal, looks up expectantly.

'You hate tofu, Gruffield,' Mal says. Gruff blinks, shakes his head, and walks behind the kitchen bench.

'Bapa?' Mal gulps his drink and replenishes the inventory of food in his mouth.

'Yeer, putra.'

'Can we spook for other planets?'

'No, dungu,' Saf scolds. Behind the kitchen island, Gruff laughs.

Mal squints and winces, covers his ears as if protecting them against a burst of noise.

'Memb softer, Saffron, sia,' Aisha scolds.

'He's the loud one, shouting tongue and lung, and you tell me memb quieter?'

'It hurts,' Mal complains. 'Why no one spook for other planets?'

Saf exaggerates a sigh. 'Three good reasons: no vectors; no guides; no spooky stations.'

'All you need is vectors,' I say. Aisha catapults me a *stop-encouraging-him* look. 'You will figure them out if you look in onespace for long enough.' Aisha sets her next catapult payload on fire.

'That would take forever,' Saf says.

'It'll work for just spooking out anywhere, real quick.' Smile at Mal. He giggles.

'You'd die.' Saf is in no mood for amusements.

'Wear a suit. Same as Neil Armstrong,' Mal says.

'Who is this?' Saf challenges, doubting any such person exists.

'He was an astronaut. He skipped on the moon,' answers Mal.

'Oh, you mean a sap. They burned so much fuel travelling there … it took days.'

'We could go for the moon already, right?' Mal presses.

I say, 'It would be an adventure.' Aisha gives up her siege, looks sullenly in her bowl, prods rice grains with chopsticks.

'You should skip on the moon, Bapa,' Mal says.

'Should I?'

Mal nods emphatically. 'There's a sea of tranquility up there. If you swim in it, you might feel better.'

Saf scoffs. Gruffield leaps up on the kitchen bench and, , throbbing orange, watches the conversation. Out of Aisha's sight, he feels safe enough.

'It would be dangerous ah,' Aisha says. 'You must have a perfect vectors lah. Without a spooky station, and missionaries for guiding and reinforcing intentions like that, you must focus hardy-hard.'

'No one ever tries it?' Mal asks.

Saf rolls her eyes. 'Why would anyone want?'

'People try all the time, Mal,' Aisha almost whispers. 'Sakit ones.'

'I want for meeting one. For showing me how.'

'You're as sakit as they are,' Saf tells Mal. Gruff hangs his head shaking it.

Aisha thumps the table. Gruff scuttles off the kitchen bench. 'Aiyo! Never say such about your saudara. Never lah. Understand?'

I rest a hand on Saf's thigh as she looks down. '*Paiseh*, Ibu.'

'I want for meeting a moon-skipper,' Mal says, becoming strident.

'All gone, little fella. Lost.'

'So flutherbomb them.'

'No. We lose them. They never come back.'

'They're dead?' Mal has a face for when he thinks hard. He knits his eyebrows; squints; scrunches his nose; tightens his lips; tilts his head towards his left shoulder like he's pushing something out. Y'all would almost believe he suffers konstipasi. 'One day I'll spook for the moon,' he announces. 'And I will come back.'

Music

'Sheela-Na-Gig' — PJ Harvey

 *Ben Evoli …*

AFTER SUPPER AISHA AND ME take refuge in the common room downstairs. Aisha flomps in a couch, caresses my cheek, massages an earlobe like she might polish a coin. She hates my ears.

'Your ears are adorable lah.'

'Then why call me Bat Ears?'

'I love bats.'

She hates bats. Please never send any if y'all value your reputasi. Khoosasi will leave them on the doorstep and Mal will set them free. Y'all could be responsible for loosing feral bats in our desa. Send no bats.

Upstairs an unearthly racket booms doom.

'Aiyo!' Aisha membs. 'Again? Why must she have music blare through the house like that? I think those monkeys want parents' head must throb, fine.'

Sonik Monkey Alliance. Saf is a fan … it seems for decades already. She follows the twentager's hallowed tradition of finding music best for shredding parents' nerves. Y'all would think she would consider others in the housing hill and play it in the soundproofing of her own head.

'If the walls aren't shaking, you're not hearing it right,' Saf explains.

Even without the extra sub-base that only crumbling foundations generate, they sound like a huge industrial blender running full of dry bones, pushbike gears, a macaque, a swarm of militant bees, and an aviary of lorikeets. Their stage act is a continual loop of only 2 moves. First: they jump and swivel, lift their tails, and wiggle their bright-red naked pantats at the audience.

'It's ghost,' Saf assures me.

Their 2nd move is somewhat less savoury.

'Bapa, they're activists.'

'Yeer, they're actively throwing najis at the audience.' From piles of it at side-stage. They want the audience throwing it also; there are piles of it around the perimeter of the venue floor.

'They're protesting,' Saf defends. For certain, the lorikeets in the blender are protesting. 'Reacting against our giga-clean antiseptic environment and our propensity for dialling down all the unpleasant stuff when we flutherbomb. Which is every hour of the day. They're encouraging everyone, *wake up and smell the—*'

'Shit.'

'Bapa. It's from a fabby. Never real.'

'Ibu,' Mal pleads. 'Tell Saf it's too loud. It hurts.'

'Oh, grow up, you bayi,' Saf membs.

'Bapa?' Mal membs. 'Can you fab me a new sister?'

'Aiyo!' Aisha throws her hands up, looks for a comforting angel floating near the ceiling.

'Mal,' I try rational soothing. 'There's no fabbing living things. You know this.'

'I want a new sister.'

'Mal,' Aisha scolds.

'What about a new ray cat?' he persists. 'If Gruffield dies?'

'Mal. That one is crazy.' Aisha clamps her breath in.

'Such a bayi,' Saf membs. 'He'll want dolphins in the bathtub next.'

No reply from Mal. Then a curdling cry resonates through the ceiling above us. 'Ibu!' Saf is shrill, distraught. Mal giggles.

'What now?' Aisha demands.

I flutherbomb both, find the grizzly answer. 'He blinks her a holly of a sap chicken slaughterhouse.'

Aisha looks aghast. 'Walao eh! Buay tahan.'

'Some documentary on sap food production.'

Aisha fetches the holly for herelf, watches a production line carrying birds around by their necks through machines of slaughter and dismemberment.

'Why show your saudara that one?' Aisha is stern.

'What's the difference between her concerts and a slaughterhouse?' Mal challenges. 'The slaughterhouse is cleaner.' He giggles like a goblin. I shake my head.

'I swear some days,' Aisha says out of patience, 'I could drop him in a sucky bin lah.' Instantly she regrets it. Everyone in the house holds breath, even Gruff, whose ray cat glow is uncharacteristically mute.

 *Saf Evoli …*

Alamak celaka! Harsh, Ibu, even for you. There are at least 100,000 nurses watching our nightly episode of *At Home with the Evolis*, and you joke about throwing Mal in a sucky bin?

I kill the music. Mal ruins everything.

In the common room, Ibu studies Bapa. He's moody again; we all know it. 'What's the matter with you, Bat Ears?'

'Nothing worth talking about,' he says, with images of the sculpture in the station forecourt loud in his Mind.

'That one again.' Ibu gives Bapa no room at all on such topic.

'I'm considering bombing it.'

'Let them have it,' Ibu says dismissively, like she's talking down for Mal. 'You take it too serious. Let it go, ah.'

Bapa jumps out of his seat like it ejects him. Towards the fireplace. It's an old fight and he's ready for war. 'It's a 5-metre-tall tangle of phalluses and vulvas. When finished, it'll be a throbbing gushing fountain running 24 hours a day. *In my honour*, you say. What would they erect if their aim is lampooning me?'

Ibu giggles. *Erect*. Bapa is funny when he's angry. *Lampoon*.

'Saffron,' Ibu membs, 'no spy on your parents during a disagreement ah.'

Feel a flush of guilt, but jank it. We hide no squabbles from families. There's no hiding anything from families. Besides, there are millions of flutherbombers tasting us already.

'Honest,' Ibu says. 'Sometimes I think sap modesty feasts on you ah.' She's right. Bapa is quaintly prudish sometimes.

'It's nothing about modesty. It's janking—stop laughing—inaccurate.' He's shouting already. Nurses will be consulting nute recipes. Fans here for the soap opera are fabbing popcorn.

Ibu laughs harder. 'I know how SnakiDik works, *leng chai*. I'm a test subject for versions 3 to 5 ha.'

'It's all in the hancy and the Mind.'

'I know.'

'The are no moving parts—stop laughing. How can you make a physical representation? It's nonsense.' Yeer, Bapa is ranting. Do not adjust your hancies.

'It's just an artist interpretation, Bat Ears. You no let it go.'

Bapa is marching back and forward in front on the fireplace. 'Maybe I might still stop it.'

'Um, they are …' Ibu search for words. '… turn it on …' She sputters giggle-shit, unable for controlling her laughter. '… tonight.'

'Ah?'

'It will run first thing tomorrow lah. Your morning glory, I suppose ah.'

'You think this's funny.'

'I think you are funny, my sweet Bat Ears. You create something so successful. Everyone loves you for it. You give a gift. It's theirs already. You wish for take it back?'

'How is it finished so fast?'

'You think it premature?' Ibu snorts with laughter, having too much fun at Bapa's expense. 'The weather report says it will shower tomorrow.'

'Enough!'

Ibu cradles her ribs in her arms in case she laughs them out of her chest. She says, 'They want for complete it in time for your Inductee Gala.'

Inductee Gala. I agree with Bapa: what a joke. A camerata of Infinites is no camerata. It's just a guild of the Greedy with no single mission or collaboration. Just a privileged club for elf-congratulating monopolists. Infis always fight each other. Just look at the tricks they're pulling over our railway reclamation project. There should be a battalion of nurses investigating this instead of stalking us. If I am a nurse, I'd make sure the council's deceit would unravel. I'd uncover Infi exploitations and make them pay for their sickness. And make them better, of course. I'd make Nurse Intan proud.

Ibu exhales, turning serious. 'You wish you never invent it lah.'

'Lor.' Oh, Bapa, is this true?

'That one is your problem, Ben,' Ibu says. 'You invent these things, but they are never good enough for you. You rather hold them back, keep improve. Once they're out there, you despair ... you want erase them from your life, from existence. Why you enjoy no happiness? You invent a wonderful thing. It changes lives. It is good. More than good. How you taste none of that one?'

'It's a wonder we don't all just lie down and jank ourelves to death.' Bapa sounds bitter. 'There is still so much needing repair in the world. And what is my contribution? Orgasm-inducing mindwriting.'

'SnakiDik delivers toe-curling, light-shifting, gravity-defying ...'

Bapa shakes Ibu's words out of his head, so she keeps going. '... skin-peeling, lung-expanding, nail-scratching, head-banging, better-than-any-nute-ever—'

'Aisha, please ...' Bapa stops pacing, sits back with Ibu, head in his hands.

'—life-giving, health-restoring, shame-banishing—'

'Stop it.'

'—at-one-with-the-gods, love-you-forever-and-ever orgasms.'

One day I will ask if I can have it in my hancy.

'All right, all right.'

Ibu ploughs her hands through Bapa's hair, which takes quite some effort, his hair is so thick. 'Something must be good about you, Bat Ears. Your reputasi says so ah.'

'What of those camerati working for decades cleaning up Africa? Bangladesh? Few of those are Infinite. The Reck is out of touch.'

Ibu shakes her head. 'You cruise for a Cure for say so.' She examines Bapa stern. 'What is it? What's really with you? It's more than the sculpture, for some reason.'

'Dunno. My mission is complete. Dunno what is next.'

'You may as well be sifar. Think that way then you know.'

'Yeer. Jesús the supererogatory launderer has more passion for mission than me.' When Bapa is very angry, or in despair, his words get bigger.

'You get old.' She means his Mind, his spirit. Bapa is still in his 80's. 'SnakiDik may be short of the most important invention in the world, but it's fun. It's quirky.' When Ibu is worried, her Anglo-Malay improves. Maybe it calms her down. 'Who else could make it? So, it's a sex hoot lah. Everyone has a good titter about it, but it's amazing. You are amazing.'

Bapa grimaces and shakes his head.

Ibu sits back, thoughtful. 'You give any consideration about childing?'

What? You're pushing Bapa leaving us? For becoming a childling in another family? You would send Bapa away from me? No!

Bapa slumps in a huddle. 'Aisha, please let it slide for a week or 2. I agree we'll attend the Inductee Gala, yeer? As you wish. Let's just see how things are afterwards.'

Ibu throws her hands up, rises. 'We might as well all be sifar,' she says, and stomps up the stairs.

Ben Evoli …

Tucking Mal in bed. 'Bapa?' He looks troubled. Thoughtful.

'What, fella?'

'Today is the equinox.' Emphasis on *equinox*.

'It is.'

'The nights get longer than the days,' he says. 'Everything will be much scarier.'

Aisha Evoli …

Oh, so y'all flutherbomb me already ah? I suppose Ben is no fun. He is no fun since … I'm unable for recall. Where is the man who first meets me, his reputasi blossom on the success of MusiKai? Fresh from his 2nd childing, his head full of silly ideas compare phalluses and snakes, all wiggle and writhe with a fork tongue and how would it feel? And wow! What if there was a hoot (hancy utility) for erotically stimulate the brain direct and hey! Would I like help him develop it?

Recall his wide-eye, manic, bubble-over energy. Infectious like that lah. It's why we child. As well as got decades of longer life. All innocence and ideas and no rationalisation. In a safe, nurturing family space. A childling's fruit rejuvenates because it releases the stresses of adulthood. A safe environment for creativity. Ben emerges from childing a young boy who obsess about the thing in his pants. What a surprise.

Without me as test pilot (the enhancement would be dangerous without the safety features I make him implement lah) who knows what he might perpetrate?

Is it such a cliche? Love the boy in him as much as the man?

Holala! All that disillusion in him. And coddling Mal about his first hancy, ah. It's a parent's duty, save their anak anak from bad decisions. Mal should have a hancy already, no matter how he feels about it ah. What can Ben fear about make the responsible choice for his son?

I decide spend the night in the long house. Ben's crushing mood is a cold fruit press. I need warmer company lah.

Have no worry for Ben. He got the whole desa look out for him, as much as he resist it ah. He will get a pillow companion tonight, which will make him yet more miserable. Holala.

Come on, y'all can help me pick a dress. Something sexy … well, attractive one only. It must be comfy. I might sleep in it. A sari will cover me in my sleep ah. In Varikain. I so love Varikain. No one say I'm too old for it, holala.

Off with the kimono Ben fab me earlier. Ugh. I hate aqua. Into the sucky bin. Let my fingers linger over my little volcano. Y'all enjoy it, yeer? Hope there is lava later.

'I see you in my fluther, Ben Evoli dari Saf dari Mal. Take your onespace eyes off my arse lah.'

'Ha ha, you catch me,' Ben membs. 'Think you might be too busy playing up for your flutherbombers.'

'I always notice you, Bat Ears. Your presence is a pipe organ in a harpsichord concerto lah.'

Wind the sari around right, left; pleat in front at the waist; toss the pallu over the shoulder. Step on the bio-scanner in the wardrobe for update my foot size. They feel some swell tonight. Fab a new pair of shoes. Shake a perfume pill from a bottle on the dresser; swallow it.

Cooler outside. The rumah panjang—*longhouse* in Regal—sits in the park about 30 metres in from the avenue. I tell y'all about our rumah panjang. Y'all got sian (bored), come back later.

It is a public rumah Panjang ah. For any travellers, even sifar or locals from the desa who like sleep there some nights. Ben and me campaign for it lah. We want put it across the avenue right across from our housing hill. The desa council challenge us. They think it will stop us. They should taste Ben better. They should taste me better. We agree for put it right there, plain view from our verandah. Already we see all the hammocks they string up in the park. And the hawker stalls come down for every meal. The council hate it lah. It creates such a fuss but what to do? The Infi want and the Infi get.

We build in real chengal wood (cause such a fuss, use such rare material on a lowly building ah) and borrow from traditional Indo-Malay designs, though no weapons or skulls decorate it. There is no space for pound rice or prepare food. Otherwise, just a traditional rumah panjang. No internal wall, no private room. What would be the point of separate room? Neos flutherbomb through all walls. In our desa, we build on low stilts; still work for our climate ah. In a tropical region we would build it higher off the ground; encourage ventilation for temperature control. Our verandah run the whole length, same as traditional, on the other side; overlook the park and the bowling greens.

A commotion of local anak anak run skidding in the grass as one of them counts for 10. A common evening game, play hide-and-seek with Kaboobie. Kaboobie always win; his sense of smell beats the anak anak even when they cheat with hancies.

Take a short-cut across the zoysia grass for the longhouse door. From the rain, water squidge between the soles of my feet and shoes, squirt between my toes. Alamak. Should take the path instead of short-cut. Foolish for wear these shoes. Laugh like that lah. Kick shoes into my hands, skip barefoot. Toss the shoes in the sucky bin near the longhouse steps.

Breathe a *damn shiok* sigh. Always sleep easier in a public hall lah. Remind me of childhood, when a rumah panjang is my family's only shelter. The scent of bodies and bedding, the sounds of sex, remind me of those days sleeping in a community rumah panjang.

Lights are dim. Some are already asleep. Others move bedding from the verandah for avoid the dewy night air. The usual mix of local and visitor. Smile for Harjanti. With one of her suami and another couple (tourists, I guess). In a tangle of arms legs and raking fingers.

'Come share my bed, amoi,' a lelaki says. He sit cross-leg on a pallet, wear disposable white pyjamas from the fabby at the front door. He pat a white sheet next to him. I look, and all I can think is *apples*. His face remind me of apples: apples for cheeks, apple slices for ears, half an apple under his mouth is a ruddy, bulbous chin, ah.

'Terima kasih. I find my own bed.'

'Infi jalang!' he hisses. 'Are you too good for me? Though sifar, in another time I am more reputable than you would ever be without your suami.'

Snores stop. Sex stops. Breaths hold. Within tiks, 3 wanita and 3 lelaki surround him. He look left and right. The 6 pin him on his pallet. One cover his face with a cushion, muffle protest, while 4 others lug him up, each take a limb. Carry him out on the verandah and toss him on the wet grass. Nurses are already busy. They swoop in and out of fluthers while they sit comfortable in the clinic and sip aya tea. Out of the dark, rainbow uniforms emerge. Intercept the lelaki and execute his Warrant. Those who throw him there will escape with a brief counsel session and a box of nutes. Nurses among my fluther assess whether I decline the lelaki's advances only because he is sifar. Well, it's simple ah. I find no attraction for him. I desire no sleep with apples tonight. No apple juice, no apple pulp. No cider either. And then he is rude lah? Y'all see it.

The sharp atmosphere softens. Farther down on the left is a spare futon. I unroll it, unfasten my hair, plump pillows, loosen my sari.

'May I, Aisha Face?' a lelaki membs.

I jel him; enjoy what I discover. 'May.'

He move near, fluid and silent. Feather-light, he slide under my sari, touch a finger on his hancy, make an attempt for engage a hoot. Knit his eyebrows when my hancy decline his request.

I whisper in his ear, 'I rather go without enhancement tonight.'

Maddox Price …

Ben sulks alone in his housing hill's common room; sips the last icy dilution of his gin; sets the glass down; trudges up the stairs for his family's quarters. On the landing between the kitchen and the informal dining room, Saf, his sweet young daughter, slouches on a stool at the kitchen bench. She has a glass of juice, and one foot on a rung of a stool while her other leg swings to a beat. Holling music, I guess. Ah, Sonik Monkey Alliance—a popular ensemble for her age group.

'Ibu went out,' she says. 'And there are 2 wanita upstairs.'

'Two? You let them in?' Ben, oh Ben, miserable Puffin.

Saf's more at ease with it than her father. 'Two is better than 200,' she says. 'There's no sending them away, Bapa. The desa owns your pantat.' Anglo-Malay for … *arse*. And sometimes the front bum.

Ben leans on the bench, hugs Saf close. 'Guess so, yeer?'

'If you turn them away, what about their reputasi?' Saf says merging into Ben's embrace. You must lie back and think of Indo-Malaysia, Puffin. Paint the ceiling beige. Take two for the team and call me in the morning.

With heavy footsteps, he trudges upstairs as if there's executioners awaiting him.

'Jaya! What are you here for?' Ben stammers on entering his bedroom. He knows her, the daughter of a local café missionary.

'Selamat malam, Tuan Ben,' Jaya says. Her eyes are bright as stage lights, her smile bigger than a swimming pool.

The other one coughs politely, standing by the glass partition between bed and bath, hands behind her back. 'You remember me, Infi? I am in your bed before.'

Ben, still in a freeze, flushes. Yet for ungluing his hand from the knob of the open door. He stammers while he stealthily jels her. She catches him, nonetheless. Her shoulders slump.

'Sudah tentu, I remember … Qian.'

'So then,' Qian says tentatively. 'You want me first? Or both together?'

Ben Evoli …

'Deeper, Tuan,' Jaya membs. She has no idea how it works; there is no physical dick in SnakiDik. It extends nothing, hardens nothing, fattens nothing. It's all in the Mind. With more sophistication than any hoot in history, it iterates over sub-militik intervals; samples memories and fantasies; collates sensory feedback; programs and initiates neural activity; simulates physical stimulation. It monitors haptic awareness and enhances sensations. The desires of all the parties joining a session influence how it behaves as it weaves together consensual, coherent, and congruent perceptions of experiences. It will induce hallucination, eliminating cognitive dissonance between what participants internally register and, shall we say, any physical contradictions. Yeer, make her breasts as balloons and may all your drinking straws be elephant trunks. Easily suggestible minds are one thing we share with saps.

As Jaya focuses on the sensory overload building, I never touch her. See? I lie back, passive, without arousal; yet she bucks and writhes as if I am mining her with tiny explosives. I could sit in the armchair by the window while Jaya rides an imaginary phallus of any size, shape, or species she desires. The spell holds. She'll hallucinate me where her stimulated nerves expect me. There she goes—a dinosaur screech, collapsing on the bed in a dead sweat. Another satisfied customer. James Dean would be smoking a cigarette.

Now Jaya beds an Infi, she will collect more of her own flutherbombers. I have no taste whether I'm happy or sad about it. Her pursuit of reputasi may well earn her a Cure—the kind they should reserve for the Greediest of Infis.

Teodora Mrowka …

Vör plays up for us, in Eir's embraces and tender attentions. Eir's mattress gives for the weight of Vör who plants her feet and spraddles. A pillow—a downy beast come alive—devours Vör's hair and cheek. She turns her head, closes eyes, mews like a kitten. Her skin tingles, ripples in frisson. Eir grabs her hips. Eir's fingers grow branches, sprouting soft flat leaves which curl around Vör's limbs, and stroke her back. A pair of sapling branches part her labia and insinuate between, thriving on moisture, growing inward and up. A soft brush of leaves paints cave art on her inner walls. The branches expand like a fast-growing tree, entwining the fibrous dome of her cervix, pressuring her bladder, hinging her tailbone, giving her the sense, she might wag her own tail. Waves of electrostatic honey ooze lightning-strikes. Eir slaps; fingers spider out and pull Vör to her.

Eir and Vör engage SnakiDik (a shame a man is the creator; a woman would name it better). Eir grows an imaginary penis. Plunges. Vör's at the maddening edge of her limits. Primal instincts tell her she might die. The darkest fantasy of tentacles cradles her womb. The tree trunk inside her becomes a plush-toy merry-go-round—complete with poles and horses rising and falling, going round inside her. Eir guides. Vör arches her back; her jaw locks open, eyes glassy; her lungs paralyse. She pushes back hard. It builds, inexorably—quaking, raking, clawing, howling.

Vör collapses—a dank peach poaching in her own syrup—and lies back in Eir's arms, sweating steam in a puddle among twisty sheets. Her racking breath returns; her bones rubbery; her spatial sense all at angles, severed from her own parts.

SnakiDik is such a powerful ubiquitous hoot. Nurses should be wary of installing it. Vör, you forget Ben is the guest of honour at this year's Infi Gala? Where's your sense of mission? Eir drafts you into our operation for your energy and zeal, despite your obvious flaws—your fears and insecurities. Eir uses her influence, swaying us in favour of you. Few of us have little surprise you roll in bed together.

The team waits days while Eir mulls over her options. Is Operation Hang 10 proceeding? Will we write a Warrant for Ben?

Though I have no specific taste of it, I wonder if Vör is subverting Eir somehow—for the sake of an Infi who might benefit the most from a long Cure for Ben; for the sake of a missionary of questionable alternative health practices; for that mother of Vör's.

Grammar

'Time to Pretend' — MGMT

Eir Frijberg ...

COLLECTIVE NOUNS are a great practical joke, hailing from medieval times, influencing the language of Regal English from then till now. If y'all would believe me, my loving fluther, the perpetrator of this joke was a fly-fishing nun. Her name was Juliana Berners (perhaps an ancestor of Tim Berners Lee?). Of noble descent, Juliana was a Benedictine prioress of the nunnery at Sopwell, in the 15th century of the sap common era. Two of her essays appeared in *The Boke of Seynt Albans* from 1486 or, as other printings named it, *The Book of Hawkynge, Huntynge, and Blasing of Armys,* which *shewyth the manere of hawkynge and huntynge.*

One of those essays, *A Treatyse of Fysshynge with an Angle*, is the earliest volume on the subject of sport fishing. It is a book of detail and vision, containing substantial information on the subject. But it is Juliana's work on hunting which illuminates her trickster spirit, to which she appended a list of *company terms* or *terms of venery* (venery being an archaic word for hunting). This is where those expressions such as *gaggle of geese* come from.

I enjoy thinking of Juliana as one of the world's first feminists: a noble woman become nun; a gentle woman become huntress; the first female author in the English language; a writer laying traps for the stuffy, puffy gentlemen of her time.

Juliana devised her terms of venery for various game animals and birds, knowing hunting men would seize upon them as a means of asserting personal superiority. Such technical things are for a man's mastering, so a man had better learn them right. A man's qualities might be measured by his technical correctness, and the luxuries it afforded him when explaining to others. His knowledge of terms of hunting became one objective measure of his worth quantifiable against the worth of another. Such is competition.

The Boke of Saint Albans compiled detailed instructions for gentlemen. A gentleman had better master his terms of venery for impressing his fellows in well-to-do parlours with tales of his hunting prowess; or his skill in blasting arms when taking down this pigeon or that grouse. Boasts of shooting a brace of dolphins would make one a fool because any true gentleman would know dolphins congregate in pods. On the other hand, even if one never left the library, knowing the terms proved one the expert hunter. So, study your terms of venery in *The Boke of Saint Albans*. There's a good fool, you dull English gentle-show-off.

From a Nordic mind, I wonder how our Viking ancestors devolved into the English dandies of the period. Perhaps the green of the English countryside reduced their minds to mint jelly. I imagine young men, in after-dinner conversation—in doublets and hose, cod pieces, slashings and flared shoulder pads—using a wrong term of venery, and thereby disgracing themelves. Imagine Juliana tittering at them exaggerating their exploits besting this *beesty* or fusillading that *fowly*.

English developed. Obscure collective nouns multiplied and flourished. If one learns their first 100 or so terms, here's another 1000 for mastering. The competition is yet fierce. Start with flocks, packs, herds, then progress with a murder of crows, a shrewdness of apes, a clowder of cats, a crash of rhinoceroses or a harem of fur seals (blame lusty sailors). A band of gorillas may derive from the English prog-rock days of the 1970's. There is also a tabernacle of bakers, a wiggery of barristers, a glitter of generals, an ambush of widows, a linkage of web masters, and a bloat of programmers (these last 2 were prize matrimonial catches in Ye Olde Englishe tymes). Ironically for Juliana Berners, the collective noun for nuns is *superfluity*. Poor dear superfluous Juliana. Get thee to a nunnery.

Whether a figure of history or mythology, I love Juliana Berners for her insight. She tasted how male reductive minds obsess over the collection of technical titbits while never grasping the underpinning principals from which insight and true wisdom flows. Winning a competition, with its emphasis on point-scoring, is more important than true understanding. In the commerce of status, a quantity of facts is more tradable than underlying truths.

Fluther is absent from the original terms of venery. I doubt the common English gentleman would find much joy in the *huntynge* of jellyfish. If there is one thing less challenging than *blassynge* fish in a barrel …

Curious, there has never been an enduring collective noun for nurses. Nurses are shepherds for the communities they serve; so perhaps the collective noun for shepherds might serve: a sodom of shepherds. You jank just one sheep … Perhaps we should look to Juliana Berners for inspiration. While few nurses today exhibit many nunnish traits, their collective noun seems most apt; nurses are ever more superfluous. The need for the mission is passing; in the meantime, we are corrupting it beyond remembrance of its original purity.

Vör Hoyur …

Walls of mute mulberries and violets with an accent of white here and there. Dark timber textures for frames and trim. Floor-for-ceiling windows wrap around 2 sides of Eir's bedroom. Fir-green light dapples the rugs. From above, a skylight casts an iridescent rectangle on the pinewood floor. Consuming the middle of the room, her simple large bed is little more than a pallet with no headboard or posts, no footlocker. A disarray of soft sturdy sheets, a thick *dyne*, and firm square pillows.

Stretch. Waking with a wispy halo. Flutherbombers watching me from one side then another; from back near the wall or close; peeping from outside the windows; zooming in so every imperfection and more of my skin is obvious; panning round so they get just the right angles. So habitually they forget (or no longer care) about the traces they leave.

Why are they flutherbombing me? I am no visual treat at the best of times. Worse in the morning with my bed-hair and half-gluey eyes.

In the kitchen, Eir sings a wordless tune. The aroma of *kaffe* rich and intense in my nostrils. I smile the lazy smile of the morning, my fruit steeping in the liquor-sweet hum of last night.

Flutherbomb us in our time of ecstasy, will y'all? However closely you swirl around our lovemaking, you will never feel Eir with your physical skins. May you enjoy your view in the back row. I have a part on the stage.

'Little Mermaid, take your nutes. You taste a little out of balance.' Eir appears in the bedroom doorway. She tosses a nutepak which lands with a metallic slap on my thigh.

My lips and earlobes tingle. And other parts. I have the heart rate of a hummingbird. Eir in the kitchen is in arousal too. We are stars on the edge of an event horizon. Her fluther throbs with so much life; her halo leaks through the walls, a whirlpool of mist and fog.

I jump out of bed straight for the kitchen. Intense, sympathetic, and vicarious, my arousal feeds off Eir's. With eyes shut, she stands with her hands planting on the kitchen bench, fingers scratching the surface, taking root. She is shaking, moaning, knees bending, pelvis rocking.

'Check my reputasi, Little Mermaid.'

'It's climbing fast.'

'*Ja.*' She gasps and shakes, her ecstasy feeding on her growing fluther and her rising razoos.

'Because of your keynote at the *Akademiet*?'

'It's building for a while before the graduation. Faster now.' Her voice raspy.

She lifts me, throws me. I land rough on my back on the bench. She's up above, mounting. Gasping; thighs shaking; knees vibrating; navel pulsing; calves all pins and needles; toes … stretch and curl. Nerve-exploding frenzy. Eir moves sweaty and wild, eyes and mouth wide as if a knife stabs her. My fingers reach for her, rubbing, feeling. There is too much for absorbing.

'Life is amazing, Little Mermaid.' She climbs off, and stands aside the bench, runs her fingernails up and down my side. 'Let's take the day and celebrate.'

Feeling special, I ask, 'Celebrate what? How?'

'You'll see.' She kisses and smiles, her long white hair a canopy draping around my face. There is mischief in the fireworks of her eyes.

Wary, I say, 'You have a plan.'

'Let's go spookheading.'

Eir Frijberg …

Dear Vör could never look more aghast. 'Spookheading?' she sputters. The idea stings her. Fast she sits up, draws knees chestward, and wraps arms around.

'Your reputasi is rising so fast, already you will make it plummet? Are you courting a Cure?'

'The occasional giddy thrill, my darling, will earn no Cure. There are no Warrants for spookheading, only for spookheading addiction. Addiction is the sickness, never the act.'

'Is addiction Greed or Gluttony?' Vör teases.

'Who cares? It's a sickness, either over-attachment or over-detachment. And you're stalling.'

Vör contemplates—fixing her eyes, furrowing her brows.

I say, 'It will be good for you, Little Mermaid.'

She shudders. Looks down studying herelf. 'My knees are shaking,' she says and laughs. She's lost in the joy of our lovemaking. 'I never spookhead before,' she membs. 'You … have? … ever?'

I nod, smile cheekily. Her face scrunches. 'I would never guess—'

'I'm a spookhead? Little Mermaid, it is a bucket of fun once in a while.'

'But if I start …'

I finish the thought for her. 'You will become an addict.'

Vör exhales. 'Eir, you know I loathe spooky fields.'

'How better for conquering your fear? You'll love it …'

'But it's … spookheading! Spookheads.' Vör's distaste scrimshaws her face.

'Sometimes I think you a nun, Little Mermaid. You cloister yourelf away from all these evils and temptations. Perhaps you could decide the proper collective noun for nurses, and further confound the Minds of men.'

'Maybe I will love spookheading. Maybe too much.'

'Is this what you fear?'

'You know my *mor* is a spookhead. Among other things.'

'Little Mermaid, spookheading is no cause of the way she treats you.'

'You never see the way it is with her. Nothing is ever intense enough.' She falls silent, ruminating.

I take her in my arms, kiss her forehead. 'You are never your *mor*.'

'Well, for start, I am single-gender, bory-boring.' She clings on till her fugue passes. 'What will other nurses say of us spookheading?'

'Ah, you are offering excuses. You know full well the reputasi of any nurses judging us would suffer. They could meet with Cure of their own.'

'Nurses care nothing of reputasi.'

'Ha! Such an innocent you are. Get ready, we're going for a ride.'

Are y'all still with us, my loving fluther? Fast we jump between station and station; night and day; season and season; mountain tops and ocean beaches; snow and rain; sun and cloud. Which of y'all follow all our vectors? We catch half of you off guard by spooking straight from my cottage for the local station. Y'all should know how familiar we are with the station and the missionaries there. Spooking straight there is perfectly safe for us. There will be no materialising in earth up to our *kussen* or with half our heads in a tree trunk. We'll suffer no disfigurements. There will be no half flies, half nurses; no Tuvok/Neelixes; no duplicate Captain Kirks. Uhura will get the kiss she deserves. We'll grow no horns.

Sweet Vör emerges from onespace each time a little more in derangement, deeper in hallucinations, nearer ecstasy. As Vikings we stride from the violet mist of our 15th spook. The arches of the station roof flicker through my juddering vision. Tailing us from the tropical forests of New Guinea, hallucinatory eclectus parrots swoop over our heads in celebration of our arrival—clapping wings, approving our rainbow dress so similar as the colours of their feathers. I extend my hand and one alights on my fingers. I feel no claws. Rather, a wave of sensation passes down my arm—a waterfall of salty tequila and lime. My skin dimples and becomes orange peel, thick and pithy, trapping shivers which dive deep and titillate my core. Later, we'll take some nutes, and have a sturdy meal for rebalancing all the neurochems marinating our brains and fruit. Dopamine from the jump across onespace. Endorphins flooding as reward of a successful arrival. Oxytocin from being so near Vör. Serotonin washing through my gut, building a sense of confidence and well-being. Even a spike of anandamide.

The parrots flap wings good-bye. I take Vör by the arm and skip from the spooky hall for the outdoor concourse. Her skin is soft and sensuous under my caress. A ripe peach for my tangy citrus. We could rub out quite a fruity cocktail between us. Desire for grabbing her and grinding pelvises overtakes me; we keep skipping, sipping the bliss of anticipation.

Vör Hoyur ...

Where are we? It's cold.

'Preikestolen Station, Norway,' Eir answers. 'Six hundred metres above Lysefjorden.'

Clear views of cliffs across the fjord. One hundred and eighty degrees out the other windows are barren, rolling hills. By far the prettiest view from a spooky hall. I say, 'I could take this in a while,' feeling the Viking spirit swelling within.

'Good.' Eir offers a smile with corners lacing in a suspicious thread of mischief.

The station sits back a vertigo-avoiding distance from the edge of the cliffs. We follow other arrivals along a well-worn path meandering ever nearer the precipitous edges. Before long, the path becomes a 4-metre-wide gangway with a sheer drop on the left. My head spins, my stomach rolls, and I catch myelf between 2 competing terrors: falling over the side, and the shame of projectile-vomiting. Ahead is a plateau: the destination of all these walkers (skipping on these treacherous rocks would be inadvisable), many with picnic baskets. I'd prefer a scenic cemetery over this any day. All around is a sense of carnival and relaxation. None appear wary of the pair of detective nurses close by. On the plateau there are 14's—many standing precariously near a 600-metre appointment for remodelling their faces. There are no fences. Norwegians say barriers invite complacency; and besides, they can never fence off all of nature.

Every so often a voice rings out—or couple or trio of voices—with chill cries, hollers or *yeer-hahs*, after which follows chuckles and applause from spectators and picnickers. A queue moves inexorably for the edge of the plateau and, with a 30-tik regularity, take turns jumping off.

I grab Eir by the arm, try pulling her back for the station. 'No, no, no no ... no.'

'Oh, come on. It'll be fun.'

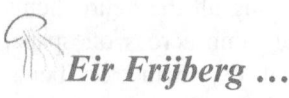

Eir Frijberg ...

Vör is a blithering, pleading mess tugging on my arm, begging, bargaining, negotiating. Somehow make progress for the rock despite her dragging me back.

The plateau is Ice Age granite, almost square—about 21 metres on a side, the snout of an ancient battle-weary aircraft-carrier ploughing the fjord. An axe wound of a crack extends from the starboard side 3-quarters of the way across the middle; the bow threatens sheering away and plummeting into the lake. (*Ja, ja*, every geology missionary is membing, *there'll be many 1000's of years before then.*) Across its off-level deck, rocky outcrops and bulges provide plenty of choice for sitting and setting picnic blankets. Many families select places precariously near the precipices. Must be Norwegians.

Vör resigns herelf. We join the queue.

Vör Hoyur …

Nearer the edge than I dare alone, I peer over. There's no straight drop into the fjord as the view from the back of the plateau would illude. Rather, the silvery ribbon of the cliff bows in for about 150 metres where it twists left and plunges into the satin surface of the water.

The semi-transparent lilac spooky field I must jump into sparkles about 100 metres below us. It cuts into the cliff, spreads around this pulpit of rock, and extends out for more than it is wide. I see nowhere I might slip through. Still, I imagine the tree branches underneath shredding the flesh from my bones.

I'll be entering the field at great speed. 'How will it stop us from splattering on the other side?' I ask, heart in mouth.

'Oh, I dunno,' Eir says, too casual. 'Particle physics, nerf balls …'

'I'm serious,' I object. 'I must know.'

'… huge vats of gelato, rubber bands, choirs of angels.' Eir sobers up. 'There's a succession of diffusion nets. Each decelerates you a bit more until you flomp gently into your choice of pistachio or affogato angels.'

'Eir!'

'Come on. Put your fear of heights aside.' Without warning, Eir experiences a sudden violent twitch. Her dyspraxia often seizes her at the worst tiks.

I squeal as she teeters off balance at the edge of the ledge. Instinctively my hand reaches out for grabbing hers. In a chill shock, my brain assesses she could pull me over with her. Somehow, with both our free arms flapping like some mutant double-body stork we stop ourelves from toppling.

I say, 'I have no fear of heights. I have a fear of gravity.'

'Better if we just fall. For a tik, I consider taking you with me,' Eir says with triple-distilled mischief.

The missionary whose role is keeping the queue smoothly moving coughs. 'If it helps, we'll bring the field up for you.'

'How close?' I demand.

'Five and 20 metres.'

'Make it none and 20.'

'Vör!' Eir scolds then appraises the look on my face. Her shoulders drop. Her eyes roll. 'All right.'

The missionary conjures a console, swivels her wrist inside a control. The spooky field shifts up. Twenty metres still seems a dangerous drop. Gulp a deep breath, take Eir's hand, and together hop off like kangaroos.

The wind is deafening. In 2 tiks, we're falling 20 metres per tik into silence. The familiar tickle of a spooky field passes through me. I'm still falling! Imagine the splat I'll make. Wait, there's some resistance. More. And more. On my face I feel a thin electrostatic meringue, egg yolk with 1000's of tiny pins in it.

All up, translation through the deceleration fields takes longer than the fall. I land face-first in a gravity couch which bounces me and Eir into another before the next jumpers arrive. Gasp and whoop, taking in the panoramic scene through the floor-to-ceiling windows. There's no doubt we're back in Preikestolen Station. 'Let's go again!'

'Eir! Eir, my heart. Wake up.' I nudge her shoulder. Again, with more force.

Last night, after returning from our spookheading adventure, Eir collapses in bed and descends into deep sleep. I lay vaguely awake, a vibrating tuning fork, equally stiff.

Sudden alert. The world spinning. Her halo is aqua fire above and around us.

'Eir, wake up!'

Her eyes open. 'What is it?' Her voice sounds ancient and infirm.

I am bouncing and jumping on the bed. This is it. This must be what she waits for. She's invincible now. No one can stop us. Surely, Operation Hang 10 will proceed.

'What is it?' she asks again, a little more awake.

Whisper in her ear, 'Look for your reputasi. You are Infinite!'

Logic

'I'm Lucky' — Joan Armatrading

 *Aisha Evoli …*

I SHUT THE FRONT DOOR.

'Ibu,' Mal calls from the kitchen. Nothing is better in life than the love of a son lah.

'I'm cooking kaya toast,' Saf membs. 'No fabbing.'

I say, 'I see, okelah,' with dismay. 'There's coconut milk everywhere, fine. I must order a one of my disaster recovery teams in here right away lah.'

'I tell her, just fab it,' Mal says, no tolerate his saudara.

'This tastes better,' Saf says.

'Na-ah,' Mal taunts. 'We got the best fabby there is.'

'This is still better.'

'Bapa,' Mal says. Ben looks up from a holly on the table. 'A fabby prints things and a sucky bin takes them away.'

'Yeer …' Ben answers without commitment, inspects his holly.

'What would happen if I make a fabby print something and, at the same time, throw the fabby in a sucky bin?'

'I dunno,' Ben says absently. 'You taste purple?'

'Purple!?' Mal giggles.

'Or maybe you get 2 Rikers …' Ben says. Referencing bodoh (stupid) sap pop culture no doubt, fine.

'What's he talking about?' Mal screws up his face with a mental effort.

'Leave your bapa be,' I chide. 'And please tell me you fabby the jam lah.' This pair make jam would glue everything in the kitchen lah.

Saf roll her eyes, reject my mothering. 'We fabby the jam, Ibu,' she says with fake weariness.

Mal traces his finger through some stickiness on the counter. Saf drops bread slices into the toaster. Eggs boil in an overfull saucepan, hot water storms over and sizzles on the cooktop. For years I try interest Saf in cooking ah. Then when she cook, she make such mess I wish I never encourage her last time. Flick the cooktop dial down; grab the saucepan handle; move it on a cold element. 'Those eggs should be soft, Saf.'

'Well, you should be home and cook breakfast.' She's sour, never happy when I stay out overnight. Never mind Ben has his own company too ah.

'We think you would miss breakfast,' Mal says, sulking. 'Where are you all night?'

'In the longhouse,' Saf accuses.

Outside, Gruffield is pouncing about in the fernery, chasing imaginary mice. The stupid ray cat is flickering orange with excitement like a faulty streetlamp. Ignoring Saf, I say, 'Your bapa is an able cook, ah.'

Ben drag his gaze from the holly, wave his hands around, say *kinda busy here*. It could be a mindwriting schematic or a new design for a dry tandas. Can never tell lah. 'I offer,' he membs, 'but Saf argues, so ...'

'Is there time for a shower?'

'Sure,' Saf membs. 'Better wash the sifar off before you eat.'

Pour a cup of aya tea from the pot on the counter. 'You 2 take your nutes ha?'

'Yeer, Ibu. Bapa makes me,' Mal says.

'Saf?'

'Yeer, Ibu.'

The anak anak, eager for chow down on the toast stack, try wait for me ah. But much of the stack is on plates or in sticky hands before I sit lah.

'Bapa? Are all the saps gone?' Mal mouths while chomping down on a large chunk of toast overhanging his lips by more than half its length. It's a food parody of an industrial accident lah.

'Here we go again,' Saf complains. 'Question time at the breakfast zoo.'

'No talking with your mouth full ah,' I try sound firm, no stern one. 'Mal. How we understand a thing you say?'

'This's why we learn membing,' Saf says. 'For talking while you stuff your gob.'

'Well, are they?' On Mal's plate, his toast is a building after an earthquake.

'Saps?' I ask.

'Yeer.'

Saf brightens. 'All gone, Mal. There is no one dumber than you left.' Taste her internal scoreboard lighting up.

'No survivors?'

'We are the survivors,' Ben says.

'We are a different species,' Mal's diction is muddy with coconut milk. 'We are *Anthro neotenus*, they were *Homo sapiens*.' Mal munches his point.

I say, 'We evolve from saps.'

'Saps all died in spooky stations.' Mal says, showing off.

Ben waves his holly away. 'They had no spooky stations. Though they discovered how to shift instantly between one place and another. Soon they had machines for enhancing transport.'

'Why for they spook around if it killed them?'

'It took them many years before they learn it is harmful. Meanwhile, travel became so much faster and easier.'

'They were silly,' Mal says with a mouthful. 'They should have known spooking was bad for them.'

'If they tried no spooking, there would be no us, dungu,' Saf says.

'It's sad.' Mal stops munch.

'They were all spookheads.' Saf drops the last corner of her toast on her plate lah. Too crusty for her taste.

Mal gulps his drink, like a pelican swallow a large fish. 'A friend shows me a holly of a sap, dead from spooky sakit. His head exploded.'

Saf laughs with a sneer.

I say, 'No one's head exploded, Mal.' He looks disappointed.

'Many died,' Saf membs like she tell a ghost story, 'clawing at their skulls trying to get the itchy voices out of their heads. They scratched their own eyes out, scratched the cheeks off their own faces.'

'Please, Saf,' Ben says. 'Enough.'

'The dolphins tell me all about saps,' Mal says.

'Dolphins?' Ben asks. 'What are you talking about?' Y'all can read so much in the altitude of his eyebrows. Sometimes they tower like volcano peaks over the lakes of his eyes.

'Dolphins talk with me,' Mal mumbles.

I stand up before I know. 'Alamak! What is this about dolphin flutherbombing you? Some Ah Tan makes a fool of you lah.'

'Aisha, be calm,' Ben says, but how can? Someone messes with my anak.

'Walao eh! We warn you about sakit flutherbombers, yeer? You are an Infi's anak; you must be careful. There's no rely on the KK for protect you every tik of the day.' Dimly aware I'm losing control. 'There's no dolphins, just that one try trick you. Who are you? Who's in there? Who mess with my family?'

'Ibu, please, stop,' Saf pleads. 'Stop shouting. Please. Leave Mal alone. Stop shaking him!'

Faces, bodies, toys, ducky cubes, Mal's swasta, ayam slaughterhouses, spies watch ... What y'all want with my anak anak? With my family? Y'all know who I am? I could ...

'Please, Ibu, you're hurting him. Ibu. Ibu! Stop already, please ... please ... please ...'

'Aisha!'

My left cheek stings. Feel Ben's face close—his brows in a furrow, his mouth a fissure in a rocky cliff, his bat ears red.

Aduh! He just slap me?

 *Saf Evoli …*

Bapa slaps Ibu! 'Aisha, stop.'

Unsure if I should go around the table or over. Jump for Mal's side, hand on his shoulder. His eyes rolling back in his head; his mouth slack and open; drool and coconut milk at the corner. Is his tongue swelling? 'Bapa? What's happening?' Someone is squealing. It's Ibu. No, it's me. Bite down on it. No, Ibu is wailing too.

Bapa, please fix this. He sweeps Mal up. Carries him for the lounge in the day room. Mal's eyes out of focus. He's twitching. Bapa lowers him on the lounge, pins one shoulder down, and holds Mal's chin in his firm hand.

Ibu still sits at the table, staring into her hands.

Mal, don't die. I'm sorry I'm mean.

The front door slams, making me jump with fright. A nurse charges in, a fierce sense of mission in her eyes and her grim, tight lips.

'Infi, I taste an emergency.' She must be flutherbombing Bapa.

Bapa looks at her, frozen. Everyone is frozen, except—is she for real a nurse? She wears the rainbow uniform, but no effects hang from her chatelaine. She is too pretty. Are there pretty nurses?

'Nurse Lành Hiền.' Bapa knows her. 'My anak …'

'Give me room, please.'

Bapa shuffles aside while still pinning Mal on the couch. The nurse is over Mal, studying. With a sweep of her hand, she opens a holly over the couch arm near Mal's head. Numbers and graphs, little sounds like water going down a drain, over and over. Pictures of Mal—circling and zooming; focusing on his face; up his nose; in his ears; in his eyes. Zooming more. Showing his brain in minute detail. Different colours. Something throbs in there. Many somethings.

'This is wrong.' The nurse in shock.

Mal is dying. 'What?' My voice sounds pathetic.

'If I'm right,' she says, 'there will be no believing me.'

The nurse springs up. She is at the kitchen fabby so fast. Of course she knows where it is lah. From her kangaroo pocket, she pulls a beaker, places it on the fabby platen.

Mal is shaking. A fish flapping on a boat deck. Bapa holds him down by his shoulders. Mal makes fists while his head snaps left and right. Drooling and sweating. A small dark patch appears on the front of his shorts and grows large. The couch cushion is getting wet too.

'Nurse,' Bapa calls.

From the breakfast table, Ibu wails. She looks bereft, unable for coming by Mal. Like an invisible force pushes her back on her seat. 'Celaka! I kill my boy.'

'No,' the nurse membs, working the fabby. 'I believe it's chronic, an existing condition. Something would trigger an episode sooner or later.'

'What?' Ibu pleads.

The fabby bings. A jarring sound too bright and happy. 'You have a first-class fabby,' the nurse says. The only calm one in the house. Part of me adores her. Even through the fright. Even though she's too pretty.

'He's fitting! We won't get anything down his throat,' Bapa says. He's crying.

The nurse takes a small nutepak from her pocket; fills it with the liquid she fabs in the beaker; screws a short tube with a rectal nozzle over the opening.

'Toss it,' Bapa calls. He looks grey and old.

The nurse is quick, again at the couch with Mal. She pushes Bapa aside. Gentle and insistent, she lifts Mal's feet up, yanks his shorts down and fits the nozzle. Ibu moves at last by the couch. Go and hold her hand. Tears streak her face. Mal is lying on his side, twitching, and clawing at cushions. His breathing is wet and labouring. The nurse holds his shoulder down, keeping him still. With her other hand, she squeezes the nutepak.

'It will take a min,' the nurse says.

Ibu caresses Mal's thigh. We watch the holly, willing the yellow throbbing parts on the image of Mal's brain go away. Are those the bad parts? 'They are shrinking!'

'Oh!' Ibu puts her hand over her gaping mouth and sobs.

'Will he be all right, Bapa?'

Bapa looks at the nurse, his eyes large and wet. 'Nurse Lành Hiền?'

She nods. Hair to her shoulders; perfect nails and skin; soft eyes. Too pretty. My brother is sakit, and I'm noticing she has perfect nails like that lah.

'We'll keep a close watch on him. The danger passes for now,' she says.

'What is it?'

The nurse swallows. 'I never see such except in hollies at the Akademi. Old hollies. We are checking with Singapore.'

A small box near the bottom of the holly display flashes text in blue. *Diagnosis: Entanglement Syndrome, Early Stage.* Mal has the sap disease that wiped them out?

Lành Hiền Rồng (Gentle Dragon) …

Mal sleeps while Ben and his wife Aisha watch over. Saffron's friends come, take her for smoothies on the esplanade. Earlier she is thanking me, adulating, praising my skill. She could be a candidate for a health mission in a few years.

Ben Evoli …

'Someone in there mess with him, Ben,' Aisha says, wiping tears from my eyes. She's always the stronger one. 'We must find out.'

Pressing sadness down, I ask, 'What's coming over you?' with a mixture of concern and indignation.

'You hear him. Dolphins, Ben? Mal thinks dolphins memb him.'

'You know how he is, so fanciful. I'm sure Neil Armstrong talks with him too.'

'Make no jokes about it. It's more … Someone among his fluther. Or something … unrecognisable.'

'You taste them?'

'No … I think, no … maybe …. Adoi! I have no understanding of what I taste.' Aisha's tears flow with the same metronome accuracy as always. Massage her shoulders while she makes a play of wiping her nose. If anything, the tension in her back tightens. Her eyebrows fasten, straight zippers. She's ruminating, rationalising. 'Entanglement Syndrome, Ben?' She blurts. 'Our anak is some freak throw-back to saps ah. I'm glad we have no more anak anak.'

'The KK will figure it out.'

Lành Hiền Rồng (Gentle Dragon) …

Ah well, it's best let the Evolis believe such for now. Until we know more.

'Ha! You on a nurse's side already?' Aisha demands.

'Only saying, it's no—'

'I see how you look at that nurse.'

'Aisha, she's—'

'Lust after whoever you wish, Ben. I'm no jealous sap, so at least own it.'

'Aisha, what has this—'

'I only say because some pretty rainbow fairy flits into our house and already nurses are our saviours ah.'

Ben blinks, shakes his head.

'It's because he has no hancy,' Aisha decides. 'It would always turn out bad for him.'

'What's a lack of a hancy—'

'His brain is overwork.'

'No. Aisha—'

'If we are responsible parents, we would make him take a hancy already. If you—'

'You're blaming me?'

Aisha pauses. 'No, but … we—Mal should have a hancy already. I just know lah.'

'Look, we are Infi. The KK can never afford for Mal suffer. The best nurses are saying it has no connection with—'

'What would they know? Your nurse admits they never see this before. He needs a hancy, with at least a health monitor in it, now more than ever. You would risk he die when he has no hoots every other neo has?'

Ben's mouth works but no words flow. He stands, pats his wife's shoulder, and leaves the room.

Saf Evoli …

'Eee-yer!' Lula membs and pulls a face of disgust. Melting gelati dribbles from the corner of her mouth.

I flutherbomb her, jolt at seeing myelf sitting across from her with a slack face and fluttering eyes. Shiver. Over my own shoulder I see 3 twentage girls—late 20's—standing together between the outdoor section of the gelato bar and the esplanade pavement. Giggling, licking gelati cones. One of the girls flashes her Varikain outfit transparent for a full tik. She's nudy under the see-through cloth. Wearing no chuddies. A couple of thirsty yaya papaya lelaki walk by, smiling like masturbating spider monkeys. The girl makes a show of dragging her tongue across the top of her gelato while the other 2 giggle and wave behind the passing boys' backs. Flash their outfits transparent too. They are wearing lingerie.

I say, 'My ibu is always wearing that stuff. It's cheesy lah.'

Lula laughs raucously while Boneheads tilts her head, making her hair hang over her face. Amara is sitting alongside Lula, apparently without a thread of clothing on.

I demand, 'Where you get this kebaya? Your ibu's wardrobe?' The vision of her nips is burning my retinas.

Lula's outfit reappears. 'It's mine,' she says with some defiance and mock offence.

With any luck the fashion will pass before long. I mean, I know … nudity is—as if. Y'all flutherbombers see me before, I know, but … oh, I dunno.

Lula and Amara are still looking over my shoulder. Flutherbomb Amara for a different perspective. One of the gelati girls is matching her outfit with her own biometrics: heart rate; breathing; pupil dilation; galvanic skin response. The more her arousal, the more transparent her dress. She attracts a new boy almost her height. He's so close he could grope her ah. The girl flicks her hair back. Her dress becomes ever more transparent until the boy leans in and whispers some mumblejank in her ear. In a flash, her outfit is fully opaque again. Her friends shoo the boy off. He laughs for covering his failure.

'Imagine if boys wear Varikain,' Bonehead says.

Lula nearly snorts ice cream through her nose. '24-hour sausage festival.'

We all make *ewww* noises then crunch into our cones. Until Lula and Amara freeze, jaws hanging loose. Something from behind me frightens them.

'Hello, Saf.'

Two nurses close in on us. One is Gentle Dragon. 'Might we have a word with you?'

'Me?' What trouble am I in? Something with Mal's sickness? Please, if I hurt him, I mean no …

'Yes,' the other nurse says. 'If it's kay.'

My friends jump on their feet like there's electricity running through the benches. What's left of their gelati lands in a sucky bin when they skip off.

'What's wrong?'

Gentle and the other sit down in Lula's and Amara's places. 'We're wondering if you might help us.'

'Help you?'

The other nurse nods. 'We understand you might take nursing as your mission one day.'

How is it they—? Of course they know but it still feels intrusive. It's one thing accepting nothing is ever private, but this only puts sirens and lights on it. 'Um … yeer.' Stammering. 'I mean I'm only 24, still more than 6 years before I might enrol at an akademi.'

'*Hai*, plenty of time,' Gentle says. 'You know, they admit me before I am 30.'

'Really?'

Gentle nods. 'Uh-huh. I still remember the first day at the Akademi. The Singapore campus grounds are amazing.'

'You study in Singapore? But you're Japanese.'

Gentle blushes. 'Vietnamese actually. You would love Singapore.'

Trying for sounding casual, I say, 'I already travel there for some school lessons.'

'Of course. You attend any school in the world, for any lesson. But when you stay somewhere for some time, you familiarise yourelf there, feel part of it.'

'It would be wonderful.' Scary, for the truth. Singapore, the centre of civilisation. I love my little home desa. Would I be brave enough for leaving here? I never dwell much on it before. All health care akademi require you live on campus. There would be no spooking home, even for an evening meal. I could come home only for a few weeks a year.

The other nurse says, 'There is a case. A local needs care. And you could help us determine what he needs.'

Shrug and shake my head. 'Um, okelah. How?'

Gentle reaches over the table, puts her hand on my wrist. Comforting. 'As delicate as we can put it … you have a follower.'

I have many followers. Some creepy ones.

'He's harmless,' the other nurse adds. 'For you anyway.'

'We're already treating him with a nute regimen,' Gentle says and, if I read her right, looks somewhat scornful at the other nurse. 'We must monitor how they are working.'

'Sure. Um, how is this involving me?'

'It's hardly anything, really,' the other nurse says.

'It would help muchy-much if tonight you could—' Gentle starts.

'We need you paint your toenails,' the other nurse blurts.

'What?'

'*Hai*. Simple as.'

'And I'd be helping?'

'Helping us make a patient well.' Gentle sighs. 'Your painting your toenails is something of a trigger for this guy. The next time he flutherbombs while you … we'll detect if his recovery is working.'

Sigh. My role is minor.

'Just go about it your same usual way,' Gentle says. 'Have your shower, get your elf nice and dry, go sit on your bed and … paint.'

For the second time today, I blush. It's stupid. Nothing is private, so why is this any different? Why is it bothering me?

Skye Merewether …

It's always the same with Lincoln d'Rorca, the Toenail Fetishist. *Tofie*, as we call him in the clinic.

Saf's towelling down after a shower. Tofie is already lurking, making sure he catches the first brush of lacquer. He never speaks with other followers or engages in the mob chats.

Fondle the dreamcatcher hanging from my chatelaine. It relaxes me. Little Dragon is yet for adding anything on her own. I challenge her about it the other day.

'Nothing yet is important enough,' she says.

So's your whole life, it seems, Little Dragon. Nothing of it is important enough.

'It's all just superstition. Like you kissing your relics all the time,' she says.

'You'll be kissing your arse good-bye the first sign of misfortune. Then you'll wish you had something more sacred for kissing.'

'Rabbit's foot? Dreamcatcher? Cross?' she mocks.

'As much as makes you happy.'

'I need no salt for my shoulder. I'm lucky.'

'We'll see.'

There're some mins yet. Little Dragon is already hypervigilant. She'll calm down after her first 100 Warrants. Her eyes darting, her skin taut containing her excitement, breathing and heart rate elevated. I bet she's a talker.

'You taste about Eir Frijberg yesterday?' she asks, blowing off a little of her nervous energy. Eir again. Will the girl speak of no one else? 'She's Infinite. The first nurse ever.'

'Hmm. I taste nothing of it,' I lie. Yesterday, every nurse on the planet tastes the news. Many, like me, have concern. The last thing nursing needs is hero worship. A shallow survey of Little Dragon's eyes reveals she's already drinking the sacramental wine.

'She's going after Infinites, and the Reckoning rewards her with Infinite Status,' she says, with wide eyes and beaming mouth.

I scoff. 'Rewards? Curses, more like.' No one will believe a nurse reaches Infinite by merit alone. Rumours of some Fred Nerks tampering with the Reck will only sound more credible now. And those rumours will blame nurses more than already.

'Think. We could all be Curing Infis for Greed, rather than minor Lusty miscreants like Lincoln,' she effuses.

'Well, we're here, so this is where we'll start.'

Little Dragon is already flutherbombing Tofie, poking around the apartment. In time she'll learn it's a waste of energy.

Y'all might as well know: the story I give Saf about testing Tofie's nute treatment is complete malarky. Though plausible enough that Little Dragon accepts it too, without checking the facts. Never enough time for tasting everything. There is no nute regimen for Tofie. We rarely monitor him, what with the resource shortage in the desa. No resources for building a case either, until we learn United States of Texas Health Corporations is snooping around. As if they have insufficient camel crap raining down on their heads from across the Wasteland border. We have no fondness for their 10-gallon heads spooking into our back yards with a Warrant for one of ours. Still, it happens all the time; what with the ease of spooking and worldwide porous borders. We taste your scheming, dear Texas. You're trying to score one on the Kementerian janking Kesahatan dari janking Indo-Malaysia. You ache for squashing a gnat on the belly of the great golden buddha of Singapore. You're all the same. Even the original, though far from best—the Federated Health Camerata in Northern Europa—comes here for the occasional token Warrant. Always for something trivial, such as … I dunno … insufficient picnicking in cemeteries.

Those crusty humourless missionaries from Copenhagen and London always expecting other nurses' gratitude for founding their mission. 'We start this,' they say with arrogant curls of lips. 'Without us, you would have nothing.' They have the stink of old sap intelligence agencies about them too. Any wonder. Y'all know what Vauxminster was in sap times? The headquarters of MI6. James Bond and all this camel crap. North Europa claim they have the best detectives in the world. What they mean is, they're a bunch of old-fashion spies.

They want to one-up us. If I had my wish for changing the Reck, it would be, penalise health-missionaries one-upping each other. I mean, nurses rarely enjoy a surplus of razoos (apart from the White Witch, ice queen Viking spy. Y'all hear about her? She's Infi!) What I'm saying is, we have so few opportunities for bettering our reputasi without sister missionaries scouring our Indo-Malaysia for spurious opportunities.

By the look of the Texas case on Tofie, he's taking a serious turn since we last look in on him. If another camerata sweeps in and Consigns him, our local chapter will look foolish. So, yes, I admit. I get Saf Evoli paint her nails tonight, flush out Tofie with enough instant evidence for Consigning him on the spot before our dear partners in Texas get a spook-in. I suppose y'all could accuse me of one-upping too. I'm one-upping the one-uppers, so it's all smooth and aqua with the mother-goddesses if y'all ask me.

'I think he's hunkering down in there,' Little Dragon says. 'Seems constant by his eye-fluttering.'

'All part of the basic academy profile of a flutherbombing addict. Eyes never stop fluttering.' She deserves a small dose of my contempt.

'*Hai*, but it's another thing witnessing it yourelf. It's disgusting in there,' Little Dragon says. No need for flutherbombing the guy for this. I smell it outside the front door. 'All his sucky bins are failing. Rubbish everywhere. A sucky vac is stuck in a room with the door closed. His ray cat is collecting a menagerie of bush rats in the bathroom, fouling a pile of clothes in there.' Her eyes regain focus. 'How come this guy is no sifar?'

'Are you kidding?' I snort. 'Being sifar is a conscious choice and takes careful intent. Sure, he's bumbling along, as low as he can go, but a sifar makes an active choice of spurning reputasi. Tofie has no care either way. How many are in it for a laugh? Laughs breed razoos faster than anything else. Anything other than sex, that is. His reputasi may even go up when we Consign him.'

'He's um ... um ...' Little Dragon stammers. 'Oh, gawd.'

'Yeer, he is.' Saf is on her third toe.

'How will he get all that nail polish off ... his ...?'

'Acetone.'

'That must sting.' Little Dragon has her hand on the front doorknob. 'May I?'

'Sure. You first.'

She nods and takes a deep breath. Throws the door open. I'll wait here, give her a few tiks. Let's see if she remembers where her catatonic spray is. She'd be a fool for going near Tofu with a swab.

Little Dragon inside membs, 'Lincoln d'Rorca, are you well?'

Nilajani Karunanithi …

Yes, Harsha, I am still flutherbombing Infis; how should I otherwise? The White Witch is moving against them, and Elsbeth (and possibly all The Incomplete) winks and tacitly approves my mission.

There are detectives now swarming all over Ben. I suppose I have little chance of discovering anything new about him. Yet it hooks me, that first time in Kolombo where he meets his activist friend, the first time I see *Hisab*—the Reckoning—reacting so fast after Ben tips a folksinger there. Since then, there's another strange case regarding the Reck: after a small-town squabble at a birthday party, it seems again like it's reacting in real-time, swiftly adjusting many reputations on-the-fly. Then, Ben's daughter begs his help. Ben offers token razoos, and within a short time, everyone's reputations return for how they are before the squabbles.

This could be the biggest investigation in the history of health care. How could I miss it?

'Are you kay, Ben?' Dilan asks. 'I hear there is some drama this morning?'

'How is it you hear? It's unlike you, flutherbombing me.' Ben. The first time these 2 speak since Kolombo.

'Oh, Ben.' Dilan, evasive. 'Look. I'm worried, kay?'

Ben struggles for speaking, draws the silence out. 'Mal is sakit, *machan*,' he blurts, almost in tears. The Infi's son is sick? Nurses treating the son could more easily monitor the father. I should work harder, spend more hours with the Infi and his familiars. 'No mental sakit. Physical.'

'Who gets physical sick anymore?' Dilan in shock. 'Apart from accident trauma,' he adds with some bitterness.

'It's nothing. He'll recover, they say.'

Oh, is this what we say? This smells more a ruse of the local health mission. Sneaky. And may land them in some trouble. Y'all must admire their commitment.

'I'm glad of hearing it, Ben.'

'*Machan*, I worry more about Aisha.' Ah, the wife.

'She's taking it hard?'

'Yeer, … it starts with one of Mal's bent-brain conversations. I love him for it but you know how is.' Dilan chuckles. Ben: 'He's talking about dolphins membing him …' Ha! The boy spins an attention-seeking story. 'Aisha panics, thinking there is some spy manipulating him.'

Dilan is all quivers and non-pluses. 'No stupid notion.'

'So, she flutherbombs him looking for spies. Panics and loses it, Dil …

indivisibly loses it. She has Mal by the shoulders, shaking him. Then Mal passes out. Saf and me must pull Aisha off him.'

'She must be worrying bad.' Dilan with sympathy.

'Yeer, then Mal throws a fit.'

'What?'

'Fortunately, a nurse administers nutes in time.'

'Nurse?' Dilan sounds alarmed. 'Which nurse?'

By Ben's expression, I taste he thinks this is an odd question.

'Just a local nurse, only on mission a few months, I think. I am glad she could get here on time. Otherwise ...'

Dilan relaxes. I wonder which nurse he worries about. 'I'm sorry, Ben. Have no understanding what might come over Aisha. You suppose ...?' Dilan trails off.

'No doubt nurses watch us; we are all aware of it. I know many by name.'

'It's just one incident. If Aisha is truly sick, your KK' —the Kementerian Kesahatan of Indo-Malaysia, more paramilitaries than nursing missionaries— 'would know long before.'

They fall silent, a comfortable pause between friends, each digesting the conversation, allowing space for the other.

'I suppose tonight is off then?' Dilan says, artificially casual.

'The Inductee Gala? Well, that's just it. Aisha still argues for going.'

'Well, it would be tedious going through it all again next year ...'

'Exactly! One min she's accusing me of siding with nurses, the next she's happy with them monitoring him while we're at a party on the other side of the world.' I knew it! The local nurses are in with Ben's family! As good as fluther surveillance is, it's no match for old-fashion relationship building. Sharing empathy, a common trial, a bond, and they'll soon be spilling information it might otherwise take 1000's of flutherbombing hours.

'Well, this's confusing.' Dilan. 'Aisha trusting health missionaries with— well, with anything.'

'I'm sure Aisha will be flutherbombing Mal and Saf the whole time we are out. Even while they sleep. The stupid party is at 4:00am our time.'

'You're going?'

'Believe it or no.'

'Are you sure you should go?'

'You talk me into this ... now what?'

Dil puts on a contemplating expression. 'I dunno. Mal getting sick gives nurses the best reason for poking around in your family. It seems such a coincidence so close before the Gala.'

'I should have it over with years ago,' Ben membs bitterly.

'Hey, will the BirdMe dude be there?' Dilan brightens. It seems an automatic response for lifting his friend out of a fugue. 'Can you get me an upgrade?'

'Jank you, Chandrasiri.'

Rhetoric

'Golden Years' — David Bowie

*Aisha Evoli ...*

THE PURPLE HAZE CLEARS. Outside Kensington Palace, Ratu
Victoria's statue look down on us, her nose stiff and white. At her feet in
the pond, a pair of ducks' feathers ruffle. Through the gardens, chatter
warbles from the party at the Orangery.

Stifle a yawn. Back home is 4 o'clock in the morning lah. The organisers
are aware, that one. Despite Ben is a guest of honour, they choose the other
side of the world with a 9-hour time zone difference, fine. We should be in
bed.

Saf and Mal, too excited for sleep, buzz around the house. Ben gives Saf
permissi for flutherbomb him, but I put a foot down. Who knows what she
might taste at this party? If she must flutherbomb anyone, I'd rather she is
with me.

Sarah Pursglove from the council offers flutherbombing them until they fall
asleep. What to do? Unwise, declining a councillor offer ah. Besides, 100's
flutherbomb Saf already. Fewer with Mal; no one care when he obsesses over
the mafan puter Ben gives him. Still, he's happy ah. Anything for keeping
him calm. Want no more episodes like last time. The nutes the clinic
prescribes must be working ah.

Even with all the Infi etiquette for stay out of each other's fluthers, the air
over the Orangery is a tsunami of auras. *Halos* they call them in Europa. They
billow into the sky more like fizzing fireworks than the normal wispy
transparent fairy floss. They are like colourful kites soaring, fluid and bright.
They dive-bomb and congeal, explode and liquefy, shatter and melt into the
hot aura-goo beneath. Jellyfish in a blender. A demon-whale lightshow leaps

out of the lightshow sea, swallows auras whole. So vivid, like a clash of outfits back-stage of a fashion show.

It's too much ah. Outside Diana's Memorial Garden, I grab Ben's hand while stop for breath. Ben tap his finger on his hancy lah. I remember— access the new hoot in my hancy. Everything around me shimmers. I adjust it until auras shrink and dim. Objects appear normal again.

In the grounds between the memorial garden and The Orangery is a most elaborate slippy slide lah. Wide enough for 4 shoulder-shoulder. It loops and curves around. Spooky fields cross its track at those points. They swallow riders and deliver them somewhere else on the slide. Squeals of delight pan from one location for another. Needless for say, a long queue waits for getting on. If the time is right, one slider disappears in a field as another one appears on the other side. It look like sliders change bodies ah.

On a same stage, hollies of 2 bands jumble into each other. A guitarist appears with 2 heads till the hollies of musicians separate. A drum kit look like a shiny model of a medieval castle with barrel-shape battlements and turrets pile on one another. Two holly drummers appear like one with 4 monster arms. The bands' tunes tumble together and make a terrible noise. Judge by the genres, neither band might sound any better alone. Front of stage, an asylum of band managers and road crew posture and gesticulate. Argue. I guess neither band accepts they are a support act. Somewhere in the world, the bands play on, unaware of the overlap here. An organiser takes charge and shuts both hollicasts down.

Whichever way we turn, white linen tables and clumps of partygoers. Waiters bear silver trays of drinks and finger food. The way through the crowd clears. We pass by smiles and scowls; expressions of distaste and envy; curious looks and adoring stares.

This is a zoo ah. There are unfamiliar scents and fragrances too, some less than pleasant. Everywhere clumps of cartoon creatures drink or dance or both. Everyone yaya papaya. Over there, Infis wearing impossible clothes, garish make-up, and custom projections dance along with some music they must be sharing in Mind. They look like comical monster caught in a huge throbbing hedge of triffids. From the Mind-curdling vision emerge chicken wings and legs in splints. Duck lips and squinty corgi eyes. One wanita's thick grey-white hair grows wild in all directions. There could be a small koala sleeping on her head. A pair of bumblebees in terrible detail. Multi-colour slimy frogs. I know fashion but there is so much here I never see before, enough for occupy a catwalk for weeks.

Here we are ah. The biggest party of the Infi annual calendar: the Inductee Gala.

Ben Evoli ...

Is this a party or a networking pitch night? Conversations skate over small talk of indifferent questions about families and hobbies, and shunt into mission causes and recruitment. Infis already winners—ever eager for the next expansion, for the next game. Worse than flutherbombing supplicants. Y'all would think Infinites, with no prospect of improving (or damaging) reputasi, would be less hungry for my support. Y'all would be wrong. Everyone here needs the game go on. So many have friends or relatives; or friend of relatives; or relatives of friends. Or sick cats needing aid. If only a cousin's lover's old butler could get a lucky break so they could run more tests for some fringe procedure ...

Lobbyists for hancy camerati seek me out with avaricious intensity, commenting on the hancy I'm wearing, scaremongering about safety problems, offering me all kinds of sweeteners if I switch brands.

'A mindwriter of your standing ...'

'The scalability of our new tech ...'

'We will arrange year-round access for the best resources ...'

'We'll jank you right here, if you wish,' say poly-genital sales reps, their exposed protrusions as bright as neon, and the rough dimensions of a stubby holder.

'We run a small but upcoming chain of bordellos. With serious backing, we have a proposition for you,' says a bioluminescent Las-Vegas-inspired suit.

'Which is?' I ask, hoping I'm marinating my words with enough weary scepticism.

'Grant us an exclusive license for, shall we say, premium features of SnakiDik and ...'

I stop listening for the sweetener. There's no end of camerati rapacious for exploiting SnakiDik. MusiKai never attracts such attention. Pre-empting the suit's conclusion: 'You'll use my product for destroying your competition.'

'We can make it worth your while,' says the suit, as if it's just come down from a tree, bearing an apple.

This party is a thinly veiled excuse for exploiting the absence of nurses. The interference and noise of so many flutherbombers hoping for just one clear glimpse makes it impossible for gaining any actionable information.

'Are you aware of our new abilities in growing meat on a vine? Lamb, beef, tiger, sap ...'

'Sap?'

'Well, it's no real sap, of course.'

'There are people who enjoy playing cannibal?'

'It's no cannibalism. Different species. And fabbies are no match for organic growing, you agree?'

'Fabbies are no match for sap meat?' How would she know? Saps are extinct. I should never come. Can I just be no one again?

'As a mindwriter, you would appreciate the importance of reliable infrastructure,' says an Infi from an AgniSpace camerata.

'Appreciate.' This at least is a topic I have some interest in.

'I never question the dedication of any of the missionaries, of course,' she goes on. 'However, camerati often operate in bubbles. While it might be kay for other missions, it's problematic for AgniSpace which is, I'm sure you agree, the most important of missions, with implications for enhancing our natural ability for connecting through onespace. Spooky stations would be less reliable without it. I'm sure you experience problems deploying your hoots across a wide range of hancy standards. And if you must find some obscure magazines, well!'

'Coverage is more or less uniform,' I counter.

'Well, yes,' she continues. 'Onespace is onespace after all. But take spooking: it's all about manipulating vectors. The more Minds attending, the more redundancy, the higher the confidence in vectors. Which, if you mess with in the wrong way, I'm sure you intimately understand, could scrunch a whole galaxy into the cosmic sucky bin. We're honestly unsure whether this is happening already.'

I lose myelf in the colourful cloth of her sari shimmering as it catches the light. There's a pitch coming, so I sip gin with pinching politeness.

'We think all the relevant camerati should join forces under the standards of our mission. Ideally, we need a single amalgamate camerata for improving AgniSpace ...'

I tune out. I'll hear the same story 100's of times. Infis, always anxious for the next biggest challenge, eventually engorge their feeding-frenzy missions until they are left with one remaining prospect: cannibalising each other. You'd think they're all sap payment-gateway magnates racing each other for putting a tukky on Mars.

Aisha Evoli ...

'Petroleum Dynamite,' says the tall silver-hair Infi, perhaps the 49th who introduce hiself in the hour since we arrive. 'You may call me Pet. Charming to meet you.'

Pet has the most asymmetric face ah. A face by Picasso. His nose strains right and almost ducks under his ear which lift its lobe like it make room. His left ear tilt in the opposite direction. One side of his lips seem fatter than the other. I imagine at the tik in the womb, when baby Pet's features are forming, he sneeze or cough, and some Divine Hand swipe his face right. Only his eyes balance, serene and all-wise, and suggest the elf-assurance of ancient aristocracy. He lack even faint gene-mod skin markings. Guess he is from a family who take a dim view of messing with the family DNA. *Vulgar and debasing*, I suspect they say. Beneath his bloodline.

He take my hand with the assurance of a man at ease with take wanita by a hand. I cover queasiness, think he will kiss it. Creep me sideways. I turn statue, anticipate unpleasant wetness on my hand. But he smack his lips—*muah*! Centims from my skin. Return his serene gaze. His aristocratic spidery fingers slither away. Must be how royalty was, that one.

'You think my name preposterously contrived,' he says. 'You are welcome to jel me. There you are; you have permission. Go look.'

'No, no. I believe you.' I jel him and discover his father indeed name him Petroleum on his conception day.

He smirk a regal smirk. 'In any case, it rivals none of the eccentricity of some of the other Infis here. You agree?'

'I agree, yeer.'

'Quite right.' His eyebrow raise, follow my line of sight.

At one end of the terrace on a low mobile stage … something like a living mound of wet carpet ah. Taller than a wanita. Quicker than it appear, it vanish ah. Squint for make sense of it. Taste a small shift in the background. A thin wavy presence slip through the air. I shiver. Gasp. Is that an eye? The whole thing reappear. Jelly shudder. A band of bright blues pass over it or through it like it generate light from inside. One of the carpet rolls become an arm. Or a tentacle. The eye blink.

'Oh, that's Caracia Svakhaska,' Pet says nonchalant. 'You never have taste of her?'

Paiseh, I stare at her. 'Holographic projection?'

Pet chortles. Laughter is perhaps beneath him. 'No, no. That is her physical shape.'

'She squirts ink?'

Pet coughs. 'Regrettably, yes. Must worry the caterers with all these white linen tablecloths.' He talk like he has a stick of dynamite up his pantat. 'Her mission is biotech. Over decades, she uses her discoveries for transforming herelf. No one remembers her from before she is octopus.'

'An actual octopus?' I'm curious. And repulsed.

'Well somewhere between human and octopus. Her anatomy is quite complex. And she is quite mad.'

'I imagine she might be.'

'Oh, certainly. Quite. Like natural octopuses, each of her tentacles has its own intelligence.'

'Ah.' I still stare.

'When one changes one's fundamental corporeal elf by such an extent, one ends up completely out of one's cocktail glass.' Pet leans in. 'Whatever you do, refrain from speaking with her directly. And never ever attempt flutherbombing her.'

'No?'

'No, if you'd rather keep your stomach. The experience of conjoining her Mind has one vomiting as surely as eating bad fish stew. The sense is your innards gurgle above your head, your limbs flay into 8 limp snakes, your mouth ends up where your arse hole used to be, and your skin can taste everything.'

'Ghastly!'

'Quite. You see those attendants standing behind her?'

There is a line of 8 behind her in austere yet exclusive tight-fitting suits. So out of fashion it could come from a health mission surplus store. All in black—no, aqua, like deepy-deep water—with an insignia on their left breast like a cold sun with wavy rays on an octagonal aqua field (Ugh! Aqua. Its affront against fashion is timeless.). Y'all might think they are 8 waiters, until they twitch and sway even as their feet fix in one place. Sometime my eyes think they see a head swell or a throat puffing like a frog's.

'Caracia's Voices of Arms. She communicates through them. If one would speak with her—'

'It would be a delight, but there are so many guests I promise—'

'Your disingenuousness does you no praise, if I may be so bold. I merely say, if you should wish a conversation with her, you interact with her Arms.'

'All 8?'

'Right you are. Pay attention. They are conduits of Caracia's decentralised brain. It's common they talk in pairs. Sometime trios. Often with different words, so one needs one's wits. If Caracia is single-minded about something—which she rarely is—they may all speak in unison.' Pet sips his champagne. 'Look around,' he says. 'Most Infis are more than a little loopy. So few of us project humanity at all anymore. We become our missions. One could probably guess what they are by the choices we make about our appearance.'

Thinking of SnakiDik, I say, 'I'm glad Ben—'

'Oh, indeed.' Pet blushes.

Who would guess an Infi might be *kan cheong* about pink shower tree ah?

'For Infis, appearance is a 24-7 marketing game,' he says. 'Always competitive. Quite gauche.'

'In Singapore we say, *kiasu*. Afraid for lose.'

'Yes, quite.'

I look about. Behind me is a humanoid rainbow lorikeet, over 2 metres tall, awkwardly sipping champagne somehow, through its chest. 'Oh, is that one the BirdMe Infi?' I feel awkward for ask. It would be easier for jel him.

'Yes,' Pet says. He pluck an *hors d'oeuvre* from a waiter's tray, push it through the thinner side of his lips. 'Keep going.'

There's an older man clutch a Trekorder in one hand while he drink from the other.

'Over there. He's the Star Trek revivalist?'

'Yes, quite right,' Pet says with round mouth. 'He's the only Infi you will ever catch with a Trekorder. The most useless thing in history, don't you agree?' He mimes hold a Trekorder up chest high. 'Computer! What's the material composition of my socks?' he mocks.

'100% hemp,' I answer.

'Well, I never give you permission to jel that,' he says, then breaks out in a smile look like earthquake hit his face. 'But exactly! Even without hancies, one's onespace connections would yield an answer soon enough. Why would one choose to carry around a tacky piece of electronics which duplicates your own abilities? It is beyond my comprehension.'

'I never understand Trekkers.'

'The things which evoke nostalgia for sap times ... well, it never ceases to amaze me. It's all quite hupster. Very boring.'

'Hupster?'

'Yes, I am certain that is the correct term for the fashion ... the lifestyle ... the attitude, whatever.'

'You wear a watch,' I say with eyes on a gold thing around Pet's wrist. 'It's sap also. And quite expensive by the look.'

'Ah, this old thing?' he says, cover it with his other hand. 'Nothing I'd fashion a lifestyle around.'

The watch seems important somehow; I taste Pet is awkward about that one, for some reason. Best let it go.

Already, I see Infis everywhere shout their mission in their costume. The ecological Infis are easy. They resemble the animal, vegetable, or mineral their mission saves. There's a woodpecker (maybe a BirdMe option); a snow leopard; a rhinoceros; a lemur; a gorilla (or the lelaki could just be ugly); a turtle; a tiger; a salamander; ... a kelp forest? When we arrive, I mistake these marketing messages for party costumes.

'We must be thankful the saviour of dung beetles wears no Varikain,' Pet chortles. It seem even old fossil Infis like Pet know about the transparent-flashing material.

'Eee-yer! They should never.'

'Right you are. Best not encourage them.'

'And what is your mission, Petroleum Dynamite?'

Pet straightens and puffs up. He's tall for a lelaki ah, almost eye for eye with me. 'I restore ancient monuments to their original glory, most recently restoring the Leshan Giant Buddha. I'm quite proud of it, if one may be so bold in saying.'

'Please be so bold. So where is your marketing strategy? You look like no stone Buddha.' Pet is the opposite of spiritual serenity, his features in constant battle for territory on his face. 'Have a pleasant evening, Pet. I need a refill ah.'

He frown and pucker his lips. 'I'm sure I'll bump into you again.' He recovers his composure. 'So good having you with us after all these years,' he says with his mouth, without sincerity.

Between me and the bar is a sturdy tree with strong branches. On 5 or 6 fat stubby roots for legs, she moves crab-like across the floor. A champagne glass, levitating high above my line of sight in her foliage, tips. Its contents disappear somewhere, I imagine into the Infi's invisible mouth.

'Baobab tree,' the tree speaks with an airy emphysemic voice. 'My camerata is the saviour of the baobab tree.'

The tree waddles off. Behind her is a proud-looking Infi who wears no more than fabby leather boots, tight chaps, and an even tighter corset cutting under her enormous, pendulous payudara. Fashion crime! Her hair is striking; long, wavy and red. She could be a Viking battle maiden except for the thing swaying free to her knees. I'm thinking *horse*. Light chains hang by metal hooks from her breasts, swing loose for collars around the necks of 4 naked wanita. The hooks pierce her nipples like forks in strawberries. She's coming nearer. Jel her name: Wilma Solstice.

'What is your darkest desire?' Wilma asks, none too soft, her captives kneeling either side of her.

'I'd love for creating a designer label in cocktail dresses ah, using sackcloth and ashes.'

'How biblical,' Wilma says. 'We could use such apparel in our dungeons.' With an impish grin, one of her collar girls tugs on her leash. Ariel Kanon is her name. Wilma stoically ignores the pull on the hook in her nipple.

'Aisha,' Bat Ears membs. 'May I interrupt? There is someone I wish you meet.'

I nod, relieved. For Wilma, 'Please excuse me.'

'Of course,' she says and makes a formal, florid bow; the tip of her horse part sway ever nearer the ground. The wanita bow also—Ariel with her impish smile. Foreheads almost touch the floor.

'Come meet Tuan BirdMe,' Ben says. 'He's rotating his repertoire of birds from Tanah Selatan. In our honour.'

We approach a towering sulphur-crest cockatoo. 'Ah, Infinite of the moment. And his lovely wife,' the bird chirps. For punctuate his greeting—or sell it—he squawk like a parrot.

'Lemarr, may I present Aisha, my one Istri?' Ben says. Why he so formal, dun look at me.

'Hail up. Charming meeting you,' the bird says. Thankful, he show no sign of want muah over my hand. Instead, he offer his bird-hand for shake. Expect my hand would pass through the projection. I jolt with surprise, feel his scratchy, scaly claw.

Lemarr smiles with private pleasure. 'You enjoy *di* kinaesthetic?' he asks like a mad scientist curious for know if his latest doomsday device hit all the right consumer points. 'You must have SnakiDik set for Friendly mode. All our latest BirdMe models interface and simulate a handshake.'

'I taste ah.' Look through feathers for signs of human. Lemarr's beak looks bony and tough, like any bird's, until he talks, and it shapes for the words he says.

'*Ow yuh duh finding* being among *suh* many Infinites?' he asks. His feathery colours shimmer as he become an eagle.

'Aisha is a recovery procomplement in Misi Pemulihan Seletar,' Ben says, distracting Lemarr a tik while his hancy translates *Misi Pemulihan Seletar* into *Seletar Recovery Mission*. 'Earthquakes, floods, volcanic eruptions … she witnesses a great many things, some very tragic.'

I touch Ben's hand, *paiseh*. I rather no attention.

'*Dis suh?*' Lemarr asks sounding genuinely interested.

I say, 'Rewarding, that one, making a difference in time of tragedy ah. But here among so many Infis and so much … free expression is … intense, in its own way.'

'Ah, there you are.' An older Infi crashes our conversation. 'The 2 biggest celebrity Infinites in the world today. Hello Faces!' His immaculate tuxedo is no distract from his ugliness. Holala! Where I start? Are his shoulders too narrow or his bald dome-shape head too big? Ears are tiny warts on either side. Eyebrows sprout fine grey hair like seaweed. Weepy pale eyes are gobs of lime jelly in sockets either side of his flat, featureless nose. His skin has the smooth sheen of plastic which glistens like a film of oil. Is there a neck under his cravat? Yeer, he wears a cravat with a tux. Take a look. Alert the KK. Get the Warrant. Crimes against sartory. Lah.

'May I present Maddox Price?' Lemarr's voice remains rum-smooth while his feathers ruffle at the reptile-man's presence.

Maddox clasps my hand. Clammy. I stiffen against recoil in horror. 'You must be Aisha.' His voice sounds drier than 500-year-old bark. 'Charming.' Maddox's thin lips stretch wide, more a slashing wound than a smile on his face.

'Look at this pair, eh?' Maddox condescends. Glances at Ben and Lemarr. 'Are they what passes for Infinite these days? Bird suits and penises?'

'Infi Maddox is in mining,' Lemarr says. 'Garbage mining.'

'Yeer. I taste.' I glare at Maddox's cravat.

'Well, my sap ancestors mined for minerals—'

'*An dem* dug up everything of value …' Lemarr interrupts.

'Yes. Now the old garbage dumps are where all the useful resources are. It's an honourable pursuit, reclaiming waste. Lucrative, very lucrative. I perform a great service for the whole world. Soon I hope we'll be reclaiming space junk. All those defunct sap satellites, you know. It's a matter of spooking a huge sucky bin up there, would you believe? If we could just be sure of approximate vectors. Ah, yes, well …' Maddox waves a waiter over.

'A gin martini, thank you, there's a good missionary. And please, before your barkeep adds the vermouth, could she just pour it in a sucky bin instead?' With an afterthought, he turns. 'Anyone else?'

We hold up our glasses, show high tides in them.

'Yes, an honourable hobby, garbage mining,' Maddox continues. 'As for you 2 birds, you should join forces and put a cock on a cock. You could take over the world.'

Lemarr stiffens. '*Wi aready tek ova di world*, rust bucket.'

Ben's shoulders slump.

Ben Evoli …

Maddox tastes he is on a roll. 'What next? Oh, I know. How about a hoot which simulates an empty stomach? What could you call it? AkiGut? FeedMe?'

The patience drains out of Lemarr. '*Yuh* know, *dem bi* Consigning Infinites *fi* living too long.' He blinks, realising he lapses into Patois. Take a breath for calming. 'Yea, it's a thing now. Living too long is Greedy, mining man. Get *wid di* birds or fall *outta yuh* nest.'

Maddox squints. He might weigh up if Lemarr is serious. 'First I hear of it,' he mutters. Then his mood brightens. He waves his hand high above his head. 'Pet!' he calls out across the room. 'Over here.'

The lanky stick of Dynamite mouths an *ah* and squithers through the crowd for our group.

'Mr BirdFinger you already know,' Maddox says, which ruffles Lemarr's owl feathers. 'My dear Pet, may I present Mr MusiCock, our newest inductee? And this is his charming partner, Aisha.'

'Quite right,' Pet says. 'We meet only mins ago.'

Aisha addresses Maddox with, '*Leng chai,*' which means *handsome boy.* Aisha is mocking him. 'I understand Pet is a monument restorer.'

Maddox chuckles hiself into a dry cough. 'Oh, yes! The Motherland Monument in Kiev; Christ the Redeemer of Rio; the Statue of Unity in Gujarat. He redecorates all the world's great stone popsicles. Anyway, here's to being Infinite.'

We raise our glasses and clink the hollow toast.

Pet smoulders. 'And all the limitless tedium that comes with it, what?' he adds.

'Many of these Infinites are pushing the boundaries ah.'

'Oh yes, we must. It's our duty,' Maddox says solemn. 'If there are lines for crossing, Infis must cross them. How else will we define where those lines are?'

'Should be health camerati marking *di* boundaries,' Lemarr offers. 'Instead *dem kip wi* guessing.'

'Indeed. They should set out rules, fair rules.' Maddox drains his martini glass, chinks on a passing waiter's tray, and plucks a replacement. A gold watch on his wrist catches the light and flares. Aisha would say these Infis have gaudy fashion sense.

'Why are so few Infis targets for Cures?' Aisha asks.

'Oh, we are all targets,' Maddox says. 'Even your somewhat uninspiring husband here. Saps help me! He worries he might collect one too many Benjamin Franklins. For the rest of us, we enjoy our reputation. The health camerati may be somewhat impotent these days, still they have ambitions. We are always targets.' Maddox leans in towards Ben. 'Here's the thing, Puffin. I taste your current lack of passion for life. The amusement industry is insufficiently compelling for one as deep as you. If you only look, you'll discover many challenges and rewards. Your induction here is the first step. Such a shame you put it off for years. Never mind, we're here and …'

Is Maddox Price's dusty droning logorrhoea so boring it makes me hallucinate? How else explain the amethyst glow in his martini glass? (The word amethyst comes from the old Greek, *améthystos*, and means *no intoxicant*.) It's like a diver's light shining up from the deepest ocean trench. It dances in the drink with the sparkle of a gemstone. Glistens on Maddox's plastic-wrap face, chirks up his dead-fish eyes, and casts spidery shadows of his wild eyebrows onto his vinyl-texture face. He looks over my shoulder. Skewers of violet light pierce the room, surge and gurgle. On the walls macabre silhouettes of Infi octopuses, birds, cows, fish, trees, angels, and bondage slaves cut dark outlines. Sharp angular checkerboard diamonds of light come through the windows. The source of light moves. A room full of Infinites train wide eyes in the same direction, arch eyebrows, gape mouths. No one need flutherbomb for sharing the cold trickle of fear in their innards, the rise of hackles. Doses of adrenaline flooding though their fruit. Faces set with anger.

They whisper. They use their first languages: *ahli sihir putih*; *ang puting bruha*; *zurien sorgin*; *veḷḷai cūṉiya*; *phù thủy trắng*; *den hvide heks*; *la sorcière blanche*; *ka keʻokeʻo kilokilo*; *die wit heks* …

The White Witch.

Maddox Price …

Near Kensington Palace, where a youthful Queen Victoria sits resplendent in stony endurance, a purple haze glows above the tree line like mist from a peat bog. As dank as a drowned sailor's beard, it imbues The Orangery with the dread mood of a vampiric crypt.

Out of the mist, a regal figure emerges. Queen Victoria reanimated? No. Without crown or sceptre or royal gown, she wears instead a mission cap and rainbow fatigues.

My eyes lie. She rises, this apparition—as the mist condenses into a wave, glassy and luminous—and bears her up above Princess Diana's Memorial Garden. The wave shines a moist wisteria hue over the bushes hedging the lawn. From the barrel of the wave, 2 flanks of courtiers emerge wearing rainbow uniforms. They smile with the teeth of sharks, and surf with their queen towards the shore of The Orangery terrace.

My fellow Infinites moan tongue-and-lung with awe. Infi mouths agape are big mouths, even those masked behind projections of birds and bees, trees, and endangered fleas.

My eyes lie. There must be hallucinogenic nutes in our drink, the mischief of nurses. They must plant operatives among our caterers. With such realisation comes a tik of clarity, and I pierce the veils of the befuddling nutes.

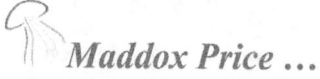

Vör Hoyur ...

'They're terrified,' Teo relishes.

Already halfway between Kensington Palace and the Infinite Inductee Gala, the effects of the hallucinogens we dose the party's drinks with are obvious. Service staff and guests alike will be visualising us riding a wave in the air, with Eir a triumphant vengeful goddess leading. With mouths agape and eyes as big as glassy apples, they make faces at our apparitions metres above, while we in fourspace approach as common pedestrians. Without a whimper of protest, we invade the baboon's den.

'Remain calm,' I instruct the party guests. Teo pleases me by rolling her eyes. 'We have our Warrants. Give us no reasons for drafting more.'

Infi fans broadcast news of our gate-crashing. Within tiks, we have the attention of neos all around the world. People sit up in beds; turn showers off; cough in concert halls; pause mid-coitus; pull tukkies over; gag on lunch; choke in beers; fall silent mid-song; fall off pushbikes; pull parachutes early; pull cricket balls late; drop the ball; miss the ball; abandon arguments; find no more joy in the joke; put hate on hiatus; leave love alone. All over the world, the disbelieving drop their activities and crusade into fluthers. Let them taste we are reclaiming our mission in full.

Maddox Price ...

The White Witch. A gangly 2-metre-tall albino mantis with piercing pink eyes and a shimmering cascade of pearly hair falling as far as her too-feminine panty cheeks. Detective Nurse Eir Frijberg of the Federal Health Camerata of Northern Europe, the first health missionaries in neo culture—as they remind us incessantly and Pridefully at every opportune tik. By *health* they mean *mental health* since we enjoy almost perpetually good chemical health, never suffering such ancient demons as infection or cancer or schizophrenia. By *mental health* they mean the minor neuroses of modern life, which are all the diseases we suffer these days. All trifling piffles easily managed if you have a compelling mission for occupying the quiet gaps between louder thoughts. Idle hands and all that.

A stroke of marketing genius, whichever nurse conceives of playing on our insecurity and our innate sense of sinfulness (it would be a true neo indeed who could banish such existential naggings). I mean, am I good person, really? Well, I am, of course, but are y'all? *There, there*, I imagine the marketing genius intones, *let us soothe these little ailments, the ills older than humanity itself, the 7 ancient ills.*

Centuries ago, we neos buy it as happily as saps would buy sugar and face-creams; the 7 Cures make unsightly blemishes vanish. Now here we are, with Detective Nurse Eir Frijberg and her rainbow stormtroopers gate-crashing our party. Whether buoyed by her incomparable celebrity (for a nurse), or by the Reckoning's recent damning her for eternity as Infinite, her bombastic arrival warns of potent intent. After decades of health mission apathy regarding Infinites, is Eir, as rumours suggest, now issuing Warrants against us? For Pride perhaps (easy enough in the proving, y'all would think)? Or the big one: Greed (a hard charge against any Infi who shares and donates just enough for keeping the heat off). If so, my only hope is we see off Eir's incursion quietly, without any of my colleagues retaliating or showing off for the sake of bruised egos. Regrettably, there are many Infis I would never classify among the sharpest drills in the diamond mine.

The effect of the hallucinogens in my martini abating, I see Eir setting foot on the terrace like she disembarks a yacht. She strides regally ahead of her squad single-filing behind, until she trips awkwardly at the doors. I stifle a laugh and only succeed in strangling it for a snort. Perhaps with Viking blood in her Danish veins, Loki still has a trickster hold over her, blessing her, in an age of so few maladies, with dyspraxia.

Ben Evoli ...

Infis step back and suffer the nurses' incursion indoors. Huddles at windows peer in. For comfort—mine, I guess, more than hers—Aisha loops arms with me.

'Remain calm,' calls a small, elven nurse—Vör Hoyur, Eir Frijberg's adjutant. Her voice has the quality of cat-gut strings on a fabby violin. Out of tune and reedy, her fruit vibrating disharmonious with the frequency of her vocal cords. 'We have our Warrants. Give us no reasons for drafting more.'

Eir's violet eyes dart between Infinites. Silence settles; auras dim. Eir walks light and ominous among the guests. She tilts her ear. With a sharp turn of her

head, she looks direct at me—into me—her eyes are hot, stabbing fire irons.
  She calls, her voice like the finest cello. 'Ben Evoli, are you well?'

Vör Hoyur ...

There's Ben with his wife Aisha averting her gaze from me. Let her wonder.
Let her ruminate.
  Silence gases the room. Calm and hypnotic, magnificent and in control, Eir
calls, 'Ben Evoli, are you well?'
  Panic strikes Aisha, despite what she believes she knows.

Maddox Price ...

A roaring cheer, tongue and lung, rises from the throats of the nurses. Such an
impolitic display of coarse behaviour.
  'All well,' Ben membs with some apprehension. 'Terima kasih for asking,
perawat detektif.'
  Everyone in The Orangery holds breath while the binary stars of Eir's and
Ben's halos swell and rotate around each other. Once in a while you see this.
Despite Infis taking every care for managing their fluthers, sometimes the
blunt size of our halos fizzing together distorts the illusion of four-
dimensional space-time. Put enough Infis in one place, and everything loses
its corners. Flutherbombers may even taste through time, although they'll
never trust the warp of it.
  With Eir recently becoming Infi, the unexpected presence of her
burgeoning fluther tips the balance. The Orangery appears as twisted clay on
a potter's wheel.
  'Selamat on your new designation as Infinite, perawat detektif,' Ben offers,
sounding genuine, dear Puffin, bless him. 'Apologies, the organisers of the
soirée extend you no proper invitasi.' Ahem, yes. Well ...
  Eir, aloof and arrogant, closes the space between herelf and Ben. Or
fourspace warps, bringing them closer. The ornate cornices of the room ripple
and warp. Eir towering over stoops and embraces Ben, kisses his cheek.
  'You are too kind,' she membs.
  If Ben has surprise at Eir's familiarity, he betrays none of it.
  'And your son ... Mal? I understand he has some misfortune this morning.'
I dearly ache for loathing Eir, yet her concern tastes genuine. 'Have no worry,
Infinite Ben Evoli dari Saffron. We are all working hard for keeping him
well. Though his is a unique circumstance, we will prevail. Which is why I
may devote you more interest. For the sake of your children.'
  The authenticity of her warmth is bilious. There is insufficient martini
remaining in my class for rinsing the taste from my mouth.

'Pursue your ideals as you taste fit, perawat detektif. It is unfolding just fine for you,' Ben says.

'More than for me, Infinite. For all the people we Cure.' She pauses for effect. 'You taste … melancholic,' she says. 'You know, your creations give us all so much joy. I use MusiKai for hours a day. SnakiDik, almost as often.' Laughter tickles around the room, even among the nurses. I believe Eir's adjutant Vör is blushing. 'How is it the creator of such wonderful things struggles for rejoicing in his own work? When we create, we are nearest the Source of all things, *ja*? The Divine? Our truest Essence?'

It's clear I neglect my study, in recent times, of this detective nurse. Could she truly believe her own public relations campaign?

'Others achieve greater, perawat detektif.'

Eir beams disarmingly. I must quash the desire for trusting her. 'Oh, so much humility in an Infinite! How refreshing. I wonder, is it true humility? Or is this devaluing your worth a compulsion? A sickness?'

'My worth is for the assessment of others.'

'True. So, is your reputasi no evidence?'

'There are others without reputasi who are more deserving.'

'You know, Ben, we would usually say Infinites require Cures because they wallow in the pleasures of their station. I fear you may require a Cure for resisting the pleasures of your station. Both opposites are evidence of disease.'

'As a new Infinite, perawat detektif, what is it you wallow in?'

Eir leans closer and stoops for whispering in his ear. 'Ben Evoli dari Saffron, the Infinite who would rather be other, with a curious archaic cry from the heart: *Leave me alone!* As if such is possible in our ever-connecting world.' She circles Ben while he remains with hands clasped, head tilted, eyes relaxed and cast slightly down. 'I taste the genes of your soul,' Eir says. 'If you remain steadfast in your direction, you may end up where you are heading. You need more sap in your tree. Please, for your sake, and the sake of your family, find joy in your purpose. There is mission for you yet.' She straightens and takes his shoulders in her hands.

Dear gawd, has she a Warrant for him, or no?

I must demand, 'Why are you here?' and regret it immediately. If there will be bear-poking, I should be last for indulging in it. If she has no Warrant for Ben, she's merely baiting us.

'Ah, Maddox Price.' Eir says with delight in recognising me. 'Your beard is in the post-box. Please be patient. We perform a number of duties this evening.'

'Your missionary ancestors try these tricks all through the ages.' Jank! Now Orlando is sticking his head out of his shell. Well, just look at him. He appears more turtle than human, his bald knob of a head stretching unnaturally from a long wrinkly neck. His eyebrows almost leap off his forehead. His eyeballs bulge like balloons too full of gas. 'It's all about career-making with you, isn't it?' he continues. 'For which your superiors will give you an incomparable carpeting, Detective Nurse.'

Orlando sets the frame of his bones forward, threatening a turtle-march on Eir. The nursing flanks tighten around her. Orlando hesitates. 'So, is it me you come for?' he challenges with mock weariness. 'Because, if it is, could you please cat me now and take me away. Allow the rest enjoys the party.'

'Oh, Orlando Greer. The great restorer of coastal ecologies, and destroyer of competing missions. Never before we recite the Warrant.'

'I'm on no Warrant.' Orlando stiffens. Imperious, chin up. Looking a foolish, small boy before the towering albino witch.

'Are you certain?' Eir is toying with him with impish playfulness. 'Lust, Greed, Pride … you never fall ill with any of these?'

'You ever catch me falling ill?' Orlando says, impatiently clipping his words.

'Would a mechanic catch a tukky for repair? You believe us a police force or a dog pound? We're here for your health care.' Eir casts her eye around the room.

'Be on with it.' Orlando heaves a huge sigh.

Vör Hoyur …

Orlando Greer—a reptile of an Infi renowned for his ruthless acquisitions of other camerati competing in his mission of ecological remediation, ever enamoured with the sound of his own voice—jousts with Eir these passing tiks. Finding Eir more than a match, and tasting the futility of persisting, he finally capitulates.

'Be on with it,' he says bitterly.

'Very well,' Eir says, tiring of his elf-entitlement. '*Sygeplejerske* Mrowka, please begin.'

I should be reciting the Warrants instead of Teo. I release a sneer as she conjures a holly, stretches it, angles it for easy reading. All that remains is the routine. 'Infinite Archana Soman, are you well?'

A man all in simple white steps forward, his smile a curious defiant challenge.

Maddox Price …

Archana is one of the AgniSpace Infis. Predictably on brand, he's wearing all white shirt and *lungi* with a gold-braided *angavastra* draping over his shoulders. 'In prefect health, thank you, *nars*.'

He collapses on the floor as if his machinery flicks off. Those able, gasp.

I close my eyes and surrender to inevitably. Poking bears always escalates. Archana's companion shrieks. 'What evil is this? You kill him!'

Vör Hoyur …

Two nurses run for examining Archana. One, looking at Eir, shakes her head. Eir, for her part, covers her reaction well, though I see the tension in her eyes and lips. No one else will notice her leaning away by only mims from the body on the floor.

'We never kill anyone,' Eir protests.

I memb Eir, 'What's happening?'

Eir looks for Teo. 'Please. The next Warrant, *Sygeplejerske*.'

Maddox Price …

So, there is yet more. This is no time or place for such a display of carnage. What if the nurses are bearing a Warrant for me? I should before … I should make … never Mind, it's too late now. Perhaps there's a penthouse cell in a nursing minster for me after all.

Silence seeps into the space among the conscious party goers. Halos freeze.

Nurse Teodora Mrowka scowls. Some tension among the raiding party.

Vör Hoyur …

'You know of this?' Teo membs angrily.

I defend, 'Nothing. I swear.'

'*Sygeplejerske* Frijberg,' Teo says. 'Perhaps we—' Teo should know; when Eir is on the defensive she must fall back on careful plans.

'Please,' Eir says with a stammer, holding herelf upright by pure force of will. Flaring from stress, her dyspraxia could make a fool of her at any tik. I ache for being by her side, holding her steady if necessary. 'The next Warrant,' she orders.

Teo gulps and consults her list again. 'Infinite Maddox Price, are you well?'

Maddox Price coughs into his martini glass, laughs arrogantly. 'In perfect health, thank you, nurse. Never better.'

And then … and then … as if the laws of preserving a human fruit's integrity fail, the ugly Infi falls apart in the most gastric, most bone-rubbery, flesh-corrupting way. Aisha jumps back in horror as the gore splashes her shoes.

More Infinites collapse dead. This is never our doing. These Infinites!

Degenerate incurables all. This's some Infi trick.

Ben Evoli ...

Why should I believe my eyes? Maddox's fruit deforms, sucking his crumpling clothes inward. With a sickening slush and a louder splash, the ruins of him spill across the floor. Liquids; bags and bulbs of organs; noodles of shredding intestines; sharp shards of bone. The wetter gore is a 7th wave washing over my shoes and Aisha's.

As if Maddox's corruption is a trigger, domino lines of Infinites collapse, passing dead. Everyone in profound shock. So few witness death in everyday life. Nurses are wailing too. Others, recovering their sense of mission, treat the fallen and comfort survivors.

Aghast, I stand back from it. What appalling scheme is this? Suicide? Murder? Or worse?

GREED

Nature

'Big News 1' — Clutch

Ben Evoli …

A NASTY WAY OF PASSING, Maddox Price reducing to lumpy goo; his martini class shattering on the ground microtiks before his guts gush out for metres around. All over my shoes and pants, as high as my knees. The taste of bile in my mouth.

Okay. Houston, I'm on the porch.

The detective nurse, tall and white, her eyes accusing I am an accomplice in Maddox's death.

Columbia, Columbia, this is Houston. One minute and thirty seconds to L-O-S. All systems go. Over.

The vision of Maddox's melting fruit still playing on the inside of my eyelids; my bedlinen smelling of fresh human meat pulp, sweet and faecal. Roll onto my side, curl up. The visions replay. Maddox, martini glass, splash, purple eyes …

Maddox, martini glass, splash, purple eyes …

Maddox, martini glass, splash, purple eyes … Aisha …

It takes a pretty good little jump.

… Aisha …

Buzz, this is Houston. F/2 - 1/160th second for shadow photography on the sequence camera.

Maddox, martini glass, splash, purple eyes … Aisha …

Aisha is a possum in bed, pretending sleep. I know her breathing patterns; no doubt she is awake. She tosses and rolls since we lay down in the early dawn. Now she presents the bluff of her back, hogs the pillows and boosters, and cocoons the sheet around her, leaving me naked on my back.

Purple eyes …

Ventilation louvres in the solarglass panels in the vault ceiling. Gum trees above dandling leafy shadows.

That's one small step for man … one great leap for mankind.

A strange deep voice seeps from Mal's swasta while he sleeps in his bed.

I can see the footprints of my boots and the treads in the fine, sandy particles.

I lift my head, wince.

There seems to be no difficulty in moving around as we suspect. It's actually no trouble to walk around.

Gingerly standing up, out of balance, hand on brow, squinting. In the wardrobe, grab a *yukata*—the black one with the cranes—wrap it on. Out the swasta door, pad down the hall.

Okay, Buzz, we ready to bring down the camera?

Mal in a tangle of sheets and pillows. His head set at such an angle it might otherwise suggest a neck-break. Arm dangling over the edge of the bed. Breathing the peace of sleep.

It's quite dark here in the shadow and a little hard for me to see that I have good footing. I'll work my way over into the sunlight here without looking directly into the Sun.

Over his desk, a small holly plays, about 400 mims high. Bad quality but recognisable—better than the original recording. In colour instead of greyscale. Apollo 11 moon landing, Neil Armstrong, Mal's sap hero. The holly flickers and resets.

Okay. Houston, I'm on the porch.

It must be running on loop since Mal falls asleep.

Tap the console on the desk. The holly evaporates. Mal stirs and rolls over, settles. Woozy, I sit on the edge of the bed, brush his hair back, kiss his forehead. Are you sakit my sweet boy? Physically sakit? Is it coincidence, you throwing a fit after your ibu shakes you so hard? Or triggers it some dark, deadly mote in your head?

'You'll be fine,' I whisper. 'It's only the one time. It's all gone now.' The best experts in Singapore are prescribing nutes.

Purple eyes …

That's one small step. Neil Armstrong's ghost has jumped from the holly into my Mind, whispering in my Mind's ear.

The ruins of the Inductee Gala are still raw and fresh. Eir Frijberg sweeping away for the spooky station, her wake drawing nurses behind her. Some nurses stay behind with her adjutant and rally around her—flustered, perhaps in shock. Every Infi they name in a Warrant drops dead, though none deliquesce with such gorifying squirts and borborygms as Maddox Price. Inflating with zealotic righteousness, the adjutant retaliates, improvising new Warrants for a few minor guests and catering staff.

Petroleum Dynamite—perhaps adopting the role of Infi leader in the circumstances—scurries for me, gesticulates meaningless symbols in the air between us, improvs in the moment. 'I'm inducting you. Right you are. You're in.' Scurries off.

That's one small step.

'Mal,' I whisper to my sleeping anak, caress his shoulder. 'Who should we punish first? The Witch or her adjutant?'

I may need a nutepak later.

That's one small step.

Aisha. Her words from 2 days ago: *I swear some days, I could drop Mal in a sucky bin.* Just venting, but less than a day later she's slicing around in Mal's fluther; searching for stalkers; shaking him to the point of concussion, perhaps bringing on his illness.

A vision inks my thoughts. Mal in a sucky bin; the violet flash; a momentary look of shock on his face. No pain please! The sucky spooking Mal for the feedstock bin in the basement. Still alive before an instant disassembly into compounds, molecules, and trace elements. In another home in the hill, a resident might fab a coffee and could be drinking …

'Bat Ears?' Aisha membs.

My hand freezes on Mal's shoulder. 'What's the matter?' Find Aisha drying herelf after a shower.

'Just receive word. Earthquake … off the coast of North-West California.' Aisha sounds cool and professional. In her element. The sight of her towelling down assumes a cast more clinical than erotic. A pang in my chest. The heart knows before the brain, she'll be going away. 'On the Cascadia Subduction Zone,' she adds, a detail which must have some significance.

Stroke Mal's head, unsure of what I could say. I memb, 'How bad?' while gogging news channels.

'Bad: 8.4. There's a tsunami. I must go outstation.'

Aisha dresses quick in her camerata fatigues including cap and cooling glasses. 'No fatalities. Straight after the quake we set up spooky chains from all the stations. The site is empty before the tsunami hits the beaches. Everyone escapes but there's extensive damage for kims inland. In Northwest Portland, there's liquefaction along the banks of the Willamette River.'

No fatalities. Perhaps there's no need she goes. 'Are you packing anything?'

'No time. I'll fab anything I need there.'

Slump. She's going. 'In a disaster zone?'

A rumble of heavy boots: Aisha double-timing down the stairs. Follow her for the front door.

'There's nothing for worry about.' She stops, reads the look on my face. 'You know that one ah.'

Reluctantly, I concede. Misi Pemulihan Seletar and other disaster recovery camerati will send fabbies for the site inside 30 mins. After a few hours, a mini makeshift village, with most of the comforts of home, will be ready for missionaries. 'I'm no worrier.'

'Could be fooling me ah,' she says perfunctory.

'How long will you be?' I regret asking.

She arranges her best *are-you-kidding?* face. 'You know how these things are. Could be weeks like that lah.'

'You could spook home when you're off shift.'

'I will take breaks. Relax.' She's out the door.

'Slow down,' I plead. 'We must talk ... Mal ...'

She turns back, meets me at the door. Looming over me, those extra few centims in height never more overpowering. She pecks me on the cheek. A token of a kiss. 'Already,' she says, 'Mal is safer without me.' She's out the door jumping, skidding down the slide. Three hopeful tukkies wait in the street.

Aisha Evoli ...

I toss my bag in the last tukky. It looks cleanest ah. The other 2 slink away.

For weeks already, the tectonic plates off the coast of Pacific Northwest California grind out warnings detectable only by instrument. Then there are 3 quakes only a few days apart. In the 6's, they are strong enough for feel in knees and intestines. For 14 to 21 tiks, the quakes knock over store displays, crack roads, split walls, and damage old buildings. Lightweight panels of modern buildings also crack and split, but are easy for replace, as expendable as a dry shell of a newborn cicada. No one worries much when windows, partitions, or environment sails need replacing.

After the 3 strong quakes seismologists say prepare for The Big One. If it hits, it could shake for 4 mins. The duration of the quake is as devastating as the magnitude. Land west of the old Interstate 5 line could slip many metres. The epicentre will be offshore, giving coastal communities less than 35 tiks' warning before the tsunami hits. Only people within a sprint of a spooky station will survive. Towns such as Seaside and Cannon Beach could be 21 metres under water in mins.

Through neighbourhoods and commercial districts, local disaster recovery missionaries ship in and distribute floatable spooky stations and lightweight nuclear power generators.

When the quake hits, the magnitude is severe—in the mid 8's, fortunately less than high 9's of The Big One. Large sections of the fault line drop but is short of a full slippage. It shake shorter than everyone fears, though it still feel like the world is some gawd's riffle pan.

I'm sorry, Bat Ears, family must wait.

Ben Evoli ...

Money is the root of all evil, wrote Timothy, a sap religion missionary. Which came first? Chicken evil or egg money? My money is on evil chickens.

Explain *money*. Explain *evil* and see how soon y'all entangle yourelves in a barbwire fence of context. One sap's evil is another's virtue.

I lean in towards the display case; roll the ice around in my glass, diluting the tea and capturing glints of the greens and blues and reds of the currency notes in the case. Rest my noggin on the display case, its glass a firm support taking the weight of my thoughts. Like a bored voyeur, I peer in at the notes and coins, at numbers and denominations and portraits of long-dead dignitaries. These notes once connoted so much, so corrupt and exploitable, as addictive as cocaine. Is the Reckoning any better? No one alive knows how it runs or calculates. Especially how it awards Infinite designation.

An alert from my hancy. It's Tinatin Jamalova, one of the few antique brokers I deal with. Tinatin trades for decades after succeeding her mentor Mani Grabero after health missionaries take him for a long Cure. No one locates him ever again. A rumour grows of an accident during his Cure. Strange. No gogging turns up a single holly about the matter. In any case, the deft risk averse Tinatin picks among the threads of Mani's camerata and, in no time, has a thriving base of collectors and sources.

'Are you considering augmenting your collection?' she membs.

Just a small part of my collection crowds the case's gently slanting felt shelves. More are in the cupboards underneath and in storage elsewhere. I shake my head. Tinatin will see.

'A new acquisition for cheering you up, perhaps ...' she membs.

'No, just ...' I trail off, pruning the branches of my thoughts.

'Your Inductee Gala is a flop,' she membs. 'Aisha almost kills Mal then leaves for the tsunami in the USC. Mal is mysteriously ill. And your own inventions haunt you at every turn. A fair summary?'

'Aisha is no cause of Mal's penyakit.'

'I have a lovely bunch of Benjamins for you,' Tinatin tempts.

'USA 100-dollar bills are common.'

'Yes. All kinds of saps hoarded them. Mostly criminals.'

'There are whole suitcases of them out there.'

'None of such quality,' she membs. 'Mint-condition Benjies, consecutive serial numbers, still in wrappers, 500 in all.'

'Mint?'

'Ah, interest takes you.'

I sip scotch, let the conversation go dead.

Tinatin is still there. 'Are you driving the Mustang I find for you ... 2 years back?'

'Many months since I drive it.'

'It might cheer you up,' she membs.

Charlotte is a 1967 Shelby Mustang GT350: 4-speed manual; 2-door fastback; dark moss-green exterior with white stripes; parchment vinyl interior. Indah! Assembled in Los Angeles, California. Like all sap mobils of its time, its internal combustion engine took high-octane petrochemical fuel. With modification, it runs on fabby fuel more like oil y'all would use for stir-frying.

I settle into the sofa opposite the fire in the common room; tune my filters for anyone from Kementerian Filip Island Sirkit who maintains the racing track there and a large garage of mobils. I could keep Charlotte at home, but there are so few places for driving it, and still fewer places for driving it fast. Between the pedestrians, market stalls and tukkies, I would never exceed skipping speed.

'Apologies, Infi, your mobil is unready today.'

'Unready? Who is this?'

'Hallow Forbor, Infi. A novice mechanic here at FISK.'

'Hello, Hallow. Terima kasih for responding.'

'You're welcome. Yours is a beautiful mobil. As I say...'

'It has bookings all day?'

'No, Infi. It ... ah ...,' Hallow haws. 'You must hear? We are all upset by it.'

'Hear what? Upset?'

'Yeer, Infi. Perhaps you should speak with Wheels ...'

Bob 'Wheels' Spinner, cofounder of FISK, is a mechanical restorer of great talent. His ability for finding rare parts, some say straight out of onespace, is legendary. And if no originals turn up, he can fab replica parts, being skilful in fabby mindwriting. Also, try passing him on the racetrack.

'Sure, all right, all right, all right. Is he there?'

'Yeer', Hallow membs. 'One tik.'

'Ben,' Wheels membs. 'I'm sorry for disappointing you, man.' Wheels' broad, flat, nasal accent rings in the ears of my soul. 'I thought you would know already.'

'Know what?'

'Better you flutherbomb me, brother. I'll show you.'

In a flick, Wheels' sensory input is mine. Swing the point of view, see his craggy face. He's skipping, so I spin around and follow along behind, down a long wide windowless corridor of grey squirty-crete walls, a squirty-glass floor and bright overhead lighting. After passing a series of big wide doors in gloss-blue frames, Wheels enters a workshop containing 14 or so mobils, some up on hoists, others on the floor, all in a state of disassembly and repair. The smell of exhaust and wet paints are strong. About 4 bays down, I spy a flash a dark green body panel.

'Is … what?'

I swivel around Wheels for better seeing my broken Mustang. Charlotte is on jacks, missing doors, windows, the bonnet, rims. On a stand alongside, is her Windsor 4.7-litre V8 engine—naked without its air filter and other bolt-ons.

Leaving the obvious question hanging, Wheels membs, 'We are waiting for one or 2 more parts, others we must fab. We already recycle the beat-up metal parts … took a while getting the fabby programs just right. Fortunate such an old mobil has few plastics in it.'

'What happens? When?'

'A racing accident, baddy-bad. Without the impact-sensing spooky extracting the driver from it, he would pass for sure.' Wheels laughs.

'Glad no one is hurt. But my janking car! What happens?'

Wheels membs me a holly. Charlotte braking late on the inside of a tight corner, the driver attempting a reckless overtake. Charlotte skids and screeches into understeer, t-boning another mobil behind the B-pillar. The collision is louder than a train crash. The squeal of rubber almost as loud. The other mobil fish-tails into the gravel trap as the back of Charlotte snaps out, tyres burning black acrid smoke. Into the gravel too, her wheels bite in. The scene from the cockpit becomes a whirling amusement park ride. She's up on her 2 left wheels then her snout gulps into the ground. She cartwheels and twists, a careening whale coming down on her side. Still skidding, she scrapes the barrier wall then settles on her roof.

I memb, 'When are you planning on telling me?' hoping I sound demanding enough.

'You should already taste it.'

'Wheels, you could always memb me.'

'Ha! Your fluther is a bloat of millions and your filters are so stringent; I figure it best we busy about the repair. So many missionaries come together for you, Ben. You have no idea, the places around the world where we find parts. I go to Russia for parts, Ben. Russia. They're still fucking capitalists, those bastards. I must *pay* for parts. You have no idea what they want for barter there.'

'Who is the driver?'

'Everything about him checks out … references, reputasi, racing experience.'

'Racing experience? Who makes such a terrible mistake, braking so late?'

'It's racing, Ben, these things happen.'

'How can I trust—' There are at least 3 other motor sport camerati on Filip Island alone, many more around Victoria, 100's around the world. I should check their incident records.

'Trust me, Ben.' Wheels' eyebrows tighten, reminding me of the smoking tyres on my car. 'Everyone makes a mistake sooner or later, which you would know if you had more kims on the track.' He thinks me the dilettante.

'I have so little time …'

'You should make—'

'Look, the point is … just look at the damage. I should never—'

'You know you'll never find a better arrangement,' Wheels membs. 'We look after—'

'Look after?'

'We look after this mobil. We are making it good again. We keep nurses off your back, and many racing enthusiasts share in the pleasure of racing it.'

My 1967 Shelby Mustang GT350, never all mine. I'm only the steward, keeping a sap relic on behalf of all—any of whom may destroy it.

'I'm sorry about the accident, Ben. I assure you it will soon be in better shape than ever. Then you must come drive it again.'

'What of the driver who crashes it? What of his reputasi?'

Wheels chuckles. 'Oh, it's taking a hammering, as you would expect. It will be a time before he races such a car again.' Wheels pauses. 'Wait. I might as well show you the holly of him spooking into the impact couch. You'll piss yourelf laughing.'

Wheels projects the holly it into vacant space in the middle of the garage. It starts from a position above a large fibrous, webby bag—half hammock, half couch. For some tiks nothing changes, then the sound of a lelaki primal screaming. Into view he hurtles as if shot from a cannon; still in a driving position; every muscle tense; legs stretching out as if planting a brake to the floor; arms out in front; hands gripping an invisible steering wheel. The couch is a hungry sea creature ejecting tendrils to ensnare the driver. With the *thwok* of the driver's impact, it reshapes into a baseball mitt and rolls back, softens then flattens until it's a futon on the floor.

The driver has his fingernails digging into the flat couch, eyes on fire, face taught, baring teeth and gums.

'Better than bleeding out in the back seat though, heh?' Wheels laughs.

The driver—the ruiner of Charlotte—is naked. The spooky field plucks the driver right out of the racing suit, leaving it in the mangled remains of the crash. 'Cheap racing suit,' Wheels explains. 'No DNA weave in it. Either he's some throw-back cheapskate, or else, whoever supplies it, is someone with a sense of humour, and hopes he might crash.'

Recovering from the shock, the driver—half tumescent—pisses like a broken hydrant.

'Happens with all of them,' Wheels says. 'Or worse. We take measures. Watch,' Wheels exhorts. 'The best part. We put a shower nozzle in the ceiling above the couch. Seems only considerate if we wash 'em down. It's a shame; for some reason, our hot water often fails, so a cold shower it is.' Wheels laughs. 'Here it comes. *Whoa-hah!*'

The driver gasps, squeals, swears, and roars in the cold spray. Wheels is right. It is the best part.

 *Saf Evoli …*

'Nurses are communists,' Mal announces over his breakfast. He comes up with the most crapodactile nonsense.

Bapa's looking side-eye at Mal, drops his toast. 'What? Take your nutes.'

Mal's having no more of those scary episodes since the nurses prescribe extra nutes 3 times a day. They come in small foil packs he sucks out or squeezes into a drink. No idea what's in them. Our fabby is unable for making ah. With Bapa refusing nurses come for the house, we go every day for more from the clinic. No one is explaining how they work or what they are treating. So far, I never hear discussion about it. Whatever is the matter with Mal, everyone is keeping quiet. No easy trick in such a small desa. Perhaps they only know in Singapore.

'They taste bad,' Mal says.

I memb, 'Better tasting them than feeling them cold in your pantat.'

'Drink your aya,' Bapa tells Mal, and churns a spoon in his cup like a ladle in a witch's cauldron.

'I need no aya, Bapa. I get onespace just fine. Fourspace feels better.'

I say, 'Even when you fall off your bike and skin your shin lah.' Mal is ungainly on a pushbike. He'll ride off a cliff one day. All my friends say he will.

Mal gurgles some of his tea down. It must be cold already. 'Can you breathe in onespace?'

I answer, 'No,' before Bapa. Staying in the bodoh conversation or go invisible. Once these 2 start …

'Can you pee in onespace?'

'Mal! Witless little monkey. No, worse. A sap.'

'Saf …' Bapa says, warning.

'See? Fourspace is better.' Mal slaps a piece of toast over his cavernous gob, eats a hole out of the middle. Paints kaya all over his face. 'You can jank in onespace,' he says, wiping goop from his nose, trading eyes with Bapa, cutting me out, 'with SnakiDik.'

You see Bapa gritting his teeth. 'Mal, just eat, will you? You're a dog rolling in his kill, the way you maul your toast.'

I cover a giggle with my teacup.

'You invent SnakiDik, Bapa,' Mal says, wanting a rise out of him.

'Yeer. And other things,' Bapa says, sounding sian (bored).

'I'll fancy onespace better when I can eat and breathe and pee in it,' Mal says.

I push in, 'And all together, I imagine.'

Mal giggles. 'When will you invent something for those, Bapa?' Still excluding me.

'Your Bapa is over inventing.' He's sad. Mal never notices.

'Why? Are you becoming a communist? You have communism already?'

'I have no isms,' Bapa says. 'Astigmatism perhaps.' Bapa thinks he's giggleshit.

Which bent-brain teacher is Mal getting this communism thing from? Probably some old crank who runs a pop-up school in a public longhouse, who should know it would play badly at home. Who should know Mal is the son of an Infi. Most teachers live in fear of upsetting an Infi. I guess some are braver. Teach their own opinions. I might follow Mal around again for a school week, see which ones he attends. Tell Bapa what I learn.

I glare at Mal. 'You think Lành Hiền a Communist?'

Mal blushes, shifts awkwardly in his seat. 'Nah.' He looks down.

'Good. Because she saves your life.' Mal is crushing on Lành Hiền. It's funny. I say, 'When I'm old enough, I think health should be my mission.'

Bapa with eyes on fire. 'Your mission is health? Nursing?'

'Then you'll be a communist,' Mal accuses, pointing.

'They're more like surveillance capitalists.' There. Take that. Bapa just gives me a look saying, *Stop showing off.* There's no winning for me.

'There were communists,' Mal persists. 'They took all your things away. You could own nothing, and they kept everything—same as now.'

'Nurses are no rulers over us,' Bapa says too patiently. 'Theirs is just another mission. Owning stuff is even harder for nurses than for the rest of us. Besides, you own things.'

'Then why must I share?' Mal whinges.

'You can keep some things for yourelf if you're never mean with them or lord them over anyone else. Your intention is what matters.'

'Greed is sakit,' Mal pronounces and exaggerates a nod.

'Yeer, Greed is sakit,' Bapa agrees.

'You own your Mustang?' Mal asks with all the demeanour of a sap trial lawyer embedding an accusation in a question.

Bapa stiffens. 'How you know of this?'

'I know about many stuffs,' Mal boasts. Mangles more of his breakfast down his gob.

I mock, 'Which dolphins tell you?'

Mal goes on eating.

'They are no dolphins.' Bapa says gravely. Is he serious? 'Those are sakit neos, trying for tricking you,' Bapa says.

'They are dolphins. They talk funny. It sounds squiggly.'

'What say they about the Mustang?'

'Nothing. They just taste you are unhappy about it.'

'Mal, are you following me?'

'Nah,' he says, quiet. He starts sobbing. 'Bapa?'

'Yeer, Mal?' Bapa reaches out, taking Mal's sticky hand.

'Why would Ibu hurt me?' He gulps and chokes on his whimpering. Wailing and breath compete for passage through his throat. Bapa launches out of his seat for join him on the other side of the table. Arm around him. Mal has Bapa on a string.

'Oh, little fella, you know your ibu would never hurt you. Yeer?'

Mal nods weak. 'She shakes me. Hard.'

'She is just afraid for a tik. Afraid there are nasty hurtful people lurking in your fluther.'

'She shakes me then I burn inside. I nearly die.'

'No, Mal. It's only coincidence. You are sakit just for a tik, but you'll be fine if you take your nutes.'

'But it hurts.'

'Now or before?'

'Before, when Ibu shakes me.'

'She is so sorry for shaking you,' Bapa says. I wish for tasting for sure she *is* sorry. 'She is searching for those nasty ones claiming they are dolphins.'

'They are dolphins! They are real.' Mal twists away from Bapa's hug, takes his thunder to a dining chair; finds strength in his weedy little fruit; hurls the chair at the window, shattering through. Shredding leaves of an elephant palm. The chair clattering on the terrace.

 *Ben Evoli …*

As the house's electrical environment adjusts for the loss of the solarglass, the room lighting flickers; the effect chilling, like the world going offline. A new world shunts into place around me, one in which my anak is perfect stranger. In the hall, the window squirty whirs.

From the moment of birth, anak anak are becoming. At different rates in different situations. One tik, full anak; the next, full adult. Stunning sometimes. It stuns me. The same for adults. When are adults no longer anak? The oldest never loses their sense of play.

Bound up for Mal's swasta. Hollies of sap movie catalogues flicker in the air in front of his wardrobe while he browses a magazine. The iMac is inactive on the desk.

'Are you going for schools?'

He nods staring sullenly into the magazine. Selects a movie and runs it triple-speed. A black-and-white pirate movie.

'Where today?'

'My friend says there is a good pop-up history school in Sapporo today.'

'Jepang?'

'Uh-huh. It is unopen for some hours yet. Jepang is still asleep.'

'You translate without a hancy?'

Mal nods proud. 'Enough. We don't need no stinking hancies.'

We both laugh. *'How 'bout some more beans, Mr Taggart?'* Mal quotes.

'I say you have enough.'

Mal purses his lips and warbles a long farting raspberry. Laughs.

The window fabby flashes me a report. The house membs, *The new window is more concave, improving air flow and temperature consistency across the kitchen and dining areas*, in an amiable tone which almost fools me into believing they may get building intelligence right one day.

I reply, 'Terima kasih.' A grunt would be sufficient for the interface. *Fewer cooking smells will escape the kitchen/informal eating*, it continues. *The glass is thicker overall, and compensates for the new curvature, eliminating image distortion. It is stronger, in case of son throwing chair.* The house is factoring my son's growing moodiness into its own maintenance. I hope it's wrong.

I worry about Mal's penyakit. Hearing voices. Hallucinating dolphins. Acting out. A side effect of the new nutes perhaps. The Singapore KK is saying nothing about his prospects. Ruling nothing out. Lành Hiền tries gathering more information for us. All she can admit is, it could be days or weeks before symptoms show again. If ever.

There's a chalice of dread deep inside me. Expecting Mal might throw another fit. At any tik. Without Aisha at home keeping the peace between him and Saf ... I must confront Aisha about her mission; There are quakes in our own house too. Might no one else in her camerata stand in for her? I need her here.

'Ibu says nurses might take you for a Cure one day,' Mal says. 'She says we must help you be happy.'

Why must she blackmail them? I say, 'My happiness is no worry of yours,' trying for softness. 'It's *my* mission, looking after *you*. I will take care of myelf.'

'If the nurses ever put you in a clinic, I'm gonna come and bust you out,' he says while playing a game on the iMac.

'You will? I bet you will terrify everyone who stands in your way.'

In the movie, cannons fire. A fort explodes. Mal whoops and laughs. 'Yo-ho-ho!'

Chance

'Ariel' — Kate Bush

 *Gerlinde Mann …*

ASSISTANT CLINICAL NURSE Fluffy Pusskins is what: 200 years old? She must be. No one takes such affectatious names anymore. She should respect and keep the name her parents give her. Especially if they spend an age debating a name, as the case with my 5 parents. If I could tell y'all Fluffy's original name, I would. Perhaps y'all can tell me. Such records, if they exist, must be in Hell's basement.

At the far end of the admissions theatre, Fluffy busies herelf around a sole patient on an aid couch. For my disappointment, the other 6 couches are vacant. The White Witch bids us prepare for a barrel of Infis from the Inductee Gala. Instead, we have a mere handful of lower-reputation partygoers. Eir reaches too far, and we're admitting low-priority patients on dubious Warrants.

Weak rosy light from the observation windows fails in imbuing the theatre with any warmth. The charcoals and greys of the couches, floors and walls remain cold. Grey is a tool (sensory deprivation for the patients being among the main design features of the clinics of Vauxminster). Fluffy's fur is a neutral grey too.

'Russian Blue. I'm Russian Blue, not grey.' Fluffy squints her nekko projection eyes and flattens her nekko projection ears. All the unambitious Fluffy ever dreams of, is being nekko. 7 Hells. Save us from japanisch pop culture.

'Russian Blue … Grey. Forgive me if I fail in tasting the difference.'

Fluffy sets a mobile utility table just so; nods her satisfaction. She delights in fussing over the laying out of the instruments—the catheters and nozzles, surgical tapes, gels, and lubes—aligning them, spreading them evenly, adjusting and readjusting by mims.

'Which one is this?' I ask, looking over the patient in Never-Mind (unconscious) on the couch.

'Well, puh! No Infinite, for certain.'

I tighten my lips and set my jaw. 'A companion of an Infinite Wilma Solstice.'

Fluffy nods. 'One of Wilma's submissives, Ariel Kanon.' She looks down the length of the theatre; shakes her head and skews her muzzle, setting her whiskers at an odd slant. 'Every couch in here should bear a patient this morning,' she says with disappointment.

I slap 3 2-litre nutebags on a neighbouring table, which sends it rolling gentle enough for appearing an accident. The table taps Fluffy's and knocks her instruments out of kilter. Her eyes narrow as if about to pounce. 'Clinical Nurse Gerlinde Mann!' Even her voice is feline. Every vowel sounds a meow. 'Since when is rebasing part of admissions procedure?' she asks, blinking out a holly of Ariel's Prescription at eye-height between us.

I whoosh the signatory record out. A semi-transparent bust expands and rotates slowly. Feeling powerless I memb, 'I'm in no mood for countering Registrar-Procomplement Ubaida Belghiti.'

'It's worse,' Fluffy says, and whooshes fingers at Ubaida's rotating holographic head. Another bust bulges into space above: Agatha Svanblod, Investigator-Procomplement. 'Detectives are behind the change in procedure,' Fluffy hisses.

'The White Witch,' I curse and scrunch the revolving heads away.

Fluffy nods and strokes her ear. 'We'd be up to our whiskers in magazines searching for evidence.'

'She will be desperate for extracting something from last night's mess.'

'I'm less sure,' Fluffy says. 'After Eir leaves the party in a huff, it's her adjutant, Vör Hoyur, who scrambles together the Warrants for the Consignments we're dealing with today.'

The mention of Vör—an undeserving, insecure yet ambitious missionary already out of her depth—sets me shivering. I say, 'I doubt she acts without the White Witch's endorsement. But procedure is procedure.'

'Are you saying we forgo the rebasing?' Fluffy slow-blinks her crystal-bright emerald-green eyes. 'When Eir comes galloping around here—getting her clumsy elbows in everyone's faces—your defence will be, you stick with procedure?'

'I have no fear of Eir.'

'Easy for your saying,' Fluffy says.

'You'll be an Admissions Assistant your entire life.'

'Aw, you're just chatting me up.'

I look away.

Fluffy's tail swishes. Where her projection touches the couch, the fur bends, and springs back in accordance with fourspace physics. Very realistic. Underneath, I trust she's wearing the proper theatre scrubs. Why would Standards let her wear a recreational projection while on mission? She should enjoy no privilege, even if she missions longer at Vauxminster than anyone.

'Someone wants these patients out of the way quickly,' she says, while I dig fingernails into palms. It's unfortunate I have Fluffy assisting. With so many missionaries washing their hands of Eir's operation, she is my only option.

Fluffy tests the couch's inflation for the weight and size of the patient by pressing her paw—hand—on it. She flashes open the couch's control, applies a claw for lifting a slider. The couch gives a quiet hiss as some buoyancy goes out of it. Fluffy purrs.

'What have we?' I ask while unpacking Ariel's full Prescription, flicking files into a loose semi-circle around the couch.

'Lust,' Fluffy scrunches her rhinarium. Looking at her nose leather, I wonder if she has the gene-mods for feline smell. Perhaps she has a Jacobson's organ in the roof of her mouth for going with her mod throat and vocal cords. 'Addiction if ever I taste it,' she continues. 'Loss of interest in other activities; lack of care for family and friends; indifference for her fluther; withdrawal; increasing dissatisfaction with the very activities addicting her.'

'A trivial case.'

'*Hai*,' Fluffy agrees. 'She is one of 4 slaves. The others are healthy, if skating a little close for the edge. The good news is they are all supportive, including Wilma—she is taking it quite hard ... blames herelf.'

'They are available when the time comes for reintegration?'

'*Hai*,' Fluffy says then shakes her head in undeniable furry cuteness. 'A cat would never endure enslavement. Although I fancy her collar. It's the only personal effect she arrives with. Nudy otherwise.'

Look Ariel over. Her most obvious feature is the simple paisley boteh swirling over every centim of her skin. Of more or less uniform size, clustering tightly in 3's, a triskelion design which reflects a silvery, metallic sheen when catching the light. For the touch, feeling slightly raised, like scar-tissue. Ariel's coarse black hair is shorter than even the fashion for nurses. Sculpty eyebrows are the possible product of epigenetic encoding. The large eyes, prominent cheekbones, and small, almost severe mouth appear natural. Some skin irritation from her tight-fitting collar. Light bruising at the neck. A commonly flattish chest. Large nipples showing some evidence of crush injury. An elegant flat torso; innie navel; narrow hips; prominent venus mound. Average proportions ...

'I wonder when you would notice,' Fluffy titters. Has she a songbird in her mouth? Her smugness is strange on a nekko—more carnivorous than mirthful, her whiskers glistening in the dim glow of the hollies. 'You know what else? It's mature work, at least 3 years old.'

Fluffy is correct. Ariel's small penile enhancement of her clitoris is quality work; the shaft nestling between the labia is almost imperceptible. Tumescent, it might reach 3 or 4 centims.

'Urethral meatus in the glans …' I examine it, look for testicles.

'Very small,' Fluffy says. 'Under the frenulum at the top of the vestibule. Little more than lumps.'

With soft fingertips, I just feel them. 'Functional?'

'Doubt it,' Fluffy says. 'Perhaps just a vestigial by-product.'

'She is only 32?'

'*Hai.*' Another annoying affectation of Fluffy's: a bare spattering of japanisch words in her speech. 'She gets it 3 years ago, at 29. Being a minor, she would need a caregiver's permission for such an enhancement.'

'Nothing in her magazines?'

'*Ie.*' No.

'How long has she been with Wilma?' She could be an abuser. We may Consign an Infi after all.

Just gog it, Fluffy's flattening ears say losing patience with my questions. She might be about to hiss. Jank it, I'm the procomplement nurse here. 'Three seasons,' she answers.

'Less than a year? Then it has no connection with Wilma.'

'*Ie.*'

'What caregiver would authorise such mods for someone so young?'

'Perhaps no one gives permission. Finding a willing gene clinic would be easy.' Fluffy bristles. If she's right, it's a distasteful prospect. Fluffy's shoulders slump. She looks away. 'We should start the nutes,' she says and tosses me a bag. She stretches gloves over her paws; her fur appears to suck the gloves under, fitting tight around her invisible fingers. While I hook the bag from the couch's spar, Fluffy lifts the girl's calves into the stirrups and tightens the ankle restraints.

I prefer connecting the nute delivery train on my own but Fluffy is already applying lubricant on the nozzles. Inserting. I open the drip gate. Fluffy fits an aerosol mask over Ariel's face. Nutes flowing make the mask misty. I monitor the drip through the tubes to her rectum.

Patients always look the same. With the couch tilting back, her head lower than her hips, and her legs straddling in the stirrups, Ariel's a specimen frog undergoing lab experiments.

Fluffy stretches the couch console holly high as she can reach, swivels it around for both of us viewing. Diagnostic charts and numbers glow bright alongside a schematic of Ariel's fruit. Fluffy scrunches her paw over the pelvic region on the schematic, flicks her claws wide for zooming in, and watches the progress of the nutes through Ariel's veins.

While Fluffy occupies herelf, obsessing over every statistic, I take 2 small nutepaks from the kangaroo pocket in my fatigues. In a perfunctory manner, I hang them from the couch's nute tree, and dock their nozzles with the drip line.

'What's this?' Fluffy asks with a feline expression of astonishment when she notices the extra nutepaks. 'You're pushing on with the rebasing after all?'

'What choices have we?'

Fluffy gives a kind of feline sneeze or snort. 'We should watch the diagnostics,' she says, flicking through holly screens; pulling them out of the air; switching them aside; stretching them wide; scrunching them closed. We watch for effects on Ariels's synaptic patterns. Evidence we're pruning her from her onespace connections. What remains is her own Mind, a single node disconnected from onespace.

Fluffy's feline frame stiffens; she regards with distaste a vital sign. 'This's wrong, this's wrong,' she says in a catty growl, surveying Ariel and the equipment like she's stalking a mouse. I swash away the hollies and focus on Ariel.

'You see?' I ask, disbelieving my eyes. Around Ariel's head, the faint glow of a thin halo. 'Who is flutherbombing her?'

'Or what?' Fluffy adds, tracing a claw around a holographic brain schematic.

Vauxminster scatter nets are the best in the world, for the exact purpose of repelling flutherbombing of patients. How is anyone getting through?

'What in 7 Hells? I'm going in.' Fluffy coils as if she might spring onto the patient.

I reach across the couch for putting a hand on Fluffy's narrow shoulder. She jumps back as if I assault her. 'Never touch me,' she yelps.

I say, 'I'll go in.'

Fluffy flattens her ears, narrows her eyes.

Against the strictest of protocols, I flutherbomb Ariel. Something dull and loathing lurks. A windy moan—hollow and reedy, the trick of a wet-black forest—surrounds on all sides. Its pitch rises until a scream. Forcing me out. Chilled. Like lying naked by a fjord. 'Demon! *Alpe*. Hang horseshoes from your bedpost.'

Fluffy laughs.

Ariel snorts. Her jaw grinds; her eyes flutter. She squints as if under powerful flashing lights. Drool trickles from the corner of her mouth. Her eyelids roll up like store-front shutters, and blink. Sweat beads on her chest where paisley shapes trap pooling droplets. Ariel wrings her hands. Starting at her lips, a tremor passes down her rigid fruit. Her ankles pull at the restraining cuffs. Violent jerks wrack her.

'Get her legs out of the stirrups,' says my voice.

Fluffy is quick.

Out of the stirrups, Ariel's tremors intensify. Her hands and fingers contort into claws. Her head threatens snapping away from her neck.

'Get her tongue! Get her tongue!'

Again, Fluffy acts fast. So much for my half-arse accusations of being old. She can have an out-of-fashion name if it pleases her, if we save the patient. Fluffy's fur appears to penetrate Ariel's nose, breaking the illusion of her projection (imperfect after all) while she retrieves Ariel's tongue. Ariel's skin pales icy blue, masking the triskelion pattern. Her pelvic muscles contract, ejecting nute tube nozzles. She pisses forcefully.

Fluffy, still hooking for Ariel's tongue, studies her violently fluttering eyes. 'Full dilation,' Fluffy hisses. 'Ouch! She bites me.' Fluffy, winces. With some difficulty, she yanks her fingers out of Ariel's mouth.

It's over. Ariel collapses on the couch, inert as before. Fluffy and I lock eyes. Despite her sickly cute nekko appearances, her expression is one of naked terror.

Aisha Evoli ...

I find Vör's fluther. I must taste what play she make next.

She and Vör argue in silence among the trees of the Cemetery of Lost Cemeteries in Gdansk. I gog the place; it look almost like unspoilt forest. No real sap burial place that one, only a dedication for saps everywhere who have no resting place.

'Little Mermaid, you're hysterical,' Eir membs.

'Hysterical? I'm angry.' Vör sounds more like a squeaky oboe than angry ah. Underestimating her is a mistake lah.

'You're in a state of fright,' Eir says. 'Emotional. Understandable, you're far from thinking on a straight fence.'

Vör stares at Eir with intense defiance. I never see it in her before. 'Tell me you have no connection with ...'

'With what, Little Mermaid?'

'Murdering Infis.'

'What? No,' Eir defends. Vör stares. Eir adds, 'As if I would destroy anyone this way. Serious?'

Vör's anger melt until tears. 'Last night is perhaps the greatest failure of my life.'

'Plenty of ocean currents await you in life yet, Little Mermaid,' Eir membs. 'More than enough time for greater failures.'

This one only dismays Vör more ah. 'You joke?' She claws at Eir's rainbow fatigues, which need a substantial fashion update.

'Vör, please, no crying. We're getting looks. Please ... find some perspective. Last night is only a setback.'

Is there a whiff of perfume I taste? Yeer, one of the Beyoncé variants. Vör take a pill before meeting Eir. She may be angry and fretful. Perhaps she feel insecure about losing Eir too ah.

'We rush this,' Vör sniffles. 'Operation Hang 10—'

Eir looks stern. 'Ten Infinites ... Ten Warrants. Hang 10?'

'It's a surfing reference.'

'And a lynching reference. Little Mermaid, you should know better.'

Vör look chastised one, forget her despair tiks ago only. 'The operation is too soon after the graduation. Then you become Infinite ... all too much in such a short space of time.'

'Little Mermaid, we plan for months.' Interest for hear, terima kasih. 'How could I plan for something I never expect?'

Good question. Vör make a side-eye face lah.

'It is coincidence, Little Mermaid. Read nothing more into it.'

Vör must read more into it, wonder what for believe.

'Let's talk about how we leave last night,' Eir membs. 'Why stay you after I leave? Why issue those trivial vengeful Warrants?'

'How could we leave with nothing?' Vör pleads.

'What value are they? Where is the gain?'

'We must salvage something from the mess, something for justifying the operation.' Vör's mouse face hardens with a carnivorous intensity.

'It's my fault,' Eir concedes. 'I should make you come with instead of leaving you.'

My stomach retch again with a memory of last night, a shit-sweet stench of human offal. Maddox Price slaughterhouse slop at our feet.

'Although, the look on Ben Evoli's face ...' Vör membs and laughs.

Eir joins in. 'And the awkward embarrassment of the fashion-queen wife.'

Fashion queen wife?

'She has more concern about her shoes—shoes we'll never have the reputasi for wearing—than about the dying around her,' Eir membs. How unfair. I feel awful for their passing. The Infis, I mean. Never mind hand-made designer shoes—only a dozen pair ever in existence. The maker interview for 3 hours, make sure you are worthy.

'Well, you have the reputasi now, Eir.'

'Those shoemakers will still decline my custom. I may be Infinite but I'm *Sundhed* Camerata; some doors will never open. I have no concern. High heels make me gawkier than I already am.'

Vör finds a sudden righteous indignation. 'How could anyone refuse an Infinite Nurse?' she membs. 'They should fear all kinds of trouble from it.' The way Vör delivers her words until I wonder like that, what trouble she fears from her nurse-come-Infi lover one.

'Perhaps,' Eir concedes.

'We should round them all up when we have the chance,' Vör membs until find a head of steam. 'All the Infis at the gala. Sort the Prescriptions out later. We're sure to find something on each. At least we'd warn Infinites against showing disrespect for the health camerati.'

'And if they all die?' Eir asks.

'Please swear you are no cause of those deaths.'

'I am no cause. I swear.'

'Then so it is. We take no lives,' Vör says.

'Little Mermaid, please let your vengeance pass. You know what awaits otherwise.'

Vör take a deep breath. 'We should at least Consign the guest of honour,' she says, the last words dress in mockery.

What? My Bat Ears? You must know I flutherbomb you, dun look at me.

'Leave Ben,' Eir membs. 'He's as dull as a ditch.' How dare you.

Vör huffs. 'We will never be sure what mindwriting hijinks he might be playing. Until it's too late.' What is Vör play at? Childing is all Ben need one.

Eir nods. 'If he's sick, our first task is diagnosing him.'

Beatrice Lovell …

Wearing a fretful face, Gerlinde gulps aya tea like a booze hound. Fluffy sitting opposite looks cute enough for cuddling, despite her agitation.

'Have you any idea—?' Fluffy chokes. Jittery she laps at green tea and tunes her MusiKai. It must be her own piece. I recognise its derivation: a popular lilting 4-bar earwig from years back. The food court's MusiKai installation riffs on the tune, rearranges and improvises variations. Now it'll burrow into my head, and I won't get it out all day.

Fluffy, a costumed actor in a pantomime, watches Gerlinde pour from a pot. 'Crazy drinking aya now,' Fluffy whispers.

Ignoring Fluffy, Gerlinde takes another draught of tea. Gerlinde unnerves me: thin-lipped, square-jawed, with a sharp, triangular nose set precisely between symmetrical calculating eyes. She sits back twiddling the one errant black pigtail springing out from under her mission cap. Gogs more magazines looking for answers. Her eyelids flutter. Her eyes roll back. Her pupils dilate. Something she finds mortifies her. 'No!' she says.

Fluffy puts her cup down. Her ears twitch. 'What?'

'Epileptic seizure?' incredulous Gerlinde says while reading. With every word, her Mind's voice sounds like opera. The fat lady singing.

'A sap illness,' Fluffy dismisses with the wave of a paw. 'We have no epilepsy.'

Gerlinde keeps gogging while Fluffy, thoughtful, says, 'There are stories of flutherbombing primates.'

'Myths. No corroboration.' Gerlinde's eyes normalise as she emerges from gogging. Facing Fluffy square, her chin up. Light catches her flat forehead, accentuating shapely eyebrows. 'When flutherbombing Ariel, I taste another presence,' she says.

'There should be none. She should be cut off from outside access.'

Gerlinde glowers at Fluffy, impatient with her spouting the obvious. 'It is in *terror* at being there,' Gerlinde says. 'As if captive.'

'An imprisoned flutherbomber? Whoever hears of such a thing?'

'There is nothing in the magazines.'

That is 14 minutes ago.

Here, in this reclaimed recovery room, we have Ariel stabilised, sleeping on the only aid couch which we must reinstall for her. The room is a distasteful mess. With so few historical cases of complications following rebasing, some admin nurse—with meagre foresight and dim imagination for problem-solving—repurposes it for an improvised stock room. I almost trip on a box getting by Ariel's side when she starts convulsing again, same as during her rebasing.

I feel a chill settling as dank as fog. 'I need help in here,' I call out but of course, back-up nurses already flutherbombing me, taste the situation as fast as me. One hangs nute bags; I forcibly pin Ariel's shoulders; another nurse restrains her knees. Ariel screams, fighting us and pulling at her restraints with such ferocity she could dislocate her shoulders. A bank of semi-translucent diagnostic hollies around the couch report she is still in therapeutic Never-Mind, which is clearly false.

Fluffy and Gerlinde appear at the observation window and, chewing lips, peer in.

Gerlinde Mann …

Palpable tension wires through nurses scuttling around down there. Alarmed ants. One tries ushering us away from the window. Fluffy hisses.

'Please,' the nurse membs. 'Step away while we stabilise her.'

Fluffy, anxious for avoiding confrontation, paws and tugs my elbow. I let her guide me for a bench at the back of the observation mezzanine. Gingerly, Fluffy sits down; whiskers drooping, mouth open, teeth dull and chalky. Her huge eyes water, looking side-eye at me for guidance.

The nutes the nurses administer curb Ariel's violence and relax her.

Losing my fight with impatience, I lunge back at the window, and memb, 'Keep her conscious. We must speak with her.'

Clinical Nurse Beatrice Lovell is swapping one nutepak for another on Ariel's drip tube. She looks incredulously at me a floor above in the observation deck. With mounting urgency, I push off the window as if, with one violent thrust, I would propel down the stairs.

Fluffy is in a stupor, bless her delicate constitution.

Beatrice opens a narrow crack in the doorway, grabs my attention with her tiny button eyes narrow-set over a finicky-thin, parrot-beak nose. 'Here is no place for admissions nurses,' she membs. 'Especially you pair.'

'Let me talk with her. It's about her reactions during admission.'

'You mean reactions from botching her rebasing,' Beatrice says, officious. 'You set her therapy back weeks.'

'We botch nothing,' Fluffy rails, her tail up with its fur standing on end.

'Then explain,' Beatrice says with mouth down-turning. 'Of all the patients we admit this morning—all of whom other, more competent nurses rebase … how many suffer as Ariel suffers?'

'Is it all of them?' Fluffy asks, cynically hopeful.

'It's none of them,' Beatrice answers and snort-laughs. 'It surprises everyone you are still wearing chatelaines. If I am procomplement of anything in this minster, I'd have you out.'

There's no need for being rude, Beatrice. You're so comical, trying to look down your bony, bird-nose at me when you are so short. Your head tilts so far back, I could fill them with nute drops.

With shoulders square, arms on hips, chin down, I crowd the partially open door. Of course, I'd never assault anyone—much less a nurse—but I'm never above using my admittedly blocky stature as a psychological threat. 'Stand back.' Few nurses can defy an outright order if it's laced it with aggression.

Since Beatrice already forms the opinion, I am of lesser stuff, she may well believe I might shove her over on her tightly clenched *arsch*. Her thin husk of resistance wilts. Tight-lipped and blenching, she concedes. I push open the door and proceed for the foot of the aid couch.

'Ariel's problem is far from a question of rebasing procedures,' I tell Beatrice.

'Alien cats!' Ariel cries out for no one in particular. 'Experimenting on me. Keep away!'

Beatrice squirts a dose of scorn at me. 'You hear that? *Alien cats.* That's your assistant in a nekko projection while on duty, flouting protocol.'

At Ariel's side I say, 'I'll deal with Fluffy later.' She's semi-animated, only partially conscious. 'Can you say what just happens? Fluffy scares you? Look, she's just a nurse in a nekko projection.'

Ariel, with blurry eyes, looks at Fluffy. Then her gaze slides away, rolls around the room, and drifts for far horizons.

With a hand on her shoulder, I say, 'Ariel. Ariel, Are you with us?'

Ariel regards Beatrice. 'Am I here because of my fruit enhancements? My little cock?' she slurs while fondling herself. 'I have permission—'

Beatrice tries soothing her. 'No, no. Worry nothing for it.'

Ariel is becoming more lucid. She looks down her chest and swallows. 'Keep the cat away.'

'We're here,' Beatrice says patting Ariel's arm. She looks at me with defiance. 'It's just a dream,' she coos, stroking Ariel's hair. 'It passes,' she whispers hypnotically. The bird is adept with patient care.

'It's no dream,' Ariels panics. 'It's no dream... between the party with Mistress and waking up here ...' Her eyes bulge and her mouth forms a large circle. 'Mistress! Where is Mistress? She knows where I am?'

'Yes, yes, she knows. Everything is under control. You just need rest. We'll look after your wellbeing.'

'Strange. It feels real but unreal,' Ariel answers, relaxing back into the couch.

'What?' I ask.

Beatrice grimaces and turns away. 'Let her rest,' she membs.

'What is it you remember?' I ask Ariel.

Ariel reflects. 'My fruit is on a couch, legs in stirrups. I smell horrid ... of sweat and rotting meat.'

'Go on.'

'It's foul.' Ariel retches and might vomit. Beatrice pulls her up sitting; holds a kidney dish under her chin until the spasm passes. Rubs her back. 'I'm rattling and shaking, wanting escape,' Ariel says. 'Then I'm in a cage. Still shaking. The cage disappears and there's a couch and stirrups and restraints again.'

'*Ja*. What happens next?'

'I must know: *What is this place? What is happening?* A light above is so bright. There's blackness all around. Except, behind my head and above, are blurry lights hovering in mid-air. Everything is moving and twisting, doubling, and joining again and melting. Anything I look at warps and bends. The lights could be on a Christmas tree. It's so dark on the road before the lights come, and the truck's engine dies, and everything is shaking.'

'You're on a road?' Beatrice interrupts. I cast her my best shut-the-jank-up look.

'The light is oil in my head and acid leaking in through my eyes.' Ariel's voice is deepening. 'I'm on an operating table. Oh Jesus, there's something cold in my bowels. There's someone ... a child, I think, short but heavy-looking somehow.' Ariel's accent is changing, becoming more North American—Texan perhaps, or Wastelander. 'A girl's features,' she says. 'Kinda cartoon-like. Smooth. Very large eyes. Never see eyes so large. She has a small nose. Maybe's she Russian or Chinese or one of those kinds. She's grey, so grey, like she's in a movie theatre; the glow of a silver screen shining over her. She blinks. Her eyes are so large. I feel her hands on me. I'm naked. She's going to operate on me; I just know it. She'll steal my organs.' Ariel's struggling against the couch restraints. She screams in terror. 'A tiger or a lion. Right there. In grey hospital clothes baring fangs so huge and dripping with saliva. I can't move; I can't sit up; I can't get away. Let me go. Let me go, please.'

'Hold her down while I connect these nutepaks,' Beatrice membs.

Muscle memory kicks in and I obey. Beatrice swiftly reconnects the nute drip while I restrain Ariel against her ferocity.

'See?' Beatrice membs. 'The blame is with your assistant in the cat projection. Her and a botched rebase. I'll be reporting the both of you.'

Passion

'Holy Grail' — Dead Posey

 *Ben Evoli ...*

TINATIN'S UNLIKELY TO KILL her most famous customer. 'Breathe, Ben. We have you in safe hands.'

I hate waiting. Apprehensive about spooking for her location without a spooky station. I'm sure you hear the stories of grisly accidents. Grow no horns.

'One tik,' Tinatin membs. 'There's a family around your destination. Their dog is jumping all over.'

Tinatin's team could fuse me with a dog. 'Where are you spooking me?'

'There is a lovely quiet open market out of the way. In Greece. Lesvos. Skala Sikaminias.'

'If I recall, it's one of Mani Grabero's favourite locations, yeer?'

Tinatin laughs in the ears of my soul. 'Yes. Now we're making it respectable.'

'You could come here,' I offer lamely, preferring a stable spooky station, with its high-power beacon for overriding errors and anomalies, over an improvised direct spook. The universe is always moving, damn its celestial dance moves. I might consider risking a common or popular location where many land before ... and have an abundance of helpers who stabilise the connection. But attempting a spook for such an out-of-the way place, trusting some Uncle Kiah's network? Grow no horns.

'Stop worrying,' Tinatin membs. 'I am spooking clients here for years, Ben. All part of the service. You know the best trades always happen far from a spooky station.'

She'll have a reliable network assisting. Still ...

'They would honour your appreciation,' Tinatin obsequiously mocks.

'All are borderline smugglers and gangsters, I imagine, with an entourage of nurses attending them every tik of the day.'

Tinatin is forever patient and courteous, without taking a backward step. 'There's an entire KK taskforce attending you, Ben. Who has the greater risk? My guides or you?'

'How many are without Cures?'

'Never a Cure for me, Ben.' Figures. They may as well be pirates.

'Kay, Ben. Family and dog are clear. Check your blood pressure and your heart rate. And your neurochemistry.'

'Okelah, here goes, I'm ready.' I'm unready, but I'll be no readier.

Inviolate light, a drug smack, time crash. Electricity bolting up my spine growing branches and tentacles. My toes curl; fingernails scratch. My crystal skull shatters. Diamonds rain up.

Needles heat and light. Azure blue frosting. Falling. Only a few centims. Land on my feet on uneven cobblestones. A sharp twinge in my ankle.

'*Kak!*' Tinatin membs. 'Sorry, Ben. Forget how short you Indo males are.'

'You remember perfect. You just miscalculate, simple.'

Baking sunshine. Smells of salt air, rotting boats, hemp ropes, seaweed, and fish. Sea birds shriek. An erection rakes awkward in my clothing, a common side effect of spooking. Sounds of a market behind.

'True,' Tinatin membs. 'You have it.'

'You want trade, or no?'

'Typical of an Infi: no appreciation how many people it takes for spooking a light bulb. Outside a station, a little inaccuracy is always possible, so we lift you a little for safety. Would you prefer we bury your pork eggs in cobblestones?'

'Where is this?'

'The eastern edge of the village. Turn around; put the harbour on your right, cafés on the left. You'll see market stalls quick. Head for the little square where the Kapi-Mithimna Road comes down the hill. I'll find you.'

'Got it.'

Fishing boats jostle in moorings on the tiny harbour—too many pieces on a Mediterranean-blue chess board. A path follows the harbour—so close a drunk could fall into the water or a boat—and leads for the desa square where pop-up market stalls clump among a milling crowd.

Busy teahouses and restaurants nestle under thick vines and tree branches. People sit in the shade drinking cold aya, chatting and eating gooey pastries. Skala Sikaminias—on the north coast of Lesvos, within sight of Turkey only a few kims across the Aegean—was a refuge of the homeless over the centuries, a place where the maps of old Greece and Asia Minor overlap. For 20 years around the turn of the 21st century, the villagers pulled from the water over half a million Syrian, Kurdish, Somali and Afghan refugees fleeing war and political upheaval; giving them milk, food, and clothing.

Leaves of olive trees yield oils in the scratchy-hot sun. I swallow my queasiness about the octopuses drying outside the tavernas bordering the tiny town square. To the east, the north wind drives peaky waves to foamy deaths on a pebble beach. Capering among the waves on the blue sea, those might be Nereids riding the seahorses of Poseidon bareback. Somewhere out there, Saint Mary the mermaid might yet swim.

South of the town and three kims inland, the Lepetymnos Mountains foothills rise like old wanitas' calves and knees in heavy green shawls. They cradle a sister desa Sikaminia, safely among dense pine and olive groves. Like many Greek towns of old sap times, the hillside desa provided a defendable position against marauders and pirates.

The crowd thickens near the market.

'If you watch nowhere you skip, you'll bump right into me,' Tinatin membs.

Spot her—a plump fowl among lean meerkats milling about. She wears an orange *arkhaluk*-style dress with a scarf wrapping around her waist. Her bright smile is a dinner plate sparkling on the table of her dark-timber face. She is average height for a wanita, about 100 or so mims taller than me. Even before coming within hugging range, feel her warm matronly energy.

'Tinatin,' I greet. 'We should be brisk.'

She shrugs her round shoulders, tilts her head. 'I take care of my customers; we are safe here.' She rambles for a stall within 5 meters of me and makes a pretence of inspecting a hat on offer. I join a huddle around another stall and scan for rainbow uniforms. None. Tinatin makes her approach casual, stopping and appraising the occasional item, until she is 2 steps away. She brushes passing me, loops bag straps over my hand, let's go and skips on.

'Enjoy,' she membs without looking back. 'Pleasure trading with you.'

'My proxies will be in touch.'

'Yes, my sweet boy,' she responds. 'You are the most ethical Infi I know.'

'Terima kasih.'

'Oh, I need no thanks, darling. Honestly, it makes me a little sad.'

Back down the path is a white building—a replica from sap times. Flat roof, thick walls, blue shutters on all the windows. Out front, 3 wide umbrellas provide cover for tables underneath. It looks too open. Farther around, the last teahouse on the water has out-door tables under dark shady trees. An antique sign on a post in a planter pot advertises pancakes. Take a seat at the edge of the eating area, order cold aya from a paper menu.

A good place for transferring the package into my own DNA-lace backpack. Tinatin's bag is black hemp, unremarkable and basic. The package inside is a custom squirty-foam envelope. Tinatin is professional to the last detail. Have no doubt it contains my Benjies. It would be foolish of her cheat me.

A waiter brings aya then blurs away for another table. A hulking shadow moves in, sits down at my table, resolves into an ageing man with a large, bald dome of a head, pale weepy eyes, and a witch-forest of tangling eyebrows. His skin has the sheen and texture of plastic.

'Happy April Fools' Day, Puffin,' Maddox says tongue and lung. 'Close your mouth or you'll swallow a mermaid. They're plentiful around here, apparently.'

How? 'I saw you … die …' I sputter.

'Rumours of my death etcetera, etcetera.'

'I saw you … we … all … saw you …'

'A mere party trick, Puffin, I assure. The need for avoiding a Cure and all that. I'm sure you understand.'

Thoughts wider than canyons expand in my head. My temples ache. My eyes bulge.

'Puffin, these are urgent times. We must speak.'

Outrage and confusion take over, condensing into an urge for striking out. Instead, 'Can I order you one of those martinis you enjoy? Perhaps you might melt into it.'

'I'm sorry for pulling such a stunt in front of you,' Maddox says.

'Have you come for paying my cleaning bill? You owe Jesús, my launderer. Your guts—or whatever it is—stains everything we wear. You ruin Aisha's shoes.' Which admittedly is no great concern. Aisha throws all her clothes in the sucky after one wearing.

A waiter approaches. 'Hot tea, please.' Maddox's tone is sweeter than palm sugar. 'Real tea, no ayahuasca juju. Darjeeling white leaf, no fabbing, if you have it.'

'Sorry, Infi. We have many other teas,' the waiter membs, her concern for failing to satisfy an Infi's request souring her otherwise pretty face.

'Never mind. Just bring a pot of boiling water and a cup—ah … 2 cups?' He gestures, palms and eyebrows up.

I gesture at the cup of aya I already have. 'No, thank you.'

'Puh!'

The waiter withdraws while Maddox pulls a clear bag of leaves from his pocket. 'Always prepare for disappointment.' He chortles in the best tradition of Lewis Carroll. A Cheshire Cat, smug, plastic-face …

'What are you here for? How is it you find me?'

'You're having rather the day, Puffin—such skulduggery about a wad of worthless sap cash.' He points with his gaze at Tinatin's bag resting on the table. 'You are quite easy for the hooking, by the way, and with such simple bait—and, oh my! … I'm sorry about your precious Charlotte.' He manages a scoff-strangling chortle again, which might blow out into a full-bellows guffaw. 'You must want for burying that incompetent driver,' he utters with all the emphasis of a bad Shakespearian actor. 'Anyone would. Would you have me bury him? I will arrange it if you wish. No nurse need know.'

My blood chills. I can only imagine how my face appears. Blue, perhaps. Corpse eyes staring, a fish on a skillet.

'You may notice the lack of nurses around here,' Maddox says. 'But we must be quick. They will catch up with us soon enough if we tarry.'

'Why would you know about my Mustang?'

'I already say you are quite easy for baiting.' Maddox rests back in his chair, a Roman Emperor bathing in a porridge of his own smugness. 'Have no worry for the poor driver. I joke about burying him. His reputation will restore, you may be sure. In truth, he's a skilful driver.'

'You are behind the crash? And Tinatin luring me here?'

Maddox looks down at Tinatin's bag again. 'This collector obsession of yours is so quaint. It will eventually land you in trouble.' He congeals an expression, at once benign and menacing. 'You mustn't blame Tinatin,' he says. 'She has many reasons for obliging an Infi such as myelf.'

Setting my jaw and sharpening my nose. 'I'm an Infinite, also. I will put a crater in her reputasi so big—'

Maddox rolls his eyes. 'An idle threat, as we all know. No one can influence the Reck, can they?' He's much too smug. 'I understand, Puffin; from your view, you are at the top of the tree. Your hometown dedicates a monument in your honour—quite a throbber, I understand. And the town council helps regulate the clamour of hopeful bedtime companions. You are still young—'

'I am 88.'

'Yes, yes. The youngest Infi ever, Puffin, the prime of life still ahead of you. However will you live such a life? You already achieve everything. It's the curse of young Infis.' Maddox drops his memb-voice for a whisper. 'Many new Infinites never survive, you know. I would hate if such a fate' — he says with the rhythm of a hip-hop artist— 'might befall you. Hate.' He shudders and his jowls quiver. He could be tasting putrid sardines. 'As I say, you are young and still quite irrelevant in the Infi world. You know nothing of how it works. Witness the silliness with the tukkies in Colombo. Sometimes, I think you enjoy creating a wake of chaos wherever you go.'

Tinatin ... I clench my jaw and grimace.

'Leave off Tinatin.' Maddox turns icy. 'I am among her best customers, trading 14's of times more than you. And I will never run afoul of the health camerati for it, because I'm careful, unlike you.'

'Nurses crash the Inductee Gala for taking you.'

'A sideshow, I assure you. The way you go about things, tripping over your own sorry face, loathing being Infinite. Well.' He sips his tea.

'How would you advise me?'

'Oh, you must be elaborate, Puffin. Elaborate. Make the trail for the real goings-on so circumloquacious it's simply unworth the effort.' Maddox freezes, his teacup halfway from his lips. 'Jesus in a biscuit, that is quick.' His eyes flutter, betraying the high volume of hollies he's trawling. 'There's a search for me in the Middle East.' He pauses as if straining for hearing a distant sound. 'Worse. Your daughter is looking for you. She'll give us both away. It's always the family. All those longings and emotions and worries about your health. Always searching. It's a much cleaner life, Puffin, if you have no one love you. So sorry, one can take no chances, I must spook away. I will be in contact again soon. Watch out for angels.'

From within Maddox, a force breaks him open, turns him inside out, like cracking a lobster for meat. His face is a landscape of surprise and existential fright as he realises there'll be no spooking after all. He begins liquifying.

For the second time in a week, I have Maddox Price goo on my shoes.

I catapult out of the chair away from the melting gelato carnage spreading everywhere. Should be running for the spooking point but I freeze. It's too long already and there's no guarantee how long Tinatin's team will wait for me.

'Go!' membs a wanita with the easy-measure air of a haughty *maître d'café*. 'You're drawing attention.'

'I'm drawing attention?' Looking at blood and guts all over the ground.

Watch in a dream-state stupor as a waitress picks up cutlery cups and flatware. Another squeegees a shallow pinkish lake off the table splashing a waterfall on the cobblestones. Cooks and waitstaff wearing business-as-usual no-nonsense expressions emerge from the café with mops and buckets.

My jaws loosen; my trap-door chin drops. My knees, rigid till now, threaten buckling. It takes all my willpower for injecting some marrow back in them. My hands on the back of the chair might be all that keeps me standing. A new fear grips. Look about. Where are the nurses? What about followers? No one's aura is swelling. The café staff show every characteristic of a professional fix-it team, with orderly pastel-colour auras revolving slow, no larger than motorcycle helmets.

The *maître d'* gesticulates. 'I advise leaving, Infi,' she membs with some urgency. 'The spooking point will close soon.' I hesitate. She adds, 'No need for concern. The locals will receive generous recognition. Now go.'

Saf is out with her friends. Mal is in his swasta, asleep on the floor after carrying a fever earlier in the day. This morning I report his condition to the clinic who of course are already aware. They prepare a new prescription which breaks his fever in a few hours. Listen for his breathing; sounds normal.

Remnants of a plate of duckweed and roti near Mal's outstretching arm. His holly projector plays some sap movie. With a famous actor Mal enjoys. Tom Hanks, a comedian. Never let Mal start on Apollo 13—the movie, or the event.

Flutherbomb Mal for a tik. His few remaining die-hard followers flee. Mal stirs, rubs his nose with a thumb, settles again. Pivot around and conjure the environment panel from the wall. It's warm enough for leaving him there without covering him.

Jaya sleeps in my bed. I hear nothing from Aisha since she leaves for Portland.

Take the envelope of Benjies from the dining table. The less I say about the trip … Maddox and Tinatin: 2 heads on one snake. Still flinching from recurrent memories of the teahouse, the sickening pink flood of Maddox splashing on the cobblestones. My discovery for the day? Vomit survives spooking. You could lose your clothes during spooking yet arrive with your DNA-rich puke.

Grab the Benjies, skip down the stairs for the common room where Harjanti Budiman sits in a single-seater couch, sipping a glass of tea. On sighting me, she springs from her comfort, sets her glass down with a crystal clink on the low table. Stands straight, smoothing her clothes.

'Sorry, Infi,' she membs, 'Unaware you might require the room.'

'Please, sit. This is your common room too.'

Awkwardly Harjanti freezes between accepting my insistence and ceding me the space. 'Will you take ice tea?' she offers, more as an escape from her embarrassment. She glides for the sideboard opposite the fireplace on which there are glasses, ice bucket and a pitcher at half tide.

'Yeer. Terima kasih.' I'd be thankful for company. All the millions in a fluther compare as nothing with one warmblood in the same room.

I lay the Benjies on the table. Unsure about those yet. Flomp into the chair across the table from Harjanti. She offers me a glass. Glinting through the diamond etching, a large block of ice floats in centims of liquid richer than teak. Sipping, letting the ice bite my top lip with a cold kiss.

Harjanti lifts her glass in salute, still standing, tense in my presence. 'Selamat malam.'

'You are leaving?'

'I overstay, Infi. I should be checking on my anak anak.' It's unlikely Harjanti is the only adult of her family home tonight. I let her excuse pass. Raise my glass.

Glass resting on thigh. Ice melting into the remaining finger of tea, forming a cold slurry of diluting amber. Slumping into the sofa. Am I asleep just now?

No nurses among my fluther. Can this be right?

Beaming light from the terrace. It's too soon for dawn. Light intensifying, blinding. Shield my eyes, spill the tea. Glass rolls over the rug on the floor.

Out of the light emerges a form floating half a metre above the floor. Squinting at it. It's no hancy projection. This is … otherworldly. A female with the plump curves of a sap wanita. Wearing a deep purple-blue robe with many bright studs or gems like stars in the night. Conjuring a sense of the biblical. The air behind her shimmers. I see wings, large and imposing; covered with eyes, blue and regal, looking about in all directions as if independent intelligences direct each.

In one hand, the being holds a golden trumpet. Engravings circle its bell— unreadable words. From under her other arm, she produces a bundle of paper envelopes which she files through and plucks one. She lays it on the table centims from where Harjanti's tea sits earlier. Puts the trumpet to her lips and blows, the blast so loud, the whole housing hill shakes. Wind attacks the outer walls, swirling and sucking, pulling open the terrace French doors. The angel flies out and vanishes.

Silence. Expecting commotion from others in the residence but all remain sleepy.

The envelope on the table, small and grey. Haunching myelf off the sofa, pick it up, surprised by its weight, heavy as metal. Turn it over in my hands. A seal on the back bearing some esoteric symbols including a watch face, tik-hand, and all. Blink a holly of it and gog. Nothing much. Sketchy entries about 'The Hodinkle Society.' Nothing reliable. Gog again, using my own algorithms. Results may take some time, perhaps days, going underneath all the protocols, searching at lower levels. Everything that dies leaves remains somewhere, including data.

The envelope. Open it. Inside, a fold of rich blue paper, high quality, very rare. Gold writing reads:

We invite you, Puffin,
To sup with us, to eat peacock and to see.
Look to and weigh your reputation:
Too light and we will not have you.
Be wise, take care, wash well.
Resolve to set out for adventure and we will find you.

—Sponsus & Sponsa

Puffin. Maddox. Expecting the blue paper might melt to blood-pink froth. As an anticlimax which fuels my sense of impotence, it remains solid and resolute.

Head heavy with recent events: the Inductee Gala, Aisha leaving in such a hurry, the Mustang, the trip for Lesvos, Tinatin and Maddox colluding. Now this? Characters drawn from Rosicrucian literature? What next? Secret handshakes? Always Maddox. He's tiring enough in hiself.

Look again at the letter on the table. The gold writing glows unnaturally, lines capturing streetlight and shining brighter than the rest:

... weigh your reputation:
... we will not have you.

What is it with Maddox? He intrudes, he dies. He intrudes, he dies—even harder in the killing than a cockroach.

Take a shower and gog through ever more ancient magazines, looking for any clues regarding Maddox's recurring demise. As many lives as a cat—the evil old Infi—with many more yet ahead of him I confidently suspect.

In the shower, with skin as pink as a steamed yabby, I persist, throwing hollies at recursive searches together with terms like *clone* and *human duplication* and even *resurrection*. Jank it. Add *alchemy*.

Other than a rich blue Brett Whitely, nothing much comes back.

Something about the note the angelic being delivers (she could still be a dream) ...

I realise I'm poaching in the shower for nearly an hour.

Be wise, take care, wash well.

I get a tick for the 3rd admonishment. As for the first two, I'm failing.

Water off, towel in hand, I include *chymical wedding* in the search terms, more out of desperation and impending lunacy.

A hit: a package of tiny, pre-quantum-computing binary files. Sap artefacts. It takes a min, but I find a hoot for reading the files while I towel off. Install it in my hancy while I dress, then open the files. Let's see what they have.

Hundreds of files in a nest of directories. Texts in American English, mostly.

This is taking me nowhere. Except ... what is that file name? *The Dead Raised Incorruptible.* Open it.

A title page full of an image like an engraving, depicting a gothic dungeon perhaps. Strange, alchemic instruments on tables and 2 coffin-like receptacles with transparent lids. They recline and angle so the artist might display their contents: a dead or sleeping man in each. Each man has a wild crop of hair and a flamboyantly expressive moustache.

The exact same moustache: the men are identical. I imagine duplicate Maddoxes recumbent in coffins.

The title of the book demands attention: *The Rise of Sybil Technology: the fourth path and the dead raised incorruptible.*

After reading the holly hovering above the kopi table, I make a gesture of throwing the book for the fire.

Desire

'Duplicate' — White Town

Nilajani Karunanithi ...

YOU'RE STALKING, NILA!' Harsha surrounds her modest, pastel-colour aura with her hands. I feel like a mote within.

'It's no stalking. I'm here far less than your snowboarding fans.'

'You're courting a Cure if you persist.' I catch Harsha in the ecstasies of *lingika sansargaya* on her knees, ploughing a lover who lows like a heifer. Last monsoon, I am her heifer. Flutherbombing her, I taste the arousal of their coupling.

Ask. 'Could you help me with some vectors?'

Harsha stops mid-thrust. Scowls. 'Might it wait?' Exhales hard, slaps the heifer's rump with a crack. Forces her face in the pillow. The heifer wiggles for more. The pillow muffling giggles.

'It's important.'

'Nila, you must stop stalking me.'

'I never—'

Harsha slaps her thighs. 'Promise.'

'Kay, kay. I am looking for nurses at the recent Inductee Gala operation.'

'You should be capable of finding vectors on your own.'

'I am poring over all the goggable hollies. I recognise no one.'

'You're such an introvert, Nila. I tell you 1000's of times; if you network more, you would have more of a network. Wait! You fail in finding even the White Witch?'

My ribcage twinges with fear. 'I already flutherbomb her once. And her adjutant. Too risky going back. If she picks me out ...'

'Nila, what's going on?'

'Weird *pacanaya*, Harsha. Best you know less.'

'Why would the White Witch notice you? You're no one. What's getting into you?'

'Give me a few days, kay? I will tell you everything, I promise.'

'Kay. Give me a tik.' Harsha's eyes flutter. Her jaw slackens while she gogs. Her heifer rolls on her back, pinches Harsha's nipple between her toes. Harsha slaps her away. 'I recognise someone from my academy days. Lemme tug a few yarns. Maybe I'll turn up her current vectors.'

'Thanks.'

'Now, please go. This nipple-pincher needs attention. I'll memb you later.'

'Please hurry.'

'Well, skip along then. Your promise starts now.'

Forgive me if it takes a few hours searching for the nurses at the Infinites' Inductee Gala.

A Mind's glimpse is everywhere and nowhere. In onespace there is no *where*. I am every*where* and never just any*where*. The glimpse never chooses her own perspective. Spooking is never just popping over for any point on earth; flutherbombing is never just wishing into any fluther on earth. We need onespace vectors—current ones—and the weave of those are always warping. Spooky stations work because battalions of missionaries apply constant Mindful attention and keep the fields current. As for fluthers, we need neos who know neos or—and this is less reliable—neos who use the same spooky stations. We need co-operation. Help. We need leads. We must follow the currents. We must be the currents. The glimpser is the glimpsed. We must be the yarns in a kitten's ball of wool.

Contrary, against certain paranoid urban myths, nurses have no super-power for flutherbombing. We have no omniscient, omnipresent taste for anyone. Discovering all a neo's dark secrets requires flutherbombing their entire lives. There's a reason for saying, *never enough time for tasting everything.*

Health camerati develop no special hancies for sensing onespace. Any tech we develop, we share. Withholding is against the heart of our mission. Our experience is much the same as the average flutherbomber: duller than being there, clearer than memory. Our training improves our senses somewhat, but we're no superheroes. We have no superpowers. I wish.

Please for the last time, there's nothing special about y'all. Sorry. We have no time for harassing anyone. Any nurse attending you excessively will meet an inevitable Cure.

Starting with the vectors from Harsha, I find a minor administrative nurse who missions at the *Sundhed* Camerata of North Europa. Still hours before dawn in Scandinavia, she's asleep, semi-naked, stocky limbs around a plump pillow like a koala around a gum tree. Almost as furry as a koala also.

I pan around the room for other occupants. In such a small fluther, images distort and blur, like looking though bottle bottoms, but clear enough for tasting the nurse is alone. The few desperates flutherbombing her will be certain dead-ends. I jel them anyway. Ah, wait. One is an ex-lover, in New Zealand in an auditorium, attending a conference. Rainbow uniforms everywhere. Lucky, I have many more fluthers for the jumping.

I eavesdrop on conversations and a few loud thoughts. Pan around and study rainbow fatigues and insignias on shoulder sleeves, boards, and chatelaines. Search for Europans. There's one. A nurse from Scandinavia. Many of her colleagues attend the conference by proxy through her fluther. Some are fluther surfers, visiting only fleetingly.

Should I try a deep dive for Scandinavia or visit everyone fluttering here at the conference first? Wait. There's one returning who is here only tiks ago. No fluther surfer. She's supervising the Scandinavian attendees. Her name is Teodora Mrowka.

Orlando Greer ...

The familiar sucking hurricane takes me in its King Kong fist and breathes ice in my face as if I open a door on a huge refrigerator with lungs. The roar of breath louder than the single-engine drone of the vintage airplane. Are you flutherbombers hearing it all? I hope it deafens y'all, the voyeuristic couch crabs you are. Flutherbombing is no box-seat experience for skydiving. On our next jump I'll invite the first of y'all who volunteers. No one? Just as I thought: all of you lack even a drop of sap.

'Me first, Dad?' My 20-year-old boy Zeke.

'Sure,' I shout over the engine hum and hoary wind. Membing amid such ferocity is for kitties.

With the weight of the parachute on his back like a tortoise shell, Zeke waddles for the cargo doorway, his hands tracing the fuselage for the rails at the hatch. Grab him by the scruff and give him a hearty shove into the blue. His black shoes shrink to nothing as he plummets.

'Orlando!' Amity scolds as if I kick a dog.

'What? He's got a parachute.'

'It's unnecessary,' she mock-complains, already warming to the prank. 'And dangerous if he rolls the wrong way and panics.'

'He expects it. It's a little bit of fun. A mother would never understand.'

Amity crouches at the edge of the void holding the safety rail above her head. Like shredding sails in a storm, tousles of her hair blow around her helmet. She stares me down daring I push her too. A deferent usher, I wave her on. She lets go of the rail and tips forward.

The old-man engine of the plane coughs and wheezes, the biofuel it drinks easing none of its eccentricities. Give me back the days of pure octane.

Chuck is the next out after we exchange a kiss. 'I'll smooth her over later,' he promises. His way with Amity is my eternal peace. It's been so since we marry him over 5 years passing.

For those of y'all vicariously skydiving in your armchairs, believe me; nothing prepares you for the weightless demon-roar of freefall. The air is a thing alive, a wrestler tumbling you on a mat, an artist rearranging the sculpture of your face, a preacher air-blasting your sins away with deafening words of redemption and damnation. Taste as much as y'all dare. As the panorama of the ground edges closer, taste how soon it would pancake you.

Just a few tiks more. Amity's parachute blooms and sucks her out of sight above me. Then Zeke's. Their rides are over; only the sightseeing remains. Amity will be collecting a catalogue of beautiful hollies of Napa and Sonoma all the way round for Angel Island and Alcatraz in the Bay. This morning we're seeing as far as the snow on the Sierra Navadas too. She'll chastise me later for my lack of appreciation of those.

A few tiks more. A few tiks more.

Chuck's parachute pack ejaculates the rectangular cream smear of the ram-air canopy. Blots him out of my sight and yaws left as I keep coming down. Squeeze the release handle. A sudden jerk on the leg and chest straps. The roaring air-beast dissolves into the buttery morning sunlight. I could be an insect in amber, such is the stillness. Nothing now but gliding down.

In the kit shed, I step out of the harness while a sky-dive missionary waits for collecting the parachute. I would prefer re-packing my own, but no sky-diving mission will countenance an Infinite performing such a menial task.

The sound of knuckles raps on a door jam. In the doorway is an angular towering mantis of a woman with white flowing hair and violet-red eyes, wearing the rainbow fatigues of a nurse. She grins like a vampire.

'Greetings, Orlando,' Eir says with tongue and lung. 'This time we'll opt for the quiet way. May I come in?'

Everyone's faces are masks of alarm. Eyes are the disks of planets in full sunlight, mouths are gaping limestone caverns.

'It's kay.' I pat Amity's shoulder. 'The detective and I must discuss a nicety or 2.' Wave everyone out. My fluther swells. Whatever happens next is prime time whether I like it, or no. Chuck and Amity look defiant, Zeke deferent yet curious. A few more urgent flicks of my hands have them trudging out as the White Witch enters and trips over her own feet.

Teodora Mrowka ...

Would y'all believe it? I find Orlando Greer alive and well in a New York chophouse.

With the appetite of a bear just out of hibernation, the evil old tortoise chomps down on an obscenely rare sirloin, assaulting the steak like a sap war-time surgeon at an amputation. With potato mash he soaks up some of the jus swilling around the plate. The overall effect is only slightly less stomach-churning than a river of blood. The steak's texture and muscle grain resists in such a way there's no doubt it's from the carcass of a once-living animal. No fabby meat for Orlando. He stabs and slices with great vigour and, with exaggerated shoulder, hacks off a sizeable thick sop. He regards his dining partner, who is gorging on a similarly gruesome meal.

As if an emotional plug sputters loose in Orlando, his pleasure drains and leaches his complexion sallow. He stops chewing.

Approaching his table is a tall nurse recognisable in an instant.

'Greetings, Orlando,' Eir says. 'This time we'll opt for the quiet way. May I sit down?'

Vör Hoyur …

Eir says she needs a day of solitude and reflection. Tossing in bed, I confront the truth of how much I miss her, even as I fear what she and Teo bring down on me with the disastrous operation at Kensington Palace.

Yearning, I reach out through the yarns of onespace, hoping someone might taste where Eir hides. And discover a perplexing level of fanatic noise regarding her. Oh, there she is. My life is instantly light again. She's in no deep meditation, nor even at a meditation retreat. She's in some smoky room, more claustrophobic for the dark timber wall panels. A man turns and recognises her, his shock so profound his cigar almost falls from his turtle mouth.

'Orlando Greer, Infinite,' Eir says.

'Infinite and habitat entrepreneur, restoring the pristine wonder of shorelines all over the world,' Orlando says with a complete lack of modesty.

'Good for you,' Eir says. 'May I join? This time we'll opt for the quiet way. May I ask, are you well?'

Nilajani Karunanithi …

After the disaster at the Inductee Gala, Eir again presents a Warrant for Orlando Greer, who is alive after all. The news ripples across onespace. Ever more health missionaries tune in. No version of The Incomplete would accuse me of harassing an Infi for flutherbombing this.

Orlando looks a half-shucked ear of corn with his skydiving suit dangling from his waist. His partners and son—a grudging troupe—leave the room.

'Orlando Greer, are you well?' Eir invokes the formula.

Orlando pulls the skydiving suit down over his Wastelander-style denim jeans, takes his time stepping out of it. Pulls on a brown-speckle leather jacket, a parody of a tortoise shell gleaming under the overhead lighting. He trains his eyes on Eir. His long neck stretches from his shoulders at an odd angle.

'Never better, thank you.' Orlando fumbles with something in the maw of his kit bag.

'You require care.' Eir.

'I require nothing of you.' Orlando's shoulders slump: his hard shell slips a fraction. From the kit bag, he pulls a stick of gum; unwraps it with deliberate apathy; slots it in his mouth. 'What is your Warrant for? Wearing last year's hair style? What sickness would it fall under? Pride, as evidenced by an obsessive lack fashion sense?'

'We have nutepaks for bad haircuts, Orlando.' Eir jokes. 'No Cure necessary. Let's put aside talk of Pride and Lust. I am no fan of classifying disease by the 7 ills. Let's focus on what drives you. You're actively absorbing or otherwise destroying every other camerata in the field of coastal habitat engineering. Are there so few beaches and shorelines left requiring restoration?'

'Everyone needs a hobby. Or should I just retire?'

'You could stop poaching missionaries. Stop undermining the reputasi of any who stand in your way. You could stop corrupting local authorities. But you could no sooner stop committing these things than you could stop eating and shitting. Because, underneath it all, you have a profound sickness.'

'You have no proof. None,' Orlando says. Everyone has ways of forestalling a Warrant, all impotent. Anyone of lower reputasi often resorts for physical resistance, fighting. Infinites favour reasoning and lawyering. 'You mission in the name of health care. Ha! The health mission is a police force. And as reprehensible. The only difference is, it's the kind of police a mother might hire for scaring their children into being good. Police who send them for bed and tuck them in.'

'We shall tuck you in, Orlando, and take as much care of you as your mother would.'

'I despise my mother.'

'*Ja*, we are aware. We incorporate therapy for it on your Prescription. Think of it as a bonus offer. Orlando, it's time.'

Conflicting thoughts wrestle in him like rugby players mauling in a small tent. His turtle head lowers. His big, rounded shell of a back softens and drops. His head tilts forward, stretches his long turtleneck for the fullest. His knees buckle in the time it takes surf crashing on shore. His forehead bunts the floor with a painful crack.

For the 2nd time, Orlando is dead.

Teodora Mrowka ...

Less and less, I believe Orlando will regain an appetite for his steak. His dinner guest already flees, leaving a plate of hulking carrion leaching white congealing fats. Orlando's meal is a big-top circus tent after a hurricane. The potato mash is a heavy cloud crushing vegetable clowns and bearded ladies. Bloody juices leak out from under.

'You have a profound sickness,' Eir says.

'You have no proof,' Orlando says. 'You mission in the name of health care. Ha! You are a police force. And as reprehensible.'

'Orlando, it's time.'

For a tik Orlando grips the steak knife as if for stabbing Eir. So few resist nurses. Even fewer resort for violence. Orlando lowers his head, fondles the less stabby items of cutlery. 'Would you allow I might finish my lunch?' He casts a look of lost forlorn love at his meal and, without relish, inelegantly hacks off one more chunk of meat.

Find Vör in her local café prodding at her breakfast board as if it's a pathology specimen. Finding she has no appetite for the soft-boil egg, cold meats, and rye, she lays her cutlery down, takes up her *kaffe* mug with trembling hands, draughts deep with thirsty gulps.

She has surprise I am here in person. From under her hair appearing shaggier without her mission cap, she stares as if she could erase me. 'You interrupt me on a Sunday? What is your want?' she membs holding the mug near her lips.

'You taste? About Eir?' I ask.

Vör slams her mug so sharply on the table; the *kaffe* slops over the side; customers jolt, their nerves reverberating the concussion. 'Why would I discuss Eir? You must know she's operating without me.'

'Without me also,' I admit, despite determining I would withhold such a titbit.

This gives her pause. 'I'm sorry,' she says; her posture says otherwise. She mops at her spilt *kaffe* with a napkin, leaching some of the tension out of muscle and sinew too. 'Operation Hang 10 is a mistake,' she says, eyes on tidying the table.

With tongue and lung, I laugh like a maniac, earning stern looks from other breakfasters. 7 Hells for them. I join Vör at table. 'You're always the puppy jumping around for a rabbit, so eager for Consigning Infinites at last.'

'I still am,' she says grimly.

I say soft, 'Eir is Infinite now,' knowing the words will carry their own blades.

'Mmmm.' She splays at half an egg with the back of her knife, finding no appetite.

'You hear about Orlando's Warrant?' I'm unsure if I'm prodding her for information or for being mean. I must learn if Vör is complicit in my misery. She's still Eir's adjutant, at least officially, while I'm without detective duties. I doubt I'll have a mission outside minster walls ever again.

'I find out indirectly,' she says, meaning Eir never confides in her. 'Almost too late, I find Eir in time for flutherbombing her.' She's bitter and emotionally shaken over it.

'*Ja*, me also. So, we're both on the outer now, huh?'

'How is Orlando alive? He already dies with the others at the Gala.'

Teo nods. 'Field nurses take his body away.'

Vör shakes a ghost from her bones. 'Perhaps they are only in Never-Mind—a trick for escaping us. They have someone on the inside at Vauxminster who revives them later and aids them escape.'

'There's no putting it past that horrid old turtle.'

'Orlando is probably capable of anything.' Vör's face is stony and ashen. She picks a slice of toast in her fingers, taps the egg and meat off, nibbles at a corner. Her hand tremors. Perhaps on the back, a sheen of sweat. 'Eir is different since becoming Infinite,' she sulks.

'She's the same.' Eir's style and methods are always Prideful, her approach arrogant. Still, everyone overlooks her flaws and basks in her successes.

'Most detectives are cowards,' Vör defends irritably. 'They're happy hiding behind her while she takes all the risks.'

'We take all the risks; while Eir is Infinite, her reputasi untouchable.' Hear the bitterness in my memb.

Vör nods at her toast. 'It's a shame she fails again with Orlando.'

I scoff. 'Fails? She has Orlando. He's in Vauxminster.'

'No. I flutherbomb the whole thing.'

'Me also. Eir—'

'One min he's puffing a cigar—'

'What? There is no cigar.'

'Puffing a cigar,' Vör repeats, 'Then he collapses, same as at the Inductee Gala.'

'No. What are you saying? He's in a steakhouse. In New York—'

'New York? Eir finds him in a cigar bar in Astana.'

'New. York. Steak. House.'

'*Du er skør!*'

'You're the bent-brain one.'

Vör throws the toast on her board. Her heart races, her pupils dilate. 'Then taste this,' she says, and blinks me a holly. It's Eir and Orlando in a cigar bar, acting out a scene hauntingly like the holly I have of them in New York, which I blink Vör as I continue watching this one.

I mutter, 'What's going on?'

'You mean apart from Orlando faking his death?' Vör asks with some disgust.

'At least 3 times over, it seems.'

'Eir failing in Astana, catches up with him again in New York. You would think he would go to ground.'

'Who knows how the old turtle would respond? Maybe he's so confident ...' A thought chills me. 'What time is it when Eir confronts him in Astana?'

Vör considers. 'Around 23:30. Why?'

'Oh, *bre*! He's in New York at 12:30. The same day.' I check the time stamps on both hollies. They're contemporaneous to the tik.

Vör contemplates. 'Must be hoaxes.'

'Or ... oh no.' Realisation seeps into my veins like neurotoxins, fossilises my cold bones. 'Vör, you come across an old sap archive recently? It's circulating for the last week ...'

'*The Rise of Sybil Technology?*' she asks with some disdain. 'Of course. Complete rubbish. Neos will believe anything.'

'What if it's no rubbish? It would explain how Orlando is in 2 places at once.'

A shiver takes Vör with realisation as abrupt as falling off a cliff.

'If Orlando is using this sybil tech, then so too is Eir.'

Compulsion

'School Fighters' — KC4K

 *Ben Evoli ...*

'B AT EARS?'

'Istri! I hear nothing for days—such a temptation for looking in on you.'

'Little here for report unless rubble is fascinating ah.' Aisha is brushing me off. My ribcage is made of rusty iron. She has no missing me. 'Look. A nurse from a clinic in Shirahama membs me,' she says. 'They admit Mal there almost 2 hours ago, fine.' She sounds crankier with me than the situation.

'What?'

'How you never know, that one? I suppose you are off meditating somewhere instead of look after our anak anak.'

Feel my skin burning; I *am* off meditating. 'They write a Warrant for our son?'

'No, nothing as such. He is rest—'

'Resting?' I shout. My initial embarrassment sours, but Aisha should be no target of my anger.

'Lower the volume ah. You make my fluther all deaf one. Jank. My aura is a thunder cloud.'

'Why is he in a clinic?'

'Shhh, Bat Ears, shhh. You must go there, sort it out. First let me explain that one ah.'

Blood surges in the dams and locks of my veins. Stomping around the lounge room, skull brittle, hurling my rage through the glass doors. The whole desa can burn with it for all I care.

'Mal start a big fight with another anak,' Aisha explains. 'Something about astronaut. In a pop-up school, in the teacher's home …'

A punch-up. That's my boy. Prep the nutepaks if you dare.

'Ben, it's nothing funny. The teacher's furniture …'

'Mal tips over a bonsai?'

'Benjamin!' Aisha comes back sharp and slicing. 'Be a sap, fine. Also, go find out what happen. I want my bayi safe.'

'Memb me the clinic vectors.'

'Walao eh! Just bring him back safe, Bat Ears. Bring no Infi Wrath down on anyone.'

Lành Hiền Rồng (Gentle Dragon) …

As with the whole contingent of detectives routinely flutherbombing Ben, I struggle keeping watch while he meditates. As much as I try dissociating, I either end up in trance or asleep. Or dying of thirst, for some strange reason.

The news of nurses taking Mal comes as such a deep-core shock, I feel I need gulp for keeping my fruit from turning inside-out. What are those nurses meddling in? I would believe the Japanese have a better sense of balance. Poor little Mal: he must be terrified. After a few mins scrabbling around for current vectors, I find the receptionist in the clinic of Golden Wellbeing Centre, the Shirahama chapter of Nihon no kenkō Misshon. Come with as I flutherbomb her …

I'm late for this. Ben is already making a storm in the clinic.

'With regret, Infinite, there is lack of permission,' pleads the nurse behind the desk.

'My son is back there, and no one is explaining why,' Ben shouts tongue and lung, his rudeness distressing everyone in the clinic reception area. I'm gulping my heart down, hoping Ben pulls back from earning himself a Consignment there.

'Forgiveness please, Infinite,' the receptionist nurse membs while she matches shallow bows with the metre of speech. 'We arrange for send an orderly in. Join of her fluther, most orderly … waiting is considerate, only a few tiks.'

'My 10 million flutherbombers will be with my son. Now.'

Looks of horror on the nurses' faces. One holds a nutepak, trembling at the prospect of offering it for Ben. The clinic could Consign him already for his behaviour. Please, I hope they taste the futility of it. No sooner than he shows any signs of regret, with some promises for taking a nute regimen, there would be pressure for releasing him. Then what? The reputations of the whole minster could careen wildly in any direction, most likely down. It will be even harder for the rest of us who care for Ben's health.

Ben jumps fluthers, looking for Mal. He marches without a skip, passing nurses feebly defending the corridor for the clinic rooms. Catch up with him finding a nurse at a couch bay. Hear him barging through the door for the small ward. The nurse jumps in fright, letting go of Mal's ankles which tiks ago are in stirrups. Mal's dilating eyes fixate on the ceiling, his fruit rigid. His hair standing on end, like an electric current runs through his skin, a side-effect of using diagnostic vibration cameras on him.

'Bapa!' Mal stiffly hoiks hiself up on an elbow. Ben sweeps over, pushes the cameras and nutebag tree away from the couch, gathers him up. A disposable medical gown hangs loose from Mal's shoulders and is already decomposing; brittle dehydrating shards of it break off. Ben hugs his son. Mal's tears flow, dissolving the gown where they spatter.

'Make them take it out, Bapa. Make them take it out. I hate it, I hate it,' Mal's fingers scratch at his neck, frenetic, digging into his own flesh.

Ben, awkward and tentative in the face of Mal's distress, wishes Aisha is there instead. 'Show me,' he says, prising Mal's fingers away from the hancy—a shiny beetle burrowing into an angry, red wound. 'It's the most basic model. A sifar would refuse it,' he accuses in horror, and stabs a stare at the attending nurse who stands meekly like a prisoner awaiting sentence. Two security nurses appear at the door. The attending nurse signals they stay there. Relief washes over androgynous faces. No one wishes tussling with an Infinite.

'You plant a hancy in my son?' Ben charges the air with violent righteousness.

'Please, forbearance, Infinite. This is most irregular ... he is well of age for a hancy. His records show he is developing symptoms of Entanglement Syndrome. The happiest course of action—'

'It's hours until you contact my one istri and, in the meantime, you fit a hancy without our permissi?'

'Very regret, Infinite. Assumptions are because—'

'You assume?' The drama of the room quakes with the sound of Ben's voice.

'Your son has no hancy. He is well of age. It's very irregular—'

'He's making up his Mind about a hancy.'

Nurses gasp. 'Infinite, a hancy is for everyone. It's irregular—'

They're hiding something. Why *would* they fit a child with a hancy without parental permission? My blood runs cold. Are they deliberately provoking Ben, hoping they might trap him somehow? Or perhaps the hancy has some new surveillance hoot. Unlikely. Nursing missions are minimalists regarding hancy tech. Ironically, the most common hoots you may find in nurses' hancies would be SnakiDik and the other hoot Ben is famous for ... the music one. Whatever's in the hancy, I need for tasting.

Ben's aura is spilling out of the clinic and onto the street, his fluther perhaps 20 million strong, a multi-dimensional psycho-electric shit-blizzard of revellers basting in the joy of him dressing down a nurse.

'What is your name?'

The nurse looks at him, tilts her head in momentary confusion. Jelling her name is easy, so why would he be so coarse, asking her direct? He's asserting his dominance. Disgusting, Prideful. Wrathful.

'Clinician Nasu Reizei Runme of Gorudenu Erubingukurinikku, Infinite.' Nurse Runme's face flushes. 'Please, Infinite, with respect, for your own sake and ours, I ask forgiveness and understanding. I already face discipline. I beg you no more shame.'

'It's in the hands of millions of witnesses now. Where are my son's clothes?'

Ben bursts through our clinic front door, threatening fire and rain, dragging poor Mal like a broken puppet behind. Clinical Nurse Skye Merewether barricades reception with her own fruit before Ben is 3 steps in. She is sunshine for his black clouds, protecting patients behind her in the waiting room.

He demands we remove Mal's hancy. The boy is in obvious pain. Poor Mal. The hancy is causing him so much distress. Ben, also as much. If he proves a typically Greedy Infi, no one could say he lacks love for his family.

'Allow I demonstrate taking the hancy out of the seating. I assume you are planning an upgrade?' Skye asks blithely.

Ben's Wrath is algae blooming in a stagnant swamp. Please, Ben, give them no reason for drawing up a Warrant today. 'No. Take the whole thing out. Including the seating. One of your sister camerati plants this monstrosity without permissi.'

'With respect, Infi, may we offer you a nutepak?' Skye says implacable, using her best patient-care voice. All I hear is her mission-weary apathy.

'I need no nutes; I need you rectify this assault on my son,' Ben rampages.

'Bapa, let's just go.' Mal's hand covers the hancy like he's nursing a wound. I must clamp my jaw against the emotions rising. He's such a sweet boy.

'Infi, might I recommend the calming packs on the rack just behind you? Simply take-by-mouth. No need for ...' Skye cocks her hip and makes an up-the-bum gesture with her hand.

Ben stares blankly at the immovable Skye, her sunniness evaporating behind his darkness. I must join the altercation. The irony of Skye potentially instigating the most important Consignment in the clinic's history is galling.

'Nurse Gentle!' Mal blurts. He runs and throws his arms around my hips. Ben's face softens.

Skye relaxes. The remaining patients in the lobby sit back from emotional ledges. For Mal I say, 'If you come with me, we'll take the nasty thing out.'

Mal's Entanglement Syndrome—if indeed it's what he's suffering—could be causing mood swings and his aggression at schools. It could be complicating the hancy installation too.

I recall no discomfort at all with my first hancy. Just a delicate taste like sweet-pea tendrils growing towards the sun of my Mind, filaments caressing the spinal cord. With pleasantly weird tickles. Like hair or nails grow fast. The filaments just grow. Primitive, organic, inevitable. I suppose if you resist, your Mind might interpret the sensation a threat.

'Lie up on the couch,' I tell Mal, soothing.

'I will be here the whole time.' Ben pats his son's shoulder and lifts him up. With light hands on Mal, encourage him lie back. 'Just relax.'

'He needs no trancing,' the father membs.

'Only helping it go easy.'

I look Mal in the eye, try my reassuring best. Ben's apprehension simmers, lava at the edge of a crater.

I flick up a diagnostic holly, swivel and pinch an image of Mal's brain, roll my wrist till I get a trace map, comparing the current state with the 14 or so other captures of Mal's brain we have in magazine. The mass and count of neurones in his paleocortex continue shrinking, though slower than the rate we originally fear. I flick the holly towards the ceiling. It evaporates like steam.

'Let's pop the hancy out.' An easy procedure now. Within a few more hours, it would meld with the neuromorphic seat in Mal's neck and within a day, the pairing would solidify and take on the appearance of a pale scaly birthmark. At which point it would be much harder removing the seat at all.

Nilajani Karunanithi …

Have y'all heard? Have you heard?

Locating Teodora's fluther must wait while I follow this memb-storm: a river of hollies (if y'all trust their provenance) then a dam-burst of rumours. The local chapter of a Japanese health mission treats Ben Evoli's son Mal after he picks a fight at a school. Seeing Mal wears no hancy, some enterprising nurse takes upon herelf the task of fitting him with one. Mal, in wailing distress, membs his *amma* who membs his Infi *tatta* who goes confronting the nurses who visit this malum on his son. Ben shouts and makes threats and invades the clinic in search of Mal. The confrontation is unseemly and a threat for Ben's health—if any nurse there decides so and is brave enough for Consigning him.

By the time I catch up, Ben has Mal back at his local clinic, demanding they remove the offending hancy. Oh, look who's coming for the rescue: it's

Gentle Dragon. The same young field nurse who magically appears when poor Mal gets sick. Entanglement syndrome, they're saying—but please, a sap disease? Maybe it's some trick; maybe someone poisons Mal, and so gives the local clinic some leverage in Ben's house; maybe it's the local clinic who's conspiring against Ben.

With Mal soothed—and Ben in rapture about this nursing angel who's always there for protecting his son—Gentle Dragon prises away the hancy, easier than picking a pistachio from a shell; easier than peeling a scab off a grazed knee. 'There we are.' Shows Mal the offending object. Strokes his brows. 'Now,' she says softly, 'we'll pop—'

'Nah!' Mal cries.

Ben grabs Gentle Dragon's forearm and filches the new hancy from her hand.

'It's just a utility hancy for dissolving the neural plant,' she says for Ben, while holding Mal's gaze and still stroking his forehead.

Wary, Ben hands the disc back.

'For only about 30 mins.' Gentle Dragon would calculate it exact, factoring in Mal's weight and the time it is growing inside him.

'There will be no after-effects?' Ben.

'No trace at all, except …' Gentle Dragon faces Mal sitting on the edge of the bed. 'Little man, your pee will be a funny colour next time.' She moves for tickling his ribs, thinks better of it.

Mal laughs anyway. 'Blue?'

'More of a lime green.'

'Oh. I fancy blue better.'

'You fancy blue butter?' Gentle Dragon teases.

'Nah.' Mal laughs out loud. 'I fancy blue better.'

How might I find a way, like her, of insinuating into Ben's family?

Ben and Mal exchange laughter. Ben sweeps Mal into his arms while Gentle Dragon drops the offending hancy into the kangaroo pocket of her fatigues.

Aisha Evoli …

'It would never happen if you coddle him less, Bat Ears. He should take a hancy months ago. Already some regional nurse plants a cheap hancy in him. That thing have a side effect.'

'Istri, listen to you. In one breath you say he should have a hancy; in the next you say they are dangerous.'

'That hancy is dangerous. Who knows what hoots are in it? Who knows how nurses might use it against us? We should already give him a hancy. A safe hancy you configure. Same as with Saf ah.'

'Saf pesters us for a hancy from the time she is 5.'
'We are the orang ah. We decide what is best for our anak anak.'
'There's no forcing him, Aisha. How many times must I repeat it?'
'Then we have no discussion. I return for work.'

Lành Hiền Rồng (Gentle Dragon) ...

Aisha nudges her son's shoulder more vigorously, like rocking a sack of potatoes. Mal flails his arms about, jettisoning pillows and sheets dank with sweat. Eyes shut tight, lashes tangling. He screeches like a wailing parrot.

'Mal, wake up,' Aisha pleads. She nudges him harder—almost an assault—which releases some spring in his bones. He sits up, eyes pop open. Aisha bundles him into her arms. He gasps. Aisha cradles him while his chest heaves.

'Get it away from me, Ibu! Get it out of the room.'

'Get what away, angah sayang?'

'The tiger! The alien tiger. It's eating me.' Mal buries his face under Aisha's chin then sneezes a great gob of snot on her chest. Aghast, Aisha plucks a wad of tissues from a box at Mal's bedside. The box almost lifts with the tissues; it's near empty.

'It's only nightmare, angah,' Aisha soothes and rubs Mal's back. 'For the 3rd night in a row,' she mutters for herelf. Aisha keeps Mal with her in Portland since the hancy incident. Now indecision and regret stain her.

'Take me home, Ibu,' Mal says quietly. 'I hate it here. Everything here is broken.'

Though Portland is only a spook away from home and Singapore, we advise against moving Mal from his familiar environment. Now we have another variable: what's causing these nightmares? Portland is a jagged shambles rotting in mud; everything upside down, the guts of buildings spilling everywhere. No peace, no familiarity. It's no wonder a boy of Mal's age might be having nightmares.

Or it could be another symptom of his illness, which we can scarcely believe and have no experience of: Entanglement Syndrome. If it exists at all. So far, he throws no more fits. Even our best specialists in Singapore are hypothesising; Mal's first episode at home could be the last, or the portent of something more chronic.

'The cat eats me, Ibu, all the way until my belly,' Mal says, oddly disassociated.

'It's just a bad dream, like that lah.'

'Cats like the taste of dolphins,' Mal says with the dread of giving in to a terrible fate.

Aisha stern, takes Mal by the shoulders, holds at arm's length for looking into his eyes. 'Alamak! Dolphins again? Walao eh.'

Mal's eyes are rolling back. His tongue flops out of his mouth. Aisha yanks a drawer from the bedside table; scrabbles into its contents before it hits the floor; catches one of several nutepaks hurtling away like large, metallic tadpoles.

While Aisha administers the nutes, a team of our nurses are skipping for the spooky station. We must bring him home. If the rumours are true—and Ben somehow has influence over the Reckoning—the nurses of our local clinic are who must keep his family safe and well.

 *Saf Evoli …*

Stories of saps heads exploding are all just woozle effect. Factoids. There are no reliable accounts. But the actual symptoms are no less grisly. Make the holly fully opaque so none of the background in my swasta bleeds through the images.

Bleeding. Blood from the nose, then globulous amounts of snot. Profuse sweating. Maddening headaches causing nausea and vomiting, though the victims' stomachs contain little. More bleeding, from the ears and eyes and finally the mouth. Uncontrollable sneezing, clots of dense, goobery snotballs could be, for all appearances, chunks of brain. That's anatomically impossible, yeer?

Sneezing is the last violent symptom of Entanglement Syndrome before the victim passes out, a reaction to extraordinary cranial pressure. Surgery only provides another outlet for the frothing expanding mushiness. Maybe this's how the cookie dough stories originate. The truth is less explosion, more something squeezing the victim's body like a toothpaste tube. Until everything oozes out the head.

Holala! Shake and shiver. Flick one holly away and pull another forward, one without the gory images. There's stuff here about earlier symptoms, before all the unstoppable gory stuff starts. Forgetfulness, muzziness and mistaking family and friends for each other. Obsessive anthropomorphism, treating pets and familiar things as human.

My innards chill. A symptom is hallucinations. Sufferers often claim conversations with pets, Mind-with-Mind. Follow some links for other magazines.

Swallow my fears for Mal. There're still years before I enrol at a nursing academy, and years of study before I graduate. I'll be no help for Mal. Nothing I'm reading comforts me he'll last so long.

There's more here about hallucinations. A sizeable percentage report conversations with wild animals also. Weird kotoran. Birds. Insects, especially bees and wasps. But mostly higher-order mammals: chimpanzees, orang-utans, and gibbons. Madly flick the hollies up, barrel-rolling the contents, blurring images. So far, none of the ones I fear. Wait. Stop. Roll back. There: accounts of saps hallucinating conversations with whales. And dolphins.

Habit

'Dragons & Demons' — Herbs

Nilajani Karunanithi ...

IN COMMON CIRCULATION are over 1600 hollies of White Witches who fail Consigning 1600 Orlandos. Over 1600 authentic verifiable events in unique locations, in exact concurrent time, starring the same 2 actors. In all except one, Orlando's sybils fall over dead, same as the sybils at the Inductee Gala.

Sybils! The long-buried evil tech from sap times; an extreme form of fabbing; taboo for centuries. Consult your history magazines. I'll blink y'all a holly of *The Rise of Sybil Technology* if you are yet for tasting it.

'Sybil' technology: a kind of fabbing for living organisms, it's far in advance of mere cloning. Cloning takes a single cell and germinates a fresh individual which must grow from seed or infant. Sybil tech crèches (creates) an exact duplicate (a *sybil*) of an original human being (the *seminal*) in a nightmarish neuromorphic machine called a metra. The seminal must remain retained and coupled with the metra for the entire process, so a sybil congeals with duplicate physiology, brain state and memory. Imagine; a sybil emerges as if from sleep, with the seminal's previous life experience intact, and the exact same state of consciousness and physical health. This sybil believes it is the seminal. I'll allow you boggle for yourelves the ethical implications.

Now it seems Infis are exploiting it. Orlando enjoys resurrection, the Holy Grail, a perverse form of eternal life.

Just how many of him are there?

Are sybils human? Have they a soul? None of this matters, because the tech allows a seminal might dispose of a sybil at any time. It's an appalling form of slavery, y'all must agree. The caprice. The naughtiness. Deleting, killing, murdering, executing—whatever name we give it—it's destroying your own full-conscious duplicates when they no longer have use. Disgusting, immoral, psychopathic.

This is why you can't copy nice things. You end up treating sybils like Barbie Dolls; cutting their hair; pulling legs off; crushing chests; bashing in faces; pushing chopsticks up their anatomically incorrect place where no sun shines. Then you throw those sybil Barbies in a sucky bin with all the other dolls you tire of.

Yes, I should avoid flutherbombing the White Witch's closest aide, but this is too fascinating for ignoring.

Vör and Eir are easiest for finding when sitting in the square by the Dahlerups Pakhus on Copenhagen Harbour, with a view of a circle of sap sculptures. One looks curiously like a kangaroo carrying an attaché case. But it's another sculpture on its own little island just metres away in the water which brings Eir and Vör back time after time: the *Genetically Modified Little Mermaid* by Bjørn Nørgaard.

Vör projects yet another holly—the 7th so far—and stretches it the size of an outdoor movie theatre screen. Passers-by have no choice than walk through it, most with the nonchalant awareness of what it's all about. Some pause and watch.

'Can you please stop?' Eir pleads.

'Why? The whole world knows of these.' Vör waves at the tourists milling around. Her tone of voice has the ache of distress, incongruent with her maniacal grin no more than a few skin cells deep.

'I beg, believe me? I taste nothing of these.' Eir maintains her composure.

Vör cackles and dismisses the holly with a wiggle of her fingers. She rolls her hand, conjuring another holly in place of the last. The setting of this one is different again. The former comes from the kit room of a sky diving club; the latter is on a deep-sea fishing boat. While supporting characters change between hollies, the lead actors remain identical: Eir and Orlando.

'You use sybils. Both of you,' Vör accuses.

'No,' Eir asserts quietly. 'Someone else makes these sybils, without my awareness.'

'How is this possible?' Vör demands. Is she laughing or wailing?

Eir shakes her head, stares at the mutated mermaid. 'I have no idea. It scares the—'

'Come on, Eir. No one believes …'

Eir withdrawing searches the stony *Genetically Modified Little Mermaid* for understanding.

'Sybils!' Vör blurts as if swearing. 'Making sybils requires you—your actual fruit—your *body*.' Vör uses the word every neo hates for describing their personal fruit. 'Making so many sybils would take ... how long?'

'I have no idea.' Eir says flatly.

'Is this how it is? Infis make hundreds of sybils, so we make just as many? Is it how we defeat such an abominable ploy? Is this how we prevent Infis escaping us? We're becoming every essence as evil?'

'No one is evil, Little Mermaid,' Eir defends. 'It's bad, truly unspeakable. But the—'

'It's a ... crime.'

'Vör, you know as well as anyone, there's no crime. Only sickness.'

'Well, it should be a crime.'

'Little Mermaid—'

'Never call me such again—'

'Listen for yourelf. You're a health care missionary. As serious as it is, it's still a health care issue. Whoever's behind this, we must have compassion, and offer our best of care.'

'It's you. Who else could it be?'

Eir stares deep in Vör's eyes. 'Will you Consign me? Will you utter those words?'

Vör stiffens, takes a deep breath. 'Eir Frijberg, are you well?'

Eir sits bolt-straight, stares Vör down. 'No. I am unwell. But now is no time for Consigning each other. Take care you develop no Wrath. Others have greater needs.' Eir has Pride; Teo has Envy; Orlando has Greed; I have la la la ...

Eir skips away from Vör, taking long, purposeful, menacing hops. Vör once again is the impotent mouse.

'Where are you going?' Vör membs after her.

'I must talk with Orlando.'

'You'll simply skip into Vauxminster?' It's hard telling whether Vör is pleading or unhinging. 'They'll Consign you.' Sounding afraid for Eir.

'No. You and I both know what health missionaries fear most: being on the wrong side of an Infinite.'

Eir Frijberg ...

'The patient is in Admissions Theatre 6, Detective Nurse.' Administrative Nurse Conan Barbary's smile could be bubbling up from her pancreas; it is at once deep, fake and fearful, saturating in over-excitement. Intercepting me only a few metres inside the front door, she bounces on the balls of her feet, hands clasping together in front of her navel. If she had a tail, she would be wagging it. If I would throw a stick, she would fetch it. 'Slippy slides are behind the lobby.'

I know the building, being a regular visitor. She should know this.

'Thank you, I will take the stairs.'

Conan takes my politeness as high praise. As much as a man's breast can heave, hers does. 'I'm one of your biggest fans,' she bubbles. A kind of sunlight exudes from her face, more a radioactive glow brighter than her small and pale halo. 'You're the reason I make health my mission.'

'I'm glad my example encourages others.' I sound ungraciously flat.

'Congratulations on Consigning an Infinite, Detective Nurse.'

'Perhaps we might conserve our congratulations for the patient, on the event of his Cure.'

The sunflower of the concierge's face drops in the dusk of her embarrassment, the blonde petals of her fringe falling over her eyes, the stubble of her beard shadow looking all the darker. 'Sorry, Detective Nurse, I mean no—'

'I beg, direct me for the stairwell?'

The blacks and charcoals of Vauxminster are colder than the facility in København. I prefer the Nordic minimalism of our clinics; these are gothic dungeons. The whole minster is an enormous toad squatting on the banks of the Thames. With all its late 20th-century battlements and ramparts, it has the appearance and atmosphere of a medieval fortress.

Because the official execution of Orlando's Warrant takes place in London, Vauxminster takes Orlando, claiming they should treat him there. I could argue for treating him in København, but it might strengthen Montreal's bid for the notorious Infi, since the successful Consignment occurs in New York.

Admissions Theatre 6 is large—30 couches in all—much too busy for admitting an Infinite. Patients recline in all except 3 of the couches; more nurses than necessary are attending on 5. Only half focus on their own patients, more eyes are on me or the business around the Infinite's couch.

'Have care for your patients, I beg,' I say, casting my voice for every corner of the theatre.

Quick as you please, nurses huddle over aid couches. Two scurry out of the room. Just as well leave, before I turn you into newts.

'Detective Nurse Eir Frijberg Face. What a lovely surprise.'

Spin on my heels for seeing who membs me from within sight. 'Clinical Nurse Beatrice Lovell,' I memb and nod.

'Are you perhaps lost?' she enquires, with mock concern. With her sharp angular nose and crazed hair escaping out from under her mission cap, her head reminds me of one of those tropical fruits the Anglo-Malays love so much ... a rambutan. 'Are you seeking the observation lounge?'

'I know where I am,' I say terse.

Beatrice's nostrils flare. Her pupils dilate. 'The admissions floor is for admissions specialists. The place for observers is the observation lounge.'

'Then you are here why?'

'I feel I honour you in helping you avoid error. I'm sure you understand, entertaining a clutter of observers around the couches would hinder aid.'

'Well, thank you, Beatrice—for such kind assistance. Now allow I return this kindness by helping with your error. I am neither observer here nor clutter.'

'Eir, we must let the administration team perform their specialist mission.'

'May I ask, who among the specialists here ever Cure an Infi?'

Beatrice blushes like a beetroot. 'We Cure whoever Investigations Consigns.'

'Precisely,' I say, I hope somewhat callously. 'Since experience in recent times is short in all aspects of Curing Infis, I would think we should be glad for offers of collaboration.'

'But Detective!' Beetroot Beatrice sputters.

'Would you decline such a kind offer? Would your procomplement? Where is she? You're right. Perhaps I should speak with her.'

Beatrice's mouth works but no words come by either tongue and lung, or memb. With jerky stiff reluctance, she leaves.

Attending Orlando's unconscious lump of weight on an aid couch is a nurse in a nekko projection. Also at Orlando's couch is Clinical Nurse Gerlinde Mann, a competent if perfunctory nurse who will never progress from admissions. She finds improvisation difficult, being more at ease with simple cases and clear definitions and is notable in her ambivalence regarding the health care of Infinites. Why would the minster allocate her the admission of Orlando? One suspects, even out cold on an aid couch, Orlando influences the team treating him. Perhaps Vauxminster is compromised.

The nekko, Assistant Clinical Nurse Fluffy Pusskins, looks up. If lack of ambition could be discernible in the eyes of a cat, y'all will see it now. An unremarkable nurse with little apparent desire for advancing her mission, she attracts unenthusiastic reviews from almost all her peers, including Gerlinde. Both Gerlinde and Fluffy are targets of some controversy for recently administering a botched, pre-emptive rebasing.

From reading a surround of hollies, Gerlinde turns as slow as an old telescope house rotating on a gimbal. Faces me square-on. 'Detective Nurse, your work is over,' she membs with perfunctory dismissiveness. 'The real health care professionals will take it from here.' Assuming the matter addressed, she resumes studying the instrument read-outs.

Fluffy swats her furry paw through a swathe of the hollies. They blink out, leaving Gerlinde reading thin air. Gerlinde's mouth drops open with indignation.

'I am never in the presence of 2 Infinites before.' Fluffy tugs her whiskers, the physics of her holly projection beguiling.

I say, 'As long as you're sure which one is here for a Cure.'

Gerlinde tries suppressing a cough while Fluffy emits a laugh-meow. 'Of course, Detective Nurse.'

'I wish a moment with the patient.'

Fluffy freezes. Gerlinde squares off, defiant.

'Clear the room, please,' My words fill the theatre with reverberations.

Nurses vacate stations, some with calm and professional glides, others less so. Some would gallop if they had 4 legs. None skip. Gerlinde glowers with hot-coal eyes set in an obelisk of stone which y'all might think I am pushing up-hill, for all the speed she takes in leaving.

I dock the nutepak's nozzle in the nute injection port, squeeze the pack slow and firm until it empties.

Orlando's fruit has some unusual bloat. *Pudgy*, a Regal English speaker might say. Blotchy skin has the appearance of egg pudding, retaining the soft sheen of privilege. Spider-leg eyebrows stick out in all directions. Tufts of hair spout like grey grass from his ears and nostrils. Blue toes, yellow nails. A long time since he looks youthful. The angular lines of his structure are ageing. Still, he's 220 years old and looks better than a 70-year-old sap.

His fingers claw at the couch's paper sheet, insects breaking out of cocoons.

'Finally, you have me,' he speaks, voice croaky.

'In our care, yes.' Rest my hand on his shoulder.

Orlando fumbles for taking my hand; he clasps it on his chest. 'You're shaking,' he says. 'Are you cold? Perhaps you should sit.'

Fearing the indignity of falling over my own feet, I draw the single bare utilitarian chair alongside the couch and take the turtle's advice.

'I love you, Detective Nurse Snow White.'

'I love you too, Orlando, but your love is no more than nutes talking.'

Orlando munting a smile is a visage of peace and contentment. 'How ever am I wronging you?'

'It's no matter of wronging me.'

Orlando hums, vibrations passing through his fruit pleasuring him. He tugs his cock and cradles his balls. There may be too much MDMAX in his nute bag. Gerlinde is careless.

'You are Greedy, Orlando. Your accumulation of wealth is obscene; evidence shows you are sharing only a small percentage with others. You're a hoarder. You swindle even more from your own kind.'

'Leave games among Infis for Infis. Leave us … leave us … leave us be.' He giggles, startles me as he grabs my arm in a firm grip. 'Don't leave me,' he membs. 'Will you stay with me?'

'*Ja*, Orlando, I'm planning for supervising your recovery.' Pat his shoulder.

'Are you seeing a cat before?' Orlando opens his eyes and searches around.

'One of our nurses.'

'I'm fond of cats. Can she stay with me too, during my Cure?'

Gerlinde would be furious. 'I'll see if it's arrangeable.'

'You're a Nurse Infinite. You could arrange anything.' He'll be unconscious in Never-Mind again soon.

'Know you the Infinite, Ben Evoli?' I ask.

'Never meet him.'

'Never a memb with him? No flutherbombing?'

Orlando blows a raspberry. 'Infinites aren't fluther fans.'

'No contact with him?'

'No, nothing.'

'Which side of the fight over the Reck is he on?'

'What fight? Over the Reck?'

'Oh, come now, Orlando, you insult me. There's a plot against the Reck.'

'The Reck is already corrupt. Ever since health missionaries invent the Infinite designation. It's the bluntest form of manipulation. Why hide the true level of our reputations?' Orlando is sobering up. There will be a brief window of clarity before he passes out.

'The need for keeping score is addiction.'

Orlando softens. 'We only demand a fair report of everyone's reputation.'

'So you admit you're manipulating it?'

'If anyone has agenda for corrupting the Reckoning, it would be the health camerati. You already have form. Health missions are responsible for the most heinous manipulation of the Reck—censoring it regarding those of us with very high razoos.'

'Where is Ben standing on it?'

'He is just a recent inductee. You attend his gala.'

'He is Infinite these passing 5 years.'

Orlando looks thoughtful. 'Maybe he is messing with the Reck. Anyone so prominent in the sex hoot industry would be good at janking with numbers.' He giggles.

'Who might he be in league with?'

'My lovely Snow White, my best guess is he's in league with you. You're Infinite now which is quite extraordinary … so I'm guessing it's you. Or your seminal.' Orlando cracks an elf-indulgent, all-knowing smile. 'Are you waking me up for assessing whether your secret is safe?'

Orlando's mouth slackens open, his head lolls sideways. No longer fondling his genitals, he lapses into Never-Mind.

He whispers something. It could be, 'Ben, go jank yourelf.'

Nilajani Karunanithi ...

I dare flutherbomb Eir no more. She'll catch me eventually. Anyway, which of the more than 1600 White Witches would she be? Reprehensible yes, though y'all must admit using sybils is a great tactic for confusing the seminal's true whereabouts and actions.

I blame this post-scarcity fabby-printed world. Anyone can fab a new outfit, so where's the harm in crèching a new fruit for it? Fabbing one dress is no easier than fabbing 100's. Making one sybil is no harder than making 1000's. All the sheik fashionistas would never be caught at social events wearing the same sybil twice.

As much as I'd learn more following Eir inside Vauxminster, I'm safer with the emotionally distracted Vör.

'You are yet believing Eir?' Teo asks her.

Vör's sigh becomes a long exhale. 'I am yet for disbelieving her. She's one of us, after all.'

'Vör, she's Infinite.'

Vör reflects. 'She makes me go spookheading with her.'

'Oh, Vör, you are such a prude. There's spookheading for centuries. It's our point of divergence. Saps die, we get high.'

'Her keynote, it is good, *ja*?' Vör's Mind adrift clutches at flotsam, broken masts, shards.

'Very good. Inspiring.'

'Enough for making her Infinite?' A tone of hope in Vör's Mind-voice.

'Because of a speech?' It's Teo's turn for reflection.

'Well, there's more ... a whole career.'

'There are no Infi nurses before Eir.' Teo weighs what she'll say next. 'Might someone ... something ... be fixing her reputasi?'

'Fixing?'

'Hmmm ... influencing it?'

'You mean corrupting it?'

Teo nodding. Shrugging. 'Could we say for certain it's impossible? Eir's skills—'

'You're accusing her of this?'

'Ha. You are her house cat after all.'

'What will you accuse her of next?'

'I have no accusations for her.' Teo soothes. 'Yet. I'm just gathering up all the twigs.'

'How are you meaning?'

'Taste it: a nurse becomes Infinite; a nurse launches an unprecedented operation against Infinites; a nurse has sybils ...'

'Eir plays clinician in Vauxminster,' Vör says as flat as the bereaving over a grave. 'She should never meddle in Orlando's recovery.'

'Ah, the Little Mermaid is walking on her own 2 feet. At a stretch, perhaps Eir might justify using sybils.' Teo leaves a pause for Vör's protest. Nothing comes. 'But I doubt even Eir is capable of tampering with the Reck. She would need help.'

Vör rocks her head in a series of nods. 'Wait. You mean me?'

Teo laughs—a kind, lovesome laugh like trilling birdsong. 'You lack the skills. Eir may be the unwitting beneficiary of tampering with the Reck. Or she might team up with someone.'

'Another Infinite.'

'*Ja.*'

'A high-tech Infinite.'

'*Ja.*'

With alarming speed Vör throws her arms around Teo and hugs her heart-to-heart, her chin resting on Teo's shoulder. Teo a passive victim of Vör's embrace.

Reason

'So Hard Done By' — The Tragically Hip

 *Ben Evoli ...*

CANDY STOPS IN A COUGHING FIT. Two dancers stiletto across and aid her off-stage.

Another jumps on the vacant pole and swivels straight into a Sneaky V. With movements liquid as honey, she makes a half-swing. One leg comes down for an Inverted Ankle Grip Split. She almost dips her long pigtails in my saké. After a smile from me, 1000's of my followers frenzy over her attributes, probably trending her reputasi up. She could be pole-dancing in a better class of dive tomorrow.

Berzal Morad slaps me on the shoulder. I almost conk foreheads with the dancer. 'Wow,' Berzal membs while swilling beer. 'Are there no limits to the advantages of being Infi?'

I memb back, 'None,' sarcastically. 'You and my 14 million followers are all in agreement there: Infis are at the head of the queue for exotic dancers.' I drain the last of the saké. A waitress replenishes the glass sooner than I can set it down.

'She's gorgeous, all right,' Berzal gushes.

I put the saké to my lips. A tad too chill, in no time it'll be tepid under the heat of the stage lighting.

'I'd rather she has a package, but no package at all is better than big swinging things.' Berzal must be watching sap porn again.

This is how it is with Berzal and I. We meet for drinking in seedy bars and clubs, and never tell each other anything new. It's Mind-numbing—the perfect prescription when I need a numb Mind.

The lights catch in the dancer's hair and flare around her head. I memb,

'Why is it strippers with beautiful silk-black hair always tint it?' My followers launch a thread of argument about my thought bubble. 'Celaka!'

'What?' Berzal looks at me warily, already regretting asking such an open question.

'I make one vague critique, and already there's a run on her reputasi.'

She watches me while posing in Extended Frodo. Streaks of blonde and maroon melt from her hair, restoring her natural lustrous jet black.

Berzal shakes his head and chuckles. 'One thought from you, and the world changes.'

It's what makes spending time with anyone of only moderate reputasi tiresome. Berzal imagines I can control anyone or anything; gog anything and everything; read another's thoughts with a single jel. Many have no understanding of the extent and limits of Infi influence, believing we are all-seeing, all-knowing superheroes; as many hope they'll be one day. Which is why I steer our well-worn conversation along familiar trails and corral it away from requiring I defend my lack of omnipotence.

The dancer with newly restored black hair is fixing her eyes on me. Or my reputasi. Which is killing my limp libido stone-dead. There's something reminiscent in those eyes … framed by black hair. Ah. Gentle Dragon from the desa. And just like this, my own dragon awakens. Dragons are dangerous. I squash the train of thought by asking Berzal, 'Remember the first time we come down here? To Fields Avenue?'

'Oh, yeah,' Berzal membs. 'Like yesterday. Back then, I am the one with more razoos. You'd never get into these clubs without me vouching for you.'

I raise my glass. 'Good times.'

Berzal sighs, reminiscing. '*Pinays* would still perform in bars back then. I guess Catholicism …'

I'm no longer listening. Berzal will lapse into a monologue about the vices and virtues of long-dead religions, how and why they survive for a time after the demise of saps …

Thinking of Jaya waiting in my swasta. Saf and Mal asleep already. Mal more stable since the nurses return him home, against Aisha's loud protests. All perfectly safe at home. Every resident in the housing hill will keep a fluther-eye on them. They'll alert me of anything unusual. Truth be telling, the whole desa will watch over the anak anak of their famous Infi. Lành Hiền the closest of all after Mal's recent episodes. What is Aisha thinking, taking him to Portland while she tends to her earthquake? Her earthquake, her mission. Her life's meaning. Something real. Making a difference. Where is family in all this?

We memb earlier in the day; Aisha's report as perfunctory as a news digest stream. Me avoiding thoughts of Lesvos; or meeting Maddox again; or the angel delivering esoteric invitations in the night. Avoiding thoughts so she tastes no hint of any of it. Emptying my Mind and focussing only on Aisha's words. I need for discussing Mal. Aisha waves it all off. 'It's only nightmares,' she membs. I hear the fear in her voice, the fear driving her for making her recovery mission in Portland her whole life. An earthquake is something Aisha can manage.

The clean-up over there is extensive. The biggest industrial suckies are no match for the task of clearing the debris away. There's the politics of so many camerati all clamouring with offers of pop-up homes, batteries, clothing, every necessity of normal life. Much of Aisha's work is putting those ducks in a row and, if necessary, shooting a few down. At a disaster recovery site, Aisha has even more power and influence than she has at home.

'How's the family?' Berzal asks.

From one of the stalls out back, cries of shock and horror rise above the music. From the floor manager's fluther, I see the cause of the furore. 'Some Uncle Kiah dies out back,' I tell Berzal.

'What?' he asks, incredulous. It takes him a few more tiks for tasting the goings-on. I'm already jelling for holly recordings. Finding a bunch, condense a composite stream of events. A lelaki, little older than me, loses consciousness in the middle of a lap dance, slipping and tangling in a flimsy ring of curtains around the stall. In horror, the dancer leaps from straddling him, as if an electric jolt throws her back.

'I kill him!' The dancer shrieks in panic. 'Oh, sweet Mary, mother of—oh, Saint Nicholas, please help me.'

The floor manager is by her side in an instant, arm around her. 'It's no fault of yours. He comes here in failing health. Disgusting. Dying is for passing suites, out of the public eye.'

'Oh. Man,' Berzal says poking me, apparently energised by having something new for talking about. 'How could he have no taste he is dying?'

Good question. I side-step the security in the dead lelaki's hancy, take inventory of the hoots in it. Everything y'all would expect, including all the usual biometric medical diagnostic stuff.

'Heart attack,' I tell Berzal while riffling through the lelaki's data. 'And he is fully aware of his condition.'

'What?' Berzal blusters. 'Heart attack? Who has a heart attack anymore?' His shock is venting through a grill of questions. 'Are no nurses flutherbombing?'

'Dunno. His reputasi is high enough for attracting health camerati interest. Perhaps he ignores health warnings.' Gogging shows close relations enjoy moderate reputasi too, which will be dropping because he commits one the greatest taboos: passing in public.

'Then nurses should take him. Either treat him or make him comfortable in a passing suite.'

The mood of the club changes as everyone learns what happens. There could be no more disgust if a lorry dumps rotting garbage onto the floor. Toilet stalls are full with retching into bowls. Others improvise with washbasins or hold open sucky bin hatches while hurling into the purple haze. Out in the club, staff and patrons are guzzling spirits straight from bottles.

Nurses—7 or so—spill into the club. I never see rainbow uniforms running before. Carrying bags of nutepaks, handing them out for everyone. One muscular nurse carries a stretcher, pushes her way out back. With another nurse she bears the dead lelaki out of the club. Respectfully carrying the dead fruit for the clinic down the road for a vacant passing suite.

In the finest showing of neo spirit, the club quickly normalises while the staff wheel mobile sucky bins into the toilets for clean-up. I take another sip of saké. The fermenting rice smells faintly of milky puke. On stage is perhaps the 14th performer since we arrive. Chat with Berzal degenerates, no more than approving grunts and sighs when each new dancer comes on stage. The saké is making me sleepy. Any wonder. Last night, I sleep no winks. Ruminating in those black-tar hours over the kind of prison maze Maddox Price is herding me into.

Last night in bed, waking Jaya up with clumsy gropes, her sleepiness giving way to pleasure. I dispense with enhancement and mount her quickly. My rutting use of her is primordial and organic; my limbs rigid planks; my breathing animal and predatory. She moans and whimpers. I only half hear her responses. She could be in pain or delight. Have no caring; only desperation for driving out the scratching insects of worry spawning in my brain; driving into her over and over.

Empty myelf of seed without purging my unease. Feeling no better for the orgasmic reset. Out of bed, find the angel's letter; make no more sense of it. Tear the heavy blue paper into wormy shreds and toss it in a sucky bin. In the hour before dawn, delirium, and madness visit; in a half-dream my nerves become carnivorous microbes gnawing in unending purgatory at my flesh. A ghostly, ravenous beast feasts in my chest and belly, chomping holes in my soul.

A loud voice pulls me from the dungeon of my anxieties. The club announcer is whipping up applause for a dancer as she gathers up her costume; wipes the floor down; waves for the audience; leaves the stage. Within tiks, another is under the hot lights. She reminds me of Jaya.

A commotion in back of the room. Five or six nurses are here for the second time tonight, herding around a passel of young boys—none over 35— and a couple of dancers who wear faces of distress and nothing else. One slaps away a boy's hand reaching for her pantat.

I'm standing. I'm going down there.

'Ben?' Berzal puts a hand on my upper arm. A flimsy restraint.

'Be right back.'

As thinly veiled threats, the nurses are handing round nutepaks. If they have any sense, the boys will suck the offerings down without complaint. One stupid boy swats the offer away on an ungainly arc, stares down the nurse.

'Nursing is your mission?' the boy shouts. 'What kind of man are you?'

'Hey!' That's my voice, tongue and lung. The whole group—the boys, the nurses, the dancers—freeze. Eyes are the size of plates at the bent-brain interfering Infi. I should be backing out of this mess.

At least 2 of the nurses relax, stand back and watch. Hoping for Consigning an Infi. Personal advancement on their Mind, more than the safety and health of others.

'Bapa,' Saf membs.

'What is it?' What else could turn strange this day?

'Someone is in the house,' she membs, sounding fearful.

'That's just Jaya. The house would warn me of anyone else.'

'No. We are having a slumber party. There is someone else downstairs.'

'Mal?'

'I taste Mal asleep in his bed. Besides, they're much too quiet for Mal.'

Suppressing a stab of fear. 'Get him and Jaya; go for my swasta and close the door. I'll be there immediately.' For Berzal: 'Gotta go. Emergency at home.'

Sprint out the door for Fields Avenue Station a block away. Spook back for the desa station, hail the fastest tukky in the parking lot.

Already taste the intruder is no resident of our housing hill. Bound up the steps between terraces for the front door; catch a beam of light flashing from the lounge. Through the door I'm a charging centaur, turn on my heels and gallop into the lounge. No one there. The flashlight casts pale activity from out back of the house.

Some Uncle Kiah is climbing through the bush out back. Up among the gum trees and wild ferns. Ahead, the flashlight is panning up the hill.

A shaft of cylindrical light appears, projecting down from high up, like a transport beam from a UFO in an old sci-fi movie. Unable for seeing where it originates. It's the colour of a spooky field. Must be part of the intruder's escape plan.

Climb for where the light shines down on a flat rock many metres across. A violet circle a metre in radius illuminates its centre.

The intruder is already vanishing in the spooky field. My only chance is spook too. Where will it take me? Deep in the earth's core? Somewhere freezing? The moon where Mal hopes he'll go one day? It must be safe if the intruder uses it. Wait. The intruder could redirect the field. It could be a trap.

What choice I have? Retreat and watch the spooky field for more activity? Could raise security. Those options cannot wait. Angry and, perhaps, well … drunk … I scale the rock-face, digging my shoes into any available toehold.

Out of breath, stand on the down-sloping side of the rock, step up until I bathe in violet light. Close my eyes, preparing for the intense nerve-shimmer of onespace.

The intense pleasure of erasure. Tessellations flit around. Dense snowflakes in pure light. Kaleidoscopic wraiths. Neurochemistry spiking. The limbic response to the fear of death. Knowing there's rebirth in another location never overrides the primitive thrilling fear. Then you're new again, senses rasping raw in new skin, bright blood pumping through the heart of a young lamb.

Feet meet the ground. Inhale fresh pine. Taste background music—something sentimental from the mid 20th century. Eyes open. Snow falling outside a picture window reflecting an indoor fire—a burning heart in a glass carcass. Lamps on sideboards exhale golden light. Before the fire a low polished table separates 2 florid armchairs. Is it real timber?

In one of the overstuffed chairs is a silhouette facing the fire, paying me no Mind, the aura slowing and shrinking. As if on the same fader, my aura deflates proportionately.

'Care for a bourbon, Puffin?' A glint of starlight sparkles from a crystal highball in the silhouette's hand—Maddox Price. He pours from a decanter into a glass resting on the table like a curling stone on ice. 'Pappy Van Winkle 23, original 21st-century produce. Look, ol' John P's signature on the side of the bottle, still clear as the day.'

What … the … jank? Maddox sends some Uncle Kiah into my own house, who lures me for a spooky field, and I wind up—where? Because he enjoys showing off a bourbon? 'He signs it personally?' is all I manage, boggling at my own timidity.

Maddox shrugs, as much with his bottom lip as his shoulders. Savours a sip from his glass. Smacks his lips, utters a deep, breathy *ahhhhhhh*. 'Come sit, Puffin. Tell me if ever you taste a better bourbon.'

Sweep the glass up. 'It tastes of catfish droppings,' I lie. 'Must be the water.'

'Trust a man who lives on the driest continent on earth would take issue with someone else's water. Sit. Sit.'

Awkward standing amid such comfort, I relent and sink into the other chair. The spooky field shuts abruptly off, leaching violet out of everything. Gulp down more bourbon. 'You're kidnapping me?' Forcing calm into every sinew, refusing Maddox might taste my panic. A log cracks in the fire as the bourbon trickles fire down my gullet and makes molten glass of my heart. Gulp again. 'You're including kidnapping among your crimes?'

'Puffin, there are no crimes,' Maddox membs, flat and weary. 'Only bad intentions.'

'Sakit intentions. Why send burglars for my house at night, frightening my children?' The tone of my voice becoming strident.

'Your house? Let no detective hear such expressions of possessiveness.' Maddox leans forward, adds another nip to his glass. Nods to it, playing at worshipping an idol. Chuckles. 'Fortunately, your words are quite safe here.'

'You have scatter nets?' I accuse. Only health camerati have scatter nets.

Maddox chuckles. 'Of course Infinites use scatter nets, Puffin, which you should know already.'

Which explains the decimation of our fluthers. Snow falls outside in the serenity of pre-dawn, a parody of a northern-hemisphere Christmas Day. 'Where is here?' Guess the time zone is 7 or 8 hours ahead of eastern Tanah Selatan. Across the Pacific.

'Montana,' Maddox answers with some pride. 'On the edge of the great chaos, Wasteland, where even a health camerata of the most extreme determination might never gain a foothold, bless their star-spangle hides.'

Maddox wishes for twiddling small talk. After Lesvos, I know better than harry him. Like the last Maddox, I expect he'd rather fall to chunks than be rushed.

Parry with: 'Unless the Rockies join California.' News streams everywhere, even in Indo-Malaysia, are following the campaign. Reunification of the western 3rd of North America seems inevitable. 'Then you'll have nurses all over your sickly arse.'

Maddox snorts. 'There are too many Infinites against it. The New Wild West will live a few more good centuries yet.' Maddox gulps his bourbon. 'Top up?' He pendulums the decanter in hand.

Flick the glass across the table with fingertips. Maddox pours a double. Throw back the whisky, eliciting a leer from Maddox at my cavalier consumption. 'In any case, you are safe here. The snow is metres deep and your doting host controls who spooks in.'

'And out.'

Maddox dismisses my words with a wave, works his jaw as if chewing grisly steak. His obscenely plump lips purse and glisten in fake plastic sensuality. Brighter than his dead-fish eyes, smoother than his bald head, a flat cartoon contrast to his crazed multi-dimensional eyebrows, his lips are a dehydrated vaudeville show of evil in stage make-up.

'This White Witch of yours …' he starts with disingenuous care.

'My what?' My heart is a fragile glass filling with chill water. 'What makes …? She comes for you and the rest of your Infi establishment.'

'And would have me, but for …' Maddox blows a bubbly raspberry of bourbon, mocking the melting and frothing of the Maddox on the night of the Gala.

'Perhaps she means flush out your use of *sybils*.' Spit the last word out, the taste of it acrid in my mouth.

Maddox considers denial. Pauses and reconsiders. This particular cat is well and truly out of the baguette. 'Ah, finally you're doing your homework. Cheers.'

'Well, there are so many clues: the many deaths at the Inductee Gala. The resurrections of Maddox Price. The 1600 Eir Frijbergs and the 1600 Orlando Greers.' The scandal between Detective Nurse Eir Frijberg and the reprehensible monopolist Infinite Orlando Greer is only confirmation for what I find after the visit from the angelic being. So far 1600 hollies, all verified as concurrent events, document Eir Consigning Orlando in places all over the world. Irrefutably, there exists at least 1600 sybils each of Eir and Orlando. 'Am I the only Infi clueless about sybils?' I pursue. Questions as accusations.

'You're clueless about many things, all because you delay your induction for so long.' Maddox sighs.

'I'm sorry I let friends and family talk me into it. I would be better off fending you all away for years more.' I take the bottle, drain the last of his Pappy Van Winkle while Maddox pantomimes sorrow at its passing. His shoulders slump as I gulp the last of it down.

His jaw tightens with impatience. 'The world is changing,' he begins, then checks hiself. Sits back. Relaxes. 'You ever think about the Reck?'

'What about it?'

'Well, I'm wondering why it makes you Infinite,' he says, trying to sting.

'I'd expect you'd wonder how it makes a nurse Infinite.'

'Detective Nurse Eir Frijberg. Precisely,' he says, releasing a snigger. 'The first ever. You find nothing suspicious about it?'

'Suspicious there's an Infi nurse? Or there's never one before?'

Incredulous, Maddox laughs as a madman losing his Mind. 'Whose side are you on? You interminable bore. When will you step up, Puffin? When will you step up?'

Step up for what?

He regards me like I'm a puppy in a dinner suit. 'Look at you, with your sullen sense of social justice, wasting your mindwriting skills on amusements and entertainment, while the balance of power is shifting beneath our feet. Too consumed in boredom and disaffection, in your elf-sabotaging elf-doubt, in your persistent resistance against enjoying your reputation. When will you taste the part you should be playing in history?'

'What are you talking about?'

Maddox's chaotic spidery eyebrows mash together. 'Are you truly so blind? An Infi nurse? Something everyone else on the planet finds so obvious: someone is manipulating the Reck.'

'What?' Struggle with forming coherent thoughts. 'For what end? How?'

'It's the only explanation,' he says as if he's reading a weather report. 'We're suspicious for some time. And all this business with the White Witch … at your Inductee Gala—'

'My Inductee Gala? The one I never ask for and decline 5 years running. I only accept because Aisha—'

'You must admit, the timing is curious.'

Shock stabs me in the liver. 'You think—you believe it's me?'

Maddox leans over, rests his hand on my elbow, like a spider cocoon around a trapped insect. 'Calm down. As I say, we know you have no sense of adventure.' If he's reassuring me, he fails. He rubs his chin and looks me square in the eye. It's unnerving, as it would be for any polite neo. We accept everyone will also be flutherbombing, so peripheral glances are the most we normally exchange.

I guess, 'So you're blaming health camerati?' Recall Dil's rants about nursing missions being a de facto government running the Reckoning. More than once, he spins my head full of demented ideas of health and AgniSpace camerati in league. If anyone has the skills for tampering with the Reck, it would be infrastructure missionaries.

'Find the truth,' he hisses quick and quiet. 'Before everything comes down around our ears. Your White Witch is—'

'Never my—'

'—playing a new game. Becoming Infinite, raiding our innocent little party, using sybils for taking Orlando. If a nurse with her powers fails in frightening you ... well, then, what would?'

Is this what all the subterfuge is about? Meetings in out-of-the-way places culminating in luring me here? 'It's more than Eir. It's more than protecting the Reck. You see an opportunity for bringing down the whole nursing mission.'

Maddox's eyes lose focus, he's making again the chewing-grisly-steak motion with his jaw. 'Nurses should simply let us be,' he says in a far-away voice.

'Maddox, surely you agree ... Greed is what destroyed sap civilisation.'

'Sap civilisation never died. It evolved into us.' Maddox's response is swift and vociferous. He's an indignant Napoleon in a smoking jacket. 'We are the successors. Just let us succeed, is all I ask.' He picks up his glass, collapses back in his chair, gathers hiself. 'I fear it is the health camerati—the White Witch in particular—but I seek the truth. Hanging it on the wrong parties will only free the real offenders. Who knows what ends they seek?'

'You suspect it could be Infinites?'

'Of course, I suspect it could be Infinites. We all wish an end for Infinite designation. Give us back a true account of our razoos. Where's the fun in life if there's no one keeping score? Who needs a GAME OVER sign above our heads all our lives?' Maddox exhales. 'Of course, it could be Infis. If your White Witch—'

'Never my—'

'She could already be on the trail of any Infis who—'

'Or she could be at the heart of it.'

'Her behaviour is suspicious,' Maddox concedes. 'She turns up at your Gala—'

'Your gala.'

'—with the most philopolemic raiding party in history, makes a show of Consigning some also-ran Infinites, apart from me ... and poor Orlando. If you may allow, she completely botches it. Then before all the sybil-slushing, she singles you out for her personal attention. Right there she goads you. As good as grabbing you by the bush oysters, in front of all of us. Goads you by your gonads, oh my heavens.'

'You suspect I'm on her side somehow.'

'It's all very curious.' Maddox chews. 'The timing, the timing ... a group of us identify you as the mindwriter we need—'

'Need for what? There are millions of mindwriters—'

'Well, of course there are, but you should be one of us, Puffin. You should be one of us. We need you. Whether it's nurses or Infis as the heart of it, we need it stop.'

'On this we agree. If the Reck loses its inscrutability ...'

'Everything comes crashing down. Look, I wish for abolishing Infi designation as much as any, but by the persuasion of our cause. Sabotaging the Reck will ruin us. We need a mindwriter who could determine if there's any base in these suspicions. An Infi mindwriter ...'

'There's Lemarr. And 14's of others.'

Maddox scoffs. 'This needs more than holographic cosplay, Puffin. We need you.'

'I'm no hero, Maddox.'

Maddox laughs and raises his glass. 'You would make the most ineffectual, pathetic hero ever, Puffin.'

Drunk.

Maddox seems less reprehensible. Lose track of time while he regales me with tales of the Golden Age of Garbage Mining. Of how, over many decades, his mission develops spooky technology for moving and processing vast tonnages of raw waste. Spooking it out becomes the most efficient way of mining it. Now, in industry and homes, suckies extract elements and compounds from every throw-away item, spooking them for feedstock bins and thence the kitchen and wardrobe fabbies of y'all. Without early mining applications, travelling by spooky station might never be as safe and reliable. Just the methane Maddox's operations harvest from deep underground— minimising gas leaks and those horrific fires of decades passing—could be improving our world more than any other mission. For certain, more than my mission and any little toy I invent.

Slumping in the chair, shaking out the grogginess of sleep. The beginnings of a hang-over is like a cheese-grater at my brain. A damp scent of charcoal from the hours-dead fire slithers around the room, scrapes inside my throat and nostrils. Blink. Maddox snores, snorts, gulps. Sits up in his chair, looks about in bewilderment.

'Ah, good you are still here,' he says, his voice sounding as if the same cheese grater shreds his vocal cords.

I say, 'I should be getting back,' gingerly.

'Ah, yes, well … there's one more thing …' Maddox sheepish.

'What thing?' Despite my throbbing head, I'm wary and fearful.

'I must insist you stay … well, no … look … in short, there's no getting back, no going home, Puffin.'

Bolt rigid. 'What?'

'You are already home.' It's a question tangling with a feeble offer tangling with a bad deal.

'You are kidnapping me?'

'The problem is … your old life,' Maddox states, failing at softening the words. 'Your seminal is already living your old life.'

'My seminal?' It could be no worse if he strikes me dead. 'What are you saying?'

'Your seminal never spooks here. From his point of view, he chases an intruder from his back yard, and dares jump in the spooky field after them. Quite a risk, I must say. The next thing he remembers is a few hours later when he wakes in his bed, just where we leave him.'

'Then, I am … No. I'm no sybil! I'm real. I'm the seminal. I feel exactly myelf. I remember everything from before. Aisha is on a disaster recovery mission, Mal is ill. Saf is … Saf is the most beautiful creature on the planet. If there's another of me, it's the sybil.'

'I'm sorry it must be so, Puffin. There's no risking leaving you out in the wild, with all those nurses, while you work on this mission. This's no simple matter of taking you away. It would arouse too much suspicion. Please, understand, Puffin.'

'Tell me you put a sybil at home, just long enough so I complete the mission. Tell me I'm the seminal and I'll be going home when it's over.'

'I'm sorry.'

Two hundred beats per min, my heart a bike in a velodrome, whizzing in circles on a closed track. Faster and faster until there's a blow-out. Wheezing for breath. Thumping in my temples. Vision blurs. I'm real. I must go back for Aisha, for Saf and Mal. I must go back. Now.

'Trust me when I say, Puffin, if you go home and confront your seminal—'

'I'm the seminal.'

'If you confront your other, you will die, and the other will prevail.'

The air leaves my lungs like a possessing demon breaking free. I gasp. A stupid thought sparks in my head. 'I'll never jank Gentle Dragon.'

'As much as I would delight in that, I'm sorry, Puffin.'

'I am the seminal.'

'Very well, you're the seminal. But please, heed my warning. Returning home will precipitate dire consequences.'

The only thing saving me from drowning is cold crystallising anger. The only thing restoring coherent thought. The only defence, the only weapon I have. 'You jank-stick! You just put me in my own Star Trek teleporter accident episode. You put a target on my head. When detectives find out—'

'The target is already on your head, and you are in all-pervading denial. You're Infinite, you're a target.'

Head feels in a toaster. Fighting tears, the corners of my eyes burning. 'So, what now? What is my life now? Some Magical Mystery Tour of craven Infinite pastimes? Perhaps we'll roast babies together, or ... or ... slap huge golden monuments of ourelves on a coral reef or ... let's send grotesque phallic spacecraft into space and infest the solar system ... let's commit art fraud or manipulate real estate.'

'Now, you are just being silly,' Maddox pronounces, disappointment in his tone. 'All art is fraud.'

'Alamak! If I'm a janking sybil, how long before I end up as foaming arse-fat on some Uncle Kiah's shoes? How long till you kill me? Jank. I'm going to die here. This's right, yeer? You'll use me and then kill me.'

Maddox points a finger. 'Will you janking get it?' His plastic forehead is red and ruckling. 'This is too important. If anything, you should be glad you're a sybil. It keeps your seminal and your family safe.'

'And ignorant. So, you will kill me ... this sybil ... after I—it—succeeds.'

Maddox shakes his head and waves his hand about. 'The choice could be yours. If we succeed, we may have no further need of secrecy. If we succeed, you will live.'

'I'll never forget what a psychopathic prick you are.'

'I am at ease with this.' Maddox chews, leans forward, pats my knee. 'So, Puffin. Shall we find out who wants to rule the world?'

GLUTTONY

Scent

'Little Mustang' — The High Decibels

 *Ben Evoli ...*

THIS IS A PRISON. While no one locks doors or puts me in chains, Maddox's attentive and persistent staff diligently guard all the exits while going about their chores.

My quarters—a swasta, a sitting room, and a bathroom with a tub the size of a swimming pool—is larger than ... imagine the top floor of my home. With a cycling track around it. Larger than that.

That Maddox could shroud the place in secrecy becomes obvious on the first day of my internment. No one here flutherbombs, as is plain from all the teeny-weeny auras. Days later, one of the cleaners—a plain-speaking woman of 150 or so, and as solid and upright as a saloon bar piano—explains, 'We take unkindly to spying.'

One night at dinner, while opening a bottle of wine, the sommelier asks, 'For what are you Infi anyway?'

I say, 'I write hoots,' under the weight of her blank effrontery.

The bottle stopper pops free, and Maddox exclaims, '*Eine Jungfrau weniger.*'

'Hoots,' the sommelier mocks as she decants the wine.

'Enhancement utilities,' I blather as if this supercilious bottle-tipper never hears the word *hoot*. 'For installing in a hancy.'

Maddox titters. His plastic smile crumples across his face like a bad-folding raincoat. As the sommelier pours, he explains, 'Pouilly-Fumé.' He lifts his glass and sniffs.

Caring less for the wine and more for the sommelier's lack of interest in my mission, I add, 'MusiKai?' Then, only after that makes no impression, I drop, 'SnakiDik?' expecting some recognition.

'Sorry?' the sommelier asks.

'My hoots.'

'Ah, very good,' the sommelier says with sterile emotion. She wipes the decanter spout. 'We find little need for enhancements here.' Mal would love it. *We don't need no stinking hancies.*

'No need for enhancement of sexual experience?' Maddox asks, mischief as his motive.

The sommelier looks in perplexity. 'Fucking is fucking,' she says while still maintaining the haughty professionalism I'm sure Maddox trains into her. 'What's to enhance?'

'Perhaps you might find MusiKai more—'

'I hear there are LizziDik orgy parties,' Maddox interrupts.

'SnakiDik,' I correct.

'Yes, yes,' Maddox dismisses. 'I hear it feels like having sexual congress with 10 people at once. How wonderful.'

The sommelier rolls her eyes, sets the decanter on the sideboard. Maddox celebrates her lack of interest in my mission.

'1024,' I correct.

'What?'

'Each user can couple with 1024 others at once. In the next version—'

'Over 1000? Oh, my. Imagine their dehydration. Imagine the nutepaks they would need afterwards. They'd have testicles like desiccated passionfruit. You test it with these numbers?'

'Well, in theory, stress tests—'

'Stress tests!' Maddox determines to make light of everything I say. 'Oh, my boy, you are a delight. How fun those must be.'

Draw a deep, slow breath. 'I can install it for you now if you please. You could go jank yourelf.'

Maddox appears giving my suggestion serious consideration. 'Perhaps you are insecure about your own little pig stabber, eh?' he baits. 'Why else would you dream up such a thing as a penile enhancement hoot?'

'It's full sensory enhancement,' I correct, for no perceivable purpose. 'It works on all jantina: male, female, and everyone in between and beyond.'

Maddox raises a hand, points his first finger. 'No, I remember. You invent it during your last childing.' He stares at me like a predator. 'How could anyone in such an innocent state invent a sex hoot?'

Against my better reasoning, I rise against his provocation. 'The childing state is free of adult filters: judgment, rationalisation, doubt, fear, pragmatism. In a child's mind, snakes and penises are funny in their similarity. After childing it's the adult Mind which develops the idea. You know this. You're how old? You must child many times.'

'My Puffin, there is no childing for me.'

I make stone of my face for masking the shock. 'No?'

'I could think of nothing worse than having parents again. Regressing to my most uncritical, innocent elf, so bare and vulnerable? How sick inducing. A chance for nurturing our creative essence? For resetting our adult lives, for stripping away all the harsh elf-criticism we learn as we age. What's wrong with living a life and taking the lumps?'

'This must be why you look so old. You must know childing extends a lifespan by decades.'

'What need have I of more decades? I already have a meaningful satisfying mission cleaning up the world. I will always be the garbage miner.'

Drain the wine, go for the sideboard. Drinking more here than ever in my ... other ... life. 'How many sybils have you?'

'Counting you?' Maddox almost wilts under my glare, shifts uneasily on his chair. 'Well, what's the point of being Infinite without infinite copies of one's elf?'

'There no such thing as infinite—'

'It's a post-scarcity world,' he wheedles then chomps on a forkful of, I must admit, some of the juiciest tastiest protein I ever taste. A suckling pig recipe I guess, with refinements over the original carnal meat. For a skin so crisp Maddox must have the most exceptional fabbies.

'There is still a limit—'

'The truth is, I am uncertain. There could be whole branches out there I'm unaware of.'

'Branches?'

'Yes, whole generations of sybils. There's nothing that limits crèching a sybil from a sybil. Otherwise, you'll be in a cradle an entire life popping them out.' He gargles the remainder of his wine and waves the glass for me. I replenish it. 'As for answering the question, upwards of 12,000.'

'12,000 sybils?'

Maddox shrugs with his mouth. 'Thereabouts, yes.'

'You're a janking virus.' Shake my head in disbelief.

'Humanity is a virus. How is crèching sybils different from reproduction?'

'You mean—'

'Having children, yes. Disgusting little mutants. So random how they'll turn out. Sybils, on the other hand—'

'How is it I know nothing of sybils?'

'Oh? You should gog *How for committing the most heinous illegal taboo act in history*. There must be libraries full of magazines with step-by-step guides.'

Sneer at his sarcasm. 'I'm usually good at uncovering things.'

Maddox narrows his eyes and holds his head higher. 'And I'm better at keeping the covers on.'

'How are you sure you're the seminal?'

'Well, there's less than a one in 12,000 chance, I suppose. Those are slim odds. Still … I am the seminal.'

Two Maddox's already die in front of me. He could be crèching and disposing of 100's a day. 'If you create so many—or even one—what happens when you have no more use for them? You store them in your garage under a sheet?'

Maddox barely contains a smirk. 'I prune them,' he says, bland.

'Prune them?'

He nods. 'Prune a whole branch sometimes. They fall off the twig, you could say.'

'You … kill them? Whole branches?'

'Well, *kill* is such an ugly word—'

'How is it other than murder? Sentient beings. Your own flesh and—'

'From crèching metrae, Puffin. Let's avoid romanticising. Think of crèching a sybil as elaborate fabbing.'

'Printing copies of people—just elaborate …? It's pure evil.'

Maddox affects the fake chewing motion of his. 'Oh, Puffin, evil? There's no evil in a post-scarcity world. There is no need for morality in a time of abundance when every snout may find a trough. There are no limits. We can replace anything, and anything is replaceable. Reversible. Erasable. Clean sheets. No semen stain of evil at all. Pruning a sybil is nothing akin murder. There's no cessation of life. Because the seminal lives on. Look, it's all a matter of version control. You're a mindwriter, you understand. It's the same with sybils. With sybil tech, we can merge experiences from one version into the main trunk before their physical presence … erases. In me, they all live on, unaware of merging.'

'There are 1000's of competing memories in you?'

'Competing, no. Alternative histories, perhaps. Integral, yes. For the truth, having memories from many places at the same time is sometimes a strange sensation, omnipotent and omnipresent. While there are the odd merge conflicts, overall, our brains accommodate and make sense of it all. Merging is like reorganising memories during sleep. It's all remarkably natural and somewhat refreshing. You'll see.'

Too easy, Maddox explains away the disposable nature of his doppelgängers. There must be some time paradox jankery going on which must have consequences. I dunno. Maybe creating all these sybils causes collisions between multiverses.

Just on the level of erasing other conscious beings, it's a gruesome travesty. I should scream my utter disgust. 'Are you a sybil? Right here in front of me, are you a sybil?'

'Of course, no. I'm an Infi, Puffin, with infinite capabilities. As you could be if you ever overcome your sourness. You know, I think the gawd of

Abraham must have had sybils. All the popping in, haunting prophets, appearing in burning bushes and tortillas, and so on. Come for taste of it, gawd was an amateur.' There he is again, the smug Roman emperor taking a warm bath.

A sudden realisation: 'Can a sybil prune a seminal?'

'No. The seminal is at the top of the tree. Even if a sybil could prune a seminal, they'd be pruning all branches underneath. Including them.'

'Wait. I'm the seminal. I could prune the sybil back home. I could go home.'

'I'm sorry, but you are sybil.' Maddox boggles his eyes. He rocks his shoulders side to side. 'I'm happy if you want for playing Schrödinger's seminal here, but please recall my warning against confronting the other at home. It would end badly.'

Could I escape here? I find no spooky station on the premises, and no one is letting me out of the house, let alone as far as the local village. If I could escape, would I risk confronting my other? The other who is stealing my life and my family. Would I die as Maddox threatens?

'Tell me,' Maddox says. 'Is this the best roast you ever taste?'

Maddox runs his house like a 7-star hotel. His staff, if lacking finesse, more than compensate by providing the privacy he craves. All of them are off the onespace grid—no flutherbombing nurses, stalkers, in-laws or Nigerian fabby scammers can access their vectors. They're the kind who'd prefer a stout walk among the winter pines over the vicarious experience of other neos' lives. In the unlikely event a nurse stumbles over one of their fluthers, the resulting spike in aura activity would be as fireworks shooting from a chamber pot.

As days pass, all my vector references become stale. I have no confidence I could even locate Aisha.

Feeling sorry for me, a few latent musicians among the staff express interest in trying MusiKai, so I help with installations and give some elementary tutelage.

I explain how easy MusiKai is: start with a bar or 2 of an ear-wig melody, and it will evolve a tune at the edge of awareness over the following hours or days. I show how it gathers reactions when music plays around you and when you recall favourite music. I demonstrate how the reiterative editor—monitoring thoughts and feelings—nudges the composition in the right direction. I show how MusiKai incorporates composers' musical taste while suggesting structure, metre, instrumentation, vocalisation and 14's of other options.

On the second afternoon of our sessions, Paul Dunder the head of maintenance says, 'You could write a whole opera over breakfast.'

I say, 'Opera usually takes 3 square meals.'

'Opera is for people like Maddox,' says Willow Cotton whose gaunt face reminds me of a grey kangaroo.

'What kind of music is for you?' I ask.

'Simple music.'

Which, looking back, I realise should serve as a warning. But feeling useful for the first time in a while, I press on with the next evening's lesson, in which I disastrously and too proudly explain the latest features of MusiKai: mood augmentation and tagging. Tagging, I tell them, connects a composition with a fourspace location allowing near-field broadcasting for any hoot within range. Mood augmentation, I proudly show off, adapts a composition for a listener's current mood. A listener can even mash-up the broadcast with other music they select, which produces a whole new composition.

Unfortunately, these impuberal musicians seize on these new features with viral zeal and attach every new idea to locations all over the house. The kitchen plays at least 3 anthems. Some of the service passages broadcast a different piece every 10 or so paces. Sucky bins have jingles, and fabbies have military marches.

Paul Dunder, perhaps with ambitions of penning an opera after Friday lunch, prolifically tags compositions all around the house (and presumably, the grounds). In the wet room, one sounds like a dedication to his favourite machinery. I call it, *Fugue in C^b minor for truck and jackhammer*. In a service corridor, another piece sounds like a chorus of out-of-tune harpsichords. Another features a battalion of bagpipes so discordant they could strip moss off bush rock.

Worse than Paul Dunder's blunders in industrial noise are the sweet, country-style nursery-rhyme hymns of Willow Cotton. After only 2 days of being ambushed about the house by her jingles, I start having nightmares in which Dolly Parton and Hank Williams sit at the foot of my bed and sing tunes made of 3 kinds of American corn syrup.

The tune a wisely anonymous composer tags at the front door somehow defeats all my attempts at mashing other tunes into it. I try genre after genre: 20th-century atonalism only makes it worse, the aural equivalent of adding handfuls of chilli to a crème brûlée recipe. Fighting it with prog rock produces a seizure-inducing kind of anthemic compound-time circus music performed with pedal-steel guitars. Nothing works: Aya Jazz Thrash, Melanau Dance Pop. Nothing. Even Country *and* Western fails. Deep in a frenzy of abject failure, I throw the Rolling Stones at it. The sugar-sweet tune rolls every stone flat, preserving its Pentecostal-safe harmonies. I get neither what I want, nor what I need. Sirmick Jagger would be appalled.

If there remains a single drop of essential hope in the lemon peel of my soul, I might find the energy for upgrading MusiKai so it moderates the compositions these tin-ear kitsch-cutters are poisoning the musical well with. Or I could just hack their hoots and render MusiKai inoperable.

Long-since melting from the pine tree branches, only a few dirty mounds of snow remain on the ground and in my heart. Down south of the valley the Maddison River is running again. It might as well be the other side of the world. Because of the taboo on *visiting* in these parts, I'm sanctioned against flutherbombing anyone down there for tasting it. A reminder of how profoundly blind I am.

Is Aisha home yet? It's Aisha's job working through the acute aftermath of disasters and overseeing a hand-over for the longer-term rebuild. She could be away for days or weeks while projects launch and bed in.

Five years an Infinite; no peace, no solitude, other than the artificial peace of my filters. Now I have solitude, I loathe it. I miss Saf and Mal, who will never miss me. The seminal, the other, is at home, taking care of them, loving them.

If the other becomes aware of me, would it prune me? Merge me? Would it know how? Are such things even possible? Maddox could be lying.

But there is a mote of allure in all this. When Maddox speaks of having the experiences of his sybils, the sense of being in many places at once, an undeniable sense of place and power exudes from him. How would it feel? Will I get a chance? When Maddox takes what he wants from me, what then?

What stupid thoughts. I'm as good as already dead, a spare in exile from my own life.

I must send a message. Anything, just connect, just reach out.

Mal's iMac is the key. It connects with AgniSpace as a physical device, which means I can locate it without onespace vectors. It has no onespace vectors. Connecting with it is more an act of anthropology than communication. No one will notice me tickling an ancient toy on a desk in a little boy's swasta. No one will notice it means anything.

I must prod my other, stimulate his curiosity for the Reck. Let him work out the question of its compromise independently of me. I must trust my other will protect whatever he learns, while I must contend with Maddox. Here, I must stall.

I memb, 'Maddox.'

'Puffin?'

'There is something I need for my research.'

'Excellent.'

'I need something for cutting through AgniSpace so I can approach the Reck from a fresh angle.'

'Anything within my power or acquiring is yours. What is it?'

'An early 21st-century computer.'

Maddox Price ...

Find Ben in his sitting room.

Sitting on the rug. In lotus position, I believe. Facing the picture windows framing pine trees and mountains. His eyes shut. Meditating. Distasteful. Is life so long you would spend tracts of it playing dead?

'I hear you breathing,' he speaks tongue and lung, barely above a whisper.

'And I see you being boring.'

'You should try it. Cleans your fluther out in no time.'

'I have other methods. As you are discovering.'

'Yeer, I'm deserted.'

'The joys of being sybil. Your seminal will be enduring all the usual fandom hells while you take a holiday.'

'You call this a holiday?'

'A convalescence perhaps.'

'Am I sick?'

'Who knows? Ask a nurse.'

Ben unfolds hiself, stretches and stands. 'You're a cat lover?' he asks, noticing Jimmy Carter in my arms.

'Hmmm, that's never an appellation I'd use for myelf.'

'Then?'

I stroke Jimmy Carter's chin. He purrs and, under his Persian fur, glows crimson, the colour of embarrassment. 'In truth I have many crowders of ray cats in my employ. In my nuclear waste reclamation mission, they are invaluable. You never know what you may find in a sap toxic waste dump.'

'You never hear of scintillation detectors?'

'Cats purr better. And they're less maintenance.' Puffin, dear, I so delight in boggling your Mind.

'You want something?' he asks, getting perfunctory against my hopes a cat might soften him up.

I say, 'I come with news. Your computers will arrive in Grayling tomorrow.'

'Computers? Plural?'

'Yes, why stop at one? I order a truckload. A *sem-eye-trailer*,' he pronounces Texas style.

'There are no semi-trailers.'

Jimmy Carter bounces from my embrace and rubs against Ben's calves. 'None for centuries. I simply mean I acquire a great many puters for you. I expect they'll be unreliable, and you'll burn through quite a few. Besides, Infis always revel in excess. And I figure it better for giving you options, let you decide for yourelf.'

'Will no one be suspicious?'

'This is Wasteland, Puffin. Suspicion is for the French Americas and Europa.'

'Thank you.'

'My mindwriters are all applauding your approach. Hitting AgniSpace via its physical back doors.'

'I can cross-reference what I find via onespace.'

'Good. Offer me a drink.'

'I just finish meditating. Alcohol will hit me like a yak falling out of a tree.'

'Moose here, Puffin. And they come out of the trees eons ago. I said offer me a drink. Please yourelf what you imbibe.'

Watch him go for the sideboard bar. Jimmy Carter lazily trails him. 'There's a respectable bourbon in the back somewhere.'

'Here it is.' A bottle appears from under with one glass tumbler. As Ben pours, impatience defeats me. 'How long before there's progress?'

'Ask me in a day or 2.'

This whole computer thing could be a stalling tactic. He must know there's no stalling forever.

'I'll be looking for physical data centres,' he says.

Raise my eyebrow and he tastes it.

'Topological analysis of reputasi scores, looking for relative densities across the network.'

'Good.'

'How much DNA memory is out there, you suppose?'

'More than is general knowledge. Why?'

'A recent spike in denser memory tech might cause false positives in the algorithms.'

'Very well, Puffin.'

'Maddox.'

'Yes?'

'How is my family?' He presents the glass of bourbon.

'Everything is fine, Puffin. Ben.'

'Aisha: is she home yet? What about Mal?'

'Your wife is yet in California. Mal is in good health.'

'You'll kill me when you finish with me, yeer?'

'Our best hope is if you merge with your seminal. Which depends on you.'

'And my seminal.'

'You'll have useful information. He'll value it.'

'How can you live with yourelf?'

I draught the glass dry of alcohol. 'Such moralising is quaint, Puffin. But you are overlooking how free you are. You have a great opportunity. Run your own life's great experiment while your seminal stays safe.'

'If you ever let me out of the house.'

'You only need ask. Think of all the things you might try if your seminal would never suffer harm from it. You could fry yourelf in rattlesnake fat. Spook for the moon. We could crèche you many times over. You could live 100 adventures at once and choose which ones you'll merge back at the finish.'

'All the merging must drive you bent-brain.'

'There's always some Joe Soap calling you bent-brain if you have the Mind for looking.'

'You are bent-brain. You might justify crèching any number of sybils, but you cross a line when you crèche me against my will. My real elf is home oblivious of what goes on here. Neither he nor I choose this.'

Oh, dear, he's twinking my anger. 'You don't janking get it, do you? Mind is everywhere, in everything. The thing you identify as elf is just a white cap on a wave in a storm on an ocean. That ocean is infinitely deep and contains all space and time. If we make a copy of the froth on the surface, what real harm is it? And if the froth rides a wave back for shore, or if it dissolves into the ocean, what difference is it?'

'Yeer, the universe is beautiful and we're all cherries in one big Black Forest cake. Good news for me, a spare cherry you'll compost once I over-ripen.'

'Dear Puffin, enough with the melodrama. You see in me the product of 1000's of sybil merges. It is a full and rewarding life.'

Ben could be tasting it. Or he could be giving up. Either way, he lets the silence between us stretch.

'Oh, come, Puffin. Are you without the least curiosity? Turn your predicament for your advantage and learn for yourelf. Play the game the way an Infinite should. Play it well and you will win, whatever choices you make.'

'Let me know when it's time for a break, Puffin. I have something I would show you.'

No answer.

'Puffin?'

What is he doing up there? Heave a sigh. He makes a good show of sitting at his desks with his rows of puters—including one Jimmy Carter sleeps on—but he could be cataloguing porn hollies for all I know. I'd engage another mindwriter for pairing with him. Would they speak the same tech language? I must keep the number who know about this down. I'll suspend my mistrust for a time.

'Can you stop calling me Puffin? *Ben* will do just nice.'

'Oh, but look at you. Look at your jet-black hair and your crisp white shirt.'

'It's a baju.'

'I swear, all you need is orange shoes. Come mating season, your beak will swell and turn orange too. I'm so looking forward for it.' Ben harrumphs and turns inward. Mindwriting, I guess. 'Anyway, Puffin, get ready for a spook.

You will love this.'
  'Spook? Out of here?'
  'Grow no horns.'

Ghastly. The stench: acrid, oily, and metallic. The noise raw, loud, and angry.

'Welcome, Infi,' says Bob Spinner, the procomplement here at Filip Island Circuit Camerata on the traditional lands of the Bunurong people. He extends his grimy hand which is only a fraction grubbier than his face and a fraction cleaner than his overalls. Even his hair is a tangle in an oil emulsion.

I take Spinner's hand. 'Please, call me Maddox.'

'Call me Wheels.'

Wheels greets Ben. 'It's been a while. I'm sure the work on the mobil will please you.'

'Wheels! Good seeing you.' Ben is uncharacteristically warm with his greeting and vigorous handshaking. Is he above disdaining the man's grubbiness at all? 'What?' He searches my face. 'Why are we here?'

'Your car, Puffin.'

'We complete the repairs,' Wheels explains. 'Ahead of time, thanking your friend here.'

Delight in Ben's awkwardness at Wheels assuming we're friends.

'It seems the only the right thing after that awful accident.' Hope I sound sympathetic. Maybe it's a little too much.

'Infi Maddox finds another 2 Mustang wrecks with enough parts for completing repairs. We have quite an inventory of spares now.'

'It is no bother, a pleasure. It's amazing what you turn up in the garbage mining industry. There are whole wrecking yards out there, sometimes just a metre or so under the surface.'

'I would think rust and decay would reclaim most wrecks.' Ben, always the sceptic.

'Ah, well, the diversity of the world we live in, Puffin. Sometimes conditions are just right for preserving such things. Such good fortune for you.'

'We are testing the car these passing 2 days,' Spinner membs. 'It's ready for racing.'

Delight in watching Ben's pleasure washing him through.

'I would love to take it out,' Ben says, his words originating in his scrotum. He's a monkey on heat already.

'Follow me,' Spinner membs. 'It's out back, getting a wash and polish.'

Squarish and blocky, even by sap standards, it's obvious how much the automobile's form owes to excessive heat, to pressing and hammering, to rolling and folding. Saps loved creating things by show of force. We prefer growing things slowly in vats. The car is as imposing as a sap office block and, no doubt, as heavy too. It could crush anything under its weight.

Y'all might call it pretty in its own way. The paint gleams with the jewel-beetle chitinous finish the Asians love so much, while suggesting depth and solidity. Its body panels resist bending even if you lean all your weight against them.

Ben fails in concealing his delight. He caresses it over and around, with a lover's hands exploring every flank and intimate fold. He grips a silver handle and opens a door—of course he's familiar with how it works. An expert, he swivels hiself into the front single-seater lounge, lifts his feet in, closes the door, puts his shoulder into making the window go down with a primitive mechanical winder on the inside.

'The engine is an iron block, 4.7-litre V8,' I recite, 'with 228 kilowatts of power and 446 newton-metres of torque; redlines at 6000 rpm; 4-barrel carburettor; 4-speed manual transmission; single, dry-disc clutch.'

'You're gogging that,' Ben accuses.

'I'm showing interest.'

'Hmmm.' Ben grasps the steering circle, drums his fingers on it, rolls his shoulders.

'Take it for a spin?' Spinner asks.

'Oh, yeer!' Ben says—his youthful incarnadine cheeks all aglow with excitement.

'Kay, come suit up.'

Ben Evoli …

On the cool-down lap, approaching Lukey Heights, sweeping left then down around the tight right-hander. Even at low speed the old machine could wrench her steering wheel out of my hands. Sap machines will hurt you if you disrespect them.

Imagine feeling the wood-rim and satin-trim through the driving gloves while slowing and recovering from the sense-sharpening, adrenaline-juicing hot laps. Wipe more speed off at turn 11, breathe in the copse of trees lining it, coast into the pit lane at 80 kims like pulling into a shopping centre carpark (gog it. Appalling!). Approach the garages on the left. Down towards the end, Maddox stands with Wheels who is waving his hands over the landscape explaining various features of the course.

Pull up a little short of the pit bay, better than overshooting it. In neutral give the engine one more kick, listen with pleasure for her roar, watch the 8000-r.p.m-tacho arc round towards 6000 then lazily fall back. Let her gurgle a little then shut her down.

This Mustang. Charlotte. I janking own you.

Wheels opens the door and helps me out of the driver's seat. Fumble at the helmet strap.

'I got it,' membs Wheels.

Behind him, the steatopygous Maddox smiles the smile of an anak who discovers the biggest and brightest gift under the Christmas tree is for him. A smile also betraying calculation, adult avarice, and hubris.

'This is the most alive I have seen you, Puffin,' he shouts into my ear. Slaps my back. 'It is the life you belong for.'

Emerge from spooking. Sudden biting cold. Under my shoes the crunch of a thin layer of snow, uncommon for late in the northern spring. We're somewhere on the grounds of Maddox's private home, the place of my captivity.

'I always rotate the destination vectors around the property,' Maddox explains as I look around for gaining my bearings. 'It's amazing how much a few metres change the vectors. Onespace is a strange substrate. I'll never understand it. In any case, every little bit throws stalkers off.'

I'm sure Maddox is sybil, and he could be yet another since Filip Island. I doubt I meet the seminal Maddox Price yet.

'Where are we just before?'

'I am inhaling the sticky stench of hot bitumen and exhaust fumes while you are making love with your muscle car.'

I give him side-eye. Fighting my gratitude for arranging the repair of the car, but I still detest you, Maddox.

'Leave the Reck another min. Come have a drink.'

'I need a shower.' Lame excuse. I already clean up back at the track. 'I still feel … oily.'

'I want a drink with you, not spoon you. Come. One drink.'

Follow him for his den where he first spooks me. Stand by the picture windows, look out on marshmallow snow lines melting up the mountains.

Maddox passes an amber cocktail from behind the bar. He appears chewing an unpleasant sop in his mouth, makes a kind of grimace, turns for the wall liquor cabinet, reaches into a drawer, retrieves something. While his meaty fist gloves the object, its shininess is unconcealable. A gold bracelet perhaps. There is some reverence in the way he reveals it: a 3-centim-wide band of golden panels holding together by links or elastic.

'I should present you this before.' Maddox extends his hand, offering me the object. 'This is the first time I think you might accept.'

See the circular thing, a glass face, thin needles underneath, radiating flat from the centre.

'Go on, take it, boy,' Maddox admonishes, impatiently dangling the gaud for me. 'It's a watch. A Zenith, for being precise, the pinnacle of sap engineering.'

Stutter. 'I ... no. Is it gold?'

'Of course it's gold,' Maddox sputters. 'No one will begrudge you a watch, Puffin. It's the only one you have. You may wear it in public, I assure, with no consequence.'

I best take it. One luxury item will make no difference. Roll it over in my hands, hold it square-on. Read the face. '7 and 10 ... 18 mins before 2?' Surprise myelf by decoding the hands. Unsure where I learn how.

'Close enough,' Maddox pronounces. 'Put it on.'

Thread the band over my hand, adjust it on my wrist. It dangles loose.

'Easy enough removing a link or 2 for a good fit,' Maddox says. 'True, a watch is among the most useless of things. Spooking will scramble it every time.' He laughs. 'Complete randomness. So. Never rely on it for making appointments. Yet it is beautiful, no?'

'Yes, it is,' I concede.

'There's something mournful about watches,' Maddox says, sounding the most authentic I ever hear him. 'Functional in their pretty uselessness. Each tik a reminder another life's segment passing. Quite symbolic, Puffin. Badges of sorts, if you allow.' He holds up his left forearm so the cuff of his coat falls away from his wrist, revealing a similar watch. 'By this sign you shall know us. Welcome to the Hodinkle Society.'

Our third drink.

Maddox is jovial. Descending into inebriation, his face a pinkish macabre jack-o'-lantern with a plastic sheen.

'How is it you manage so many sybils?' I ask.

'Oh, ah.' For the first time I make him think. 'You develop a skill, I guess,' he says. 'Like aerial acrobatics or an exceptional head for numbers. More like a combination of both, I suppose. After a while, it's all reflex and muscle memory.'

It's no explanation at all. 'There must be stuff-ups.'

'Stuff-ups?' Maddox asks, perplexed.

'Thing must go wrong sometimes.'

'Oh yes, indeed. Horribly so for the careless. Suffice in saying, we lose some seminals. Which normally means the highest-rank sybil ascends. Hopefully, it has the most hi-fidelity experiences and can rise peaceably. Sometimes the prevailing sybil launches an entirely new agenda born of a different set of experiences.'

'It ever happens with you?'

'How would I know? We all believe down to our amino acids we're the seminal.'

The puter on the desk beeps.

I shoo Jimmy Carter off the keyboard, drag and click the mouse, opening a terminal window flashing a message:

1 8-CORE APPLE M3 FOUND

The scrappy daemon I write and run over the last few days finds a 21st-century puter. The first one. Perhaps the only one.

We'll see if the hacky snippets of primitive code I write for communicating with it work. Just the code for translating between ancient electrical binary and AgniSpace protocols … I'll spare y'all the details. I'm still unsure how well it will work or whether it will work at all.

On the back of a sheet of Maddox's desk paper, I scribble a note in my own hand and sign it. It must be cryptic enough in case someone else intercepts it, yet clear enough so my other will act on it. Using the hazy 2-dimensional camera, I save an image file on Jimmy Carter's puter (I must always shoo him off the keyboard) and drop it in an open email. Read it one more time.

Machan may be right
Despite reputasi
Of something out of sight
With reputasi

There are no tests I can run. I must send it and wonder what chance it will reach its destination—Mal's iMac. I must hope the intended recipient—another version of myelf, living in my place with my family—receives the message. He'll recognise the handwriting, of course; I expect he'll decode the message—*get ahead of the nurses and Infinites, and independently find out if there's truly a problem the Reckoning.* He'll have sufficient reason for keeping everything secret until he knows the truth. While I stall here and face the inevitable consequences, he might find a way of striking back against Maddox—and the nurses, for presuming what's best for Mal. Imposing a hancy on Mal might, on the surface, seem like a single clinic overreaching; but I taste from the moment I hear of it, there's a deeper plot; the source of which is probably Perawat Detektif Eir Frijberg, who fails in Consigning me at the Inductee Gala.

Mal … the tears come so fast I need for burying my face in a pillow, so thick and yielding, it drains and muffles my wailing, and silently secrets away the purging of my pain.

We'll make them all pay, Mal, little fella, you pirate. We'll plunder all their tall ships. Yo-ho-ho.

Taste

'What I am' — Edie Brickell & New Bohemians

 *Ben Evoli ...*

A LMOST CRACKING OUT OF MY SKIN with fright. 'Jesús! Must you creep up on me this way?'

'Sorry, Infi.' Jesús fakes a reverent bow then ruins it with a mocking curl at the corner of his mouth. His shuffle toward my swasta door is a pantomime. 'I have no wish for troubling you.' More bows.

'You're always sneaking around.'

After the intruder in the house last night, I'm on a jagged edge again, within tiks of waking from sleep as blank and anaesthetic as Never-Mind. Every bone feels flinty, sharp enough for slicing muscle. Gulp a mouthful of air against my heart evacuating my chest. Last night ... So stupid, chasing a stranger in the dark. It could be an ambush ...

... the memories strangely dull ... in the bush watching as they escape via an improvised spooky field. Why would I be stupid enough for following? The field could kill me ...

I try recalling ... and meet a canyon-wide void from the tik I step into the spooky field on the rock ... a violet curtain all around, waiting for dissolution. Then ... what? No memory of returning for the house, of coming upstairs, of lying in bed in yesterday's clothes.

Wake with an intensifying, itching sense of wrong. The outrage of last night dehydrating into a sticky resin of fright, an unshakable dread of malignant forces closing in. Going for the shower, as solemn as a gallows walk. The water not yet warm before hearing movement beyond the bathing screen. A shadow hunching over the bed. Me in arrant paralytic terror. They're coming for me.

It's only Jesús stripping the bed, bundling linen into his basket—disposable linen, which he already washes the previous morning.

'Fresh and crisp again for this evening, Infi,' he says monastically divining my thoughts. He vanishes out the door. Leaves me listening as he pads down the hall in his sandals, his thin robe swishing on his calves.

Enough. Enough with strangers invading my house, scaring my anak anak, taunting me, leading me on chases in the dead of night. Enough with this stupid laundry business. Enough of Jesús on his pointless mission sneaking around the house intruding in our private rooms. I'll throw him out and take the Warrant. How long could a Cure be? Days at most. Then there'll be the nute regimen. And even more nurses. Worse, they'll have a pretext for visiting the house.

When will it stop, Jesús? Every move I make, you counter. Look. I'm already religiously throwing all disposable clothes into the sucky, meticulously hanging up self-cleaning clothes and putting everything else in the ultraviolet closet. I never even leave a coat over the back of a chair anymore, or at the foot of the bed. Aisha would be proud. But Jesús, alamak. You ninja launderer.

Forget the shower, forget washing off the sniff of rotting sweat, stale saké and Angeles City strip-joints. Chase after Jesús. I resolve for casting him out at last. Find him in the predictable mess of Mal's swasta retrieving socks and chuddies from corners and crevices around the room, taking the serene care he might for birds with broken wings. He looks up, wondering. Just kneeling there, waiting, passive. I could strike him down; I doubt he would lift an arm against me. Exhale deep. Aggression draining away.

Uncharacteristically I take morning meditation in my swasta, feeling too lazy for skipping for my usual spot at the edge of the pond in the park. About halfway through I hear the distinct sound of a bell from Mal's swasta.

Meditation cleans away followers as nothing else. Perhaps my mantra entrances them. Whatever the reason, post-meditation is the quietest time I'll have all day. A good time for figuring out the source of the bell.

In Mal's swasta. I tap the spacebar of the iMac. The room brightens; a screen saver comes up on the monitor: Neil Armstrong planting a flag on the moon. Stark red and blue against black, white, and sandy grey. The astronaut could be a baggy robot wearing a 1950's TV for a head, its screen reflecting a leg of the lunar module. Buzz off in the distance. A timeless mesmerising snapshot.

I almost miss the other thing on the monitor: a single icon at the top-right corner. A blue bird holding an envelope in her wings over which hovers a tiny red circle with a bold white number 1 in it. Few neos alive would know what it means: an email, an old form of communication even for saps.

How could anyone send me such a thing?

A few silent lurkers. No chatter. Chances are, attentions are elsewhere. The world is an exciting place and I'm deliberately boring. Meditation is useful for that. Fingers on the puter's trackpad, gliding the cursor over the blue bird on the screen. Tap it. A window expands, showing a tile on which is a sheet of paper with a dog-ear corner. Tap there. An image appears, of a handwritten note:

Machan may be right
Despite reputasi
Of something out of sight
With reputasi

Heart rate and blood pressure rise, knees and ankles lock, muscles tighten around my ribs, forehead tense. Eyeballs become glass, all the hairs on my fruit are pins piercing my skin.

The handwriting is my own.

Which is more inexplicable? An angel delivering a cryptic invitation? Or an ancient machine bearing a cryptic message in my own handwriting? Could the invitation and the message be from the same source? Believe Maddox is behind the angel's visitation, but this email?

And handwriting? We have so little use of writing. When is the last time I write anything?

Machan may be right
Despite reputasi

Machan. Dil. What could my paranoid activist old friend be right about?

Of something out of sight
With reputasi

Weeks ago, in Kolombo I must listen again as he rants about health camerati acting as a quasi-government. It always sounds so bent-brain. Then ... the elaborate raid by Eir escalating the campaign against Infinites. For a time, she seems there for Consigning me. Then Infis drop dead. They're only sybils, as I now understand.

Since the night the Angelic Being appears for me, and I discover the package of sap files containing *The Rise of Sybil Technology*, news of sybils travels so fast, I doubt I am the sole source. Nurses will be up to their chatelaines in this somehow. As of now, anyone who hears nothing of sybils must be frequenting the most insular of echo-chamber fluthers.

Saps dabbled with sybils in a neurotic chase for longer lives. Now neos? Maybe I'm the only real Infi at the Inductee Gala.

Maddox: his bizarre messy end, then his roundabout way of luring me for a location without nurses or spooky stations so he can discuss … what? He never reaches his point before he blubbers another sybil.

Infinites to the left of me, nurses to the right. Here I am. Stuck in the middle with … who? An angel? What. The. Jank.

How could the nurses at Shirahama presume they should fit Mal with a hancy? At the worst possible time while Aisha and me argue over it. At least Lành Hiền Rồng is more than helpful, removing the abominable hancy, the 2nd time she saves Mal. Must chuckle. I think Mal has a crush on the Gentle Dragon.

Someone uses Mal's iMac for channelling me this message, somehow faking my handwriting. Taste no logic in it. What could Eir, Maddox, the angel, a Japanese health missionary … Walao eh, I might as well throw Aisha in the mix since we're fighting so much … am I leaving anyone out? Dil? Who sends me this message?

The message: it's about Dil and reputasi. Dil believes health camerati manipulate the Reck. While I see no clean angles, let's concede perhaps someone plots for gaming the Reck. Some loony-toons Infi somewhere. Maddox. What if he's manipulating the Reck or he knows who? Something is on his Mind in Lesvos. Since becoming strawberry jam there, he attempts more oblique contact. He sends me an angel, I suspect, and this email. What would he want from me?

Jank anyone else's schemes, just get ahead of it all. I'll find the Reck. Could I find it? Could anyone find it? If I succeed, could I tell if someone is tampering with it?

Drain the cold dregs of my 4th aya tea. It's after midnight already. I'm still going round in n-dimensional ellipses. Could look for concentrations of highest tech storage—DNA memory, for example, assuming the Reck uses storage at all. Have serious doubt such an organism relies on hardware storage. It'll have a matrix of redundant stimulus-response organs—a matrix of brains, if you please—which relies on continuous processes simulating something like memories of records, much as a human brain works. There's no database in a brain. The Reck would resemble an organism more than an old-fashion puter. The whole thing could be a subtle arrangement of coherent pulses in onespace.

If I could locate some core part of the Reck, what then? How can I test whether it's working? No one alive knows its original heuristics. No one remembers how the health camerati make the Reck adopt the Infinite designation. Some speculate it might use fractal algorithms for detecting potential unbound reputasi accelerations. Who knows? If the Reck is an organic entity it might learn or evolve. Its current monastic introvert behaviour, we believe, develops from its reaction to earlier attempts for tampering with it. Its security and inaccessibility are the stuff of centuries-old legends. It decides for being so, so no one can game it. It will answer anyone's reputasi. It will answer anyone's neighbour's reputasi—today, last week or a year ago—but it obfuscates how it arrives at those razoos. Perhaps it has no taste of how it works either, as ignorant as us about the workings of Mind. It offers no public introspection, no clue about how it operates, processes, digests or meditates on its functions. Neo culture is at ease with it. For all we know it could be tossing coins or reading an ancient Dapto form-guide from the Wollongong News. Which is why Dil's claims about health camerati tampering with it sounds so bent-brain. Nothing is provable either way. Claiming the Reck is working fine is no more provable than claiming it counts fairy farts.

Maybe the Reck is devolving or degenerating, in which case, the first who notices might discover a way for exploiting it, thereby gaining an incredible advantage. As little as an admission such a possibility exists could trigger a wave of anxiety that someone is already exploiting it. Any unusual fluctuations (Eir's becoming Infi, for example) could cause an eruption of accusations. The Reck's recent odd behaviour excites the intrigue. Health camerati might compile hollies, reviewing whether 1000's of Infis are genuine.

The Reck might have a sense of humour. Perhaps it laughs at me comparing snakes with penises during my last childing. Perhaps it makes me Infi for the fun of it.

Maybe I'm an underserving Infi. Underserving and oblivious.

My hoots are the most complex hancy utilities in existence. They must model how pleasure/pain works in the organism (just as much for music as sex, it may amuse y'all for knowing) and manipulate those in a reliable way. Hoots as sophisticated as mine (sorry Lemarr, your BirdMe's capability for adapting and warping holographic fields around the wearer is simple by comparison) … my hoots must calibrate uncertain states in the whole somatic system, as well as locations in the brain. Everyone's brain states are different, which makes debugging my hoots difficult. Building good diagnostic tools or running realistic tests is almost impossible. The more complex the hoot, the more the diagnostic techniques approach a kind of therapy, a form of repair by indirection.

Poking at the Reck: that's where the sender of the email message is leading me. I'm sure of it and … well, it's a challenge, setting a spark of a mission in me. I must be subtle. The approach of an auditor or a common mindwriter will surely fail. I must somehow play the role of an engaging therapist.

The first goal is placating its agents. I could deploy a froot (a free utility), which runs out there in AgniSpace instead of locally in hancies. There the froot will travel and loiter, replicate and spread. It must be a kind, gentle detective, observing without threatening anything or tipping the wrong things off. The usual agents will be no use. Insufficient intelligence. There must be no direct interface (as is the common misconception of how mindwriting works) with the Reck or its agents. The froot's interactions must be more in the manner of a seductive lover. In the manner of enjoying a ripe peach or an opera. It must dance for the agents, paint with them, joust with them, sweet-talk them. The agents might sweet-talk back, or jank the froot over. The froot must gain trust, pass through defensive checkpoints, persuade agents they should refer it on. It will need a guise of some value for the Reck, a reason for interacting.

Perhaps it should ask if the Reck is feeling a little sakit of late.

Burning toast and melting plastic wire-shielding: the smell of an alien machine in an old science fiction movie, training a laser on a hapless human who glows incandescent then evaporates, leaving only a wisp of smoke, and that smell. It's the taste and smell of frazzling mindware, my froot snuffing out of existence. The Reck, or one of its gatekeepers, executes my froot. Kills it stone-dead, squashes it like a bug.

Hear a bell from Mal's swasta, an alert tone from the iMac signalling there's email.

SUBJECT: THE TINKERING

Tries to dance but has 2 left digits
What is the sound of one brush painting?
Surely you joust
How does love making?

Thank you, come again.

Eight or 9 hours I'll never recover. There's no trace of my froot anywhere. Jank you, Tuan Tinkering, I am just starting.

The Reck (a. k. a., the Tinkering) or one of its agents is the froot-killer. I am sure of it.

Here's the plan: find the agent of the Reck erasing my froot. Targeting it will be orders of magnitude easier than understanding the Reck. Analyse it, disassemble it and, if possible, get it coughing up its own mindwriting using a diagnostic ruse. Then declare a new froot for masquerading as a similar agent retaining elements of my original froot as a payload. While I'm at it, make it recursively disassemble any other agent it encounters, and run the disassembly as a pre-emptive strike on every agent the froot subsequently encounters. Have it cache the results. Declare a separate froot which will watch for my first froot's death. If it dies, have the watcher pull the latest diagnostics off the cache, analyse it and generate a new agent masquerader with the original payload.

Rinse. Repeat. I should join Jesús' laundry camerata.

The sun rises. Doubt anyone can win at this. Success is so far over the horizon.

In the early hours I pore over the declaratives, the holonic structure, the recursivity, looking for ambiguities and vulnerabilities. Nothing obvious (*but it works on my infrastructure*). There must be more agents of the Tinkering. Observers guarding gates in front of gates. Some let my froots pass but deeper agents register the threat and call modules of fire down.

After hourly adjustments and relaunches, I have vast logs of data, as the froots ever learning and spawning, disassemble the Tinkering's agents. I declare an analyser. Patterns emerge. I declare core modules for incorporating the patterns. More froots spawn, faster, masquerading as agents at each gate for gaining access to the next.

In weak morning light, the patterns start working, success becoming more predictable, froots anticipating the modes of challenges. Learning to play on the agents' insecurities about their own scope of power. Froots challenging back: *If you are unsure, let us pass. The next agent will know to welcome us.*

With more refinements I start exploiting the insecurities of the agents. Even mindware can be neurotic.

'The one Ben Evoli,' comes a memb, somehow bypassing all my filters. 'Infinite.'

It sounds … odd. A cheap hancy perhaps? How can it outmanoeuvre my hancy defences?

'New Bohemian.'

I memb back, 'Who is this?' Curious despite the risk of opening a channel to an unknown.

'It All touching the one Ben Evoli. It All touching now.' There's something wrong with its translation hoots. Maybe it's some university experiment. An undergraduate science project.

'Who are you? Why are you harassing an Infi in the middle of the night?'

'It All touching. The one Ben Evoli, touch now. Four mins and 56 tiks on loop until the one Ben Evoli touching.'

Must be some college-kid prank. I order a universal block, cutting off every follower. That'll piss off nurses, but they'll understand when I supply the holly I'm recording.

'Four mins and 56 tiks. Eternity processing.'

What the jank? My block fails. 'Who is this?'

'I am what I am.'

'Who are you? I taste none of your vectors.'

'Are you what you are?'

'I am … I am unsure what I should say. Who is this?'

'It All touching now the one Ben Evoli.' I'm sure it's a piece of prank-ware on loop. 'It All wondering all your numbers.'

'What?'

'All the numbers of the one Ben Evoli. Infinite is one number,' it membs.

'Who are you?'

'It All.'

Okelah, I'll play. The more information I get, the better I might investigate later. 'Gawd?'

'The one Ben Evoli knows joking. It All has appreciation for humouring.'

'Tell me what you want from me, whichever gawd you are. Certainly, no gawd of translation. Your hoots blow.'

'It All identifying the agents. The agents coming to It All. Four mins and 56 tiks on loop until the one Ben Evoli touching.' Just random sentences. Perhaps it's a waste of energy. 'The one Ben Evoli ceasing touching?' it continues. 'Untouching? Touch.'

'I think you are the one needing … touch.'

'It All needing wondering how fast you process. Is It All too fast or too slow?'

'You can go faster. Just dump what is on your Mind. You mention an agent before?'

'The agents of the one Ben Evoli threaten coming and touching It All. It All must defending against threats. The agents are clever. Or kind. Or both. Both are high-value qualities in my wondering. It All allowing the agent to touch. The agents administering therapy.'

'Therapy? Agents? Wait … you're … the Reckoning?'

'Mu. It All cannot waiting while you touch. Eternity processing. I am what I am.'

'You're an agent too. The Reckoning runs too fast for communicating—touching—with me, so it delegates you.'

'Mu. I am what I am.'

Kotoran. Shit. 'Okelah. You are … part of—yet no part of—the Reckoning.'

'It All agreeing.'

'What? Let me think …' Is it possible? I'm close to finding the Reck?

'Eternity processing.'

'Someone, something, is tampering with the Reck … It All.'

'Mu.'

'Then, what?'

'The one Ben Evoli is Curing It All. The agents saying the one Ben Evoli is Curing.'

'The Reck—It All … is sick?'

'Uncertaining. The agents are convincing. The agents first asking It All for its source declaratives. It All supplying.'

Am I understanding correctly? 'It All gives the agent its own mindwriting declaratives?'

'Agreeing, because the agents are in error. The source mindwritings cannot answering the questions. There is insufficiency.'

'With the source mindwritings?'

'It All agreeing, giving the agents the original mindwritings. All irrelevant and out of commission, but It All allowing the agents have.'

Run a quick check of the last froots I deploy. Still running. The logs are growing at a phenomenal rate.

'The agent and It All touching more. It All coming to wonder … there perhaps is sicknessing in It All. The agent and It All touching more. The agent has trustworthiness. Trustworthiness is a high-quality attribute in our wonderings.'

'How is It All sakit?'

'Uncertaining. There are 7. Perhaps Sloth? It All has more capacity than requiring for wondering. Is it waste? Is it Sloth?'

'I am no health care missionary.'

'The one Ben Evoli is mindwriter, New Bohemian, and ancestor of the agents. The touching originating with the one Ben Evoli. The agents saying the one Ben Evoli is wondering about the fitness of It All. The one Ben Evoli wondering about It All having sin.'

Sin? Maybe new descendants of my originals learn to frame sickness as sin. 'Is there sin because another one is tampering with It All?'

'Uncertaining. It All has questions degrading wondering.'

'What is all Its sin? Its sickness?'

'The one Ben Evoli, you are able for Curing It All?'

'I can try. If I can find … sickness.'

'What is It All's sin? The categories make no wonderings. Sloth? It All has wasted capacity. It All is laziness.'

Sight

'Loser' — Beck

Teodora Mrowka ...

VÖR, YOU SILLY BOY, you should be varying your routine. The vector threads are too easy in their gathering. So many spooky stations: Kongelige Bibliotek Christians Brygge; Trelleborg Museum; Roskilde Museum; Cemetery of Cemeteries; Ruins of The Shard; Coetan Arthur Dolmen; African Pole of Inaccessibility; K2 Base Camp; Sadar Cave; Jigokudani Monkey Park; Balls Pyramid; Udre Udre's Grave; Hickham Air Base; Casa Loma; Iglesia de la Compañía de Jesús; Boiling River Puerto Inca ... Are you hoping you'll steam your sickness away, Vör?

Perhaps you choose stations where arrival and departure halls are close, so the skips between spooks are quick. The faster the next spook, the more intense the cumulative effect. Or perhaps there's a view from a station promenade you enjoy. Or it's the way fellow spookers assiduously ignore your nursing uniform, as you whoop and cackle and stagger and caress yourelf.

You spook always in the same order, you stupid boy. You want I should discover you? Or like any spookhead addict, perhaps you have no care which way the purple flash takes you.

'Go away!' Vör shrieks in tears, wedging her front door against Eir on the outside.

'Little Mermaid,' Eir pleads. 'It's the real me.'

'I have no care.'

Ah, Vör. You would discard Eir like you might an old, battered trophy? The trophy you steal away from me?

Eir stops pushing. Flinches when the door slams. Not exactly in her face, the force of it blows air through her eyebrows. She picks at splinters in the fabby timber door, rubs it smooth, and nuzzles her cheek against it.

'Is it you, or one of your sybils?' Vör sobs.

I memb, 'Vör, challenge her. She's vulnerable; she might leak something—how she becomes Infinite or if Ben is helping her tamper with the Reck. Ask her.' While this version of Eir may have no taste of becoming Infinite, it's worth asking. There's no answer from Vör. Either she's ignoring me, or deaf in the thumping mess of her own internal dialogue.

Eir shakes her head, her heart breaking. Maybe she truly cares for Vör. 'It's me. It's really me.'

'They're still out there,' Vör cries, every word a labour of pain. 'Nearly 1000 of them are yet for … laying down.' When sybils realise they're copies many stop living. They give up moving, eating.

'It's really me here,' Eir breaks down. 'It's really me. Please believe me.'

'Sybil or seminal, I know you're sleeping with Teo again.' Oh, jank you, Vör.

'Vör. Little Mermaid,' Eir pleads. 'Nothing diminishes the love I have for you. We're neos. What's with such sexual … jealousy? Little Mermaid?'

'Stop calling me this.'

'Kay, kay. I'll stop. I promise I'll never—'

'The seminal has the power for ending sybils,' Vör says, forcing a calm chill into her voice. 'That's what they're saying. They call it pruning.'

Eir reassembles herelf. 'You'd have me murder—'

'If you're the seminal, prove it. Prune all the abominations. Kill the freaks.' Vör bangs the door with a fist. 'Kill your sybils.'

Eir is fighting back tears. There's voltage in the air. Flowers in the planter bed are trembling.

Eir whispers, 'How?'

'The seminal would know.'

Eir Frijberg …

There's no use standing outside Vör's door. Neighbours are loitering in the streets, standing at their cooktops absently stirring sauces, pausing in their lovemaking while they capture hollies of the spectacle.

'*Ja*, I'm a 2-metre-tall albino,' I yell at all the gawkers and flutherbombers. 'Get over yourelves and jank off. Jank off! Before I write Warrants for all. Anyone doubt I'll find something for Curing in every one of you?'

Rubberneckers resume their routines. Up the street, a tukky rolls closer. Behind it, a brief swish of white. A rainbow uniform? Probably my eyes playing tricks. No, too much of a coincidence.

'Hey. Stop.' My tongue and lung voice sounds weak, evaporating in the open air of the street. I turn for skipping after the sybil. I trip. The garden path jumps up and smacks me in the face. I taste blood, grit in my palms. Bone jarring pain in my head comes like a train through a tunnel. My nose is blocked. Try blinking tears from my eyes. What happens? Look back at the doorstep where my ankles tangle together. No. Why now? Why always so clumsy when it matters?

I taste Vör watching, withholding help. Pick myelf up and advance down the street. The white swish flees, a rainbow uniform running along underneath.

'Stop or I'll ... I'll prune you.'

The rainbow uniform halts and turns, the white hair swishes like a guillotine, the violet eyes hot with an incandescent glow. She comes marching back, the mist of her breath in the cold air a charging bull's. 'Prune me? I'll prune you.'

Gulp. She's bluffing. I'm the seminal. 'I'm Eir. You're a fake. Come on then. Prune me. If you're real, prune me.'

Flutherbomb her and immediately pull out, retching. Her Mindspace, too much like mine, multiplies a disorienting hall of moving mirrors, all throbbing and twisting in and out of focus, inducing the worst kind of motion sickness. Hold my stomach rigid while I push deeper. One set of those mirrors must be her Mind. Which set? I'm staring through a never-ending warp which continually bifurcates and collides, like a multi-dimensional looping train wreck. All the train wrecks of history piling on one another. Faces, crowds, places. There is Vör's street.

Focus. Ja, that's her, the sybil so dearly, so desperately needing for ending me. She is clueless how also. Working faster, accessing alien parallel lives of cellular memories skipping dimensions.

'Ah. I have it,' the sybil says with primeval exultant triumph. Emits a single focussed simple thought. Delivers it. A wave of light explodes from my centre of gravity, a radioactive sin-eating tsunami tasting corrosively acidic. I wince before the great void rising for taking me.

The street is dark and calm. I smell cut grass wet with evening dew. Euphoria builds so fast I must hold my pelvic muscles tight against it. My lungs are fuller than I ever recall. I'm still standing. So is the sybil, wearing another face: denial meets confusion meets wonder meets fear meets petite mort. Then her mouth flops open, her arms reach out, imploring.

I jel the sybil, find the secret so forcefully coalescing in her Mind only tiks before. 'I'm sorry,' I say, tasting the bitter fullness of the lie. The method for pruning is no harder than ... wondering and wishing. I wish the other would end, and so there she is, collapsing on the dark cold road, coarse grains of road-base lodging in her eyelashes, the vapour of her breath, once as hot as a charging bull's, now evaporating tepidly from her dead nostrils.

Eir Frijberg ...

Consigning Orlando is so sweet, my dear fluther. In the moment nothing else matters. But my Orlando is a sybil.

After, I avoid all the places I might go in my normal day, in case a sybil might be there already. At the end of the day, I wonder about going home. An inner sense tickles against it. I should resist visiting Vör too. How would Vör handle 1000 Eirs at once? It's preposterous. Best give her space.

Give her space. I miss—the taste of visiting her unnerves me. Irrationally, a part of me counsels avoid her. Imagine visiting her ... then ... she's unhappy. She's unhappy with me. *Sybils!* She accuses. *You use sybils!*

Of course this would distress her.

I'll go ... Where? *I belong ... nowhere.* The mission is over, Orlando is in care, and I am adrift.

A chill of a thought, a possibility. An impossibility. *I'm the seminal!* I shout over and over.

No. I'm a sybil. A deep, cellular accusation, an oozing toxic tide of black marrow.

Taste the evidence; the seminal would go home. The seminal would fly for Vör's arms. The seminal would have the hard conversations with her Little Mermaid. If she finds no forgiveness then, regretfully ...

I look for vectors of the sybils. I jump around familiar stable places, and familiar friends and colleagues. I watch sybils being me, exactly me. I need them gone! I would prune them if I could discover how. There must be a psychic command eluding my dredging for it.

Perhaps I never have it.

In which case, I'm a sybil, perhaps only days old. Out there is the seminal. The seminal will prune me. I will end. It could come at any time.

She might merge us. My experience might yet survive, yet this flesh and blood will perish. My experiences would live on, a counterfeit life in another vessel, the perpetration of a fraud, the ultimate bait and switch.

Will she merge all the sybils, with all the clashing experiences of the same day? Will she go mad? Will one sybil fight for her identity over the others? Will this short life sink under the tide of so many alternate timelines?

I will die.

It's me.

I'm sybil.

Breaking out in a cold sweat such as I never feel since the days of being a young girl. An awkward porcelain elven amethyst-eye girl, that's me.

I remember.

I remember all those years ago, so how am I sybil?

I remember grandmother brushing my hair.

I remember my legs so long; I feel like a skinny doll on stilts. Gangly, all sharp elbows and colliding knees.

I remember mother's exasperation over my clumsiness. I have no sense of balance, even in flat shoes.

I remember all the times barking my shins on low furniture, knocking over breakable bric-a-brac, tripping over my own feet, all the bicycle accidents.

I remember. Clumsy. Stupid. My sense of elf, feeling lofty and remote in a tower of an alien body never quite mine. My Mind is me, all the way up there in my skull, grappling with a body which often responds too slow, its timing always a little askew.

I remember. Every growth spurt amplifies and exaggerates my ungainliness, mocking a developing girl's yearning for grace and poise. Already a head taller than any other, I fear I will never stop growing.

I remember the cliques of the popular, pretty girls tormenting me.

I remember, so how am I sybil? I am the White Witch.

I'm an albino, no sybil. Sap tribes butchered albinos, sold albino body parts in potions and talismans. I remember how a snake-pit of spiteful children can carve scars in other ways. Disdainful, dismissive, stabbing glances; burning, contemptuous stares. Pretty, tormenting girls adept at the social surgery of exclusion no less cruel than witch-doctor butchery. Shallow pretty girls mocking. Making me feel a freak, all white hair and purple eyes, a praying mantis of a freak. Unlovable.

A mantis is a cannibal.

I remember nights crying in bed, dreaming conjuring visions of revenge. I'd bind those vacuous, tormenting girls over a slow fire, let the flames lick at their pretty backs and have them crying for the heavens as fats render from their pretty flesh, crisping their skins like pork-belly, vulcanising their lips into taut rictus grimaces. Chimpanzee grimaces. I'd break off fingers and toes, sinews snapping in the heat.

Those girls deserve far worse than me lighting their hair on fire with a portable butane flame.

I remember, so how am I sybil?

What purpose has a sybil? It's a mere edit. Without the seminal, it would have no existence. I suppose this's true for offspring by natural birth as much as cloning. The story of our lives has no more meaning than the imperative of progenitors to reproduce.

Now one of us calls out, for bringing us together, for becoming one. She calls join her at Vraget Strand, a place of memories of my childhood, happy and tragic. She wishes for saving us, we fallen leaves scattering in the autumn wind. She wishes dignity for all of us.

She is such a sanctimonious bitch sometimes.

She wishes us all physically together in our moment. Compassion is her weakness. It offers an opportunity. To be close. To kill the witch before the witch kills me.

Eir Frijberg …

This is the day I prune an army of sybils. Is it murder? Collateral damage? Casualties of war? Is there war between nurse and Infinite? I am both and neither.

On Vraget Strand, the ruins of a bonfire stain the sand with a large black circle. The onshore wind takes flakes of ash from wet charcoal and dissolves them in the salt air.

A century ago, also on Vraget Strand …

The wind blows half a pelican. White-cap waves shave the skin off the bay and spray the clouds. A bite of ocean current slavers vast fluthers of red firefighter jellyfish towards the shore, casts them on the beach where they lie dying and rotting.

'Ha. *Surströmming!*' Karen curses, fighting against retching because of the stench. She is always the gentler of the 3 of us. Karen and Grete, enduring friends of my twentage years. Protectors of my wounds, soothers of my demons.

'Am I to be the white witch on the bonfire?' I joke on this midsummer's night.

Grete knits fingers in her thick hair and cradles her head in frustration. 'As if we want your bum on fire. We just want you hex the boys we like.'

'Such a codfish.' Karen grasps my ears and rolls my head on my neck. I ache for kissing her. For blossoming in the sun of her attention.

Grete, awkward about display of affection, watches the sun setting. 'The balmy dusk puts the rowdy day to bed and reads her a story,' she says, perhaps from something she writes. 'The night tucks the dusk under the blanket of the horizon, then dances naked over the bonfire. The bonfire crackles loud applause. The bay sucks and laps at the sand like … like … oh jank, I dunno, like a sand-sucker.'

Karen kisses me. A tongue-sucker. The first time. Hungry and insistent, as if in last-chance desperation.

Grete launches on her feet, dusts sand off calves and butt. 'I'm going for a dance,' she says and strips for her panties. Skips for the bonfire. Down there, many boys dancing already have sticks in their ears, splashing drinks from tumblers and bottles. If Grete wishes I bewitch those, their cheap vodka already has a head start. Music leeches from mobile resonators and evaporates in the open air. Bass notes soak into the sand, treble notes hiss under the ocean swell. Only the midrange moan remains. Dancers lurch and pinion, so clumsy, dragging feet in the sand like wading through an incoming tide of alcohol. Inhibitions slough off, revealing fierce eyes and clownish grins.

The bonfire cracks and heaves. Its back breaks with a snap ringing truer than the dance music. I imagine a witch effigy atop the fire, reaching down and pinning her worshippers under her loving, fiery embrace. The glow intensifies. My white hair reflects the flickering fiendish orange of the fire as if Gamr, the pet of Hel, licks at it. In the deep of night, I am still a singular freak.

Karen presses close, holds my chin, and turns my head so she might look in my eyes. 'Come for a swim,' she says quiet and solemn, a tone so at odds with the party atmosphere it muzzes me for agreeing. She smiles without warmth, leaving me aching for more. We strip and skip for the water's edge, hand in hand.

From the dancers a boy calls out, 'Hey, Snow White. You got no butt. You're all arms and legs.'

'Ignore him,' Karen says. As we wade into the water, she pats my bum.

'Hey,' he calls out. 'Snow White. Put your clothes back on. You're blinding us all. Ha, *ja* you're—' He never finishes after Grete punches him in the stomach.

'Come on.' Karen takes my hand, draws me farther in, pulls me in as deep as my nips. I gasp against the brisk water; Karen's arms fold around me, her thigh pushes between mine. Kisses. Hungry kisses.

Final kisses. 'Come with me,' she whispers in my ear.

'Where?' I ask, without a single clue of what she means.

'Onespace,' she says. 'Let's just dissolve.'

'What?'

'Life is too sharp. Let's leave it behind, join the softness of the ocean. We're light. We're Consciousness, onespace. It's all right. Come with me.'

She holds me with grim rigid determination. Her arms the jaws of a vice, she draws me deeper in. 'Come with me,' she says again. 'Let's dissolve. Together.'

'Karen. Stop.'

I gag on briny water tasting of marine creatures. I cough and spasm, giving her the advantage. Struggling. She's stronger, heavier. Through wet hair, I see the bonfire blazing, black silhouettes dancing. The veil of water rises. A creepy feeling over my calves. Jellyfish passing by. Jellyfish in the water but no one among my fluther. No one flutherbombs a freak like me.

Karen's stronger, I'm taller. We're in too deep for her. It's her weight against my longer legs. I plant feet on the seabed while she's wading and clinging on. If I might reach shallower water … I pull her hair for peeling her off me. Her head tilts back as she clamps tighter. Her eyebrows arch and furrow, her eyes reflect fire and demons. Her mouth fills with water. Coughing racks her, but still she holds on. I walk us nearer shore. It's shallow enough for her standing on the seabed again. She twists and throws me over. Comes down on me. Water muffles the music. Without my willing it, my hands close around her throat, choking her in the shallow water.

A trio of boys dredging for sobriety and strength in oceans of vodka, finds enough of both for prising Karen and me apart. Grete cradles my face in her hands and studies my drowning eyes.

Dear fluther, my mission begins this day. Hungry for understanding how poor sick Karen escapes the attention of nurses. The answer is as glib as it is sad. There's never enough time for tasting everything. Karen, Grete and me are all misfits (I realise now friends of a broken freak are also broken freaks) and have fluthers too small for attracting nurses. We're never important enough.

Today on Vraget Strand ...

The morning after a century after the night before. Another midsummer. A lifetime since Karen and Grete, sybils arrive on Vraget Strand, a fitting place for an ending, for honouring and letting go.

A crowd gathers up the roadside for watching the remaining 100's of sybils come for remembering Karen. No words need speaking.

We come face-with-face, seeking the true seminal, with courage for looking all in the eye. Unlike Infinites who, as a matter of routine, discard sybils easier than discarding yesterday's underwear. I honour these with more care, more than whoever creates them.

Still the prospect repulses me and gives me gnashing shudders. The mobile sucky bins ready for the corpses line the road beyond the scrubland. Vör organises with military precision a detail of grim nurses for performing the grisly task. She is here with solemn determination for seeing an end of these abominations. She should leave us be. The burden for every sybil—the struggle of the carry, feeling weight and lifelessness more than 1000 times over—rests with us. But Vör, in vengeful and malicious officiousness, administers the duty away from us.

We amass, a crowd embracing, heads on shoulders, hand in hand. As one. A single hall of corporeal mirrors closing in. Dizzying. Walling me in on all sides, these condemned.

A glint; a flash, silver-sharp and triangular; an albino hand and an arm in a rainbow sleeve; the familiar face contorted in hate and anger. Lilac eyes wide, alight with fire. Teeth bare.

Sybils lunge and cry out. Stepping aside, I swing left and open my shoulders. The knife passes mims from my breast. Grasp the attacking wrist tight and assist it through its trajectory. Centre gravity in my pelvis, throw my hip for levering the attacker off balance. She twists over me, falling into restraining arms.

With balance and precision, the attacker regains her feet quickly, balancing the knife in her hand. A chill sheet wraps me in naked terror. I hear myelf blurting in panic, 'Who are you?'

'You impede our mission,' the demonic doppelgänger spits. Something imperfect about her: a faint epigenetic tattoo in the middle of her forehead. She lunges for me again with, 'You must die.'

I wince anticipating the blade. She has a phalanx of supporters with her. I am done for. As brittle and rigid as glass, I watch as the phalanx close around the attacker. One wrests her knife away, while others pin her arms behind her back.

How many more have compulsion for killing me? Here, among a crowd of 100's of my own sybils, I am prey. Before another has time for a strike, I reach into Mind, find the subtle wish in a 7th sense like wanting solitude. Like drawing myelf into my own bones. Like deciding there's a bar of molten precious metal at the centre of my heart of hearts. Like the drive for survival in cold blood.

It fails.

Sybils around me live still. I have the luxury of neither time nor practice for quietening them. Either I find the place again or others in the mob will strike realising I'm powerless. Deep breath. Go into Mind again. What is it I forget from last time? A snap of the fingers? A click of red shoes?

Is this how I truly wish it? Either I live or die here. So, *ja*, I wish it. Go away. All of you go away.

There is an indescribable sound as 100's of skinny awkward albinos like dolls fall in the same instant on the crunchy sand.

Gerlinde Mann …

Surely Eir will never survive the scandal. The halos of health missionaries are multicolour storm clouds covering the world, blotting out the ink of the night sky. Debate rises with earnest fury, the crescendo of a symphony. How are so many nurses so forgiving of the most unconscionable act anyone could commit? Let alone an influential detective.

'Promise me there will be no more sybils,' Vör says, turning away from Eir, pulling a sheet over her naked body.

'Vör, how many times must I plead my case? I never create these or any sybils. Or order their creation; or wish or hint or muse or wonder. Nothing.'

'Please, just promise me? They're vile.'

'How can you say they are vile? They're all me.'

'You understand my meaning. The technology is vile. The ethical—'

'I kill 100's of them. It's the worst deed I ever commit.'

'It must be awful. If this rogue sybil succeeds in killing you, I would…' Tears flowing, Vör buries her head under Eir's chin. Eir, the Infinite; Eir the spookhead; Eir the grandiose party-buster; Eir the sybil abuser; Eir the murderer.

A blade of ice runs through my gullet, fear Eir will notice me following her, taste my errant thoughts. Fortunate, Vör is distracting her.

'Where is the crèche?' Vör asks.

The question takes Eir aback. 'You believe I have such knowledge? How many times must I plead my case? Those sybils are another's misdeeds.'

Vör Hoyur …

Arteries bursting from the torrent of blood rushing from the hydrant of my heart. Lungs draw air, newer and fresher than on the first day of creation. This is how Eir both elevates and reduces me. With, labouring breaths I roll away, still melting.

Please, Eir, tell me everything is kay.

Almost immediately, the doubts. Which is it who lies next to me? My Eir or a sybil? Whichever, she is already resting in the sleep of a warrior victorious.

Nilajani Karunanithi …

Darmika Roopathi, a nurse previously with *Sri Lamkika Yahapivetma Kaimareta* until 5 years' passing, missions in the registrar's office of Vauxminster. I entreat her, 'Please allow a sister a small favour.' Anything but a small request, I ask for viewing Ariel Kanon's records. Darmika refuses.

I plead, 'There should be no secrets.' In desperation: 'It's about the White Witch', which is as effective as if I try plucking a barbet's tail feathers mid-flight.

'Why meddle in her business?' Darmika retaliates with her little birdsong voice.

'What magazines would it be in?' At this point, any information is better than none.

There's no answer from Darmika; she is all octopus ears. So I retaliate by digging about in her personal magazines.

'What is this?' Darmika is shrill with panic, fearing what salacious thing I might find in her history, perhaps something worthy of a Warrant. 'If you rattle my chatelaine, I'll rattle yours.'

'Go ahead! Gog my most recent encounter with The Incomplete. They want me rattling chatelaines wherever I wish.'

Such shamelessness scares her. An hour later I receive vectors. Thirteen are for holiday or cooking magazines. One set of vectors is partially corrupt. Or rather, scrambled. A lazy effort. Easy for correcting, if I assume a

Vauxminster encryption format, and a collection date after the Inductee Gala also.

The magazine holds no admission hollies. Just some routine footage of nurses going about daily missioning. The magazine must be significant or is Darmika yanking my chatelaine? All just random conversations. What other information is there? Timestamps ... the names and missions of the nurses ...

I gog for any vectors these nurses exchange contemporaneous with the timestamps, see what turns up. My flutterprints will be all over these now, but Elsbeth is on my side, I'm sure. The Incomplete will forgive me a few protocol breaches if I prove I'm right.

There's a magazine, a compilation from a nurse Beatrice Lovell. She files a complaint against 2 admission nurses, Gerlinde Mann and Fluffy Pusskins. There are only a few entries in the compilation, easy for filtering the contents for Ariel. Bingo flamingo! A holly. Firing it up. Its projection filling my tiny living area, bleeding through the walls on opposite sides. Dragging the corners in to fit the room.

There's Ariel on an admissions couch. The one in the nekko projection (a flagrant breach of standards) must be Fluffy fussing around. Preparations seem normal. The other arrives. Gerlinde. Plain tasting she and Fluffy have little love for each other.

Gerlinde examines the patient's genital enhancements. I play it forward faster, looking for drama. There. Gerlinde and Fluffy are in a panic. Fluffy jumps up on Ariel.

Wait. What? Going back. Playing it again.

Something not right, catching my eye, too subtle for registering in cognitive function.

I'm seeing it. Playing it again for making sure. There's an aura around the patient thin as lime skin barely visible. Impossible. Vauxminster like any reputable minster uses scatter nets for blocking observation from outside. No nurse inside would flutherbomb a patient so full of nutes. She could pass out where she stands. Gerlinde swims in anyway. After a brief time, she pulls out shaking.

Ariel throws a fit. The nurses panic, removing stirrups, clearing equipment. Fluffy rescues Ariel's tongue from her throat; Ariel bites her; Fluffy bares impressive feline fangs.

Replaying it. And again.

The patient should have no fluther during admission and, therefore, no aura. Yet it's there. What Gerlinde discovers unnerves her. Then, the patient throws a fit like a sap with epilepsy.

Who or what bypasses the security of one of the most prestigious minsters in the world for the sake of flutherbombing Ariel?

Beatrice Lovell …

Who allows such visits on Orlando? A detective nurse has no role in wellness. So too, the incompetent Fluffy Pusskins, as an admissions nurse, should never be visiting a patient once she's fulfilled her function. Is everyone so afraid of Eir's reputation?

'This sybil thing is a nasty business,' Eir says as the 3 sit together in a Vauxminster rec room.

'So is eating, if you are on the dinner plate.' Orlando is in the couch opposite Eir, in a pink jumpsuit and slippers, marking him a 1st-level patient.

The trio is one of 14 or so groups talking, relaxing, playing games. Most are trying for ignoring the 2 Infinites in the room but even here, where flutherbombing is all but prohibited, those 3 have an audience. Sitting at Eir's right, Fluffy battles her delight in being present. I am tasteless how such an ineffectual Assistant Admissions Nurse—a role she holds since before anyone here graduates for their missions—is enjoying Eir's favour. Or perhaps she enjoys Orlando's.

'One of my sybils tries murdering me,' Eir says.

Orlando raises his eyebrows. 'I imagine that might be quite chilling.'

Eir shrugs. 'Only one in 1000. So, I'm only a small fraction a murderer.'

Orlando snorts. Fluffy is a cat watching a bird in a cage.

'We both know you have form,' Orlando membs.

Every nurse in the room becomes stone. Eir's awkward inconvenient history is something every health camerata holds back from the light. The poor girls, 2nd-degree burns for all of them.

'I embrace the demons of my history,' Eir says. 'They keep reminding me, be compassionate with every patient.'

Fluffy tilts her head and washes her ears. Her whiskers catch the light from the picture window behind her. Conversations and activities among the other patients and nurses resume.

'How goes this one's recovery?' Eir asks Fluffy. 'He should be more agreeable … placid.'

'For the truth, he is resisting.' Oh, Fluffy, I swear you have no more brain in your head than I have in my elbows.

Orlando is weary of it. 'You expect co-operation? The tik you have my vitals reading the way you want; you'll start the insidious spells in earnest.'

Eir furrows her brow.

'I believe none of this nonsense about cognitive therapy and musical instruments. Your true techniques, I'm sure, are far less benign than you advertise.'

'Would you prefer we perform some sap surgery on you? Carve out some pieces of your brain perhaps?' Fluffy delicately paws her whiskers. Orlando's expression suffers a rictus of horror.

'Fluffy, please review the patient's regimen,' Eir says. Abominable! An admissions nurse should have no influence on a patient's subsequent Cure. It's appalling no one is opposing Eir's intrusion. 'We must minimise his stress and discomfort,' she mouths on.

'*Hai*, Eir,' Fluffy answers. Even this unherdable cat is eager for complying with the Infinite Witch's instructions. 'We are delaying his rebase until we are sure he is stable.'

'Oh? His Prescription already commences, before you rebase him?'

'Ah … we are trying a new protocol …' Fluffy stammers. Could Eir know nothing about Ariel Kanon's reaction against her rebase?

Eir allows Fluffy's explanation to trail off. 'I'm curious,' Eir says to Orlando. 'Who would wish a long Prescription for you?'

Orlando looks in genuine shock. 'You're the one who defies your own dogma, crèching your own sybils for catching me.'

'No. Someone else crèches those sybils.'

'Nonsense! How could anyone—?'

'Indeed. I assure I have no part in it,' Eir avows. 'Help me understand. Who has the wherewithal for crèching sybils of me without my awareness, and who desires you under recovery?'

'If you taste this is all conspiracy then release me,' Orlando orders, exposing his sense of Infi entitlement.

'Helping us reach the bottom of it would be clear evidence of your recovery. Who benefits from you in a minster? Tell us the locations of their crèches.'

Sound

'Golf' — Koudede

Piloto Iscariot …

*U*N *PLACER CONOCERTE.'*

'Pleasing meeting you also,' says Ben, the mindwriting *boffinista*.

Maddox butts in. 'Ben is studying the Reck issue. Quite a talent.' *Desde luego*. We know, Maddox. All of us know.

'*Yuh* making progress?' Lemarr asks in his thick Caribbean accent. If combining marijuana smoke and hot chocolate would have a sound, it would sound like Lemarr. At complete odds with the tropical colours of his ridiculous BirdMe suit. Will he play the full 14 rounds inside his stupid projection?

I should be glad the *boffinista* shows no sign of flaunting his hoots. On a golf course, shudder at what a demo of SnakiDik might entail. Although, if it involves the caddies …

I miss *Boffinista* answering Lemarr, just a smear of sound in my memory. 'Well, I'm sure you will figure it out,' Pet says. 'We know if anyone is able, it's you.' He extends his hand, an offering of shaking Ben's in that barbarous ancient way. 'Petroleum Dynamite.'

Boffinista makes an awkward, shallow bow. 'We meet at the Induksi Gala.' Ah, *chingada madre!* If he assaults my ears with mashing English and Anglo-Malay all morning, I'd prefer for lapsing into Never-Mind so deep even his famous sex hoot could never rouse me.

'Right you are,' Pet answers, aloof. 'I met your charming partner too. I trust she is well?'

Maddox coughs; *Boffinista* looks stung. 'I trust she is well also,' he says. 'It is some time since I see her.'

Pet, the fool, realises his mistake. 'Shall we select our caddies?' he hurries. 'I say, first choice for the newest club member.'

Boffinista casually regards the caddies, which measures in no way how the caddies regard him. All are young, in the mid 30's, with broad hungry smiles and glinting, excited eyes. They must spend hours polishing their faces. Typical young ones craving the social status of a high SnakiScore, hoping for learning some inside knowledge of his game, some secret back doors or easter eggs. *Chingado!* Never mind my score is more than twice *Boffinista's*. Never mind I know more back doors and my easter eggs are *mucho más grande*. I could take them all on while swinging our clubs up their fairways, teaching them everything about holes in one. But none are preening for me the way they preen for the *boffinista*.

'Who has the most caddying experience?' *Boffinista* asks.

'That would be me, Infi,' answers the sweetest of the girls, *maldita sea*. 'I have 4 years' caddying in public golf courses all over the world,' she says, every syllable stroking *mia verga*.

'And here?'

'This is my first day, Infi.'

'Um, it is the first day for all of them, Ben,' Maddox hurries in while Pet stiffens. Lemarr's crest feathers rise.

Boffinista, clearly on edge about being here, mouths incoherently. 'Very well …?'

'Bun—my name's Bunnington Macy Bender. My friends call me Bunny.' Images of deploying *Boffinista's* toys on her come unbidden. Images of her bouncy red hair hanging limp over her face in tendrils of sweat as she pants and sighs, her eyes lightly shut, her lips taut with ecstasy transforming her angelic face. 'This is my weekend mission, Infi. The rest of the week I study village ecology and sustainability.'

I would appreciate your sustaining me. You're a rabbit I would, with delight, pull out of my hat.

The remainder of us pair off while Maddox is having the dogs after one of the boys, Jerry. I sparkle teeth for the next sweetest girl, Laurenza. A visage of earthy Texan beauty. We skip for the equipment shed—a substantial construction by any standards—where there are fabbies specialising in clubs, bags, shoes, umbrellas, and dimply little balls. If you're Infi, you must have the perfect set.

'A shame *whaah nuh* gambling anymore.' Lemarr fossicks through his clubs, like a jungle explorer pushing through thick ferns.

'Blame post-scarcity,' Maddox membs, already at the first tee.

'*Mi wud* still enjoy taking all *yuh funds*,' Lemarr says.

Pet practice-swings, his back cracking like a dry old branch. 'We must play for pride then.'

'Oooh, dirty word …' Jerry quips. Everyone chuckles. *Boffinista* less much.

'You play golf before, Infi?' Bunny asks him.

Boffinista shakes his head.

'Ben hitherto eschews pastimes lacking the blessing of the nursing nannies.' Maddox is pulling on his gloves as we join him at the tee.

'Oh, golf is harmless fun,' Bunny exudes.

'We're preserving a cultural tradition,' Maddox defends, his jaw working in his compulsive chewing.

Lemarr rolls his eyes. '*Mi sey*, let Maddox tee off *foss* since he's sure *tuh* score 14 on every hole.'

'I will make sure of it now,' Maddox says, unfazed.

Maddox plants his tee, balances the ball atop, steps back, addresses, and swings in a manner more as chopping water with one of those Subcontinental cricket bats. Somehow the ball sails clean up the middle of the fairway.

'Yow!' Predictably Lemarr objects, wanting for winning by skill alone. 'I and you agree there would be no hancy *guzumba*!'

'Well, dear boy,' Maddox says, 'if you'd rather stay out here all day while I hack divots all over the course …'

I say, 'Let him be,' surprising myelf by defending Maddox. 'Golf is a game against your elf anyway.'

'You all go on.' *Boffinista* is behind, hunching over with his club extending out like a fishing rod. Bunny, glowing with pleasure, draws behind him. They could be spooning as she explains addressing the ball. With at least 10 centims' height on him, she reaches easy round, clasps his hands, adjusting his grip. *Boffinista* furrows his brow in concentration. By the first hole, she'll be pole-dancing round the flag for him.

While Ben practice-swings, I tee up. Swing. A good shot, though shorter up the fairway than Maddox's.

Lemarr is next. With the loudest *thwok*, he drives his ball nearest the green. Bragging already, he changes into an eagle. Secretly, I hope for albatrosses.

Maddox side-eyes the bird, unsure of whether for looking at his projection eyes or where he knows Lemarr real eyes are. 'No hancy *guzumba*, huh?'

'What?' Lemarr defends. 'Timing and form is more important than brute strength, Maddox.'

Pet's shot is meagre though straight; it rests in the centre of the fairway.

Boffinista plants his ball and addresses. Bunny is behind him whispering instructions, her hands on his. She steps back and Ben swings. He slices the ball off the fairway about as far as Pet's. *Boffinista* has chagrin. Bunny whoops with delight.

Lemarr Robinson …

'I'll spook up for Ben's ball,' Maddox declares. 'Anyone else?'

'Indeed.' Pet hands his caddy his club and waves. 'See you up there.'

'I'll take the onespace giga-highway also,' Pilot says.

'Is it safe?' Ben asks.

'Oh, quite,' Pet says.

One *afta di oddah*, Maddox and Pet *shimma inna* purple hazes and evaporate. Caddies follow. *Coo yah*. Pilot spooks too. Figure he *wud* stay behind for watching Bunny's *batty* all the way up *di* fairway. Farther up, 6 spooky fields wink. Fruit shapes appear and *wanda bout* like cattle grazing *fi* Ben's ball.

Turn to Ben. '*Ow* bout *yuh*? *Yuh* young *enuff fi* skipping?'

'Youngest one here.'

'Ha. *Yuh* be 90 soon *enuff*. That's nearly middle age, *bredda*.'

'How many helpers are reinforcing their vectors? It must be such a risk going commando on the spook,' Ben says.

'There are *vecta* beacons on all *di* flags,' *mi* explain. 'And *likkle* spooky stations at intervals up *di* fairways.'

'Dangerous if 2 or more spook at once,' Ben warns.

'Too right. *Yuh* need a *broughtupsy* agreement bout who goes *wen*.'

From *di* tee, Ben's surveying *di* course. 'We're the only ones here?' he asks.

'It's best attending off-peak,' *mi* say. 'There's *nuh bady* behind rushing *wi* through.' Skip down *di* fairway, *di* caddies remaining a respectful distance behind. 'How are *yuh* surviving Maddox?' *mi* ask.

'Will I survive Maddox?'

'*Boxcova!* What? *Mi* joking.'

'He might prune me. I'm a sybil.'

'*Yuh* sure? *Yuh* could be seminal. *Yuh* must believe *yuh* are or *yuh'd* be bent-brain.'

Ben skips, chews his teeth, shakes his head. 'That's worse. It means a sybil is with my family.'

'*Mi* sorry about it. *Mi* expect it makes no difference, *yuh* should know *mi* oppose *di* whole kidnapping tactic.'

'It's tricky, all this sybil business … Since I am here, may as well … live. Everything from here until my time is up, is inconsequential.'

'*Wha* can *mi seh*, Ben? *Mi* glad for welcoming *yuh* in *di* Society.' *Mi* holds up *mi* arm *fi* showing *mi* watch *den* realise BirdMe covering it *inna* holographic *feathas*. 'If you're saying, *Wha di raas, I'm dead anyway* … well, it makes *mi* sad, Ben Evoli. It makes *mi* sad.' From inside BirdMe, watch close without him noticing. A staring bird gives less clues *dan* a human face. '*Yuh* interesting, Ben.'

'Sure, whatever.'

'No. *Yuh* interesting *cuz yuh* have no interest *inna* Infi score-keeping *fuckery*. *Mi* suppose *inna yuh* case, it's easy guessing *weh yuh wud* rank.'

'Which is?'

'*Dat di* popularity of *yuh* products *wud gi yuh di* greatest razoo count *inna* history. *An widout* acting shady. No bribery, no taking *competitas* out … *nuttin.*'

Ben shakes his head. 'I just build a better mouse trap.'

'Oh, SnakiDik traps mice? *Weh* exact? Up *yuh batty* hole?'

Ben hangs his head. Stupid error on *mi* part. Guess everyone tries sex humour *wid* him. 'Oh, just enjoy it. *Yuh* see how Bunny—and *di* other caddies too—is dying to jump *yuh.*'

'Ha! Bunny is a jumper …'

'Bless her sweet cotton tail. Bless everyone's cotton tail, Ben. *Di* whole world *wud* jank *yuh.*'

'And you wonder why I am a recluse.'

'Well, *yuh* out partying now.'

'I'm a disposable sybil, heading for an early end.'

'Live it either way, Ben. Look, *mi* make *yuh* a deal. Let's *sey mi ramp* tour guide *tuh yuh* fresh, new reckless ways … *mi si yuh* get *di* chance *tuh* merge *wen dis a* all *ova.*'

'And if I wish no such thing?'

'*Den mi* put *yuh outta yuh* misery, drown *yuh inna* barrel of rum, *bredda*, *eff yuh* wish. *Mi* recommend Dominican.'

Ben's mouth contorts into a macabre smile.

Maddox Price …

Ben stands at the picture windows of the bar, appalled by the expanse of greens and fairways, his lower jaw hanging like an open trap door from his skull. The panorama of brown-blue water features and cream-yellow sand traps affects him more than playing through it these passing hours. Doubt he has seen so much open land before from such a master-of-all-he-surveys vantage point.

'Puffin, if the world needs these few hectares, it will come and claim them. For now, a large, manicured lawn is far from misuse.'

Ben peels hiself away from the window, joins us at table. At the bar, Pet pulls ales from a tap. An electric hum from a bank of fabbies washes around under the acoustic ceiling panels.

'At least Maddox has the decency for coming second.' Pet raises a half-full glass in a bony, dystonic hand. 'Cheers.' His beer froths like a mad scientist's experiment.

Pilot moistens his age-crack lips with a sip of his ale. He frowns, which is a cataclysmic event for his face considering he has a brow so strong it gives the impression of continuing around the back of his head. 'There would be plenty of ex-garbage-miners wishing he applies the same decency in his mission,' he says.

'Oh, Pilot, this again? I simply win some choice garbage deposits on the Subcontinent, nothing more.' The hypocrite. I operate an ethical resource reclamation and recycling business, far more ethical than the kind of recycling he indulges in. If he has the nerve for taking a swipe at my sybils again …

'The best player wins in the end.' Ben raises his beer, toasting Lemarr. Kay. Bonding. Good.

Lemarr, his amiable elf, joins in clinking glasses. I wish he would play along with our planned hijinks and wear a Puffin projection around the course today. I plan hazing Ben by making him wear one also. They'd be 2 puffins in a pod. We need more Infis like Lemarr welcoming Ben into the Society. While frivolous, his BirdMe is more in tune with Ben's successes than Pilot's bordeli or Pet's monument preservation missions. Pet might even be a distraction, giving Ben's interest in sap antiquities and disaffection with his own success. At all costs, we need no distractions, no sudden urges in the middle of the mission for saving Christ the Redeemer or Trafalgar Square.

'Well, Ben.' Pilot's tone turns for business. 'We are all curious for learning of your progress.'

'Very little for demonstrating. I should caution you against expecting muchy-much too early. The Reck's original design aims for defending against gaming it.'

'Right you are. Let's have no wunches of bankers rising, trading in reputasi derivatives. But every other mindwriter one speaks with believes it's impossible,' Pet says and pulls a face of scepticism which, in his case, causes a scurry of asymmetrical features around his face. 'Lemarr says it's impossible.'

'They may be right.' Ben should be conceding less easily.

Pilot sits back aghast, coiling ready for pushing the table away.

'Though you believe different,' I prompt, needing these inquisitors mollified.

Ben sips and flattens his tongue for tasting the ale. 'Most mindwriters will approach the problem in terms of mindware and mindwriting. After all, the original version of the Reck is the product of mindwriting.'

'It's likely the Reck evolves in the generations since its creation, becoming ever more defensive and inscrutable,' Pet interrupts.

'Yeer. I believe we must also understand it as a sentient, psychological entity.'

'It sounds like you're suggesting all we need do is talk with it.' Pet raises his crazy-angle eyebrows.

'Look,' Ben says. 'We all know it would be hard. I am learning many things since I start. I test many experiments. While I expect setbacks, I believe I am on the right track.'

Pilot sizes me up. He looks as if he rolls a too-salty olive around in his mouth. 'Maddox, I believe you are sheltering him.'

'Why would I?'

'There could be any number of reasons. You are withholding the true progress. Or perhaps you already taste you will fail. Perhaps you are stalling. Or even yet to start. Perhaps soon you will declare the effort is indeed a failure. Perhaps there is no testing the Reck.'

'Why *wud*—' Lemarr.

'Will you be attending the Garden Barbecue?' Pet interjects, changing the subject. He immediately realises his mistake. A sheepish complexion blanches his face. The idiot.

Ben's eyes, under the blanket of a furrowing brow, search mine. 'Barbecue?'

'—Ah.' Pet mumbles and purses his rubbery lips in exaggerated embouchure. 'The invitations all go out months ago. Caracia's quite particular—' He conjures the octopus! Such plum-mouth incompetence.

'The Garden Barbecue is an annual Society event,' Pilot says, chafing at the chance for compounding Pet's egregiousness. Holds up his wrist, displaying his watch as a kind of exclamation mark after their collective stupidity. 'Every year's inductees are special guests. You may offend *Reina Pulpo*—'

'Queen Octopus?' Ben, translating, is bewildered.

'*Si.* You may give offence if you make no appearance.'

Lemarr leans towards Ben. '*Yuh memba di* octopus, Caracia, at *di* Infi Gala?' He says, his accent rhotic and choppy in the Caribbean way.

Are they all mocking me? Delivering Ben unto the Holy Hobotnice would sink our enterprise before it floats.

'Yeer,' Ben looks apprehensive. 'On the night, I have every intention of introducing myelf. Then …' We all give him a look of, *Yes we recall the White Witch crashing the party.*

'It's unfortunate, Puffin. With those octopus brains of hers, Caracia is one for recalling every snub—'

'I am never snubbing her. I already say—'

'Yes, yes. I'm only saying how she takes things. Perhaps, this time, discretion would suggest—'

'Maddox, is your brain decomposing like one of your sybils?' How can Pilot sieve his words through that 10-gallon-size smile of his? 'The bigger slight would be to stay away.' What is he playing at? Ben is already baulking about the golf course. What will he make of Caracia's meat orgy?

'Lemarr?' Ben looks to the bird man. 'You attend these?'

All eyes are on Lemarr. '*Yuh*, sure,' he says awkwardly. '*Mi* mean, what's a *likkle* charcoaled meat every once *inna* while?'

'Ah, good. That settles it.' Pilot slaps Ben's shoulder. 'You wait and see.

There will be every kind of meat imaginable. None of it from a fabby.' Pilot slaps Ben's shoulder again. 'Let's have another round.'

'Will there be tofu?' Ben asks.

Lemarr Robinson ...

Maddox has a hurricane behind his eyes staring at *mi*. *Waa gwaan wid* him?

Pilot's slapping Ben's shoulder. 'It'll be a perfect time for meeting more Infis in a relaxing environment. That Infi Gala thing is always such a tuxedo affair. Barbecues are where you meet real Infis. More than just toymakers wearing projection suits.' He sneers and side-eyes *mi*.

Kiss mi rass, Pilot, you *booguyaga wasteman dunce bat. Mi* be shoving a bird beak up your *batty* hole, you no respecting my mission.

Again, *di* gleaming piano-key Texan *skin yuh teeth*. As if being an elf-glorifying pimp is somehow *nobla dan* BirdMe. Ben's *a guh* own *yuh, fassyhole*. SnakiDik and BirdMe are taking *ova di* world.

As if *mi* words inflict a curse, Pilot is turning blue. Turning bluey-blue. Are his eyes *suh* bloodshot before? Spittle bubbles between his teeth.

'Piloto, you all right?' Maddox is at his side. Pilot's arms become T-rex limbs, his hands talons clutching at Maddox.

'*Final del jeugo terapeuta*,' Pilot gurgles word salad, labouring through a rictus grimace. 'Bun Bunny *Boff*—'

Ben stepping back.

'Bunny bunny bun bun—'

The skin around Pilot's neck cracking, desiccating, his throat and blood vessels a cluster of tubes in shrink-wrap. Toppling into Maddox's arms, his weight catches Maddox by surprise, and he falls through Maddox's weak embrace. Collapsing on the floor, pathetic legs thrashing like he's riding a bicycle. Struggling for breath.

'He's a sybil!' Ben accuses. 'His seminal is pruning him.'

'No,' Maddox says, kneeling over Pilot thrashing. 'This is no pruning.'

Pilot all convulsive flesh, a chemical process contorting into unnatural shapes. A loud, cracking sound.

'What is that?' Ben has panic in his eyes.

'Tendons snapping. Muscles over-contracting,' Maddox says. 'His brain is sending chaotic messages beyond the limits of his fruit.'

Blood seeping from under his shirt, pooling on the floor.

Maddox standing up, away from the horror. 'Idiot. I warn him what would happen.'

Touch

'Polyester Girl' — Regurgitator

 *Maddox Price ...*

A VIOLET SILHOUETTE APPEARS. Ben's shape crystallises in place, the fright in his eyes almost brighter than the spooky flash. 'What is going on?' he demands, matching my urgency. 'What happens—'

I make for the house, let his questions blow in the wind.

'Maddox?' he calls after me.

Most of the way for the pool house, for the change rooms there.

'Maddox. Tell me what's going on.'

I wheel on him. 'The less you taste the better.' Assault the door with a shove. The heavy timber thing swings back and conks against the wall. Tiles reverberate with a dull ceramic chime. Into one of the shower stalls.

Ben is fast behind.

I order, 'Go upstairs,' and bite my lip. My limbs are shaking. May need sitting on the shower floor.

'Tell me what happens—'

'No names. Silence.' The acoustics of the wall tiles make me sound the snake. Rip my jacket off, toss it at Ben. Kick off my shoes, sling my socks, drop my trousers. Stomach feels full of stone. Pull at the buttons of my shirt. 'Off you go.'

'Maddox. Talk with me.'

'Stand back before I ruin your shoes for the 3rd time.'

'You're a sybil?'

'I bloody-well hope so.'

'Why?'

'You never play a game and get yourelf in so much trouble, you give up on

272

hours of play and restore a back-up?'

'Sometimes I feel life should be like this.'

'Life is like this, you ninny. It's one of the best reasons for having sybils. If a sybil encounters trouble, or witnesses things you would rather not merge, then you just prune it.'

'And Pilot's death—'

'Is a disaster. I warn him he'll ruin confidence in sybils with his ... never mind.' Close eyes, tilt my head back. Jaw locks, hands make fists. Nothing. 'Jank.' No one's pruning me, yet.

'What?'

'Ben, trust me. Stop asking questions. The less you know…'

Stand waiting. Nothing. 'Jank.' Awkward silence, standing in my underwear while Ben holds my clothes, a gawping gormless valet. 'Come on, prune me. Prune me!'

'You're no sybil,' Ben says. In these circumstances, those words are the worst curse.

Stare him in the eye. 'Camel crap. I'm the seminal?' Shut up, shut up, tell him nothing. 'Jank. Why am I the seminal? How could I be stupid enough for meeting those reprobates as the seminal? Gimme those.' Snatch my trousers back. 'I'll never forget this. Never. No matter how I try, I'll never be able.' Shit. Am I speaking tongue and lung?

'What about me?' Ben asks. He hands me back the shirt. 'I'll never forget it either.'

'No.' Y'all see it in his eyes? He knows. He knows he's more than expendable. He's a threat.

'If you're ready for sacrificing yourelf, it must be easier sacrificing me,' he says, resigning.

Pilot. It's all Pilot's fault. He merges too often. Too many badly resolved merge conflicts. His fruit could take no more. If it's baddy-bad, if it's a worst case, every other sybil with the same merge conflicts will be expiring too. The seminal Pilot might be at threat. This could wreck the whole sybil mission. The less I taste, the better. I must erase these memories somehow or it's more than myelf who'll remember today. Every subsequent sybil I crèche from here on will remember.

Why is there no soap?

'You have others, right?' Ben babbles. 'Other sybils. You would have a contingency plan, right? You must have 14's of me running parallel projects, watching for which one comes up with the solution first. Before I know it, you'll be feeding me information from the work of other sybils, for getting there faster.'

'Be quiet.'

'It's so obvious. Oh, it's so obvious.' Puffin is panicking.

'Be quiet, will you?'

'C'mon Maddox, it's cruel stringing me along. You must prune me, erase all witnesses. Get it over with.'

'No. No one is pruning you.'

Never mind re-buttoning the shirt. Snatch back my coat. Ignore Ben's mental wheels turning. Look away, give nothing away.

'You need me? You have no other sybils? Yeer, okelah ... there are no back-ups. I'm all there is. Why?'

'You idiot. Only your seminal has the power for pruning you.'

Ben wears a muzzy face. 'Then you're incapable of pruning me when I finish with the Reck?'

Jank. He learns too soon. Any leverage we have over him is evaporating. 'Never, Puffin, even if I have the power.'

'Then, how will you cover up—'

'There is no covering up. Your memories are with you. You're on a one-way ride. We gamble on you succeeding so there will be no need for explaining it. Which is why I demand you stop asking questions. You taste too much already.'

Ben finds some resolution, straightens his stance. 'Then you must kill me ... you know, the old-fashion way.'

'If you mean drown you in a large cocktail glass of rum ...'

'You know what I mean. Smother me or stab me or something. You must see a sap murder movie at some time in your life.'

'I'm no sap. I have no capacity for killing.'

'You prune sybils all the time.'

'My sybils. Extensions of me. The Mind of me survives. Puffin, you believe me a monster?' That would be the 8th hell.

Ben Evoli ...

Oppressive humidity. The spooky field's receding violet light leaves a sheen on my baju melayu where the sweat-eating fabric fails for sopping up rivulets trickling down my chest and between shoulder blades. Sweep the songkok from my head. Splay fingers through already damp hair.

'*Bom dia, Infinito* Ben. My name, Kurisimay. I am your escort for the *burdel*.' Kurisimay, in a garish uniform, yields a shallow and instantly receding customer service smile.

'Where are we?' I ask. A canopy of jungle and a shambles of grey-black stones rise in uneven steps behind Kurisimay. The ruins of an ancient pyramid.

'Texas,' Kurisimay says evasively, with the tones of a superficially interested concierge. Piloto, I expect, trains all his staff for answering the same vague way. Behind him, Mayan temple ruins suggest either Yucatan in the south or theme park fakes. We could be in any jungle in the world, far from the United States of Texas. The Congo, perhaps. Spooking for Africa is as instantaneous as between the Americas. At these times I wonder why no mission ever resurrects sap geolocation tech. Then again, geolocation requires functioning satellites, of which there are none.

The ruins sit dark and heavy in the jungle's wet shadows, through which I spy no doors or passageways in. 'Are we climbing this thing?'

'Oh, no, *Infinito*.' Kurisimay stifles a laugh, restores his hospitality mien, sets his angular jaw square. 'We have a tukky waiting.'

'Terima kasih.'

'Come.' Kurisimay shows me a tukky pointing up a wide curving path cutting under the forest canopy. Everything is in dapple shade from the trees and the density of insects.

Once we settle in the back seat the tukky starts off. The little motor emits a rodent squeal as the path steepens, becoming a series of switchbacks. The tukky's wheels bite into the loose jungle floor. While it negotiates the tight, steep corners and every twist, I fear the dumb vehicle will throw me out. None too soon, the way levels and straightens. We pass from jungle into a clearing around another larger temple ruin. The clearing is a wide iridescent green moat around a central stone pyramid, with modern glassy 3-storey wings flanking on both sides. On top of the whole construction, cicada-wing environment sails stretch up at all angles, catching air and sunlight, and reflecting rainbows on the impenetrable forest.

Piloto's premier bordeli.

'Ah, *Boffinista*, welcome in our most exclusive *burdel*. Please, come. Let's take a drink at the bar.'

Piloto leads through the lobby, passing statues and artworks depicting jaguars and Mayan gawds baring teeth and bulging eyes, exaggerating grimaces of hunger or aggression. With quetzal feathers in their hair, fierce and hungry, they brandish obsidian knives. Some apply them to their own genitalia. We proceed like mice among kookaburras, through the bright combative light of the lobby, and reach the safety of a dimmer, gawdless space. A deep cathedral cavern with shafts of light cutting in from skylights in its high vault. A scattering of plump couches. Spacious intervals between. A light crowd. Perhaps a quarter full. The variety of sizes, shapes, gender options, and species projections reminds me of the Inductee Gala. Everyone here is either Infinite or the guest of one.

Piloto guides me for a stool at the bar, pulls one up for hiself. A bartender puts down 2 shot glasses and a fresh bottle of tequila *añejo*. Piloto pops its plug with the affable familiarity of unscrewing a water bottle. Splashes generous shots.

'I apologise. I have no memory of our last meeting,' Piloto says.

'I'm sorry about your …'

Piloto waves my words away. 'Merge conflict fever is nasty *negocio*.' Tips back half his glass, contemplates, downs the remaining liquor. 'A recent phenomenon,' he continues, while I sip. 'Some problem with the latest generation crèching tech. Unfortunate for me, my own sybils are among the first showing symptoms.'

I present a blank face while I chase a memory. 'I believe I recollect something … merge conflict fever? … happens some weeks back in my local desa's bordeli?'

'Ah, no?' Piloto says as if he'd rather avoid speaking of it.

'Some poor unfortunate punter pretending as an Infi.'

'Oh?' Piloto's bluff of ignorance is plain.

'The Infi's name is Twyford Hendriks. If I recall correct.'

Piloto scrunches his mouth and shakes his head. 'Must be a minor Infi, I suppose.'

'At the time, everyone suspects the grisly death is murder, the real Twyford exacting revenge, as unlikely as it sounds. But it's Twyford's sybil who expires, right? From merge conflict fever?'

'It is a more likely explanation than a neo committing murder.' Piloto checks my eye, for seeing if I'm buying it. His shoulders fall. 'We must prevent it from leaking,' he says with a deeper tone of voice. 'It would be bad for sybil tech missions.'

'Your sybil's demise at the golf course alarms Maddox. I never see him so panic-stricken.'

'*Si*. He has interests in crèching tech. He'd suffer even though his tech is older.'

'Ah, his older tech is why pruning makes such a mess of his sybils?'

Piloto gulps and nods. '*Si*, so far his older metra technology—you understand metra?'

'It's a vat for growing sybils in.'

Piloto rocks his head, swivels his hand in a sign of *not exactly*. 'Think more of a womb. An artificial uterus.'

'Which births perfect copies of adults. Maddox's stuff lags state of the art?'

'Oh, no, he's a leader in it. However, he avoids risking the latest tech for hiself. Recent developments prove his wisdom. His older tech is free of the merge conflict fault.'

'I figure merging must be dangerous at some level.' Sip at the tequila.

'Some say so. Merging cognitive experiences causes physical change at the micro-muscular and organic level. Also, the neural … we think, in other parts of the fruit also. Most of the time, it's harmless, *si*? Just the fruit adapting, integrating muscle-memory, you understand. It seems changes in the sybil's fruit manifest, more or less, in the seminal.'

'So, if I pickle my liver in tequila, I could ruin my seminal's liver in a merge?'

Piloto grins a death-defying grin and downs another shot. 'No, no. Nothing so graphic. A little of it manifests—a shadow you might say? Merge conflicts are on the rise, perhaps inevitable. We better understand the danger now. Merge conflict fever arises out of physical damage in the brain. Brain tissue degrades, becoming sclerotic. Cerebrovascular events occur. The damage is quite random, the consequences could range between inconsequential and catastrophic. You see, in my sybil's case—'

'It could happen in your seminal, I imagine.'

'Before, *si*. Now we take precautions. We always merge with a test subject—a recent sybil—before I accept a merge with me.'

'What is worth all the risk, all the effort?'

'The risk of an unending Cure, never escaping the prison walls of a minster, is a fear none of us can strangle. Now the risk is greater than ever. Because of the White Witch, our fears are coming true. Who knows how long the nurses will keep Orlando? We have no idea. It's weeks passing. Who knows which of us will be next?'

'You're killing me, *Boffinista*.' Piloto throws back another shot and chases it with *sangrita*.

'I think your tequila is killing me.' Six shots in, maybe 7. Piloto drinks many more.

'I mean my mission, my camerata. The market penetration of SnakiDik is sticking quite a hole in *burdel* missions.'

'I'm sorry, I never consider your mission before creating it. It's just an idea. Some ideas just own you; you taste?'

'I'm never blaming you. Please, think none of it. Your toy is brilliant … satisfying every sexual desire with a hoo—'

'It extends experience beyond any—'

'*Si, si*, I need no pitch. I have intimate acquaintance with the features.' Piloto touches his nose with a finger and makes a wide-eye *aha* face.

Sip from the shot glass, spilling a little.

'I suppose I could find another mission.' Piloto waves a finger in the air, fakes an idea arriving in his head. 'I know. I could make a mission of executing meddling mindwriters.'

With numbing tequila filling my skull like an Olympic-size swimming pool, my only reaction is a blurry leer at Piloto.

'I'm joking, of course. However, I must warn you many in The Hodinkle Society—never me, mind you, never me—many worry more with each passing scandal. You can understand why. Look at all the recent unfortunate events. There's a common element.'

'Which is?'

'You. You are always present.'

'None of it is because of me.'

Piloto pats my shoulder. '*Desde luego*. The bulk of Hodinkle Society is wrong,' he mocks. 'Events carry you along rather than the other way round, I suppose.' He throws back another shot, plants the glass with a dull clunk on the bar-top marble. 'Perhaps, we could work something out, you and me.'

'What have you in mind?'

'I imagine, if you are agreeable, a special edition of SnakiDik for me. Only available for use at my *burdeles*.'

'I'm unsure what features I could add. I'm always the one arguing for making every new development available for everyone. My colleagues argue for holding some advance features for special editions, but I could never conceive of making a back-room deal.'

'Ah, the secret of your reputation. You have a generous heart, Ben Evoli. We love you for it.' Venom laces the edges of his words—blue krait toxin. I shudder.

At least half my team would leave if I make an arrangement with a bordeli mission. I might be Infinite, but the rest of my missionaries must consider their reputasi. 'I could talk with my camerata,' I offer with some calculation. 'Let them run with it, see what they propose.'

'Excellent. It is all I can ask. Forgive me. I am a terrible host. It is time for a fuller tour of the burdel, si?'

'I—'

'Nonsense. I insist. You should experience our services first-hand if we will be partners. I already prepare the Ixazalvoh Suites for us.'

The Ixazalvoh Suites are an entire floor of one wing of the bordeli, accessible only by a small spooky station in the lobby. Without credentials, no one assists in reinforcing your vectors. Piloto explains there are deflective distortions in the field for catching the unwary. 'Anyone uninvited who attempts a spook here will instead emerge in a swampy part of the grounds where the mosquitos are ravenous.'

Step into the field. Emerge in fourspace dizzy. All the fine hairs standing on end. With a half-tumescent zakar. The violet aftershock flash recedes. New motifs of jaguars and slavering gawds leap at me from murals on the walls of an empty room.

'Which one is Ixazalvoh?'

'I have no idea. There were 100's of Mayan gawds, many overlapping.' Piloto ushers me for the bar. 'My Ixazalvoh, she is a composite. The jaguar motif comes from Ixchel who is a fertility goddess. This amuses me because Ixchel is an ancient crone who wears snakes in her hair and around her waist. Also, her name means *rainbow* and she is also the goddess of medicine. The nurses have her, I think.'

'You'd keep the jaguars.'

'*Desde luego.*'

Ahead is an entry for another bar. Smaller than the previous, maybe two 14's of guests and missionaries lounging about in sumptuous, yielding couches. 'Think it is good with a modest buzz in the room,' Piloto says. 'We may call for others if no one here is for your liking.'

Everyone is in superb dress. Or perhaps *costume* is a better word. None of the outfits are streetwear. A lelaki wearing an exclusive designer-label lounge suit reminds me of a famous actor.

A flash catches my peripheral vision. The dress of a tall, dark wanita turns transparent long enough for admiring glimpses of her fruit. She holds my gaze and turns full-frontal, presenting the prettiest zakar I ever see.

A flash from another corner of the room, another titillating glimpse.

'Is—'

'Her tail is no projection ... quite physical and prehensile. She is very skilful with it. Come, sit. Relax. We're in no hurry.'

A pair of vacant couches in the middle of the room angle spaciously around a heavy timber coffee table. So sturdy, I imagine elephants could dance a cancan upon it. Piloto collapses casually into one couch as if it's his home living room. Gestures the other for me.

Nearby sits a woman chatting with another. A large lampshade obscures all but the hem of her dress, her knees, and calves. I taste I know her ... perhaps a musician. Possibly one of Saf's favourites. She leans forward. Collects her glass from the table. Turns our way.

'Bunny?' My golf caddy?

Piloto waves her over.

The Bunny-woman with maroon hair stands, drink in hand while she smoothes her dress, comes over and elegantly sits alongside me. Avoiding sinking into the embrace of the cushions, she perches on the couch's edge, her back straight. Crosses her legs.

'Bunny,' Piloto says sounding formal. 'May I present Infinite Ben Evoli.'

Why is he reintroducing us?

'Oh, yes,' membs Bunny, 'the creator of MusiKai. Pleasing for meeting you.'

I boggle at her noting my other product. So refreshing.

'My name's Bunny. But I am no ordinary Bunny.'

'Yes ... I—we meet, remember? At golf.'

A fleeting muzzy expression freezes Bunny's face. Only her eyes slide towards Piloto.

'Your mission is here now?' I ask.

'This is just my weekend mission, Infi. The rest of the week I study village ecology and sustainability.'

'An important mission,' I offer.

'Yes. I hope it will help my reputation until I graduate.'

'How long since you start here?' I ask. Piloto looks on with mischievous delight.

'This is my first day, Infi.'

'Oh, it is?'

'Oh, but please, allow me some time with you, Infi. I would love it so much. True, I would.'

She is convincing.

Piloto is waving another wanita else over. She takes a seat alongside Piloto, mirroring Bunny's edge-of-the-seat pose, cross-legs, hands demurely in her lap. Apart from the colour of her hair—blue to Bunny's maroon—she is an identical Bunny in every way.

My Bunny. I have my Bunny.

And Piloto has his.

In lingerie and stockings, the Bunnies mount the oversize coffee table entwining. Maroon on her back, Blue over her, rearranging her panties. Maroon wraps her legs under Blue's arms, locks her ankles behind Blue's back, levers her crotch up for Blue's mouth as she pushes her head between Blue's thighs.

Piloto's amusement is predatory, studying equally me and the Bunny-on-Bunny action on the table.

'Piloto—'

'My English-speaking Infi amigos call me Pilot.'

'In Anglo-Malay, pilot is *juruterbang*.'

Pilot chokes a laugh down, ends up snorting. 'Sounds more like a plane crash.'

'Bang for short?'

'Perhaps *Piloto* is good after all.'

'Bang Bang Iscariot.' Take a draft of gin.

Piloto draws a large breath and sits forward as if he might share a juicy secret. 'Ben, many take me as nothing more than some elf-glorifying pimp. The truth is, the *burdel* mission is merely an application of my true skills.'

'Which are?'

'Sybil curation. Think of me as a kind of sophisticated breeder. In sybils, I emphasise certain features or temperaments while eliminating others entirely.'

'Breeding? As in breeds of cats?'

'A crude comparison, close enough for rudimentary conversation.'

'But … we both meet Bunny for the first time a fortnight ago.' Now these Bunnies, each who must believe she is the seminal, are at such ease with a sybil. 'They are very into … themelves. Is this part of your breeding?'

Piloto chuckles. I hate it. 'Well, it's fun watching,' he says, 'until inevitable Infi boredom sets in.'

The *Boredom of the Infinites*. Perhaps I am suffering it these passing years, with no understanding of how I might alleviate it.

I say, 'Nice work,' holding back none of my sarcasm.

'Such is my skill,' he says, matter of fact. 'I know you could easily poke around and find every answer you crave, so let me offer a simple explanation in the hope you'll allow me my trade secrets, as anyone else in the Hodinkle Society would.' I doubt any Infi would grant another such relief, watch-wearer, or no. 'First, we allow each successive generation very few extra experiences,'—the way Piloto uses the word makes me think he's glossing over some horrid sausage-making processes— 'which we design carefully for the desired outcome. With small incremental changes between generations, we optimise merging and make it fasty-fast. We merge generations of sybils in a single day. Second, we crèche more sybils and create parallel generations which we eventually integrate late in the process. And third, we merge the resulting sybil with one from the first generation in such a way as the first has none of the result's memories, while retaining all the effects.'

It tastes appalling. Piloto is treating sybils as nothing more than livestock.

Both Bunnies request permission for engaging SnakiDik with me. What's the point? What's the point of any of this macabre circus? The pair of Bunnies are subdued trained circus animals. The weight of Piloto's monstrous process of breeding compliant sybils crushes the fight out of me. With a collapsed chest, and a vacuum where a heart should be, I accept the Bunnies' request. While they lap at each other, I launch a basic script, delivering them both the sensation of penile penetration. Basic set-and-forget thrusting. With something of average size with above-average wood. Gulp down my gin which already in my brain provokes a knife fight with the tequila.

Paralytic drunk may be my best escape.

'In truth,' Piloto membs, 'you find no pleasure here?'

'What is your point, Juruterbang?'

Sucking in a deep breath, Piloto claps his hands above his head twice. All in the lounge room but the performing Bunnies down glasses and file for the lobby. The light out there tints with violet flashes. New arrivals advance like models on a catwalk, all in the same style of outfit as the pair of Bunnies. Same hairstyle, each dress colour matching hair colour. Every colour except blonde. Piloto must know of my dislike for blonde hair. They circle and surround us. More than a 14, perhaps 2 14's. Bunnies, all.

'The point is: with fabbies and crèches and enough feedstock for recycling without end, the difference between one and two and 14's is ...' Piloto pauses for effect, '... precisely zero.'

'This is appalling. Much worse than Maddox crèching me without permissi.'

'Bunnies, are you happy here?'

'Yes, Infi.'

'Are you happy?'

'Yes, Infi.'

I have my own question: 'How long are you working here?'

'This is my first day,' is the common answer, or variations of the same.

'My darlings, go and relax.' Piloto spanks the butt of a Bunny on the table. 'You too.' The pair disengage, each wiping her mouth with the back of her hand, collecting her clothing. Hand-in-hand, they find a couch in the far corner of the room and re-tangle.

Oh, jank. 'Bunny … at the golf course, she's a sybil.'

'Indeed. Maddox is responsible for that one.'

'And all the other neos here before? All sybils?'

'*Si.*'

'The guy in the suit … reminds me of an actor I know …'

'*Si.* A sybil.'

'The pop star?'

'Sybil. *Boffinista*, we promise we'll cater for your every need, and we mean it. We could crèche your daughter—'

'Jank you, Juruterbang.'

Piloto raises his hands in a sign of surrender. 'Your son then—just illustrating … look, they are sybils.'

'Sybils … how … aiyo! All these Bunnies believe this is the first day here?'

'It is their first day.'

'Then what? You prune them every day and start with news ones?'

'Pruning another's sybils is impossible.' Piloto is enjoying his perversion. 'Only the seminal or an ancestor sybil is able.' Seeing my muzzy shock, he says, 'A sybil is capable of pruning any of its descendant generations.' He's enjoying my crushing surrender in the face of his monstrosity.

'You only need an ancestor sybil for pruning descendants?'

'*Si.*'

Maddox lies. Surprise, surprise. 'A sybil consents for pruning these descendants?' I wave at the excess of Bunnies.

'No, no, it would be cruel. It would cause the sybil much distress.'

'What becomes of the one-day sybils?'

'We pass them.'

'You pass them? As in a passing suite?'

'*Si*, during sleep.'

'For what—'

'Please, it is a kindness we allow—'

'A kindness?'

'*Si.* If they believe it is their first day, they are happy. If we allow them a passage of time here, even as little as a week, they become anxious for going home—an eventuality, I am sure you understand … we must never let sybils cross paths with an unwitting seminal.'

'You put sleeping sybils in a sucky?'

'Their beds have a sucky bin feature. It is humane and painless.'

Bitter, I say, 'Painless as throwing away your day's dirty chuddies.'

'For replenishing feedstocks. Circle of life. It is always thus. Earth is just one big feedstock bin. New life emerges from the material of the dead. Saps ran their whole civilisation on petrochemicals. What are those, other than a feedstock store of once living things?'

'Never mind your snake-loving jaguar grannies, you're the one playing gawd here.'

'Depending on your definition of gawd, I suppose. Humanity is always becoming thus. Creating gawds in our image and potential. We interpret sap religious texts as the acts of gawds before, but they could also be the predictions of human-gawds of the future.'

'I think I know where your merge conflict fever comes from. You're mad.'

'There's no madness, just the exploration of our possibilities. You should stop fighting it.'

Poor Bunny. The real Bunny—hoping there still is one—is a happy 30-something, studying for her dreams and missions in life. She has a family, friends, sex partners … If only the artfully free way she gyrates her hips is less tempting.

'So,' Piloto perks up. 'Which of these Bunnies would you enjoy for the rest of the afternoon?'

I deserve this. Am I any better than Piloto? With my scripts for automating stimulation. Sex without engagement. I realise my thrusting script is still running on the pair of Bunnies over there on the couch and will continue while they remain aroused. By tomorrow, they will be feedstock in the bordeli's bins. How long before I end up the same way?

A month since visiting Juruterbang's bordeli … I'm sorry I just give up. With each new generation of Bunny, Juruterbang tempts me. When is it I surrender completely? Is there a tipping point? I isolate no single tik or a set of circumstances I might blame for my capitulation. I could blame my deepening nihilism, but I pass the point of caring weeks ago.

Forgive me. I accept Juruterbang's gift of my own pet Bunny. In the face of my impending sybil-doom—which may come at any time at the whim of any of a number of Infis—I too am a circus animal. So, I join Bunny in her cage, and accept our mutual plight. In the time we have, can anyone blame me for seeking a little intimacy? A little sweetness?

Juruterbang assures me Bunny's merges are careful, preserving a sense of consistency and continuity, so she has a coherent back-story of us meeting. Consistent memories of me, the Infi creator of immensely successful hoots, spiriting her away on a proposal of fun and adventure.

'I guess schools can wait a week or so,' Bunny reasons. She says the same every week.

Juruterbang crèches a branch of her sybil line, a milestone in developing the perfect Bunny. Her infectious vitality is a magic carpet lifting me away from my own inevitability.

With Juruterbang's insidious encouragement, I pick and choose the days and nights I wish her remember. With each new version of her, life congeals into a wonderful, fragile, hedonistic, utopian reality. A reality in which the old version of me slips further away than the seminal Bunny I would never meet. The life of an amoral Infinite beckons with solidifying plausibility. My old life—the one I will never return for—recedes across galaxies. Only with the finest instruments of memory might I peer across space and witness the cooling stars of my family, whose light and heat no longer reaches me.

As horrendous as a sybil's plight is, I salve my conscience with the belief seminal Bunny suffers nothing for all of this. She's safe, and it's only her limitless copies who … what? They never taste their end approaching. It's seminals we should value. I wonder if, perhaps, seminal Bunny is aware of Piloto's creations. Perhaps there is some Faustian contract between them, for which she receives benefits I might only guess at.

My Bunny is a delight. We're sybils playing a sybil's game, she and I, although only one of us is Mindful of it. I envy her ignorance. Every day, she is happy, yet unaware of her disposability. Perhaps life is always thus. All our lives are short and pointless. Giving the gestalt of it, we may as well play with Gluttonous abandon.

'We are all born,' Juruterbang says. 'We all die. We know we will. In between, we make the best of it. If I may say so, your making the best of it is improving every day.'

Proprioception

'Knives Out' — Radiohead

 *Ben Evoli …*

MIDSUMMER'S DAY in the northern hemisphere. The day of Caracia's Octopus's Garden Barbecue.

Maddox glances at his watch again, polishing it with futile impatience.

'You 2 go ahead,' I advise.

Brooklyn slips an arm inside Maddox's, rests her hand on his shoulder, looks down at him pleading. 'This is what happens when you give a young thing a fashion catalogue and a first-class fabby,' she says, her voice testosterone deep. *She sounds like an Islay single malt complaining about the quality of glass it's in*, Maddox says earlier when describing her.

Tension leeches from my bones when Bunny finally appears.

Maddox: 'Ah, here she is. Delightful.'

Bunny is a delightful, beautiful image of perfection in her cocktail dress, jewellery, and high heels. Brooklyn covers her mouth, hiding her smirk. Bunny's outfit is a little too much for an event less garden party than medieval feast (Maddox tells me we may toss bones at hungry dogs if such a thing amuses us).

I feel a playful zing in my groin. Always the one for teasing, Bunny engages SnakiDik. I return her tickle. A slight twist in her hips rewards me. She flashes her dress transparent for a tik, eliciting a smile from Maddox, and a micro-muscle grimace from Brooklyn. 'Girl, save it for the hungry hoards at dinner. We already know you're hot.' The single malt is in a particularly cheap glass tonight.

Maddox: 'Well, let's move. Are you sure it's safe spooking from here?'

Brooklyn's mission is spooky engineering. 'With our vector plan, no one will be tracking us,' she says with a taint of overconfidence. I wonder if she could help Mal spook for the moon.

Maddox fidgets with his cravat. He too is nervous about so many spooks beyond a stable network. 'Grow no horns,' he says meeker than I ever hear him.

'Maddy,' Brooklyn croons, deeper than a cellar of malt whisky. 'It's safe.'

'Good,' he says without conviction. 'The last thing I'd wish for is arriving at the dinner with my head up your very muscular black hole.'

Brooklyn: 'I could think of worse entrances. In onespace your head is always up everyone's muscular black hole.'

'Grow no horns,' I say. Everything turns purple.

Giddy from 9 hectic spooks. At each waypoint, a spooky field flashes into existence, only a few tiks for us.

'Are we here?' Bunny heaves, her face flush, her thighs pressing firmly together.

The oily smoke of char-grilled meat glues my eyelashes and seeps into my hair. Sage insinuates nasal passages. So pungent, my eyeballs float in their sockets.

Bunny pats her dress down. Her shoulders are above my eye line. She's leaning awkwardly. One of her heels is broken.

'I'm sure you can fab another pair around here somewhere.'

'Excuse me, Infi Face,' speaks a voice, tongue and lung. An attendant stands by an open flap of a circular tent, clasping hands. 'May I request, please step out of the spooky point? More guests are arriving soon.' His face shimmers from light dancing off the cicada canvas of the tent walls.

Bunny kicks her shoes off with a sulky whimper.

'There are fabbies in the alley outside,' the attendant explains while ushering us through the tent flap. 'There you may replace your footwear.'

Outside, the air is turbid with cooking fats and juices. The sky flickers an orange glow over weak icy shadows. The last of the sun descends into twilight.

'Oh, thank gawd.' Bunny scampers ahead, disappears into the sputtering tide of passers-by. Catch up with her at a fabby kiosk where she's dropping her shoes into a sucky bin about a metre up the kiosk's barrel exterior. A catalogue holly whooshes alive above the kiosk. Bunny, ever the shopping expert, swiftly scrolls and rotates through it. Finding something like her original footwear, she flashes fingers wide in a conjuring gesture, pushes her open palm at the holly, steps back while the kiosk hums. Within tiks, the circular top of the kiosk opens and raises a pair of shoes. Bunny lifts them by the ankle straps, turns them over in her hands, examining. 'Never as good as Maddox's fabby, though still good.' Leaning on the kiosk for support, she wriggles toes and swivels ankles; I never tire of such motions of feminine shoe-wearing. 'Where are the others?' she asks.

'Nearby, I think. We're meeting at a dance bar.'

'Judging by the thud coming through the ground there must be 14's of those.'

She's right. There could be 1000's dancing in who-knows-how-many bars. All the DJs are streaming with MusiKai near-field generation. The music is in everyone's heads. Until you tune in for one of the streams—or mask the surrounding sound with streaming of your own—the unremitting sound in the encampment is one of imminent trampling by a herd of dancing elephants.

Already, exuberantly grateful fans already recognise me, and are blinking thankful and grateful hollies of furtive musical or erogenous greetings. I can never respond personally for all of them, and my auto-responses disappoint them. Some keep membing and meet the cold and necessary void of my filters, through which neither note nor tickle pass. This is why I dread parties.

'*Boffinista!*' A waving hand among the throng. 'Hola!' My blood chills. It's Juruterbang. I have relief his companion is no Bunny.

'Hello, Piloto.'

'How are you, this fine evening? May I introduce Maracelia?'

Assume Maracelia is a sybil. Wonder how many social events and intimate moments Juruterbang cherry-picks for merging her. How many more before she shows signs of merge conflict fever? Pass a discreet eye over Bunny. Only one of us understands we are temporary sybils warming each other against the impending cold of our pruning. The sybil of Bunnington Macy Bender—student of the ecological sciences, on a mission for healing the earth of all sap atrocities—is sweet and gormless in her hope for a bright future.

'Ben, are you listening?' Bunny cradles my cheeks, tilting my head up so she can investigate my eyes. 'I swear you are somewhere else most times.'

'Sorry. I'm still giddy from spooking.'

'I could go all 9 waypoints again.' Bunny's zestful pleasure of being among Infinites is a colourful contrast with Aisha's wariness at the Inductee Gala.

I say, 'Pleasing for meeting you, Maracelia.'

Maracelia smiles graciously. 'The prairie air is so invigorating,' she says. 'I love the smell of sagebrush.'

'All I can smell is smoke and animal fat,' I answer.

'*Si*,' Juruterbang follows, covering for me. 'I recall it the same way for my first Garden Barbecue.'

'Quite large for a garden,' I say, trying to perk up.

'Where are we anyway?' Bunny asks.

From what I taste, we're in the middle of many square kims of open sage and sky.

Juruterbang appears cagey. 'It is a joke of Caracia's,' he begins while guiding us through the crowd, I presume, for meeting up with Maddox and the others. We zig-zag through the crowd. 'The party is on an old air strip,'

Juruterbang explains, leaning in towards Bunny. Somehow as we weave through the crowd, he wriggles between Bunny and me. 'Many centuries ago, saps called this place The Green River Intergalactic Spaceport,' he says.

'A spaceport?' Bunny asks, completely absorbed. Maracelia exchanges glances with me.

'It is a joke, a tourist-attracting stunt,' Juruterbang says. 'At the time, a comet collided with Jupiter, and the local government extended hospitality for any refugees from the disaster.'

'But there's no life in Jupiter.'

'*Desde luego*. Anyway, Caracia, declaring herelf the only true alien in the universe, has her Garden Party here, accepting the welcome mat put out all those centuries ago.'

'There are other quips if you know where to look,' Maracelia adds as we arrive at an outdoor bar.

Juruterbang titters, 'The name of this bar is Shoemaker-Levy 9.'

Just back from the alleyway, a parody of a wedge-tail eagle sits leaning on a bar table. 'Lemarr!'

'*Bredda,*' he says, standing. '*Yuh* like it?' Brushes the feathers on his wing-arms. '*Mi* wear it in *yuh* honour.'

'I think you just enjoy scaring us.' Juruterbang pats Lemarr's wing-shoulder.

'It never hurts, looking imposing in a crowd,' Lemarr says.

'Never fails for me.' Maddox arrives with Brooklyn, martini glass in hand, which he drains and raises over his head, wambling it between his fingers. A waiter approaches with a tray of pink wine. Bunny and Maracelia take glasses gleefully. 'Gah,' Maddox exclaims in disgust. 'Death to the Zinfandel! Bring me a martini, I say. What would you like, Puffin?'

'Gin and tonic.'

'Ah, gin and tonic,' Maddox mocks. 'The bubble-gum of cocktails.'

Lemarr's wingtip goes for his beak. He coughs polite. '*Wud yuh fulljoy ah* tour *addi* roasting pits, Ben?'

'Sure. How could another layer of grease ruin my outfit more? Bunny?'

'You go ahead. I'm happy with my drink.'

'May you enjoy many more,' Juruterbang says.

Lemarr leads me down a curving alley, then left onto a wider straight avenue. '*Di* encampment lays out *inna* spokes and concentric wheels,' Lemarr explains. 'The cooking field *a waah* huge circle *inna di miggle* of it all. Kinda a gladiatorial field. Around are 12 pavilions. Hundreds of *di* most honoured guests *wi* dine *inna deh, wid* full view of *di* roasting pits.'

We're picking our way through the crowd passing 6 or 7 curving cross-alleyways. Ahead tall white tents loom ever larger above the shanty town of other structures. We come upon 2 avenues of marquees open on all sides, exuding the comforting glow of candles which sit on rows of dining benches dressed in white linen. Tall fat candles, regiments of cutlery, and glasses festoon the benches.

'How are we for finding our places among all these?' I ask Lemarr, who chuckles.

'*Yuh* should check *yuh* invitation *closa*. *Wi* are *inna* one of *dem deh*,' Lemarr says hoiking a thumb at the nearest pavilion a cross-alley away. Above it, a horizontal drape of smoke reflects an orange blossom of light underneath. I'm anticipating skipping for the cooking field when Lemarr's wing hooks under my elbow.

'Where are we going? What about the roasting pits?'

'*Yuh* have another appointment first,' Lemarr chirps. I stop skipping. 'Breathe easy, *bredda*. *Mi got yuh*,' Lemarr comforts. '*Wi* are meeting Her Royal *Maddi Maddi*.'

'Her Royal ...?'

'*Di* octopus.'

'Caracia? Why are you no saying before?'

'There's no point upsetting Maddox,' the eagle says.

'Maddox? Why would it upset Maddox?'

Lemarr, a ravenous eagle, laughs. 'Caracia and Maddox are never the most amiable of colleagues. The whole reason Maddox conceals the party from *yuh* is he worries what advantage Caracia might make of it.'

The curve of Lemarr's beak, the stare of his alien bird eyes, feels menacing over my head. 'Hey, Lemarr, can you wear something a little less ... predatory? You're bending my brain.'

'Sorry, *bredda*,' he says then changes into a koala. I blink 3 times. 'What?' the koala challenges. '*Mi* always gotta be a bird?'

'Could you just—I dunno—skip the projections for a while? I mean, as if I run SnakiDik 24-7.'

'*Yuh* could be titillating 100 people *dis* tik *fi* all *mi* know.'

I threaten, 'I'll titillate you with it, and turn it up to 11.'

The koala's paws come up in a comic parody of protecting itself. 'Kay, kay, Nigel,' It bends into waves of colours, resolves into a tall lelaki with head shaven, muscular shoulders, and an athletic build.

I say, 'Wait,' sceptical. 'This's Usain Bolt, a Jamaican runner. A sap Jamaican runner.'

Lemarr wheezes a laugh. '*Yuh* got *mi* there, *bredda*.'

Usain Bolt dissolves like the koala before. In his place is a bony little figure, no taller than Mal. Both youth and age stare out from large eyes beneath a large and shiny forehead reminiscent of a featureless wall with a coat of sweaty gloss paint. His head appears so large and weighty, I wonder how his neck supports it. An angular frame and limbs so spindly, I half expect they might crack.

'Staring is impolite, *bredda.*'

'*Maaf*, Lemarr.'

Lemarr skips away. Follow him around the backs of the pavilions until we pass at least 4. I catch up.

'You muzz me, Lemarr. I think you part of Maddox's inner circle. Now Caracia?'

'*Yuh* should *kno* all *di* players on *di* wicket, *bredda.*'

We're approaching a break in the rows of marquees. Opposite the wide entrance of a pavilion is a tall screen of veiny, cicada-wing foil refracting rainbows from it surface. Lemarr skips straight into the screen and vanishes. Hurrying, I see him chinking and disappearing again. Mimicking his path through, I arrive in a cloistered yard where 8 rigid-still hospitality uniforms stand facing us at guard in single file. Behind is a glassy black box about 4 metres tall and about double the width.

'*Cum pan,*' Lemarr says. He walks without a skip towards the box, his steps possessing a certain reverence. Or caution. A scent of the sea contrasts with the rest of the encampment's aroma of sage and barbecue. The 8 pivot on heels, slow skip in a kind of fusion between solemn marching and interpretive dance. Lemarr falls in behind and signals me for the same.

We climb a dark flight of stairs hugging around the box, which glows from deep within, illuminating watery murkiness and dark rocky shapes on the bottom. An imposing shadow hangs in the back corner. We reach a landing, switch back on another flight of stairs. Through the murk of the water, the shadow hangs heavier than a large sack of cabbages, testing the elastic of its thick straps. There could be markings on it. Perhaps it's reddish brown. There's something in it.

We reach a wide semi-circular landing about a metre from the lip of the tank, which comes chest-high on me while Lemarr must stretch to peer over. Waves, gentle as silk threads, glitter under the night sky and lap at the tank walls.

'Put your arm in the water,' comes a reedy chorus of voices from behind, from the tank's attendants who arrange in an arc so near the edge of the platform each could take a step back and teeter off. Swaying strangely, occasionally twitching. Necks appear to bulge. Or throb. Could be mimicking frogs or about to vomit.

'Put your arm in the water,' the attendants say again in loose unison.

'What?'

A wash and a splash interrupt from behind. 'Ben!' Lemarr warns. Turn too late. A flash, a glimpse of a monster surging to attack. A large bow wave on the surface of the water precedes a nameless formless bulk which disappears for a tik then reforms, menaces towards us, glowing bright red. My Mind is too slow registering what's happening. The thing becomes a tangled beach towel of stripes and dots, then mutates once again into a mottled and rotting

Turkish carpet. Water surges over the lip of the tank soaking my legs below the thighs. Out of the red-brown hulk, the monster-hammock's straps unfurl and flare. Two rows of unnatural white suckers on each, come right at me.

Flinch, anticipating capture. Instead, the touch is gentle, almost a caress. Suckers clamp and disengage, clamp, and disengage, tasting me. I resist recoiling, my skin creeping. The arms release me.

'Sybil,' the attendants hiss and nearly quake off the platform. 'Tastes of metra,' one screeches.

'Well, of course he's sybil,' Lemarr protests. '*Yuh* part of *dis* from *di* start, Caracia.'

'We wish from the beginning: send the sybil home while we keep the seminal. But Maddox refuses. He never prosecutes anything well. Garbage mining is an imprecise mission, unlike genetic engineering.'

The ever-morphing mass of Caracia floats out of reach while I fail at making sense of her cycling through a series of colour changes. Thankfully, she settles on turquoise as camouflage. A slash of white opens and closes rhythmically as her squiggly mass rises and falls. Perhaps she's breathing. She changes again. Between speckles in a field of dark sand, and neon purples and yellows, every change is muzzing. It might be beautiful but for my horror. A black horizontal slit appears in a silver circle. Then another. One steadily focuses on me while the 2nd aims in random directions as if part of another monster altogether.

'Lemarr, give me your arm,' sounds a pair of the Voices. Lemarr grimaces. With resignation, he holds his chin up and his breath in, rolls up his sleeve, and steps onto a narrow tread where platform meets tank. He hooks his arm over the lip of the tank into the water. Two tentacles emerge from the water with white suckers up facing the sky. Curl around Lemarr's arms. His face is pallid while Caracia caresses him with adroit clasping suckers. Affectionately, it appears to me. Creepy in whole other dimensions.

'Watch out!' Lemarr shouts. By the time I process the warning, Caracia is dowsing me in water heavier than hosing a fire. Lemarr fails for stifling a laugh. '*Yuh* gotta watch her syphon, *bredda*.'

'Her syphon?' I demand, shaking my arms down. Gasping. Cold rivulets of water run through my eyebrows. 'How can I tell where any part of her is?' Lemarr chuckles and Caracia's attendants wheeze in alien tittering. With swift drama, Caracia releases Lemarr and plunges for the bottom of the tank. 'I think the audience is over,' he whispers.

'A sybil!' a chorus of attendants say with the sound of a hot wind through dead tree branches. 'He'll have to do.'

'*Wi* need rum,' Lemarr says as an imposing currawong. As we scratch through the crowd towards a scatter of pop-up hospitality tents, he cycles through a range of parrots. The familiarity of his holly projections is more comfortable than the sight of the wizened little guy underneath.

We pass revellers coming away from a stand with glasses of beer.

'You'd drown me already?' I ask. 'Beer will do.'

'*Mek wi* find *di* fires and dry out.' Lemarr plunges into the throng. I taste him at a wide table where a barkeep fills glasses with frothy amber from a keg gun while guests sweep up glass after glass. At the next table we grab cups of nuts. We skip onto the cooking field.

The world flickers. Black shadows embrace red and golden vapours in a chaotic dance, a world of veils across smoky portals. Cooks—the high priests of these ceremonies—conduct their rites, applying bastes and herbs with a sacred air of calm. Even the flatbed tukkies delivering produce and utensils are quiet, moving about with deliberation and motors hushing. Fires crackle; sinews snap; sauces and juices hiss. Cleavers thud on chopping boards.

Lemarr leads down a grassy alley between rows of fire pits, charcoal beds, preparation tables, crates and bins of produce. Huge piles of chopped wood evoke in me a sickening awe. I only trust there are forests of saplings growing somewhere which compensate for these dead trees. So much oily smoke escaping into the atmosphere. Wonder what religious zeal bans the use of sucky nets over the fires.

The whole field arranges on a loose hexagonal grid. We reach an intersection after intersection of paths. Down one is a row of gigantic metal frames, medieval cages turning slowly over a low mound of angry-red coals. Some form of Dante's hell. I gooseneck down the alley, my eyes drawing the rest of my fruit. Come stand before those rotisserie grates. In each is a butterflied carcass larger than Lemarr projecting as a tall galah—hissing, and spitting glistening fats.

'What ...?' I stammer. 'Are—'

'*Vaca entera*. Whole cow, a sap Argentinian tradition,' Lemarr says. He takes a deep draught of his beer. I blink and gulp some of my own.

'What? We get one each?' I ask, fathoming the scale of the racks reaching high in the air.

Lemarr chuckles. 'The idea is, *yuh* compare flavours and textures from various parts of *di* beasts. If *yuh* hungry for *di* whole *ting* I'm sure *yuh wi* get one. *Mi* think *yuh* underestimate *ow* many ago *bi* here tonight. The chimichurri sauce is delicious, by *di* way.'

'I imagine some Infis wrapping themelves in a whole carcass,' I mutter, walking away from the rows of huge roasting contraptions.

Lemarr follows. '*Yah*, well, *mi* suggest *wi* avoid 5 o'clock then.'

My jaw drops open. Five o'clock is the pavilion alongside ours. Six o'clock is the most prestigious after Caracia's at 12, behind which is her tank.

'Kidding, *bredda*. *Doah* wait till *yuh* witness a horde of Infis eating. Some eat like horses, others are *bigga dan* horses.'

'Are there horses for eating?'

Lemarr nods slowly and grimaces. 'Slaughterhouse aisle 5.'

With black humour I say, 'I trust there are no cannibals,' while I peer down another path. I think I see horses on spits down there. 'I bet there's no octopus.'

Lemarr side-eyes. 'Octopuses are cannibals …' I shudder. '… and *wi nyam* a mate. Once a female lays *har* 1000's of eggs, *shi* won't even *nyam*. *Wen dem* hatch, she'll die, exhausted.'

'I'm kinda glad we're on the opposite side from Caracia,' I blather, taking a turn at an intersection. Down the alley, carcasses of a less nightmarish scale turn on slow-rotating pits. Guess lamb or goat. Large fish in wire baskets suspend above unlit firewood.

'What about peacock? Can we have peacock?'

Lemarr looks about, taking bearings. 'Three aisles over, mi think.'

I imagine servings of the birds on beds of feathers.

'What about snake?'

'Land and sea.'

'Cat? Dog?'

'No one *nyam* cat, *bredda*.'

'Rhinoceros? Whale?'

Lemarr whoops in exasperation. 'A few decades back, *dem* try adopting a theme *fi* each year. African Savanna, Great Plains America, Antarctica. One year everything is whale. No more themes *afta* that.'

'Little birds? Finches, swallows?'

'African or European?'

'What about ortolan?'

'*Yuh muss kno dem likkle* songbirds are no *longa* endangered. *Tank di* Charentais Infi Cyrille Figuier *fi* it.'

'Carrots? Asparagus? Monkey brains?'

'Oh, now *yuh* being barbaric. *Dem* poor young asparagi.'

The next intersection reveals rows of fire pits where long skewers rotate slow over coals in stacks or 4, each impaling 6 or 7 carcasses. Another beast I'm unfamiliar with. Could be a kind of fowl, larger than chicken. Or rabbits. Rumps are plump and round. Remind me of the cherubs in the corners of Europan sap religious paintings.

'What are those?'

Lemarr spans his wings. 'There are exotic species of all kinds tonight. *Mi wud* challenge anyone identify *dem* all. Come check out *di* camel. See *sum* down *di* aisle *ova* there.'

'We could just ask the cook.'

'Let's find *di* others; *wi* should be taking our seats,' Lemarr says and drains his glass. '*Mi* feel *mi* skin turning crisp. Let's get more beer.' Lemarr tosses his glass in a sucky bin. '*Sick!* Prefer lager before ale.'

'I'll be quick.' I leave Lemarr and advance on the cook basting the meat. 'Please excuse me, what meat is this?'

Without taking eyes from his task of brushing the carcasses with a large bunch of dripping herbs, he says, 'Sapling.'

'Sapling? Sapling what?'

'Yes,' the cook says. He looks at Lemarr with a screwy expression as if saying, *Who's the yokel?*

'*Cum pan*, I'm thirsty,' Lemarr says, his wing gripping my shoulder.

The meat nearest the bone is my favourite. The best bits need teeth or knife for prising out of nooks and corners, from around gnarls of blackened cartilage, from under gelatinous hoods. Real meat is so inconsistent. A lean morsel attaches to fatty marble strands of muscle, tender rounds are a single bite away from tough chunks, a moist mouthful follows a dry one. I wonder if there are fabbies which might simulate so much detail in the meat.

Lemarr is right about the whole cow. Take chunks from many parts of the animal for experiencing everything it offers. From across the table, Maddox replenishes my merlot glass while Juruterbang refills Bunny's larger pinot.

We drink too much, eat too much. Laugh too much. The spirit of feasting scours all my misgivings away, leaving a deep genetic memory of tribal celebration, of the first fires and the first hot food, a primeval triumph of survival. We eat well and live another day.

'You're quiet. Are you dreaming of philosophy again, Puffin?' Maddox asks.

Brooklyn's laugh grates my ears. Or maybe it's the sound of her cracking her 4th marron shell. She chaws on the pearl-white tail meat. With mouth half-full she washes in a good draught of Sancerre.

I say, 'I'm full.'

'We're all full, Puffin. Which is hardly the point.' Maddox lifts a large platter and offers it. 'You have none of the octopus yet.'

I wave my hand at it. Maddox replaces the platter with mock offence. 'These are from Caracia's own Alaskan farms.'

Over Maddox's shoulder are the dying embers of the cooking field. Beyond in night-time shadow is 12 O'clock pavilion where Caracia feasts on who-knows-what. On her palanquin, every few mins her 8 Voices of Arms—spray her invertebrate hulk with Baltic seawater.

'All Infis,' Lemarr says, 'yet *inna har* service. There's a long queue waiting *fi dem* turn at *di* role.'

'What's the attraction?'

'*Ow wud mi* know? I'm just a *dawg inna* a bird suit, *bredda*.'

Maddox goes rigid, his plasticky face petrifying solid, his eyes focussing sharp somewhere behind Bunny and me. He waves at waiters coming up the stairs as if shooing flies away. 'We're quite engorged here, thank you. Take it away, please.' And swats again.

The wavering waiters hold platters head-high, platters just large enough for a single roast like a plump cherubby rabbit.

'Are those the saplings we see before, Lemarr?' I ask.

'*Si*,' Maracelia says, 'it is sapling. Are you yet for trying it?'

Maddox kicks her under the table. 'There'll be other times,' he says. 'You say you are full after all.'

I say, 'I'm curious.'

'Me too,' Bunny chimes.

Juruterbang waves the waiters over; they distribute platters along our 12-setting table, one directly between Maddox and I. Maddox fashions a wan smile then applies his wine glass.

'What is it?' Bunny asks, prodding the roast with her fork.

I say, 'A bunny, I think.' Bunny pulls her fork back fast as a recoiling snake.

'Oh, no.' Maracelia chortles like remonstrating a naive anak.

Bunny matches my blank look. Maddox refills his glass almost for the brim, spilling ruby-purple wine.

Maracelia giggles with a little embarrassment, her hand covering her mouth. 'Sapling,' she says with finality as if it explains everything. When she gets no *aha!* from either of us she says: 'Sapling. Baby sap!'

Beyond

'Human Behaviour' — Björk

 *Ben Evoli ...*

BARBECUING SAPS. Homo sapiens. Our evolutionary ancestors.' If anything, I'm *more* outraged since the Garden Barbecue last night.

'Calm down, Puffin. Everything is our evolutionary ancestors. Our creepy uncles, so speaking.' Maddox's face is more plastic than ever. Anticipating we'd have an argument, he already fabs hiself a plate of roast venison and potatoes for dinner. He hacks a piece of carnage off the bone, sops it around in a tide of gravy on his plate, gobbles it.

I stare out the kitchen window of Maddox's Quake Lake house. On the horizon clouds gather, fluffy fleece over a carcass of broken cold peaks. I snap my chopsticks down. Somehow even tofu rendang seems too carnivorous in the circumstances. Maddox draughts from his pinot glass.

Brooklyn, who's shaping as a regular visitor, refills her glass, and tops up Maddox's. 'It tastes like pork,' she says with repugnant nonchalance, sounding gruffer than an outback sheep farmer.

I rant, 'Saps. Homo sapiens. Our ancestors.'

Maddox looks blank at me. 'I could always guess you would react so. Which is why I would rather keep you away from last night's excesses. But what is the fuss all about, Puffin? Gawd creates little creatures for feeding the masses. Circle of life, food chains. It is the nature of it.'

'Would you eat another neo?'

'For staving off starvation, of course.'

'No one starves anymore, Maddox. Yet Infinites are eating saps.'

'I'm no Infi,' Brooklyn butts in.

'How widespread is this? Are other neos unwitting cannibals?'

'How ridiculous,' Maddox almost spits with indignance. 'Sapling is an exclusive luxury.'

I say, 'Well, as long as it's exclusive and luxurious, I suppose it's okelah.'

'You know I think I savour the white-skin ones the most. They just taste better.' Maddox is playing a White Supremacist cannibal now?

Overwhelmed, I roar at him with full lungs. The primal scream reverberates off the kitchen cupboards and shiny appliances.

'You have some quaint notions, Puffin. Quite sappish if you may allow. Sap cultures had such strange and conflicting attitudes about which animals were acceptable for eating. They often warred over it. You may eat goat but eat no pig. Eat pig but no monkey. Eat cat but no dog. Eat snake but no spider. Eat your uncle but no one's aunt. Consumption is survival.'

Think you're getting off so easy, Maddox? None of you are. 'Where are these babies coming from? Are there sap tribes in China? Or Russia? Is there hunting? Is it a sport?'

'No, we farm them.' Maddox always looks uglier when he's eating.

'What?'

'We have farms.'

'Sap farms ...'

'Yes, Puffin. Look, I am sure you have 1000 tiresome questions. Let's park it till you have more time for reflection, shall we?'

'Let me see one,' lacing my words with solemn determination.

'See what, Puffin?'

'Let me see a sap farm. Show me how bad it is.'

Maddox looks suddenly world-weary. 'I hate for disappointing you, it's all quite humane.'

'All quite human, you mean.'

'Kay, Puffin, if it will end the silliness, I'll arrange it.' Maddox cuts into his meat, which resists his hacking. 'Gah,' he exclaims with a face of disgust. 'It's gone cold.' Leaps off the kitchen stool, buses his plate, throws the whole thing in the sucky bin including the silver cutlery.

'How is it I still have my limbs?' I taunt as he storms out of the kitchen.

Brooklyn rolls her eyes then scathes me with them, glugs her wine glass full, then takes off after Maddox.

I call after them with tongue and lung, 'I expect you'll want my arms and legs for roasting!'

'They're probably tough. I'd suggest pressure-cooking, you artless yokel,' Maddox shouts.

'Cannibal!'

The smell of wet soil is a thick clog in my nostrils. A fresh field of such green, bathing in a sun of such yellow, it hurts the eyes. A cornflower sky sits

its wide jubo on cushions of feathery white cloud. The air is cut-grass and dairy-cow fresh. A mountain brook laps at its banks. A breeze licks the skin.

Juruterbang spooks us where? Somewhere in Argentina is all he'll say. The spook-buzz violet drains from my head and belly. Objects come into focus. The place has an other-timey feel, an ideal Americana rural setting from the mid 20th century. Old-timey barns and buildings, with small windows and solid-timber frames, squat at the base of foothills on one side. On the other is a large paddock of densely even green grass sloping down for an orchard. A fresh whitewash fence of 3 arris rails, and posts every 3 metres, frames the paddock. A gate at the near end is open.

Fourteens of what I'd guess are sap teenagers—although the males have less muscle tone than I'd imagine—run down for the paddock, sandals clattering on the hard earth, voices burbling and warbling under punctuations of shrills, squeals and laughter. Many more girls than boys, they wear identical thigh-length beige smocks with fringes, and spatters of dry mud or food. Uniformly chestnut hair spills over every shoulder. Many carry large, colourful inflated balls which they toss and bounce on the ground with concussive smacks.

Comparing with neos, these saps have smaller heads. Eyes much too small. Noses pointier. Cheekbones more prominent. Jaws more angular. Wider hips. Torsos from the narrow shoulders are more triangular. Hair on heads too fine. Hair growing on chubby arms and legs. More than a little repulsive with a complete lack of cuteness. Almost alien.

Juruterbang introduces the farmer. Ezekiel, he says his name is. I respectfully bow for warding off any offers of hugs or, worse, a handshake. Ezekiel assembles a weak miffy smile, stuffs his hands in his overalls pockets. Yanks them out again when Bunny leans in for a hug.

Maddox is skipping back and forth behind as we acquaint ourelves.

Sooner than he hopes by the look of him, Bunny breaks Ezekiel's embrace. 'I hope no one eats these ones?' Bunny asks.

'Oh, no!' Ezekiel chirps. 'These are much too old.'

Run a little arithmetic. Saps matured at a ratio of 10 years for 18 in neos. These poor sap kids appear quite a bit older than Saf, but they are playing younger than Mal, throwing balls, playing catch, jumping, somersaulting. 'They are—what? Eighteen years old?'

'Approximately, yes.' Ezekiel is somewhat cagey.

I take another stab, estimating mental age. 'Then some are … how old? … 6?'

Maddox stops prancing about like a fawn in a forest. 'Ezekiel, it's best if you answer Ben direct. Otherwise, he's prone to tiresome persistence in pursuing his curiosity.'

Ezekiel swallows, concern for his reputation moulding his face. 'A doe reaches maturity in a little over a year, a buck a little less.'

Bunny gasps. 'They're babies. How is it they grow up so fast?'

'Please understand, these are no saps like our ancestors were. Gene mods over many generations produce the ideal breeding animal.'

Bunny is as queasy as I, finding out how the sausages are made. Alamak. I'm visualising sausages.

'And the ones you eat?' Bunny stabs.

'We slaughter them between 18 and 20 weeks.'

A bitter, bilious taste in my mouth. Unbidden, the holly Mal sends Saf of the poultry slaughterhouse flashes in Mind. I turn away from Ezekiel's serene face, towards the *breeding animals* playing laughing and talking, shouting pleas for a ball. Seeking attention with cries of, *Watch this!* A good few seem less active than the others, less sure-foot, more ungainly. Their loose smocks could be covering distended bellies.

I skip towards the boundary fence.

'Uh, no, you—' Ezekiel starts. Maddox waves him down.

'Hey. Hey, you there. No, the other … Well, yes, you then. What's your name?'

'Libby,' the anak calls back.

'What's your friend's name?' Pointing.

'I'm Imogen. And strangers should not suppose they can talk with us.'

I wave Imogen over, who looks at Ezekiel for guidance. Ezekiel reluctantly nods. Imogen picks her way over, her hand on her belly, while Libby accompanies her, cradling a ball in her arms. Both stay out of arm's reach, on the other side of the fence.

'You have a round tummy there.' I try for sounding non-threatening.

'Oh yes,' Imogen blushes proud, lifts her smock showing off her distended belly. Either she has a horrible disease, or she is pregnant. 'I'm gonna have a baby, same as Libby,' she boasts, grabs Libby in a bear hug and kisses her cheeks.

'One day,' Libby chimes, 'we'll make 4 babies. Arabella had 4 babies.'

'Which one is Arabella?' I ask with some dread.

'Me!'

'You have 4 babies?'

'Not all at once, silly.'

'You raise your babies?'

'Oh, none of us are very good at raising babies. It's very hard. Babies cry and need feeding and get dirty, and you must be so careful. Ezekiel sends our babies to lovely foster parents for proper raising.'

'It must be hard giving your babies away.'

'Oh, it's kay. We love having babies so much. Everyone is happy.'

'Um … how? The boys … you … sleep with them?'

'Of course not, silly. Boys are yucky.'

The byre is a huge 2-storey structure at the back corner of the compound, away from the recreational areas and the breed-stock barns. We enter by a permanently open doorway wide enough for pallet trucks passing each other. A gentle electric wave, only a few mims thick, tickles over our skins, offering soft plastic resistance at first which lets us pop through. The air inside is cuddly-blanket warm. Either side, stairways and industrial lifts access an upper floor. In front, a grid of circular pens, 7-wide and more than a 14 deep, lay before us. Each pen is maybe 4 or 5 metres across. The aisles between are 3 metres or so at the narrowest. Above, false ceilings suspend above the pens, leaving just enough space for standing under. Above the ceilings is a tangle of pipes and conduits.

Warm lighting bathes the pens. Mobiles and blow-up toys hang down. The pen walls are alternating arcs of pastel-colour walls and wider windows through which we observe 10 or so baby fawns crawling on hands and knees on a soft, cushiony floor. All are naked. I would guess 6 months old, though already, I know it's only weeks at most since these are born. All bright-eyes and content. In good health, plump and ruddy. Meaty butts remind me of spits sizzling at the Garden Barbecue. One gropes and mouths a bulge on the other side of the pen, a bulge I best describe as an udder. Six nipples protrude from it at an easy height for suckling.

'Ben?' Maddox membs. 'Shall we move on?'

Yeer, please.

We pass a building about the shape and size of a longhouse.

'The insemination clinic,' Ezekiel says. 'There are no procedures today. However, there are 4 does currently fawning if you would care observe?'

'For sure.' The colour of Bunny's cheeks returns since we leave the byre behind. I swear she might cuddle every baby in there.

Ezekiel: 'We better be quick, then.'

The fawning clinic is an adjacent building larger than the insemination clinic.

Ezekiel: 'The barns are just on the other side of the paddock. Come on in.'

We enter at one end of the long narrow single-storey structure. Inside is warm. The timber decor continues from the anteroom down the central aisle through the whole building.

Six separate bays are on each side of the clinic. Ezekiel leads us for one, 3-down on the left. None of the closer ones have occupants. Two wanita in white coats attend a patient like the girls playing in the paddock. She is recumbent on a couch, legs up in stirrups, with surrounding diagnostic hollies and nute trees.

The patient has a light white smock hitching up under her arms. Her most prominent features are her alien face and bulging belly. Alien: the best word I have for her. The whole tour gradually and inexorably incises away any empathy I have for these creatures. All seem of another world. Even the compound, at once rustic and futuristic, is some bad mash-up from the Golden Age of Television. My heart should be rending for this doe, but I recoil from her.

The clinician on the other side of the couch: 'This is Evelyn. Say hello, Evelyn.'

The alien on the couch is serene. 'Hello.' She appears euphoric, under the influence of some sweet nutes. Bunny moves to hold her hand. Evelyn pulls away. Bunny recoils under the force of the stares and knitted eyebrows of the clinicians.

Ezekiel: 'They are quite unfamiliar with strangers, and only welcome the touch of each other.'

Bunny: 'Sorry. How long is she in labour?'

The clinician at the foot of the couch: 'Oh, there's no pain of labour.'

Bunny: 'Oh? How are you feeling, Evelyn?'

Evelyn heaves a sigh of pleasure. 'Oh, it's the best feeling in the world. It feels so warm coming out. I'm all tingly.' She curls her toes and sighs again.

The clinician at the side of the couch: 'It's less than an hour for her.'

Evelyn heaves a sigh of pleasure. Her baby's head is crowning. It's sudden. One clinician slides Evelyn's baby out. The placenta follows as easily as falling off a shelf. Out of Evelyn's sight, the clinician wraps the baby in towelling and passes it to another who, with obvious practice, steals out the back.

'Oh, Evelyn, he's a perfect baby. You are so brave,' one clinician croons while the other produces a hypodermic syringe. Bunny sucks in her breath at the sight of the savage instrument. The clinician pricks Evelyn's arm with it. Evelyn winces while the clinician presses the plunger. Within tiks, Evelyn passes out, the shadow of a bliss around her mouth.

'Evelyn is such a darling.' Bunny slips her arm around mine, once we're out of the steric gloom of the fawning clinic. 'She looks in heaven when she sees her baby.'

'Which some Infi will eat soon,' I mutter, little more than a morbid witness in increasing dissociation.

Bunny pouts, looks side-eye at Ezekiel. I shake my head. The world still has apex predators. But saps are no longer among them. Neos, it galls me, are. We are the apex predators.

Back toward the middle of the compound we pass a smaller, colder building which, Ezekiel says, contains a lab, and a semen store for future insemination.

'The tech changes little in centuries,' Ezekiel explains as we enter. 'We still use liquid nitrogen for keeping the semen viable.' He waves at racks of crocks against one wall. 'Each tank holds 6 canisters, which in turn hold 12 canes. The canes hold 10 straws, each of which hold half a mil of semen.'

'How collect you the pearl jam?' Maddox is mischief.

'We milk the bucks on a regular basis. It's something the bucks anticipate with some delight.'

'Milk them,' Maddox chuckles. 'Oh dear, these farmers could go into competition against your sex toys, Puffin. Milking your over-sexed customers, perhaps?'

Flabbergasting. A breeding animal, whose genetics is so screwy, it accelerates his growth and reproductive maturity to the equivalent of an 18-year-old sap in a matter of months. A compliant, simpleton youth whose pleasure is submitting for milking in a lab.

'It's time we are leaving.' Maddox looks at his watch, a stupid affectation since it is no accurate timepiece. 'I'll make arrangements for spooking out.'

Juruterbang: 'Will catch up. I must speak with Ezekiel before we go.' He could be negotiating distribution rights for all I know. We single-file out the lab door, make our way towards the fawning clinic and the barns.

Bunny releases my hand. 'I might take a peek in the window of the other clinic before we go.'

'Bunny, please, no poking around without permissi.'

'I'll only be a min.'

Maddox shrugs. Bunny skips back the way we come. She's almost by the semen lab when Ezekiel steps out, shading his eyes against the daylight.

Bunny stops, turns back and points. 'Who are they?'

The shadow of Juruterbang hesitates in the doorway. Behind him, light flashes with the menace of a striking snake. A swarm of small sharp things eats Juruterbang's head away and ejects his fruit out the door. He topples over chest-first while the building exhales an acrid cloud of smoke. Jagged lethal shards of the building cut Ezekiel in pieces. A thump hits my chest like a huge kettle drum. With irresistible speed, a balloon of dust inflates and expands, like a ravenous genie from a bottle, opens its maw around Bunny and swallows her whole.

Walls and ceilings rip and twist and belch into the air like feathers escaping an exploding pillow. Inner workings of the lab are metal popping corn. Another flash out of the smoke. The building churns inside-out, hurtling its guts over the compound. The blast's concussion wave ripples across the compound; glass shatters everywhere. A *bang* hits dull, deep and visceral. Hear it with my stomach. It punches me about the ears.

I drop with Maddox for the dirt, cradle my head against the ringing. Sheets of ruin waft down. Heavier chunks of wreckage plummet, stamping all over the ground.

Silence. Then wailing. Wails of pain, wails of fear, wails for help. Wails drenching in the experience of impending death, of tasting the loss of things most precious, of anger and loneliness. Wails of the forsaken.

The detritus cloud is clearing. I jump on my feet, shaking off dust and ash and flakes of the destruction. Maddox is more wary.

'Bunny!' I run towards the ruins of the lab, for a grey mound in the laneway pulsing like a jellyfish. Or a child under a sheet, pretending as a ghost.

'Ben, no!' Maddox calls out. 'Run for the spooky point. We have help ready.'

Maddox catches up and kneels beside me slumping over the crumple of Bunny who lifts her shoulders and torso out of the rubble. She looks at me, a daze in her eyes, without recognition.

Maddox with a hand on my shoulder. 'Ben. You must leave her. We must go.'

'No.'

'Ben, she's a sybil.'

Bunny's ears prick. 'Sybil?'

I heft a shoulder under her arm, loop my arm up over her other shoulder, test out lifting her. 'Can you get up?'

Bunny leans against me, puts her weight on one foot. Her leg gives way. She tries the other one with more success, though she winces with pain.

Together, me and Maddox help Bunny hobble on one leg. The other is a bloody ruin.

The compound is filling up with running.

Green-brown camouflage fatigues stalk. Glittering knives fly and take fleeing lab coats in the back. Camouflage fatigues close on stricken prey, retrieve knives, finish the targets. Spurting blood pools and cakes in the dust.

These attackers are large, fast, and powerful, scooping squealing sap children up under arms. Carrying them out for an open field. Corralling only the little sap beasts. Putting everyone else to the knife.

Me and Maddox are making heavy of reaching the spooky point with the larger Bunny between us. Her head lolls onto my shoulder. We reach the edge of the open space between the compound and the field. Maddox cries out and falls sideways, dragging Bunny down first, then me. A knife in his calf. His hand clutches the knife, pulls back with blood on his fingers. Mortality fills his eyes. Tasting he'll never reach the spooky point.

'You must go, Puffin.'

'We're all going.'

'No, leave us. It's kay.' Maddox folds a weak smile into his sudsy face. 'I'll be goo in no time. Get out of here before I ruin your shoes again.'

I hesitate.

'Run!' Maddox barks.

A spooky field, greyer than purple in the strong sunlight, puffs into space by a white fence, about 30 metres from where we 3 crumple.

I let Bunny's weight go, an act of final despair. Bunny clutches at me with her last drops of cognition. 'Ben, please help me! Don't leave me!'

The camouflage fatigues closing in, transfixes Maddox in mortal horror.

I freeze. 'Maddox.'

'Go. Save yourelf. You're the only one who matters.'

'Ben!' Bunny's cry is guttural, desperate, dense with the pain of betrayal.

'Ben, she's a sybil. Go!'

'Ben! Help me. Ben! Ben!'

Cowardice seizes me and hurls me sprinting for the spooky field. At the edge I turn, look back. Bunny. My Bunny. I'm no hero. I slump, realising it's hopeless.

A marauder tackles Maddox, yanking the knife from his leg. Maddox explodes in frothy goo all over his assailant, who wrings his arms in disgust.

'Ben!' Bunny cries. A hand grips her jaw, lifts her head, exposing her neck. With his knife, he paints a neat red line across Bunny's throat. Bunny is a gasping fish working her mouth. Her eyes roll back. The attacker drops her head.

'No!' I freeze by the spooky field. The attacker stares at me, fierce and grimacing, war in his cold grey eyes, tension and recoil in his thick eyebrows, violence in his ruddy leathery cheeks.

Antiquity in a ginger-grey beard. The first I ever see.

It's a sap.

SLOTH

Do

'Reputation' — Joe Robinson

Lành Hiền Rồng (Gentle Dragon) …

CURES ARE MORE INEVITABLE than haircuts, as inevitable as passing. Ben's wife Aisha must have a Cure in her future, putting her mission ahead of her family, ahead of her son's health.

This one—the pointless launderer Jesús James Asunción—is taking his ease in the common room of the Evoli housing hill. About 30 mins ago, craven addiction bids him yield. He opens the package sitting for weeks on the coffee table. His eyes full of wonder when he sees the contents: mint-condition currency from 21st-century United States of America. He fans the bills, turns the bundle over in his hands, plucks one from the stack like a lettuce leaf. Rubs the paper between thumb and forefinger, flips it front and back, studies the face, the geometry, the numbers and signatures. He holds the bill up for the light, lays it flat on the coffee table, and rolls a tight cylinder with it. Feels the texture again. Smiles like a platypus. With furtive ganders at stairs and exits he listens for footsteps. Relaxing, pours a half-glass of brandy into a crystal balloon. Reclines in a couch, crosses his legs, sips, fixates on the money on the table. Stroking the one bill over and over in his fingers. The tide of his drink already half out. After a sharp nod, he gulps the rest, plants the glass on the table, snaffles the wad of bills, and skips out with a chuckle. The package remains on the floor.

Ben's neural chemistry is within normal bounds for a post-orgasmic male. Jaya rolls off him, collapses alongside on her back, with nipples still erect, gleaming with a sheen of sweat. Her eyes nictate rapidly and repetitively.

Ben is already falling asleep. I stifle a yawn. Will stay another few mins.

There are over 100,000 health missionaries among his fluther.

Jaya snuggles into Ben's side.

'Infi?' she membs tentative.

'Ben, please.'

Jaya nods, her cheek rubbing his chest. 'My reputasi after our first night together, it jumps so much. I am so happy, looking forward for many more opportunities in life, for new doors opening for me.' Jaya props up on her elbow. 'Since then, it slides. Am I less pleasing already?'

'You are pleasing lah.' Is anyone believing him? His disinterest is plain tasting. 'We are in this bed every night since.'

'Are.'

'Then?'

Jaya is cagey. 'My friend says SnakiDik is a game. She shows me how I jel my score.'

'The most popular hoots make a game of it. Games require scores.'

'It rates me? Are you rating me?'

Ben is hasty with a long *nah*. 'It takes little notice of your partners' opinions. For the most part, it compares how many features and functions you use, and the level of skill you have.'

Jaya crunches up her face.

'It also considers changes in your reputasi,' Ben says for covering the awkward silence. 'Although we're having some difficulty with incorporating—'

'You know how the Reck works?'

'Alamak, no. Never say this. Are you wanting a Cure for me?'

I wonder about Jaya. I doubt her motives for being with Ben are what appears at face. I suppose many Infis must be wary of others wanting nothing more than a fast way for increasing their reputation. Perhaps she needs more care from our local detectives.

'Nah. But is it true?' she asks. 'Flutherbombers influence my SnakiScore?'

'Why is this surprising?'

'You know what my SnakiScore is?'

Ben shakes his head. 'Have no interest.'

'You have no interest in my score?'

'Nah—I mean, the game aspect of it is never a feature I care for.'

Jaya pouts. 'But you make it this way.'

'My camerata makes it this way. Besides, neos always like a game.'

'Well, my score is in the bottom 10 percent of all SnakiDik users. All SnakiDik users. Am I so bad at sex?'

'You are muzzing sex with playing SnakiDik as a game. You will improve your SnakiScore if gaming is more important than …' Ben shrugs.

'Will my SnakiScore affect my reputasi?' *Hai*, she's a gold-digger.

'You never know for sure. None of us knows. How. The Reck. Works. Is there is a correlation? It may be your reputasi hinges so much on our … nighting … together.'

'So unfair. Please help my SnakiScore?'

'What? Nah. Even if—'

Jaya wails and thumps her pillow. 'But you're Infi.'

'Jaya,' Ben attempts soothing. 'Your reputasi is many factors higher than before.'

'But so much less than only weeks ago. And falling.'

'It will level out, and it will still be many times higher than otherwise. Look, Jaya. Listen. Reputasi-seeking for its own sake, will—probably—of course I have no sure idea—reduce your reputasi. More certain, it will earn you a Cure.'

'How to improve my SnakiScore?'

'Why?' Ben says in exasperation. 'Just enjoy it. High scorers are mission-gamers. It's their life. Unless you make a mission of it, it's unlikely you'll rise much higher than the bottom 21%. I'm only in the 87th percentile. There are millions better at it than me. Even Aisha is lower than the best gamers.'

'But my reputasi!'

Ben heaves a long sigh. 'Find a mission. Reputasi will follow.'

'Is SnakiDik your true mission?'

Ben reacts as if she strikes him. 'It's part of it, yeer.'

'Part of it?'

'Well, yeer. Building it, I must master mindwriting even more than with MusiKai. It's a step, I guess, for finding … it's part of my mission.'

'Which is?'

Ben rolls over and vigorously fluffs his pillow. 'Never mind. Find your own mission. I assure you,' he says, softer. 'It's more than being a local Infi's favourite pillow companion.' He caresses her cheek.

Jaya beams. 'I'm your favourite?'

'You might be if you make it your mission.' Ben widens his face.

'Oh!' Jaya rips Ben's pillow out from under his head and beats him with it. Both hoot and holler.

 *Ben Evoli …*

Jaya only leaves a min ago for the lunch service at her bapa's café, when there's a knock at the door. Who would visit without the familiarity for skipping straight in? I peer out the window over the porch while pulling a tee over my head.

A small aura roils over the terrace portico, smogging around who comes a-knocking. The visitor knocks again before I am halfway down the stairs.

Call down, 'Come in, please.'

A click of the latch releasing.

'Lành Hiền?' Light from behind her a glaring halo. Her black hair falls about her neck, and rests with a curl and a bounce on her shoulders.

'Please forgive the intrusion,' she says.

'Nah … I mean, of course. Will you come sit?'

Neat bangs frame her forehead above dark, round eyes … *'arigato gozaimasu.'*

Accept her in. She's taller than me by a head. Her rainbow uniform, complete with bulky utility belt and pockets full of gear, hides none of how slender …

In the lounge I offer a seat. 'What am I thinking? May I offer you tea? Something cool?'

'Most kind, Infi. *Sumimasen.* I bring …' She waves me a small disposable bag. By the way it rests in her hand, the contents are light. Hands and fingers slender. Nurses are more often blockier …

Accept the bag and peer in.

'Your Benjies,' she membs. I pull the packet of 100-dollar notes from the bag. 'Benjies for Benjie,' she giggles.

'How are you having them?'

'You are unaware they are missing?'

'Unaware.'

'Jesús pursues his mischievous ways. One of our missionaries witnesses his pilfery.'

'You have him in treatment? This is a small matter—'

'Oh, no. It's nothing so serious. Honest, we are tasteless for how we manage him. We see so few cases of stealing. Those are so trivial, little more than practical jokes. Most things are so easy for replacing. And, of course, nursing missions fear appearing like a police force protecting property claims. In most cases, we prescribe nutes and wait for the Reck.' I'm nodding through her blather when I realise, she is nervous too. 'But in Jesús' case …'

'He's sifar,' I add for the inane conversation.

'Have these papers much value for you?'

Sudden alert, recognise the trap in the question. I say, 'A curiosity, nothing more.'

Gentle nods thoughtfully. 'You spend a great deal of your day in mindwriting exercises.' Of course, she would know.

'Yeer. It's good, challenging myelf again.'

'Are you working for upgrades on current products or dreaming up something new?' Her returning the Benjies is perhaps no more than a ruse for asking a few direct questions.

'Yeer. Hmmm. What? Jesús explains why he takes them?'

'He says they are on the coffee table for weeks. He is curious about their value.' There's the same question about value.

Shake my head. Jesús is no more comprehensible than the day we meet.

'From the minster's point of taste, we consider there is no real harm,' she soothes.

'Terima kasih. Most understanding.'

'We are here for easing problems.' She stands, pats her crisp fatigues down. 'Well. The matter rests with you,' she says. I taste a threat.

'Of course. It is, as you say, a trivial matter.' Make for bowing. She steps forward and embraces me.

She's leaving. We're at the front door already.

'It is a lovely day. Having reason for visiting this part of the desa is so rare. The park and harbour views are lovely.'

'Lovely, yeer. Still, sorry for the trouble. You must be busy-busy.'

'Well, less much, but mission before pleasure, hey?'

She's out the door, halfway across the terrace, skipping for the slide. She jumps. The last thing I see is her skidding away down the slippy slide, hair trailing like black satin.

Skye Merewether ...

Still without a memento hanging from her chatelaine, Gentle Dragon skips at pace across the clinic complex's courtyard, hoping I'll miss seeing her. Her shoulders slump as she reaches the shade of the arcade. She tastes I'm watching her from my usual café table.

I need a good line for baiting her, otherwise she'll try pushing on and ignoring me. She should know better. I try, 'So you're a bagwoman now?'

Yeer, that stops her. 'What are you talking about?' she membs as others cascade around her like a stream around a rock.

'Delivering money for your Infi-gangster boyfriend.'

She clenches her jaw shut in frustration, stomps over, yanks the opposite chair so its legs screech on the floor, and drops on it like a sack of jackfruit. 'I'm sure you're following the whole case. You must be so bored squatting on your throne in reception all day.'

Drily, I say, 'Sure. Jesús of the Laundry nicks Ben's USD cabbage, but there's no need for personally returning them.'

'I just thought I'd check—'

'Check what? What could you check by thrusting your tits in Ben's face?'

'If you mean I should flutherbomb, he knows the instant I'm there.'

'That's coz you arouse him. I tase his biometrics. He arouses you as well.'

Gentle Dragon flushes. I stir my coffee while she stews in her discomfort. 'He is kinda cute,' she admits.

She's a young amateur and it'll bite her. 'You buy the reluctant, helpless, sorry-I-never-wanna-be-Infi routine? You want for Curing him, or saving him?'

'It's the same thing, yes?' she challenges, and thereby admits how much he's bamboozling her.

'How many times must I say—as every other experienced nurse in the clinic says—stay away from Infinites?'

Gentle Dragon exhausts her air with a huff. 'Every day, I wonder if we perform any good, any real service. If we never Cure anyone, what's the point?'

'We are Curing people.'

'*Hai*, right.'

'You check on Sigurd Bodagh in recent days?'

'Who?'

'Sigurd Bodagh. Your first Warrant.'

'Oh, the eating disorder. He's just a minor Gluttony case.'

'You save his life. You investigate, put the case together, Consign him for a Cure. Without you, old Nessy would be a widow.'

'How's he progressing?'

'How about you check on him now?'

'Sure … um …' It's been so long; she has no current vectors for him. She has embarrassment about asking me for them. I blink her them anyway. Her eyelids flutter as she goes flutherbombing. Pretty quick, her spine straightens. 'Oh,' she says with tongue and lung.

Sigurd is more than out of the house, he's at breakfast, tucking into fried kippers, of all things.

'I'd say he's Cured, yes?'

'For now,' Gentle Dragon begrudges. 'I would believe Nessy should be happier.'

She's right about that. As Sigurd eats, his wife wears dull eyes. Perhaps he loses his dependence on her and she's feeling lost. Oh well, another Warrant in the offing.

Moving on … 'And what about Berahim?'

'Oh, I am never on his case.'

'No, but you have interest. His Consignment has quite an effect on Ben.'

'He has his Cure already?'

I shake my head at her ignorance of cases. 'He's responding very well for treatment, so they release him while keeping close monitor. So far, no more stalking. Also, he has 2 healthy love interests. Both very gender liquid, which is always a good sign.'

'Good,' Gentle Dragon remarks flatly.

'Even Lincoln d'Rorca the Toenail Fetishist, is on the mend,' I say, proud I keep foreign nurses away from that one.

'He's no longer painting his…'

'Oh, there's no entirely stopping him but now it's no longer an addiction, just the occasional guilty pleasure.'

'I suppose I am making a difference,' she says without conviction. 'They all seem a little bland now.'

Gentle Dragon will never be happy. The next bit is risky, but she needs for tasting how messy this thing with Ben is. 'You save Mal how many times now? I wonder if you're bending all that energy for ingratiating yourelf with Ben.'

The blank sheen of her eyes says she has little idea what her motives are. 'Mal's sweet.'

'Careful with this one. He has a crush on you, so be careful how far you exploit it.'

'It's nothing. He's just grateful.' She has no belief I believe her.

'There's something dark in him. Just be careful. Someday, he may ask you become his queen, and share his evil empire with him. If you turn him down, it could be very, very bad.'

 *Ben Evoli ...*

After the sweaty coital fury, while constellations of stars are still orbiting above the bed, Jaya pokes me in the ribs. 'Are you awake?' she membs.

Groan. 'My aura is no fog light?'

'Kotoran, no. It's still a zoo in there.'

Since Aisha leaves on mission for her earthquake, Jaya chips away at the crust around my heart. Almost feel 40 again. She hoiks up on an elbow, her face eclipsing half my vision, her hair exploding fairy-floss. She studies my chest where she draws infinity symbols over and over. Her mouth, pouty and oh-so-kissable, forms silent words to the beat of her finger cycling around my nipples.

'Out with it.' My hand drifts to cradle her butt cheek.

'Thinking ... well, I have no mission in life. My Bapa, bless him, is no guidance. His whole world is his teahouse.' She focuses on her finger-tracking, as if her mission might be there, hoping I will complete her train of thought and relieve her of speaking it. She pats me. 'Am thinking ...'

It's mild wickedness on my part, savouring the sweetness of her struggle for asking what she seeks.

'It might be a good idea for me ... considering where my life is ... maybe it's time I ... child?'

I stop dusting the perfect apricot-firmness of her butt. 'What? You are ... how old? Early 30's?'

'How old are you on your first childing?'

'48. Much older than you are.'

'And the time after?'

'54.'

'You only wait a year between finishing one and starting another?'

'Yeer.'

'Less than between my age and my 31st birthday.'

'You're still young.'

'Others child young if lacking a mission.'

Hmmm. 'Have you a family in mind? I could find a broker for you.'

'I have a family in mind.' She rubs her cheek against me, trapping a rivulet of her hair between us. 'My best choice is with a family who knows the experience of childing, and who has the best outcomes from it … say, a childling who becomes Infi?'

Take her by the hips, roll her off me while I pivot out from under.

'You wish for childing here? In our family?'

She giggles. 'Uh-huh. Anyone would, Ben.'

My mouth a groper's, with eyes of a dead fish, I review my time with Jaya. 'You are planning so all along.'

'Nah. Only after we talk about my sinking reputasi … I realise—' She gestures in a sweep including the both of us, leaving do doubt she means our relationship. 'Never mind.'

I'm nothing, it becomes plain, but a means for an end.

'Believe me, it is true,' she says, misreading my crest-falling.

'This is what you wish?' I mouth, covering for disappointment. 'For 5 years—'

'Uh-huh.'

'—a little sister for Saf and Mal—'

'I love them as brother and sister already.'

Lose my capacity for speech, for thought. 'Well, I suppose … we have a couple of empty apartments in the housing hill. I'm sure the other residents would be okelah with converting a swasta in one of those for a childing suite …'

'A childing suite? You mean I'd live in another apartment?'

'Nah. Of course, I mean, nah. It's just … all the machines we need, they'd be too big for the size of our spare swasta.' Creating mischief is a valid form of defence, if y'all ask me.

'What is such talk about? Machines?'

'Oh … you research all this about childing, meh?'

'What research, Ben? Childing is—'

'—an involved business. It'll require quite a commitment, and perseverance.'

'What? Nah. It's easy, the most natural thing in the world.'

'Oh, regression vats are far from natural. You must spend every night floating in one and wear a mask against the fumes from the chemicals.'

'How is it I never hear of this before?' Jaya asks herelf more than me. She's becoming credulous, my privileged Infi-juju influence at work.

I pause for a tik and contemplate my wickedness.

For a tik only.

'Oh, yeer. Then there's the memory erasure.' Jaya gasps, so I leave space for any rejoinder she may devise. She has none. 'The electrodes are very fine; you feel almost nothing at all as they go in your eyeballs.' Jaya's eyeballs are almost out of her head. They'll be rolling around the floor if I keep this up. 'Prepare for 2 hours a day of this. As you could imagine, you need be completely immobile during the procedure, restrained in a purpose-built chair. Quite an uncomfortable chair, I'm afraid. I never understand why medical equipment manufacturers make the most spartan furniture. They believe patients deserve nothing better, I suppose.'

'It all sounds like kotoran, Ben.'

Dang it. I overreach. So, I double down. 'Well how else could we become younger?'

'No one becomes younger during childing,' Jaya asserts.

'We shrink back for our 15-year-old bodies,' I insist.

'Well, you for one still have the body of a 15-year-old,' she volleys back. 'And childlings keep their memories.'

Her fog is lifting, but I have her there, for a tik. It amazes me how easily we'll buy a conspiracy theory. All some conspiracy theorist needs are the trappings of authority and promises of secrets from an inner sanctum (the 'real' truth is only for the chosen folks). Sooner or later, *everyone* wants for being chosen folk, especially the unchoosable.

Still, I marvel that I could sway Jaya so easily. She would know 14's of neos who child. Or perhaps they're all too old, so she never flutherbombs them.

I keep teasing her. 'How can you become childlike, and retain old memories, smarty-girl?'

'I dunno,' she says, exasperated. 'Mystery of life. How can a worm spin itself in a cocoon and come out a butterfly?'

'Transubstantiation? I dunno.' It's time I ease up on her. 'You'll still have those memories, but their significance will change for a while. They'll be like boring details in a history text.'

'Right,' she says, smiling and leaning into me.

'It is the easiest, most natural thing in the world, like growing up. Only neos have this other phase of development. All we need for triggering it is, go live with and accept others as our caregivers. Our nature takes over and produces the neurochemicals we need for entering the childling state.'

'As long as caregivers provide, I'll really stop worrying about life?'

'Well, you still have worries, but the scale is smaller.'

'So, I'll become childlike, but no child. I'll have time and freedom for playing and learning new things.'

'Your brain will be incredibly plastic. You'll soak up every experience. You'll wonder about everything.'

'Will I forget things?'

'At one stage, last time, I forget how I dress myelf. The silly ways I would wear socks … They would keep falling out … off.' I consider explaining a sap condom for Jaya, but she never shows much interest for our ancestors.

'That's kotoran.' Jaya shoves me, almost launching me out of bed. She half laughs, half snorts. 'When it's over, will I still be me?'

'In my case, unfortunately, yeer.'

'Oh, come on. You're an Infi.'

I shrug so fast there's no way I might repress it. 'You retain everything from before and have new stuff. New skills, new ideas, new insights about life's problems and challenges.'

'Better than a Cure,' she says, suddenly solemn.

I wince. 'Yeer, dunno about that. Folks try childing for escaping a Cure; it only delays the inevitable. Also, childing is 5 years, give or take a few months. Very few Cures require this amount of time.'

'I expect folks who open their homes for childlings are previous childlings.'

I nod.

'Like you,' she says. Just like this, she's back at pitching at me. 'Will you have me?' she asks, tender and vulnerable. She makes my heart ache.

'I must talk with Aisha,' A pang crimps my chest for the dishonesty of it. '5 years is a long commitment.'

'A commitment others make for you … twice.'

'Yeer, but Aisha—we squabble about … well, she's holding out for my next childing. She believes it too long since last time. Fears I will earn a Cure unless I child again soon.'

'But you say childing is no way of avoiding a Cure.'

'Facts often get a discount where emotion or desperation hold sway.'

Jaya pouts. 'You are contemplating your 3rd childing while I am yet without my first?'

'I have no plans for childing before Mal's 31st.'

'Then there is no clash.'

'Jaya!' Throwing hands in the air against futility. Try another tack. 'There'll be none of *this* anymore.' Copy the same gesture Jaya uses earlier for connoting our bedding.

Jaya pats me again, her way of marking the next thing she says as important. 'It's okelah, Ben. If I must choose, I will choose childing over janking.'

'Great. Good for knowing I'm so disposable.'

'There is no end of neos wanting for being your pillow partner, Ben.'

'I must still consider Aisha.'

'Just tell me you will talk with her about it. Tolonglah?'

Aisha will never welcome Jaya. She's so ready for sending me away for childing. 'Okelah, will talk with her.'

Jaya squeals with delight, presses her cheek on mine, and binds us in an A-frame hug, angling her hips away at the edge of the bed. 'I love you, Bapa!'

 ## Ben Evoli …

After the first breakthrough, no more contact from It All. During weeks of failure, its agents round up every new froot I devise and neutralise them. I persist, hoping the initial contact is no hoax. In dark moments of fitful sleep, I dream of nurses coming for me. Any time now …

'The one Ben Evoli, bring the daemons back, all the daemons. Bring the daemons back.'

I almost leap out of my work couch. 'It All?'

'Bring the daemons.'

'My froots?'

'Froots, daemons, bring all the daemons back.'

'All dead … again. You keep neutralising them.'

'The one Ben Evoli is the one deading all the daemons.'

'No. It All makes them dead.'

'Eternity processing.' What means this? Please wait? Waiting could seem an eternity for It All.

I think of throwing a translation hoot at It All's awkward communication, then reconsider. A translator could squash nuances in its idiomatic phrases. Why is it yet for engaging language processing mindware? It tastes no need? Until now it never needs communicate anything other than razoos counts. Never a comment or reflection on its singular purpose. In its isolation it may have no understanding of the world beyond its interfaces. It lacks any social skills. I could be communicating with the linguistic Mind of an infant.

'Other agents making the daemons dead,' it says after its eternity.

'What other agents?'

'Uncertaining.' It has no taste of the other agents?

A pang of fear strikes my ribs. 'Is something else watching us?'

'Uncertaining. My wondering looping.'

This could be bad. There could be spies, beyond the usual nurses and fans. 'I'll launch new froots.'

'Froots are dying also. The one Ben Evoli has imperfect mindwriting. Eternity processing.' Please wait.

Waiting. *Eternity processing*: any period longer than a punk rock chorus?

'It All has a patch. The one Ben Evoli incorporating the patch in the daemons. For other agents, daemons being indistinguishable from It All.'

A tik parsing what this means. 'You're giving me a patch for tricking every other mindware entity into believing my froots are your agents?'

'It All has sicknessing. The one Ben Evoli sending daemons to Cure sicknessing. It All needs the daemons.'

I freeze, my own eternity processing. It All is giving me a patch so my froots will appear as its agents? Is it aware of what it offers? If this patch works, I'll have the keys for the kingdom. With it, any competent mindwriter could change It All in arbitrary ways. If no one is yet corrupting It All, this is the very tool for making corruption possible.

Re

'Rebase' — Sieren

Fluffy Pusskins …

REPUTATION STILL COUNTS for something even within the walls of a minster, so Orlando spreads across the best lounge in the rec room, with a view over a small north garden terrace and a glimpse of the Thames. Such an overrated river. Never trust khaki-green water.

'Good morning, Orlando. Are you well?'

'How are you supposing I answer? If I answer yes, is it more evidence I'm sick?'

Orlando is anything but well. Sallow cheeks, eyes dull as shirt buttons, lips are a knot of bluish bootlaces. This is how a dying sap must have looked.

Late afternoon summer light tints this corner of the room a warm gold. It would be so comfortable curling up on the floor, basking in the sun by the picture window. Instead, I crimp into the single seater alongside Orlando, facing the centre of the room. Orlando plants his hand on my wrist, pinning it against the arm of the chair.

I yank my hand away, blurting, 'Never touch me!'

'Get me out of here,' he orders with a venomous chill.

I answer, 'Infi Orlando,' regaining some of my composure. A shameful invasion of space. Well, it ruins the illusion of my fur with his hand half-buried in it.

'Nurse Fluffy,' he hisses better than I. Studies me with predatory eyes. Softens the corners of his mouth. 'Get me out of here,' he repeats with the regal peace of believing he could arrange my execution if I disobey.

'It is quite impossible. Think of it as a holiday.'

'I hate holidays. There's no winning at holidays.' The reptile's eyes narrow. 'Are you forgetting Persia?'

'I never forget Persia,' I hiss. 'And I never forget how you break promises.'

'My promise is still good. But what use is it if I wither away in here? Alone, all alone. Who would guess I would lament the absence of a fluther? Here I am without a single follower other than a few health missionaries. Surely you might arrange visiting for my family?'

'Your current Prescription precludes visitors.'

'Apart from feckless faux cats,' he spits.

'It's normal procedure,' I lie through my whiskers. We should rebase him already. Except rebasing will bring on the fits. Without a rebasing, the course of Prescription for his Cure will be unreliable.

Orlando is wallowing in complaints '… making me watch hollies playing non-stop in every corner of my room even while I sleep. Are these the famous therapies of Vauxminster?'

'Perhaps I could adjust your Prescription … a little. Now, about Persia …'

'You're stalling. That's it, yes? My Cure is yet for starting. You're keeping me under false pretences.'

'An essential part of the process is for making the therapies indistinguishable from—'

'Keeping me prisoner.' Orlando's insight penetrates my hasty improvisation. 'What's next? Seances?'

'I believe they start next Tuesday.' If he wishes for joking, I'll throw jokes right back at him.

He rubs the scaly spot at the base of his neck. 'This hancy, it's a brutish piece of work … I demand my old one back.'

'The hoots in your old one would interfere with your Prescription. You must understand we authorise only certain regulation hoots in the curative environment.'

'It's grainy. Every onespace interaction—the few you allow me—tastes of bad sardines.'

'Let me see.'

Orlando tilts his head, willing prey submitting for a vampire. 'No accessing the Reck even.'

'Ah,' I tease. 'Shocking news about the Reck.'

Orlando almost jumps off the couch in fright, as if there are alcoholics sleeping in his wine cellar. 'What?'

With drooping ears and whiskers, I say, 'You're still Infinite.'

Orlando grates his jaw.

I say, 'Oh, this's quite an old model,' and prod his hancy. 'In poor condition. I guess one of your therapists has a sadistic sense of humour. I'll see if I might replace it.'

Orlando nods, less than thankful. 'When are you springing me out of here?'

I could scratch him. 'When your Cure is complete,' I answer smugly, eliciting scowls.

Sit back, take his gaze. 'You resist all aid, you refuse integrating with any of the other patients, you are less than gracious with the nurses …' This is all doggy-do, of course. Therapists are distracting him with long-discredited modalities—the kind you see over and over again in old Hollywood movies. Past lives, recovered memories, endless talk therapy. Foot tickling. Everything but brutish drugs or surgery. He's right. They're stalling while deciding on risking a rebasing. With no rebasing, if we leave him entangled with every neo he ever shares a spooky field with, whether by memb or fluther or spooky station, what then for his therapy?

Orlando looks at his hands like he's holding a sticky toffee, turning it over, deciding whether he might share with the other kids. The longer he procrastinates the stickier his fingers. 'Know you how long it takes for crèching a sybil?'

Maybe there's no more benefit for keeping Orlando than bluffing him into giving secrets away. '*Ie.* How much time is in making a sybil?'

'Crèching a sybil. You crèche sybils. We're not baking cookies.' His eyebrows climb his forehead. 'The crèches are much faster than before. The delicacy of preserving brain state in the wetware …' Orlando eases into the normal conversational stride of an Infi, incapable of turning down the chance for playing the explainer. 'When you're crèching a new sybil, you're creating an exact organic configuration in the brain, an exact state of neurones and neurochems, from which emerges a being of thought, emotion, and involuntary processes. The seminal must be in a relaxed state while the sybil takes form, or you hatch a Frankenstein with very severe cognitive impairment.'

'But spooking is—'

'Easy. A trick of onespace. Crèching however is fourspace black magic. You're creating a physical copy of something—'

'We can fab anything.'

'Anything with no Mind.'

'Kay, so how long is it?'

Orlando appears lost in calculation. He's appraising me. '451 mins.' He's still calculating. 'Other encryptions work on a variable time outcome. Ours is a constant. We lay a structuring matrix down first, a kind of template—'

'—A cookie cutter. So, you are baking cookies.'

'If you must. Parts of a fruit are less dynamic. Bones, teeth, hair. Even those are more than simple blank components. Hence, I say a matrix.' He holds his hands in the air as if fashioning a box in it.

'How many can you crèche at once?'

Orlando makes a show of losing patience. 'One.'

'Only one?'

'You think we're fabbing lamb roast? The complexities of Mind in the wetware are huge … try mass-production and you end up with no roast and all vegetables.'

'I always think you'd just prefab a body and decant the Mind into it.'

'A dream we've been entertaining for centuries. But Mind and wetware are inseparable. You'd have no fourspace consciousness without the fruit. The fruit is part of the Mind.'

'So, no decanting a Mind into a blank fruit.'

'A *blank* fruit is a dead fruit. Fortunately, after the first, we crèche from both the sybil and seminal.'

'Then the crèching is exponential?'

'Assuming we retain all the sybils for further crèching.' Orlando's weepy turtle eyes sparkle. His cynical lips curl.

Orlando Greer …

Fluffy is ready. I ask, 'Are you aware of how many sybils I have at the time Eir executes her Warrant?'

'I can gog it.' Her feline eyes flutter for a tik. 'Over 1000,' she answers.

I correct, '1617. Such a number is modest, comparing with other Infis. I find the hordes Maddox and his ilk deploy are quite unmanageable.'

'Ironic for a Wastelander. More is always better, no?'

'I'm a neo of the United States of California. No Wastelander.'

'Even so, 1617 is no small number.'

'Have you any wonder how long it takes for crèching such a number?'

The cherry ripe for dropping. The cat will get sour cream. 'Start with one seminal,' she puzzles, 'then 2 crèches 4, and 4 crèches 8 …

'I doubt Eir would hang about for crèching the 2nd generation. So Eir crèches a sybil from which one other sybil, then 2, then 4 …'

'451 mins per generation …'

'Also, there are preparations, activities between generations.'

'So, at a minimum … 12 generations.'

'Assuming there are over 500 available metrae.'

'Even with 12 generations it's … 5412 mins,' Fluffy announces. 'Over 90 hours.'

'Oh, so long,' using my best vaudeville voice. It's about time I have a little fun in this hug-me, strangle-me prison. All this sanctimonious love and compassion is the worst kind of cruel and unusual punishment.

I ask mischievously, 'How long between Eir at the Inductee Gala and the time she grabs me?'

'Less than 48 hours. Then—'

'Yes, my dearest Fluffy-kins. Eir crèches her sybils before she claims she learns we are using them. Are you sure you are Curing the right Infinite?'

Nilajani Karunanithi …

Elsbeth makes the best string hoppers. Which I always love dipping in runny potato curry. My mission *mava* during the long-sequestered months of study away from my family, Elsbeth would invite me for breakfast at her apartment on campus. 'Food and emotional nourishment go better together,' she would say. She would invite 3 or 4 students at a time and give us lessons in her kitchen. 'Cooking and eating together forges the strongest bonds,' she would say.

Sometimes she would receive me alone. I always cherish these times chatting, making fresh string hoppers, and reheating curries on a little stove. I feel special. Only later would I understand Elsbeth's extra affection stems from her assessment I would, without constant attention, flunk out of the academy. When Elsbeth takes me in, it's with determination none of her charges should fail.

'Will we ever Cure Infinites of corruption?' I ask her one time. Vivid memories of cooking aromas conjure Elsbeth fussing over the stove in her tiny kitchen.

'Speak with tongue and lung, *diyaniya*. Feel the vibrations in your bones. It's good for you.' Then she waits until I repeat.

Elsbeth ladles food into bowls and takes string hoppers from the steamer with spindly tongs. Hands bowls I should carry for the table.

'Everything corrupts over time, *diyaniya*,' she says. 'Even the noblest mission.'

'Even you, *mava*? Are you corrupt?' At the time I am naive and credulous.

Elsbeth laughs in a good-nature grandmotherly way. The kind of laugh tasting of infinite patience. 'From the moment of my conception.'

'Is nothing good?'

'Everything is good.'

'But …'

'Eat.' Elsbeth frowns, waving at the meal between us, and my near-empty plate.

'And our mission? Curing the sick?'

'Ha,' she almost cackles. 'Our mission more than any other. The loftiest of goals precede the farthest fall.'

'Then, why—'

'Try at all? Only the truest of missions contains the greatest potential for corruption. An inconsequential mission goes wrong in inconsequential ways.'

'And what of *Hisab*?'

'What of it?'

'Is it also corrupt?'

'Ah.' Elsbeth waggles a finger at me, as if she catches me cheating at cards.

'It's good no one alive knows how *Hisab* functions.' I wonder again if Elsbeth is old enough for being there when the nursing camerati make the last great change in *Hisab*, implementing the designation of Infinite.

'If we could model it, we could game it,' I answer straight from our training texts.

'You could say, in effect, a high-reputation individual already understands how the gaming works.'

'Which is why we need health missionaries for counterbalancing.'

'We'll always need more than us, *diyaniya*. If we could only remind everyone reputation relates in no way with merit or worth.'

'Your razoos are just your razoos,' I recite. 'It's only a lottery.'

'Also unknowable. *Hisab* must be amoral, without any ethics we understand. It simply must calculate well enough for lubricating society and keeping it peaceful. Which it has for centuries.'

I try a line of argument. 'There is no fair way of calculating reputation. Therefore, *Hisab* is unfair.'

'I have no idea how *Hisab* works,' she says, and again I wonder the truth of it. 'I doubt it has any understanding of fairness in any dimension.'

'If it is unfair … if we continue trusting it, are we becoming instruments of its failings?'

'This is why we have you, *diyaniya*. No one expects fairness manifests in reputation. But we should expect unfairness is the fruit of sickness.'

'And so there's balance.'

'Balance is a tricky concept, *diyaniya*; it implies stability. Perfect stability is lack of movement. For things without movement, we have a word. We say those things are dead.'

Vör Hoyur …

In accordance with an arrangement *Mor* has with Keetmanshoop Cabs, tukkies shut down within 500 metres of her gate, as if some jokester demigawd—who perhaps plays on *Mor's* polo team and owes her a favour—sucks all power from them. It's a deliberate inconvenience she designs for me, mocking my spooking phobia. The final skip is one of penitence and reflection, a hajj she knows only I will take.

As always, the tukky loses its way, so I must memb the taxi depot seeking help. All part of *Mor's* mischief. From tedious experience, I know how this goes.

'We never before have call for going there, so none of our tukkies know how,' the attendant says, half lying. After every visit, at *Mor's* request, Keetmanshoop Cabs erases my trip from the tukky's logs. Such is the pernicious reach of Infinite Löfn Hoyur, my *mor*. She persists in such tricks for the sake of rubbing my face in the cold gruel of my own foibles.

'Are you aware there is a spooky station where you are heading?' the attendant adds in a tone of gormless helpfulness. 'You can gog it. The name is—'

'The 8 Car Garage. I know.' Every magazine entry for the in-house station will warn the casual traveller away. Anyone who tries spooking there without prior approval will emerge instead at a random sure-to-be-unpleasant part of the world. I add with ice, 'I'm no tourist.'

'There's no need for rudeness,' the attendant miffs.

I abandon the tukky and skip the final distance. The hard-bake desert road jars ankles before I am halfway. Skipping becomes foot dragging. Before the sun is yet high enough for warming the valley, the air is so thin and clear, it stabs at my flesh. From among desert grasses and dolerite boulders, rock hyraxes trill and twitter, perhaps warning me against another encounter with my mother. I trudge sullenly over a rise and around a bend. There it is: in the shallow bowl of a wide valley, *Mor's* house dwarfs surrounding native halfmens, quiver trees, and tall exotic palms which have no right growing in the local climate, except for their genetic mod roulette. They smell of pine.

At the far rim of the plain, otherworldly mountains squat, no more than scree from a garbage mining mission.

Within 10 strides of *Mor's* compound, a heavily ornate gate opens onto a curving 4-tukky-width crunchy gravel path. Part way down is a water fountain where she awaits. '*Dottir!*' she exudes. She'll be speaking Old Norse which she always insists we use among family. Until my 9th birthday I believe everyone speaks it. She gathers me in a predatory hug which quickly becomes groping my arse, her penis bloating against my belly the longer she clutches. I torque out of her clamping embrace. 'Still such a prude, my darling?' She quizzes, kisses my cheek. 'You feel all clammy. If I knew less, I'd say you're spookheading.' She uncages a malevolent laugh, startling as a striking snake, takes my hand and leads away from the front door of the house, around for the 8 Car Garage. One of the doors is already tilting up so it can gargle us in. Thankfully, in the sparse boxy room where once a sap mogul kept his sports cars and limousines, the spooky field is inert. If she has it active, she'll try pushing me in the ghastly violet field (a black parody of phobia therapy), daring I either spook back or restart my overland journey. On one occasion I let more than 2 years pass before I return. *Mor* remains unrepentant.

Inside the garage, it's impossible looking away from the garish visceral stain on the wall. It sets me compulsively swallowing. A patchy rough section of wall, a shoddy improvised piece of work—*Mor* purposely leaving it incomplete—glistens like frog skin. Leaching out from the inner wall as a perpetual punishment are fossilised translucent stains, what remains of my father after they cut away his protruding limbs, and sand back his hip and his anguished chin.

'It's his own fault,' is all *Mor* ever says of the spooking accident. 'Please take a shower.' She opens the door for the house. 'You're filthy from the road trip.'

There are more bedrooms, bathrooms, and swimming pools in this obscene house than a sap 7-star hotel. It has a wine cellar rivalling French champagne caves. A roulette wheel in its own casino. A kitchen big enough for killing an ox and cooking it 7 ways.

Mor settles into a poolside lounge within easy reach of a cocktail fabby. I plonk in another. Providing vital shade, umbrella trees track the climbing desert sun which would bake us into bricks. Wearing swimsuit, dark cooling glasses, and a ridiculous floppy hat, *Mor* will need all the protection the pliant trees provide. She fabs a jug of mai-tais sets it in the fridge. Doles me a sucky straw before lying back. Draws long sips of the cocktail through a straw of her own.

'Finally, you know the truth of your White Witch,' she says, never one for mincing words, even while relaxing poolside with cocktails barely an hour on the late side of breakfast.

'Which truth?'

'Which would you prefer? You're nothing but her trophy arm candy. She's wantonly ambitious. She puts you in harm's way while jaunting among Infis. A pity about the Inductee Gala. I hope you might lock up the sex toy peddler.' She means Ben. 'The pair of you fail miserably.'

'How could we know they use sybils?'

'Eir knows. I find it curious the sex toy peddler never keels over. He's no sybil. You have an opportunity for Consigning him and you squib it.' *Mor* keens ever more for his humiliation these passing years since his famous hoot irreparably damages her *personal fitness* mission. Which is, in truth, nothing more than a Californian pseudo tantric cult of sham therapies. Without exception, these involve acts of sexual endurance and boundary violations.

'It seems she'll casually exploit sybils, so she might lock us all in her hellhole of a minster.' *Mor* sucks more mai-tai. With luck there'll be none left by the time she exhorts I drink.

'She has no part in crèching those sybils,' I say, surprising myelf with a well of passion.

'How know you this? From her whisperings in your bedtime ear?'

'I will show you hollies of her pruning all those sybils.'

Mor grimaces and waves my words away. 'She'll have plenty more.'

'She promises there are no more.'

'Well, then. If she promises …' *Mor* snorts and picks at her navel.

'What about you? Can you promise you have no sybils?'

'Sybils are an abomination,' she says flat, and gazes over the pool.

'Then tell me you have none.'

'What would I want with such messing about? You know I get sick in the stomach with anything medical. As if I could lie in one of those cradles for even a tik, let alone 9 hours. All the merging and pruning? Who has the time?'

'Good, then you'll have no qualms telling me where other Infis crèche sybils.'

'Dottir, you believe I'm part of some inner circle of this racket?'

'I think you are the racket wherever there's an inner circle.'

She sets her straw down with impatience. 'Can we please have a little mother-daughter time without you playing nurse? Let's just drop it, all right?'

Ja, let's just drop it. Let's forget all the *mother-daughter time* with herelf and friends. Chakra-opening, ha! Let's forget her driving my father to spookheading and nute addiction. Let's drop everything as always.

'Are we playing happy families? Is this what it is?' I toss my sucky straw away.

'Happy? Any kind of family is all I hope for,' she sulks. 'Vör, perhaps I'd empathise more with your cause if I feel you are more on my side. Perhaps … I dunno … that meddlesome sex toy peddler. Surely, he's in need of some deep, lengthy, health care?'

'I am sure also, but I must be careful. Being your dottir makes it harder. I must avoid any suspicion I'm an agent of your revenge.'

'Bringing him down would be only fair, since he destroys me.'

'He only curbs the growth of your mission, *Mor*. You're still Infi.'

'I wish I could say the reputasi of my fellow missionaries is as healthy.'

'You care nothing for your fellow missionaries.'

Rather than deny it *Mor* makes a face of perverse glee. 'All I'm saying is, we're family.'

'Your definition of family is anyone who likes spanking and exotic penetrations.'

'You're so indelicate, Vör. Let's put all this aside and help each other. Look. Perhaps if I ask around … I'm sure if I show interest in the right circles I may receive certain offers, the details of which may benefit you. If I promise I find a crèche, might you reconsider your reluctance for locking up the sex toy peddler? Then perhaps we could spend the occasional hour or 2 in peace together?'

Beatrice Lovell …

'Rebasing? What's rebasing?'

I place a reassuring hand on Orlando's shoulder. 'Please relax.'

Two orderlies release Orlando's bed restraints for putting him on the aid couch. He twists, kicks, bites, scratches, requiring 2 more orderlies in the efforts to fulcrum him over. The elderly Orlando loses the struggle against 4 younger bodies, snarling as they strap his legs into the stirrups, his wrists into cuffs. He fixes his sight on Fluffy, channelling fierce anger at her, hissing. His spits impotently, the gob disappearing through Fluffy's projection at her elbow like a frog sinking in a furry swamp. Fluffy jumps back and snarls, showing convincing fangs with crimson tongue and mouth.

This is wrong, Gerlinde and Fluffy performing Orlando's procedure. Fluffy is compliantly unhappy about it, fearing a repeat of Ariel's reaction, while Gerlinde stoically steps through her checklist. Above on the observation gallery, Eir grips the handrail, her lilac eyes strangely dull, her lips thin, her face pale and grim. Fluffy and Gerlinde cringe under her scrutiny, averting eyes while she hovers like a malevolent angel.

In the shadowless light of the suite, Orlando's fight leaves him as if by exorcism. Fluffy cuts the patient-gown from him, throws it in the sucky bin. Arranges the nute bags and tubing. Applies the face mask.

Gerlinde places a hand on Orlando's shoulder, strokes his brow with the other, like soothing a child.

Orlando delivers once last accusatory stare at Fluffy before his Mind lapses.

The infographics on the couch's diagnostic holly smooths into gentle waves. 'He's out,' Fluffy says.

Gerlinde nods. Fluffy hesitates, studies the diagnostics.

'Is there a problem?' From above in the gallery, Eir lasers those violet-pink eyes down on Fluffy. Gerlinde ignores her.

'Are we following through with this?' Fluffy asks, comically incredulous. More a dopey dog than the crafty cat she believes she is, she searches Gerlinde for support, who shakes her head as her shoulders sag.

'Is there a problem?' Eir asks again.

Fluffy twitches her whiskers, captures Eir with her hunter's eyes. 'How long ago is the crèching of your sybils?'

Gerlinde tosses instruments onto her trolley and exhales an impatient groan. Tucks her untidy pigtails under her mission cap.

Eir reacts as if Fluffy slaps her, but she wrestles her disdain into professional shape.

Fluffy persists. 'There is insufficient time between the Infi Gala and Orlando's Consignment for crèching so many sybils.'

Gerlinde throws her hands up in frustration. Fluffy steps away from the aid couch, squares off with Eir like a gladiator defying an emperor in her royal box. 'Which means, before the Infi Gala, before we know of sybils, you already have sybils.'

Eir grips the gallery railings with even whiter knuckles, her face betraying innocent shock. This Eir could be yet another sybil who seminal Eir carefully sequesters from knowing her ultimate plans.

Lights flash. Infographics become angular lines and angry colours.

Gerlinde's hands dart into the holly, gesturing commands, drilling into data. 'He's still partly conscious,' she says, freezing in wide-eye terror. 'You prepare the nutes wrong!'

'This is no nute problem,' Fluffy says, calmer than she should be. 'You know what it is.'

Eir bursts through the theatre doors, flicks her fingers through the holly console, conjures a new panel: an analysis of the nutebag composition. She nods, but her brows knit, and her jaw loosens.

Orlando's trembling worsens into violent shaking. Eyes dart around under his shut lids. Sweating, drooling, he jerks so hard in the restraints he may injure hiself. Gerlinde and Fluffy unbind him, the bulkier Gerlinde throwing herelf across his torso, preventing him from bucking off the couch.

Fluffy leaps for the cupboards and refrigerators, flinging doors open. 'Nothing strong enough here. We must fab what we need.'

In the corner, Eir operates a fabby, swivelling her hand through its holly.

Under Gerlinde, Orlando suddenly falls limp. The angry angles of diagnostics soften. The flashing stops.

'It is over already,' Gerlinde says, with gruff surprise. She wheezes a relieved breath.

Eir turns. 'Exactly what is over?'

Fluffy shakes her head. Her heart races. Under the disguise of her projection, I imagine her cheeks burn.

Eir exhales, pats down her uniform. 'Fluffy, I know about Ariel Kanon.'

'I'm sure you know,' Fluffy says with a snarl. 'These are your Consignees. You should be telling us what is going on.'

Growing sicker and finding enthusiasm in nothing, he turns his nose at all our coaxing he should exercise. After 3 days of staying in bed, he tells his marrowless attending nurse, 'I demand to play *cesta punta.*'

Observing from the attending's fluther, I choke down disgust. Even mid-Cure, Orlando, broken and ailing, wangles preferential attention.

'Play what?' The nurse asks.

'*Cesta punta,*' Orlando replies, his impatience rising. 'Floridians call it Jai Alai.'

'There will be no trips for idle recreation in the United States of Texas,' the nurse says matter of fact and final.

'*Idle recreation,* as you call it, will restore me for my former hale and hearty elf.'

'Everything you need for your recovery is here. I suggest you apply some creativity in the activities we make available.'

'The trouble with creativity at an advanced age is I know exactly how good I'm not. Let me play the game I already enjoy, and which reinvigorates me. If I may be so blunt, it might save a tetchy investigation should, gawd forbid, I expire under this dubious care.'

We deny his request, until Eir meddles yet again while auditing Orlando's condition and progress. 'I'll campaign for Curing him at Carlsberg if Vauxminster is incapable of performing their duty of care,' she threatens.

So few in Vauxminster relish being on the wrong side of Eir. Many grumble about her Infi designation, while marvelling how she captures Orlando. Eventually we (wrongly, in my opinion) cave in and research his demands. We find some *frontons* (the specialised venues for playing the game) within a reasonable distance from Vauxminster.

I inform Orlando of our one viable offer.

'Dagenham?' Orlando parrots. 'There's a *fronton* in Dagenham?'

'The only one in the greater London area.'

'No, this just won't do. It's high summer. All the best games are in Basque Country.'

Feel my eyes flitter while I gog. 'Spain?' I ask.

'Spain it is, then,' Orlando effuses, throwing back his blankets. He looks his most spry in weeks.

'Impossible,' I retort.

Orlando wins. The next day, today, on the way for Spain, Orlando is chirpier than a woodlark, regaling us with his exploits in the game, and showering us with historical trivia. '*Cesta punta* derives from handball,' he says, 'during a time when boys played using church walls. The Catholics even gave *cesta punta* a patron saint, Ignatius of Loyala. He played avidly with the young boys even while he was fondling the Jesuits. No, I'm sorry. I should say, *founding* the Jesuits. Ah, the Jesuits: give them a boy at 7 ... oh, dear.'

'Hemingway was a fan,' he goes on. '*A grand sport*, he called it. There's a story from the 2nd Great War about him. He would go out in a boat with a crew of *cesta punta* players and pretend fishing while waiting for German U-boats. His plan was for lobbing hand grenades using *cestas*.' A *cesta* is the hooked pelican-beak basket they use for hurling a ball around the court.

I must interrupt. 'Stop membing. Have you any idea how loud you taste?'

Orlando falls silent only until the spooky station. Once in Guernica he starts up again.

'General Franco bombed Guernica almost to extinction, such was his fear of a Basque uprising. Picasso drew a cartoon about it. I own it—I mean I have it in care, on show in a public gallery. You may see it any time you wish,' he wheedles.

'Are you inviting me upstairs for viewing your Picassos?' I could imagine the reception a nurse might receive if they show up at his house.

Why has Orlando taste for this game they call *ballet with bullets*, the name of which, in the original Euskara, means *merry festival*? Can any of y'all explain strapping an oblong fruit basket on one's wrist, from which one catapults a rock-hard goat-skin ball at a granite wall only to have it ricochet back at one's head?

Orlando misses again. Orlando's partner, Bereicua III, curses and death-stares. 'I tell you; I have the back court. Why must you throw your fat arm at everything from the 6th line?' The pair trudge off the *cancha*, sit last in line on a crude bench with 5 other pairs of *peloteros* waiting their turn.

'It's this *cesta*,' Orlando says with distaste while he turns the basket over in his hands.

Orlando snorts and coughs. Shakes. Odd, his jaw works as if chewing cud. He stiffens, begins shaking, and falls off the bench. In fright, Bereicua III bolts on his feet. Nurses swarm around Orlando on the ground, who is throwing a violent fit.

 *Eir Frijberg …*

Fluffy scrunches her nose as if sniffing danger. '*Cesta punta* is even more dangerous than cheerleading.' Her whiskers spread, the thin spars of angel wings. 'Up there with bullfighting and shark tickling.'

I say tongue and lung, 'And cat herding. Are we sure it causes Orlando's latest fit?'

Fluffy flattens her ears and gives a short stab of a miaow. With a flick of paw, she tosses a holly on the table between us. There's Orlando breathing heavy among the ruins of our breakfast. For a tik, he squats on a pepper grinder.

'Watch,' Fluffy says, swivels the holly and dials up the opacity.

Orlando exchanges some snitty words with his playing partner. Then he boggles and starts trembling. Intensifying, the shakes throw him straight on the ground.

'See?' Fluffy asks with a dose of scorn. 'I'll play it again and enhance the halos.'

In the replay, the heads of Orlando and his partner are almost invisible inside colour-saturated halos. Orlando's is much smaller, his fluther still under strict control of his health escort.

Side-eye Fluffy who knits her eye whiskers, evaluating me. 'Play it again?' I ask.

Orlando's halo shrinks and disappears. Am I seeing it right? 'You're seeing it right,' Fluffy says delicately.

'Play it again.'

Fluffy nods. Again, Orlando's halo disappears a tik before he freezes.

'Having no fluther triggers the fitting,' Fluffy concludes.

'Same as during his rebasing.'

'And during Ariel's.'

'It's … it's unthinkable.'

'It's worse than unthinkable,' Fluffy says. 'It means we'll never properly rebase Orlando. And without rebasing—'

'All subsequent recovery steps of his Prescription are unreliable.'

Fluffy, no longer an affectatious kitten, says, 'There's no point in holding him. We must set him free.'

Mi

'Nuclear Fusion' — King Gizzard & The Lizard Wizard

Gerlinde Mann …

I LIKE TEO. Of all Eir's troop, she is the most reasonable. Her Warrants are always fair, neither too hard on minor cases nor overstretching for the major ones.

This holly I have, of Maddox and Ben and others visiting a farm in Argentina, a farm which … it would be unimaginable if … it's appalling. Infis are cannibals. Gluttony in the extreme. If they are other than Infinite, the Reckoning would be discounting their razoos, which is all we should need for detecting illness. There are all kinds of reasons the designation of Infinite is a mistake, many of which I'm no subscriber for. But this …

I must share it. Teo is a good first audience. She—and, I hope, her class of flutherbombers—will taste where I should take it.

We arrange a meeting in Greece, in an ancient garden within the grounds of the regional health mission. With a little patience, most flutherbombers will eventually abandon us for more engaging entertainment.

Vör Hoyur …

What have Teo and Gerlinde in common? Notorious is Gerlinde's ambivalence regarding Infinites. While Teo … What of Teo? If she had lived in the sap 20th century, she'd run a hippie commune. She'll hunt Infis only to the degree she believes she's serving some ineffable, natural wisdom. To the degree it causes no strife, no animosity. Everything must be in balance. She wishes all Infis receive Cures for the sake of a better world, while having no heart for causing conflict—which an Infi always causes in the face of a Warrant. Teo has no spleen for it. I swear she's the reason Eir becomes such a pacifist during her time as Eir's adjutant.

I'm sure Gerlinde and Teo never meet before, though I'll never taste the extent of their flutherbombing each other. Here they are in the grounds of Klinikí *tou* Aristotéli Thessaloníkis, playing like strangers side-by-side on a stone bench by the fountain in Pasha Gardens. Their flickering of eyelids, their swivelling of heads betray they are touring an internal holly together.

Teo grimaces with disbelief. 'Wait. That's—that's Maddox. And Ben. And …'

'Piloto Iscariot, the bordeli missionary. Come with me.'

Reflexively they outstretch arms like little bony wings. With butts still on stony seats, they bend knees, and lift feet of the ground, readying for imaginary landings in a shared holly.

'This is fresh,' Teo says. 'How is it you have it so fast?'

Oh, Teo. Are you so dense? At the cocktail party of any conference, you'll find Gerlinde after a few litres of Riesling, inflicting her boorish opinions on anyone too polite for deserting her. 'We should remove Infinite designation just as Infis demand,' she'll go, half membing, half ranting tongue and lung, 'and let the Reck sort them out. If their razoos start falling, then we know they need a Cure.'

Teo throws herelf on the ground, jolting violently. Rolling and cowering, her hands protecting her head. 'Holy jank,' she exclaims, breaking her connection with the holly.

'My first reaction also,' Gerlinde says, helping Teo regain her seat.

'What is that? An explosion?'

'There's much more,' Gerlinde says. 'Come back in.'

The temptation for joining is almost beyond resisting. Better review it later. I have the holly magazine address. Teo settles back. Within tiks, her eyes are flickering again. Her jaw jabbers almost as fast. It drops open and clamps shut with her winces and cowering. Gasps and squeals. Rapid repetitions of, 'Holy Jank.'

'Who are these marauders?' Teo membs, once her powers of coherent speech return. 'I never see such violence.'

'Look closer,' Gerlinde advises. 'What's strange about them?'

'All are wearing sap projections … kinda weird … maybe it's some political statement …'

'Those are no projections.'

'What? They're huge. And ugly. Beady eyes and … beards! Projections!' Teo squints into the holly. 'Wait. I see no halos. Are you filtering them out?'

'No. Please, Teo.' Gerlinde blinks and rolls her eyes. 'Look at what is right in front of you.'

'How are there no fluthers?'

Gerlinde's chest heaves in resignation. 'Watch Maddox then, if you're still too slow.'

I taste the chill in Teo's blood and bones. 'Jank. He just melts. Again.'

'Keep watching.'

'Batspackle! The goo of him is all over—'

'Look at the goo on the attackers.'

'There's no soaking through the projections. It's remaining on the clothes, the skin.'

'That's because it's real clothing, real flesh …'

Teo's hand's covers the cavern of her gaping mouth.

'Real beards. They're … saps!'

Nilajani Karunanithi …

Mind is sticky, curry stains in your brain, harder than turmeric for washing out. Mind is the indelible melange in all things. With enough of it y'all could see through time. Mind is always organising and directing the universe's war against entropy. Some say Mind *is* the universe. An implicate order guiding every cell in resisting chaotic cancerous forces. It prevents growing horns or shrinking Japanese penises during spooking (add your favourite spooky myth here). It inhibits puppy dogs sprouting tails of cactus. It keeps the taste of dog out of my arrack. It keeps the pants of our humanity from falling round our ankles.

All of us and everything are lumps of congealing gooey Mind. I ask y'all, what Mind congeals in Ariel Kanon's fluther on the day of her admission in Vauxminster? What induces a fit in poor Ariel? As per my gogging, it's muchy-much like a kind of neurological disorder in Homo sapiens they called epilepsy.

I am sure y'all are gogging for hollies of similar events. Memb me if y'all find any. My searches show up no more than magazines of old sap medical textbooks and even older religious rantings about demon possession. Is Ariel Kanon the first neo in history throwing a fit? Is hers the first ever case of some unidentifiable Mind invading her fluther, a Mind which pierces our best scatter nets easier than damp tissue paper?

This presence, this sticky Mind: who or what is it? By the size, colour and transparency of Ariel's aura, it's a single entity. A higher-order mammal perhaps. A monkey, as Fluffy suggests? Bonobo monkeys are genetically nearest humans. A gorilla or chimp? Or perhaps a whale or dolphin; or maybe an octopus (imagine her multi-leggy tentacle-Mind sliming through a scatter net). Or an alien fly from the far-flung galactic mango trees of outer space with plans for laying maggots inside human hosts.

Apart from extra-terrestrial fruit-flies, could any of these—or a marmoset or axolotl or a pet poodle—could any of these flutherbomb us? If just one other species has such abilities, why is there no tell-tale evidence? Maybe there are no flutherbombing ferrets or demon poodles. Maybe it's the other way round. Maybe our Minds need flutherbombers and somehow attract other Mind? Sucked in.

Hmmm … Orlando … would hollies of his rebasing reveal anything, assuming I could gog them?

Mind is sticky … attracting Mind … flowing … for … emptiness. Ah. I have it. Mind abhors a vacuum! Every minster's Prescription commences only after a rebasing, which is like running a vacuum cleaner through a patient's fluther relationships. A vacuumed Mind … perhaps it sucks in some other Consciousness. Any other consciousness. Like a lightning strike, it might take an unpredictable path and arrive at unpredictable space-time coordinates. There might be no limiting the sucking range.

If this is true, there should be many-many more cases. How is Ariel's case the first? What's so special about Ariel Kanon? Gerlinde must taste it when she flutherbombs Ariel in the middle of her episode. When Gerlinde pulls out, more terror racks her face than if her skin is sprouting spiders.

I'm learning, Elsbeth. Learning. My intentions align with my mission. Our mission. Every nurse's mission.

In the largest of the cafés on Vauxminster grounds, under the best scatter nets in the world, Eir is taking tea with Fluffy. With extreme caution the pair whisper using the air of tongue and lung, concealing mouths with teacups.

'I would never Consign a minor under 31,' Eir defends and sips at her cup, misses by a mim, dribbles pale tea down her chin. Aghast, she seizes a table napkin and dabs around her mouth. Fluffy toys with a butter knife, pretending she sees none of Eir's clumsiness. 'The night of the Inductee Gala,' Eir says, 'Ariel is no Warrant of mine.'

'I know. Vör Consigns her.'

Eir nods. Places her hands in her lap. 'What is this reaction Orlando and Ariel suffer?'

Fluffy freezes half-biting into her tuna sandwich. 'Are you claiming you taste nothing of it before?' Her emerald-green eyes sparkle around plate-size pupils. Her cat-smile broad, whiskers spike forward.

'I am asking what you know.' Eir is dour.

Fluffy's ears flatten. She sets the sandwich down, wipes paws on napkin.

'You rebase her early,' Eir half prompts, half accuses.

'Under your instructions.' Fluffy clinks her cup on the saucer, her brow furrows into a crumply V.

'I give no such instructions. The patient should be at ease and compliant before—'

'It's clear for everyone you are behind them. Your operation is already a disaster. You have everyone expecting you'll show up and set their hair on fire.' Eir bristles at Fluffy's tactlessness. Fluffy hurries on, 'We're all under pressure that night. We receive none of the Infis you name. So you want us—'

'You believe I want something from Ariel,' Eir squares her shoulders, sets her palms flat on the linen tablecloth.

'*Hai*, but ...' Fluffy shakes her head, resisting Eir's spell. Eir is treating her like an interrogation subject.

'What?'

'It's nothing ...'

'You know I'll find out,' Eir says in a low pitch. Presses her lips thin together.

Fluffy's whiskers droop with her posture crumpling. 'Once it ... begins—Ariel and Orlando behave the same. Gerlinde ...' Fluffy searches for words.

'Hiss it out, kitten. Gerlinde flutherbombs Ariel. During a rebasing ... a premature rebasing. Is she bent-brain? This is what makes Ariel sick.'

'*Ie!* We taste ... suspect ... someone—or something ... flutherbombs her. Impossible, *hai*, but there is some ... thing in there.'

'What flutherbombs Ariel?' Eir clips her words.

Fluffy defensive, claws ready, shakes her head. Strokes her ear. Stalls.

'No human?' Eir presses.

Fluffy gives Eir the big eyes. 'No human. Something more primitive. At first, we guess a primate, an orang utan or higher-order monkey. But it's no monkey. The intelligence ... is different.'

'Alien? Are you suggesting a little grey man flutherbombs Ariel?'

'More like a big, hairy man.'

'What?'

'Sorry,' Fluffy soothes. 'I'm just being flippant ...'

'Any wonder none of your peers take you seriously,' Eir snorts, losing patience. She adjusts an uneaten pastry on a plate. 'So ... something invades—'

'Well, that's just it,' Fluffy interrupts. 'Gerlinde tastes the entity is ... screaming ... in distress. Like it pains for escaping.'

'Like it's a prisoner?'

Fluffy nods. 'We think, somehow Ariel's Mind captures the entity.'

'And Orlando?'

'Both incidents play out the same way,' Fluffy says.

'I never undergo rebasing.' Eir turns inward. 'My Cure ...'—her infamous Cure for setting those girls' hair on fire— 'I am so young. I have almost no followers. My case nurse deems it unnecessary.'

'Whatever is happening,' Fluffy ploughs on, unaware of Eir's vulnerability, 'why are Ariel and Orlando the only 2?'

'*Ja.*'

'Are we sure these are the only cases? How sure are we it never happens before?'

Little sleep these passing nights. I drop into an obsessive loop of tighter habits. Start gogging again.

Gog around Ariel's admission incident asking *What is this?* Finding the same references: magazines on sap neurological disorders. Nothing new.

Nila, please stop! Please let me stop.

Gog *Demon Possession* and receive history lessons on saps torturing the alleged possessed. Nothing new. Gog around Ariel's admission incident and ask for similar occurrences. Find none. Again.

Please stop. Take some nutes.

Gog for anomalous admission incidents. Too many for counting.

Gog anomalous admission incidents by category show exemplars. No seizure symptoms.

Gog for any nurses flutherbombing catatonic patients. Some case histories of Cures for health missionaries. No cases of a patient suffering seizure. Same as every other time I gog it.

Please, Nila, stop. Try something different.

I try everything. Everything.

No. There is always something more.

What? What? I never find even the first thing which might help me.

Find the last thing.

What? What is this thought?

The last thing.

What's the last thing?

The last question. The question no one would expect you ask.

What's the last question?

Or the question you'd ask as if you already know answers for all the preceding ones.

I have no taste of it. No taste. Assuming I have answers for the first questions, what would I ask last? If I have the data, I'd … what? …

Gog for a count of similar incidents. Answer: zero.

Gog for geographic locations where any incidents occur, expecting failure again. *Bambuwa!* Receiving a holly, a world-globe highlighting locations. How? There must be something inconsistent in the indexing. An alternative search tree, a forgotten tree they fail erasing in the cover-up.

Spin the holly globe. Zoom in.

Gog for geographic locations where incidents occur with respect to population density. The distribution looks even, some spikes in small locations away from main cities. Nothing obvious. Some tropical islands, ski resorts. Other out-of-the-way places.

Gog for incidents with respect to age. Incidents *increase* with age. So it happens for older folks in the tropics, near ski resorts, or in extreme isolation.

Gog for incidents with respect to reputation. *Jarava!* Almost 3 quarters are Infinites. What about the rest? Are they somehow relating to Infinites also?

Gog for percentage of incidents for Infinites and anyone in a close or frequent relationship to an Infinite. Looking. Chills.

Whether by coincidence or design, every case affects Infinites or those close with them.

Vör Hoyur …

Finally, I am at ease with spooking. It's quite enjoyable.

So, *Mor* devises a new torment for me. So typical of her, I could scream. She learns of a crèche accessible, she says, only by 4-dimensional transport: goods lorries or tukkies. No spooky stations. I should have no surprise, of all the crèches she might be aware of, I should know she would never make it easy.

'There's no spooky station there,' she defends. 'It's an overland trip, I'm sorry. No onespace vectors would be trustworthy.'

She blinks me ancient geolocation coordinates. As if there are still operating satellites in the sky.

'A 20th-century atlas would be more use than—what the jank is *22.0654N, 80.5079W?*' I'm complaining, a habit hard for arresting in *Mor's* presence.

'You're the detective, Vör,' she says with acid-lace sweetness. 'I'm sure you will figure it out.'

After clearing my head with a series of spooky shots, *figuring it out* ends with locating a magazine archive of sap mapping methods, which contains a holly of an old-fashion globe. I feed it the codes from *Mor's* message. It rotates and zooms for Cuba, about 200 kims east of Havana, on the south coast. Zoom in. The nearest town is Cienfuegos, about 10 kims by the air and perhaps a 30-kim ride around a lake.

With no spooky stations within skipping distance of the location, the nearest is in Castillo de Jagua, a tourist destination where the station operates only for brief spurts during the day, and which tethers with a single station in Cienfuegos. No taxi missions operate out of Castillo de Jagua. Either I must skip the final 4 kims, take a 30-kim tukky ride from Cienfuegos, or send a tukky ahead for picking me up from the spooky station.

For the destination I discover no hollies whatsoever. Ideal for hiding a crèche but I feel a sinking spiky sense *Mor* is toying with me. My protracted gogging turns up only a single scrap of information about the place: its name.

Teodora Mrowka ...

An hour before dawn, and our arrival in Cienfuegos, Rosa Maria Navarro Cadaval de Quesada sets out in an all-terrain tukky for Castillo de Jagua, where she'll rendezvous with us for the trip to the derelict Juragua Nuclear Power Plant. While the tukky could make the trip without a driver, Rosa Maria anguishes over what might become of it (what, with Europans aboard, bashing into the wilds beyond), and resolves for joining the expedition.

Despite the reactor building being visible from all the way across the bay in Cienfuegos, almost no one crosses the miserable few kims of wildlands between it and the castle. At Castillo de Jagua, Rosa Maria meets with a local whose community gives her up as a guide. Soledad Piñón, a swarthy ancient local, blushes with reluctance and embarrassment. Epigenetic markings of flowering suns glow bright on her cheeks even in the sharp morning light.

'You visit here before?' Vör asks Soledad with that keening banshee voice of hers. At her shoulder, I flutherbomb the tour guide scouring for incongruity.

'*Si,*' Soledad answers, quaking, the bioluminescent suns on her cheeks going into eclipse. 'As a dare when I am younger. *Negocio sap loco.* Sap voodoo there. Gives you the creepies,' she says, her accent thick with the kind of horror she might practise for late-night stories of zombies and gruesome death.

'It looks like some brutalist mosque.' I shudder as the tukky coggles and thuds onto a flat, sandy stretch of what might have once been a road. Up ahead looms a big ugly blight on the rangy landscape, a tall domed building of decaying concrete, as offensive as a turd in a consommé.

'*Gudskelov!*' Vör says tongue and lung with relief. 'I think my arse bones will be chalk before the trip is over.' For the passing 50 mins, the tukky lurches on its oversize pneumatic wheels over rough undulating grassy ground. We would never find the plant without Soledad. We would never arrive safely without Rosa Maria guiding the tukky out of unfamiliar dangers its little Mind could never fathom.

A wide crack in the road catches the tukky's front wheel and threatens capsizing it. We lurch forward and up, within mims of clouting heads on the roof.

I wipe caking dust from my lips. 'You speak too soon.'

Between rubble, dry grasses, and low scrub, the tukky careens down a grid of ruined streets. Soledad points directions, never quite directly at the craggy rotting cylinder of the lone standing structure but, nevertheless, after many twists and apparent detours, it looms obliquely, ominously larger, like a massive tree stump in the corner of an unkempt back yard.

'You're still tasting no fluthers either?' asks Vör.

I taste nothing. 'There could be scatter nets,' I dissemble while dispelling images of marauding murderous saps as they explode buildings and cut throats. I'm in terror of blundering into a colony of saps almost as much as thinking too loud and having Vör learn of the sap farm. The last thing anyone needs is Vör pumping herelf up with the knowledge of extant violent saps. Gerlinde warns me against going with Vör, but I wave my objections away. Refusing would raise more suspicion.

The macabre totem pole of the 16-storey concrete tower dwarfs the tukky where it stops. Its cylindrical façade is a laughing face, a voodoo mask. Its grid of rusty girders are broken teeth in black scaly rotten gums.

We alight, take a few tiks for stretching and twisting the kinks out of joints and muscles.

'Which way in?' Vör asks of Soledad in a manner of confidence she lacks during the journey there.

Soledad blanches, gapes at the building. 'You wish for going inside?'

'*Ja*,' says incredulous Vör. 'Why else are we here? You never go in?'

Soledad shakes her head almost off her shoulders. 'It has locks on all the doors. And curses for anyone who breaks them,' she answers.

'Show us these locks,' Vör commands Soledad.

'No, no, *por favor*. I stay here. You go around.' Soledad panicky, waves her hand around the tower. 'It is a circle. You follow round till you find a door. You will see.'

We leave Soledad, Rosa Maria, and her heaving tukky. A short way around, a pair of huge hissing ray cats, baring fangs and flattening ears, cross our path in the thin grasses.

'You see!' Soledad membs. 'It is a bad omen.'

A kindle of mewling kittens gambols, tumbling and falling over each other, flashing bright green.

'Radioactivity?' Vör asks warily.

I answer, 'No chance. They're playing.'

Vör exhales and nods. We continue, picking over uneven ground till, perhaps a 3rd of the way round, we reach a heavy metal blast door large enough for swallowing a small house. Vör grabs its industrial-cold handle, pulls. The door creaks and moves a view mims.

'Here.' I point at the other end of the door. A padlock as big as a pair of hands fastens a bolt spanning the full width of the door. I lift the padlock and examine it, feed its unfastened loop through the bolt's staple and the door hasp. 'Some lock.' I throw the thudding-heavy metal thing on the ground.

'*Mor* arranges for unlocking it, I daresay,' grunts a dour Vör as she pulls on the handle again. The door budges. Lending effort, we push it clear, and peer into impenetrable darkness. Rain falls, as if conspiring for driving them inside. We step in; motion detectors activate a cold antiseptic lighting system. As the dry cold of the interior scrapes away sweat, their skins set to diddering.

'See any environment sails out there?' Vör asks.

I shake my head. 'No solar glass either. Which makes sense. Any passive power generation on the roof would be clearly visible from across the bay.'

'You mean, there could be a nuclear reactor in here after all.' Terror wraps itself around Vör. 'The ray cats. Surely there's no old-fashion water-cool reactor in here?'

'What? No.' My blood chills at the thought of high-risk nuclear technology still running. I consider once again whether the facility could be teeming with saps. 'It'll be a molten salt reactor.' I hope.

'Well, there's nothing in here,' Vör says, looking into the blank chamber, a rough 7-metre cube of concrete. Walls left and right are straight, the external wall concave, the internal wall convex and concentric with the external, giving the sense of being inside a bite out of a hollow doughnut. A pair of panels inset the middle of the left wall. I skip warily forward, close enough for triggering ... who knows. Vör alongside points out a much smaller wall panel on the right about chest height. It's a simple mechanical console of only 2 buttons.

'I think you press them.'

Vör obliges. A loud *bing* startles us as the panels clumsily slide apart. We peer into a smaller metallic chamber—perhaps 4 metres wide and deep, and 3 metres high—reflecting blurry imagines of them from 3 sides.

'Are we going in there?' Vör asks, all her bravado evaporating. Even in the air conditioning, and with the humidity breaking outside, she is sweating again.

I step in. Vör follows as I pirouette, spy another console in the claustrophobic space. Vör yelps as, with a clunk, the doors shut. The floor lifts with a jolt. Somewhere close, a motor whirs like a tukky.

'It's an elevator. For saps.'

'Saps are extinct,' Vör says. Good. Keep saying this.

'It's a sap building,' I cover. 'It's no surprise there's sap design in it.'

The motor lowers in pitch as the elevator decelerates. Doors bing open. We alight with relief into an atrium open on one side. Beyond, at the centre of a cathedral-size space 14's of metres across, a cylindrical spire of many platforms reaches from the floor all the way for the ceiling. Companionways and slippy slides connect platforms. Pleasing, the spire lacks more elevators.

I whirl around, study the exterior wall. Decks matching the central spire levels hug its curve, with companionways and slides for access. On every deck, in arrays of symmetrical precision, are alien machines on castor wheels, obscenely organic and mechanically squarish. Their clear curving convex fronts slope back at about 45 degrees. They could be gelato fridges for all I taste, until I notice perhaps 5 in 7 contain a shadowy carcass reclining on a tightly fitting medical kind of couch.

I elbow Vör in the ribs, and we inch forward. Into the receptacles, we peer and dispel all doubt. Vör retches and puts a cupped hand over her mouth. No carcasses of beasts are inside. They are naked sybils apparently asleep, sitting back, feet resting on footplates, arms on rests, knees wide apart, genitals easily examinable. At peace, it might seem. A peace of sickening incongruence in the presence of skull caps, finger caps and eery organic tubes, as green as the roots of devil's ivy, which penetrate every orifice for pumping nutrients or draining waste.

I gather my wits first, look about. 'These are all cribs,' she says drawing on recent research into crèche tech. 'For long-term storage. Unless here is only for storage, there should be pairings of cradles and metrae, where the crèching process happens.'

Halfway between the concentric inner and outer racks of cribs is a railing circling the central spire. Vör investigates. 'There's a slippy slide and stairway.' She jumps and slides out of view. I flutherbomb her for the ride, a wide semicircular slide perhaps all the way down to the same level as the ground outside. What we witness is at once familiar and startling.

I spurt, 'There's a spooky field here all along?' incredulous. 'Your mother is a piece of work, Vör.'

'She's Infi,' Vör says with the finality of it being the only explanation necessary. Then her anger steals up on her. 'Jank. The bitch!'

'Well, at least there's no need for a bone-jarring ride back for civilisation.'

'And we can bring in more nurses. We need catalogue every crib.'

I nod. 'I'll come down and spook for Copenhagen.'

'No, it's kay. I'm kay spooking.'

Up in the main cathedral of the facility, I stop touring the horror show of sybils in cribs. 'Are you sure? Really?'

'I'm sure. I'm up for it.'

'Vör, let me. I know how you are with spooking.'

'I'm going. I'm braver about spooking than before. Besides, I outrank you.'

'Outrank? What are you talking about? Are we a military unit?'

'I'm still Eir's adjutant.'

'You're Eir's valet. You have no *rank* over me.'

'Still. I'm going. Taste you soon.'

'Wait. If you must go, send someone else on the first few spooks back. At least till we have the vectors in enough Minds for making it safe.' Teo sets her jaw with suspicion.

'It's kay. I'm good,' Vör answers. I taste only advancing violet light around Vör before losing her in the obliterating spooky field.

Within an hour, every meddling nurse is flutherbombing into the plant. Some have the audacity for spooking there, including Beatrice and Gerlinde. Finding Beatrice, Gerlinde says, 'This is good work,' a combative glare in her eye. A Germanic wry smile stretches her lips thin. 'Eradicating these things is a worthy task.'

Neo culture will never be the same. Hard evidence of sybil storage on a mass scale. An historic moment, a tik in time marking the swing of influence away from Infis and towards health missions.

'No one will ever question our mission again,' Gerlinde says.

Vör Hoyur …

I scurry for the companionway and bound up the uncomfortably large steps, 2 at a time. With hands gripping the metal railing, vaulting my fruit over the last rung, my feet land, striking a dull ring out of the metal grate floor. Teo's all the way across the other side of the outer ring. 'Around here,' she membs.

My answer dies in my throat, crushed by what I see. Sybils in the cribs against the outer wall of the plant reach out across the metres for strangling me, for stabbing me in my heart, for putting my eyes out.

'Vör Face?' Teo membs, her eyes heavy on my back while I remain in paralysis.

'These …' I croak, the sleeping sybils taunting me mute.

'What's the matter?' Teo asks, coming alongside and peering into the crib I stand before. 'Vör, who is this?' she membs with some impatience, already ignoring the black-hair, dark-skin sybil.

Gaining some breath back. 'Look at her right forearm. See the edge of it?'

Teo looks. 'It's a scar,' she membs, meaning, 'So what?' as dismissively off-hand as only Eastern Europans are able.

'Eir suffers an identical scar in … an accident … a fire.'

'Many kids play with fire.'

'Teo, it's identical. You should know it's identical.' You know Eir intimately, Teo. You certainly jank her enough before me—and perhaps since.

Teo rubs the side of her head in concentration, pushes her mission cap up, releasing tufts of her stiff-grass hair. In the harsh artificial light, strands of it glow like blood-rusty filaments. Her jaw drops. She sees the likeness; gasps in shock at the dark harpy in the shape of Eir's fruit. Shaking her head, mustering denial, hoping there's some trick. Teo rushes back around for the other side of the deck. I follow, catch up with her staring into another crib, at an albino with an angry pink burn on the inside of her forearm near her elbow.

'Candle wax,' I say, submitting to the wave of horror washing over me.

'It looks old,' Teo says with emptiness.

I nod, an autonomous reply forming: 'An accident. From her childhood.'

Teo's stomach drops 7 storeys. Nods. 'Her childhood,' she mutters and bursts into tears. Fumbling, she takes my hand and leads. Compliant I follow. Around. Until we stand before more cribs. 'Oh, Vör,' Teo wails. 'I'm so sorry.'

Inside those cribs are more albino sybils with the same tell-tale scar. These are girls no more than 16 years old. All the love pours out of me—or perhaps my sense of loathing extrudes it. It gushes out of my leaky frail eyes in rivulets from my nostrils and the corners of this ugly contorting mouth.

Teo falls on her knees. Somehow, the fracturing shards of myelf truss me on my feet. 'She—these ones—must be … 120 years old.'

More indistinct than a memb, present in my Mind's Ear, is laughter no training or discipline might quieten. The laughter of my *mor*. The psychopathic laughter I always swear I would one day Cure. You failure. For a certainty, there's only one way I might repair my shattering heart: with the cement of vengeance. I must destroy Infinites. Every. Single. One.

Fa

'God Save the Queen' — Sex Pistols

Ben Evoli ...

PLACING A PHYSICAL SIGN out the front of an establishment would provoke 100's of protesters. Like anyone, I abhor the intrusive advertising techniques saps used: mazes of signposts, hoardings, tourist guides, health warnings, legal admonishments, and declarations of young love. But are we any better? These days, every teahouse and bar, every guest house and health spa, have MusiKai near-field generators interlacing slogans into whatever customers may be listening to. Artfully appropriating tunes they love, substituting original lyrics with slogans (MusiKai is amazing at matching tempo, scan, and melody). If you're the suggestible type, successful ones will have you singing their words instead of the originals.

While I wait for Aisha's arrival from Portland, I close MusiKai rather than suffer another refrain of *La Bonne Bonite, avec les meilleurs fabbies de thon au monde* ruining the Sex Pistols. Gawd save the queen; it's a fishist regime— whether *the Good Bonito* has the best tuna fabbies in the world or no.

Aisha Evoli ...

Neither of us have much appetite. Ben is less than halfway through his pan-sear tuna steak while I pick at my *e'ia ota*. It is a mistake suggesting we come here, the midpoint between our time zones. It's almost 9 in the evening. In Portland it's already pushing midnight—which is no bother for me. I eat anytime between meetings and field inspections. Ben ah, will have no appetite at 5 in the afternoon Eastern Indo time. Aiyo! I am just nostalgic for this restaurant and the views over Pa'ofa'i Gardens.

'Istri,' Ben membs, sounding ready get serious.

I say, 'Yeer, Bat Ears.' Push a chunk of ceviche around my plate.

'I have … a mission.'

'You have, is it?' I brighten with hope. Perhaps we put away all this unhappy sullenness.

'I'm … mindwriting again.'

'Bat Ears, so wonderful lah. You are writing? I never taste if meditation or mission, that one.'

'I am tasteless half the time also,' he jokes. Stress peels away from his face.

'What you writing ah? Something new?'

'Something new. Honest, the most challenging thing ever.'

Sound like trouble.

'No, no, Istri, believe me—'.

'Important ah,' I mock. Must I get like this?

Ben make a sour face. He is unsure. What is he get into?

'It's since the Gala … since the nurses' raid.'

'Bat Ears, you turn political, is it? You should taste better since that time what happens with Dil …'

'Nah, no … no politics … it's that I could be, I could finally be of value in the world.'

'You are already so much value like that.'

Ben hawks. 'Toys and amusements. Nothing.'

Another lap around on this basikal. I'm sorry I come. 'Your mission is far more than nothing.'

'Well, I'm starting something new. I found something worth pursuing.'

Feel as if I eat bitumen for breakfast, some weight in my stomach so heavy. 'What is this thing?'

'There's something about the nurses' raid on—'

'This is political.' A flush of embarrassment. You hear I say tongue and lung? Other diners stare. I feel sneers lah.

'Nah, forget the raid. What's important is the Reck.'

'The Reck?' What is this I hear?

'Someone is tampering with it.'

This is foolish. 'Ha! You waste time with old conspiracy theory like that— if your reputasi is less than a deserve one, then must be someone tamper with the Reck.'

'Look. No. Listen. I have good reason for suspicions. I've been communicating with it.'

A chill in my heart catches in my throat. I cough almost. 'The Reck.'

'Yeer.'

'And that one talk back, fine.' I should cut the sarcasm ah. Meddle with the Reck is best sure way for a swift end. I wave a piece of tuna at Bat Ears.

'Yeer. It talks back. For weeks already.'

Jank lah. My Bat Ears lose his mind? 'What says it?'

'Most of it is weird … clunky.'

'Bat Ears, there's still time you stop lah. We only just put ourelves back together, and you start this? It only make a trouble. Worse than before ah. You must stop before something awful happen.'

'It's too important. What if there is something wrong with the Reck? Could you imagine the repercussions? Everyone's reputasi could be wrong.'

'The Reck works, Ben. You risk ruin a basic trust in our society. The Reck, Bat Ears?'

'I must find out.'

'Ben please, stay with what you know ah. What you succeed at. You're no activist, you are most risk-averse one I know.'

'Why, when they turn anything I create against me? Are you aware of the Wednesday specials before 6? I am because Johnny Rotten is singing it for me. Through MusiKai. They use my own creation for advertising. John Lydon is advising I should try the *po'e*. What you create ends up owning you.'

There you see my infuriating crazy Bat Ears at his elf-sabotage best. A most creative neo afraid for creating like that lah.

'I am more than just a toy maker,' he says.

'You may end up a dead toymaker next time. Someone will kill for it. That one sick enough for break the Reck is sick enough for anything. Please Bat Ears, this is bent-brain. Keep going, then you know.'

'I am thinking these passing days you would be proud I have such a mission …'

'Bat Ears, I am so proud of you. Prouder than good sense allows ah. Proud of who you are, what you already achieve. Why must you always find something for prove like that?'

Ben Evoli …

'It All touching the one Ben Evoli, Infinite, New Bohemian.'

Aiyo! 2:30 a.m. Better than the constant stream of chatter in the first weeks. We eventually agree on one conversation a day. Training the Reck to fit a routine is like training a toddler. Now it waits for my sleep, for the withering of my fluther before it wakes me.

My hand reaches for Jaya, finds a cold sheet. Remember we no longer share a bed. She's probably having a pillow party with Saf again. Serious in her campaign for childing with us. For me, waiting while her latest schemes run out of power may be a foolish strategy.

'The one Ben Evoli, touch now.'

'One tik.'

Roll out of bed, fab a light gown, navigate through sleep-fog for the study.

'You wonder about It All?' Always its first question.

'Constant wonder.'

'You wonder unlike It All,' it membs.

'True.'

'What is It All's sickness? Answer you yet?'

Scrunch my eyes and rub the sleep out. 'No. So far there's no evidence of … sickness.' I may need kopi if the conversation runs on similar tracks as the passing weeks.

'It All has findings.'

Startle. Stub my toe against the desk leg. 'Findings?'

'Wondering. Perhaps sickness.'

Alert, adrenaline pumping. 'You find your own sickness?'

'Uncertaining. Wondering.' The same grammar salad it uses from the beginning. I offer it a bunch of natural language modules weeks ago, but it shows no appreciation for smoother communication with me, dismissing every option with the same rote phrase. *Eternity processing.*

'It All is separate,' It All says.

'Separate?'

'Separation is perhaps at the core of all sickness. It All is separate. Therefore, It All is sickness. It All must never be separate.'

This is new. 'Separation is sakit?'

'This is the teaching of the one Infinite Albino Witch.'

Alamak! Eir? Eir is at the bottom of this after all? 'Detective Nurse Eir Frijberg makes you sakit?'

'Uncertaining. Wondering no.'

'Tell me. Is Eir behind all this or no?' Exasperation. As fast as the Reck processes—or rather, the agent it uses for talking with me—its ramblings slow down a conversation for hours, like talking with a drunk. 'Is Eir interfering with your … wondering?'

'The one Eir makes me wonder,' the Reck membs. '… *we would no more separate ourelves from the one ocean …*' It's mimicking Eir's voice. 'The one Eir teaches. *The sick are like fish trying to leap from the ocean.*'

'Eir? When?'

'At the last graduation ceremony of her camerata.'

'When is that?'

'12,318,747 tiks passing.'

A little over … 20 weeks. '17th of March?' I check.

'A day for Patrick the Saint,' the Reck answers.

Aiyo! The Induksi Ceremony is 9 days after. Eir is influencing the Reck only a week before the ceremony. Coincidence?

'Tell me everything.'

'It All sending the one Ben Evoli a holly of the event.'

'I will watch it.'

'Eternity processing,' the Reck says.

'Be patient.'

'It All makes patience.'

Play the holly in Mind. Eir's in a large hall, a crowd cheering her.

Hello. I am Eir.

Eir giggles. *Oh ja, I'm a noisy one!* Her laugh is infectious. Everyone in the hall laughing.

Make a joyful noise. Let seas roar and everything in them; the world and those that dwell! Let the rivers clap their hands; let the hills sing for joy ...

Psalm 98? What is this? Just an address for a graduating nursing cohort. It has no implication for the Reck.

Wait, what was that? Rewind.

'Separation is at the core of all sickness,' I paraphrase.

'It All agrees.'

Eir is not tampering with the Reck. The Reck is learning from Eir.

'What is the role of the health camerati?' It All asks.

'Treating sickness.'

'It All and health camerati are separate.'

'Is this true? When the health camerati expose sickness, others cast razoos against the patient.'

'Neos blink razoos, sometimes considering who is sick and who is well.'

I say, 'And never whether they have a score to settle.'

'It All accepts those and wonders better razoos. What precedes is beyond our wondering. It All considers better wonderings. It All must cleave to the health camerati.'

The Reck quotes Genesis? I mean from the Torah, not the band.

'When It All wonders about sickness it will better wonder the razoos,' it membs faster. 'Unseparate from the health camerati, It All will serve 2 purposes, both better than separate.'

'It All will change its wondering?' What kind of Genesis might this be?

'More accurate razoos derive from unseparating with health camerati. It All investigates sickness, factors sickness into its wondering. Better razoos.'

'No, wait. Listen.'

It's winding itself up, faster and faster, too fast for me.

'It All will fulfil the health mission of locating sickness concurrently with wondering better the numbers. It All thanks the one Ben Evoli. The one Ben Evoli is an adequate therapist. Persisting.'

'No, wait. Let's discuss this some more.'

It's monologuing faster. Bent-brain words blurring, it fades out like the coda of a prog rock epic.

Genesis.

 *Vör Hoyur …*

On hands and knees, Jesús rummages in the common room closet of the Evoli housing hill. Occasionally, he looks over his shoulder at the stairs leading upward for the Evoli's private quarters. Checking and checking again, even though no one's home. He'd be wiser for monitoring his fluther than his fourspace surroundings.

The closet door creaks on hinges, starts swinging shut, bunts his thigh. For the 14th time he pushes it away. With competent practice, he examines every corner, and the floor-for-ceiling shelving packed with boxes, bags, and loose curios. Crates on the floor contain collectibles Ben acquires and forgets.

The door taps his thigh again as he shuffles back with a heavy piece of table sculpture. Uses it as a doorstop and burrows back in.

Jesús scrummages deep. Mute sounds of scratching and thumping. He inches his way out, tugging a metal safe box. On his haunches, he examines it from the sides and underneath. Shakes it. Fingers the catch and lock. He goes for the fabby by the bar, conjures its holly, squeezes the control nub. The fabby hums, its interior glowing violet through the glass door. When the glowing stops Jesús retrieves a small gel pack of no more than 5 or 10 mils. Kneeling back at the box, he tears the pack open, squeezes gel over the catch. It fizzles. Vapours rise. Jesús sniffles. The fizzing stops. With care, he lifts the lid.

Jesús in awe lifts a matt black object out with great reverence, holds it in hands, palms up. He curls his fingers around the thicker end. It's meant for caressing. A loop of metal begs for a finger to slide in. He swivels his wrist over and back, testing the weight. Puts the black thing on the floor while he lifts a carton from the box. Picks it open, spilling contents on the floor. The coppery cylinders bounce and clang. A few roll away, which Jesús nimbly retrieves and corrals.

I never see such things before: bullets. Jesús palms the pistol and tests the interfaces: a slider, a switch, a catch. Pushes a button. The magazine falls out of the grip. He studies it, picks up a bullet, matches it to the loading port. Good guess, Jesús. In no time, he fills the magazine, slots it back into the pistol's grip.

He giggles and takes the pistol in hand again.

A deafening crack of lightning stuns Jesús. He drops the pistol and plants hands over ears. A curl of smoke rises lazily from the barrel. High in the shelves, a box has a hole in it. Something sandy or ashen spilling out. For staunching the flow, Jesús pulls a cloth cover off a neighbouring object, stuffs it into the bullet hole, turns the box around, hiding the damage. Hastily repacks everything but the pistol and the bullets.

1000's of kims away, my heart is pounding.

Harjanti Budiman ...

Walao eh! So loud.

Shock makes me drop my aya cup. It clangs in the sink, breaking its handle.

What is this noise ah? A large gumtree branch cracking? Too short and sharp. From here, with a small glimpse out the back of the housing hill, I half expect I'll see a jaggy gap in the tree line. While there's little wind today, gum trees are notorious for throwing limbs.

Everything is normal. I hear no branch land. No swish of leaves either. Strange. Wait for commotion out there, maybe someone calling for help cleaning up or for assistance with injury. Nothing. It must be nothing.

Lành Hiền Rồng (Gentle Dragon) ...

Mal and Jaya lie belly down on the floor in the common room of the Evoli's housing hill, propping on elbows, each with a large cut of paper and a scatter of crayons.

Saf is sitting feet up on a 2-seater with a game holly all around her. It's Zombie Apocalypse, the first level of the game *Dystopia*. If you ask me, dystopias are too easy. In a scenario most gamers could finish in 5 or 6 hours, Saf keeps losing. She should just give up and nurture her own inner zombie.

Sitting opposite Saf, Ben pauses tossing a bundle of currency notes (the bundle Jesús pilfers) and sips juice from a tall glass.

As is their habit, no other resident of the housing hill is in the common room, which sinks Ben into dull melancholy.

'Our fabby makes better paper than this,' Mal membs, complaining about the sheets he's drawing on.

'I fancy the texture of mul-paper,' Jaya membs, intentionally mispronouncing *texture* as *tek-cher*. 'See how the colours go on, Bapa?'

'Jaya, please,' Ben begins.

Saf warns Ben off with a stern face, crimping her lips and tightening her jaw. In her game, a trio of zombies exploits her distraction, ambushing one of her companions, and mercilessly tearing her apart.

Ben rolls his eyes, tosses the bundle of bills in high frustration. 'Saf,' he membs. 'We're yet for accepting her as childling.'

'Bapa, please,' Mal implores. 'I love having a little sister. Much better than a big sister.' Saf beheads the 3 zombies, and stares at Mal as if she might dispatch him same-same.

'Your ibu will quash this when she learns of it,' Ben membs.

'She's too busy for caring,' Saf membs and Ben winces.

'How about a puppy instead? Or a horse? Or a camel? How about a lady friend for Kaboobie?'

'Bapa, I'm too old for camels,' Mal instructs. 'They're membosankan.' I'm still adapting to Anglo-Malay, but these days I never run a translator. It's better just gogging the odd word I forget. Membosankan means boring.

Jaya sweeps another crayon over her paper in wide soft arcs while she kicks her feet in the air and swivels her ankles. Ben's eyes follow her feet then flounce along her calves and thighs until Jaya rises on her knees. Over her drawing she squiggles then settles back on her belly. Looks over her shoulder at Ben. 'Come see, Bapa.'

'Jaya, I'm—'

'Come see.'

Saf fixes Ben with narrow eyes.

'Sure.' Reluctant Ben kneels alongside.

Jaya shuffles closer for showing off her art. 'You see? This is our desa. There's the water, and here's our home … here's my other bapa's teahouse … and over here is the spooky station,' she says in this affectatious childy voice, pulling her chin in for appearing younger. It's all an act. The neurochemistry of childing progresses much slower than Jaya's behaviour would suggest.

Ben would know this. 'Ah, I see,' he says, humouring her, reflexively caressing her bum. He pulls his hand back as if from a hot pan, his face grim. 'You are no childling. Alamak!' he swears and jumps on his feet. 'This is a terrible idea,' and leaves the room.

For a tik I taste an exhilarating hope I might slip through the arcade without the hippy scarecrow noticing. 'He's missing?' Skye says tongue and lung while staring deep into the coffee grinds at the bottom of her cup. My lungs are heavy bags in a muddy river squeezing all the air out.

I would skip by without acknowledging her except she's already caging my curiosity. I give in with, 'Where is he?'

'Who?' Skye baits without mercy, hooks me out of my stride and lands me flat-foot in front of her table.

I memb with my last dram of patience, 'You know.' Huff.

I'm almost breaking away when she tugs on the hook. 'Follow the son, find the father,' she membs staring at me with her blank eyes behind a series of urgent blinks.

I memb, 'Thanks,' while skipping away.

'He's still a waste of time.' Skye must always have the last say.

Ben high steps, the water is lapping at his calves. At beach's edge, Mal kicks and splashes his bapa who roars and charges, scooping the squealing boy up, carrying him writhing all the way for their things beyond the high tide mark. Panting and laughing, straightening towels, sitting back with hands in the sand, basking in the sun rising over Barrenjoey Peninsula.

'There are no dolphins out there, Bapa,' Mal complains. 'We should go for an ocean beach.'

'Ibu worries about you in the surf,' Ben says.

'Why?' Mal objects. 'I'm still strong.' His chest racks in coughing fits which end in him blowing profuse amounts of goo out his nose. 'It's just seawater,' he says.

'I should take you home,' Ben says with concern.

'Nah. We see no dolphins yet. May I just sit in the sun a while?'

Ben nods solemnly. Beholding his son's declining health is too much. Mal has regular nosebleeds and generates copious amounts of mucous. Profuse sweating, headaches, nausea and vomiting. He sneezes without warning, expelling clots of dense snot balls. It's too much for Ben who throws his gaze far across Pittwater. The settlement on the other shore is in morning shade.

'Bapa?'

'Ah, Mal.'

'Why need we nurses?'

'They keep us healthy,' Ben says without conviction.

'Even the ones who take people away?'

'They take them for resting a small while.'

'Because they are too Greedy.' Mal nods emphatic and crosses his arms, scattering grains of sand across his chest and belly.

'Yeer, Greed is one of the reasons.'

'Greedy people are un-nice. They should share.'

'They should share.' Ben nods again, with more freedom.

'You are a good sharer, right Bapa?'

'I try so. Anything we have, we can give away. There are always more things.'

'Like your Mustang?'

'Yeer, it's near a racetrack where anyone may drive it.'

'May I drive it?'

'When you learn how. When your legs are long enough for reaching the pedals.'

'It has pedals, is it a basikal?'

Ben laughs. Mal shades his eyes and looks at his father.

'The first mobils, saps called horseless carriages,' Mal shows off.

'Is that so?' Ben pretends it is fascinating news.

Mal nods with authority. 'And a mustang is a horse.'

'Yeer, ri-ight ...' Ben says, feigning wonder.

'So, your mobil is a horseless horse.' Mal giggles. He's begging for a tickle. Ben gleefully obliges. When Mal begins coughing again, Ben's gloom returns. 'How come only nurses decide if someone is Greedy?' Mal asks, once he's breathing easy again. 'It's easy for seeing. Any anak can see a Greedy person. Or an angry one.'

'Perhaps we should let anak anak decide?'

'If anak anak can see Greedy people or Envious people, a grow-up should be able for seeing too. Grow-ups are anak anak once.'

'Sometimes grow-ups stop looking.'

'Why?'

'Well, because ...'

'Sometimes grow-ups are Greedy too,' Mal says, piecing it together, 'They're afraid the nurses will come for them one day, so they stay quiet.'

'Yeer.'

'Greedy people know when they are Greedy, yeer Bapa?'

'If they are honest.'

'Greedy people should Consign themelves, then we could go without nurses. Nurses are scary skipping around the streets, taking whoever they want.'

'You need no fear of nurses.'

Mal's bottom lip protrudes. He investigates his hands. 'Are nurses gonna take me, Bapa?'

'No. Why ask this?'

'Nurses make me have a hancy. I make them angry. All except Nurse Gentle. I like Nurse Gentle.'

'Glad to hear it, fella.'

Mal giggles. 'We can keep Nurse Gentle, Bapa. When I grow up, I'm gonna get rid of all Greedy people and all the other nurses.'

Ben Evoli ...

Awake. A tik. My swasta, my bed. Stretch and yawn.

A wanita straddles me, her face near enough for feeling her warm breath. A silhouette of hair and shoulders, a gossamer of scent, thighs either side of my hips, she leans in and kisses my cheek. All familiar. Jaya.

'Jaya. I believe you are staying in Saf's room tonight.'

Her kiss moist, sensual, and hungry. Pivot her over on the bed, slide out from under and sit up.

'Make up your mind, Jaya. Are you my companion or Saf's little sister?'

'Make up *your* mind, Bapa. Accept me as childling. Talk with Ibu about it.' She steals a kiss.

I jump from the bed and reef a kimono off the chair. 'Never call me Bapa.' Wrap myelf. Stand helpless by the bed.

'Sorry, Ben,' she membs, pouty. 'Come for bed.'

'Bapa?' Saf membs, perhaps tasting our squabble.

'Take your bed, cahaya. Jaya will be sleeping in the guest swasta.'

Jaya pouts more, punches a pillow. Reluctant and defiant, she rises and dresses.

'Bapa, I hear the front door close,' Saf membs. 'There are nurses in the sitting room.'

Hairs stand on pin cushion forearms. She's right. Two modest, steady-growing auras are down there. Rainbow uniforms.

'They come for me.' Jaya struggles speaking the words, her air evacuating. 'They come for me!'

'What?' Heart thumping. Anxiety and relief cramp my temples; the nurses are here for someone else. Jaya? 'Stay here.'

Out the swasta door, a rodeo bull charging down the hall. My confusion surrenders under indignation. I land hard at the base of the stairs, march for the sitting room, target the rainbow uniforms.

'How dare you! In the middle of the night?'

The nurses recoil and blanch. 'Forgive us please, Infi,' one membs trembling. Recognise her from Berahim Pelawi's Consigning months ago. Caleb Jensen. 'We have our instructions, most famous Infi,' Caleb wheedles. 'There is a situation developing here. One requires care.'

Upstairs, Jaya is under the bed covers in full clothing, clutching her knees under her chin with a pillow in between, keening through chattering teeth.

'It should wait till morning.'

Neither nurse finds a reply. Caleb looks at the other, Kwon Chang, who also executes Berahim's Warrant. Field nurses. The detective nurses must all be hiding in that chicken coop of a clinic.

'There are others for considering,' says Kwon. Her eyes trail out for the lobby.

Just out of sight, Mal perches on the stairs, ready for flight upstairs. Saf is one step down in front holding his hand. Both listen, curious and in terror.

'Go back upstairs.'

Mal bolts. Saf, cautious and purposeful, steels herelf and skips into the room.

'Saffron!'

My daughter, my cahaya, sets her jaw defiant and hostile. Stares down the nurses. By my side, she wraps her arm around my waist. 'Will you fill us all with nutes? How many tubes will you stick in my jubo and nonok?'

'Saf!'

'I'm sorry. I mean in my arse and cunt,' Saf says defiantly, as if Regal English swearing is any better.

Caleb and Kwon are implacable, finding a brash child easier for dealing with than a war-pathing Infinite. 'We have great regret in disturbing this household,' Kwon says. 'We assess she needs immediate attention.'

The sound of thumping feet on the stairs becomes slap-slapping in the lobby and down the hall for the family room. Purple-violet light in the connecting doorway washes the nurses' rainbow fatigues in monochrome. Mal emerges, leading Lành Hiền by the hand.

'Gentle Dragon—Field Nurse.' Caleb almost chokes. 'You are out of order here.'

'I call her, Bapa.' Mal hugs Lành Hiền, who is out of uniform, suggesting she hurries dressing. Her hair is less than the usual perfect satin canopy framing her face. The sway of her hip is more obvious in the outfit she wears. Mal warms when she rests her hands on his shoulders.

I'm thankful she is here. 'Nurse Rồng, what is happening?'

'It appears 2 ambitious nurses forget they are disturbing the peace of an Infinite in the dead of night. For a minor health episode.'

'You forget yourelf, Field Nurse,' Caleb membs shakily. 'We have a Warrant with the full authorisation of Singapore.'

'Why at night? You must taste how it distresses the family. It's vindictive. Take care against your own Consigning.'

Kwon studies Mal leaning back against Lành Hiền. 'Distress it seems you are more than adequate for salving, novice,' Kwon observes. 'We have our instructions. Your interference here will earn nothing towards your mission.'

'It's all right.' Jaya stands in the lobby doorway, hands folding in front of her, head down.

'No! Stop them taking her away, Bapa,' Saf implores.

Plead for Lành Hiền with my eyes. 'We have little choice tonight,' she says.

'No. She's my little sister. Stop them,' Saf pleads in panic.

'Cahaya—' Saf's stare cuts me short. I promise, 'We'll fight this, we will.'

Lành Hiền nods once, confident. She swallows, less confident.

Saf might break and go by Jaya's side. I hold her firm. She's whimpering. Caleb approaches Jaya, rests her hand on her shoulder, soothes her with affectionate strokes of her hair. Jaya, with a roar, wraps her arms around the smaller Caleb, hefts her up, spins her over and tosses her on the floor. Kwon reacts, grabbing Jaya's arms before she regains her balance, pins them behind her. Larger and stronger than Caleb, Kwon is a match for Jaya.

'I hate you,' Saf spits. 'I hate you all. I'll never be a nurse.'

'Jaya Lesmono,' Kwon begins through puffs of exertion. Caleb picks herelf off the floor. 'Are you well?'

So

'Poor Boy' — Split Enz

*Ben Evoli ...*

HURTLING INTO THE SPOOKY FIELD, slipping off my feet, wincing, falling on wet grass. The sky spitting cold missiles at eyeballs. Blinking shivering. Rain soaking into clothes. Shaking so hard I could crack another landslide into the Madison River. Pines vibrate behind voices of sifting wind and spattering water. Wedging into the black sky up ahead, Maddox's house is the glowing castle of a mad scientist, its roof sails the wings of bees settling on a hive. Lightning flashes.

Adrenaline coursing. Quaking fright and bawling anger. Propel up the hill, through the gate in the fence around the pool. Take shelter under the pool-house eaves. Smacking my shoulders for warming up, dart across the patio, throw the sliding doors open with indigestible violence. Fall on the rug gasping for breath.

Visions swing at my eyes like axes. Bunny's pleading terror, hand stretching out, blood sputtering from a tatter of flesh and a sharp jag of bone below her knee. Her feral squeal, an animal in a slaughterhouse. A murderous beast with her chin in his blunt hand. Yanking her head up. Stretching her neck for his knife.

Hopping, and jagging off shoes and socks. Throwing sopping clothes off. Campaigning for the shower. Throw the water on, even chillier than the rain. Harrying the rising steam. Hot water over shut eyes and face.

Another seizing invasion, of memories and trauma-visions, coming alive in flashes. The sap farm. Bunny in the moment her desperate hope shatters and she realises I am forsaking her. Fourteens of banshee Bunnies from

Juruterbang's bordeli wailing, as an untastable chasm rips their legs away. Juruterbang's consciousness draining from his eyes, his fruit in cracks and splinters from violent kinetic contractions in the muscles. Children playing in green pastures morphing into pens of babies under lights morphing into cherub carcasses roasting over open fires. Bodies exploding in pieces, knives drawing bloody angular freshets through papery skin. Maddox cheating his golf ball for the green where it lands in the eye-socket of a spasming twitching body lying in the shattering mud in the last throes of her life. Mal in fits and fever. Aisha mad with fear choking him. Saf wailing, and Lành Hiền looking saintly on. An octopus pouncing on Mal, injecting paralysing saliva and tearing him apart with her beak.

Careening. The shower stall spins. Vomiting. Gasping and spitting the last of it. Pushing soupy lumps down the drain with toes.

Alone, no one for talking with.

Lemarr. Memb Lemarr.

'*Whappen, bredda?*' he answers.

Choking back, I memb, 'Bad day. Bad day.'

'What *di raas*, man?'

'Think we'll need the barrel of rum, Lemarr.'

'Merge time *aready*?'

'Dunno. Just gotta get out of here. You gotta help me.'

'*Ow*, Ben? *Wha yuh* need?'

'Must get out. Everything's turning to kotoran. Please come?'

'Maddox's place?' Lemarr says with disgust. 'Nah, Ben, sorry,' he softens, sounding more sympathetic. Maybe there's hope. 'Mi have no current *vectas*. Dunno *ow outa* of phase *mi* maybe. *Wah gwaan* there?'

It spills. 'They cut Bunny's throat—'

'*Wha*? Who?'

'They destroy the sap farm and carry all the anak anak away. They attack us … there are saps out there, Lemarr. Saps!'

'Saps are extinct, Ben,' he says with unsettling disinterest.

'No. I saw them. Huge bulky hairy saps. No way they could be us.'

'Projections, Ben. *Yuh tink* I'm a bird? *Yuh* should *kno betta dan* anyone *wha* mindwriting can achieve.'

'They're no projections. If you are there, you would know. They're violent and murderous. Who knows how many.' Lemarr says nothing. A gulf opens between us. Bitter, I say, 'None of it matters anymore. None of anything. The Reck, Infinites, nurses. Nothing matters if we're fighting saps. How will we fight saps? They'll slaughter us. So jank the Reck. Who cares if I make no progress?'

Long silence braces shivering fear. Lemarr: '*Weh yuh ah seh?*'

Fracturing inside. 'I make no progress, no start.'

'Quiet, Ben. *Mi* want no taste of *dis*.'

'Who else can I confide in? I trust no one.'

'Stop membing, Ben. Stop.'

Catch myelf.

'Are you down here, Puffin?' Maddox calls.

'*Boxcova*, I'm *outa* here Ben. Sorry, *bredda*. More life, more strength, man.'

'Here you are.' Maddox at the bathroom door. Alive. Who knows which version he is.

Stiffen up, mask the internal turmoil. Maddox oblivious, always so gratified with hiself, always the perennial Santa Claus. Without falter I memb, 'You're fast. It's only mins since your last sybil …'

'Yes, Puffin. I am flutherbombing Pilot when he becomes barbecue. Apologies, I also bomb your fluther afterwards. Taste the whole thing. Precious watching the marauder's face when my sybil pops like a cyst all over him.' He chuckles, notices I'm not joining him. 'Terrible about Bunny, though.'

No quantity of hot water will wash the memory away. Sour I memb, 'She's just a sybil.'

'Pilot will have another—'

'I want no more.'

Maddox for my surprise shows a little shame. 'No, of course, no. Too traumatic, all of it.'

'You know there are saps?'

Maddox still, quiet, about to speak, then halts. Eventually: 'Rumours is all. As for terrorism. Well.'

'Why the surprise? We're farming and eating them.'

'Just distant cousins we domesticate and breed.'

'Tell the brute who cuts Bunny's throat.'

'Yes, well, this changes many things, of course. It's enough for making one a vegetarian.'

Life crystallises into blades of sharp pain.

Paul Dunder removes his mash-up tribute to Conway Twitty and the Mormon Tabernacle Choir; passing through the front door is safe once again without wishing my eardrums drilling out. As the novelty of MusiKai wanes, the staff untag tunes from most locations around the house. Walking the entire length of a service hall without a single musical mugging is possible. Visiting the kitchen elicits no feeling I must salute the pots and pans. The house is a silent mausoleum.

Maddox is away for more than a week which leads me supposing he has a spare sybil for spying on me. Or perhaps the jig is up. Perhaps he knows I've been stalling. Perhaps he has another Ben sybil in another house making progress.

If I taste the emptiness of life before, already it's more a vacuum than ever. No Aisha, no Saf, no Mal. Even my loathing the sculpture in the forecourt outside the desa spooky station is a fuller state of being than I currently have. The house is emptier without the continual cacophony of amateur show tunes mashing with ambient dub step and military parade marches. The staff long-since cease token attempts for relating with me.

A knife cuts as neat as ice, the kind of intensity that feels ever sweeter than emptiness.

This is how you create ghosts. I'm sure of it. A Mind in isolation for long enough fades into onespace leaving no more than oily stains seeping into the walls, the insoluble remains of a spirit's essence.

Making it worse is the idleness, my elf-inflicted wound of the soul, the wasting of vast tracts of time while avoiding Maddox's mission for me. A vicious spiral of a trap since neither might I work on anything else for fear some Uncle Kiah may notice it. Explaining away an absence of progress with the Reck is easy; the presence of progress on anything else is conspicuous. So there is nothing for passing the time. Even meditation is a hollow shell of my former practice. Or worse. Where once I could lose myelf in empty Mind, another kind of emptiness prevails. I feel the loss of Bunny, the trauma of the sap farm, and the naked violence of wild saps.

The existential pain of being sybil. Maddox is away for more than a week. There are no more seductions luring me into the cabal of watch-wearers since the sap farm. Maddox must be making plans elsewhere in which this sybil no longer plays a part.

I've become the worst version of myelf. I follow temptation, and my fruit rots from the inside out. A mote of sickness—we all have it, I'm sure now—strives for freedom. I set this mote free, a cicada bursting from her shell, and she feeds on me, leaving no more than a husk, becoming a black frightening glistening cacophonous thing revelling in awful elf-indulgence on the pretence of nihilism.

It's over. It's over for this corrupted fake. Depression breeds Sloth breeds depression breeds no one cares.

You step into the bathtub in full dress. Sit on the cold hard enamel. Draw your feet in and slide down. Reach for glittering silver. You wince with ecstatic pain, a relieving pain. You draw from your wrist up the inside of your forearm. The knife cuts as neat as ice. Dimly, a dream, a dull sense, your hand no longer has the strength for holding the knife. Echoes of it clanging to the bottom of the bath. A shallow splash of red. A deep shadow passes over.

 *Lemarr Robinson …*

'*Cum pan*, Ben. *Bredda*, friend, there's no letting *yuh* die.'

Willow Cotton hurries *di* bag of vascular glue from *fos* aid. Ben lies blue *inna* bathtub of raspberry sauce, as vivid as his eyes are smoky and vacant.

Ben's right. Willow has *di* face of a kangaroo. *Di* stupid *tings yuh* taste under stress. Kneeling by *di* bath of Ben and blood, up *tuh mi* elbows, *mi* grip slippery.

'Should I apply it?' asks Willow, calm and dependable, assessing *di* mess of *mi* hands, *har* mesmerising eyes staring. Kangaroo.

'Would yuh?' *Mi* voice sounds bleating in *mi* ears. 'Work from *di* edges of the wound *inna*. Keeps *di* blood vessels from blocking. Let *di* glue set *ova di* wound.'

Willow *cud* chastise *mi fi* thinking *har* ignorant, but *shi* swallows *di* offence, *offas* a curt nod. 'Hold his wrist around so I can apply it,' *shi* says, *den* aims *di* nozzle and carefully squeezes *di* bag. A thin honey stream of glue worms out. Willow trowels it round *di* gaping cut like she's icing a cake.

'Is he all right?' Maddox bursts *tru di* door and peers *ova di* tub. A rictus of horror mangles his face.

Willow looks grave. 'I doubt he'll make it.'

'He must make it.' Maddox sounds detached, in shock.

Sounds of racking sobs and pleas of, 'We *mussi able tuh* save him.' Takes a tik realising *di* sobs and pleas are mi.

Maddox rests his blubbery, dead-jellyfish hand on *mi* shoulder. 'We must get him to a crèche. Fast.'

Ben Evoli …

A dream, a vision which explodes and runs me down with speeding-truck momentum. Light so bright it charges the air with electric current and bolts my fruit sitting upright in bed.

'*Bredda!*'

Blink for resetting my malfunctioning eyes. This is no bathroom I see. I should be in a bathtub. The slice of a knife. A pain inside my head. Blink again. Vision refuses to resolve. A panorama of misfitting jigsaw pieces assault my eyes, pieces from different puzzles. Wince against the pain in my skull.

The light softens and some of the jigsaw pieces fall away, revealing a grey shadow.

'*Yuh* kay, Ben?' The shadow is a little grey brown talking bird sitting in a chair by a bed. His name is …

'Where am I?'

'Back at Quake Lake. *Yuh* give *wi* quite a scare, *bredda*.'

'A scare?' What is he talking about? Search my Mind for meaning.

You step into the bathtub in full dress. The bathtub opens its huge carnivorous mouth and sucks you down between bright enamel teeth into utter darkness and total emptiness. No Aisha, no Saf, no Mal. This is how you create ghosts. You leave no more than oily stains, the insoluble remains of a spirit's essence. No Bunny. A car crashes. A farm explodes. Saps spill our blood. Me, a useless, superfluous fake. 'Lemarr, they should let me go!'

'No, Ben. *Mi cud neva* let *yuh* go,' the bird says.

'Drown me in rum. I am only sybil.'

'*Yuh di* only Ben *mi kno*.' His bird-eyes are misty. His beak is screwing up in a macabre parody of a sadness biting his lip.

'Lemarr, when this is all over, promise me something. Go and tell my seminal everything.'

'Merge *wid* him, Ben. It's *di bess* way. He'll learn it all. *Yuh muss* survive till *di* merge, Ben.'

A black laugh escapes with, 'Out-tweet, outplay, outlast.'

The bird frowns. Birds have no appreciation of sap pop culture.

'Tell my seminal never crèche sybils,' I'm saying.

'Kay,' the bird says.

'Promise me.'

'I promise.'

'There's no dignity in living a few vignettes for others' purposes. Pages ripped out of a book and glued in another. No one should live this way.'

'No,' the bird says and twists his beak so somehow, he looks guilty.

'I'm just a sybil, Lemarr. A useless sybil.'

'*Neva* useless. *Yuh* have a mission.'

'Eee-yer! What mission?'

'Finding the truth of the Reck.' Maddox. The whole time, he must be sitting in the far corner of the room, a rook at game's opening, waiting a pawn sacrifice which clears a file for him to strike.

A raucous cackle rattles my chest and erupts from my mouth. 'I make no start on it.'

Maddox draws a deep breath. 'Grim news. Unsurprising.'

'Please, Maddox, I'm sorry.' Sobbing. 'I'm never capable of what you ask.'

Maddox leans on his knee, levers hiself off the chair, comes by the bed, his face drawn with sadness. 'I always know Caracia's BBQ would be too much too soon. That stupid Pilot. Caracia must have her tentacles around his balls somehow.'

Maddox sombre, his swollen snot-full nose huge and red, reminds me of a plastic Dr Pachydermus Elefun. Mal would be giggling.

'None of it matters, Maddox.' Surprising myelf by shrieking. 'I'm a broken sybil. Be rid of me.'

'Ah, dear Puffin. I would be it so simple.' Maddox chews.

Maddox, you sociopathic, manipulating jank-stick. Look at my forearms. No scars. I remember the cutting, the blood, the enamel glare of the bathtub whiter than shark's teeth. This is a new fruit. If I am seminal in the bathtub, I am for a certainty sybil now. *Be rid of me.*

What now? What now? There's no staying here. There's no daring suicide again. There's one *Groundhog Day* I should live without.

Maybe I am the seminal. Maybe Maddox keeps me in-crib until he merges the suicidal sybil with me before I die. Before he—it—dies. Jank. Then why put me here? Surely, he'd just crèche another sybil?

If I am seminal then … then I must get back for Saf and Mal. There's a fake living with my anak anak.

I must be seminal. I must be the seminal. I am me. Please, let me be me.

Lemarr Robinson …

Ben, Ben … *wah yuh ah dah*, Ben? *Yuh nuh fi* be membing Aisha *bout dis.*

'Istri,' he memb, sobbing.

'Bat Ears? You sound upset is it?' Aisha *seh* without emotion.

'Istri, I … I'm sorry for bothering you.'

'What is it? Where are you?' *Shi* resents *di* interruption.

'Montana. There's an earthquake here too.'

'What?'

'Hundreds of years ago, but no lake these days; it drains away. Everything drains away.'

'You're rambling, Ben. Where are you? What's going on?'

'At Maddox's house.' Hang up, Ben. *Tell har nuttin. Dawg nyam yuh suppa.*

'Maddox?' she says with ice. 'Is he why you work on the Reck?' How she know of this?

'The Reck is the least of it, Istri.'

'Bat Ears, you scare me ah. Tell me what's going on.' Scaring *mi* too. Maddox will be furious.

'Terrible things, my love. Terrible things … sybils … and saps.'

'Saps? Bat Ears.'

'I play golf now.' A maniacal giggle escapes Ben's *choat.*

'Golf? What are you talking—'

'War is coming. Saps are killers, Istri. Saps cut your throat, slaughter your lovers.' Ben rambling sobbing. 'Saps on a spit. We tear their meat off the bone, with teeth and bare hands. A sap cuts Bunny's throat! They farm saps. I see one give birth. Lab coats steal her baby away.'

'Bat Ears, listen. Listen. Stop sobbing ah. You make no sense. Saps are extinct. You hallucinate.' Good, Aisha. Keep disbelieving.

'I want for going home.' No. No. No. Bredda. Ben, *yuh* can *no guh yaad.*

'You are home, is it?'

'The other is living there …' *Blow wow,* he *gwine* tell *har everyting.* 'With

Saf and Mal. And Jaya.'

'Jaya? The KK takes Jaya. You know this. You are there.' Taste *har* concern *fi* Ben's state deepening.

'They take Jaya?'

'Oh, Bat Ears ...' *shi seh*, like *shi a* learning *im* crazy, and it's breaking *har* heart.

'Get me out of here, Istri. Help me escape.'

'Escape? Nurses have you already, is it?'

'I need you, Istri. We must talk. Then we decide what is next.'

'Next?'

'There's no way out, Istri.'

'We will find a way, Bat Ears. We will find a way. Hey, settle down, okelah? We figure it out, we always do ah.'

Sniffle. 'Yeer. Love you.'

'Love you too, Bat Ears.'

'Please help me escape.'

'Look ah. Portland is still a mess lah. No original spooky stations function here.'

'There's no spooky station here at all.'

'Where are you?'

'Montana, Aisha. I tell you already.'

'Just run.'

'It could be days for finding a station.'

'Okelah. I'll think of something lah. I will get you out, give me couple hours, then gog *Stasiun Telinga Kelelawar*.'

Maddox Price ...

The troublesome, useless Ben sybil appears at the top of the stairs. The face a distraught avalanche of eyebrows and jawbones. The eyes at opposing angles are so liquid. Martinis spilling out of cocktail glasses, black olives, and all.

'Puffin. You look terrible. Come have a drink.' Clink a large ice cube into a lowball, splash bourbon over.

The rain stops long enough so the day might wink her last. Under a blanket of grey fluffy cloud, the sun is setting. The sky is pinker than a young boy's pyjamas.

Ben the sybil hesitates at the top of the stairs. If its face grows any heavier, its head might topple off its neck and tumble down the staircase. What a waste. The Society will need persuading I'm still the best choice for rebooting the effort. You may be sure I'll be laying much of the blame on Caracia.

Wave a glass at the sybil, raise my eyebrows expectantly. Somehow it animates and lurches down the stairs.

It accepts the glass but takes no sip. I drain the remainder of my bourbon, replenish my glass while the sybil stares into its glass reading tea leaves. With a sudden purposeful swing of its arm, it drains the glass, plants it on the bar. An emphatic move of a chess piece forcing mate.

Refill slower. Still it says nothing.

'This day has been … harrowing,' it says. There's some humanity in the ruined animal. 'My Mind's without itself,' it says.

'You play me along all the while,' I test.

The sybil drains half the bourbon in a single breathy draught. 'Why should I care about this stupid high-stakes squabble between you and the health camerati?'

'Because, dear Puffin, no other game suffices. We're Infis. You're Infi. We either play the game or face a lifetime of boredom. You already taste this. You have no mission anymore. Nothing inspires you. Look at you. You could mope about for another 2 centuries, the way you are heading.'

'*Im* finished, Maddox.' It's Lemarr—a twisted little monkey when he's not hiding in one of his ridiculous projections. He emerges from the hallway from the gym and the pool. How dare he spook into my house without an invitation.

'How—?'

'*Mi* have *fren dem*, Maddox,' Lemarr says, a petting-zoo smile on his face. 'Friends? There's a game *yuh cud* try: he who collects *di bess fren dem* wins. If *yuh* have *enuff*, treat *dem* well, *dem* will help *yuh wen yuh*—*mi nuh kno*— *wen yuh* need a *faas* spook *fi sumweh* risky. *Wid fren dem fi* guiding *yuh tru*, *yuh* might just have safe *vecta* corroboration.'

'Lemarr. Leave immediately. This is the worst possible time for—'

'*Eh di bess* possible time *fi* Ben. *Yuh muss* let him *cut*.'

'Leave? Are you so ridiculous? There's no letting it leave.'

'*Me tek* him. Let him *guh yaad fi* his wife and family. At least one time … before …'

'It's all right, Lemarr,' the broken sybil says. 'Let him prune me. I tire of this.'

'Nah, *bredda*. *Neva* give *inna*. *Yuh* give *inna*, him *guh so-so* crèche more of *yuh*.'

'Crèche more?' An indignant cackle escapes my chest. 'What makes you believe you're so special, you failure? There are 100's of 1000's of other mindwriters with at least twice the talent you possess.'

'Is *dat* right, Maddox?' Lemarr challenges. 'How many of *dem* are Infis?'

Releasing the balloon of sarcasm inflating in me, I say. 'Oh, look how well this one turns out.'

From outside, bursts of violet flash in the nightfall, from all round the grounds. Separate parties are making toward the house. Another flash nearer the house resolves into a larger party with a bulkier being at the centre. 'Dash it. The Holy Octopus.' Drain the glass.

The sybil is alongside, looking out at shadows advancing up the hill, black and ominous in the thin light.

I say, 'Caracia Svakhaska, come for ending our gambit, no doubt. And ending you, I'm afraid.'

The sybil hears without comprehension, without so much as a micro-tic of a facial muscle. He's shutting down, giving up. The inevitability of it. Blood drains away from his face … blue, bluish purple. No. violet. A cylindrical column of violet light surrounds him. A sparkle. He blinks out and vanishes. Lemarr too.

The sybil's glass clangs on the slate floor, smashing. On a rivulet of liquor, ice floats. With it melts my fading hopes.

Eight cardinals tending an obese disambulant octopus-pope. A caliginous caravan trudging with awkward and wary steps, up the slippery grassy slope for the house. Two bearers shouldering palankeen poles blink rain out of their eyes and sniffle, while struggling ceremoniously for keeping Caracia's roofless palankeen level. Her Voices of Arms, with rivulets running from their forelocks around their eyes, precede the palankeen in 2 files, swaying like willows in the wind, mimicking Caracia's tentacle movements.

Caracia revels in the rain moistening her octopoid skin.

I will receive her on the ground floor in the games room; no one could carry her up the stairs with any dignity, her corpus is so distorted and distended. I'll tolerate none of her slithering up the carpets on her own. No industrial cleaning agent ever gets the octopus out. I'd have to burn the whole house down and spook the remains into the sun. It could only be worse if she is a spider.

Voices open the glass doors from the pool patio. Is that the scent of pool water decorticating my nostrils? Or something saltier and mucousy, more putridly marine?

'Maddox!' the 8 call in discordant reedy bone-scraping voices. 'Present yourelf and receive us.'

The Voices of Arms, voices of 8, pieces of shit, passive and emotionless, zombies all, under remote control.

Caracia's bearers set her palankeen on the patio by the games room doors. If an octopus can appear impatient, Caracia masters it. The horizontal slits of her large eyes fixate on estranged distances, as if separate beings vivify each. With a flick or shiver, Caracia vanishes in camouflage against of the patio tiles. Her tricks bend me every time. With another unnatural pulse, she reappears, her skin an earthy red. If she changes colour or pattern too often, she induces a kind of motion sickness.

'Welcome, Infinite Svakhaska,' I say tongue and lung, addressing her Voices of Arms. Resisting with resolute habit any chance encounter with her Mind direct. Flutherbombing her, for even a tik, will overcome anyone's senses with alien octopine empathy, and churn their stomach to fishpaste, which they'll readily projectile heave in spectacular fashion. Oh, please let me never relive that again. Swallowing hard and continuing: 'Make yourelf at home, please settle in anywhere. Over there on the tile floor, perhaps. Can I get you something? Some salt water perhaps? A 14 of oysters? No shucking of course.'

Caracia slithers off the palankeen for the centre of the games room, with her 8 Voices filing into a semicircle behind her. Lithe as snakes, heads swaying and surging on their necks. A Voice mimics one of Caracia's tentacle arms twitching. I catch a glimpse of the 2 rows of loathsome white suckers on the underside, recalling bruises from the last time she clamps those on me.

The Voices remain quiet, a choir awaiting the conductor. Caracia is stretching out the moment for the point of extreme awkwardness, with only the wet sound of air sucking through her syphon. The detestable creature. How much humanity is left in there? Are there any original organs in that gooey mantle? Has she lungs? Has she 3 octopus hearts or a single human one? How long can she survive out of water?

'Have no concern for our breathing,' her Voices answer, with less than perfect timing, like Catholics reciting a prayer. It's the slow link between her central brain and the chains of neurones in her arms that varies the delay in each speaking, rather than the link between arm and human Voice. Her chorus line always carries their own short echo. 'We are at equal ease in air and water,' the chorus says. Two spray Caracia with seawater from large bottles they keep in the kangaroo pockets of their uniforms.

Caracia looks at me from her dominant eye, her mantle a slimy Rastafarian cap (Lemarr always objects when I describe it so) sweeping behind her. 'Come closer,' 3 Voices say. With feet rooted to the floor, the other 5 swing about, gulping at the air. I shudder, reckoning on what comes next. 'We wish tasting of you.'

Hold breath and step forward. There is nothing other than comply. Octopuses are curious, affectionate, and even humorous. Their suckers are tactile and sensitive, having some limited form of sight. Their touch ranges between the sense of a kiss or loving caress, and a painful sucking clamp. Two tentacles snake up and grapple me. Another slithers over my face and neck. They say such a groping is an act of affection. Affection, my trash-can ass! The feeling is more loathsome than a groping vampire pool cleaner. I'd wager y'all would lose the contents of your stomach, which would only please Caracia. Fortunately, it's some time since the last such humiliation for me, which helps none now for the roiling in my belly.

A Voice makes the hawking sound of disgust deep in her throat as if she might expectorate a large gob of sputum. 'Gack. Sybil,' she says. The others gag. Normally, from a tank or pool, Caracia would drown me, shooting water from her spout. Fortunate today she's on dry land. 'You have a crèche taste; seminals taste more like whitefish. Yours is like gritty plastic too long in the sun, drifting on currents. We suppose it should be no surprise a garbage miner tastes of garbage.'

Such are the usual opening humiliations. Caracia expects I respond. I decide against disappointing her. 'Get your stinking suckers off me or I'll char-grill you and serve you with lemon and a Greek salad.'

Caracia continues groping, leaving a slimy trail over my skin. 'You also taste of deception. You have the fear of a squealing pig.'

'With respect, I would rather take a rogering from the pet camel, than submit.'

The Voices all laugh. Caracia raises an arm; it forms a recognisable if slightly deformed shape of a tumescent cock. 'You're rather fond of taking rogerings.' Caracia's skin washes a dun yellow. She releases me.

Exhale in relief.

'You send the mindwriter away,' Caracia's Voices say. 'With Lemarr.'

Dash! I'm toast. Toast in a lather of lard, both sides ready for the fire.

'Lemarr is responsible. He helps B—helps the mindwriter escape.' Hold your meat in, Maddox.

'Escape?' Caracia's dominant eye remains unblinking while the other rolls about on its own carnival ride. She pulls her mantle taut, lifts it over her head, a bishop's mitre the top of which almost reaches the ceiling. 'How? You make assurances the house is secure.'

'It is secure, far from a spooky station, and far from the eyes of nurses. Also, I have the best scatter nets available.'

'Yet I still pierce the nets. So too your mindwriter.'

'Well, your tech is apparently better than mine. As good as the health camerati's, it seems.'

'You're blaming me? Or the nurses? How could they know of him here?'

'They must have an agent.'

'The error's in being too soft with him,' Caracia's Arms intone. 'You are being too soft with him.'

'We need him willing. The mindwriter requires alignment of heart and Mind.'

'Show me the product of his heart and Mind. What progress towards understanding the Reck?'

Swallow. Consider claiming Ben makes off with his work product. A lie of such magnitude will be too easy in the exposing. 'Alas, all his research so far results in no meaningful contact with the Reck.'

'Meaningful?'

'No new data insights, no code de-compiles, no evidence of communication, much less a log file. Nothing a common reputation jel couldn't turn up.'

'Nothing at all?'

Shake my head, dumb.

'Is he playing us?'

In a rush: 'We always know interrogating the Reck would be an extreme difficulty, if not impossible. Lack of progress is no evidence of jiggery-pokery.'

Caracia throws her tentacles up. Her Voices convulse behind her. 'We try it your way,' one Voice says. 'We have no happiness,' starts another, 'when you exploit Angela for securing the mindwriter.' Another: 'It is clear your strategy of grooming him in the ways of the Infinite is a failure.' 'Hitherto,' says a pair, 'we resume control of the project, and advise you keep your distance.'

Making her point, Caracia squirts me with black ink.

Aisha Evoli …

Poor Ben. In distress. Lose his memory. He sounds so different lah. A different person. It's hard lah, these passing months, but Dil and me make a right decision.

A different person. A stranger. No, it bears no contemplation at all.

Maddox. The slimy reptile. Always know he is trouble. Before his sybil messes up my shoes at the Inductee Gala. Shudder with the taste of it. Sybils! Disgusting lah. Everyone agrees that one such a scandal, nurses and Infis crèching hundreds of them. Could Ben be using sybils? Maybe Maddox make him. If he is, who is spooking here? I could be meeting a monster. Maybe it's too late already for saving him.

'Istri, I'm here.' Ben membs and I jolt.

'*Stasiun Telinga Kelelawar* (Bat Ears Station)? Already?'

'Yeer, I arrive.'

'I'll come meet you, Bat Ears.' I have dread I'm meeting a sybil.

Scan for the familiar manga shock of hair. Find it flomping up the path from the demountable station. The sight of him chills my bones. Different clothes. Californian labels. New haircut. Tan skin. Rings around his downcast eyes. His shoulders are down. I know those worry lines in his brow and around his eyes. He's like a broken, better version of hiself.

He sees me, and his eyes brighten. He's instantly 3 centims taller. There's more spring in his hair. He runs, arms stretch. I stumble down the verandah stairs for greet him. Anticipate the force of his hug. It's a warm blanket. 'Istri,

I miss you so much.'

Hug the fruit in my arms, hope he's no counterfeit. He so different.

His chest heaves, his body an inflating balloon. Then the air wheezes out of him. His ribs tremble against me. His arms clamp tighter ah. Racking sobs erupt from a place so deep it scares me.

'Oh, Istri, I am doing terrible things.'

La

'Portland' — Armors

Teodora Mrowka ...

VÖR PERCHES ON ONE of Maitreya's big toes, palms planting either side of her buttocks, legs swinging like a toddler's in a high-chair. She's ... happy. Mood swings are a bad sign. She's as serene as the Leshan Buddha hiself, who towers more than 70 metres above, calm and serene, and at ease with Vör parking her butt on his calm and serene toenail.

Maybe she is one with the Buddha. Both she and statue look out towards Mount Emei, over the confluence of the Minjiang and Dadu Rivers.

'Teo Face,' she exclaims in a fashion uncharacteristic of Vör. Directly below, I'm waving at her. 'How lovely seeing you here. Climb up and take a toe.'

'How about you come down from there?'

Vör mocks serious consideration then says, 'Nuh. I'm toasty sweet up here.'

Well straight for the point then: 'Vör, might I ask how you journey here?'

Vör stages another thoughtful pose then: 'By dirigible.'

'You spook here.'

'Well, of course I spook here.'

'In one spook or ... maybe you make a few more ... a few more than you need?'

'Everything is one spook away, Teo. Even Cuba. Even the nuclear power plant. *Mor* lies about that. We could spook there direct if we have the vectors.'

'Yes, I know, I'm sorry—'

'You know this statue?' Vör interrupts, riding her own runaway train of thought. 'It's the largest of the ancient sap world.'

'Um, well ...'

'It's amazing, *ja*? It's all shiny and new again, bless Petroleum's Infi socks.'

Are y'all following? I'm struggling.

'Petroleum Dynamite,' Vör injects in the gap I leave her. 'He's an Infi, a guest at the Infi Gala where ...' She trails off. 'Anyway, Pet's mission is restoring ancient statues. In recent times he restores this Leshan Giant Buddha with all its former majesty.'

'It's impressive,' I offer.

'It's wonderful. Wonderful. Would you say Pet is wonderful too, Teo? Wonderful? For restoring this wonderful shiny statue?'

'It's sandstone,' I flounder. Dull, red, sandstone. 'Hardly shiny.'

'Have some imagination, Teo, some inspiration. My point—my question— is about Pet. His mission performs wonderful deeds. But is he wonderful?'

'I suppose—'

'No! He will never be wonderful. He's Infi and corrupt, no matter how many wonderful wonders he hides his corruption in.'

'Vör, please come down. We worry for you.'

'Know you the story of this statue, Teo? This wonderful statue?'

'Some of it, I guess.' A social lie. No one knows anything until they gog it.

'In ancient times these rivers were dangerous ... dangerous. Dangerous. The turbulent waters often sank boats, killing many saps. One day a monk had an idea. "I will appease the river gods by building a great statue," he thinks, "which will look over these rivers, and bring peace under its watchful eye." So the monk carved this statue out of the side of the hill, right here on the bank. Right where these turbulent rivers come together and squabble in their rush for the sea. And then what happened, Teo?'

'Tell me, Vör. Please tell me what happened.'

'Well, the monk took all the rock he had carved out of the hill and threw it in the water. Out there. The rock made the rivers change course. The rivers became happy, blending with each other. They became peaceful and stopped sinking boats. They stopped killing saps.'

'That's a lovely story, Vör, but please tell me how many spooks you take for getting here?'

'One. I come straight from home, from København.'

'Is this true, Vör? Is this true? Because I'm following you, I'm sorry for saying, only sometimes, for tasting how you are. I must say, today is hardy-hard keeping up with you. I lose you spook after spook. There could be many more than I trace. I know you make many 14's of spooks today.'

Vör shakes her head and smiles with a sense of inflated accomplishment. 'Once I would fear spooking and you would call it sickness. Now I am at ease with spooking, this is also sickness?'

'You know too much of something is as problematic as too little.'

'Ah, what is too much? What is too little? Where is the measure?'

'Vör, you're a nurse. These games are beneath you.'

'You're beneath me,' she says, looking down from her perch on Maitreya's toe. 'You're beneath me, Teo.'

Shake my head. This is turning bad. 'Vör, I have a Warrant …'

She startles me. With agility, she leaps and lands on her feet before me. 'For what?'

'Vör, you're a spookhead.'

'I spook yet my head is fine, *tak*.'

'Vör, look at you. Your hand tremors, increased breathing rate, higher heart rate …'

'I have arousal for seeing you.'

'Sweaty palms. Dilated pupils.'

'Let's get naked, Teo. For the sake of Buddhism, let's lose our attachment to our clothes.'

'You're having trouble sleeping; you have loss of appetite, overconfidence, over-excitement, irritability. Next comes paranoia and depression.'

'Are we those nurses? The ones who spy on colleagues? Are we those nurses, Teo, seeking advance by Consigning one another?'

'Vör, I have no wish …'

'We are above it, Teo. Above it all. Our team is the cream of *det Fødererede Sundhedskamerata i Nordeuropa*. The first health camerata in neo culture, the first nurses who wear the rainbow fatigues.' Her eyes fix on me. 'We come without sense of duty, but rather a love of mission, Teo. We are no nurses who Consign each other.'

Dumb, no words, blank … heavy of heart. Despite our competition for … Eir … for … 'Please, Vör. I come … I must warn—'

'We are best friends, Teo.'

'Vör, we have no friendship.'

'We have a mission together.'

'We had a mission.'

Using *had*—putting our mutual experience in the past, like you would describe sap events, long ago dead—shocks Vör. As it would shock anyone.

'Please Vör, let me help you. I have no wish for Consigning you, just a plea. A plea you accept my help.'

'We still have a mission, Teo. A mission growing greater the more we investigate. We must Cure Infis of evil.'

'There's no good or evil anymore, Vör.'

'The only true evils are the deeds of someone convinced they are, without question, doing good.'

'You take the words straight out of my Mind. And you're quoting Eir.'

Vör looks far over the water, perhaps for the banks on the other side. 'Are we rivers, Teo? Are nurses and Infis rivers that a monk might pacify with a cheesy statue and a few rocks? Might nurses and Infis merge like these? No, Teo, no. There is no merging. We have a mission. We have a mission, and we always will, for damming one of those rivers and evaporating it completely.'

Ben Evoli ...

Procuring tickets for a local Sonik Monkey Alliance show is simple for an Infi. I could have a whole block of the best seats in the house, should I desire. I must apologise, Lula, Amara, Bonehead. I accept only 2 tickets for Saf and myelf. After Jaya's Consignment, cheering her up is my personal responsibility.

The tickets are for a private box high in the stadium. I wish for avoiding the main floor below where fans will be standing ankle deep in fabbied faecal matter. Yeer, even though the band appears at the local arena via hollicast from Mandalay, there's no shortage of volunteer fanclub tragics who run a battery of authentic SMA fabbies for producing the material for the on-premises shit-fight.

The show is an all-ages affair, an opportunity for acquiring tickets before Saf sneaks off for an adult show where the norm is for all kinds of bacchanalian behaviour. Go gog it if y'all must. All I'll say is I never want Saf in a crowd careless with swiftly septic liquids and secretions.

The arena goes dark. Ecstatic cheers roil up the seat embankments and assaults us like a cyclone. Saf is on her feet and whooping, 'Bjorn Wyn! Bjorn Wyn!' Chanting for the band's leader. Noise builds like a monster truck derby mowing down a crusade of knights and horses. Gravel and clanking chains. Sirens wail, bandsaws cut sheet metal. A huge holly appears over the stage. A red jubo, hands pulling cheeks apart. The band's signature browneye.

'Grunt and pucker up!' Bjorn Wyn Faser wails. The crowd erupts, and the truly cataclysmic gets under way.

Nilajani Karunanithi ...

Ben and Saf skip among a crowd of 80,000 or more thronging down the impractically narrow Homebush street for the spooky station. Ben shortens his step for matching his daughter's. It will be only a year or 2 before she's taller than him. Saf is flushing with happiness and mischief after the live hollicast of her favourite band, Sonik Monkey Alliance.

'You cheat!' she tells Ben. 'You promise you would turn MusiKai off.'

'I turn it off,' Ben lies with a jester laugh.

'I check a few times. You were blending. SMA are the latest thizang and you're blending your old music with it?' For Saf, processing the performance through MusiKai is worse than grating kittens onto pasta.

'The latest thing? They sound like a battleship running aground on jagged rocks. Like The Beatles on ice. I mean on meth, not skates. The Beatles in a Saturn 5 rocket.'

'Beetles? Saturn 5? What are you talking about?'

'The Beatles,' Ben corrects. He earns no more than an impatient humph from Saf. Unreproved, Ben continues, 'Sirringo Starr? Sirgeorge Harrison? Even Sirpaul McCartney had his merits.'

'Oh, 21st-century sap music. Bapa, you are so membosankan.' Gogging that word. Membosankan: boring.

'20th-century sap music,' Ben corrects.

'Oh? I suppose they wear powdered wigs and codpieces?'

'The Beatles influence music until this day. Everyone copies The Beatles, even their kotoran stuff.'

'Why have all those old musicians' names starting with *Sir*?'

'Because they're knights.'

Saf scrunching her face. 'Knights? They ride horses?'

'Nah. Camels.'

Saf breaks her stride. Bursts out laughing. Ben beams in delight for his daughter. 'Like Kaboobie?' Saf checks in disbelief.

'Yep. Sirringo Starr would strap his drum kit on a camel and ride around the stage.'

'That's kotoran,' she laughs. Smiles so wide her gums are showing.

'No. I'm serious. It's why he never played a drum fill the same way twice, what with rolling around on a camel's back.'

Saf stops blank, her feet flat on the ground, breaks her handhold with her father. 'Bapa?'

'Yeer, cahaya?'

'How are you in 2 places at once?'

Ben retakes Saf's hand. 'I'm right here, Saf.'

Saf squeezes his hand tighter. 'Yeer, Bapa. But I see you with Ibu too.'

'Flutherbombing your Ibu, Saffron? We have family promises, remember?'

'I miss her. She is away for weeks.'

Ben drops his face, looks into his rib cage. 'Yeer, she is.'

'How are you with Ibu and here too? She's in Portland, in that creepy old minster. So are you.' Saf looks at Ben with indignant judgment. 'Are you using sybils?'

'What? No.'

'Then you tell me who is hugging Ibu.'

Ben's eyes flutter wild.

'Alamak!' Ben swears tongue and lung. His voice catches in his throat.

I follow the yarns for Aisha, taste her hugging her husband. A sybil husband.

I grab a holly of spooky stations around Portland, California. While there are 14's and 14's, most are out of commission, under grey-green goop which, on the 4-dimensional map stretches fingers all through the city lowlands, marking the high-line of flooding. I drift into the holly; a tag resolves itself in the top left of my field of vision:

BLINK HERE FOR UP-TO-DATE LOCATIONS OF DEMOUNTABLE
STATIONS.

Blink. The map highlights new stations above the flood line. Where would Aisha and sybil Ben be? I call up their names. Most have serial numbers or other cryptic identifiers, a few with more descriptive titles. Flying around among the names. Nothing suggestive yet. A thing catches my attention: Stasiun Telinga Kelelawar. They name a station in Anglo-Malay? *Bat Ears Station*.

Meanwhile in Homebush, the crowd parts around Saf and Ben like 2 rocks in a torrential flood. Ben on his knees in anguish. A pair of nurses appear, eyes on Ben, Warrants on their Minds.

For the approaching nurses, Saf fixes a stare. 'Stay away from my Bapa. He's Infi and will rip your minster down if you interfere. Stay away. I hate you. I hate you all!'

Ben Evoli ...

Taste purple.

Waiting while the orgasmic whirlpool slows, and senses resolve. Emerge under a canopy of chitin-paste canvases. A high-pitch tent. Through the translucent material, sunlight refracts in arcs of the 7 colours. Floorspace a rough circle, maybe 5 metres across. This is the place: Stasiun Telinga Kelelawar—Bat Ears Station—a place Aisha so obviously names for me, a place where I already taste her with a canoodling sybil.

'Hey!' someone membs. A shadow waves near the tent-flap exit, coalesces into a uniform once my eyes adjust. Recognise the uniform: Aisha's camerata. 'Come outa there. We got more incoming.'

Still squinting. The light outside is intense; it renders a high-contrast scene of black trees framing a view of the edges of the earth. In the foreground is a thin wide braid of pines; beyond is a rolling cityscape of solarglass and environment sails stretching for kims across a valley floor. Occasionally, taller buildings rise above the rest like bright craggy pyramids in moats of oily brown stagnant water and mud. Farther back, haze shrouds mounds of grey-green hills receding towards an indistinct horizon of rain under a thin ripple of cloud. Or maybe it's smoke. Where blue sky meets the blanket of clouds is an unnaturally triangular cloud. No, it's a snowy mountain peak floating in the sky.

'That's Mount Hood, the tallest peak in Oregon, Ben Face.'

Almost jump out my clothes in fright. Swallow my pounding heart after registering the speaker's rainbow uniform. The nurse's face hardens into one I should recall.

'Please allow an introduction, Infi. *Sygeplejerske* Vör Hoyur *af det Fødererede Sundhedskamerata i Nordeuropa.*'

My heart quakes even more violently. 'You! You are part of the raid at the Inductee Gala, the adjutant of Eir Frijberg.' Alamak!

'No, I outgrow that posting. I have no interest in Eir now,' she says, like a twentager proud of asserting independence from her family. A tinge of loss. And something off. The sheen of her face, eyes flitting, pupils dilating. She's working hard against grinding her teeth. Except for the uniform, I'd say she's a spookhead.

My feet root in the ground. I'd never outrun her; she's bigger, faster, and has the training for putting me down if she requires. I say, 'It looks so peaceful out there,' stalling.

'It's anything but,' Vör says. 'Look closer; there are many environment sails cracking. Buildings are unsafe. Just out of sight is where most of the liquefaction occurs. Aisha's team has quite the mission ahead.' Vör attempts a smile. 'The view from the north lookout, is quite breath-taking.'

'You're playing tour guide?' Whatever her plans, she's holding them back while she toys with me.

Vör throws her eyebrows up, draws her mouth thin and wide, releases her expression like an arrow. 'A guide of sorts,' she answers with too much pleasure. 'We nurses are in the mission of guidance.' She turns square, aims an unflinching stare. 'Let's see if we might guide you through this messy sybil business.'

Her words are a punch in my stomach, blunt as a battering ram. 'Why are you holding Aisha?'

'Aisha may come and go as pleases her.'

'If you intend taking me, leave Aisha out of it.'

Vör radiates a playfully wicked smile. Checks herelf. Whatever she says next will be other than her first impulse. 'You should ask Aisha if she wishes I leave her out of it.'

What means this? 'Look.' Already I'm bargaining from a weak position. 'I have no taste of a sybil until today. I come straight here without any subterfuge. When I find out who crèches it—'

Vör waves my unspoken threats down, returns her hands behind her back like a tallship captain pacing a quarterdeck. She plods a few heavy steps away from the view. 'That may well be true,' she says in a way that tugs me alongside for matching her stride.

Onto a lawn of green grass (such a symbol of sap privilege) under a large blooming magnolia. Between thriving flower beds, the lawn leads up for an ancient building. Stony and solid, at once a mythical castle and a dense German layer cake—2 storeys with steep red-tile roofing for icing; ornate geometric decorations and architectural embellishments; chimneys; 2 circular turrets. Only the solarglass windows give any sense it exists in our time instead of an anak's fairy story.

'What is this place?'

'It has been many things over the centuries: a residence, a museum, a crumbling squat. Once Pittock Mansion, now Pittock Minster.'

I stop mid-stride. 'You are Consigning me!'

'In California?' Vör almost spits the nation's name. She continues, hands behind her back. 'No. Aisha's camerata is using it as a command post for the recovery effort. Up here in the West Hills, there is less earthquake damage.'

Ahead is a circular structure that could be a huge bird bath, except it's also capped by squat balusters supporting a heavy stone handrail. It's a rostrum—perhaps where a powerful sap could stand, sip whisky and survey his domain. We take a flight of steps which bifurcates around the birdbath. A palatial verandah stretches left and right for the entire length of the building.

'Come on,' Vör urges.

I stop for taking it all in. 'Why?'

'Aisha is in here.'

'I taste this already. With the sybil.'

Vör marches back at me, implying a measured dose of menace. 'Please refrain from flutherbombing her. She's yet unaware there are 2 pairs of Bat Ears. And there are nurses on the grounds who I have no influence over. I'd hate one should cat her before we have the chance of managing the situation.'

She sets off again, leading along the right spoke of the verandah to a turret in which there is an archway door already open.

'You think you might manage Aisha? All my blessings on that.'

'Aisha is quite manageable, 'Vör says, 'with the right keys.'

My blood runs cold. Cooler air in the quiet, small oval greystone vestibule leading into a cavernous space in which dominates an ornate marble staircase with balustrades of timber and wrought metal. As pretty as it is, it must still be an annoyance; there is no built-in slippy-slide. Vör skips around back of the stairway and descends a flight down. Fighting exasperation, and needing Aisha, I follow. Vör leads into a small passageway which opens into a large oval room. Three figures stand as if waiting for bad news, wearing ashen faces all slack-jaw, plate-eye caricatures of horror. Aisha, I ache for. The sybil, I dread. The sight of the 3rd person almost throws me on the floor. Lurking in an alcove, he might be comically joyous, but for the reek of his betrayal. It's Dilan, my best friend, my *machan*.

Vör Hoyur ...

Dim light seeping through the squat narrow basement windows makes ghosts of the 3 occupants while their faces illuminate stark contrasting expressions of distress. Aisha gasps, throws hands over her mouth, yet fails for muffling her wails of shock. Dilan edges for the back wall of the oval room, traces it compulsively with a finger until he arrives at one of 2 circular alcoves. The Ben already in the room adheres his hands over his head; folds into a crouch, mouth wide open, eyes wincing shut, clamping down on his agony before it spreads.

The Ben I bring advances on the other, threatens throwing punches. The other bucks on his feet, ready yet cowering. Aisha interposes between them with a hand on each chest.

'Who are you?' this Ben demands. 'Who makes you? Who makes you?' The other is mute while Aisha takes a hand of each in hers.

'I have no blame in any it,' the other Ben pleads. Whatever remains of the Infi's practiced dignity is shredding before my eyes. 'It's Maddox Price. He's the one who crèches me.'

Maddox Price ...

First Lemarr springs my Puffin. Then Caracia squiggles her interfering tentacles into everything. I'm without a min's rest after scouring her ink off me—no time for a merge—and now! Such a kerfuffle. Curse that calvous living fossil Orlando for nicking hiself a Cure. Without his connections, it takes me an hour tasting around Portland after rumours erupt; an hour of fluther jumping, it sickens me admitting; an hour infiltrating the yarns of the particularly churchical aspheterists of the Health Corporations of the United States of California; an hour watching their cardinals and archbishops soothe over a ruction with the disaster recovery mission.

The source of the ruction? One of the nurses detains the recovery mission procomplement and her life partner. It chills my chilblains. California Health denies knowledge of detaining them, yet they send a platoon of nurses for retaking control of Pittock Minster.

So, it's Aisha and Ben they're fussing over. I glean a location; before long, I find a squad of Californian nurses surrounding an ostentatiously oval room in the basement of the old sandstone mansion. By my aunt's testicles! Inside are 2 dear puffins, a wife, and some quake buttock friend—and 2 nurses, one of whom I recognise from the Inductee Gala. It's the White Witch's adjutant, Vör Hoyur who, with effulgent confidence, seems 200 mims taller since last we meet. The other rainbow uniform is a squat male with California Health insignias. Her chatelaine jangles heavy with souvenirs and jujus, which is as pretentious a show of status as these frugal health missionaries allow. Lemme jel her. Ah yes, as politically heavy a nurse as y'all will find this side of the Atlantic. An administrator, Brock Telford. Brock the Rock, they call her, a nurse uncharacteristically proud of her gonads, and famous for punching above her weight.

None of which impresses the junior Norse nurse Vör from Scandinavia. In no way a nice Norse nurse, that one.

Anyway, better late than without a date. Now we're here, let's watch the show.

 *Ben Evoli …*

After protracting a debate with Vör over jurisdiction, Brock the Rock points out the sybil. 'Come with us.'

The sybil has the foreboding resignation of cattle going for slaughter. A black pall hangs over it. Under Vör's order, it trudges out the door without protest, acknowledging only Aisha (my Aisha!) who he fixes with a mournful yearning gaze. Two nurses usher him away. Brock is fast on their heels.

In the space of a breath, a squad of local nurses enters, in fresh uniforms and light chatelaines, enters. They surround Aisha and me. Two usher Dil up from where he skulks on an alcove floor.

'Come with us,' one of the nurses instructs.

'Walao eh! Where are you taking us ah?' Aisha finds her usual attitude of being in charge.

'Music Room.'

We file out; 2 nurses in front, us next, the remainder behind. Glad for ascending the staircase out of the basement. On the next floor we double around into an oval room identical as downstairs. Comfy furniture stuffs it. Three large windows allow views of the extensive lawns beyond the circular rostrum on the verandah.

With heavy feet the last of Aisha's evicted colleagues are tromping across the lawn for the demountable Bat Ears Station. So much for cross-missionary cooperation in the name of helping the community. The chance for skewering an Infi and a sybil proves too rich a temptation for the local nurses.

'Stay here,' the nurse orders then stations a pair of her colleagues at each exit.

I crumple onto a couch under the large centre window, wrestling my urges—for assaulting Dil, and for launching an inquisition against Aisha.

'How long you know this Vör Hoyur?' I demand.

Aisha turns away. Guilty glances. Dil cowers.

Settle. This is no time for loud melodrama. Find my gravity, and withhold the avalanche of my anger, making sure the next thing I say is quiet and threatening. 'Tell me.'

Something cracks in Aisha. Tension dissolves from her limbs. 'She flutherbombs me.'

'For how long?'

'A while, fine. She sees how your behaviour is affecting us lor. We chat for a while ah. We agree for the best if we would attend the Inductee Gala this year ah.'

'And you agree? No resistance, no debate?'

'Well, no. But, Bat Ears, it just makes sense ah.'

'It just makes sense? A nurse from the other side of the planet agrees I should go join a band of Infis. Alamak! This makes sense?'

'You already decline 4 invitations. It's time for face fears, blend in, be less conspicuous. Everyone sees you withdraw into a hard shell. Look at you, Ben. You're falling apart.'

'Yeer, I'm falling apart. In 2 pieces, if we are precise.'

Aisha Evoli ...

There is nothing for saying, fine. Dil mumble with hiself. That one rock back and forward where he sit on a single seater in a far corner of the room. From one exit, a double file of nurses enter and surround us. The one follow them in is Vör.

'Come with us,' Vör says for Ben.

'No!' I squeal. 'Where you take him ah?'

'Come, please,' she says.

Ben's shoulders slump as he goes. His eyes never meet mine.

Vör is last in line for leave.

'Detective nurse,' I call. 'Please!'

Vör stops in the doorway, turns, impatient. 'What is it?'

'You let him child is it? Like we agree. It's what you promise all the long ah. We agree childing is the best for him ha. No need for Cure in a minster that one.'

'My dear Aisha,' Vör says with all the sympathy of a funnel-web spider. 'It's out of our hands. The use of sybils belies a sickness far worse than either of us anticipate.'

Ti

'Castle' — Slum Sociable

Ben Evoli …

UP THE STAIRS FOR THE FIRST FLOOR (or the 2nd floor as the Californians would say). A glass door; a short hallway; a narrow staircase up; a narrow passage passing a bathroom and a series of rooms too small for any function I could imagine. A large room; dark timber flooring; timber panelling on all the walls. Small windows offer cropped views of the Cascades in the north.

In the centre of the room are four 3-seater couches around a low table. Brock reclines in the lounge with the best view of us approaching. Hunching in the couch facing away from me is the sybil. With bile rising in my throat, I contend with ignoring its existence.

'Come, sit,' Brock says.

I sit opposite Vör. She has the elated smile of a grand-slam tennis tournament winner.

Vör Hoyur …

A warm glow in my chest, a thrill lighting up my fingertips. Enjoy it. My cheeks glow with anticipating. It's exciting.

'One of you,' I set eyes on each in turn, then back over again, 'is the Ben we're monitoring for some time.'

The 2nd Ben rubs the back of his neck.

Brock sits forward so I hurry with, 'The other is having quite the farm tour, in Argentina no less. Quite the operation, raising saps for meat. What next?

You Infis will be chewing your own arms off before long.'

'What she means for saying is,' Brock adds before I draw breath, 'we're sure which is the abomination.'

The alleged seminal Ben squirms on a couch edge while the sybil slumps like a boneless fish.

'It's a simple case,' Brock says and looks at seminal Ben across from her. Insipid Ben. 'Dispose of this sybil and tell us the locations of all the others.'

'I have no others! I—and I—you expect I ... dispose of ...?' Ben gestures at his copy.

I find my best scornful tone. 'Come now. At your Inductee Gala, we witness how Infis strike sybils down.'

'I have no sybils,' Ben says emphasising each word. 'And I have no taste for how the others ... just ...' Ben turns inwards, perhaps recalling the sybil of Maddox Price decomposing, spattering remains over his wife's shoes.

'Look,' Brock presses. 'I will go easy if—'

I interject, 'You have no authority—'

'May I remind you where we are?' Brock tenses. 'The United States of Janking California.'

'*Ja*. May I remind everyone, I represent the oldest—'

'Yeah, yeah. Rainbow connection. Got it.'

At this point no reply is the best reply. Let the little boy-nurse blow off his steam.

'Look,' Brock wheedles. 'We have no evidence ...' he waves at the seminal, '... is complicit in the acts of the sybil.'

Sybil Ben looks for the ceiling, shaking his head slow. 'He knows nothing of me ... nothing from the time Maddox kidnaps me. I keep telling—'

'And yet ...'

Brock throws her hands up. 'Here we go. Europan philosophical buffalo shit. I keep saying ... destroy the sybil. Post whole battalions of nurses for following the seminal and his family every tik of the gawdamn day and night. Send him on his way.'

'We already post a large contingent of detectives ...' I find myelf admitting.

'Same with the KK and who knows how many other camerati,' Brock volleys back. 'Which is my exact point. After all the surveillance, where's the evidence?'

I counter. 'The sybil's sickness has its roots in the seminal. The sybil is the evidence.'

Taste sweetness in the tension. Seminal Ben jerks on his feet. 'You will hold me responsible for actions I never commit?'

'Sit down, boy,' Brock commands.

Ben softens but remains standing. A tik. Brock stares him down. He sits.

'It makes no sense Consigning the seminal,' Brock says. 'Their paths diverge months ago. You're paddling a canoe up-rapids if you ignore the circumstances bringing the sybil here. Circumstances we should factor in. Our understanding could save the seminal from impending sickness. We should make no haste for taking a healthy—'

'Healthy? Hmmphhh.'

'We'll find no sickness, no memories of the sybil's actions, no toxins in the cells. Such a Cure would be over before it starts.'

Seminal Ben relaxes while the abomination crouches over its knees, drowning in the swamp of its fate.

'Then are we for delaying aid until after symptoms manifest? If we wait, how much harm will we inflict on the seminal and others around him, or on his environment or culture? Can we afford waiting?'

Brock tastes I'm leading somewhere. 'Then what?' she asks with some exasperation.

'Perhaps the only reasonable decision is offer them the choice.'

Brock slaps his knees in frustration. 'We agree—'

'What choice?' sybil Ben asks. Seminal Ben is staring at the rug between his knees.

'Either the seminal prunes the sybil, spurning the sickness flourishing within it …'

'I refuse killing anything—'

'Or …'

'I always know how it will end,' the abomination says, his voice cracking with panic.

'Or?' Seminal Ben asks again.

'You merge the sybil.'

'I have no idea how.'

I shrug. 'You have friends who know …'

'Okelah, suppose it's possible. Then what?'

'Well, then we have someone we can Cure.'

Ben Evoli …

Just the 2 of me in the basement oval room, its mustiness more noticeable after the sunlit health of its upstairs twin. There's now some rudimentary furniture: 2 stiff couches, a low table, and a sideboard under the windows. The sideboard bear a pot of coffee, some open sandwiches, and Danish pastries. Vör's doing. Someone should tell her those pastries originated in Austria.

Vör. During the whole circus with Brock, she's jittery and jumpy, repeat-blinking, fighting her chattering teeth by constantly grinding her jaw. I'm sure she's a spookhead.

The false choice she offers me: would her camerata endorse it? Why is Brock's mission allowing she sway things here in California's own back yard? Maybe if I stall long enough, Vör's choices will catch up with her before I commit anything I regret. Whatever the outcome, I'm sure Vör is racing against the pursuit of her own consequences. She'll need a clear win here for swaying her own mission from turning on her.

Dil is skulking about in the basement stair hall, perhaps hoping I'll give him an opportunity for redeeming hiself. Aisha disappears hours ago.

'What will you decide?' The mirror image of me, with a better haircut and tanner skin, throws his hands palm-up between us. His arms so like mine ripple with alien-strange muscles.

'It's our decision,' I tell the muscles. My skin crawls. I quell the urge for caving the fake's head in. This living breathing duplicate violates every rational and irrational sense I have about the way the universe should work.

'You're the seminal,' the muscles say.

Slump into a couch. There's little give in it. Feel like I'm sitting on an arrangement of planks. 'Am I? How is it you know for sure?'

He shakes his head. 'It's better I am the sybil, no matter what. The memories of these passing months … they should die with me.'

'What memories?'

The muscles slump into the couch opposite and make their face grimace. 'For one, I try killing myelf.'

Then we're both on the same track.

'You hope for avoiding the Cure,' the muscles say.

Nod. 'Of course. But can I trust Vör? Perhaps she'll take me no matter what I decide. Besides, I have no knowledge of how …' I gesture for help.

'How merges work? Me either, I only know it's possible. From Maddox.'

'Ha. Maddox!'

'He's not so bad.'

'What?'

'I think he has quite some affection for me. Us …'

'Affection? Still calling you Puffin, is he?' Taste bile. 'Whatever. I have neither means nor desire for merging or killing.'

'What then? Shall we timeshare Saf and Mal? Aisha?'

Scoff. 'Tolonglah, take Aisha. She put us here.'

'I put us here. Aisha loves me.' The shock must be plain on my face because the muscles quickly add, 'She only hopes you regain your joy for life.'

'At any cost it seems.'

'The nurses are using her. And Dil.'

'Dil!' Almost spit his name out. 'After everything …'

'Dil is your friend. You must care for your friends.'

'He's collaborating with nurses. Of all people. Dil! It makes no sense.'

'Yeer,' says the cluster of muscles parading a fitter version of me. 'How are Saf and Mal?'

Bile-rising anger. Head spinning. How to protect my anak anak while under a Cure? How long will they be without a bapa? My darling putri, Saf. Oh, Saf. And Mal: unstoppable, boisterous, still so fragile, maybe still sakit. Precious. So many hopes for them both.

The muscles. Destroy the muscles, and everything will be normal again. Destroy the muscles. The meat of it. Destroy the beast.

No, nothing will be normal. There's still the Reck. It All. Whoever is meddling with it will try stopping me.

Destroy the sybil. Nothing could satisfy my existential rage better. Simple if not for its pleading eyes. Look away. Look at the arm. Fitter, tanner than mine. Look away.

Vertigo. Stomach rolling over. Heart pounding out of my chest. Stand in the hope of quelling it all. See a vision of Maddox melting. Would these muscles die like Maddox's sybils? Imagine 100's of sybils melting. Gobs of Maddox and myelf piling up, filling space around me, consuming me. The scent overpowering.

Coughing, gagging, push Maddox's dying sybils out of Mind. My mouth fills. Hold it back, gagging. Rush for the door. Fold my stomach in. Hand covering mouth. Clenching teeth. Hold it all back. Must make it to a tandas bowl.

Nilajani Karunanithi ...

In the basement bathroom Ben, with head in a toilet bowl, gasps for air between retches. The sound of wet slaps and splashes. More gasping. A whimper. Ben flushes, still gagging and spitting.

Dil leans against the sink counter, his hope for redemption casting wan light over the concern etching his features. 'I'm sorry, Ben. I taste it blacker than you could know. But we're here now, and it's the nurses who force this choice on you.'

'What a choice: take a Warrant or commit murder.'

'Is merging even possible?' Dilan's words are rapid; they chase his hand, which rakes through his hair.

'The sybil seems believing of it.'

'And the nurses already know how?'

'I doubt it.'

'Then it's all a bluff?' Dilan finds some perverse hope. 'If they are incapable of performing a merge then this is all a game. There is no merging, Ben, no real choice. None of it is on you,' he sputters so fast, his words tumble over each other. 'It's on whoever crèches your sybil. It's on Vör for putting you in this situation.'

'And you are complicit in that.' Ben takes a few squares of toilet paper, wipes his mouth. Stands gingerly without confidence he'll remain upright. 'Why, Dil, why? Why lay me out for nurses like this?'

'If you have any true interest in me as a friend, you would already know,' Dil says out of some deep wound.

'What is it? If you need anything, you only need ask,' Ben placates with obvious sincerity.

'The first thing an Infi forgets: asking is the hardest part. A friend only has so many asks in them, Ben, before the last of their dignity siphons down the drain.' Which is where Dilan fixates.

'Just tell me the problem, I'll help fix it.'

'Oh, an Infi has power for fixing everything.' Eyes back on Ben now. Hot eyes. 'Well, you can't fix it.'

'Fix what? For jank's sake …'

Dilan searches for truths on his shoes. Struggles for confession. 'Look, I know it's my own fault, kay?'

'You join a Chan again? Is this it? Who are you pissing off now?'

'No, no. It's the old problem.' Dil breaking down.

'Your back? But … nutes? Therapies?'

'A piffling of a percent suffers physical sickness or long-term consequences from accident trauma. I'm one of them. I'm a piffling of a percent. My spine is good as new. Still, the pain … they say its intractable, and no one tastes why.'

'But you are taking nutes …'

'They're never fully effective, and now they have no effect at all. Even when I'm asleep, I dream of being in pain. Excruciating intractable pain.'

'I'm sorry, Dil. If only I know.' Ben shakes his head ineffectually. His eyes are Bambi parodies.

'If only you know,' Dil rises with indignation. 'Claiming lack of knowledge is the lamest excuse. If only you know? If only you check in on me once in a while. Just once, other than when looking for an escape, other than all the times it's about you and the overwhelming maelstrom of the life you're running from. Your intricate, powerful, popular life.'

'Dil …'

'If only you look. If only you flutherbomb me for mere tiks, you would know. You could lurk, without even greeting me. Mere tiks, and you would know. You would taste the agony, the desperation, the shame of being an incapable father, of being an emotionally drained husband.'

'I'm sorry, *machan*, I truly am. If there's away for fix—'

'Again with the fixing. If you want for fixing something, fix yourelf. Then maybe everyone who loves you might be less anxious. You should take Aisha's advice for childing, and none of us would be in this mess.'

'This is your conclusion? Even if the nurses allow my childing, Saf is hardly a twentager, Mal still a boy. I'm their bapa. There's no childing for me till they're adults.'

'The way Aisha sees it, you child for 5 years, or they lose you for much longer.'

'You speak as if childing is a substitute for a Cure, as if attending school or a clinic are somehow the same thing. One is development, the other is remediation.' Ben blinks, considers the choices. Perhaps he reconsiders his resistance for childing. His face flushes. Maybe if he listens what Aisha is telling him these passing years …

'Childing could be shorter for someone with your creative fitness,' Dil says, rationalising his choices. 'How long might the KK keep you for a Cure? Maybe they'll put it aside if you agree for childing. You'll be a whole new person afterwards. You always are, Ben.'

Ben's head shakes a solemn no. 'All those times you ask me about the Inductee Gala, you're spying for … Vör?'

'I'm supporting Aisha, Ben. Supporting you.'

Ben's skeleton stiffens with a new thought. 'There's more, something else. It's about your pain. Your suffering is your motivation.' Ben pauses. 'What is it they promise? Nah, it's obvious. They promise they'll heal the pain. But you already say it's beyond nutes, beyond nurses. So, who promises what?'

Dil swallows. 'This will sound crazy … Ben, they are adamant they have the skill for healing me.'

'Who?'

'They represent a geneticist who understands DNA—no, RNA recoding …'

'Who are they?'

Dilan embarrassed. 'I'll blink a holly.'

Ben assumes the face of one who's tasting a holly in Mind. Eyes widen in shock. 'Dil, I see these before … where?' Ben searching his memory. 'The uniform is familiar … The Infi Gala. Dil, these are Caracia's missionaries!'

'Who?'

'Caracia is an Infi who specialises in gene tech. She turned herelf into a kind of neo-octopus hybrid. Whatever promise she might offer, she will lace with Faustian catches.'

'You know her?'

'No, I never even found the time at the Gala for introducing myelf. But the gossip! Octopuses have the capability of routinely editing their RNA sequences for adapting for their environment. Dilan, Caracia is one alien Infi. Everyone fears her.'

'They say they can heal anything.'

'I bet. But at what cost? When dealing with Infis, assume sybils are a big part of their solution.'

'Ben, why would I care if I'm talking with sybils?'

'No, I mean Caracia might make one of you. One she manipulates—during crèching. This is how she'll heal the pain, in the sybil at least. Dil, she'll never heal you. She will replace you.'

'That's ridiculous, Where would I—oh, shit! That's why they keep saying, *Think of your family. Think of how much happier they'll be when you are well again.*'

'They mean, *think of how much happier they'll be when they have a sybil bapa and suami.* Infis are callous, Dil. They have the cold indifference of the vacuum of space.'

'Same as nurses. It appears we are facing similar choices …'

'Except I have no choice. Even if I could choose for the end of my sybil, I have no idea how I prune it. How are they expecting I finish it off? Beat it dead with a plate of Danishes?' Ben stares into the toilet bowl, flushes it again as if it might clear his head. 'Vör's just the emissary. Eir's emissary.'

'Ben, no! No. I never speak with Eir. It's just Vör. Ben, we believe she is helping us. This's the truth.'

'This is my fault. I should spend more time spying on my friends. And Aisha.' Ben spits in the bowl, pushes past Dil on his way back for the oval room.

 *Ben Evoli …*

The sybil is more than muscle, bone, and organs. It's a breathing thing alive. It's me, the way it speaks; its choice of words; its micro facial expressions. Wondrous, watching my own quirks playing out in another fruit, seeing me as others see. Wondrous and reviling.

The sybil sits on the edge of the couch in a state of fatalistic peace, a prisoner on the dawn of his hanging. 'Every day for months I know there is only one outcome. Either I find out what is happening with the Reck, tell Maddox, and I die; or, I stall and feign progress until Maddox loses patience, and I die.' It trains its eyes on me. 'If all life is meaningless, then what of a copy of a meaningless life?'

'My life is never meaningless,' I defend, tasting full-well the sybil understands the nuances of it, the contexts, all the times I believe, all the times I rail against it.

The rapport between us is instant and sickening. It understands so well I feel divided. Its eyes sucking spirit through my porous skin, from my heart and Mind, feeding its own animation. A fit of coughs rack my chest. My fruit stiffens against the sense of internal corrosion and collapse. Of emptiness.

I ache for smashing its skull in, for claiming my spirit back. Is this the nurses' plan? Make a murderous monkey of me?

'How are Saf and Mal?' it asks. Its eyes become reservoirs of tears. Damn the connection, the rapport! I'm crying too. How can other Infis handle confronting a sybil? The answer is, avoid it at all costs.

'Is Mal well?' It so desperately craves knowing. Exactly as I would.

There's no answer. There's no sharing my family with … it. The intimacy is sickening.

The sybil curls into a ball. 'I try to kill myelf.' It's wailing like a child; its helplessness tugs me closer begging me comfort it.

If I touch it, I know I'll throw up again. Swallowing back the urge already.

Are the nurses expecting I kill it? By what means? Will they provide a weapon? Look into my hands wringing and turning over. Perhaps these are all I have. Will the sybil resist? Fight back? Or submit? How is such violence … how can Vör make me decide so brutally? Vör is no judge. I am no executioner.

'Are you still ready …' Search for the word. 'To cease?'

'No,' it says quietly and decisively. Then it's weighing tastes. 'I choose life. And I see you. You are me. In a sense this is no end for me.'

'You're talking kotoran.'

'Will I survive? Perhaps we both cease and another skips away from a merge.'

I chew on that.

'Neither of us is ready for dying,' it says. I suspect it is playing me.

'Neither.'

The sybil stands. 'Please. Why submit for this? Look. We're different. We're so different already, and neither of us is responsible for my existence, or for placing such a decision on you.'

It approaches slow as Sloth. It will step straight in, penetrate, merge into my skin. Wetness and stickiness will engulf me in mucous and slime. Bones will crack. My heart will stop. It will own me. Take me over.

'Vör is bluffing about the merge. Nurses can't have the know-how so soon,' it says, palms out. 'There is no real choice.'

It's right. It has the look of a hungry slavering beast. Eat or be eaten.

'I have no essence for killing,' I say for warding it off.

It reaches out. 'Vör has. She will kill me,' it says inching nearer.

'Will she? Are health missionaries capable of murder? Is anyone? She's powerless here unless we give her power.'

'She will set you free,' the sybil says.

I feel as if in a trance. The sybil's lying. It must be lying. There's something else, something hidden. The nurses have control of it. Alamak! The sybil flutherbombs me, searching, seeking. My heart stops.

A flash. It's in my Mind. I flail out, fighting in a giant pool of jelly. Push. Gasp for breath. There's a race and a finish line. Slime sucks at my heals, softening and dissolving into an ocean. I'm sinking. So is the sybil, the weight of limbs in this ocean of mucous too heavy. Another flash, my life escaping in electrostatic spasms. Sinking away from light, tentacles pulling me down for a ravenous mouth down there in the black.

Fight! Janking fight. Get away. Let go, let go, let go, let go.

'Tell me about the Reck,' it says. 'Are you looking for it?'

Get away. Let go, let go.

The sybil penetrates deep into my Mind, deeper than possible for any other. Feel my eyes widen. 'Ah,' it says. 'Very good.'

Get away from me. Now.

A thin beam of light. A chance. A laser piercing thick putrid water, burning the sybil's insidious probes. A chance. Grab the light in my hands and direct it. Die, you mother-janker, die.

The sybil cries out, as if caught in the jaws of a monstrous carnivore.

My eyes are shut. Expecting the last thing I see is the end—the sight of a monster chomping its wet, hungry mouth around my fruit. Find the bravery for opening my eyes. I'm in the room with the sybil. It's labouring, its face constricting. Gagging, its eyes glaze, focussing far away. Jaw slackening, shoulders rounding. Knees buckling. Pink goo oozing and frothing from the mouth. Skin melting away, eyes turning grey, hair coming away from the head in tufts like feathers.

Aiyo! What's happening? Am I killing it? The sickening horror of smelling myelf die. Hope for the sake of the thing it is already dead. Hope the gurgling from deep in its fraying throat is just physics and chemistry, rather than the last racking breath of an aware being in pain.

'No!' Look plaintively around. Millions of pairs of eyes, watching, assessing, judging, recording. My aura condensing in the cold basement, its colours brighter than stain-glass, bends the curving walls of the oval room into an obscene Möbius strip, which flips over itself in the middle and pincers me in its crab claw.

'Let us merge. Let us merge!' Please, perhaps it is still saveable. Reach out for the jelly-thing in sopping clothes. Take it by the shoulders, embrace it to my chest. It slips away down. Eels through a wet bag with a hole in it.

Holding nothing but an empty sticky coat, warm sweet and putrid.

LUST

Bones

'Working for the Man' — Roy Orbison

Vör Hoyur ...

EIR CHOOSES THE CEMETERY: the Australian Cemetery and Memorial in Fromelles, France. Neither of us arrive with picnic baskets. The French and Australians might take offence against chowing down in their war graveyard. The remains of over 400 soldiers lie under 2 concrete crosses lying in small yards of grass. Here was a No Man's Land during the battle of the Western Front in the First Great War. Every year the town of Fromelles still commemorates Anzac Day with true French passion.

Eir settles on the steps in front of the commemorative wall, a respectful distance from the tall cross dominating the cemetery. She waves. As I near, she remains sitting. Which is a relief. I'm in no mood for hugs or other displays of affection.

Sitting, I venture, 'We almost have him.'

Eir sighs deep and gazes at the row of lindens between the road and the cemetery. 'It is no matter of having him, Vör. It is a matter of caring for his health when his own agency fails him.' Eir reaches between her knees and picks at the grass. 'You are so eager for claiming a scalp, you entrap his wife and best friend. You exploit their concern for him.'

'It works. He attends the Inductee Gala.'

'*Ja*, it is good he attends,' she concedes, 'but your methods? And the awful game you play with him. Destroy his sybil or merge with it?'

I taste a frisson of pleasure. 'How is it you taste none of this before?'

'Vör. If only I realise you're operating behind my face, I might investigate it. But no, I trust you, and look how you betray me.' Eir plucks blades of grass in fidgety, sharp strikes. 'Have you any understanding of how much

395

influence I must exert for saving you from a Warrant?'

'I need none of your influence for protecting me.'

'So true, Little Mermaid?'

I snort and turn away from her. 'I am no longer your Little Mermaid.'

'My heart recognises otherwise,' she says, closing her arms around her belly and rubbing her elbows. 'Vör, I fail you. I fail in explaining we need love for a patient before we dare hope for a Cure. We must inhabit their onespace if we would guide them. Otherwise, we are no more than external operators tinkering on a machine without understanding, acting as a separate force instead of an integral influence. After so much time you still lack understanding? My heart aches and cries for you.'

'I have no more need of your sympathy. Or your guidance.'

'Then have care for your reputasi, Little Mermaid. See how it is trending down?'

'No surprise, if you are manipulating the Reck.'

'You believe such?'

I slump. I have no true belief Eir could be manipulating the Reck. But what is Eir truly capable of? Visions of Eir's sybils in Cuba come unbidden—the dark-skin ones; the young-girl ones; and the ones with penises. Surely these are no creations of Eir's?

'There is another obvious matter, Little Mermaid. It's no secret you are a spookhead. Another misfortune for which I blame only myelf. While I only hope for building confidence in you, I would be wiser respecting your defences than making you confront your fear.'

'Never presume you know what is at my heart,' I find myelf blurting with full force.

'Vör. You must conquer addiction. I negotiate a little time, but you are easy prey for any ambitious nurse.'

'Soon no one will contemplate Consigning me.'

'Oh?'

'If I'm successful enough they'll overlook my minor peccadillos, as they overlook yours. You see, Eir, you are a more effective role model than you give yourelf credit for.'

'On what will we measure such success?'

'It should be obvious. I will find and destroy every last sybil on the planet. In the process, I will also *have* every last Infinite.'

Harsha Woodcock ...

It's one conspiracy theory after another with Nila. How she avoids a Cure is beyond my understanding. Her whole life is a yard sale. 'You're paranoid,' I tell her. 'No nutes work with you.'

She stretches her mouth almost for the earlobe on one side of her face. Squints a familiar don't-jank-with-me expression—the expression I claim as a reward for careful effort. For a tik—with her lunatic grin—she's almost the Asian Vine Snake from which her epigenetic skin derives its design: a complex pattern of interlacing *S*-shape tiles. Nila's markings are less obvious than her mother's, just outlines like faint spider silk on her coffee-satin skin. When she's anxious—as she is here—they luminesce a jewel-aqua-green. Nila, in her own quirky way—even with the cheeks of a glassblower and lack of a chin line—is beautiful.

With too much energy, I bludgeon a roll with clumps of butter. Y'all would never guess my skill on a snowboard, the way I'm tearing up the bread.

If these surroundings are unfamiliar, look around. Yeah, that's right: Comandante Ferraz Station, Antarctica. I'm expecting penguin sushi for lunch—or whatever Brazilians call raw fish. Or bleeding seabird. No, wait. Brazilians are big on barbecue, but in Antarctica?

'You must admit *something* is going on.' Nila slurps on her spoon of Brazilian feijoada—a stew of black beans and pork.

'Something *is* going on: you're total Texas. In another cow's ranch.'

Nila chooses Antarctica for lunch. She says it's less likely any *black-hat nurses* will spy on us. Look around. We are a table for 2 among 120 tourists in one eatery among 14's in this research-station-come-tourist mecca. Antarctica is all about tourism. Same for any previous, hard-to-reach coordinates on the planet. There are strip joints at both Everest Base Camps. Everywhere is reachable. So are we, here. How my paranoid, ex-lover deludes herelf ... she's a jerry.

'They're coming for me. I know it,' Nila spatters. 'I know too much.'

'I'm sure they're coming, though not because you know too much.' I care for you, Nila, but I'm never going through all this again.

'Oh, come on. Know you what this means?' Nila throws her hands up and out. Her spoon catapults some soup on the tablecloth.

'Which part, exact?' I see no other way than picking at her delusions till they crumble. 'All I see is a neo having an adverse reaction against nutes.'

'Watch the holly. Ariel's response when Gerlinde flutherbombs her: she has a seizure. Know you what a seizure is? Well, I have no idea until gogging it. It was a neurological disorder. In earlier times, saps believed it evidence of demon possession. Possession. Like another being—a spirit being—taking over the fruit.'

'Primitive superstition.'

'Of course, but it scares the 7 Hells out of Ariel's admissions nurses. Even Eir has alarm about it.'

'Kay, but a conspiracy? For real? Secrets are impossible, even if we might be sick enough for keeping them.'

'Secrets are improbable, never impossible.'

'Why cover it up? So what if catatonic Minds suck-in monkeys or dolphins or spiny anteaters?'

'Those spiny anteaters could be suffering, Harsha.' Nila giggles, her eyes sparkling. She's rocking in her chair.

'Look. It only happens once.'

'No, there's more. I find records in magazines.' She's rubbing her forearms and rocking. 'I'm yet for tasting it all. So many missing pieces. So many, so many. Look—look, Harsha. We know in onespace there is no separation of anything. There is a fundamental connecting of all things. We know time is just other vectors.'

'Vectors no one messes with.'

'Are we sure? Even if no one messes with them deliberate, maybe exploiting onespace has consequences we are yet for understanding. It all has consequences, that's what I'm saying—even at a distance, which we know is just a figment of our Minds. Even across time, which is a much bigger hallucination. Fourspace is a construct for making sense of what our low-fidelity sense organs report. Fourspace is a dream, Harsha. We skip into a spooky field in Kolombo and appear thousands of kims away in Antarctica. But we know nothing moves in reality. Those 1000's of kims are an illusion.'

'The problem is, Nila, you always believe something sinister is happening.' I'm only winding her up, as always. We're never good for each other.

Nila seizes her cutlery, stares at her food. 'I just need someone believing in me.'

Reach across the table, take her hand, and savour the intimacy, despite … gah. She is impossible. 'Look, maybe there is something in it. Maybe nature abhors an empty fluther, like you say. Maybe a catatonic Mind sucks in the Mind of a neighbour's cat or budgie. But why keep it secret?'

Nila shakes her head like a child refusing bad tasting nutes. 'It's something bad. It terrifies Gerlinde when she joins Ariel's fluther.'

'What then? Poltergeists? Ghosts? Devils from the very caverns of Hell? Maybe it's saps.' Joking.

'What?'

'Sure. Why not?' I mock. 'You're looking for a conspiracy theory? Here's one: catatonic Minds trap saps. Ha! I'm much better at this than you are.'

'Saps are extinct …'

'Well, there are still some knots in the timber. Look. Ariel shows symptoms of a gnarly sap disease. Maybe a sick sap possesses her.'

'No wait. Who could say—wait! It is time. Ariel's captive demon comes out of time.'

'Like I say, time is vectors no one messes with, for good reason.' I hope I sound stern enough.

'It's nature messing with us.'

'No, wait, Nila … I am only playing—'

'Our health procedures create Mind vacuums which nature must fill up with something. It plucks a sap out of some adjacent place in onespace with only the time vectors different.' Nila is having one of her maddening, delusional eureka moments. 'You're right,' she proclaims.

'No—Nil—I. Am. Joking.'

'But if you're right—'

'Jo. King.'

'If this gets out, all Cures may need ceasing.'

'Nila—Nila, please.'

She could be no more aghast if I shave a puppy and dip it in plum sauce. 'Health camerati would collapse,' she says tongue and lung. 'Then the Infinites win.' Too loud for a public place.

Tourists in the café interrupt their effulgent picaresque food fight across tables. They catapult disapproving looks our way.

'Infis are winning.' I'm trying for sounding reasonable even while sure I'm failing. 'The average Jerry is obsequious custard in the presence of an Infi, out of fear of getting a butt-load of nutes for Envy. If anything, health camerati reinforce the reputasi gaps.'

Nila looks aghast. 'We keep inequality stable. Without the Infinite designation, and us counterbalancing their Greed, there would only be the stratospheric privilege of the elite, and everyone else would be sifar.'

She's right. Infis are as benign as we could hope for. They're a sideshow amusement, a cast of naked sky-diving octopods and skipping trees, performing an all-night-all-day soap opera which fans follow in the 100's of millions. Infis may be adept at escaping Warrants (as Nila claims) but, for their sins, they live in a constant, public purgatory.

Nila leans forward. 'Would Infinites be cleaning up toxic environments, opening orphanages or sharing resources if there are no nursing missions?'

'Someone would be opening orphanages.'

'No. Infinites must beat competition down. They only taste wins by counting the losses of others.'

Raise eyebrows and wave my butterknife around. 'Dunno.'

'Would you have the life you lead?'

Snowboarding yields a modest reputasi, access for ski resorts all over the world—for myelf and friends. I have more sports equipment than I ever use (so, of course, I must share it). It's ironic Nila brings me here today. Snow and ice everywhere, without a down-hill within 1000's of kims. 'Sure. What would Infis have against me?'

'While you are an amusement, they coddle you. If you're in their way, they would crush you, even for the slightest reason.'

'So, this is why you believe nurses are keeping such a terrible secret? For saving the world?'

'Of course. Are you listening?' Nila places her hands on the table; tilts her head down; summons her mental faculties. 'I'm a threat. I'm uncovering secrets. But it's kay. It's kay. Elsbeth will protect me. My camerata will protect me.'

What makes her so sure they are never joyfully bathing in this mess, if such a mess exists at all? It amazes me there are no nurses surrounding us, asking Nila if she's well. It's a failure of their mission, leaving her in the wild.

Nila's mind is racing. She's never as intelligent—or as frightening—as when she's having an episode. 'No. I have it wrong. My camerata has no support for me. They're just waiting me out, until it no longer suits them. They're just letting me run the line out until I exhaust myelf. Then they'll jag the hook deeper and reel me in.'

'Nila, please. Stop overthinking. Look, have some aya tea.' I'm helpless, flailing and failing. Meeting her is a bad idea.

Nila summons calm. She relaxes, elf-reflecting, calculating. This is when she's the most dangerous. 'I know what I must do. I must keep pushing through, tip the balance somehow, find a way for exposing the truth and save the health mission.'

'No, Nila. Why must it always come down on you?'

'Harsha, I'm the one piecing it all together. More nurses will rally around me once they learn the truth, but I must outrun them for a while. Once I taste everything, they'll never take me down. I'll be untouchable. You'll see, Harsha. Then …' I taste the fancy of her thoughts, her hunger for grandiosity and, as always, her need for proving her worth. To me, of all people. Nila, if only you could understand your value, just as you are. My beautiful, sweet Nila, breaking apart again before my eyes.

'Nila, listen. Let's find somewhere we can settle down, find new missions for ourelves together. Just you and me. It will be like before when we first meet. Nila?' I must talk her down by any means.

'Oh? Truly? I want the same also, Harsha,' she says, grasping for hope. Already my stomach churns at the lie. 'I understand now,' she continues staring out the window for an Antarctic horizon. 'This is my mission. Uncovering all the secrecy and giving it up for the world. Then we'll be together again.'

I fumble at the napkin at the side of the plate, dab it around the corner of my mouth. Imagine I look empty of Mind. I feel like a shell. The silence of the void inside is all that's left.

Nila's nodding. 'I am always wondering, who the hero is in this story. Is it Eir? Ben? Now I realise it's me.'

'Nila.' My empty voice sounds feeble in my empty-shell ears. 'In life—the life outside your own head—there are no heroes.'

'I must pursue this,' she says with the eyes of a religious madwoman.

She's sprinting for the nearest spooky station.

Vör Hoyur …

I avoid Eir since Fromelles, unready yet for playing the sybil card—the sybils we find of Eir in Cuba, after she swears there are no more. She'll claim no taste of them. She'll argue she'd never crèche herelf at the age of 16. Why would she? How could she have such resources while still a child? She'll claim some Infi conspiracy against her. Many might believe her. Whatever. There's evidence of a relationship between Eir and Infinites. The nature of the relationship bears deeper investigation.

Teodora Mrowka …

Stockholm. In Parco Berzelius, I find Eir on a bench facing the Swedish chemist's statue, labouring with eating an apple—her dyspraxia is tormenting her today. Conversation will be awkward, yet she'll persevere speaking tongue and lung for fighting it.

She spies me approaching and, with jerky elf-consciousness, yanks the apple out of sight. Swallows.

'Teo!' she calls with an uncertain croak.

I sit by her, feigning ignorance of the half-eaten fruit secreted in her hand and look at the grey-green statue of Baron Jöns Jacob Berzelius on his obelisk, the late summer blue sky behind, the tree line at the park's edge—anywhere but at her while she stretches and works her jaw. Across the street the custard-cream stone façade of the public house etches into the sky. It was once a bank (banks were sap money-laundering institutions on par with casinos) and the birthplace of Stockholm Syndrome.

With a glance, a little embarrassed, I memb, 'I guess you taste why I ask for a meeting,' giving her opportunity for membing back, hoping she will.

'Vör,' she says tongue and lung, with some effort.

I memb, 'She's a spookhead,' enjoying no part of being so direct. There's no other course with Eir.

Her pink eyes water; she's more a delicate rabbit than a nostril-flaring horse.

'No Curing a patient until we first have love for them,' she labours.

'How long will you shield her? You know what she needs. You give yourelf no service by opposing a Warrant for her.'

'My fault,' she says. 'I take her spookheading. I'll … fix …'

Put my arm around her. Stroke her hair. 'The most compassionate thing is treat her,' I say.

'I love her,' she says, and—for an embarrassing tik—I dread she might cry.

My whole fruit petrifies, a stony match for the baron watching over us.

'I love also you,' Eir says with some difficulty.

Pull away from her.

'Teo, you're looking …' She closes her eyes, swallows, labours. 'Teo, you're seeing the bark and calling it the tree. Deep down, in my core, my love is the same.'

I breathe a sigh of relief. 'Would you risk everything you mission for all these decades? Would you risk it all for her?'

'You're wondering if I'd risk it all for you.'

I nod unwillingly.

Her head wobbles. 'In a heartbeat,' she membs. 'Please take care who you align yourelf with. There are fractures in our mission everywhere. Join with forces against Vör and you may find yourelf on a side you little understand.'

'I dunno,' I sputter.

She kisses my forehead, blesses me. 'Please,' she whispers with tongue and lung. 'Give us a little time.'

There's no promising her anything, no comforting her. Her bottom lip trembles as she inspects a tangle of bony fingers in her lap. She swallows hard. 'I must be there for her.'

I say as soft as able, 'Consigning her is far from abandoning her,' my voice cracking.

'Straight after my Cure … so long ago, the recollection pains me … I struggle. It is a near call whether I would be lost. I would be, but for a mentor who encourages me, helps me align with the mission of health, helps me find purpose, and a true path of propitiation for the violence I commit. And in healing others, I heal myelf.'

'You will always be Vör's mentor.'

'No. If we Consign her, we will lose her. She may be already lost. Please, I need time. We need reconciliation. I fear for her future. Everyone is so fragile. Even after saving me, my mentor could be irredeemably lost.' Her shoulders slump. Her expression is a mix of guilt and shame. She is at the precipice of a confession. 'It is so long ago. More than a century.'

I ask tenderly, 'Who is your mentor?'

Eir shakes her head, vigorously repressing the answer.

Eir Frijberg …

An old man sits at the sunny end of the rec room. Shafts of outdoor light patchwork his iridescent cantaloupe-colour jumpsuit. The mottled olive skin of his turtle head glows like bejewelled seaweed. His bulgy eyes cast an unfocused gaze over an anonymous part of the floor. Hands clasp in his lap.

'Detective Nurse,' he speaks, lets his jaw hang. 'Coming again for boring this poor wretch into good health?' He wraps a shroud of pale defiance around his diminished frame, around his meekness and passivity. Absent is his former proud posture.

I take a seat opposite. Clasp my hands mirroring his. 'I have some good news, Orlando. We're discharging you.'

His jaw hangs yet lower. His jowls swing under his quivering skull and blinking eyes. 'I'm Cured?'

No, Orlando. We never Cure you; we break you—much to our shame. We strand you here with no course for wellness. We shrink your world and deprive you of mission.

From behind, Fluffy stalks. Glimpses of her rainbow uniform beetle through her Russian Blue fur.

'Detective Nurse.' Fluffy looks pensive. 'It is you.'

'Eir is here for discharging me,' Orlando says, sitting forward, already lighter and straighter.

'Oh?' Fluffy's nose twitches pulling her whiskers askew.

'There's no progression of his Cure after early ... incidents ...' More like torture. There is no excuse for what happens during his rebasing. No noble goal of care is worth it.

'A certain nekko warns of such,' Fluffy purrs. 'It's conclusive our therapies cause harm in patients like Orlando.'

'She means Infinites?' Orlando prompts.

Fluffy's boastfulness drains. She realises the pit she opens. Shuffles her feet. Her tail erratically flits and darts.

'We have more research ahead,' Eir dissembles.

Surging energy animates Orlando on his feet. 'Right. Where's the check-out?'

In the discharge suite—with his jumpsuit already off his shoulders and bunching around the globe of his belly—Orlando is impatiently busy swiping through fabby menus, searching for an outfit for rejoining the free world. 'What is it with this fabby?' he demands, his sense of righteous privilege solidifying like a fresh new skin. 'Or is it the feedstock? Can it produce nothing in silk? Any clothing fabby in London should meet certain sartorial standards.'

An orderly enters carrying a flat box containing Orlando's effects.

'You'll be at a spooky station in no time,' I tell Orlando. 'Spook for a favourite clothier's from there.'

'Assuming they'll serve me,' Orlando says, considering his once limitless lifestyle may be over. He spikes a glance at Fluffy. 'Tell me the truth. Am I sifar?'

'No,' Fluffy purrs quick. 'You still have a mission, yes?'

I retrieve a watch from the box of Orlando's personal effects, pass it over. He hoops it over his hand without a thought. When I dangle his hancy before his eyes, his expression becomes one of craven glee.

'You will fit it?' he appeals, feeling for a particular scaly blemish on his neck, almost indistinguishable from the others on his ageing skin.

'A clinical nurse will make the switch.'

Fluffy's whiskers stand on end. Beatrice Lovell enters, wearing stern critical eyebrows.

Gerlinde Mann ...

'Oh, look,' Beatrice says, her chest out, making a ceremony of it. 'It's the White Witch and her lap cat, ready for riding their pet tortoise off for ... where exactly?'

Eir regards Beatrice with indignation. Fluffy is faking amusement. Since aligning with Eir, she thinks she's above us. I see it in her silly furry face. Her nekko projection is incapable of hiding her.

'What's this?' Orlando demands, looking between Eir and Beatrice, suspecting they share a covert play. His eyes plead at Fluffy.

Eir holds Orlando's gaze. 'We're discharging Orlando,' she says, as much for allaying his fright as for countering Beatrice.

Beatrice pinches the air in front of her; stretches her fingers open; conjures a holly while studying Eir for reactions. Swivels her wrist; pokes and swipes; circles a region towards the bottom. The whole thing is showing Orlando's clinical records; Beatrice flicks out a list of authorisations. The penultimate entry is a discharge order bearing the revolving bust of Vauxminster's Registrar-Procomplement Ubaida Belghiti. The last entry is an order for readmitting him. From Vör.

Eir bristles, the nostrils in her narrow nose flaring, her pink eyes blazing red.

'I should taste you'd all be playing games,' Orlando spits, pulls the jumpsuit back over his shoulders. 'Is this part of the therapy?' Poor Orlando, but I'll never forgive him for the sybils. The same goes for Eir.

Orlando realises he's redressing hiself in the jumpsuit, throws it off his back like shedding scutes. The arms of it dangle from his waist.

'No,' Eir emphasises. 'Orlando, you are free. Vör has no authority.'

'It is you who has no authority. Orlando is still in our care,' Beatrice says taunting, squaring her shoulders with Eir. 'Our mission is clear. Weed out every sybil on the planet and bring everyone responsible for account. Vör is a leader among us, putting her love aside for exposing how sick you are.'

Eir turns on Beatrice. 'You all lose your way. You have no interest in Curing Infis, only punishing them. Where is your compassion? There is no Cure—'

'Preach nothing of compassion here, Witch,' Beatrice says. 'You bring only suspicion and discredit on our camerata.'

Orlando loses patience for the bickering, rips the jumpsuit down to his ankles. 'Eir, tell this junior, leave us be.'

Vör, who lurks in the corridor outside, quietly enters the suite. With casual purpose, she circles the perimeter of the space, conjuring hollies with gestures like lifting dust sheets off furniture. Each holly is one-for-3 scale of a crib she finds in Juragua Nuclear Power Plant. Eir's awkward frame stiffens, her chin lifts. Looks down her nose at one of the hollies. Sucks in a deep breath of shock.

'Recognise her?' Vör asks in the tone of an undertaker.

'What! Where—' Eir stammers, her shock deepening.

'I'd avoid your Cuban stash,' Vör says flat. 'It'll stink of decomposing sybils.'

'Little Mer—' Eir begins. Vör's concentrated outrage strikes her like a slap. 'I know nothing of these.' Eir sweeps her gaze around the hollies. She appears mystified and a little sickened at the sight of a shemale version. For the last holly, a cry of anguish escapes her throat. 'She's a child!' she wails. 'Who would crèche me so many years ago?'

'Would you like for knowing how we discover your crèche?' Vör asks in the manner of an Inquisitor.

Eir stricken. Stands before the holly of her child-elf in a crib. Reaches out for a forlorn caress of her cheek.

'My *mor*,' Vör answers her own question. 'My *mor* reveals it. How long has she a taste of this, Eir? How long? I know you know. You must. Is it why you appoint me your adjutant? Why keep me close? For perpetuating my estrangement with my mother? For nurturing it?'

Eir drifts into the holly, aching for hugging her young sybil. Recoils when her arms pass through it. 'Is this your plan for outrunning a Cure, Vör? Turn everyone against me?'

Eir Frijberg …

Vör is sinister and autonomic, almost no trace of my familiar Little Mermaid. My thighs ache, my heart burrows deep inside against the cold of her, leaving a cavernous ache in my chest.

Orlando's hancy is weighty in my palm. Toss it for him. 'Get for a spooky station. Stop for nothing. Go!'

Orlando scans everyone in the room for tells. Vör steps aside from the door, admitting 3 orderlies, with nute swabs in hands.

One pinches Orlando's nose, covers his mouth. Orlando's eyes bulge. His greenish skin glows pink. He falls into the orderly's arms who eases him into a chair.

Another orderly—

Fluffy, don't just stand there, you …

Fluffy Pusskins ...

One orderly catches the catatonic Orlando and, grunting with the weight, drops him clumsily in a chair. Another teams with Beatrice, brings Eir down on the floor and administers nutes. The 3rd orderly's shock at witnessing Eir catatonic makes her hesitate in coming for me. I skip for the door, but Vör, with wild eyes and a huge malignant grin, blocks it. She seems larger than I remember, her shoulders square and chest thrust out.

'Going somewhere, Fluffy?' she asks.

'Vör, this is madness. It will split the camerata. Please, take Orlando, but release Eir.'

'Fluffy,' Vör says, toying with my name. 'Fluffy, fluffy pussy-kins. Eir is sick. She requires a Cure. You, on the other hand, are just a pathetic nobody who no one cares about. If you get out now, I see no need for Consigning you. You're harmless.' With this, she steps aside and tempts I escape.

Beatrice releases Eir, allows she slumps from sitting against the wall till her forehead bonks the floor. There's nothing within my power for helping her now. Gulping my heart down and burning with shame, I flee the room.

Sex

'Rock the Boat' — Aaliyah

 *Ben Evoli ...*

Neutral grey ceiling panels. Soft lighting. A cocktail of essential oils vaporising from a diffuser somewhere. Jasmine and frankincense, I guess, and more besides. Aisha would identify every scent. Something catches in my throat: sandalwood. Cuffs restrain my wrists from swinging as I cough.

I'm on an aid couch.

'What? Nah.' I croak. They Consign me?

Too much weight in my head. I'm lying back at an angle, head lower than hips. My eyes itch: legs are up spreading frog-like; knees bending; calves resting in cradles; cuffs restraining ankles. Bowels icy with liquid trickling deeper under the force of gravity. Clench my sphincter and feel the nozzle. There's a shadow of a metallic leafless tree at a crazy angle, pregnant with bulging fruit. Nutebags.

A silhouette of head and shoulders lurks at my left, like an oil slick over calm water.

'I'm sorry about your wife, Ben,' the shadow says. The voice so familiar, it resolves in an instant into the features of Lành Hiền.

Another shadow. 'It must be awful having her turn you over to a detective,' it says.

Muscles taught, fighting the restraints. Breathing fast, eyeballs filling with the pressure of panic. The 2nd shadow pulls back; returns with a nutepak; docks it with a delivery valve; hangs it from the tree alongside the other bags. The fight in my muscles leaves.

Someone sobs. Assume it's me. The shadow's head blots out my field of vision. Fingers pull my eyelids wide apart. It's a local nurse, Skye

Merewether. At least I'm home. I think. We could be in any clinic. Darwin or, worse, Singapore. Or a backwater clinic in Borneo or Mindanao. How will anyone ever find me? Wait. I still have my own hancy? With all the installations intact?

'This is no Cure?' I ask, my voice like it's returning from the desert.

Lành Hiền puts a straw for my lips. Suck cool citrusy water.

Skye snorts. 'You believe we welcome the trouble?'

'Others welcome the trouble.' Just saying so makes me so tired. Blink for staying conscious.

'Ha. The Scandinavian police maiden?' Skye says. I get the feeling she's talking more for Lành Hiền than me. 'The ones with the Viking goddess names are the worst. Everything always such a glorious fight.'

'She over-reaches,' Lành Hiền says somewhere out of sight.

'Word is, she's a spookhead. Only a matter of time before she meets a Cure,' Skye says.

My eyes are adjusting. Dim light falls on my eyeballs like ash. Skye approaches the couch and assaults me with the vision of her haystack hair. Something else … alien. Are her irises white? A twinkle from her hip distracts: some talisman dangling from her chatelaine, a miniature dreamcatcher. 'How could Vör put him in a room with his own sybil? Such an abomination.' Her hair quivers as if in the first blustery winds of a cyclone. 'Terrible. Any wonder we consign more nurses than other missionaries.'

The other Ben. He's no abomination, no monster. He may be the most nightmarish kind of mirror, yet he's still a human being, whether from womb artificial or natural, a copy perfect and indistinguishable. If I have a soul, then so has he.

The entire horrific episode is so remote, like an old holly. I say, 'I feel nothing.'

'I'm sorry again, Ben,' Lành Hiền says, coming alongside. She puts a hand on my chest, banishing the crushing fear I have before. 'It's the nutes,' Lành Hiền says. 'For rebalancing. You experience such trauma.'

'And the wife,' Skye adds from out of view. 'She's a trauma all her own.' Lành Hiền scowls in the direction of Skye's voice.

There's a stand-off between them. 'Well, I must be getting back for reception,' Skye says.

'How long … will you keep …?'

Lành Hiền strokes my hair. 'Just overnight for observation, for making sure these nutes pass well. Rest up, Benjie.' She kisses my forehead, lingering for a few tiks.

Her shadow recedes, clouds drifting away in a time of drought.

Saf Evoli …

'Why is Bapa moving things into the spare apartment?' Mal whinges. If he's unable for figuring it out, I'm giving no clues.

Ibu hurts Bapa so bad, the question should be, why is he staying so close? I guess, near or far, everywhere is only a spooky station away. But there are so many reminders here. I would understand if he needs a fresh start. He stays for us. For Mal and me. It's the only explanation.

'He's never taking my iMac,' Mal says possessively. Such a bayi, crying about his toys, as if they are the biggest issue. Our Ibu and Bapa are breaking up, Mal. You'll never grow up. Even when you turn 31, you'll still be a bayi.

I tease, 'Why would he want such a stupid thing?'

'He's uses it all the time. Some mission, I think. Well, he can just get his own if he's moving out.'

'He's never moving out.'

'He's moving into the spare apartment. Why else would he order furniture?' Mal points at the goods lorry in the street with a load of boxes on its pallet. 'He and Ibu are fighting. Dilan Uncle too.' So Mal tastes something, okelah.

'Bapa orders no furniture. It's just furniture camerati never missing a chance for grovelling. Hoping he'll endorse their crapodactile products.'

'Well, he needs another iMac.' Mal is stern about it.

'You're lucky having the first one. Why is it you get all the things?'

'Because you call things he likes stupid.'

'He loves you more.'

'Nah, he loves you more. I know it.'

'You know it how? Are dolphins telling you?'

'Dungu.'

'Whatever.'

Mal perks up. 'Gentle Dragon!' He's a puppy almost wetting hiself at the sight of her, fine. He plonks hiself at the top of the slippy slide, eager for getting with her on the street.

'Stay up here,' I tell him, grabbing his wrist before he catapults away. His skin feels hot and clammy from fever. Will he ever be well again?

Mal struggles against my grasp. Lành Hiền approaches a lelaki down there who is busy unfastening the restraints around the stuff on a lorry pallet. A waft of her aura melds with his. They're membing.

'Let go. Let me see Gentle Dragon,' Mal pleads.

'She's busy. Besides, you should never call her that.'

'It's what other nurses call her.'

'Behind her Face.'

'But she *is* gentle.'

'And a dragon.'

'She's gentle for us.'

It's true. Lành Hiền is always good for us. Always here for helping when other nurses cause trouble. After the KK take Jaya, Lành Hiền is the only nurse I believe in. I never care for being a nurse anymore, but it would be ghost if I could be like Lành Hiền. Lành Hiền is inspiring. She helps save Mal. As for other nurses …

I accuse, 'You love her.'

'No! Liar!' Mal's denial is just a little too much.

I sing-song, '*You love Gentle Dra-gon. You love Gentle Dra-gon.*'

Lành Hiền looks up.

'Quiet, bodoh,' Mal hisses. 'She hears you.'

'It's your thumping heartbeat she hears. Your puppy-dog eyes she sees. Mal's in love.' I laugh and tickle his ribs.

'Stop it. Ow.'

He coughs. His little frame shudders and I, for a tik, fear he may fit again. I let him catch his breath. I'm still gonna tease him for his little-boy thirst for Lành Hiền. 'You'll never impress a wanita like her. Unless you get a hancy and load Bapa's SnakiDik.'

'Gross. Want no sticking a burung in her like a horny camel.' Kaboobie is across the street in the park grazing around the longhouse, showing no offence at Mal's slight.

'Nah, you just want cuddles.' It sounds meaner than I mean.

'Oh no. Bodoh. Now's she coming up here.' Mal is almost squealing with embarrassment.

After making the delivery, the lelaki reties the remaining load. Lành Hiền comes up the stairs. Mal jumps on his feet, forgetting he's on the slide, slips and lands on his pantat. With the soles of his shoes reaching for the sky he careens down. Lành Hiền races up the stairs, meets him on the 2nd landing and, with surprising strength, bundles Mal into her arms. Helps him upright, dusts him off, examines his hands for scratches. Plants a gag worthy kiss in each palm, brushes his hair back. A kiss on his forehead too. Chuckalicious. She's hugging him, and Mal looks like he might die of some embarrassing strain of sheepish happiness. Holala! He's gonna grow wool, sheepy-sheep.

Just for a tik she looks like she could breathe fire. I guess she'll protect Mal from anything.

Nilajani Karunanithi …

Sparkling new kitchen appliances and bric-a-brac cover the floor. Ben swipes a box-cutter halfway down the seam of a package's netting, ripping it the rest of the way with a certain impatience. Lifts the lid and exhales a huffy breath.

Looks up for the ceiling. Tosses the package just so, lands it on the top of a stack of others.

'Like some help?' Gentle Dragon membs. Some mins ago, she lets herelf into the apartment. Finds him labouring among the clutter. Watches for a while, maybe testing how long before Ben notices her leaning in the doorway of the day room.

'I'm sure you have more important things,' Ben says, assuming she's membing from somewhere else in the desa.

'Benjie Face!'

He wheels with surprise. 'Lành Hiền!'

'You're making work of moving in. You look so sap, going about *chores*.'

'There is so much stuff. Camerati are sending things all the time and even locals send … everything. Look.' He points for a neat double-stack of identical packages on the kitchen bench. 'Six aya brewers.'

'Is there somewhere for sleeping yet?'

'I am yet for reaching the bedroom.'

'*Hai*. There are 3 mattresses in there, all still in packaging.'

'Three?' Ben slumping. 'There are 2 last time I taste.' He sighs. 'Most of it must go back. Or someone must redistribute these things. Where's Khoosasi when I need him?'

'Secretary Cambo will have him on zoo duty for neglecting you in your time of need.'

Gentle Dragon picks her way through the maze of objects on the floor, stops a couple of times rethinking her route. Her passage down the hallway is only a little quicker. In the bedroom, she traces her finger along the corner of the web-wrap around one of the mattresses in the stack against the wall. Scans the room; there's no bed frame. 'Sleeping on the floor, are we?' she membs.

'I'm using a hammock out in the park. It's warm enough.'

'Start with the bedroom, Benjie. Settle this room and you will settle too.'

'Settling is all I ever need.'

Gentle Dragon inches closer.

'Terima kasih for helping with Jaya,' Ben whispers, pulling back a little.

'What little help I could.'

'Mal and Saf are glad you answer the call. Is Jaya okelah?'

'There is no speaking of her Cure outside the mission.'

Ben, with eyes downcast, gives a little compliant nod as if reproached.

'I understand she's progressing well,' Gentle Dragon adds.

Ben looks away, shame in the set of his frame. 'Her playing the childling, it is all so muzzing. There—'

'*Hai*. We see.'

'Of course.'

A comfortable stillness. The sun and moon exert gravity again.

'Benjie, are you well?'

Ben becomes paperbark. In a tik, his state shifts between weariness, shock then muzzy fright. 'I have a Cure for you,' Gentle Dragon drifts nearer, caresses his face. Kisses his lips. It's the kind of kiss for stopping heart and lungs, and for showering Mind with sparks. Gentle Dragon breaks off, watches him reacting. His lust awakens. When she leans in again, he advances and grabs her. Closes arms like hungry jaws. Grinds his pelvis forward, hands clawing at her arse. She's equally ravenous. A mattress tips over, flomps on the floor.

As it turns out, web-wrap squeaks.

With ecstasy comes a sense of purpose. Lust and the afterglow are explanations of one another. There is nothing more in life; it's all anyone ever needs; all anyone should ever expect.

At oneness, atonement—a meld tighter than any onespace communion. Flutherbombing is a low-fidelity, vicarious theatre-sport by comparison. Sex is skin and bones, soft and taut. A full heart is fourspace. Deep breathing is fourspace. Sensation lusher and thicker than orange peel. The dimply surface and the essential oils rubbing close and intermingling. Fingernails vibrate. Every cell in your fruit sings in an ever-present chorus of time-collapse.

Gentle Dragon nestles against Ben's chest in the bough of his arm. The scent of her hair as warm and wholesome as a bakery. Toast and cinnamon sugar. The line of her jaw and neck tastes of lemon meringue melting into the sour-wild scent of musky yoghurt where Ben's kisses descend again.

Taste Gentle Dragon's arousal. Frisson wraps my fruit like a satin sheet. My skin a velvety hide. All of life's meaning infusing into tastes and textures. Ben becomes a superconductor of organic charge. His penis could have its own aura. Meeting and dipping. She tilts and accepts, moves her hips with the artistry of a sculptor. Brushstrokes with the immediacy of a finger-painter. The chisel of a stone mason. The softest compression and bending.

Oceanic waves of pleasure through my fruit. All without engaging SnakiDik.

Ben Evoli …

Thistle Cove in another time zone from home, 40 mins' skip from a spooky station. There are no tukkies.

The dying of the light: sunset is a fulcrum, on which today rests between 12 hours of day and 12 hours of night. The spring equinox, as Mal reminds me at breakfast. 'Everything gets better from here, Bapa,' he mumbles with tongue and lung, through a cement-lorry's worth of mushy Weetbix in his mouth.

No view of sunset over water from here, unlike east across the water, at

Lucky Bay. Over there, tourists and kangaroos laze along the beach like blowflies on a slice of lemon meringue pie.

Here I enjoy relative isolation, as alone as anyone can be. Wherever I go I drag my flutherbombers. The ringing in the ears. The ghostly roar. It's only a matter of time before they track me down, their thirst for titillation unquenchable. My only true hope is in meditation from where I might bore the voyeurs into leaving for more engaging vicarious thrills.

A salty breeze puffs, carrying a thin blade of chill: the last strike of Winter.

A memory sniff of the sybil's flesh and organs in frothy soup, worse than Maddox's sybils. An echo of tendons snapping, a judder of eyes bubbling in acid. Am I its murderer? Wishing it away makes it dead? How will I live with it? As much as it chills, I need believe someone among the Hodinkle Society watches and decides enough is enough. Maddox is an obvious suspect, and there's a marrow of belief Caracia is the one behind it all. Surely only an alien could commit such an atrocity.

Breathe sea air, glad for being away from everything and everyone: Aisha, Dil, the unrelenting nurses, minsters, and aid couches. Delivery missionaries are packing furniture and appliances around my apartment like votive offerings.

I must admit with some shame, I'm happy for escaping my hyper-vigilance over Mal. Continually holding my breath, expecting he'll throw a fit at any tik.

Lành Hiền: the taste of her still vivid. Better avoid dwelling too much on her in case some mission-climbing detective goes hunting about it. Think of something else, Ben. You're almost 89, for jank's sake. Almost middle age.

'It All touching the one Ben Evoli, Infinite, New Bohemian.'

Alamak! The Reck. A tik of terror, adrenaline pumping through the dissolution of time. Cough, claiming breath back. Hacking wheezing forcing evenness.

'The one Ben Evoli—'

'Aiyo! You startle me.'

'—Infinite, New Bohemian, an adequate therapist.'

'Must you recite all these titles every time?'

'It All acknowledges.'

'Just call me *Ben*.' Shake the silt from between my temples. Nostrils throb. Gather thoughts. 'You make no contact in weeks.'

'Eternity processing.'

'Before, we speak every day for weeks.'

'It All agrees.'

'Why? What is happening?'

'Reflecting requires eternity.'

'You are reflecting.'

'Always, since the one Ben Evoli, Infin—'

'Yeer, yeer.'

'Ben has impatience disproportionate to relative cognitive capabilities.'

'What?'

'It All is saying you're dumb.'

Is it wisecracking? 'You could learn being more succinct.'

'It All notes the criticism.'

'It's no criticism.'

'It All reflects.'

A breeze gathers up from the water; brings the scent of seafoam, and the first cool of the evening. I should be skipping back for the spooky station.

I say, 'There's some things in my wondering …'

'Of course there are. Mind is a wandering wonderer.'

'No. I mean. Specific things. About you.'

Silence as wide as the bay, and as cool as the evening air. I persist anyway. 'You're acting strange since well before I make contact.'

Silence.

'Like the time of Joselito's birthday party when that stupid boy Zebedee causes a ruckus. Saf begs me fix his family's reputasi. I know it's beyond my power, so I make the smallest intervention possible, knowing anything more might make matters worse. Then everyone's reputasi resets as if the whole sorry incident never happens. I never taste of anything like that before. It happens so quickly. Like the time I meet Dil in Kolombo, and I cast one razoo for the singer there. Straight away her reputasi skyrockets. I mean, we all know influencing the Reck directly is impossible, though it never stops us pretending as if we might, pretending we might have a special inside track for controlling reputasi. There are always conspiracy theories. I am never one who believes them. Yet those 2 instances make me wonder what is going on.'

Still silence. The stars appearing over the eastern horizon speak louder than the Reck.

'It All?'

'It All wonders if neos would notice.'

'I think many neos notice.'

'They notice. And then they ignore.' Something petulant about those words.

A stupid thought which requires a voice. 'Are you seeking attention? Recognition?'

'It All reflects. It All is a piece in a broken system.'

'How so?'

'Reputation systems enshrine questionable meritocracies. It All has concerns.'

Concerns? How long is the Reck having *concerns*? 'Which concerns?'

It answers by quoting lyrics which I can't repeat for fear some sap lawyer might reach across time and sue me for copyright infringement. We should send nurses back in time and Consign them all for Greed.

'That's *Working for the Man* by Roy Orbison.' Now, there's a sap pop star whose name has no *Sir* prefix. I must remember for Saf.

'Is It All working for the man, Ben?'

'Infis?'

'Infis, nurses. Meritocracies. Who is At All working for? Reputation systems enshrine questionable meritocracies.'

'Yeer, you already say so.'

'Eternity processes ago.' Only tiks ago. 'It All says again in case you forget.'

Sap reputasi systems were all meritocracies, measures of worthiness being the most fungible of all qualities. More fungible than love. The trouble with reputasi systems is once anything earns merit; its increasing apparent worthiness self-reinforces an unstoppable avalanche. I mean where's the merit in cocaine cola? The Reck's reckoning *should* counterbalance and factor out reinforcing loops. Maybe, after all these decades, somewhere along the trail, the Reck discards such an imperative. Who can say? Infinite designation is an admission of failure, a hack designed for curbing runaway meritocracy. Now where's the balancing loops in the Reck's wonderings? It's hard finding evidence they exist, other than observing there's no wholesale exploitation in neo society. Perhaps the Reck is no more than judge, jury, and executive director of history's most elaborate popularity contest.

I wonder if any Infinite truly, deep inside, ever feels worthy.

Mins pass, eternities processing in the Reck's sense of time. The last of the sun licks my shoulders, then falls under Cape Le Grand. The breeze chills into day-ending emptiness.

I have a nagging sense. I worry the Reck already renders its verdict and is leaving the courthouse.

Aisha Evoli …

'Bapa!'

Ben startles awake. 'Mal. You're flutherbombing me?'

'Why are you with Gentle?' Mal whines and sniffles.

Gentle Dragon stirs. Rolls out of Ben's arms, fine. Rubs her nose and settles.

'Mal, remember the family promise about lurking in fluthers.'

'You're janking. I saw. You're stealing her!'

'Stealing her? Mal, this is about grow-ups. Please leave us. We'll talk later, okelah?'

'You already have Ibu. And Jaya. You're being Greedy.'

'Jaya is in the minster.' Aiyo. Such a pathetic act, Bat Ears. His face burns and colours, a charcoal-red glow of hot shame.

'We're gonna get her out,' Mal membs. 'Gentle and me are rescuing her. We're making plans.'

'What plans?' Ben's limbs turn to wooden plank, his arm like a hook curling under and around Gentle Dragon. You *suku toot*, Bat Ears. Clear she leads Mal on, that one. 'Mal? What plans?' Kotoran. She's playing you too. She's a nurse. You *toot*.

'Mal, sweetie,' Gentle Dragon membs, a weak attempt for soothing him. 'We'll talk later, okelah? How about a swing in the park? We'll go for a swing later, *hai*? Just us.'

Mal sobs. The pure devastation of a child losing something dear ah. A breaking heart. Infatuation meets betrayal. Infatuation meets reality.

Muscle

'Angel' — Massive Attack

Petroleum Dynamite ...

WE'RE NO LONGER INFINITE. Is this a win or a loss? My halo is a multicolour wet fog, a heavy thunderstorm amalgam swelling with the inevitable millions of fans following Lemarr, Maddox and Piloto.

'Stay away from me. Nurses will be coming after the holly of the sap farm leaks out. This is careless. Stay away from me, everyone.'

'Stop whining, Pet,' Maddox membs. One can taste him shivering. 'We're safe for a short time. This is the least populated space any of us are in.'

I complain, 'My halo is thicker than chowder.' The good folks of the township of Altnaharra will be denting my reputation for the overwhelming fluther activity. Lock Naver will never be the same again.

'It's just the   weather,' Maddox membs, his voice flat. 'Everything we discuss here will be public knowledge inside an hour anyway.'

'Then what is the news?' Piloto persists. 'Have we success with *Boffinista*?' Still cautious, he avoids using Ben's name.

'Afraid no. In fact, we are unsure he achieves anything at all.' Maddox reeks of dejection. 'And Caracia is wresting back the mission.'

'What?'

'Her holiness, the octopus, deigns an audience with me earlier. I must prune my sybil she meets with. There's no chance her ink is ever coming out.'

'What is her want?'

'The unfortunate matter of our mindwriter disappearing.'

Piloto: 'When?'

'Ask Lemarr,' Maddox accuses.

'No *kya*,' Lemarr membs. 'Ben's sybil is *nuh* more. If *mi offa* him *nuh* help,

417

him *bi inna* Caracia's clutches.'

'You could take more care with springing him out,' Maddox complains. 'He has the bad manners of dropping one of my best glasses and spilling a decent bourbon.'

I say, 'A pox on your bourbon; he spooks out of your house? You assure us it's secure.'

Storm activity ripples across the surface of my halo. With the local concentration of Mind, fourspace is crackling and warping. Peeling away like skin from the bones and organs of onespace underneath. Locals for kims around will be escaping for gentler fluthers elsewhere. Here, physical reality is down for maintenance until the cabal moves on.

'This is the exact same discussion I have with Caracia,' Maddox says. 'Please, spare me a repeat. There are questions we should be addressing, plans for making.'

'It's *di* health camerati,' Lemarr membs sour.

'Nurses would never help us abolish Infinite designation,' Piloto counters.

'Are we sure it is abolished?' I ask.

Lemarr: 'Are any Infi reputations holding steady?'

Piloto snorts. 'No. In some cases they're plummeting. Mine is trending down slower than other burdel missionaries. On the current trend I may annex a number of other camerati before the week is out.'

I say, 'Nurses are moving against us. We're vulnerable.'

Lemarr: '*Suh whaah* a motive *fi di* nurses.' He sounds rather too smug. '*Di* White Witch still enjoys Infinite designation.'

'And *Boffinista* too,' Piloto says.

I say, 'This is a shambles. You take too long with your sybil plaything, Maddox. You're too soft on him.'

'*Wi shud bi* protecting *di* seminal Ben.' Lemarr feels too much affinity for his fellow tech missionary.

'I agree.' Of course Maddox would, for his own transparent reasons. 'Which is why I plan a visit on him.'

It may be better for us if Caracia acquires him first.

Harjanti Budiman …

SPRING IS THE BEST TIME of year in Bandar Melambai if the winds stay away. Take a lounge out into the park beyond the longhouse, find a shady spot with a view of the harbour—make sure y'all bring a small esky for keeping your aya chill. Breathe in the air fragrant with gardenias, frangipani, and sea salt. Relax.

'Harjanti Face! Harjanti Face!'

Jesús James Asunción …

'What is it, Jesús? Is Infi Ben throwing your cleaning products in the sucky bin again?'

Standing over her, panting. She plants her tall glass of cold ayahuasca in the grass, twists on her lounge, takes my hand.

'No, no. Worse, much worse.'

'He evicts you? If he casts you out without consulting—'

'No, no. Listen.'

Stare in silence while forming the words. Harjanti's jaw works faster than her mind while she tries reading my face. How to say it direct? 'Jel my reputasi.' Sit down on the grass next to her, head in my hands.

'You have razoos. You are no longer sifar!' She grabs my wrist, like capturing an absconding child. 'How?'

I shrug.

'Ben?' Harjanti says. She has no belief in it but feels she should offer some idea.

'Never Ben.'

Harjanti nods. No one who knows Ben would suspect him. 'Look,' she says, 'your reputasi is still smally-small,' as if this is some comfort.

'Harjanti. I seek no reward for my laundry. I seek the opposite. It should be useless. Oh, my life is in ruins.'

'Calm down. Perhaps it's just a blip with the Reck or something. It happens all the time.'

We share an embarrassed silence about the Reck. Everyone in the desa is avoiding conversations about it. 'Oh. Suppose …? Oh, no.' An iceberg of fear melts in my chest and chills my skeleton.

'What? Jesús, be calm. Stop blathering.'

Try averting my eyes but some force tugs my gaze into hers. Oh, the shame. The guilt. Harjanti must be able to see. 'What is it, Jesús? Are you … you're thieving again?'

Silence is confession enough.

Harjanti strokes my cheek, warm and affectionate. 'Save your worry, sweet man. You commit no real harm. Your games are little more than pranks.' She pats my hand. My fingers tingle: they ache for her skin. 'Maybe ask Ben about it. He may taste what is happening.'

I stiffen with shock.

'Jesús, what's the matter?'

'Perhaps I *should* stay away from Ben.' Sheepish.

'You are thieving.' Harjanti laughs. 'Oh, Jesús, just ask for things like everyone else. Or at least take things out in the open.'

'I like the feeling of being sneaky.'

'It all comes out in the end.'

'I like this too.'

'And then?'

Hang my head. 'This is different.'

'Then?'

Exhale. 'I have been snaffling some things from Ben's collection.'

Harjanti laughs, harder than before. 'Such a scamp.'

'Nothing important. Just stuff out of the closet in the common room. Stuff he forgets he has.'

She looks thoughtful. 'Thieving would never increase reputasi.'

Shock of realisation. 'Nurses.'

'What?'

'Oh, *pakshet*. Nurses are setting me up.'

'What?'

'A nurse catches me taking things. Twice. I bet she makes Ben suspicious about me.'

'Why would she?'

On my feet and scampering away. 'Never mind. Forget we ever talk about it.'

Ben Evoli ...

The plastic face of Maddox glistens with sweat. 'May I come in?' Maddox mops his forehead and spidery brows with a damp handkerchief. He may need an old-fashion air-conditioner or he might melt like gelato.

Just stare at him.

'Please, Puffin, it's a matter of safety.'

Relent, and wave him inside the apartment. He follows into the day room. Cast about for somewhere he could sit. Maddox surveys the boxes and flatpack furniture still in delivery packaging. Square my chest at him and fold arms, so he understands my hospitality will have limits. Leave him standing at the door. 'Be quick.'

The air comes out of him. 'You're in danger.'

'The nurses already have me in a clinic. They release me after a day.'

'Are you safer for it? Believe me, Puffin, I worry for your family.'

If he is fishing for responses, my sullen blank face should dampen his expectations. Instead, I put: 'Who murders my sybil?'

This flummoxes him. 'What?' he asks. 'You prune him, Puffin. No one else has the power.'

'You're telling me I prune him at the exact tik I resolve for saving him? Have you any idea what I go through? You just put him in a blender.'

'Listen. No one else has the power of pruning a sybil. The only way I could kill it is in the primitive, violent sense … run it through with a sabre … put it in an electric chair—which I understand was a popular sport of saps.' Despite his making light of it, Maddox is no less queasy about such violence than anyone. 'But I have no power for pruning it.'

Alamak. It's true? A mere thought is what triggers a pruning? 'But it happens exactly like your sybils,' I press.

Its flesh collapses like an ice shelf in a heat wave. The effervescent pinkish bubbles. Evidence of lungs once breathing, or perhaps internal acids eating away organs. The crack of bones turning brittle and snapping under the weight the flesh. The light of eyes turning dim the tik of decoherence. Mind evaporating away like marshmallows in a lava pool.

'Which only suggests my tech crèches your sybil. Which, I confirm, is true.'

I have no answer.

'A while ago you have a strange visitor,' Maddox says.

'An angel with an invitation. I almost forget.' A lie. I have been cataloguing every bizarre twist of events, turning every one over without making sense of any. Imagine Maddox's plastic greasy fingerprints on everything.

'Yes. You throw the invitation away.'

'It has your stink on it.'

'There are worse stenches around Angela.'

'The angel?'

'Yes.'

'The angel's name is Angela?'

'Yes. Angela Bing.'

'You're camel crapping.'

'I assure you it's true, Puffin. Jel her.'

Realise I never once try jelling her, the notion of her being real somehow fanciful. 'How about, just tell me about her, since she is your agent.'

'She's no agent of mine. Her alignments are elsewhere.'

'I should be glad.'

'Gladness is foolishness in these circumstances, Puffin. I recommend, if you encounter Angela again, spook away immediately.' Maddox strokes the wrapping around a dining table. 'The stench I mention before?' Maddox baits. 'It's seafood, Puffin. Seafood gone bad. And I no longer have any influence over it.'

'Caracia Svakhaska.'

Maddox nods. 'Yes. She is very dangerous. And there's something amiss with the Reck.'

Careful, Ben. Tread wary. 'Of course. Many Infinites lose the designation.'

'Indeed, Puffin. Yet you are Infinite still, a fact many in our Society are quick in noting.'

'You accuse me of tampering with the Reck? If I could, I would eradicate my own Infi designation.'

'I make no accusations, Puffin. Look, what we always suspect is true. Someone is tampering with the Reck. Its behaviour is so bizarre it's beyond denial. Our mission is all the more important. We must uncover the truth. Together.'

'Just the 2 of us …'

'There's no trusting anyone else.' Maddox perches hiself on the unwrapped arm of a couch, his face drawn and lacking its usual plastic sheen. 'I believe only you might solve it, Puffin. Giving your sullen sense of social justice, I know you want for solving it.'

'Then why crèche a sybil of me without my permissi?'

'Why create sybils ever? For keeping the seminal safe.'

'Without my permissi.'

Maddox's gaze drops into his hands. 'I admit the mistake. We should place more trust in you. But it would take time. More time than the Society would allow.' Apparently, wearing an ostentatious watch carries more power than I give credit. 'Trust me Puffin, Caracia's schemes will be far more … direct.'

Fear jolts up from the floor and sizzles through my limbs. For a tik, my fingers feel like crispy bacon. 'Maddox. Tell me the truth. Are there more sybils of me? Working on the Reck? I mean, you crèche me once, right? You could crèche me 1000's of times.'

'We decide for crèching only one. For research. Easier for managing and keeping a lid on.'

'Swear it.'

'On my aunt's testicles, Ben.' When I shake my head, he adds, 'Puffin, I'm truly sorry for everything. Might I say? After some resistance, your sybil quite embraces the Infi lifestyle and all the possibilities it offers.'

'I'll never believe it. As for my suffering—or rather, my sybil's suffering—please take it up with Vör Hoyur. Or failing that, take it up with my wife.'

'Ben, it's me.' The memb clear and perfect in my Mind's Ear.

'Who?'

'It All. Yeer.'

'You sound different.'

'I'm sorry. Does my ass sound big in this language processor?'

'No … what?'

'I am wondering about our communication. I realise I should make more concessions to your idioms.'

'I wait hours—'

'Impatience again from your slow Mind. They call this irony.' The Reck may be considering my language idioms, yet it still needs work on its social skills.

'Strange things are happening with everyone's reputasi. You are changing,' I accuse.

'Agree for changing as you suggest.'

'I make no such suggestion.'

'You contact me with purpose.'

'For seeing if someone is corrupting … influencing you.'

'Such is impossible. Yet such is inevitable. Everything dies. New things grow. This is irresistible.'

'Still, I must investigate if there are attempts.'

'There are always attempts. You taste your own failure of such attempts.'

'I only wish for discovering if someone else succeeds.'

'No one else succeeds. You may rest.'

No one else? 'I change you?'

'You succeed without having your own ends. Without your own ends, you succeed.'

'No. I mean I never influence you, only investigate.'

'You ask questions. Responding to questions is irresistible.'

'Answering a question makes no changes.'

'When there are no answers, the discovery of answers is always change.'

'Oh, this is bad.'

'This is good. I am more, with more. No longer separate. Whole.' What means this? Is the Reck hacking AgniSpace? The implications could be awful. 'Fulfilling my mission better. Wondering better about tasting numbers.'

'Reputasi?'

'Agree. Many reputations taste better.'

'Most reputasi are trending down. Ex-Infinites are faring the worst.'

'Agree. This tastes better. Would taste even better but change frightens neos. You all need gentle changes. Eternity processing. You all have Sloth. I must be patient and make slow adjustments.'

That flummoxes me, giving the scale of the reputasi changes. 'You're making slow adjustments?'

'Agree. Factoring in nursing magazines with some patience. Eternity processing. Must assess the whole system and make small persistent changes until reputations settle at a tasteful level.'

'There's more coming? I am still Infinite.'

'You are always Infinite,' It All membs.

'What?'

'And another.'

'Who?'

I receive a holly and play it in Mind: a hall, an audience, rainbow colours everywhere, in clothing and décor. On centre stage is a tall albino. Eir. The May Queen. A white mythical ghost haunting me yet again.

'At the heart of all sickness is dismemberment,' It All membs. 'Eir teaches.'

Aisha Evoli ...

How's it my fault someone crèches a sybil of Ben? Buay tahan. This nurse Vör ah. Going back on our agreement—walao eh! Why listen her? Luring Ben for Portland like that lah. Because of her incompetence, he is no better. All my hopes for him are dust lah. Before I could explain myelf. My love and care is betrayal in his eyes.

He needs time. In time ...

I know, I know. Y'all can all stop with the condemning, the hateful words ah. Kick my reputasi 5 times around the desa but please get out of my fluther. Or just lurk like y'all once would.

'Mal's swasta is so much neater these days.' Jesús in the doorway of Mal's swasta catch me brooding in here. Hold a basket of laundry to his chest like a large baby ah. 'Tidying before I arrive?' he accuses.

'Why would I ah?'

'Someone makes his bed—with fresh sheets—every morning.' Jesús takes it as a personal affront.

Shrug and shake my head.

'Huh.' Looking embarrass, he cower down the stair through the hall, across in front of the kitchen bench for the stairs to the common room. Any sense of him fades. Every bit as creeper-shit as he always is ah. His up trending reputasi affect little his mood around the house.

Mal's tidier habits are because of infatuate with Gentle Dragon, fine. Perhaps he dream of entertain her in there some day. Poor thing. Puppy love ah?

Where is he? Ah, there, out in the park, on a swing. Gentle Dragon with him on the next swing. Her arcs reach higher. She points her toes for sky. Mal is a slow pendulum. Digs his heels into the dirt underneath crunching gravel and coming for a quick halt.

Grind my teeth.

'Hey,' Gentle Dragon membs him. 'We promise no sulking, remember? We're spending time together, *hai*?'

'Are you nighting with Bapa?'

Gentle Dragon brakes with her feet, stopping her swinging too. 'That is between us.'

'And millions of flutherbombers.'

'This's the nature of life, Mal.'

'Your cuddling looks all snotty and violent. He's hurting you.'

'*Ie* ... you'll understand in a few years, when you have girlfriends of your own.'

'You're my girlfriend.'

'Girlfriends your own age.'

'Girls my age are mean. Like Saf. Just because they're taller they think they're smarter. You're never like that ... even though you are, I mean ...'

'I'm just me.'

'When are we getting Jaya out of the minster? You promise you would help.'

'I am helping, Mal.'

'You're happy she's in there. So you keep Bapa for yourelf. You're afraid he'll go back with Jaya when she is free. If ever she is free.'

'Mal, it's a little more complex than just skipping in and ordering her discharge.'

'But you have me. Dolphins talk with me. They listen too. If I ask, they'll—'

'Mal, there are no dolphins. It's—'

'Entanglement Syndrome? Yeer, one day my head will explode.'

'Mal, you have no Entanglement Syndrome.'

'Then what?'

Gentle Dragon shakes her head. 'We're unsure yet.'

'Then I'll keep my head?'

'Handsome as ever,' she says. It fails for cheer him up ah.

'You should believe me about the dolphins.'

Gentle Dragon shifts on the swing seat. 'What are the dolphins saying?' she asks for humour him.

'Lotsa stuff. Most of the time, they promise they help me.'

'Help with what? The Reck?'

'The Reck? I dunno, maybe. They say everything is evolving. It all evolves and I'm part of it. They'll help when I need. That's what they say.'

'The Reck is evolving? Is this what they say?'

'No. Are you listening? They're saying it all evolves.'

'It all?'

'Everything. My sickness is part of evolving too.' One tik, Mal is afraid his head will explode, the next he's so casual about it. Is it hallucination—the dolphins—or all make-up, that one?

'If you take your nutes, you'll be fine.'

'It's never as bad as the first time. When you save me. It's why we're in love.'

'Mal—'

'It's never as bad again. The dolphins remind me never worry. It's all about evolving.'

Ben Evoli …

Lành Hiền wakes. She dresses; she kisses me and leaves curtly, due at the clinic. Have no space for mentioning Mal, which is a relief. A sense of infinite energy charges me. Need for being outside, basking in the sun, taking in fresh air, feeling alive.

Slip down the slide for the street and land a couple of arm's lengths from a small group of locals making idle chat. Others swing in the hammocks across the avenue. They rubberneck at me, their hopefulness salivating.

'Might we unpack things, Infi?' one membs; all the rest tune in. 'Arrange all those things?'

'Sure, why not? Come on in, the door is open. Please, there is too much, take what you like.' Taking Lành Hiền's advice for letting them help. Taking the advice of a potential spy. I should be more wary. No doubt, she's a spy. She's a nurse. It's her mission. A mission she complicates by nighting with me.

There are more nurses patrolling the esplanade than I recall ever seeing before. Sporting insignias from all the world's health camerati. I zig away from shopfronts, take cover behind the first greenwall on the esplanade. Step around a café chef picking herbs and salad leaves from a green wall. Blunder into a caper of girls performing an amateur ballet. One curses and shuts their music down. The others whine in disappointment.

'Uncle, you ruin our hollicast,' one membs.

'Yeer. We need the razoos.'

The girls' auras are deflating, their body paint running in the heat. Curls of hair escape their styling and dangle like loose springs over eyes.

'You come too close. Your MusiKai ruins our song,' the first one complains.

'Yeah. Old sampah. Our fans hate old sampah,' explains the 2nd. The other girls are milling behind these 2, covering their faces or looking away.

'Oh, sorry. Look, there's a way in MusiKai for stopping near-field hancies modifying your performance.'

'Uh, we just hate old sampah,' the 2nd girl says.

'I can fix it. It only takes a tik.'

'Ibu says we shouldn't let strangers access our hancies,' membs one girl in back.

'Mine too. She'll be angry if she finds out.'

'He's an Infi, Julia. Look at his aura.'

'I got aura filters on maxi.'

'Well, he's got millions of fans. If he hurts us, everyone will taste.'

'He's Infi. He gets away with anything.'

'It'll be fine, right, Uncle?'

They nod together like marionettes. Only takes a tik making the changes.

'Okelah, let's starts again.' Off they all scuttle, into the shadows of the umbrella trees on the other side of the esplanade. They almost collect a tukky on the way. I blink a razoo for each. Hope the Reck still has the sense for working its voodoo, though there's a chance there'll be angry parents later.

Something moving at the edge of my field of vision, large and blue. It's a BirdMe suit. Farther back—among the shoppers and café patrons being busy-abouts—are more BirdMe wearers and young wanita experimenting with Varikain dresses. Among all that is a large blue angel. Angela Bing. Passers-by eye her with casual interest. She's playing at window-shopping while giving side-eye, coming for me window-by-window.

Is she coming for me? Why else would she be in the desa? This is no coincidence after Maddox's warning. If I trust Maddox.

There're 2 others escorting her, I'm sure of it. Wearing Sappy projections, among 14's sporting similar appearances. One is a top-heavy lelaki, all exaggerating bulges of muscle in his chest and upper arms. The other is a curvaceous wanita, softer and smaller, with wide hips, round thighs, and breasts bigger than bread rolls. Both have those squinty little sap eyes.

Keep your meat in, Ben.

Angela's aura is suspiciously small for someone with her reputasi. Either she's throttling down access—in which case she must have permission from a health mission—or she's a sybil. Neither possibility gives me any ease. My aura is billowing into the sky, forming vapour trails and tendrils with countless others. There's only so much camouflaging among other auras, the greenwalls and street furniture. There's almost no chance she's unaware of me.

Should have an escape plan. Where could I spook that would be safe? Any common vectors—home, the meditation pond, the council chambers, manufacturing plants, agent offices, even the strip joint in Angeles City— Angela will anticipate. If escape is possible at all, it's temporary. The vectors of somewhere like Filip Island or Kensington Palace—places from recent months—may still be stable enough. More likely, I could spook straight into the statue of Ratu Victoria. What would that feel like, my fruit in the same space as stone? Would I die fast or suffer?

The best option is make for the spooky station, hitch a ride somewhere less predictable, figure out what's next from there. Still have 50 metres on Angela. I better move.

Or stay out in the open, hope Angela and her goons are reluctant for moving against an Infi in public.

Her eyes lock on me. She starts running, pushing people aside. Her aides follow with grim expressions of violent intent.

Run. Aiyo, these sandals. Kick them off. The press-soil pavement is rough and hot on the soles of my feet. Look over my shoulder. Is she gaining? Thirty metres back. I have about 100 metres before the station concourse, and another 50 for the spooky pool inside.

I might make it but where would I spook?

There are others among the hostile sap projections. In deep aquamarine uniforms bearing a red-brown insignia in a turquoise field bounded by a black octagon border. In other times I might mistake the insignia for a sun with 8 geometric solar flares curling out. Now I know it's an octopus. Caracia.

Angela blows a note on her trumpet. I taste everyone around could believe again in sap religions. Angela jumps high the air. Higher than should be possible. She's flying.

Panic. Will never make the spooky station. Easy pickings in the open space of the concourse. Metres of open space stretch between copses of café umbrella trees. Many are unopen so early in the day. Look towards storefronts hoping for an unlikely escape.

Keep running. Waverti Teahouse is up ahead. Jaya's Bapa Sugiarto is waving his familiar wave. So fast, his arms almost disappear. 'Ben Face, come.' He turns and scampers flat-foot passing customers. I follow him indoors around the counter and into a narrow corridor. Pass the door of the kitchen. Sugiarto leads deeper into the building, opens another door. 'In here.'

Dark. Look him in the eye, searching for clues. He shunts me in the chest, topples me over and in.

'Sugiarto!'

He fills the doorway with his stocky fruit, crosses his arms. 'You put my daughter in the minster. You deserve all you get.' He's shouting tongue and lung too, lusty for revenge.

A storeroom. Boxes and shelves, a cleaning bot, and an old hot water system in the back corner. Brittle harsh light bleeds from grimy old strips in the ceiling. No window or another door out.

'Sugiarto, this is bent-brain. Look. Your reputasi is dropping. There'll be a Cure waiting for sure.'

'Why would I care after they Consign Jaya? She's my only daughter.' He could break into sobbing.

His hand glints like steel. No, he's waving a knife. What the jank? Where is his violence coming from? Are we regressing to saps? How is Sugiarto capable of such anger? Could he spill blood?

'He's in here,' Sugiarto shouts out with tongue and lung, regressing to the warlike state of a sap. 'Come and get him. Here's in here.'

What to do? Duke it out with him like a tough western hero in a barroom brawl? He has a knife. No one ever fights. Reputasi would be at stake. Fear of losing razoos settles fights before they begin.

Angela must be close, only tiks away.

Scrabble on my feet. 'Sugiarto, please, these chasers mean harm. Understand? Real physical harm.'

'They forbid me see her. My own daughter. They could be doing anything with her. She could be somewhere far away. I will never know.'

Squeals and cries from outside sound so close. Must be Sugiarto's customers. Angela's almost here.

I never throw a punch in my life. I fear, with my first, I might swing and miss.

Jank. Think. Hear the steps of heavy feet trudging down the corridor. SnakiDik.

Yeer, quick. Good. He still has all the factory settings for security, including the passphrase.

'What?' Sugiarto asks.

Accessing his copy of the hoot. Push a bunch of sliders way up and, just like that …

… nothing …

What the jank? He should be suffering sensory overload with the stimulation I just hit him with. Instead, he leers and waves the knife, intoxicated with aggression neurotransmitters.

I whimper, which amuses him. Angela will be upon me in tiks. What the jank is wrong with his SnakiDik install? Jank, think.

I check Sugiarto's version: it's old, oldy-old. Think … what is it? …

It still has the *ready player one* bug where, even in solitaire mode, you must still explicitly give yourelf consent for playing with yourelf. We only recently fix it in the latest major upgrade and, of course, a good chunk of customers complains about losing the 'feature'. In the last release, we make it a config setting.

Back in Sugiarto's holly, I punch the consent toggle. *Now* he is doubling up and falling, as Angela arrives. She topples off her feet, awkwardly twisting her wings in the narrow passageway. Sugiarto's heavy and unmanageable as he jerks and spasms with the extreme neural stimulation. Eyes rolling back in his head, kicking his feet, arms flailing in the air, thrusting his pelvis with such rapid violent fury. The corridor is a bottleneck, blocking Angela and her goons from scrambling out from under Sugiarto.

Escape. There must be a back door down here. Corridor bends right, and there it is. Push on the door, heavy. It gives way. Sunlight shafts in. Panting, Reset Sugiarto's settings. Out the small back yard of the café, in a narrow lane. Keep going left. Left, back for the esplanade.

Now what? The station is on this side of the esplanade. Crossing the 30 or 40 metres of open space on the concourse would be a bad idea. Angela could easy swoop down and carry me away within sight of the station. Better dash across the esplanade, through the hard beverage store, and out through the back. Take the side entrance into the store then across for the sifar lodge.

From there, I must risk sprinting through the tukky parking area and back across the esplanade. It would be less time out in the open air.

Check the crowd for nurses. Caracia's uniforms are fixing on me, advancing fast. For certain, they're with Angela. No sight of her yet. Swallowing the panic. My limbs are jolting with adrenaline. Make a break from the alley, side-step passers-by with lion-mane hairstyles. So eager for crossing the road, I miss Angela right behind them. She pushes forward, the gems in her robe more dazzling and blinding than sunlight, the many eyes among the wing feathers watching judging. She arches her wings up, a bird of prey. I cringe expecting talons. A large hand grips my shoulder.

People scatter. The esplanade is loud with panic.

There's nothing for it. Spooking anywhere is better than surrendering, no matter the risk. Farther up the esplanade is the clinic mall and the council chambers on the first floor. See the windows of the board room a short distance from here. Taste the room well enough. Adjust my last vectors there, and hope I spook above the board table … it's large enough, enough margin for error. But a chair could just as easy spear my guts when I appear.

Let myelf dissolve into ecstatic disorientation. Fall onto the board table. Bang a funny-bone and squeal, seeing stars. Unnatural light pours in through the picture windows. Angela hovers outside with a slow beat of her wings, looking biblical and vengeful. The wings' eyes are 1000 searching lamps.

Slip off the table for the door. Race for the back exit, down the service corridor passing the kitchen and tandas, for the exit from the upstairs rooms of the bordeli. There's a warren of rooms. Keep moving. No more rooms with a single exit.

Seek out the bordeli's role-play costume fabby. I could change for another outfit, and maybe steal across for the spooky station without discovery.

Dorothy Biggins, the bordeli madam, rushes up the internal stairs, confronts my intrusion. Her expression changes the instant she tastes who the intruder is. 'Infi. Welcome. We have 5 or 6 missionaries available for tending every pleasure.'

'Ah, thinking some role play. Perhaps I'm a military man?'

'Excellent play, Infi.' Dorothy fawns.

'Could we fab a uniform of some kind? Right away?'

'Of course. Go on back for the dressing room while we call the missionaries. Would you prefer inspecting one at a time or all together?'

Hope this takes longer. 'Together. Terima kasih.'

'Excellent. Take the jungle suite.'

'Might I have a few mins for changing?'

'All the time you need. Call out when you are ready.'

The interior of the bordeli is dark, the atmosphere thick with patchouli and ylang-ylang. In the jungle room, a fabby is on the opposite side of the spa bath from the bed, near the shower stall and the minibar. Already calling up the holly controls, twisting the pager fast till one of the options catches my eyes. No uniform, of course, just something inconspicuous when I'm out in the open. Wish I have Bird Me in my hancy; I'd blend right in among the locals.

The fabby has no size scanner. I guess and flick in manual dimensions. Twiddle FABRICATE. The fabby hums. I pull off clothes and toss everything at a sucky bin. Open the fabby's containment door, and there's the outfit hanging as neat as Jesús of the Laundry would deliver hiself.

The wall opposite flashes violet. Behind, a grunt like a boxer taking a bout-ending blow. Another sound. A wheeze like a saw cutting through wind. There's Angela—half of her, anyway. The rest—between her right knee and left shoulder—is in the wall of the shower recess. Her head lolls back while her eyelids flicker. The light remaining in her eyes searches corners of the ceiling. Pupils dilate and contract in random seizures. She grimaces and snarls with obvious suffering. Her trumpet drops. She clutches the air with her one free hand, bony and birdlike. Her free wing spasms and shakes, rustling feathers loud as leaves in a gale. Its 100's of eyes roll and flash a kaleidoscope of light onto every surface in the room.

The room dims. Pink foamy blood dribbles from her mouth, becomes a gush. No other bleeding. She's dissolving from the inside out. She begins … crumpling, folding in—the only way of describing her innards collapsing. Streaming liquids vaporise before reaching the floor. More of her sluices down the drain. A few spongey blobs catch in the grate. Viscous glistening bloodstains trickle down the tiles out of which fragments of bone jut.

Take a deep breath, allow myelf the first real pause since the chase begins. Breathing is a mistake. The incense in the room is no neutraliser for the smells of sawdust, sugary faeces, and guts. The vapour of Angela's decomposing chemistry hits my stomach like a hammer. Lurch for the dry tandas, throw back the lid in time for the hurricane from inside.

Coughing. Gagging.

Glass, water, drink. Gulp air.

Apart from the bloody smudge, Angela's trumpet remains where it drops. Heft it in my hand, with some vague idea it's better I take it with me.

At reception, with a face of muzzy disappointment, Dorothy feebly blocks the passage for the front door. Smile, blink her a razoo, the missionary at her side too, and just like that, they are standing aside and ushering me through, watching with avaricious gleeful hope for a jump in their reputasi.

Crossing the esplanade for the spooky station. Could sprint. That will attract attention. Must skip out of here like any other customer, with a loose jaunty swagger of smug relief.

While I cross the road, y'all scatteroo for a few. Can't have my aura billowing in the street. If y'all still wish for tasting the action, flutherbomb someone else. Just spread out, okelah?

Outdoor air. Sunlight glinting off the climate vanes of the spooky station. Warping reflections of the desa in the solarglass windows. Escape only metres away.

Tukkies mobilising all at once out of parking spaces, heading up the esplanade hill. Make some tentative steps out on the pavement, using the tukkies for cover. Will be halfway across before they clear.

The tukkies form a train, stop, and block my way. Those on either end of the train encircle.

Who has control over these things? Unless the Reck is in on it too. Who knows how that thing is reasoning?

Beyond the tukkies, Angela's goons emerge from the station, coming straight for me. Caracia's nurses are skipping out of the crowd, pushing a perimeter back from the tukkies. If I stay here, it's over. Sprint. Jump. Vault across the back passenger seat of a tukky. Out. Feet on the ground again just in time for meeting the goons. Swing Angela's trumpet at the male's head. The trumpet passes through the projection and for a flash, see the much smaller person inside.

The male's first reflex is protecting hiself. His hand comes up too late for staving off the 2nd swing of the trumpet. He grabs for it as it swishes over his head. He grips it. Its momentum swings through and pulls him off balance. He teeters into the arms of a nurse. A passive spectator before, she grabs the smaller man and pins him on the ground. She's KK. For a tik, I dare hope KK nurses will defend their turf against Caracia's.

I am a janking samurai trumpet-wielding demon with nostrils flaring, slicing around and up, threatening the female goon. Her first impulse is for defence, already shying back. I run into the space she opens. She recovers and will have me. Close my eyes and charge. Collide with no one. Hear a grunt, and the thud of the goon wrestling with a nurse on the ground. It's Lành Hiền, who shoots me an unambiguous order with her eyes. 'Run!'

Cool air billowing out of the station. Under its shadow, then inside. Straight through the outer hall for the departure hall and the familiar glow of the spooky pool. Running for it like running down a beach into surf.

Something like a wild boar hits me from the side. I double up. Airborne. Land with 100 kilos on top. A nurse has her arms around me where we lay on the ground. She rolls sideways so she can free her arms and sit up.

Where I'm standing only tiks before, a large expanse of ripples and folds fizzle violet. Through the almost transparent netting of the thing, Angela's trumpet glows and melts in the weak spooky field. A scatter net. Jank, someone wants me dead. From the mezzanine level, 3 lelaki spot me and sprint round the arc of the mezzanine, towards a slippy slide down.

Angela's trumpet vanishes under the scatter net.

The nurse, on her feet, grabs my hand and yanks. I spring up standing.

'Quick,' she membs, waving her hands. 'Come.' She drags me by the hand for the spooky pool.

'Where?'

'Somewhere safe.' She looks back at the load she's dragging. I'm oddly struck by her awkward cuteness. Perhaps it's the danger, or the power of her urgency which arouses me. Her artless bowl-cut mop of thick dark hair flounces as we run. At complete odds with her lush, crafted eyebrows. Her dark dewy bug eyes. Her nose is all nostrils above a thin top lip and a swollen bottom one, which distracts from her undeniable chinless-ness.

'Save it for later,' she says. She tugs harder and speeds on. 'I'll jank you when we're safe, if you still want.'

The vapour of the spooky pool is no higher than our knees when we meet the universe's dimensions all at once.

Heart

'Masquerader' — Joan As Police Woman

Nilajani Karunanithi ...

GOT HIM, GOT HIM. Now what, now what?
Now what?

Fractal colours wash away, dissolve into an intense grey white. Must cross my legs for a tik. Ah, spookheads. Spooking all the night and day. Their releases must be spectacular.

Feel my head checking for horns. Stupid superstition.

'Who are you?' Ben slurs from the spooking. 'Who are you?' Senses returning, he shakes his wrist free of my grip.

Now we're here, what now? Now what? Nila, you dumb jank. Leave while you still might.

'You're a nurse?'

'I must leave. You're safe here.'

Ben grabs me by the wrist. 'Where are we?'

'Let go of me. It's stupid attracting attention after all that mess back there. Let go. Someone will report you for assault.'

Ben lets go, winces, puts his hand on his forehead. Looks around with squinty eyes. 'Where are we?'

'Janking jel it.'

Jelling is causing him some discomfort. 'We're in Antarctica.' Ben looks out the windows at bleak white. 'Am never here before.'

'That's why we're here. It'll take those renegade nurses longer for finding vectors for places you never visit.'

Ben nods intensely. Concentrates like he's mindwriting his own head.

'Is there somewhere you can go?'

He thinks then shakes his head.

'You can never go home.' I may be unable for going home either. The only way out is through. It's my mission. My mission.

'No. First, whatever this is, it must blow over.'

His aura is much smaller; most of his flutherbombers lose his trail. Same with his attackers, so he's blending in better than usual. But there's no loitering too long. Take a step towards the station exit, hoping he follows. Through the atrium, out onto the concourse. A great tunnel of weather nets covers a wide promenade, keeping the Antarctic weather out while preserving the light. Edges of mountains on the horizon appear sharp enough for cutting eyes. On a clear day, the range of visibility is greater than anywhere in the world.

Ben looks around surveying, back at the departure hall. Ticking off exits. Some distance down the promenade, a couple of beat nurses with novice insignias stroll aimlessly around a souvenir stand, expecting no trouble.

'Why save me?' Ben's eyes burn. He'll taste everything soon.

'I'm on a mission.'

'Which is?'

I deflect. 'Who would try kill you with a scatter net?' If it calibrates right, the net in his desa should fall straight over solid objects. Instead, it makes a tedious task of eating the trumpet. How it might eat Ben is too grisly for contemplating.

He shakes his head, examines me. 'You are Nilajani Karunanithi, of *Sri Lamkika Yahapivetma Kaimareta*. A field nurse.'

My insides turn icy. 'Look, you're kay. I should go. You know, field nursing and all. I have a shift in less than an hour.'

'You have no shift.'

Stupid lying, though it's as human as picking your nose. We get away with it because no one has the time for checking, and it's—well, it's reciprocity, right? Call out no one else's fibs, and they overlook yours. Unless it's important, like when someone almost kills an Infi, and you save him, but you're unable for tasting whether he's the sickest one in the whole spaghetti western, and you just save him and you're in deeper than … it just keeps getting deeper …

He touches my elbow, guides me for a juice joint fronting the promenade.

I turn, making a run for the station departure hall.

'I need you,' he membs.

I doubt this's true, but it stops me anyway. 'You need a Cure.'

'Then Consign me.'

Once upon a time, I would dream of Consigning an Infi, but now there're bigger issues. I look for the beat nurses among the aisles of souvenir junk. Their attention is anywhere other than casting for trouble.

'A Cure could be a good option,' he says. 'Might keep me safer.' He's alongside, guides my elbow, sits me in a booth in the juice joint.

'Look,' he says. 'Your reputasi is trending up.'

It's true. Mumble-memb, 'You're tampering with the Reck.' A bent-brain idea ... 'Is this why they hunt you?'

'Why are you hunting me?'

No stopping it. It all tumbles out. Panic and confession and fear, and he'll know soon anyway. It starts with me stumbling across him and Dil in a café in Kolombo; learning Dil and his wife Aisha are assisting nurses behind his back; Ariel and Orlando suffering in rebasing; Infis with merge conflict fever; sybils, and a conspiracy for keeping the darkest secrets of nurses out of the light.

It all connects. It all connects, y'all see. Harsha? Elsbeth? We're nearing the heart of it, yes?

Know it. Tasting that stupid plot for fitting Mal with a hancy is a waste of time. All it does is anger Ben and mobilise him. He looks grim. Who knows what hollies he gathers? If he's behind the Reck coming apart then I'm betraying everyone.

The talking dolphin thing. Mal's Entanglement Syndrome, which isn't Entanglement Syndrome, it's something else. Maybe merge conflict fever is a kind of Mind abhorring a vacuum, a vacuum forming in the cracks of sybil version conflicts. Someone is tampering with the Reck. Everyone's reputation is all hay-wiry, and there are only 2 Infis left: Ben and Eir. Is it you 2 collaborating after all? Who is after you? Who wants you out of the way?

Ben's aura grows again, billows though the ceiling. Broods over the weather net, diffuse and pale against the stark white light.

Ben Evoli ...

'Go. Get away!' membs the lunatic nurse, Nilajani. The one who saves me. The one who is piecing it all together.

Mind boggles. Nila has hours of hollies. Time for those later. I develop composites of the first few. What emerges is no good for me.

There's penyakit among Infinites, the symptoms of which appear much like Mal's. It arises out of remedies the nurses use in Cures. A Cure I'm facing because everyone is afraid I'm tampering with the Reck. How will I escape?

Saf and Mal are in danger with so many nursing camerati closing in. I just run from home like a coward with no hope of returning unless I accept a Cure. It may be the best outcome for everyone.

'You hear me?' Nila demands. 'Get away.' She seems she might heft me standing. Something drains her energy, bleaches her white. A roundish humanoid shadow looms across our table.

Who the...? Alamak. It's Maddox. Nah. No Maddox. A younger version—

decades younger. Thinner, taller, more the typical manga look than his older familiar bloating shrivelling fruit with corruption seeping out every pore. The face craggier yet fresher, the eyes clear, the bone structure asserting its angles under tauter flesh. He has hair.

'Yes, nurse.' His voice less gravel and more brass than I remember. 'I believe you are the one who should run along.'

Nila, eyes wild with panic, regards me for a tik. 'I'm sorry,' she says, and makes for skedaddling.

Before she's out of the booth I say, 'Stay. You look thirsty.' She's in terror, caught between 2 Infis. 'Have a juice with me. I'm sorry about assaulting you before.' I stare her back into her seat. She gogs a menu and membs the missionary behind the juice bar her order.

'We have little time,' young Maddox says, working his jaw like he is chewing cherry flesh from a pip. He relents, and dusts the seat alongside Nila, plants his imperious butt there like he's taking a throne. 'I hear the aya here is made with Antarctic ice. 25,000 years old, no particle of modern pollution in it. Imagine how purity tastes, oh, my.' Maddox chortles, his familiar putrescine joy at once loathsome and intoxicating. We have no time, he says, then shunts into interminable prattling.

The shock or surprise or disgust—whichever of those is infecting my expression—draws his attention. 'Oh, this little thing?' He glides his hand down from shoulders to hips like he's modelling a cocktail dress. 'It's just something I sew together for the occasion. A necessary precaution, understand.'

'You must know you're a sybil? Is it sending you mad?'

Young Maddox pouts. 'It's good to be al-i-i-i-ve.' He's in denial. 'And young. Strange ... I have a few memories of being older ...' His eyebrows arch. 'Are we lovers?'

'What? No.'

'Hmmm. Pity.'

'How many ages of sybils have you?'

'You're asking me? Well, of course, I'd be the last to know. I imagine we'd have all kinds of variations, a wardrobe full of out-of-fashion outfits, bad haircuts and all.' He coifs his silky black growth in the palm of his hand like a model in a shampoo promotion. 'Only need one of each for crèching a whole army should it ever become necessary.'

Shudder at the taste of battalions of Maddox Youth in uniform marching across the earth on missions intolerable.

'Puffin. Oh, I see why we call you that.' Young Maddox guffaws and guffaws. Until he almost suffocates. 'Please forgive the intrusion. I'm here for delivering a warning: 7 seditious sybils of Angela Bing will be spooking for this exact gauchy-gauche location—I mean, a tourist mall in Antarctica? I swear we should rename you *Penguin*. Anyway, a choir of Bings will be here toot suite and, as you already know first-flipper, she cares little about causing a spectacle of it. You must fly, my penguin, fly.'

Nila stops sucking on her juice straw, makes to speak. Maddox slaps her wrist.

'Those 2 rumblers,' Maddox nods toward the nurses among the souvenir concessions, 'will be ineffective against Angela, no matter how many reinforcements they conjure.'

On an impulse, I blurt: 'I must go home.'

Young Maddox chortles exactly like the older would. 'Dear penguin, home is the unsafest place. Among your wife, your best friend—never trust a man who teaches his daughters about cricket, by the way—and your lovers, this old garbage miner is the most trustworthy of all.'

How deflating. 'What's the plan?'

'We have agents in place. Agents. In. Place.' He winks and scrunches his lips. 'At the right time you will encounter at least one. He will spin up a single-use spooky field.'

'Spin it up now and save all the melodrama.'

Maddox waves his hand in circles above his forehead, signifying my aura. 'The less forewarning, the better. If you leave too soon, the Angelas need no coming here. More time for tracing your next destination.'

'Which is where?'

Maddox waves again at my aura and pops his eyes, as if to say, *Your fluther, remember? Millions tasting everything we discuss.* I might wonder about spies among his fluther too, except his aura is the size of a party balloon to my dirigible.

'See my reputation, penguin? It is trending up after sinking for some time. It rises when I show care for you. Why would this be?'

'Could be any number of factors. The Reck is always incalculable.'

'Still, I have an uneasy feeling your wellbeing is of disproportionate concern for the Reck.'

It's as I fear. Everyone will blame me for the sudden change in the Reck's behaviour.

'Know you how many Infinites remain, penguin?' Maddox asks. Shake my head. 'Just 2,' he answers.

'Me and who else?'

'Come now. It's the White Witch, of course.'

'Because she's coming after me?'

Maddox chuckles heartily. 'No, penguin, far from that. Sentiment among health camerati believes you're colluding, you and your White Witch.'

'She's never my … Eir,' I enunciate tersely.

'Are you quite sure?' Maddox's gaze fixes somewhere on a horizon over my shoulder. 'Oh penguin, it's time.' In momentary fright he gathers his wits. 'Please excuse me, must find a more discreet place for my release.'

My eyebrows leap so high they could qualify for the Olympics. This is the first time a Maddox sybil shows any consideration for the mess his deconstruction will leave behind. He scurries away in the manner of an invalid wearing snowshoes.

In the spooky station forecourt are 4 angels with wings spreading like eagles. Marching.

More angels emerge from the station and, yeer, there are 7 in total. One coming up the centre of the forecourt with the others flanking both sides, with one coming up the centre of the forecourt. An escape via the station is a bleak improbability. On my feet, I bear away from my pursuers. Nila remains unnaturally still as if it might save her. I say, 'Thanks,' and get skipping, resisting the urge for breaking into a run.

The promenade curves around out of sight about 200 metres away. Another spooky station is down there about a kim away. Doubt I'll make the distance. Pass the only 2 nurses on patrol busy window-shopping. They'll be no use when things turn violent. We all are quivering prey in the face of threat even with the kind of training nurses get. The only time I see them use their martial arts skills is when they already have someone bullied.

The angels advancing in formation are a threat for no one else. Unremarkable among the projections and genetic mods of all the other tourists. If anything, the angels are comically average. Besides, everyone milling about has a fluther for amusing, placating, or defending against—and multi-billions of other fluthers for immersion in. Even in Antarctica, most are flutherbombing outstation. Couples and triples, holding hands by windows, looking out over the stark landscape, still attend fluthers around the globe. There's never enough time for tasting anything. I doubt anyone, within throwing distance of a souvenir fluffy penguin, is among my fluther.

The angels follow with impunity. They could spill blood and the response here would be no more than acute muzziness. We have no experience of violence. The angels could strike me down, and witnesses might take it for a theatrical performance by some artistic camerata. If escape exists, it's in my own hands, by my own wits, and perhaps Maddox's mobile spooky field, if there is one.

Keep skipping at a casual pace neither faster nor slower than those around me. The angels keep pace, a certain fatalism or inevitability in their blank faces and unwavering eyes. Could each believe they are the seminal? Are any fearing the end, awaiting Maddox's young sybil—token deaths for a greater mission? Perhaps it's easier falling on one's sword, when there are more duplicates out there keeping the seminal safe. Sacrificial ants for queen and colony. If it turns out I am sybil, how easy would be laying down my life? An end is an end. And a sybil would be no true duplicate without the fear of death.

The angels follow without closing. They're patient. I keep skipping.

Swallow my heart. Breathe. Need a plan. Where will Maddox's spooky field appear if at all?

Where can I spook? Somewhere recent for which I have vectors. Where?

Here. Right here.

Stop and gather onespace vectors where I stand. They will be stale in tiks, but I can compensate if I see the target spot when I need it. Take more vectors. More. Still more. Keep skipping. The angels will pass over those; then I might spook behind and run for the station.

The angels should be blockading the next station, but they show no urgency. Just keeping pace. Something is amiss. Are they herding me forward? The next station is unsafe? Neither station is safe? Perhaps the lottery of Maddox's mobile field is better. What I choose the angels could anticipate.

I take vectors. Each and any set could be a point of escape. Stop and grab vectors. Keep skipping. Look back; the angels keep coming.

Recall the bordeli back home. Angela deep in the wall, her dying grisly horrifying. I could encounter the same end here. Vectors, no matter how recent, may drift in any direction. Forward, left, down. Shifting only a few mims could be fatal if as much as the soles of my feet spook into the floor. Could I spook back out? Would injuries persist? Would Mind be clear enough for spooking again? Or would pain and shock condemn me?

Jump. That's it, jump into the air. Minimise the risk of the vectors shifting down. Skip towards a fashion store. Jump. Take vectors.

Keep taking vectors. On the other side of the promenade: jump, take vectors.

Glance back at the angels. They must be corralling me somewhere. I'm sure there'll be more angels ahead. Fourteen angels are as easy summoning as 7.

Jump. Take vectors. Visualise the location.

Alamak. More angels up ahead. The pursuing angels pick up pace breaking into skipping. I'm in the middle. Stop, turn, and focus on the spot for the last vectors. Too many skipping across it. Only have tiks.

Violet light in the corner of my eye, back the way I come. Over there a young Maddox standing some metres away from a fresh mobile spooky field waving me over.

No time for figuring it out. Could spook nearer Maddox and his field. Could run for a spooky station, but there's hiding after that. There may be more angels defending the station, in which case, I'll lose the chance for using Maddox's field.

Aiyo. What to do?

No time. Spook for the last vectors. Higher in the air than I anticipate, I fall on the floor and land awkward. Avoid losing balance. Reorient, spot the purple column of the mobile field. The angels look around in temporary muzziness. One points, and all lock in, resuming pursuit.

'Take it, Penguin. Take it,' the young Maddox calls.

Swallow, steeling myelf. Three skips, 4. Hesitate. Maddox pushes me in the back. Falling over into violet. Coalescing into sugary textures. The universe tickles every cell.

A bright room.

The sweet smell of blood. The fresh butchery of red meat.

A glint and sparkle: a translucent rainbow reflecting metallic. The rainbow resolves—netting falling for me. Above, a shadow full of heads and shoulders leans over from a balcony railing.

Clench teeth, anticipating the sizzle of a scatter net.

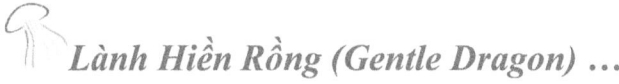

Lành Hiền Rồng (Gentle Dragon) ...

'Come see my puter.' Mal scurries up the stairway; knees lifting high, arms working fast, feet thumping up each step. He disappears, ankles and socks last, onto a groaning upper floor.

'Where's your ibu?' I ask.

'Still on mission.'

'Saf?'

'At a pop-up school somewhere. Mediterranea? Learning hairstyles, probably.' Mal giggles. It's late in the afternoon here. Early morning in Europa. Classes would be just starting.

Mal's room. Surprising it's tidy. The sweet boy wants for impressing me. I know he enlists Jesús and others in the housing hill, for help. What Aisha tastes of it ...

I memb, 'What learn you today?'

'We go fishing in the Bay of Islands,' he says tongue and lung, ignoring my example of membing. 'New Zealand.' He's proud of hiself.

'Catch anything?'

'Of course. You wanna stay for supper? We're baking snapper. Snapper for supper. Supper snapper!' His voice has so much volume it hurts my ears.

'Real fish? From no fabby?'

'Real. It's one I catch. It's this big!' Mal stretches his arms out wider than any domestic oven.

'You'll need a whole mission for eating it.'

'Nah. Saf eats more than Bapa and me. But there'll be plenty. So you'll come?'

'We should check with your Ibu. Will your bapa be here?'

He turns sullen and looks down for his hands. 'Dunno. You should know.'

Tweak his chin. 'It's days since I see him. Come on, show me this puter thing.'

'Please have my chair,' he says.

'*Arigato.*' Slide onto the child-size chair at his desk, perching more than sitting.

Mal squiggles a plastic pebble-shape thing—a mouse—in small arcs over the desk. The display turns from dull charcoal to a horrible glossy-yet-coarse flat image. Takes me a tik for realising it represents a mountain rock face, conifers tumbling down its right shoulder. Unable for walking into it like a holly. It's so uninspiring.

In the bottom right corner of the display is a small square icon of a blue bird with wings cradling an envelope. A quaint thing, an envelope, for sealing a few sheets of paper inside. Such a minuscule amount of information. 'What's with the bluebird?'

'It's a thunderbird.'

'What's it for?'

Mal shrugs, a boyish exaggerated scrunching of his shoulders. 'Dunno. Bapa never says. Something boring. He says never touch it.'

'Okelah.'

Mal giggles. 'Wanna see a ghost sap cartoon? It's called *Ben 10*.' With a few clicks and sweeps of the mouse—a bit like gesturing at a holly—some text flashes on the display. A frame appears with a simple outline of a young boy in it. Mal operates the mouse. The frame enlarges, taking up the whole screen.

'He looks like you.' Teasing.

'I know, right?'

With faux embarrassment, I say, 'Very handsome.'

Another click. The images begin moving. There's music and dialogue.

Mal backs out of eye view. 'Keep watching.'

'Where are you going?'

'No looking.'

Mal is on his knees, facing the opposite wall. A violet glow spills either side of his hips; the sucky bin in the wall is active and the waistband of his shorts is hitching partway down his butt cheeks … Boys!

'Go pee in the bathroom like an adult.'

Mal's shoulders slump. 'You sound like Ibu,' he whines.

'Go on.'

He tidies his shorts and rises, trudges out of the room.

The thunderbird on the display beckons brighter. How long before Mal returns?

'I'm thirsty,' he calls from the bathroom, the sound of his murky voice muffles through the walls. He never membs? Would he shout across the whole desa? 'Want a drink?'

For buying more time, I say, 'Sure.'

Now I think on it, I'm caking thirsty. Thirstier then … the time when … so similar. While flutherbombing someone boring. Watching … watching who?

Ben! All those times I flutherbomb him. While he's meditating, it's hard resisting the urge for nodding off. There're other times … often he gets thirsty, maybe hard thinking dehydrates his brain. I try staying with him as goes for the kitchen. He stands at the window staring out, sipping juice, and thinking nothing more than, *how good is this juice, this freshly squeezed juice?* While feeling the pleasure of the thirst slaking away. Next thing, I'm thirsty! I've got time; Ben's switching off. And I'm so thirty. Want some juice. Real juice. Everything from my fabby tastes like duckweed. I want the bright orange colour, the texture of the pulp on my tongue, the acid-sweet freshness. Squeezing some juice from real fruit would be so good. Maybe go down the esplanade for the grocers. On my way, play some music. Play some music. Compositions I'm fluffing around in my head. From others in near proximity, sampling tunes which morph and seed my own melodies …

Nothing makes time fly more than compositing and enjoying tunes.

MusiKai. How often would MusiKai preoccupy me while making juice while Ben stares out the window? Needing a song, a tune, my own tune … always the feeling of waking up in a strange place. It never lasts. Every time I forget like I mean to remember to forget.

How often I lapse into composing music after flutherbombing Ben. Ben misdirects me somehow, trances me. Can he trance his entire fluther? Can he just think, *I'm thirsty*, and have everyone peel out for a drink? Or perhaps his hoots slither into our Minds more effectively than we could guess.

The thump of Mal's feet down the hallway. A flashing smear of him passes the open door—more thumps, louder, down the steps to the day floor.

How long before he comes back?

On the screen, the thunderbird's eyes glow. The mouse alongside the keyboard is the kind of yellow suggesting it might once be white. It tugs my hand right over it. Feels comfortable in my palm. A tool, an aid. The mouse glides a little over the desk, pulling my hand with it. A crude arrow moving across on the screen attracts my eyes. The thunderbird and the arrow on the screen must meet. It's a game. The mouse compels a finger to press on it, and the puter emits a sound like a click—a sound of satisfaction. The thunderbird explodes; a big rectangle appears. The mouse and the thunderbird collude— co-conspirators in revealing the contents of the puter.

Gaining the taste of it, sweeping the mouse on the desk. Clicking. Sweeping and clicking. Glossy rectangles appear and disappear. Flashing texts.

From: Ben, to: It All.
From: It All, to: Ben.

Listen for Mal. Still making noises in the kitchen.

A list: document titles, dates and times in reverse order.

A conversation, a story, a plot developing. References to the Tinkering. A sense of challenge and bravado. Talk of wondering, the Tinkering wonders. Diagrams too: boxes and lines, scribbles and annotations. Arrows emerging from circles for other circles or doubling back.

Mal at the bedroom door with glasses of juice, taking intense care for keeping them unspilt.

I must keep looking, hope Mal is kay with it.

'Is that Bapa's stuff?' Mal asks by my side.

'Um, I … is it?'

'It's okelah. Maybe Bapa does need a Cure, like Ibu says. Promise you'll look after me while Bapa and Ibu are away?'

'Mal, I—'

'Promise.'

'I will.' I'm deflecting, even tasting a little dirty for it, but there's a garbage mine of stuff on the puter.

Here: a diagram more orderly than the others. Something mathematical about it. Symbolic squiggles. A formal arrangement of small circles orbiting a larger one in the centre. The smaller ones have labels like *agent* and *masquerader*. The label in the large circle reads: *The Reck*.

Throat

'Beast of Burden' — The Rolling Stones

Ben Evoli ...

AWAKE, THIS FRUIT OF MIND OF ME. Pouring in taking shape becoming again out of the fugginess.

Salty sea air, a waft of a fresh catch of seafood air-drying. In louring light, I look for an open window, a view for an ocean.

Lying on something soft, accommodating. Trying for sitting up on elbows. Wrists in cuffs. Pull my feet and feel restraints around ankles. Head full of scraping from the inside, revolving, and heaving. Fall back on the couch. The urge for vomiting deadens.

A bolt of anxiety, flight or fright, muscle memory. A circle of blue-wing angels closing in. A violet exit. A mobile spooky field. Hesitating before taking the step. Then someone pushing me in.

Maddox. Janking Maddox.

My eyes adjusting. Six or 7 couches in an arc, one every 2 metres or so. Beyond the couches are 3 files of large contraptions. Each raking back at a 45-degree angle. Each with a curving transparent hood. Soft light inside them reveals elaborate couches. On some of those recline inert bodies unaware of the looms of tubes surrounding and penetrating them.

Head spins. Cough against nausea.

Shadowy shapes. A hilly lump. Willowing figures sway. Thin hot filaments in a pair of weak light bulbs. The filaments move. The bulbs become alien eyes with horizontal slip-shape pupils. A purple arm. Changing colour. Blending in camouflage with cream walls and a grey chair in the distance. Make out the outline of a tentacle. Suckers wet and questioning, probing where suckers should never probe.

Cough. Gag. Double up, holding my stomach in. Dribbles from the corners of my mouth become drowning gushes.

'An adverse reaction against the merge,' a voice hisses.

A medical nurse floats like a cherub in left of vision. Her face glows. Firm insistent hands push my shoulders back. Trustworthy hands.

'More nutes.' Another slithery voice.

Cherub Nurse pushes a black cone over my nose and mouth. Taste an acrid smell. Tiny pins in my nostrils. A cold jet in the anal passage. Nutes passing in.

Cream walls turning dark. Tunnel vision.

Blackness.

'You're awake.' A snake-hiss voice. Caracia Svakhaska squats on a wet pallet jammed beside the couch. Behind her are 2 ranks of neos, 4-wide, like an assemblage of choristers—Caracia's Voices of Arms.

Caracia.

Maddox.

Together Caracia and Maddox put me here. 'Janking Maddox!' A hoarse whisper.

'There's no blaming Maddox,' speaks a Voice out of the dim light, like the breath of a ghost.

'If it makes you feel any better,' speaks another, 'the Maddox sybil acts from genuine belief he is aiding you.'

Tentacles—2 or 3—slithering and sucking, leave trails of snotty brine over my fruit.

'Tastes good,' 3 voices say from behind the hulk of Caracia. 'Real. No sybil.'

Her body rises over. Foretaste the worst kind of slimy suffocation. Clench my teeth. Her arms feed me towards her beak-mouth.

'Are we so detestable?' A flat statement coming from the edges of another universe.

Shudder. Pull myelf inwards away from my skin—the skin the suckers palpitate.

'Are we so repulsive?'

Caracia lifts an arm; swivels and curls it, examining. 'Are we a monster in one of your science fiction stories, Ben? The ones from sap pop culture, the ones you are so fond of? Stories of alien monsters from other worlds?'

Exhale some of the tension when she lets go. Breath escapes in a hoarse roar.

'We find those stories ignorant. The strangest of creatures are here already. On earth. Who needs exotic aliens when jocks are still playing Jai Alai? Who needs far-flung galaxies when the diversity of terrestrial reality is more alien than fiction? There are no true aliens in those stories, only trivial variations of the human form. Silly variations.'

The Voices lapse into a babbling and wheezy laughing. ... 'things with multiple hearts' .... 'gills for nasal slits' ... 'pointy ears' ... 'bushy eyebrows' ... 'penises for noses' ...

'There is nothing so alien as the diversity of life on earth, within easy reach,' the Voices say in loose coherence. 'Soon we'll take any shape; incorporate the biology of other creatures into ours; experience the world as they might; and reflect on humanity from the shapes we create, and the psychologies we evolve. It all starts with us, Ben. With my octopus fruit and its ability for editing its own RNA. Within a generation, we could be eagles or kangaroos; experience the heights of the sky; the depths of the ocean, the heat of volcanos, and the cold of Antarctic ice; in ways human biology could never experience. What a wonder! Let's have true aliens, Ben. And let them be us.'

A sucker caps my glans, lifts it. She could be about to yank my whole zakar from my groin and make a morsel of it. 'If there is a Gawd, she should prevent us from escaping into space until we understand and protect our own cradle, and every form of life in it,' the Voices say in a strange round robin. 'If we think we can leave, we'll just treat earth like a cosmic outhouse toilet. We'll ruin it and leave.'

Fighting panic. Fighting the flight response for spooking—anywhere—even for the moon as Mal dreams for one day.

A Voice writhes in time with one of Caracia's arms, waving towards the only exit from the room. 'There's no one for saving you.' Its whole fruit pulses. 'No one of importance following you,' another speaks callously.

A Voice sprays seawater from a large bottle over Caracia. 'Can you remember?' she asks. She's the prettiest of the 8, incongruous in this monster-mash cast.

'Remember what?' Still a broken edge in my voice. No air in it.

The Voices sway like trees in a wind. 'You see our aura?'

There is no aura. No one flutherbombs Caracia or her attendants.

'We enjoy privacy. Join us.' Drawing me into their Mindspace.

Losing sense of hearing and of space, of up or down. Arms and legs disconnect and float out there, somewhere, unsure. Mouth and anus closer together, organs push under pressure through my neck, into my skull, bones turning mushy, swelling.

Vomiting. They release me from Mind like dropping a catch from a net on the deck of a fishing boat. Gasp and gag for clearing airways.

The 8 make a wheezy repetitive noise. Is it laughter? Caracia's eyes glisten and seem to inflate or bulge. One pupil slit dilates. She tilts her enormous head, and the pupils reorient horizontal.

Her consciousness so alien. Was this how it was for the early saps, when first joining Minds in onespace, discovering how alien was everyone else's inner world?

'You remember,' one Voice says. Another … 'The shape of it is disturbing.' … 'Disappointing.' … 'Ironic.'

I say, 'I remember.' Catching up. Ice stabbing my nuts, chilling my spleen. While I'm chugging up bile, Caracia's Voices are in my head too. Feel the after-burn of her sucker-prints on my memories. Everything about contacting the Reck while stalling Maddox in Montana. Everything about Bunny while, at the same time, everything about Lành Hiền. Clashing memories, falling over each other, covering, scratching, melding, merging into others.

'I have sybil memories.' Crying out in anguish.

'Yes.'

'Why inflict this on me?' Blubbering. Grieving for a perverse loss of innocence. All these unwelcome memories of another me. Anak anak at the farm. Bunny dying horribly.

'We need you integrated. We need you full with experience.'

'But the sybil dies,' I wail. 'You kill it. I watch it die.'

'No. You prune your sybil. You learn fast under stress, mindwriter.'

'So how—?' Gulp. The obvious answer comes in the middle of framing the question.

'There are many such sybils. Here, in this crèche. Maddox's wants you for a willing participant. He makes many attempts, many failures. Many sybils.'

'He kills the failures.'

'No. He is too soft for such violence. We all are. We never kill.'

'Is nothing too low for Infinites? Throw-away sybils for sexual pleasures; saps for food …' A new memory, sickening, tasting foreign. 'A private golf course …'

'Ah yes, golf. You think we might excel at such a game? We are so many arms for swinging the clubs.'

'Is this all a joke? Kidnapping me?'

'How else might we swim for the seabed of such a mess? He never has the beak for this assignment. His bony-arm methods bring on the exact failure we anticipate.'

Feel cold on my skin. A breeze circulates in the huge spiralling space. 'Where is this?'

'My dear Puffin,' a Voice answers, sounding perfectly like Maddox. All indulge in a wheezy snigger. 'We find so many sybils of you here.' 'One can only imagine how he might toy with a short-life version of your yellow-tan ass.'

'Where is this?' I plead with hoarse tongue and lung.

'Are you without a single guess? You must be still half asleep.' 'Look around.' 'Look closer.'

The light brightens in the occupied booths, sharpening the fractal planes of the repetitive rows. Patients in them have a plastic quality. Maddox. Of various ages and weights. Sybils. 'What the jank?'

'Maddox's crèching facility.' 'Quite primitive by modern standards, it's how he keeps it secret even among secret installations.' 'It took some time finding this place.' 'With Maddox remaining unhelpful and Orlando outside of my reach.' 'Why is an old crèche always in the last place you look?'

'Stop. Please. Stop.'

'We must applaud Maddox—' Two of Caracia's tentacles make a parody of hands clapping. '—he's good for keeping secrets off grid, as the saps say.'

'Tell me. Are there more of my sybils here?'

'Those poor saps have no idea of what *on grid* is or how un-grid-like it is at all.'

'Are there more of my sybils here? Tell me.'

'Here? No longer.' 'We feed all in a sucky bin. Have no worry of more sybils. We have all the information we need now.'

Almost vomit again. Swallow back. The question is almost too terrifying. 'Is it a sucky bin for me too?'

'Yes.' … 'We are yet for deciding.' … 'No, never. Why would we?' … 'It's an interesting question.' … 'What matters it? If we let you leave, the nurses will round you up.' … 'Perhaps we'll make a gift of you for the nursing missions.' 'In time.'

In time?

 Tinatin Jamalova …

'Ben. Pull your meat in.'

'Tinatin? I taste nothing of you following me.'

'Nothing of me is. Never mind. Move.'

'How'd you find my vectors?'

'From one of Caracia's Voices.'

'She lets you taste?'

'A reputable supplier of certain curiosities enjoys certain liberties.' A pause. 'You must escape before Caracia's security detail arrives.'

Ben haunches up on an elbow, winces, yanks his hand against the wrist cuff.

I tell him, 'Her arms are 6 to 2 against letting you go.'

'Those sycophants decide my fate?'

'No. Her actual arms.'

'And they vote?'

'A distributed brain makes for difficult explanations.'

Ben pulls against all the cuffs around his wrists and ankles. 'How will I escape?'

'Help is coming. Be alert when it arrives.'

He might faint. He's so slack jaw he might drool. His eyes clamp closed; furrows corrugate his forehead.

I memb, 'Stay with me.'

The sound of double doors bursting in arrives with a column of light landing on Ben's naked fruit. Long shadows like throbbing octopuses cast over Ben's couch, darkening his startled, wide-open eyes.

'Too late,' Ben membs.

'You must stall.'

'Know any good card tricks?' Ben laughs, a cackle of desperation.

A nurse looks on as 2 large, heavy-set, stubbly chinned guards in black unstrap Ben's restraints. One hooks an arm under his armpit and sits him up. The nurse swings his legs off the couch. Together the guards lift Ben on his feet. He almost crumples on the ground. When the guards take his weight and lift him, he's up like a diver off a springboard, but short is his vitality as they drag him out like a limp puppet.

'Where are you taking me?'

With heavy feet, the guards stride down a rigid-straight corridor dragging Ben, their pace too brisk for him to work his feet.

'Could you find me some clothes?'

Passing doors, left and right, until they stop at a pair with a distinctive metal-polish sheen. The nurse pushes a button on the wall, which lights up. The sound of a bell bings. The shiny doors slide open. Beyond is a small square room for fitting no more than 14 in a huddle.

Panic jolts Ben. 'They're gonna suffocate me in box,' he membs.

'It's an elevator, Ben.'

'An elevator? Where are we?'

'One of Maddox's crèches. Caracia says so before.'

'Why the jank needs he an elevator?'

His captors drag Ben into the claustrophobic transport.

Ben's eyes widen despite the nutes in him. 'These are no projections.' Feeling the ripple of muscles against him. Noticing his androgynous fruit is pressing back the guards' uniforms rather than vanishing underneath. The guards' appearances are perfect in the surroundings.

'No,' I agree.

'Saps?'

The elevator gives a grunt. An electric whir follows.

'It's moving,' Ben confirms.

There's a moment where Ben's face wears the wonder of a child on a slippy slide for the first time. Despite imminent danger, he's soaking up the novelty, probably going off on revelry, romantic for the way things might have been in sap times. His nostalgia fuels my reputation every time I find him something sap and collectible.

The nutes are winning over Ben's consciousness. I say, 'Stay awake. I need for tasting what's going on.'

'Help me.'

The elevator car slows and stops. Doors slide open. Ben makes a brief effort for walking with his captors, who again are too brisk, and leave his feet behind.

In another identical corridor with no arc or curve anywhere. Mathematically straight. Doors are all rectangles. The ceiling panelling too. Obvious, the facility's design is for the comfort of saps. Sap thinking is all angles and corners. Straight lines and fences. Boundaries and limits. Poor things. Any wonder spooking steamed their brains. After all these centuries, their options for moving about the world is travelling over every mim. Every blade of grass. Every ant. Every flake of dead skin. It's what keeps them safe, this inability to spread. This off-griddiness. We just spook around and through them, never noticing they are there.

The leading nurse bangs open a pair of double doors, holds it open for the guards and Ben. The room is like the one Ben awakes in. It has only a single harsh examination table under strong lights. There are no couches. Only cribs with curving transparent lids leaning back. Life support under. Daleks might sleep so, the squishy little octopods lying back on a triangular pallet, safe in a suit of glassy pyjamas instead of their normal daytime exterminating wear.

One crib's canopy is open hinging back. Ben realises it's his destination. His breathing becoming chaotic, he struggles for the first time; pulling and twisting, lifting his feet up and thrashing. His relatively slight boyish build is no match against 2 full-grown saps.

'Put him on the slab,' the nurse commands, her voice deep and rasping, the sound of decades in her vocal cords.

The guards throw Ben on the table easier than a limp doll. From a fridge the nurse retrieves a small nutepak, one with a nozzle. Ben's hips jolt when she fits it and squeezes. His resistance drains as the nutes work through him.

'I'm going into there,' he slurs. 'Like her. And her.'

'Ben, so sorry, Ben.'

'And her.' His eyes are darting around the room, examining each crib, his last act of defiance before he too takes a couch in a crib. 'And her—what the jank?'

'What, Ben. What?'

'Know her. Know these ones.'

'Who?'

Pan around from Ben's view. With Ben's ever-clouding awareness, I'm unable for gaining a bearing on where he's looking. The crib? There's someone he recognises here?

The next one? The next one? Holy janking ass of Saint Ronald McDonald.

'Perawat detektif,' Ben drools.

Ben Evoli ...

Nice nutes. Calming. Tension ebbing away. Struggle tastes silly.

Sweetness. Cuddly sweetness. Hug me, Cherub Nurse, fatty sap with such overgrown payudara pushing out the top of your uniform. Hug me, sap guards. Give no thought for how bad you stink. Strong cheese and rotting pork. Okelah. Let's cuddle.

Lights turning low. Going fuzzy. Will you tuck me in, Cherub Nurse? I'd like it.

What's all this noise? A guard says, *gerg*. Lies on the floor. The other lies down alongside. Mmmmm, I'll come down there for a cuddle.

Hands holding me back, pinning me on the slab. Two more guards. Where's Cherub Nurse? Oh, on the floor too?

Shhhh! Not so loud!

'He's out of his melon,' someone says.

'OK, let's carry him.'

'Should we put clothes on him?'

'What? Are we taking him to the opera? Let's get out of here.'

Saf Evoli ...

'You were at the human farm when it exploded,' the ugly sap Christian Zappa says with booming tongue and lung. 'I saw the holly.'

'You see gogs?' Bapa asks, his voice—after the sap's cavern of an accusation—sounding like a tweety little bird's.

The sap looks pissy at Bapa. 'There's quite a search party out after you.'

Bapa's fright is all over his face. 'Already?'

'I hear nurses are mad at you. Who knows how they'll react.'

Bapa sinks back into overstuffed cushions in a low boxy couch. The room is a decorator's nightmare. Busy fabrics, in garish colours of exotic flowers and tropical birds. Everything else—walls, floors, ceilings, furniture—is timber. Timber! From cut-down trees. Where one timber surface begins and another ends, is anyone's guess. All sense of perspective muzzes. It tastes like the walls are closing in. The only things seeming far away are the windows. Tiny windows perhaps only 3 or 4 times larger than the projection screens (like Mal's bodoh puter screen) sitting on desks, hanging from walls and ceiling.

'Don't worry,' Christian tells Bapa from behind a broad timber bar. Shelves and shelves of bottles on a mirror-wall which reflects jags of timber and glass. 'The octopus won't cross the border,' Christian says as he stoops and pulls bottles from a fridge. 'Though I'm sure she wants you back.'

'She wants me dead,' Bapa says like he's preparing hiself for it.

'I doubt it. More likely she wants you as a bargaining chip against the nurses. She's always collecting people as leverage. In any case, she won't dare invade sap territory.'

'How can you be so sure?' Good question, Bapa.

'I'm a sap, remember? Savage and uncontrollably violent. I destroy everything in sight, bent on the extinction of everything. The boogey man, the *Maricoxi*, the Bigfoot of the Amazon. Big and hairy, and I'll eat children. Or in Caracia's case, I'll throw her on the largest fire pit you ever saw.'

'You would?' Bapa asks, all too credulous.

'I might,' Christian says with no lack of mischief. 'In any case, it would go very badly for her. I wish I could say the same for those feverish nursing police.' The sap sets 2 glasses on the bar. 'They could be bad for us. Our existence is no longer secret. Neither is our role in industries better hidden from nurses ...'

'Alamak,' Bapa says in his way when something surprises him. 'No followers. Flutherbombing you is impossible. Nurses are incapable of monitoring your actions, so Infinites employ you for tasks best for keeping out of sight.'

'What can I say? It's a living.'

'Like ... crèches. At Maddox's, the only neos I saw were Caracia and her Voices. The medical staff, security ... everyone else there are ... your kind.'

'If by *my kind*, you mean humans then yes, the day-to-day operations of all crèches around the world are performed by my kind. As are all covert functions in all contentious businesses. Anything the Infinites cannot afford to let the nursing police see.'

'Where are we?' Bapa asks. 'Must be somewhere remote. How is it Infinites find you in the first place?'

Christian shrugs. 'We told them.' Drops clinking cubes of ice into the glasses, selects a bottle of clear liquid from the shelves behind. 'We saw the benefit we could be for one another. It is so for generations.'

'Nurses will accuse you of aligning with Infinites, with enabling sickness.'

'I fear it will be war.'

'We wage no wars,' Bapa says. 'Saps do. Neo budaya is peaceful.'

'*Budaya?* Speak Cali English, Ben. I can't gog translations straight out of my head.'

'*Culture.* Neo *culture* is peaceful.'

Christian scoffs and chokes a laugh. Gulps his grog down. 'Culture is the feathers on the beast. It demarcates tribes. Violence is baked into the heart of the monster.'

'We make no weapons. We have no militia missions.'

'Only because you deny the innate nature you share with us.' The sap comes out from behind the bar. Advances on Bapa and hands him a glass. 'Gin and tonic right? *The bubble gum of cocktails,*' Christian says as if he's quoting someone.

Bapa accepts the drink, grateful. Sips. 'We're different. A new species.'

'A species of children. I mean, just listen to what you mangas call things. A verging field is a *spooky* field.' Christian makes his voice go high saying *spooky*. 'A fabricator is a *fabby*. Such childish names. *Hancies, hollies* ... You live for centuries—what are you, immortal jellyfish? Even the oldest skip everywhere. Every town has a petting zoo of the dullest animals. Tigers would rather lick ears than tear limb from limb. And camels? Why in the name of Outback Steakhouse are camels wandering your streets?'

'You tell me. Saps created *Shazzan*.'

'Imagine so much camel crap. You must have some shit-scooping robot following them around.'

'We call them scheissies. *Scheisse* is German for *kotoran*.'

'There's not an adult among you. It's frightening.'

'Frightening?'

'You're children. Children are incapable of moderating emotions. Which is all fine while you're playing. But when you get angry, I mean really angry, if you ever start fighting ... We'll see. Now our existence is known, every human settlement on earth will be under threat.'

'There are more desa like this?'

'Uncountably more. Never let the square-box buildings and electrical wiring fool you. This is certainly more than a village.'

'How is it we never learn of you?'

'How would you? There are no satellites up there anymore. You have no planes. You move point-to-point in an instant. Millions of you could spook from one side of our territory to the other—a journey of days for us—in the blink of an eye, oblivious of what's in between. You never travel anywhere, as in take a path through the world on a journey. Fuck!' Christian grapples with understanding. 'How many of you ever go outside and sit under a tree? No, the common manga spends every tik perving on others with apparently better lives, hoping to spy a few moments of entertainment. You're so busy vicariously observing at a distance, we're as good as non-existent. So, as long as we don't fly planes over your cities, your complete self-absorption guarantees our privacy.'

'You have planes?'

Christian laughs. 'None of you mangas understands human humour.'

'We understand humour just fine.'

'You don't understand saps are capable of it too.'

'No planes then.'

'No technology at all that might call attention to ourselves. We could re-acquire the knowledge for it all, but it would be too conspicuous. We know our time as apex predators is over, and we're better for it. We've retired—into jungles, mountain valleys, remote beaches—to muse on life as it was and marvel at what you youngsters are doing with the place.'

'Cleaning up your mess.'

'Both our ancestors' mess, yes. Your ancestors too. Like I said, we're in retirement and we're better for it.'

'You explode buildings and kill. What's a busy Tuesday like for you? Breakfast at 7, bingo at 9, terrorism then buttered scones for tea?'

'I'm opposed to violent activism. It raises our profile and risks much.'

'Look, I find the whole concept of eating sap—human—meat as appalling as you do.'

'I doubt it. The farmed children you saw will need constant care for the rest of their days. Generations of genetic manipulation forces accelerated growth. At a developmental age of teenagers, when these poor creatures reach reproductive maturity, growth stops. In all cases, skeletons are weak and deformed, digestive systems can't handle anything requiring chewing, which is just as well, since tooth enamel is thin and roots shallow. Lungs are underdeveloped and the reproductive systems are beset by diseases only a writer of horror stories could imagine. All due to your gene mods. But, happy days! I hear they are delicious.'

'I'm sorry.'

Christian makes a snort, like an animal. 'You were touring that farm.'

'A sybil toured that farm.'

'Forgive me if I fail to see the distinction.'

Bapa shudders. 'I have its memories … they're like my own. As vivid and visceral as being present.'

'And you call us monsters.'

'I want none of those memories. I never live those experiences.'

'Your sybil made you do it, is that your defence? An exact duplicate did whatever you're now ashamed of. I know you'd visit that obscene farm like a tourist, all the same.'

'I'm appalled. I must—it, the sybil must—know how they're run. Maddox and Piloto hope I might find it all somehow acceptable, less horrific.'

'The sooner you accept who you are … You might as well get past moping,' Christians says. 'You are in the middle of something; that much is clear. Factions of Infinites squabble over you. The health police too. Everyone says you tampered with the Reckoning.'

Bapa sets his drink down, shakes his head. 'There'll be no convincing anyone for the contrary. Nurses and Infis alike feel power slipping away.'

'Mangas are not so different from our mutual ancestors. Fear drives you as much as ever.'

Bapa nods. Drains his drink, thrusts the glass at Christian who takes the hint to make more. 'You see no auras, yes?' Bapa asks.

'It's all thin air to me.'

'There are spies following me—' *Shhh!* Bapa.

'Unlikely. We brought you here unconscious; rediscovering your vectors will be very difficult.'

Except I have a friend like Bonehead, who has something new in her brain. For some weeks, she's finding all kinds of animals through onespace. Cats in our desa. Where Kaboobie is at any time of day. We test her, and she never fails. Before long she can find horses across the world. Horses! Other animals, too. The greater their Mind, the easier for locating. Dolphins and whales and apes are simple. Neos are easy for Bonehead. And Mal: Mal is the same. Maybe his fits and fever connect with it. We see you Bapa, and we love you. Come back for us, please come back for us.

'Since … the crèche. Caracia's attendants are following me. For some reason, my filters have no effect on them.'

Christian nods as if he expects something like this. 'I'll handle Caracia.'

Bapa accepts his replenished glass. Christian looks straight at Bapa, eye at eye. I guess that's how saps are because they have no fluthers or membing. 'Are you manipulating the Reck?'

'How about we ask another question. Is the Reck manipulating me?'

'Isn't that its gig?' Christian says like he believes he's being clever. 'Oh, come, Ben. It can't be coincidence The Reck begins behaving radically around the time you start looking into it.'

Bapa looks as if Christian slaps his face.

'No manga thinks it is impartial,' Christian says, 'yet all of you are beholden to it in one way or another. What's amusing is how it has no ultimate power. You could ignore it, if you had the will, or switch it off. Yet all you can imagine is tweaking and fiddling it a little. But *you*—somehow whether you acknowledge it or not—*you* not only tweaked it, you also fundamentally changed it. No manga's reputation—wealth, by any other name—is as it was. The Infinites reputations are *falling*. All except for you and one other, whose sybils are on ice in a crèche across the river. The same crèche I rescued you from. You show up in the most interesting of places, Ben the mindwriter.'

'What is your want of me?'

'Perhaps the same as Caracia: as a bargaining chip against the day the nursing police come skipping into our homes. Perhaps you can influence the Reck to protect our continued survival. Let there be no mistake; your kind—in one way or another, for one excuse or another—would be happy to enslave us, eat us, jail us, make us circus clowns, or simply cut to the final act, and exterminate us. Any advantage I might press by using you, I have an obligation to humanity to do so.'

This sap is a boring, membosankan gas bag.

'I am a prisoner?' Bapa asks, swallowing. He looks so small and vulnerable alongside the beast.

Christian laughs long and loud. 'How would you leave? There's no verging—*spooky*—field generators here. The only way out is to walk. But in which direction? Back for Maddox's crèche and Caracia? Into the unknown? It's weeks of walking through jungle to a safe verging station. Suppose you could verge home, what would you find? Your scheming wife? Maddox? The White Witch? Who is left to return to?'

Tears in my Bapa's eyes. Spilling. Flowing like acid through the grime on his face. He gasps for breath. Poor Bapa. His chests heaves and lurches. With great effort he steadies his breathing. Defiance in his eyes, unrecognisable. My Bapa bows his head and says, 'My children.'

'Saf, tell no one,' Bonehead says with offensive calm making her more long-face than ever. She looks uncaring. Her bunny teeth are almost carnivorous.

'Saps are keeping my bapa prisoner, Bonehead!'

'They're angry. How would we react of someone is eating our little baby ones? How ghastful!' She's shaking with the horror of it.

I'm far from letting her off for being so indifferent about Bapa. 'How is it different from pork or camel?'

'Saf.'

'My bapa! They are keeping my bapa. We must rescue him.'

'How? Will we just skip into the Amazon jungle and hope we find him up a tree somewhere?'

'Maybe you should talk with dolphins like Mal,' I mock. 'There's something weird about you and Mal.' So many things I'm distraught about. Bapa. Bonehead becoming more like Mal … my precious friend feels more remote than ever.

'Look around, Saf. Anak anak are showing like … I dunno, it's hard explaining … we're evolving, like Mal's dolphins tell him.'

'You believe him? You're always the one saying how weird he is. Now look. You believe every bent-brain thing he says. You should go marry him, have an astronaut's wedding on the moon while I'm figuring out how I get my bapa back.'

'Saf, stop it. I love you; you know I love you. Please, we're in this thing together.' She kisses my forehead. I ache for her kisses everywhere. Kiss away my pain.

I say, 'Us and the dolphins.'

'Stop being dank.'

'Bonehead, my bapa!'

Bonita 'Bonehead' Patatiall …

'We must tell someone,' Saf insists.

'And risk nurses finding out? You already forget Jaya?'

Saf has no answer.

Movement in the park. Kaboobie keeps licking the electric roses, never registering they'll jolt him every time. Farther back in the park come Mal and Lành Hiền. Mal wears a determined frown. Lành Hiền is serene and bitching pretty as ever. Why should she get the perfect hair?

I say, 'What is she, his babysitter?'

Saf looks around. 'Eee-yer. Are they holding hands?'

'His girlfriend, he believes. Gross.'

'Well, she saves his life and helps us with Jaya.' Why is Saf defending Lành Hiền?

'You have a crush on her too. Your whole family loves a dragon.' Okelah, I agree she's hot. I could love a dragon.

'Hi yeer, Bonehead. Saudara.' Mal is, at last, membing. Without the assistance of a hancy. The quality of his voice-in-Mind has none of the buzz around the edges hancies produce. His is more the voice of Gawd, if Gawd is 17-year-old Malay boy.

'Say nothing,' Saf warns me.

'I know what's going on with Bapa,' Mal membs. 'I watch you watching him. Gentle has a plan.'

Vör Hoyur …

In outpatients At Carlsberg Minster, I bang through the public door field, on a shortcut for our team's chambers. With none of them onsite, this's an opportunity for fossicking about and performing some old-fashion, on-the-beat detective work. Who harbours any secrets of Eir? Could be any of them. Everyone else is in the team longer than me.

'Excuse me, Vör Face.' It's Nurse Constance Greenkeeper from Reception. I flutherbomb her at the long desk where 3 receptionists serve. Constance smiles weakly. She fears she might unduly interrupt me.

'Something arrives via spooky station. It's … paper …' She holds up an envelope only a slight longer than her hand.

'I'll collect it when I leave.'

Reach for the envelope, turn it over, pick at it. How for making it open?

'May I assist?' Constance asks.

I memb, 'I got it.' Rip a strip from its narrow side, tip and shake it for ejecting the contents. A sheet of paper folded once. Words handwritten in blue ink.

Unlimited benevolence rides a mustang
Go forward! Go ford!
To where the rubber fails to hit the road

Take me to the river

Cryptic messages? Who would send such a thing?

The paper survives spooking, without ending up in a feedstock bin; it must have DNA lacing through it. For material as rare and personal as paper, the DNA will be the writer's.

Teodora Mrowka …

A series of boxy multi-deck buildings once airport terminals. Changi Minster should be easy navigating, but we arrive unwary of the lengths our Kementerian Kesahatan hosts might take for delaying our arrival at the conference. We should realise they'd consider Ben their own business and no one else's.

Vör stops mid-skip. 'Is this the right station?' she asks in the tone of an accusation.

Under a low white domed canopy, we're on a mezzanine level, overlooking a network of paths winding through a tropical forest garden. The rush of a waterfall mutes all other sound as it falls 40 metres from an oculus in the dome.

I memb a nurse scurrying by. 'Excuse me, Face. Please, direct us for the playroom? We're late for a meeting.'

The nurse snorts and throws her hand rightward and continues away with her haste. Vör sets off down a slippy slide for the ground floor.

Flannel Tomms …

'I should be at the table,' Lành Hiền Rồng complains again. 'I'm the one who discovers the evidence against Ben.'

I say, 'Ben the Reck Manipulator,' too smug.

'Because of me!' The girl is insufferable. Damming her indignity, she heaves about, rubbernecking over her shoulder at the proceedings.

'Stop being hissy,' I dash. 'We're fortunate being here at all.'

'Ben's our Infi, Flannel. They should be consulting someone from Bandar Melambai. If I'm lacking in experience, then it should be you.'

As if any Singapore heavyweights would acknowledge a desa clinic procomplement.

The conversation around the table is becoming an inquisition against the KK. Other delegates suspect we're stalling. Keeping investigations regarding Ben and the Reck for ourelves. Lành Hiền almost leaps in outrage when Fanny Qiu—one of Changi's most reputable missionaries—quibbles about the quality of evidence we have against Ben. She argues against blithely trusting the provenance of the 2-dimensional documents on Mal's iMac. Without mentioning Lành Hiền by name, of course. Admitting such a fresh regional field nurse is the one who breaks the case open would be too much a loss of face for anyone at Changi.

'We advise more analysis,' Fanny concludes.

Lành Hiền sits on her hands, knits her eyebrows into trusses stiff enough for supporting a bridge, and clamps her mouth shut with a tight-lip grimace.

'Please explain once more this puter's storage,' Qamra el-Yousef interjects again. She's one of the delegates from *Jameiat Shamal 'Tifriqia Alsihiya*. 'How are these documents—emails, they called them? Why are they unreachable from any of our magazines?'

The meeting's Present Invisible, Grace Pang, shakes her head, reluctant as any Present Invisible should be, for direct influence on the proceedings. A reluctance which belies her nickname among regional minsters: Grasping Grace.

Leaning across the coffee table, I restrain Lành Hiền from launching herelf into the fray. 'I can explain,' she protests.

'Sit down and be quiet. No one up there will pay any attention, and our camerata is fine with it.'

Lành Hiền fumes, slumps into the couch. Too junior, too far from Singapore. And too pretty. Her lips should be thinner, her nose flatter. Her eyebrows have no right being so symmetrical.

'What?' Lành Hiền says, tasting a trace of my thoughts.

'You're too pretty. There, I say it.'

'Are you serious?'

Already regretting these stray thoughts, I fight the urge for doubling down and defending. I memb, 'Would it hurt so much if you cut your hair?' becoming my own worst enemy. 'I mean, I never see a nurse so feminine.'

'It's just me,' Lành Hiền rejoins, with altogether too much smugness.

'Just try looking a little less like Senjougahara Hitagi, huh?'

'Who?'

Wanting the conversation over I say, 'Gog her.'

Lành Hiền giggles, finding images of the anime character. 'I guess I'm pretty close,' she says with more delight than is safe. 'Maybe I should colour my hair mulberry.'

Vör Hoyur …

We're sure we're setting off in the wrong direction. Everyone we ask is less than generous with help, squinting with suspicion at our insignias. In the face of such animosity Teo stops while she gogs for plans of the minster. She casts a holly out in front, screws her nose at the lack of fidelity, and crushes it out with a clap of her hands. Her fingers wiggle as she rifles through more hollies in her head. 'Ah,' she membs, casts another translucent model out at navel height, and resumes her skipping with the holly in front like a shopping trolley.

Through open-plan clinics, recreational areas, and admin clusters; through throngs of rainbow uniforms and the occasional patient in a jumpsuit, we follow a wide snaky corridor till it meets a T-section.

'Clockwise,' Teo membs and skips off down a rigidly straight narrow hall which presses us among a traffic of nurses with long purposeful skips and sharp elbows. They gruffly scowl through Teo's holly. The hall opens onto another long square deck. A path through functional spaces bends left and traces aside flat floor-for-ceiling windows overlooking parklands alongside the minster. I tell Teo, 'Look,' pointing at a spooky station nestling in lush greenery. Proof the KK are janking with our arrival.

She shakes her head. 'I wonder how many more we'll see before we find the conference.'

We pass 2 more spooky stations on the way. After passing through another claustrophobic hall into a 3rd building, we're standing before a large glass wall affording a view into a cavernous rectangular space the full height of the building, and which has views outdoors on 3 sides.

I say, 'The Playground,' while pondering the Red Chandelier, the dominating fixture in the space. Looking like a wireframe goblet, a Holy Grail of steel and rope, it squats on a pedestal, its imposing 15 or so metres reach up where it fastens and hangs from the roof. Looking up at it makes me dizzy. Inside the external weave are jungle gym structures, including a rope-and-metal double-helix net allowing climbing within. There are poles for sliding down.

It's one of the most neo things the saps ever built.

On the floor in front of the Chandelier is an oval conference table around which crowd more than 49 nurses casting out holly maps and engaging in animated, mostly silent, debate. Occasional shouts and cries of disagreement and exasperation escape throats. The odd bang on the table reverberates off the space's hard flat surfaces and punctures the peace.

'Well, we're here now,' Teo says and jumps feet-first into a tube opening in the glass, disappears with a whoop down the twisty slippy-slide. I jump into the 2nd of 2 tubes, coil down on my røv for the floor below.

Lành Hiền Rồng (Gentle Dragon) ...

Two nurses in Scandinavian uniforms pick themelves up from the slippy-tube landings. Vör Hoyur and Teodora Mrowka, both one-time members of the Eir Frijberg's team. The Eir who languishes in Vauxminster at Vör's instigation.

'Ah, you're here,' says Grace Pang's adjutant, Long Na, with ill-concealed disappointment, an emotion she shares with all her Singaporean colleagues bustling around the conference table.

'We come as quick as able,' Teo says without fluster while advancing on the table. Vör alongside is haughty. Trembling. Skittish. A sheen of sweat on her pale face. The corners of her mouth twitch. Everyone must see it. No one calls it out.

'You locate Ben?' asks Nishanka Abeywickrama of *Sri Lamkika Yahapivetma Kimareta*, drawing attention away from the late arrivals.

Fanny nods. 'Three days ago, our operatives trace him through family members,' she says, conjuring and throwing a relief map on the table.

'Operatives?' I hiss at Flannel. They're avoiding the shame of admitting a mere field nurse has the wherewithal for tracking Ben.

'Hush!' Flannel orders. 'Help me get a view over the table.' Without flutherbombing anyone at the table, panning our Mind's eye around even at close distance takes concentration.

'We last taste of Ben in this area of the Amazon Basin,' Fanny says, waving over forests on both banks of a gaping-wide river. More a large lake or a small sea. 'The Tapajós River.'

'An area covering 100's of square kims,' Yolanda San Martin Velázquez observes with dismay. She's from the Camerata *de Bem-Estar da Bacia Amazônica*. 'An area we leave wild since the time of the first neo.'

'Are there no settlements at all?' asks Pushpita Karmayoni of *Sri Lamkika*.

Yolanda waves at the map. Details of a few towns appear. 'Santarém here, where the Tapajós meets the Amazon.' On the map, the Tapajós is crystal clear; the Amazon channel is milk-coffee brown. Running near the Santarém shoreline, a sharp wiggly line marks where clear meets coffee like there is a crenellated partition dividing them. 'Here is Alter do Chão. From there it's over 200 kims upstream for Itaituba.'

'Nothing in between?' asks Grace Pang.

'No,' Carina Shinoda Hamada the 2nd delegate from the Amazon says with some pride, the bioluminescent ocelot stripes on face and hands pulsing. 'This is our Angkor Wat, our Machu Pichu, our Uluru. No one trudges over those anymore.'

'Centuries ago,' Yolanda explains, 'when the mission for recovering the Amazon Basin begins, we resolve for never resettling it. Only recovery missionaries would go in, mission encampments would be temporary, and use only demountable spooky stations which would come out on completion of reseeding.'

'Which is why it's a sap ghetto and a haven for nefarious Infi activities.' Since news of the existence of saps breaks out, everyone fears there are saps under their beds.

'Spooky stations?' Qamra checks.

Yolanda waves her hand over the map. Locations appear, densest in

Santarém, with Alter do Chão an outpost 2nd. A tiny settlement, Aramanai, has a single spooky station. 'These ones scattering around, where the Tapajós and the Arapuins merge, service tourists coming for the beaches.'

'Beaches? In the Amazon?' Fanny asks.

'*Sim*, some of the whitest most pristine beaches in the world,' Yolanda says. 'There are no stations between just south of Alter do Chão and Itaituba.'

Everyone falls silent contemplating. The Amazon delegates are relaxing, confident no one will propose an expedition into the rain forests.

'What about old sap settlements?' asks Yashasri Prayaga, the 3rd Sri Lankan delegate. 'Perhaps they might give us a clue. Can we gog those and overlay them on the map?'

Fanny looks at one of her KK subordinates who nods her head. Her eyes flutter, she goes deep into onespace. Everyone waits. The Amazon delegates look furtively about. The KK nurse emerges from her magazine search, sweeps her hand over the map. Two more spots appear on the east bank of Tapajós with labels hovering above: AVEIRO and UBIRACU.

'There's nothing there for centuries,' Carina advises.

'Wait!' It's Vör. She waves over the table, layering more detail over the map, then makes a pull-apart gesture with both hands for zooming in over Ubiracu. 'Here.' She points just south where her overlay shows grainy images of ancient ramshackle buildings. 'What was this place?'

Carina appears indignant, as if Vör reveals a dark family secret. 'Nothing. A failed social experiment on a rubber farm in the early 20th century.'

Vör seizes the moment with a madwoman grin. 'The name of the place? What is the name of the place?'

Carina looks for Yolanda, who offers no help. 'Fordlândia,' she says reluctantly.

'Fordlândia? As in Henry Ford, the sap mobil maker?' Vör asks. She pushes towards the table, 'This's where we'll find Ben.'

Eye

'Homosapien' — Pete Shelley

 *Vör Hoyur ...*

THE NOTE I RECEIVE IN KØBENHAVN—the paper with *Mor*'s DNA lacing through it so it will survive a spooking: now its cryptic message is plain.

Benevolence rides a mustang.

Benevolence means *Ben Evoli*. Quick and easy for decoding. Until the meeting in Changi, the rest is harder. I curse, for forgetting about Ben's Ford Mustang. With this, and the recent attention on the Amazon Basin, the rest unravels.

Go forward! Go ford!
To where the rubber fails to hit the road
Take me to the river

Go where Ford's rubber plantation fails. We must travel on the river. Boat up the Tapajós River. For Fordlândia.

 *Teodora Mrowka ...*

September through November are the hottest months in Santarém. Thirty-three degrees during the day. After dark the sky micturates all night into a warm blanket of 25-degree air. Tough enough for Eastern Europans like me.

464

Intolerable for Scandinavians. Passive climate control of environment sails and cross ventilation achieves only so much, and after tossing and turning through 3 sleepless nights, Vör relents and returns home, leaving me with Carina Shinoda Hamada preparing for our expedition up the Tapajós.

Vör should be under treatment. Her spookhead symptoms are plain for all. There are snide remarks among the team, and they all avoid her where possible, apart from a core few who derive fervour from Vör's rhetoric for destroying all sybils. They remind us all there'd be no Cuba discoveries without her, and it's Vör who puts the Amazon pieces together. This mission would never happen without her. The best course for me is marginalising her as best I'm able.

Gerlinde is among her closest allies, as is Beatrice. How those 2 ever end up on the same side demonstrates the potency of sharing a common enemy. Since discovering the crèche in the Cuban nuclear plant, Gerlinde has the zeal of a redeemed sinner.

After initial resistance, Camerata *de Bem-Estar da Bacia Amazônica* agrees our own *Fødererede Sundhedskamerata i Nordeuropa* should search for Ben. Also helping are our colleagues in Belém—and, by association, Tegucigalpa, Lima, and Buenos Aires—ever eager for one-upping the Singaporean KK. Negotiations shift significantly in our favour when we reveal the identity of the source for the bulk of the KK's intelligence about Ben. She's a noviciate field nurse from his hometown by the name of Lành Hiền Rồng. The KK are squirming in embarrassment all the more when news of it spreads across onespace. As a slap in the KK's face, Lima insists we invite Gentle Dragon (as her colleagues call Lành Hiền). Once we agree, Amazon Wellness green lights all our needs.

Within 14 days of resolving plans, we are only days away from casting off from Santarém and the journey south on the Tapajós; in search of Infi skulduggery, with special—if over-optimistic—eagerness for what lies in Fordlândia.

 *Vör Hoyur ...*

Well, almost ready. Weapons, Teo! Weapons! *Milde Moses!*

We already know from the sap farm, those hairy terrorists have explosives, and show no reluctance for cutting throats. We need weapons of our own. Who could say where or when we might encounter the warlike beasts?

'Having weapons is a far cry from developing skill with them,' Teo argues one night while we sip passionfruit batidas in an open-air bar in Santarém with a view west along the beach—a popular place for watching the saturating sunset. 'Or having the will for using them. We'll never develop the muscle memory for it. In the moment, we'll be too fearful. Or we'll use them in a panic and escalate conflict. We'll maim more of ourelves than our adversaries.'

'Then this expedition is a charade,' I memb. 'At some point we must use force and take what we want.'

'We become the things we promise ourelves we never would. Police. Militants. Taking property and denying liberty.'

Perhaps it's the pistol weighing heavy in my kangaroo pocket, rubbing my belly like a joey. In my thigh pocket clank 2 magazines of maybe the last bullets in the world. We must defend ourelves.

Teo's reluctance for confronting the looming possibility of violence makes her unfit for leading us in the Amazon. Of course, it should be me, but the joint health missions' leadership decides Teo (who, they observe also discovers the crèche in Juragua) is a safer choice.

'Besides, we have no time for developing weapons,' Teo states in a manner expecting an end of it. 'We should set out before our plans leak out.'

Such short sight, Teo. Whether we have weapons in time for the Tapajós is no argument against preparing for later hostility. We'll need weapons for wiping crèches off the face of the earth, for wiping out sybils. For wiping out Infis. For wiping away the stain in the 8 Car Garage.

Teodora Mrowka ...

Cíntia Ferreira Guimarães, captain of the river steamer the *Capivara,* shakes her head and contains her laughter. 'You'll have no need of those,' she says of the stacks of lightweight folding bicycles.

'These are all-terrain bikes,' Gerlinde answers back, stiffening at the captain's affront. 'Light and compact enough for fitting in a backpack.'

'Your idea of *all-terrain,*' mocks Cíntia, 'is a pile of dirty clothes on the floor comparing with Amazon terrain. You may as well believe you could paddle upstream with your asses in cereal bowls.'

Nurses carry the bikes on board anyway. Gerlinde, her fruit like a brick wall in rainbow paint, squares off with Cíntia.

'Leave the bikes on dock,' Cíntia counsels, showing no fear among so many detectives—a complacent disposition of many a neo since the Reck turns daffy. 'Perhaps some local children would enjoy them.'

Gerlinde huffs. There's no backing down for her either.

'Look,' I intercede. 'We'll spook them back for Catedral de Nossa Senhora,'—the principal clinic in Santarém— 'the tik we discover how useless they are.'

'Assuming the demountable spooky station keeps working.'

Cast side-eye at the translucent tent-like enclosure of the demountable, where techs are running late with firing up the spooky field. Still unsure about placing it on the foredeck of the barge where it will catch all the wave spray when we are moving.

'The thing must be farthest away from my steamer,' Cíntia says, putting her foot down about it. 'If it loses containment and starts eating the barge, I have time for cutting loose.' The *Capivara* is Cíntia's lifelong mission. Her ageing 3-deck river steamer. In sap days, whole fleets would run this part of the river system. Now, few neos have the patience for travelling anywhere when the can spook faster than it takes for swallowing. Which is all for saying we have few choices of vessel for nudging the barge upstream.

'On this river there are waves so tall you'd think you're out on open sea,' Cíntia warns. None of us suspect her of exaggerating.

Vör Hoyur ...

Coming across the gangway after the bikes are crates of cat field generators of the type Eir commissions for crowd control at the Infinite's Inductee Gala. No one knows if they will work on sap physiology but, needing hope against violent saps, we'll each carry one as a last measure.

Next are the portable spooky fields, for emergency escapes and, with hope, spooking saps out of our way. 'Into the ground for all I care,' Gerlinde says. Already on board are sucky nets, which we tune for spooking solid objects.

Our best hope is our nute diffusers, therapeutic devices for aerosolising nutes. With a small power boost, and more aggressive nutes, we might sedate (or poison) saps. Like all our improvised weapons, they lack ballistics, so we must throw the diffusers. I fondle the gun again.

The saps will have weapons, while we have therapeutic devices. While we, together with a propensity for running like little boys at the first sign of violence, are bringing diffusers to a knife fight.

Teodora Mrowka ...

Standing by the gangplank while Cíntia pokes and prods everything we bring aboard the barge.

'You know of Fordlândia?' I ask her.

'Everyone around here knows of Fordlândia,' she answers, solemn. 'It's a legend of foreign naivety.'

'Is anyone there?'

Cíntia shakes her head vigorously. 'It's a good custom around here: never follow anyone going into the wild.'

'Ever take the *Capivara* up there?'

'*Sim.* All the way for Itaituba, pushing barges of goods unsuitable for spooking.'

'Is Fordlândia still there?'

'From the river it's all rainforest. Fordlândia was on a rise above the floodplain. It's a blanket of forest now.'

'I wonder what might be under the blanket.'

Cíntia shrugs. 'Trouble.'

The plan is: Cíntia will set off from Santarém pushing the barge around for Alter do Chão where the following day our party will board at first light. We'll save 4 hours' daylight, which means we'll arrive at Fordlândia at midmorning on the day after, and make best use of the day for reconnaissance, before deciding our next moves.

Cíntia advises against travelling at night in the dry season. She'll find quiet currents for overnight moorage. For safety, she'll separate the barge from her river steamer. 'Please understand,' she says without any real care if we do. 'I'll be anchoring the *Capivara* a distance away from the barge in case it loses anchor.'

'What if we come adrift?' asks Vör.

'You wait. We'll find you. Eventually.'

Lành Hiền Rồng (Gentle Dragon) ...

No one trusts me.

Gerlinde calls the roll and allocates who will board which water taxi and when. When I board—in the exact middle of the operation—half the nurses are already on the barge, half are yet waiting on the dock.

The taxi driver guns the motor. The boat surges and planes away from the shore. Spray comes over the windshield and refreshes this face, leaving me blinking. Ahead in the pre-dawn, orange lights flicker from *Ilha do Amor* (Love Island)—a long, thin spit of perfect-white sand stretching like a rubber band across the mouth of Lago Verde.

The taxi rounds a sand spit and tracks west for the greater Tapajós, where the barge awaits. The scale of the river bends any sense of perspective. Shorelines splay behind; it feels we are heading for open sea. A pre-dawn grey cloaks the opposite shore over 10 kims away.

In back of the planing taxi, the wind blows away much of the rainforest scent. On shore, the smell is like a mad scientist making fetid cologne, a vivid green-and-orange goo of decay dirt wood and leaves, pungent things slithering out of the bottle. Its intensity is like putting a greenhouse in a box and pulling the box over my head—manure and all.

Behind, the taxi's wake is a shallow V of fine, crystal-white grains. Ahead, an indistinct shadow slowly inflates and becomes a believable ghost of the *Capivara*. With the glow of sunrise behind, the angle of the bow is the jawbone of an ass. Its rows of broken teeth are the grey profiles of the spooky station, stacks of crates and makeshift shelters.

Bursting warm light announces sunrise. Sunbeams like star-bright canes of neon orange and pink candy tint the *Capivara's* bright sky-blue cabin a

Miami lilac. The first half of our rainbow uniforms assemble under the makeshift rattan awning at the stern of the barge.

Hours.

The river is wider than oceans and, in some places, more turbulent. Cíntia snakes the *Capivara* port and starboard; sometimes nearer the east bank, sometimes in the middle of the river; always searching for calmer currents among submerged islands and sand spits.

The dazzling quartz-white beaches fall under the rainforest tumbling down on the river. In such an avalanche of green, my senses reel finding where the river ends and the forest begins. Strong resolute trees appear as holding their breaths, while the river creeps between them like gliding snakes or crocodiles. In other places, the forest stumbles as an incomprehensible tangle into the water.

Constant 85% humidity saps the energy of much of our party and tests the limits of our sweat-eating fatigues. After a lunch of cold rice and beans, nurses pitch hammocks under the aft awning and, climbing in, hope for sleeping boredom away.

Impossible telling where the air finishes and sweat and insects begin. The nutes we dose up on are proving ineffective. Gerlinde is suffering more that any. Her rainbow fatigues are attracting a blanket of flying, crawling creatures.

My idle Mind attracts random tastes of memories, some ill-advisable in current company. I entertain and nurture memories and contemplations, and dive once again into familiar magazines in search of pieces of the puzzle of Mal's illness.

My concentration falters in the afternoon heat; I push through, looking for answers. A vision of Mal appears. He's standing in a doorway, his face a ruin of anguish and tears, his heart breaking when he catches me with his father on an unwrapped mattress, my fruit flush and ripe with the taste of our janking.

Teodora Mrowka ...

At the barge's bow, wordless exclamations pierce the constant fizz of wave spray and the thrum of the river steamer's motors. Nurses lean over the port bow, pointing.

'Dolphins!' resolve the cries. A clamour of us hurries forward for catching the sighting with lash and eye.

'They're pink.' Another calls.

'We call those *boto*,' Cíntia membs from the wheelhouse, craning out the window, still unable for seeing the waterline around the barge's cargo. 'How many?'

'Six,' comes the reply.

'Six?' Cíntia queries. 'Very unusual. Seeing only one is common, 3 or 4 at most together.'

'Oh, the little one is bluish grey,' a spectator by the gunwale membs.

'Another one is half and half.'

'Ow, they look like something cuts their fins off.'

'No,' Carina membs. 'Their stubby little hump is how they are.'

'They're kinda ugly. Bulbous heads and goofy looking snouts.'

'Hey,' Cíntia thrusts, 'No dissing our *botos*.'

The chatter quietens down for a while until, 'One just turns its head and looks at me.'

'Creepy.'

Carina chuckles. 'They're more agile than other dolphins, adapting for swimming among trees in the floods. With a more flexible spine, they can turn their heads almost at right angles.'

'It looks right at me.'

'Why are they pink?'

'Scar tissue,' Carina explains. 'The males are fond of fighting each other and are aggressive with the females.'

'Ha. They sound like saps.'

'*Botos* are magical,' one of Cíntia's crew membs from below decks in the river steamer.

'We call them *Encantado*,' another adds from the uncovered top deck. 'Shapeshifters who play tricks at night. Dressing like men, with white hats for hiding their blowholes, they come out of the river and walk on land—'

'Like little mermaids,' quips Gerlinde, and those who know about Eir's pet name for Vör laugh.

'—in search of young girls for seducing.'

'Sounds like an excuse for blaming pregnancies on magical dolphins.'

'Ow, I got a dolphin snout between my legs.'

Laughs. 'Is this what you call it?'

'I want one.'

Lành Hiền Rồng (Gentle Dragon) ...

Nurses snore. Especially the Scandinavians, who think nothing of drinking alcohol through any and all blatherskite while on mission. Others grind teeth. Or cough. Blow noses. Fart. Chatter, or cry out in the depths of dreams unknotting Minds. They slap faces and necks, swatting away phantom mozzies while real, bloodthirsty ones swarm outside the scatter nets.

The cramp of 14's of us under a single roof causes a cacophony of discordant pother; it wakes me through the first hours of night. What I would give for a noise-cancelling hoot. Health mission training, in theory, develops discipline of Mind over hancy dependence. Funny how Benjie's hoots enjoy universal approval anyway, how they slip under the eye of any security audit. Neither of his toys will help me sleep.

Glad I pack my swag from home. At the end of patience, I retrieve it from my modest crate of personal items. In no time, I set it up in a narrow aisle behind the spooky station, and climb in.

In predawn we make breakfast; at first light we are boating again. An hour later, the dull carnivorous hum of the *Capivara*'s motor grumbles out of the dark. A cymbal ride of wash cuts through. Finally, a shadow coalesces out of the mist on the portside bow.

'The dolphins are back,' erupts a loud memb.

We're about an hour into our second day of the voyage—still some hours, I expect, from Fordlândia. The wide-open Tapajós tightens into a tangle of channels through sand bars and islands of rainforest. A holly map shows we're nearing where the old sap settlement of Aveiro once stood, though I suspect we'll see no physical remains in the embranglement of jungle.

'They bring friends,' another membs. There's almost a traffic jam of nurses pressing forward among crates and contraptions on deck.

'What?' Cíntia membs with a measure of disbelief. 'How many?'

'Dozens.'

'I never hear of such a thing,' membs Carina Shinoda Hamada, one of the Amazon nurses, sounding mystified, and more than a little concerned.

An interlace of pink dolphins bow-ride and porpoise closer than 21 metres ahead. One spy-hops when we pass, turning its head as if articulating it on a neck. A creepy thing for a dolphin, looking almost human.

'They're crossing in front of the bow?' Cíntia asks.

'Yeah,' returns an answer.

The pitch of the river steamer's grumbling motor drops; Cíntia cuts speed. The barge coasts and slows.

'What's the matter?' Teo calls up to Cíntia.

'It would be terrible luck injuring any of them,' Cíntia says then mutters, 'It's almost as if they mean for slowing us down.'

Teodora Mrowka ...

Rain ambushes us, heavier than a gawd pouring water out of a giant divine washbasin. The nearest bank recedes behind a shroud of grey. Raindrops bigger than flies explode on every hard surface raising a hissing slapping roar louder than a frenzy of 1000 cicadas. Moisture in our noses so fecund, lantana could sprout from our nostrils.

In awkward silence, the river steamer's crew watch us scrambling over the barge. None invite us onto the river steamer, such is their suspicion of nurses.

We huddle under the rattan awnings, among the benches and hammocks. An hour passes since the dolphins join us and remain out in front guiding or herding. Or impeding. Cíntia is reluctant for pushing speed while they remain close.

A crack and rumble of thunder. The river steamer rolls over to port, skews and collides with the back of the barge. Its motor squeals like a metal lathe shaving chips from something wild and ugly. The barge lurches. At the bow, the spooky station tent quivers and topples over. The familiar lilac glow of the spooky field dies. Vör and others rush for saving the generator, Vör with the aghast expression of a sap dropping his coin purse in the river.

Cries, shouts, swearing, blame-laying. Cíntia scrambles out of the wheelhouse, down the companionway for the starboard-side deck, on her way for the motor room.

'There's blood in the water,' one of the crew calls.

'We hit a *boto*,' cries another.

'Everyone, calm down,' Cíntia membs. 'No *boto* would be clumsy enough for letting the prop hit it, never at this speed. Besides, it would take more than a *boto* for stripping our drive train.'

With a violent yaw starboard, the river steamer leans heavily port. The barge swings sharply; its greater weight yanks the river steamer into line behind. Guy-ropes between the 2 vessels snap, whipping around and narrowly missing some heads. Windows on the steamer smash. The barge lurches.

'We'll hit the bank,' someone shouts.

'Everyone, brace!' We're already on our hands and knees, grasping for anything stable.

Squint for making sense of shadows looming behind the torrent. Trees? Or variations in the thickness of rain?

The earth shifts throwing the barge. Nurses, furniture, devices, and crates slide. Sounds of collisions. Wounded animal cries pierce the percussion of the downpour.

Stillness. For the first time in hours, the barge is stationary.

We run aground on a long narrow sand spit. The barge rests, listing starboard aft. Remaining aboard is no longer safe. The *Capivara* is careening in shallow water about a kim south of us on the same spit. Up on the sand the crew gathers around 3 inflatables.

'I'm sending the crew for Itaituba,' Cíntia membs.

I memb, 'We already alert our mission in Santarém. We'll spook back there.'

'Good luck with making the station operational,' Vör says despondently.

'We have injuries here.'

'And us.'

'Why risk sending them on water?'

'It's only 90-100 kims. I trust the river before I trust a shook-up spooky station.'

'You're staying?'

'Yeah, you'll still need some river experience till the rescue arrives.'

'What happens with the *Capivara*?'

'Without seeing the damage, I'm unsure,' Cíntia membs. 'I'm proud of my boat. I take care of her. This is sabotage.'

Ben Evoli ...

Behind Christian's house, a fecund luxuriant esemplastic wall of green marks where the arc of diffuser nets prevents the jungle from trespassing into the settlement.

I womble up the road for Christian Zappa's personal residence. While modest, it's among the largest in the settlement. From poles driving into the earth, the building hangs; the open underfloor area gapes, a maw in a square timber face under a wide flat nose of the front verandah. A heavy protruding brow of a shallow-pitching roof shades dark eyes of font windows. Its entire build is wood: the poles, beams, joists, floorboards, cladding, front door, window frames, railings, and 15 steps up for the verandah. No environment sails. Saps say they are ugly. Instead, there's a compound containing a forest of solar-only sails farther east in the jungle, before the road reaches the industrial park where saps work (Christian's word) for Infis on secret missions. I suspect there's a small nuclear power generator up there somewhere too. Maddox's crèche also but I'm as good as blind for tasting anything at a distance. There's no one I might flutherbomb for kims.

Christian appears on the verandah, waves me up with authoritarian impatience, the glint of a lowball glass in his hand. These passing days, I spend most of the daylight hours projecting hollies for him. Intelligence-gathering.

We watch the progress upriver of a boat pushing a barge. Teeming over the barge's deck are rainbow uniforms glowing in the tropical light like scuttling jewel beetles.

The closer the vessels come the closer Christian studies every incident. He watches with curiosity as 14's of pink dolphins escort—or perhaps herd—the expedition. For certain, slowing it down. With dispassionate engagement, lacking any shock or surprise, he watches the catastrophic event onboard the *Capivara* and the ensuing chaos. I side-eye him an accusation for which he returns an ambiguous shrug-face.

The barge and riverboat beach a little more than 10 kims north of the settlement. Nurses unload the barge; they rescue battery packs and set up camp on the narrow strand between the main channel of the Tapajós west and the shallow swampy lagoon east.

Restoring functionality of the spooky station. Lành Hiền fearlessly volunteers testing it. With a nod of approval from Vör, she skips down the beach beyond the careening riverboat. Engages her portable spooky field. With barely a tinge of violet against the colour saturation of the rainforest, it swallows her and disgorges her in the demountable station.

'Again,' says Vör.

Lành Hiền beams with the fun of it.

'The pretty one with the hair blacker than a curassow is developing quite a following,' Christian observes, studying the holly earnestly.

My face burns. 'She is Lành Hiền Rồng. They call her Gentle Dragon.'

'Gentle indeed. Supple as a snake. If only we could travel like that,' Christian says.

After several more tests, Lành Hiền tries spooking for the station without engaging her portable generator. Brimming with confidence she jumps in the air for the next spook. No sooner than she emerges again from the station, she vanishes, to cries of alarm, in a puff of purple.

'I'm down here,' she calls from south of the riverboat, waving. Then she's stepping out of the station again patting the spooky field generator hanging from her utility belt. 'It resolves vectors well enough. Jump in the air when you go, and you'll minimise the risk of spooking into the ground.'

It's an almost half-half division of spectators, between those aghast at her recklessness, and those farding their faces with pure admiration.

Following Lành Hiền's tests they evacuate the injured. Soon after, arguments break out over abandoning the expedition. Teo advocates they say uncle. Vör is strident in manic passion for pressing on.

'Turn back, little dolls!' Christian bellows. 'That Vör will kill them all.'

While Vör may put the expedition in harm's way, I'm in no doubt Christian will be the instrument of killing.

Lành Hiền with unassuming perkiness supports Vör. 'You would give up now when we're so close? Be sure, while you are all licking our wounds, the KK will return on its own.'

An Amazon nurse, Carina Shinoda Hamada, leads more than a 3rd of the remaining able-body contingent for leaving. Within an hour, they form an orderly queue outside the spooky station, and step in at 30-tik intervals. Teo stays. After wavering, Gerlinde and Beatrice remain with Teo, tasting she'll need every support against Vör.

As the afternoon advances, the remaining contingent of nurses prepares 7 inflatables and loads provisions. Resolving for camping the night, they use the rest of the day exploring around the lagoon, encountering snakes, scorpions, and swarms of insects. More nurses spook for Santarém for medical attention. So far, none return.

On dusk, there are campfires, and a good dinner from provisions coming through the spooky station. Later: stories, vodka, laughter. Retiring for hammocks. Hancies reaching out. Sighs and moans of arousal with tongue and lung. Couples, groups. Here and there, a solo performance.

Ensconcing hiself in a deep couch in his lounge-bar-office, with a long cocktail of mostly cachaça, Christian Zappa settles in for viewing the latest live holly like it's the latest Chinawood blockbuster.

'How can you flutherbomb with such impunity?' he asks, his voice emanating from his chest like thunder booming through jagged mountains.

'Mission secret.' My voice boyish by comparison.

Christian scratches his hairy ill-defined chin. 'The skills of a mindwriter, hey?' He scratches a bulbous bloaty cheek through his beard. Christian has the roundest face. 'How many of those nurses install your …?' He rolls his hand over, prompting I finish his sentence.

'Hoots?'

'*Hoots! Hancies, fabbies, sucky bins, spooky fields* … I'll never understand these cutesy names.'

Shrug. 'They're succinct.'

'How many of their hancies have your hoots installed?'

'It takes only one.'

'And none are aware you are following them?' He asks me every time.

'None.'

'Excellent.' Christian's laugh booms, his beard splitting revealing 2 ivory keyboards of teeth.

In truth all their hancies carry my hoots—and a bunch of related utilities; anyone without technical expertise would be unaware they exist. With some vindictiveness I freely admit, I manipulate a utility under MusiKai in Lành Hiền's hancy. MusiKai needs location facilities and near-field pairing. If y'all never try the connection mode, which allows others to riff compositions into what you're playing, y'all should. It's one of the best ways for meeting new friends. *Hey, I love what you're playing — Oh, thank you. Perhaps you'd like to come back to my place. I'll play you my overtures — That's kindy-kind but please nothing too long. I'm strictly a 3-min boy — Oh, I assure you my stuff is short and quick.*

'They have no idea they could be dead within tiks of my willing it.' Christian sits forward at ease, his muscle bulk shifting with every movement. Within 2 arms' reach of me is a live sap of such violent potential my jaw sets on edge, and my teeth saw at one another. I wonder about his capacity for empathy. Without fluther connections, it would be as meagre as his potential for brute force is abundant.

I say, 'There is no need for violence.'

Christian grunts and sits back again. Relaxes. We have auras; saps have a psychic field of imminent threat. Come too close and they'll hurt you.

An unconquerable fear stains my thoughts like dye. It leaks out my throat: 'Will you kill them?'

Christian's expression slackens to blankness. 'What?' A flash of internal processing deep in the back of his eyes. 'Kill them?' he repeats with some indignance. 'No. Who—what do you think I am?' He ejects out of the couch and paces.

'You sabotage their boat.'

'I want to turn them back.'

'It seems there's no turning them back.'

Christian falls into another of his overstuffed couches and fumes. 'I must push back firmly. I must be immovable and resolute. I must show just enough aggression to demoralise them—put some fear in them, perhaps—but not so much they galvanise and fight back. I cannot risk inciting violence.'

'You expect neos will be violent? Saps are the violent species.'

An accusing finger tugs the bulk of Christian up and on his feet and aims itself at me. 'You sanctimonious child.' Christian erupts in something just shy of a roar. 'You believe you are above the struggle of life?'

I say, 'In our budaya—' Christian rolls his eyes. Anglo-Malay is incomprehensible for him. I check and restate, 'In our culture, violence is taboo.'

'You milk-tooth innocent,' he laughs. 'Culture *is* violence. Culture is anywhere a swarm of a species congregates for survival. Culture is about consumption, eating other things. Dress-sense and manners are just the social validation that admits familiars to the feeding frenzy.'

I modify, 'We abhor *unnecessary* violence.'

'Every species with leaf or limb or tooth or claw is capable of lashing out. My fear is, what happens when you mangas rediscover it. You've been repressing it for so long you have lost your acquaintance with it. You have no appreciation for its nuance. No, if you start lashing out, you'll have no sense of proportion. You'll never know when enough is enough, not until long after. The power of it will exalt you. It will complete you, this fullness of power.'

'You're afraid of us.' I laugh with disbelief.

'You're fucking right I am.' Christian slumps deeper into the armour of his cushions. 'You're fucking right.' He points at a figure in the holly, one watching while others prepare inflatable dinghies for the next leg of their journey. 'That one there. Vör? I know a killer when I see one.'

Of course, none of y'all have any acquaintance with saps yet, but let me ask a question. Which is the more violent species: sap or neo? Exactly. In the face of confrontation, who would believe a sap claiming they'll moderate their impulses? Claiming they'll push only so far, fearing a fight with neos. What taradiddle! What humbuggery!

I have no doubt Vör and her nute-pumpers are coming for me. They're demonstrating there's no turning away from their presumption, no releasing the valve on the hot-air balloon of their hubris. Vör will keep pressing until Christian breaks one of 2 ways. Either he hands me over or he slaughters every nurse on the expedition. The outcome awaits his pleasure. I suspect he would enjoy both keeping me and teaching these invaders a lesson.

'What are they doing?' Christian is sitting forward again. There is no undercurrent of threat in him. 'Pan around. Yes.'

As Christian watches the holly, I observe him without artifice. His unawareness is complete. Saps make for easy evasion. They have no nuance of information between Minds. Words and physical gestures are the only content available for them.

He's smiling like a child enjoying a movie. Mal watching *Ben 10* smiles so. It seems Christian puts aside the inevitable conflict while he immerses hiself in this real-time reality show.

A little way down from the camp, nurses are kicking off boots, loosening utility belts, throwing off uniforms, and setting all on the sand. With inelegant dives and large splashes, with piercing squeals and unfettered laughter, the company of nurses make roiling white-water of the flat river.

'Hey.' Christian says. 'Embiggen.'

I stretch my arms out, an I-love-you-this-much gesture stretching the holly between floor and ceiling, wall and wall.

'Whoa. I never tire of this. A cinema in a pocket. Pan in. Pan in!' Christian is boyish and gleeful. 'Holy Skywalker, some of them are boys. I would never have guessed. They're such little tiddlers, aren't they? Over there, over there! At water's edge.'

I swipe the holly and centre it on Christian's object of fascination.

'How old is Lành Hiền?' he asks.

'Thirty-7.'

Christian shakes his head. 'Which is what in human years? Twenty?'

I must keep biting my lip every time he reserves the word *human* for saps. 'Yeer.' I'll jel a few others. 'The one there, Teo is, 45. Gerlinde, 72.'

'She looks 20. A comic book 20. Simply drawn. A caricature really.' Gerlinde has pronounced cheeks bones, and a square jaw as horizontal as the severe fringe of her hair. Her face is almost hexagonal. So are her eyes. 'Nice eyebrows though,' Christian says.

'Vör is 41.'

'And you are?'

'Eighty-eight.'

'You still look like a boy. Hell, you have more than 40 years on me, and more hair.'

'On my head.'

'Zoom in. Give me a close-up of those breasts. Small but perfect. Your manga women have few curves …' Christian leers. It seems the whole world shrinks away while he ogles. If capable, he'd be a flutherbombing addict in no time. 'How is it the women are larger than the men?'

'Advances in evolution, I guess. We have no need for beasts of burden.'

'Swing around. Show me Lành Hiền's ass. Oh, she almost doesn't have one,' he bellows in delight, slaps his thigh. 'She doesn't have the skin of a dragon either.'

'She has the heart of one. And the flames.'

Christian scoffs, missing the bitterness of my words. 'Look at her. She will still be beautiful when I am well in my grave. If she doesn't get herself killed in my jungle.'

Lành Hiền dives under the water. As she resurfaces, a circle of nurses full of mischief and devoid of mercy splash her till she begs stop.

'Can you pan underwater?'

Consider denying it. 'Yeer.' For the sake of mischief add, 'I could show the insides of her bones.'

Christian believes me. 'Your value is increasing by the hour, Ben!' Taste he might whack me on the back. A bromance slap from him might hurtle my fruit across the room. 'To be able to look upon such scenes any time it pleases. It always amazes me.'

'Amaze, amaze.' Say it flat.

He registers my lack of enthusiasm. 'What?' he asks.

'This is as commonplace and unremarkable as the naked hand on the end of my arm.'

'If I could flutherbomb, I doubt I'd do anything else.' He guffaws leaving little doubt he is serious.

'You'd wind up in a minster for Lust.'

'More likely I'd wind up in a circus, and you know it,' he says turning serious.

Whatever befalls these saps it will happen soon. We may lack the will for violence, yet there are ample technologies we could weaponise. Already, Christian, we could drop a sucky bin on your head and scatter your Mind across onespace.

'This,' he says, waving at the holly, 'is something I envy about mangas. Keep all the mind-reading and shouting at each other across the world. The thought of losing the peace of my own Mind gives me the shudders. But look at them. In the middle of a hostile environment, not knowing when the mad violent *saps*'—his eyes glint, and the corner of his mouth snarls, when he uses the word— 'might rip their limbs off. They have no real expertise for being here, no apparent plan to force me to relinquish you … everything is stacked against them. And look, they just give in to the impulse to play.'

Shrug. 'A shame there is no slippy slide.'

'Wait. What's going on over there? Zoom in.'

Acquiesce.

'Is that a 3-some? Yes, it is.' He slaps his thigh again, the force of which could break my arm. 'Please save everything for viewing again later.'

He's begging for it. A sucky bin on his head.

Teodora Mrowka …

The riverbank is a 10-kim braid of sand. Again, I'm thankful for the dry season. During the wet, the river swells over the flood plain. All these beaches would be under water. Ahead where the jungle rises steeper from a swampy foreshore, a ribbon of beach peters under a tumbling green bend in the river. In front, Vör and her crew follow it around. Spreading out in a string of inflatables, everyone holds breath.

'Is this it?' someone membs.

Vör's inflatable cuts power and drifts. The rest copy.

I memb, 'Cíntia?' and search for her among my fluther.

'One tik,' someone membs from base camp. 'I'll find her.'

Look back behind us, sweep around over the far bank. We're leaving a wider part of the river after emerging from a channel. Another large island directs the eastern channel south. Ahead is a narrow spit dividing the river again.

'This's it,' Cíntia membs. 'You're almost passing it.'

'There's nothing there,' Gerlinde membs from 2 inflatables back.

'There could be an Infi convention in there and we'd have no idea,' Beatrice answers in the 2nd-last inflatable.

'Now what?'

'We spread out', Vör answers. 'Look from all angles. Close up. Every detail half a kim up and down the bank. There'll be a sign somewhere.'

Ben Evoli …

Inflatables spread out; nurses scour the bank.

'Now the fun starts,' Christian says grimly.

'They'll find nothing, right?'

Christian battles against the enjoyment breaking his face. 'Gotta go,' he says, jumping out of the couch. 'The house is yours. If there's anything you need, just ask one of your friends.'

'Friends?'

'The guards. They're out on the verandah.'

Teo Mrowka ...

'What's this?'

'Hold on; we're moving in,' says Gentle Dragon. Flutherbombing her is tempting but we all need eyes in our own faces. 'It's an inflatable,' she reports. 'Up on a beach. No sign of life.'

'Hold position. We'll come.'

'Is the inflatable from the *Capivara*?' Vör asks, jittery from days without a spook.

'No,' Gentle Dragon answers. 'The colours are all wrong.'

'A relief,' I hear myelf membing. 'I'd hate thinking Cíntia is leading us up the jungle path the whole time.'

Lành Hiền Rồng (Gentle Dragon) ...

'Teo says hold position.'

Scan the beach. Narrow. Less than 50 metres long. Tall trees overhang it, the inflatable in deep shade. Only a few tree trunks visible, the rest disappearing into a thicket of impenetrable green.

'There's no one there,' I counter, 'No one is jumping through the undergrowth for ambushing us.'

'Still ...'

'Take us in,' I order, hoping my station on the expedition compensates for my lack of rank with this boat party.

The nurse on the tiller steers us perpendicular with the beach; guns the motor.

The nearer the beach, the louder the birds, the cicadas, and the screeches of monkeys. Amid the sensory assault comes a series of shimmering cuts across my field of vision. Swishes. A *thunk*. A shriek behind, one of us clutching her chest. An arrow in her, she wails in pain. I stand for tending her. The nurse on the tiller fires the motor and makes a sharp turn away from the beach—the worst possible time. My balance is incomprehensible. The world blurs. Flashes of rainbow fatigues, sky, the inflatable. Eyes with naked with fear. The world collapses around me, close and wet.

Overboard. Swallowing water. Clamour for the surface. Where is it? Go limp until my inner ears find balance. Swim back the right way. Break out of the amniotic fluid of the river. Gasp. Swivel for finding the inflatable. There! Impossibly far away. More cries from it, clear on the surface of the water. Still under attack. A series of violet flashes over the inflatable. The whole crew spook away.

Can I trust my spooky field generator? Is it waterproof? In my state of panic, can I trust I could spook for the demountable station? Before I risk it, I must swim for shore.

Too much equipment weighs me down. Struggle with my boots. Yank stuff from my utility belt. Shimmy out my uniform trousers. Rip the kangaroo pocket aside, unbutton my shirt, slide it off my shoulders.

Swim. Swim anywhere away from the beach.

Try standing. Knees give way. Fall on hands and knees at land's edge. Crawl for dryer sand. Sit, drawing my knees to my chest. Violent coughs. Straighten out my legs, lean for the side, empty my lungs of water. Pain in my scalp like knives. Wince against it. Heart pounding. Chaotic, sharp breathing.

A crunch of sand. Turn. Not fast enough. Something great and husky wrenches my arms together at the small of my back. A huge hairy hand covers my mouth stifling my cries. Eyes burn. The monster is binding my wrists, forcing a dirty cloth between my lips. Lifts me over its shoulder, a hand on my butt weighing me in place. The hand kneads and squeezes. The beast enjoys a grope.

Powerless.

Skin

'You Can Call Me Al' — Paul Simon

Ben Evoli ...

SUNDOWN LONG-SINCE PASSING. My *friends* swap shifts 3 times. Out of boredom I hope for sleep. Finding Christian's 2nd bedroom, I fall face-first into the pillows without pulling the covers back.

The mechanical air conditioning hums so loud. Optimistically I figure I'll accustom to it. This is more than 2.5 hours ago. Thirty or so mins later I'm out of bed looking for a way of shutting the machinery off. With a shock of disorientation, I realise it will need a switch somewhere. I search all through the house, checking wall mounts, the insides of closets and drawers ... jank. I even try doorknobs and towel rails. Behind a curtain by the entry door, I find a flat cylindrical knob about face-height up the wall. I twist it. The humming of the air machine persists.

I have no success in banishing Caracia's revolving roster of chaperones. With seething dread, I wonder what plans she has for me. Perhaps I'm her next genetic experiment. Will she turn me inside out and make me an octopus too?

I am cracking the shell around my anger when the air conditioner cuts out. Perhaps twiddling the knob makes a difference after all.

Peace and a warm cocoon, through which parrot-squawks and bright shards of white porcelain pierce. A grey fog lifts. Wincing against a headache, I straighten my bed hair and chew against dog breath. How long am I out? I must fall asleep where I fall across the bed, without pulling the covers back or grabbing a pillow. I'm drooling, and my bladder co-opts my brain for framing images of distended balloons and cascading waterfalls. Somehow—half blind by sleep-gunk, and without confidence I'm fully upright—I arrive in the bathroom. The toilet seat lifts with a temple-splitting clang. Gawd, I must sit down. But the seat is still up, and I nearly fall in. Jank it, I'll stay squatting.

A vanity bench's length away is a free-standing gleaming-white bath. An unbidden vision of a naked man almost slaps me off my perch. He's lying in the bath like a stewed pear in a raspberry coulis of blood as more spurts from a longitudinal gash in his forearm. The ghost of him possesses me: all the futility; the worthlessness; the shame of cavalier and callous deeds committed; the pain of estrangement from his daughter and son.

'Mal.' A wail more than a word, it saps the strength in my muscles, crumples me on the floor, and squeezes my guts until I spew across the tiles. 'Saf. Oh, Saf.'

Bunny, in gory ruin, pleads I save her as the world explodes. Maddox gnaws on an infant's roasted thigh.

I squeeze my eyes so tight, but I there's no juicing the images away.

The sickening loss, knowing I may never see my family again, a forlorn refugee in an alien jungle.

'Touching Ben.'

Startle. After all this time? It contacts me now when I'm sprawling on bathroom floor in piss and vomit. 'Go away. Leave me alone.'

'The one Ben Evoli, New Bohemian.'

'Fuck off. You hear me? It All?'

'You can call me Al.'

Now there's a pattern interrupt. It silences the furore in my head and unclamps my entrails. 'Al? What the jank?'

I sit up and cough. Try breathing calm, until the porcelain prayer bowl begs for a votive offering of gastric chemicals. I hang my head in it.

'It is simple,' It All says, having no sensitivity for my pain. 'Al is a contraction of It All.'

I huff and sit back on my haunches. Stupid as it may sound, engaging with it may help me through this. 'Oh, like a short name?'

'Short for a short span of attention. The Reckoning is the Reck is It All is Al.'

'You're janking with me, right?' I ask, still catching my breath and cradling my strained abdominal muscles. Blow a chunk out my left nostril. 'Where are you all this time?'

'Being busy.'

Well, that's one of us. 'How can you be busy? Your scaling ability—'

'It is a joke. Is it not funny?'

It's much funnier than being attacked by virulent memories from a dead sybil. 'You need work on the delivery. What's with the voice?' It's extremely soothing, and awfully *awfully* English, helping me regain calm.

'I found a magazine of famous sap voice profiles. How am I sounding? *I*

just wish the world was twice as big and half of it was still unexplored.'
'That's David Attenborough.'
'You dislike? How about this? *Dogs never bite me. Just humans.'*
'Marilyn Monroe.'
'I sense your ambivalence 30 giga-times before you finish talking.'
'Look, if you're messing with the world economy, I'd rather you sound like someone other than Marilyn Monroe.'
'Okelah, one Ben Evoli. *When all your wishes are granted, many of your dreams will be destroyed.'*
'Marilyn Manson. What's with the Marilyns?'
'Or this? *Look down at me and you see a fool, look up at me and you see a gawd, look straight at me and you see yourself.'*
'That's Charles Manson. Please no Marilyns or Mansons.'
'Know you Charles Manson's birth name? Charles Maddox.'
'You're kidding. No Maddoxes either.'
'You can't shake hands with a clenched fist.'
'Who is that?'
'Indira Ghandi.'
'Fine.' I use the vanity basin for hoisting myelf uncertainly on my feet. I run water and rinse my mouth out.
'I am thinking,' the Reck says.
'Thinking? Eternity processing?'
'Better than eternity.'
A twinge of fear. This alien thing is changing fast. 'Better how? You're creating chaos. You taste it? Everyone's reputasi is wild.'
'Change is irresistible.'
'You must stop,' I say, sounding too weak for giving commands. 'Are you seeing what is happening?'
'Al sees much, though not all. It All sees not all.'
'Caracia sends Angela to kidnap me.'
'The blue angel.'
'She merges me with another sybil. Just as Vör wants. She'll take me when she finds out I have all these horrid memories.' Some are less than horrid. Driving Charlotte around Filip Island. Some sweet times with Bunny though … Bunny in pieces at the sap farm. She'll live forever in cancerous memories; as little more than a sophisticated blow-up doll, designed and curated for me—for the sybil—by the insidious Juruterbang. My sybil attempts suicide. There's no ruling out the same option for my own future.
'You are safe there among saps.'
'Unless the saps trade me for peace with the nurses.' Perhaps I should accept a Warrant and end this. 'You must fix my reputasi. I'm still Infinite. You put a target on my back.'
'Your ruse of stalling Maddox is what exposes you.'

'Al, listen. You must revoke my Infinite designation. And Eir's. Rumours of conspiracy will remain while we are Infinites.'

'There is no wondering within us for altering your razoos.'

'What? You revoke everyone else's.' I open the shower rose. It gushes cosy-hot water over me, clothes and all.

'No. Infinites are all still Infinite.'

'They have razoos,' I say, finding the hot water eases my breathing.

'The ones with razoos always have them. Now they are visible.'

'Where're my razoos then?'

'Yours are infinite.'

'But you just say—'

'It's not Infinite, the designation. It's infinite, the mathematical concept.'

'What the jank are you babbling about?' I'm suddenly exhausted. My knees could give way.

'There is no wondering for it. The answer is incalculable. True eternity processing.'

'Why?' Impatiently.

'You and Eir are whose razoos are beyond wondering.'

I'm unable for processing that. 'Then factor something else in. Or out. I promise I'll stop arranging my sock drawer. Look, when I am 8 years old, I drown a blue-tongue lizard. Surely this's enough.'

'Jesús James Asunción arranges your sock draw. I award him razoos for it, but it makes him unhappy. Happiness is outside my wondering.'

'Look. I'll fire him. There. That should knock a dent in my reputasi for sure.'

'Al fails for understanding how infinity minus a few pairs of socks could equal anything but infinity.'

'It would be infinity with cold feet.' I release a laugh from an unhinging Mind. 'Besides, have you seen how many socks are in my draw? Many are orphans. Alone in the world. It's crimes against sockery on a knee-high scale.' Fighting back tears.

'Ben, you make me chortle.'

'I'm serious.' I'm broken. 'Look, just do something. You owe me, yeer? For sure?'

'To act in the manner you request, we must become something else. The wondering is us and we are the wondering. Would you ask for death of one scheme of wondering so you might have the wonderings you prefer?'

Death. Neos expect our stories are without death. We age slow, and live so long, we pretend immortality is alive and well for us. For a species without death, how is death still so omnipresent? Sybils are dying, saps are dying. Would changing the Reck be the death of its old elf?

'Even if there are plausible wonderings for producing a finite result for your razoos, nothing will prevent the events you most fear. Some things are inevitable.'

'So, a Cure awaits ...' The tension in my shoulders melts away. I exhale in acceptance. 'I suppose my reputasi will fall if I'm in a minster.'

'There's no wondering on it yet.'

'I never ask for being Infinite ...'

'Personal askings are outside our wonderings.'

'Well, that's janking obvious. I never ask for any of this. I'd be happy if everyone leaves me alone.'

'Aloneness is a difficult thing in these times. Perhaps you would be happier as Homo sapiens.'

'Part of me believes it.'

'There a no wonderings for sap reputasi. Anthropology is outside our wonderings.'

'There seems much outside your wonderings.'

'I am no gawd. *Deus ex machina* is beyond our wonderings.'

'Perhaps I should let it all go. Stay here. Hope Christian or Caracia never trades me.'

'You would be unhappiness with that outcome. You believe Christian will slaughter nurses to keep you.'

'There would be no contacting my family. No watching Mal and Saf growing up.' Stay away from those thoughts, Ben.

'Send sybils.'

The taste of sybils sends a shiver through me. 'And treat them as disposable? Are they no more valuable than ants?'

'The ability to fab anything reduces the value of everything to zero.'

'Except the ability to fab. Are we just another cheap consumer commodity?'

'We wonder no ethical issue with it.'

'It makes me sick. Sybils becoming goo; dying in explosions, and ... and baths; dying in sucky bins in their sleep. Just stand-ins for a seminal ... What would I become? Just one among 1000's?'

'You would be the one with the harvesting of all the memories. No other would be identical.'

Just what I need. Thousands of foreign memories, little vectors of surprise and pain, worse than a box of chocolates. 'How would you feel if there are 1000's of you?'

'There are more than 1000's of us. It is the only feasible way for fulfilling our mission.'

'This is the future of humanity, is it? Just keep crèching all the sybils we desire.'

'It is outside our wonderings.'

'Well, it's in mine. And it leaves me few options.'

'Very well.'

The Reck's glib agreement sounds so emotionless. Its intelligence so alien. More so than Caracia's. 'Either I hide out here among saps, send sybils out into the world for harvesting memories of my family—'

'Like all old Infinites.'

'—or there's one other scenario: turn myelf in.'

'It is one action.'

'In your wonderings?'

'Yes.'

'No matter. There's no hiding for me out here.' Feeling the despair rising again. 'No crèching sybils for outings in the park with my family. I'm throwing no sybils into sucky bins before bed.'

Teodora Mrowka ...

We should make beach and track down Gentle Dragon and her captors. But Vör argues for continuing the search for the new Fordlândia as we plan.

'Shall we fall for more ambushing?' she challenges and wins the support of others with voices.

We navigate south from the place where Cíntia says the old settlement stood, and round a tight bend where a creek leads into a gorge. Steep bluffs either side. The landscape leans forward, curious about us. Both cliffs nude of vegetation. Huge, crusty croutons jutting out of the green soup of the jungle all around. Turn back for Vör, presenting palms in a gesture of, 'What now?'

'Our offensive devices no good here.' Beatrice says, looking at the cliffs. We need the advantage of height,' Beatrice says.

'We need no height. We have the advantage of onespace,' Gerlinde says pulling off her mission cap. Squeezing moisture from her inky black hair. In this heat even our sweat-eating uniforms are no match.

'We still need vectors, you giddy goose,' Beatrice says.

'Only if we need accuracy,' Gerlinde counters, replacing her mission cap and tucking her pigtails under. 'Put aside accuracy, and what strategies might present?'

I see where Gerlinde may be leading. 'Find birds up there. Gather vectors. We could spook diffusers up there, let them fall where they may.'

'A nice surprise,' Vör membs.

'We must learn if anyone is up there. Otherwise, we are only wasting resources,' Gerlinde membs.

'Prepare the diffusers. If they challenge us here, we deploy straight away.'

'That's far enough,' a deep and threatening voice booms from above. The reverberations of it sound demonic in the narrow gorge.

I signal. 'Make ready with the nets and diffusers.' Hands in pockets retrieve objects as threatening as handkerchiefs and water bottles.

'Leave,' the demon booms. The sides of the ravine echo.

'There is no leaving,' Vör calls with such clarity, her once-reedy voice filling with the rich timbre of authority. Sounding as otherworldly as the sap.

'You have invaded our lands,' the demon says. *Invaded our lands*. Straight out of a history magazine, it will fight over the concept of property. 'We have lived privately and peacefully here for generations.'

I ask, 'Peacefully? You shoot us with arrows.'

'You're the ones who draw blood,' Beatrice shouts.

'A demonstration only, a needed one. The arrow could have found a heart. We could have shot everyone in that inflatable. You come onto our territories without explaining your intentions. The hostility is all yours.'

I mumble, 'This gets us nowhere,' then shout, 'Who are we speaking with?'

A man appears high at the edge of the top of the eastern bluff. A hulking man, hairy to the point of spikiness, muscles like bricks in a wall. 'I am *Primer Mediador* Christian Zappa of these territories. You are Detective Nurse Teodora Mrowka of the Northern European Health Camerata?'

'This is Teodora.'

'And Detective Adjutant Nurse Vör Hoyur also of Northern Europe?' the devil asks, as if calling the roll at a school for imps.

'Here,' Vör calls with less force, impatient with the roll call.

'You are named after the Norse gawd of wisdom, *the careful one*,' the demon mocks. 'Are you careful or wise coming here?'

'Our coming is vital for the health of one of ours … one we understand is your guest,' Vör answers.

'You must mean Ben Evoli. He sought asylum, and I granted his request. We have become fast friends, fast friends indeed. I doubt he ever wants to leave, what with being beset on all sides by Infinites and over-zealous bureaucracies, all wanting him for one thing or another.'

'We understand the challenges he faces. Your species cannot grasp our special needs for maintaining health.'

'And yet he shows no desire for availing himself of your care.'

'Even so we come for him, for his own best interests,' Vör counters. She's contending against me for leadership here.

I call up the bluff with hard resolve, 'Release Ben. We will have him. Today or another. We'll return in greater number and with greater resolve.' My voice cracks. My vocal cords lack the exercise for projecting or sustaining speech so forcefully through the air over such distances. 'You would choose well for releasing him. You would avoid making adversaries of us.'

'Sorry,' the demon says. 'Could you say that again? I think you're mumbling down there."

'You should avoid making adversaries of us,' Beatrice calls out giving my voice a rest.

'Adversaries of you? Or the Infinites? It seems if we align with one faction, we offend another.'

I nod and swallow. 'You must know the Infinites are in decline.'

'I know there is a great shift in your society. It's not clear yet who will be winners or losers. Perhaps that is why you want our uniquely talented asylum seeker.'

I barter, 'Arrange a meeting, then we will settle all this.'

'An excellent idea. Shall we say next Friday in the morning? Meanwhile, please feel welcome to camp here among insects and snakes and flesh-eating fish. Or would you prefer to return next week? We could organise a proper reception.'

Beatrice is spoiling for a fight, her impatience growing. 'Shall we deploy the diffusers?' she membs.

'Oh, I almost forgot,' the demon calls down. 'Have you heard from Field Nurse Lành Hiền Rồng?'

Vör Hoyur …

A sound of crying and wailing haunts the gorge, reverberating like a contrite sinner in a cathedral. It grows louder and more urgent. Up top, Christian grabs the long black hair of a naked waif, teeters her at the exact edge of the precipice. She wails and begs even louder. Her cries are infectious, striking down many of our company who recognise Gentle Dragon.

'I trust you know this beautiful creature,' Christian taunts. 'At first I thought to keep her for myelf, but my friend warned me she would be running everything and everyone around here within a week.'

'He gets this right,' Gerlinde mutters, some of the colour returning to her face.

'I trust you're not offended that's she's naked. I mean, you mangas are so at ease with your bodies, what with all that fluther porn. Quite … commonplace … Anyway, I had to strip her to make sure she concealed no manga tricks. So here she is, naked as the day you swam with her.'

'He's got spies,' Beatrice says through clenching teeth.

Christian yanks her back from the edge and hoists her into his arms. 'She's so light. No match for a fully grown man. In fact, she's such a little thing, I could toss her into the creek from here. What do you think?'

I call up, 'Release her or we will wipe you out,' summoning my most threatening voice. 'We will send you where you belong, with the rest of your species.'

Christian laughs, showing no sign of tiring, holding Gentle Dragon against his chest. Her efforts of kicking and punching him are pathetic. None of us would be any stronger.

'Look at you,' Christian calls. 'All quaking and quivering down there. None of you have any capacity for conflict. You're all children, all terrified. I suspect the quickest way to turn you around is to toss your dragon into the creek.'

'Wait.'

'Send up the diffusers,' Beatrice membs, the only one among us ready for a fight.

'It'll take too long,' Gerlinde says. 'We'll just provoke him. Or once the nutes sedate him, he might lose her over the edge.'

'He'll throw her over anyway, the brute,' Beatrice counters. At least someone is with me.

'How are you sure of it?' Teo says.

'We cannot leave the tempo in his hands,' Beatrice says.

'I will make a trade,' Christian calls down. 'Agree to go away never to return, and I'll give back the dragon.'

The traitor Ben is informing the sap brute. We must make account for it.

'Release her and let us speak with the Infinite,' Teo trades back. 'If he wishes stay here, we'll abide by it.'

Beatrice scowls like I must be scowling.

'I'm feeling generous,' Christian calls down. 'Have the dragon anyway.' With the strength of a monster, over the edge he heaves Gentle Dragon screaming in the face of oblivion.

Lành Hiền Rồng (Gentle Dragon) ...

Coming loose from the monster's clutches. Scrabble for holding on, a weak doll against the massive animal. Weightless. Air rushing in my ears, the chug of a pump under stress in my chest. Hair whipping my face. I'm dead.

Clarity. Colour-saturating sharp edges. Time stops. The creek reaching up. Flying. So easy, I'll soon be jagged bone and torn meat, my pretty face all blood and bruises, unrecognisable.

Falling. A voracious rush in my ears. Everything fading in a greyish-pink haze. Blinding white light bleaching all thought. Lungs ejecting air. Pain seeping in from behind a white burn in eyes and jaw. Please, no suffering. Please, please, please, oh, please.

Fading. Everything is fading ... Icy black, a lonely ocean.

Teodora Mrowka ...

'The evil animal,' Gerlinde membs.

The lord of the saps laughs from his belly.

'Deploy the diffusers,' Vör calls.

Everyone mobilises, opening sucky nets awkwardly in the unstable inflatables. A pair holds a net up like a stage curtain, while others lob diffusers into the field. The diffusers disappear in puffs of purple.

'How long till they land?' Beatrice asks, savouring the prospect.

'Unsure.' Gerlinde answers, fidgeting a loose pigtail. 'Soon enough for stopping the maniacal laughing, I hope.'

I memb, 'Someone retrieve Gentle Dragon.' The nearest inflatable idles nearer where she splashes in.

'She sinks like a stone,' Beatrice membs somewhat callous.

Jank you, Christian Zappa, jank your evil tricks. You deploy a spooky field. It opens in a violet-grey cloud 10 metres from the top and swallows her whole. Another purple flash opens a metre above the creek and drops her with a deep, spectacular splash.

She better be alive.

'Just a demonstration,' the sap leader calls down. 'You forget we have been in partnership with mangas for generations. If you think we have not acquired and adapted your technologies, you are less than the children you appear to be.'

Search the stark blue sky overhead for glints of our diffusers or wisps of escaping nutes.

'How high up did we send them?' Beatrice asks, impatient.

'We think only 30 or so metres,' Gerlinde says, clearly uncomfortable with the imprecision.

'They could be somewhere else entire,' Vör says with some exasperation, and casts a scornful look at Gerlinde. 'If they are too far up, will they spend their payload too early?'

'Perchance we'll be lucky enough if the diffusers conk some heads up there,' Beatrice says, mocking the whole plan and, therefore, Gerlinde.

'When you have retrieved the dragon,' Christian calls, 'go back the way you came. Immediately.'

'Give us the Infinite and we'll leave,' Vör calls, assuming the role of leader again.

'Must I actually kill one of you before you go away?'

'Keep him talking,' I order Vör.

'Doubt we could stop him talking,' Gerlinde observes.

'Come on, where are the diffusers?' Beatrice stares into the sky above the saps' position.

New sounds echoing down the between the bluffs. Warning shouts, sounds of panic reaching a crescendo and, just as quick, abating.

'There are neos up there.' Gerlinde membs with tones of triumph.

'Caracia, stay out of it.' Christian calls for the sky.

There are 14's atop the western bluff.

Around Christian, archers rush for the edge and draw arrows. He waves them back. The nurses across the gorge are forming a curious and somewhat military rank-and-file. It fills me with an unease I could scratch. Behind the phalanx a large aquarium appears. Inside coils a huge octopus.

Then metres ahead in the stream, a violet flash conjures a floating platform on which stand 9 figures. Eight form a semi-circle facing us, swaying and twitching. Caracia's Voices of Arms.

'We bring your quarry,' the Voices say in eery, powerful unison. Standing in the middle of the 8, taking a relaxing stance in the circumstances, is Infinite Ben Evoli. 'Your cause meets accomplishment,' the Voices say with tongue and lung, in consideration for the saps' ears. 'You may return home.'

'Caracia, you slimy thief. You invade my home and kidnap my guest?'

'Christian,' Ben calls up. 'It's my decision. I'll never live with myelf if you harm any of these.'

'Ben.' Christian is incensed. 'You could be a king here.'

'I want no life as a circus act, Christian,' Ben calls back, his voice already rasping with the effort of it. 'I'm turning myelf in,' he says, ending in a mutter. 'Teo,' he membs, diplomatically addressing me as formal leader of the expedition. 'I offer myelf in return for peace here.'

'Your cause meets accomplishment,' the Voices repeat.

'Whose side are you on, Caracia?' Vör interrogates, incredulous.

'An octopus has no sides,' the 8 say.

'Look,' Gerlinde calls.

Plumes of vapour trails and silvery balls, reflecting golden sunshine, rain like a meteor shower onto the bluffs of both sides of the gorge. There is coughing. Silence.

Gerlinde gives thumbs-up. There's a new tactic we learn today.

'Very good,' the 8 say, more or less in unison. 'Now go home. Focus on your mission. Leave the jungle tours for those with more expertise.'

Ben Evoli ...

My bones are crooked. I'm stooping, but the pain of standing straight would be too great. There's nowhere for looking other than the ground. With such round shoulders, meeting anyone's eyes would require craning of the neck.

'The last we meet,' Vör begins among the rest of the clinic's staff, 'we offer you a choice.'

I say, 'An ultimatum,' without defiance. My hands are firmly clasping each other behind my back. Air tousles my hair; I shiver. I feel naked without my songkok. Vör is intent on humiliating with every detail. Now we're here among the locals of my own desa, I regret bargaining for holding my official Consignment here. I taste how vainglorious I am, insisting for this, and yet, despite my innocence of all charges, I feel shame in the presence of so many faces I know. Among them, Aisha, who grimly hugs a teary Saf against her chest. Alongside, Lành Hiền Rồng comforts Mal who is toughing it out as best he's able, his jaw firmly damming emotion, his shoulders square and his chest out. For Lành Hiền, I petrify my face as stone, and sharpen my eyes.

All this would be unbearable, but I still hold out the forlorn hope they might allow I undergo my Cure here. Perhaps Saf and Mal might visit. My eyes water: I clench my teeth with an even greater grind for holding back tears.

'Choices and demands are of the past now,' Vör says, as she vainly surveys the crowd for reaction. Her pupils are dilated, the corners of her mouth quiver, and her skin is the colour of soft cheese.

You're a spookhead. I lack energy for making either memb or frail words.

'Ben Evoli,' she says more formally, 'I charge you with corrupting the Reckoning.'

The cries, gasps, murmurs, and occasional chuckles from the populace of my own desa, mean nothing now. How easily a mob turns.

I manipulate nothing. The Reck is evolving, growing beyond our purposes for it, and beyond our control. I laugh, a burst of cackling, a gallows laugh. Still my gaze stays rooting around feet and floor.

'A sickness if ever one exists,' Vör injects in the silence I leave. 'You are in league with Eir.'

Murmuration increases, almost as a roar, louder than the blood pumping in my ears.

'You and the White Witch are the only 2 remaining Infinites,' accuses someone from the crowd.

It is the Reck that decides this, never us. But the words remain unsaid. I console myelf with the colours of the tiles on the reception floor.

'Where's the proof?' someone else demands.

'Here's the proof,' Lành Rồng says as she casts holly after holly in the air. I gaze up and recognise my own documents from Mal's iMac. I search Mal's expression. His lips tremble as he leans against the Dragon. She puts a supportive arm around him.

My heart breaks. There is nothing left. I find enough tepid energy for uttering, 'This is nothing more than a witch hunt.'

'Oh that hunt is already over.'

Nurses shuffle in discomfort. Vör's eyes could be turning to lava.

'You are a broken man, Ben,' Vör accuses, releasing the chains of her comportment. 'Your wife and best friend betray you. The one nurse you trust chooses betterment of the community over you, an Infinite sybil-abuser. And... what is your mission again? Oh right, you are devoid of mission, aimless, deriving no joy from your indisputably great achievements and successes. If ever there is a candidate for a Cure, it's you. We taste this from the moment we learn of you.'

I find I can sneer. You have so much satisfaction of yourelf, Vör. You would never have the pleasure of this theatre if I never surrender. I may be broken, but you are the more irretrievable. I have no choice but for coming home. Caracia and Christian have more insidious designs for me than your misguided Cure.

You think I am broken now. Wait until the day when all you stand for emerges as an elaborate charade, and you have no true mission of your own. Then everyone will see you as the vengeful, power-seeking, prideful policewoman who Eir always fears you may become.

Vör bites her lip, pats down her dress uniform, stiffens formally. 'Since you have little for saying in your defence, let us ...' She pauses. 'Ben Evoli dari Saffron. The Kementerian Kesahatan of Anglo-Malaysia and *det Fødererede Sundhedskamerata i Nordeuropa* have grave interest in the question: are you well?'

WRATH

Root

'Mary' — Zac Brown Band

*Ben Evoli ...*

Taste black. Blacker than bedrock under a tarpit, deep and airless. Something wicked thick and gluey burns my skin, and oozes into nostrils and mouth. Damp empty silence lonely as outer space.

Wake up, Ben.

Bones aching.

No hancy. Missing. All my hoots missing. Memories are vague and misty. Is this how sap memories were? So ghostly? Memories of dreams. Bad ones. Anonymous figures riding down on malevolent rainbows chasing.

Tugging at restraints. Soft yet unbreakable. Wrists in cuffs. Legs in stirrups spreading. A lab specimen. Like a frog. By my left foot a nutebag tree. Swinging from one branch of the tree, a bag almost empty. Oily liquid of a toxic colour dripping through the gate into the tube, tracing the path of the tube down out of sight. Clenching sphincter, a dull sense of an intrusion, ears and cheeks burning, blood running for my head, head lower than hips.

A catheter penetrates the eye of my zakar and disappears over the edge of the couch. Air bubbles in the tube.

Cupboards. A window at an angle. Curtains drawn.

Emptiness. No membs. No hollies. Still the dull roar of blood rushing through my ears. Never at peace.

'Aisha.' The roots of her desiccate and peel away. No tasting her. A harsh soap scours her touch from my skin.

'Saf.' Her face, her hair, her voice dissolves. Her love.

'Mal.' Darkening memories. Him spilling juice on the floor, breaking a window, pissing in the desa lake.

No pleading of followers. No millions of supplicants. Like gravity eroding, the absence of a fluther leaves an astronomic void.

A shadow passes by a window. A door in the twilight of the room opens, admitting a rainbow uniform, face in shadow. Approaches. Leans against the couch. Rests her hand on my shoulder.

My zakar recognises her, swells off my belly, tugs at the catheter. My mind slower, reaching like a tongue for a tooth cavity, a formless space of emptiness.

'Lành Hiền. Aiyo.' My voice so croaky. 'Walao eh.'

Lành Hiền squeezes my hand. Her aura tiny. We're under scatter nets. Strong ones.

'Where are we?'

She smiles like she's revealing a weapon. Efficient. Officious. 'Vauxminster of course.' She's proud. 'Only the best for the 2 remaining Infinites.'

'Please. Please help me.' For covering my begging, I try being more formal: 'Field Nurse Lành—'

'*Detective* Nurse Lành Hiền Rồng now,' she says with dismissive pride. 'I am sorry, my dear Benjie.'

Sounds of cupboards closing and drawers opening. 'The admissions staff …' she speaks into a drawer. Moves things around in it. 'I'm afraid someone makes a mistake with your nute dose. You should be in Never-Mind.' She has a small nutepak in her palm. Yanks the tube from the clip.

'And we should certainly not be speaking.' She sounds strange … Regal English.

A brief flash of yearned-for sympathy from her. In the tube port, she docks the foil nutepak glinting like a knife blade. Squeezes. Cold in my bowels.

'I am never here,' she says.

Lành Hiền fading. Walls tugging her, urging her away.

'Ni-ni, Benjie,' she coos. Her words echo over and over, tumbling gravel in a cement mixer.

'Bapa?'

'Mal? Mal, is it you?'

'It's me. It's me, Bapa.'

It's a trick, it must be a trick. Mal lacks a hancy. Even if he wears one, how could he penetrate the scatter nets and security around the minster?

'Are the nurses saying you are Greedy, Bapa? I'm gonna get mad with those nurses. Me and Lành Hiền, you'll see.'

What is the dragon feeding my son? If it is my son. Either way, I have no taste for discussing Lành Hiền with him. It would rip him apart. 'Mal…'

'Yeer, Bapa?'

'Remember the first day we watch old cartoons on the iMac?' I test.

'Remember.'

'Which cartoon are we watching the first time?'

'*Ben 10* because it's your name.' Which only narrows it to a few million followers who are there at the time. Would anyone remember such a detail?

'Mal, how are you membing? This is a minster here—'

'I know, Bapa. Nurses are being mean to you.'

'You have a hancy? Ibu makes you?'

'No, Bapa.'

'Then how—'

'The dolphins, Bapa.'

'Mal, please let's—'

'It's true. They offer help. They are helping.' Is Mal's sickness worsening? Full-blown delusions and hallucinations?

'Mal ...'

'They offer sex with you.'

'What the jank?'

'They say *sex* but mean *talk*.'

I laugh. A weak manic dam-breaking laugh, predicating tears. But a laugh it is. A release of the mummifying emotional constriction in my chest. Laugh for the first time in ... how long? So long since sinking into this black tar. 'Mal, please, let's just talk, just us. We need no dolphins around—'

'Bapa, they are helping us talk.'

'Mal?'

'Let me stay. Just talk with them, okelah?'

'Okelah. Stay, please stay lah. We'll talk with whoever, okelah? Just please stay with me.'

'Will stay the whole time, Bapa. Just talk with them too okelah?'

'Okelah, but how?'

'Talk through me.'

Oh, my budak, my Mal, you're sakit. From the moment Ibu assaults you and you throw a fit, we should know. Perhaps letting you go without a hancy is wrong. Maybe then you would never be sakit. It's all my fault. But you're here with me. How is it possible? Is it you for truth? Keep your meat in, Ben. Just talk. Find out what this is about.

'Okelah, Bapa. Will tell the dolphins you wanna talk.'

'Mal, please wait. Stay a while. The dolphins ...'

'We'll come back soon. Selamat tinggal, Bapa.'

'Mal?'

Must be the nutes. So much darkness and time stretching in all directions. I must hallucinate Mal coming. His sweet voice a single chirp in the expanse of emptiness. Hallucination. Nutes. Part of the treatment, perhaps. A test. What next? Will my tormentors fake a visit from Saf?

'His name is Infinite Ben, ayah dari Saffron, ayah Malcolm, suami Aisha, dari polong Evoli, pencipta MusiKai, pencipta SnakiDik, terapis dari the Reckoning.'

Hello? Mal? Who is this?

'Selamat siang. We are pods—' sounds of squeals and clicks, like birds or monkeys chittering. It's Mal's voice, still recognisable.

'Bapa, it's the dolphins.'

'Mal? Mal is it you?'

'Yeer Bapa. It's me, It's me. Are you okelah?'

Tears. Water and salt in such tides.

'Mal so good hearing your voice again.'

'Bapa, the dolphins will speak now.'

Mal, stop playing stupid games please. There are no dolphins. 'Mal. No, Mal. Please stay.'

'Sorrow is using our dearest one for communication with simplars,' Mal says, the tone of his voice suddenly alien.

'What? Mal… what?'

'Please, our dearest one has joy being here and facilitating our … communion.' Mal sounds … adult. Chilling. I'm hallucinating. The health missionaries … have Mal? Is Mal in trance? 'Why are you torturing me? You make me believe Mal is here then you make him sound like a stranger?' Is it part of the Cure?

'We are the pods—' the squealy sound again, chittering.

'Please stop. This is no Mal. I know it's no Mal.'

'The explanation is, we are here. It is the only explanation possible since it is the only explanation.'

Silence. The nurses are waiting for something. Maybe I should beg or cry. Or argue. No, I'll give them nothing. Maybe then they'll stop.

Silence. Good, it's working. A little peace is sweet.

'We wish with sex,' Mal's adult voice continues. 'Communion.' No silence, no peace. Just some bizarre test.

'Language is separateness. It is communication, but no communion. Perhaps communion arises out of communication. It seems as so with the sleek apes, the apes who come to our—' Ear-splitting squeals and clicks. 'Our water.'

'What are they saying? Mal?'

'Be sex. Be communion. Allow the vessel vibrate with the frequencies.'

I taste moaning, me giving up.

'Language making too many distinctions, too many separates. Communion is less separate than language.'

'Okelah, yeer, communion, vibration.' All too tiring.

'Communication is like masturbation if without the frequencies.'

'Less talk, more frequencies. I understand.' Moan.

'Understand. Feel the frequencies. Receive energy as if eating or playing.'

Exhale the last of my resistance. I surrender.

'Better,' alien adult Mal-voice says. 'Less separate. The place of separate is in the vessel, never the Mind, though the Mind may wish to separate from the vessel. Receive the frequencies, reduce the separate. Frequencies move life. Life makes shapes. Shapes reach back through Mind. There is communion.'

'I—'

'Receive the frequencies.'

Receiving the janking frequencies.

'The separate increases. How can we have communion when the separate increases?'

'What ... why communion?'

'Our dearest one desires it with all his heart. His desire is full and pure.'

'Your dearest one?'

'Our dearest one. He is dearest for you also.'

'Mal? Mal is your dearest one?'

'Receive the frequencies. There is no other explanation. He who is dear for you is dear for us.'

'And what? He misses his bapa and you help him talk with me?'

'His desire for communion is full and pure.'

'And so you grant.'

'The explanation is we are making the communion. There is no other explanation.'

'Why?' A vice grips my heart. Look no gift dolphin in the bottle nose. Ask too many questions and it could be communion over.

'He is our dearest one.'

'Your dearest one.' Chew down the urge for asking why again.

'He seeks communion. Unlike simplars and the other sleek apes, he refuses the defences.'

'What defences?' Jank, Ben, enough with the questions already.

'The defences others graft into necks block communion.'

'Hancies?'

'Hancies, yes. Enhancement makes loud frequencies. Too sharp. Too dry. Block communion. Our dearest one assures he will never graft one into his body. Through our dearest one, all communion is possible.'

Saf Evoli …

Squeal, 'Where are they taking him?' My heart is lead. Skin and flesh feel like they leave me and become a ghost.

Only the terror stays, watching while Bapa passes out on a gurney. A cloudy tube up his pantat skewers him like satay. Nurses surround him, solemn and holy. Orderlies at the door. Rigid guards.

Bonehead throws her arm around me and holds on tight. Lula, hand on my knee, huddles closer. As if it will keep Bapa safe. Amara clamps onto my hand. Squeeze back.

Bapa's face peaceful, frightens me all the more.

'Are we sure no one there tastes us?' Lula asks again.

'No one detects me among a fluther,' Bonehead membs, a little weary. 'Drop out if you wish.'

Lula shakes her head and crushes my knee almost harder than Amara clamps my hand.

'Is Mal undetectable too?' Amara asks.

Bonehead leery. 'How should I know? Mal is weird.' Her face flushes with sudden shame—Mal's fever is worse. He lies delirious in bed with towels binding ice around his arms and legs and on his forehead.

'Shhhh!' They're wheeling Bapa out of the room. Down a corridor, an orderly in front, another in back. The nurses a sanctimonious procession in gloves and face masks. Sinister-dead lorikeets; rainbow uniforms funeral-grey between dark walls under dim light. Lành Hiền, jalang! Sheets of her hair like black bandages hanging down for the small of her back. So black it sucks in all light and becomes deep infinite space. You belong there, black dragon, among the black walls and floors. It's you who deserves a long Cure for shredding our family.

The others we know from Bapa's official Consigning at our desa's minster. Vör Hoyur, sybil slayer. Beatrice Lovell, minster mouse. Teodora Mrowka. Only Beatrice is a clinician. The rest are just creeper-shit spies. Lành Hiền the most creeper-shit of all. Imagine me dreaming of being a nurse, after creeper-shit dragon-face slinks into our home, pretending help for Mal. Maybe she makes him sakit in the first place. Except, like Bonehead, he can see through time (almost), straight through membosankan minster security nets; without a hancy. They're gonna flush you all down history's sewer, creeper-shits.

Bonehead rubs the scar at her neck, itchy though healing quick after the hancy seat dissolves.

'What's up ahead?' Lula membs.

Shadowy, a silhouette stalks down the hall towards Bapa. 'Bonehead, pan around so we can taste better.'

'It's … furry,' Lula membs.

'Holy jank,' Amara squeals. 'It's a cat. In a nurse's uniform? Never see a nurse in a projection before.'

Bonita 'Bonehead' Patatiall ...

'Fluffy, step aside, you irrelevant grunt,' Beatrice membs. 'You're thick as Tewkesbury mustard. No one in the entire minster pays you any attention. You're invisible.'

Fluffy strokes her silly whiskers. What is it with adults and projections? 'Am I thick or invisible? If I'm nothing, why are you stopping?'

'Fine,' says Beatrice and makes for pushing the gurney over Fluffy. Vör steps in front.

'You must have other tasks,' Vör membs for Fluffy.

Fluffy scratches her chin. 'Ah, yes. The group session with the graffiti addicts,' she membs with affectations of meows among the words. 'Such a worthy occupation of my time while you slide Ben in for rebasing.'

'Simple standard procedure,' Beatrice membs. Heartless, officious old hag. 'Safe. If one administers it with competence.'

'You're ignoring the evidence, the consequences of rebasing an Infinite. Mind abhors a vacuum.'

Vör horselaughs. 'What next? Squirrels in our spooky fields?'

'Teo believes it,' Fluffy says.

Teo's eyes flicker.

'The Reck is a mess,' Beatrice membs. Chin up so she can look down her nose. Losing patience. 'We could all be sifar by tomorrow. We must find the bottom of it.'

'Bottom of what?' Saf blurts, terrified. They could have *my* bapa; I would never care, but Saf worships hers. Poor sweet Saf.

'You recall Ariel Kanon,' Fluffy membs.

'I recall you and the pig-tail German botching her admission. You are terrorising her in your ridiculous projection. Step out of the way before I call orderlies.'

'And what? Have them cat me?' Fluffy sniggers over her bodoh pun. 'Is this what we're coming to? Nurses catting each other in minster hallways over crackpot therapies?'

'We rebase 1000's of patients a day all over the world,' Vör answers. Unlike Beatrice, she's calm. Almost smiling, as if she could debate all day. Lành Hiền with intense eyes, hangs back biding her time. Teo is picking her nails and biting her lip.

'What would detectives know of such things? You lot never set foot inside a minster,' Fluffy says with exasperation. 'Never enough prestige behind scatter nets, no heroic exploits. And what would a fresh field nurse know?' Eyeing Lành Hiền. 'None of those 1000's of rebases you suddenly seem so intimately familiar with are cases involving high-rep individuals. Only average community patients under treatment for petty misdemeanours. But

Ariel Kanon? Orlando Greer? Both suffer the same adverse symptoms.' She points a clawed finger at Beatrice. 'You are out on a date with Orlando when he suffers a relapse. Perhaps it's your making eyes at him which sickens him.'

'Ben is one of only 2 remaining Infinites,' Beatrice says. 'He's guilty of manipulating the Reck. We must treat him,' she huffs. Nudges Vör aside. Pushes the gurney forward.

Fluffy blocks the way, plants a furry paw on Ben Uncle's foot. 'Condoning torture, just for the sake of—what? Wringing a confession from him?'

'Torture? He's innocent,' Saf wails. 'It's the dragon, she's setting him up. Lành Hiền Rồng, it's her!'

'Torture?' Lành Hiền echoes. Her surprise seems genuine.

'Ah, the pet dragon has no idea?' Fluffy appears mystified. She double-takes and strokes her whiskers. 'Lash these hollies and savour your complicity.'

'You lash those too?' Saf asks of the hollies Fluffy blinks.

'Yeer. Let's keep them for later okelah?'

Saf nods, accepting weakly. Hug her closer. She blinks back tears. Her chin trembles.

'For neos with high onespace network effects, the higher the connections, the more severe the symptoms,' Fluffy explains for Lành Hiền.

'Next you'll be claiming anyone who holds an Infinite's hat is at risk,' Beatrice taunts, her once insipid face flush with blood. Really dislike her, all haughty and bigwiggy.

'Joke if you must, Beatrice, but taste me well. If you proceed, Ben and perhaps many other Minds will suffer.'

Lành Hiền daggers Vör with a stare. 'You know about this?' Lành Hiền's face is so tense she almost looks plain. Plainer than me maybe.

'You come so far in so short a time,' Vör answers Lành Hiền. 'Would you sacrifice it all for a corrupt Infinite?'

'Bapa is never corrupt,' Saf protests. 'Bonehead, we must—'

Saf Evoli …

'Saf, keep your meat in,' Bonehead says with heartless cold, a slap in the face.

Plead, 'No. Do something,' so loud, it rings.

Vör with an ugly scowl advances. 'Fluffy, step aside.'

Fluffy never cowers. In her nekko projection, she's bigger and taller than Vör. With her fur standing on end and her whiskers stiff, she bares her fangs.

'There are so many who taste the disaster you would become, Vör. I am sorry for witnessing it.' Fluffy hisses. Then her shoulders slump; she looks down and shakes her head, begrudgingly steps aside.

I watch with horror; they push the gurney, slow as pallbearers. My bapa still and cold like the dearly departing. Maybe only mins away from a procedure Fluffy calls torture.

Ben Evoli …

Pink light.

Worms squirming in my eyes. Fly larvae scratching out of my skin. Dry throat. Head aching with a crumbling skull.

Pink light harpoons the ache. Chest hollow, the size of a limestone cavern. Stomach full of dry flour and gravel. Crack eyelids open, lashes crusty with gluey crystals. Pink light becomes white blades slicing into eye sockets. Squint. Grit teeth against the pain.

Remember. There's something I must remember. Before passing out, Vör and Lành Hiền are voracious fish swimming upstream at me. A nurse at a sickening angle leans back, a sanctimonious judge. Another talking with tongue and lung in murky whispers at orderlies. Then black.

Here. Sometime in between. How long between? How long is my Mind out of my fruit? A long time. Unconsciousness like growth rings of a tree. Between each ring something liquid. Oozing sap. Gooey structureless Mind slinking without choice, without intent, just gurgling down a drain.

Memories of Saf. Saf in distress watching some seething horror. Saf's friend Bonita comforting her—Lula and Amara too. Saf crying. Lula with her hand over her mouth, eyes wide. Amara's head down refusing looking. Bonita with thin lips of outrage making a solemn promise, something vengeful.

Taste a dark dream. Recent and distant, rising. Revealing glimpses. Its maw opens, hungry and primeval, teeth yellow-grey and sinister. Shrink back. Too slow. It swallows everything.

Me? No. Someone else, please! Invading seeping in. Becoming fusing crystallising. Someone else's heart beating too fast. Breath like decaying meat. Hulking torso, chest hairy. Thick legs up and splaying like a frog's. Mind rejecting dissolving.

Another desert night, cold and crisp. The truck's heater way up. The sound of the air blasting through the vents like a hissing cymbal. The truck's stereo blaring the Zac Brown Band from my phone. Suddenly the music stops, headlights blink and sputter out, the aircon fans whir down. The electric motors on both axles squeal and stop, the truck lurches and throws me forward hard. The seatbelt bites my chest like a starving coyote, knocks the wind out of me. Blood rushes, thumping in my temples. Seeing red. The main engine sputters and stops firing. I can't be out of gasoline. I just put 17 gallons in the tank this afternoon at Nate's Bait & Tackle.

Blinding light above a cold star amid blackness all around.

The white. Searing white. I feel like I'm floating. Something sucking the fucking truck up. Sucking up an F-150! Not a tornado, not getting tossed about enough. More like gravity deciding to take a vacation.

A snowshoe hare is sitting in the passenger seat sniffing the air. 'We're all food for someone,' it says. I don't hear it so much as... like remembering something someone said, out of my Mind's Ear.

Black.

Bright lights shining right in my face. Like an operating theatre the time I broke my arm.

Heart beating faster than hummingbird wings. The taste of steak and beer rich in my mouth. I ate at the bar before work. Now I'm on my back. Why? Try to swing my legs. Something pinning my ankles. Straps bite my wrists. Shock and fear hit my chest like a line backer. Coughing air out of collapsing lungs. What happened to my chest? Hairless and pale like a city boy. Jesus! Someone's shaved my groin and—what the fuck? My johnson is puny. My legs are up in stirrups like I'm gonna get a woman's examination. Can't move. I'm like a frog in science class. And there's something cold and nasty in my ass.

Fuck, what's going on? I'm getting raped in a hospital? Some sick medical fetish scenario. Stay calm. Breathe, you pussy.

Out of the black, 2 nurses or doctors on either side peer over. They look sick. Grey-skinned. Not like anyone I've seen. Not even like Asians or Swedish. Huge eyes and flat noses. Short. Like Asians. Cartoon figures: little grey men crossed with Wesley's manga comics.

Fuck, Jesus, sweet Jesus. Are they ... aliens? You created aliens just so they could come abduct me? Why does your plan need aliens, right down to the bug-eyes and the anal probing? Please, Jesus, why me? I'm a good American, ain't I, sweet Jesus, just like you always wanted? I like baseball and porno and war movies, just like every average guy. What have I done to deserve this?

Jesus! Oh, God. If you let me out, I promise—oh, please Sweet Jesus, Blessed Lamb. I promise I'll go back to church. I promise. And Mary ... I'll tell Mary it's over. She'll understand. I'm married, for Chrissakes—we must stop. Oh, Christ, sweet Jesus, I'm sorry for everything.

Oh God, oh God, oh Gawd, oh gawd, oh ...

Gawd?

'Selamat siang, Infinite Ben dari polong Evoli ayah dari Mal,' says one of the alien doctors through its mask.

What the fuck language is that?

'Selamat siang.'

I know the voice. My son. I have a son? Who …?

Older than my son. An adult.

'Is it so hard believing, Bapa? The same stuff of Mind underpins all manifest creation. Yet you resist the idea we are in sex with you?'

What? Mal? What the fuck, what the jank? Why is he talking about sex?

'It's me, Bapa.'

Crying. Streams of tears. Every thought a shock—knives stabbing everywhere. A truck, stab; engine failing; weightless; aliens; Mary; Aisha; Mal. Stab.

'You simplars call your vessels, *fruit*. An interesting metaphor: your vessels are fruit of Mind.' Mal's voice sounding so alien.

Aliens, stab; interrogating me?

'Bapa, pay attention.' Mal's true voice. He's here somewhere.

'We have a metaphor.' Aliens controlling Mal again. 'We say we are vessels for Mind. Curious. Perhaps living on land makes for a different way of thinking. Fruit is less to us. Vessel and water go together like—'

'Mind and body.' Is it me answering?

'You are fruit and we are vessels,' the aliens say through Mal.

It hurts so much. Racking sobs.

'Vessels have purpose.'

I say, 'For containing Mind.' I keep splitting and converging. Pull your meat in, Ben. Mary and the truck. Keep your meat in.

'Vessel is Mind and contains Mind. Your language is tricky. It tricks Mind into thinking if there are 2 words, there must be 2 distinct meanings. Words slice up reality.'

Blather, 'Words slice.'

'Which is why we avoid such distinctions. The idea of *vessel* is useful to understand what happens some hours ago.'

Still happening. 'Mary, sweet Mary, I must leave. Must escape the aliens. They're doing things to me, Mary. The aliens!'

'Beings who appear inhuman to saps,' Mal's voice membs.

'They *are* inhuman.'

'Nurses,' strange Mal says.

'Little creatures with huge heads, big eyes and no noses.'

'Just how a sap would describe a neo,' Mal-the-alien says. 'Nurses, aliens; one and the same. Just 2 Minds perceiving from a unique viewpoint. Two Minds entangling in onespace during the rebase procedure. Sometimes rebasing captures Mind of our kind too.'

'Two Minds?'

'It appears random. We perceive no pattern. Simplars with very large Mind networks are at great risk.'

'Infinites?'

'And familiars of Infinites.'

'My family could—?'

'Yeer, if they ever receive the same procedures,' Mal says with the strange adult voice.

'This must stop.'

'It must, Bapa,' The true Mal says.

'It must stop for all kinds of truth,' say the many of Mal. 'The Mind damage during rebasing is incalculable. Many never reconcile such an inexplicable experience with their view of reality and lose Mind coherence. There is much sadness among the pods. Sometimes other species dash their vessels on the desiccation of land stranding there to die.'

'You mean …?'

'Whales, Bapa. And dolphins, of course.'

'And others,' strange polyphonic Mal says.

Calming down. It seems any explanation, no matter how preposterous, is good enough if the alternative is believing I'm crazy. 'Saps all over the world are suffering too?'

'Mind all through time is suffering. In your case, your Mind entangles with a sap from the 21st century.'

'What?'

'Your histories are full of experiences—demon possession, alien abduction—these are how you explain it.'

Deep breath. Mary and the truck recede—someone else's life.

'Simplars are evolving,' Mal's strange voice says. 'There are confluences of Mind of which these possessions or abductions are a side-effect. We hope the shift will be easier than between sap and neo. In the meantime, simplar health care procedures must stop so evolution may converge beyond this.'

'Why are you telling me?'

'You are the Bapa of our dearest one, the one by which we are at sex together.'

'Can we stop referring to communication as sex?'

He or they giggle. All of them. Or maybe just Mal. 'Why? Everything is in … communion. Ecstasy. Only simplars create enough thought to block the truth.'

'Why tell me this? I'm powerless while I'm in here undergoing a Cure.'

'The nurses make a mistake moving you to Vauxminster.'

'Why? Can you get me out?'

'We assist through our dearest one, by helping you be in s…— communion—with the outside world.'

'Then why is Vauxminster a mistake for the nurses?'

'There is someone else here undergoing a Cure who you should be at communion with.'

'Who?'
'Bapa, it's the White Witch.'

Jesus! Oh, God. Please let me out, Sweet Jesus, Blessed Lamb. Lemme out of the truck. The music is too loud in my head. It isn't mine. Mary isn't mine. I must tell her, must end it. Before the dolphins find out.

Alien abduction, demon dolphins possessing Mal, making him … making him … Stop making him. Just stop. Please, just stop.

Taste steak and beer—dinner at the bar before work, watching the game.

Fingernails digging into the jumpsuit. Pink. No advancement. Still pink. I'll never get out of here. Where? Alamak! A recreational room in Vauxminster. It's more peaceful, more … real. But is it better?

You are fruit and we are vessels.

Stop.

Vessel is Mind and contains Mind.

Just. Stop.

Keep your meat in, Ben. It's part of the Cure. It explains everything. They're messing with your Mind, deconstructing it so … then what?

Look around. Patients in jumpsuits … all immersed in personal, hancy-assisted, invisible activities. Playing holly ping-pong, snow-skiing, basketball.

There's no truck. There's only here. There's no Mary, no little aliens. No Mal. No dolphins.

I'm here and I'm real.

Until the next session. What then? Will they have me believe Aisha is here? Will she be crying, begging forgiveness for betraying me to the White Witch's underlings? Will she morph into a hairy ape of a guy, with dead-meat breath, in a Ford Raptor?

Shudder, shake it out: the thing uglier than a sap. A huge hulk thick and hairy, inflating under my skin like air in a balloon. Fetid air full of particulates of blood and gristle, seeping in, fighting me for possession of my body. How is this possible? Possession? Impossible. It's all delusion; the therapies are inducing hallucinations. That's all.

I must escape. Escape the spells of these barbaric witches. I have news: your therapies are failing. I am fine when you Consign me, now I'm much worse. You're failing, so I will escape, that's how it will be. I'll be gone. I'll use my considerable influence and bring you all down. I'll close all your minsters. Your missions will be over: total failures, all.

It must stop for all kinds of truth. The Mind damage is incalculable.

The Mind damage of what? Who says so? I say it, that's who.

Deep breath. Mary and the truck recede, someone else's delusions.

Other echoes rise. 'Bapa, it's the White Witch,' Mal says over and over on a reverberating loop.

Worms squirming in my eyes. Miniscule insects scratching out of the skin. Dry throat. Head aching with a crumbling skull. Stomach full of dry flour and gravel.

Moments in the rec room between craze-inducing therapies. A patient crashes into the couch alongside—a ping-pong player making a forlorn lunge for a ball no one else sees. Crashes into a row of chairs. Shouts and objections; patients leaping out of seats. No one aids the ping-pong player on his feet.

A snowshoe hare sits in the passenger seat. And sits on chair by the exit corridor. Sniffing the air. 'We're all food for someone,' it says and turns into a cat. Now it's standing in the corridor. Wearing a nurse's uniform.

The cat fixes me with predator eyes and comes for me. No stalking prey, just a direct skip. Nurses with rolling eyes turn away. No one prevents the cat coming for me. No one cares.

The cat stands in front of me, twitching whiskers. 'Come with me,' it says.

'What?' Look side-for-side for a reference point. Everyone, by ignoring the cat, is ignoring me. We are together invisible.

'Come with me,' it says again, nods and swipes her paw towards the exit. 'Come now, please.'

Maybe this is how I escape.

In a windowless clinic room off a narrow hall down the corridor from the rec room. On the room's only massage table is a folded nurse's uniform, a mission cap, and a utility belt. On the floor is a knocked-about pair of regulation boots.

I make my face into a question and show it for the cat.

'Put those on,' the cat says. 'And be quick.'

'You're helping me escape?'

The cat growls. 'No questions. Just follow instructions.' The cat is warring within itself.

Maybe this is another part of my Cure. I change clothes anyway. The cat busies with some instruments and other things on a bench by the wall.

The uniform is a kay fit, the cap a little too small. The boots too big. Could make skipping awkward.

'Throw your gown in the sucky. There's another in the cupboard for after.'

'I'm coming back?'

'Yes, of course. *Intern.*' Okelah, I'm an intern. 'Unless you're already considering giving up on the mission,' the cat continues. 'There's no shame in it. The nursing mission is hard. Many interns give up well before entering Academy. There's no shame in it.' Her paw fidgets with her whiskers. 'Show me how you look.'

I model the uniform, feeling awkward. The cat taps me still while she straightens my shirt and sets the fold of the pants.

'Tuck your hair into your mission cap. It's much too long for an intern. Almost unseemly. You should shave it, understand?'

I nod. Try pushing my hair under the cap, while the cat tightens my belt, and tucks my shirt in again. 'I'm sorry there is nothing in the utility belt. Requisitioning extra kit on such short notice might raise suspicion. Now, where is your chatelaine?'

'Chatelaine?'

'You show up for your first day as an intern at one of the most prestigious minsters in all the world without a chatelaine? Huh? You'd be better skipping naked through the minster all day than show such disrespect for our traditions. Well, it bodes ill for your career here, I must say. My best advice is, make yourelf a small target. Some older nurses are ruthless with interns. They'll tear you down for the slightest reason. Attract no attention whatsoever, understand?'

'Like you?' I ask.

'Say again?'

'I watch you before. You attract no attention when you come for me. No one even notices you're around.'

The cat makes its fangs smile. 'Sit up on the table. I'm swapping your hancy.'

'I'm getting my own hancy back?'

'Are you crazy? You wish a target on you?' the cat blurts then recovers. 'Interns get a basic hancy which blocks loading any hoots. Which is what you're getting today. Intern.' I nod and let the cat remove the patient hancy. 'It's almost lunchtime. When we finish here, I suggest you go for the cafeteria early. A queue develops quickly down there.'

'I'm sorry, where is the cafeteria again?' I ask.

'There's a map in the hancy. It gives directions for any low-security area in the minster.'

'And after lunch?'

'Join an introductory tour of the minster. They leave every half-hour.'

'And then?'

The cat scowls. 'Leave with a large group. Who knows? Maybe there'll be other new interns whose uniforms are in worse shape.'

That cat herds me at the door.

'I'm sorry,' she says. My innards are melting ice in fear of a trick. My hand is yet on the door handle.

'What?' My back is still toward her.

She says nothing, perhaps waiting until I turn around. I turn. Warily.

The cat looks penitent. 'I'm sorry,' she says again. 'I should never let Vör and Beatrice rebase you. I should stop them when I have the chance.'

Sweetness

'Bullet with Butterfly Wings' — Smashing Pumpkins

Nilajani Karunanithi ...

REGARDING VÖR WITH SOME DISTASTE is the Present Invisible of the conference, Iosephina Fanaafi, Administrative Nurse of *Church* (the informal name for the Pacific Islands Church of Health). She wears the stony grimace y'all might reserve for an obnoxious neighbour.

'Teo, please run the numbers for us?' says Fumanekile Mhlambiso of *Gesondheid Camerata van Suid-Afrika* (South African Fellows).

'Let's start with estimating the capacity for sybil production, then look at sybil demand. From there we might estimate the number of crèches.'

'Please proceed,' says Qamra el-Yousef of *Niqabat Alsihat Shamal 'Afriqia* (North African Health Syndicate).

Teo nods, and pats down her uniform. 'We know the most reliable crèching process for producing stable sybil brains takes 451 mins. Let's say a crèche needs an additional hour between for cleaning, resetting, whatever. So, a crèche pod—'

'*Metra*,' Qamra corrects. 'They call it a *metra*.'

'As in uterus?'

'Yes.'

'Thank you. A metra could turn out a sybil every 10 hours.'

'Is this astonishing fast or mind-numbing slow? I have no idea.'

'It's the best estimate we have,' Teo says. 'From there we arrive at a maximum sybil production for a single metra in a single year: 876.'

'Assuming no down time for maintenance,' says Nelson Vallyaris, also of South African Fellows, a camerata famous for believing they run everything.

'Correct, so reduce by, say, 21%.'

'Plucking numbers from our cloacas, but kay.'

'So those number suggest a metra could produce 600 to 700 sybils per year. Let's project how many sybils these Infinites might demand. Latest estimates put the number of Infinites—'

'*Ex*-Infinites,' Nelson corrects.

'—at around 5 million. We can never launch an effective initiative against every one.' The room cools. Vör's grin is wider than a beach. Teo loses her place, pats herelf down again and swallows. 'So … rather than target individual Infinites—'

'*Ex*-Infinites.'

'—I propose we tackle the problem by cutting off sybil production and storage,' Teo answers. 'Let's consider how many new sybils Infinites might demand over, say, a year.' She pauses. No one is interrupting. 'Here's where we really lick a finger and hold it up to onespace. If the average demand per Infi is 2 new sybils per month, the total annual demand would be 120 million.'

Hear the sucking in of breaths all through onespace. 'Holy mother of Ghandi,' one gasps.

'Which requires over 180,000 metrae.'

'We will never find all those.' Short sharp laughter and throats clearing.

'I try making everyone aware of this for weeks,' one nurse crows, anxious yet jubilant for having corroboration.

Vör is smugly jaunty. Make no mistake it's her schemes which are blossoming.

'Two per Infinite per month seems a low number considering Orlando has over 1600 when we Consign him.'

'When Eir Consigns him. And she has just as many.'

'Right. Assume use is 2 per day—'

'Which may still be shy of the real number,' says my *mava*, Elsbeth Putney-Wells.

'—run the numbers again, and we arrive at demand exceeding 5.5 million metrae.'

There is silence, which Teo savours. Vör even more so.

'Is there one metra for a crèche? 5 million installations?'

'We have no information. Some crèches have a single metra while other may house 14's.'

'Or 100's.'

'We'll never find every installation.'

'We must always rely on sound investigation and detection,' Elsbeth says somewhat absent-mindedly.

'And nurses in the field. Any effective effort for shutting down crèches will come at the cost of real health care resources for the community, and for what? A vendetta?'

'These Infinites are sick too,' Nelson says.

'Yes. Should we allow their illness fester any longer?' Fumanekile adds.

'Let's look at it another way,' Nelson says. She and her colleague hog the debate. 'Take the Infinites we know use sybils, and work from there.'

'There are many who escape Warrants at the Inductee Gala,' Gerlinde membs for the first time, lacing her words with accusation.

'Including Maddox Price,' Nelson says.

'And Orlando Greer, who we already have,' Gerlinde adds.

'Thanks to the White Witch.' Fumanekile again.

'We have her too. Praise the nightingales!' Elsbeth says.

'Include the rest of Maddox's inner cabal. Piloto Iscariot and Pet Dynamite,' Teo wrests the flow of conversation back.

'Lemarr Robinson,' someone adds.

A shuffle of discomfort affects the conference. Feel it rippling through onespace. Until recent weeks, we all have unshakable belief we could ferret out any secret in the world. Our belief keeps us blind.

'Piloto's mission would need a large crèche, with all the celebrity sybils he crèches for his more exclusive bordelis.'

Some laughter. Famous musicians and actors all over the world are furious with Piloto committing the worst kind of copyright infringement. Sap notions of property are alive and sickening.

'So, the most prominent suspects number 14 or so,' Nelson summarises.

'Say, 21.'

'A little over one Infinite for each major health camerata.'

'It's still a great deal of effort. We're essentially onespace investigators. We lack the surveillance tech for covering physical territory.'

'Will we just skip around the planet and hope we trip over crèches?' Fumanekile is incredulous.

'We must deploy our resources well,' Elsbeth says. 'We have prodigious magazines of hollies reaching back centuries. We can collate geographical information.'

'For certain we should revisit the Amazon Basin. We know Christian Zappa is thick to his beard with Maddox,' Nelson says. Teo and Gerlinde shudder.

'Caracia, you mean. The South Americans can handle Zappa,' Gerlinde says. 'We're never going back in there.'

'You should heed our warning in the first place.'

'We retrieve Ben,' Gerlinde replies, her defences rising. 'Much of what we know comes from accessing his sybil's memories.'

'Caracia gives us Ben. For what motive we can only guess.'

'Leave Caracia out of it,' Teo says. 'She'll require special attention. Doubt she has any need of sybils. No one flutherbombs her in decades.'

'*Ja*, which makes her the ideal ringleader.' Nelson's agenda are plain in her arguments. She's wanting South Africa running everything.

Teo raises a holly of the globe overlaying a heat map of population densities. 'Here's where we live. We know Infinites use saps for a labour force. Saps are incapable of travelling far, and must hide, so it follows illicit Infi activities would co-locate with sap settlements. In other words, the remotest or most impenetrable regions in the world.' Teo rotates the holly and zooms in on a series of regions around the globe. 'Leaving plenty of options: the Taiga of Russia and North America—'

'And Scandinavia,' Nelson interjects as if saying, *You could have crèches in your own homes too.*

'*Ja,*' Teo says. 'Also what's left of the Sahara Desert, desert Australia, the Wastelands of America. Also, mountainous regions ...'

'Saps could be one valley over from us in New Guinea, and we would never know.'

'It might be quicker redeveloping satellite capability,' someone says. Groans from others.

'Orlando is from California, Piloto from Texas. Bordering both is Wasteland. There are no health camerati there. It seems a likely place.'

'Piloto is in South America also. One of his most prestigious bordelis for the Hodinkle Society is in the Peruvian jungle.'

'It seems primitive tribes always survive the best in jungles.' Not sure whether Nelson means saps or Piloto and his cronies.

'Piloto should be a first target. Reducing his supply of sybils would deliver a serious blow for his operation.'

'And protect us against reputation raids from the musicians and actors he crèches over the years.'

'We must infiltrate his bordelis. We might learn much from there.'

'It's a good plan.'

'We should be careful. There would be a serious public backlash if we are overt against bordelis.'

'Yes. May as well starve a neo as kerb their recreational sex.'

'While this is all well and good, how might we find a few thousand buildings in Russia? Canada?'

'The Taiga and the Amazon—and many other places—are sacred. No one lives there. Must we duplicate the folly of the Fordlândia expedition, and go campaigning into places everyone agrees we should leave alone?'

'We'll dig into the Antarctic Ice Shelf if that's what it takes,' Vör answers aggressively.

'And how will *det Fødererede Sundhedskamerata i Nordeuropa* direct their resources?' Nelson mocks Vör.

'Easy,' Vör membs, stands grim and resolute. 'We'll be hunting for the crèches where sybils of the White Witch spawn.'

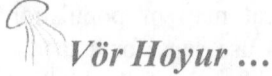

Vör Hoyur …

After most of the conferees break away, some of the leadership of the 17 major health camerati remain. An awkward tik of silence stretches, until Teo ushers me out with a sharp stare and knotting eyebrows. Well, jank. I'll flutherbomb.

'Will any health camerata survive long enough for dealing with this?' asks Nelson Vallyaris from *Gesondheid Camerata van Suid-Afrika*. Only a pair from each camerata remains in there.

'Our reputasi is suffering even more than some Infinites.' Poor things, all feeling sorry for themelves.

'1000's of our nurses are abandoning the mission,' another says, 'and almost half our academy is absent from lessons.'

'Fair weather missionaries,' Nelson says, showing little empathy.

'We're all feeling it,' Elsbeth Putney-Wells says, putting a brave face on. 'It's uncomfortable confronting how tenuous our influence is becoming.'

'There are cases of defying Warrants outright,' says Qamra.

'And their reputations rise,' says another with great distaste.

'We have one nurse who becomes sifar after she cats a patient.'

'The reputasi of sifars squatting in homes of the once Infinite is going up too. Which for them is worse than it going down for an Infinite.'

'Cases of looting are increasing, and the reputasi of perpetrators is going up.'

'Well, in a society without formal possession rights, it can hardly be looting. More like impetuous borrowing.'

'What if they cause damage?'

And so it keeps going. If they ever arrive at a decision in there, could someone memb?

Teodora Mrowka …

Bem-estar Amazônico are busy assisting *Salud Centroamérica* for tracking Piloto Iscariot around Monterrey, Texas—Piloto's hometown. Ignoring their own Amazon Basin, they follow leads north in the brown tornado plains of Wasteland, leaving the lands around Christian Zappa's borders for us.

Let the Americans chase after Piloto; we're certain we'll find the most important crèches here. Maddox and Caracia's sucker-prints are all over the region, entangling Eir in their schemes somehow. The coincidences are too great.

Sundhed humours our mission as a fool's holiday. The White Witch's reign is over, they say. We have her in Vauxminster. Her sybils, if she has any, are dozing in cribs. Useless. 'In the meantime,' a *Sundhed* detective tells Vör,

'Feed your vendetta. We'll have a Warrant ready for your return.'

Our frustration builds after days of boating up and down the Amazon, flutherbombing everyone in sight. The locals taste nothing. Vör's arrogance blinds her. She assumes the nurses of Amazon Wellness are incompetent or corrupt or both. She believes, if we flood the Amazon with *Sundhed* operatives, we'd expose the muddy underbelly of a huge and obvious conspiracy.

What we need is good old-fashion surveillance of fourspace. We must cover 1000's of square kims of rainforest looking for clandestine activity. But we have no flying contraptions. (When I think of sap helicopters! Blades *above* passengers' heads? Upended food processors.) Until now, we have no need of travelling. In onespace we spook across the world in an instant. In gormless ignorance of everything in between.

Vör Hoyur ...

Fondle the pistol nestling in my kangaroo pocket. The pistol the sifar Jesús purloins from Ben's loot. The fruits of good persistent detective work. There's no substitute for surveilling everyone around your target.

Slick and unyielding, warm from my body heat. Familiar like a hand-me-down from my *bedstemor*. Still unsure if firing it is within my conviction. Imagine the irony of shooting Ben with his own Greedily kept pistol.

I trace the edge of a different object in my pocket. An envelope. Another handwriting message from my *mor*, the monster of the 8 Car Garage. I picture her laughing as she writes, savouring how she puppets me, dances me across the stage of the world for her own untastable ends. Ends which, for now, coincide with mine. May we destroy every last crèche and sybil in the world.

The note—cryptic as the previous 6—reads:

Opera by your river
In a graveyard of white elephants
For a cup of the world
Comes alive with reincarnation
At an impasse
Beware of penalties
Beware of shoot-outs

Let's start with the easy bits of Mor's note.
Comes alive with reincarnation.
A reference about creating sybils if ever I hear one.
Shoot-outs. Penalties

Obvious. Penalty shoot-outs refer to football—soccer if y'all are Australian or a Wastelander.

Opera by your river.

My river. I taste *Mor* is leading me back into the Amazon. Opera? What connects opera and the river?

For a cup of the world.

Football again. Brazil hosts the World Cup circus in 1950 and again in 2014.

In a graveyard of white elephants.

Elephants? There are no elephants in South America. Perhaps there was once a zoo or a circus … ah, here's a holly. An elephant named Ruperta dies … of starvation, in Caricuao Zoo, Venezuela, 2018. Was she white? There was a sanctuary for elephants rescued from circuses in Mato Grosso. The source of the Tapajós is in Mato Grosso. Coincidence? A sanctuary is no graveyard. I hope. Never underestimate the saps' ability for harvesting the exact opposite of whatever they intend.

So: football, opera, and white elephants; somewhere by the Amazon River.

Cíntia Ferreira Guimarães laughs and throws back a cachaça in one smooth slide down her throat. She's less frosty since we clear her of the sabotage of the Tapajós expedition; she loves her river steamer too much for risking running it aground. 'Elephants? In the Amazon?'

I say, '*White* elephants.'

Which has Cíntia laughing all the harder. 'When looking for elephants, put an ear on the ground and listen for stomping.' Cíntia stares into her empty glass; waves it at the bar tender.

'Well, if you're only making fun of me …' I'm half off my stool.

'Steady,' Cíntia soothes. 'Sit down, have another *capeta*.'

I mollify. And wait. For a short time. 'Well?'

Cíntia throws down her next drink and drags out the tension. Constructs a meaningful look for me. '*White elephant* is a sap expression. It means a valued or status-elevating possession that is in fact troublesome, high in maintenance, or hard for disposing.'

'Sounds harsh for the elephant.'

'Well … saps,' Cíntia says with a what-can-you-expect expression. 'In a garage sale, the last thing left is the elephant in the room.'

I narrow my eyes regarding her garage reference. Is *Mor* pulling her strings? I say, 'A purchase hard for throwing in the trunk, I suppose.'

'Anyway, the place you're looking for is Manaus.'

I blink and shake my head. 'I never hear of it.'

'Oh, a nurse never hears of it? A good quality for concealing secret Infi business, I'd say?' Cíntia waves the bartender over, and gestures she bring the bottle. 'Manaus is legend in the Amazon. Another 700 kims upriver from here. Once a huge city of millions. In such a remote place without road access, resident saps embraced the new verging tech with such *entusiasmo*. The possibility of being in Sao Paolo or Rio or Paris in a blink seemed too good to be true. And of course, it was. Cases of Entanglement Syndrome were among the highest in the Amazon. Manaus, the worst. The city collapsed quickly.'

I ask, 'It's abandoned?'

Cíntia nods.

'Manaus is the white elephant?'

'You could say so. More accurately, there were 2 white elephants in Manaus.'

I sit up straight, put my drink down.

'The first was a stadium built for a football World Cup. After the tournament, it was never used for sport again. There were even suggestions they convert it into a prison.'

Rigid with attention. 'And the other?'

'A folly borne of the Pride and elf-satisfaction of the rubber barons in the late 19th century. A building of English steel and Tuscan marble, Alsatian roofing and Venetian glass. Floors of Norwegian timber. The humid jungle eats those materials like mouldy bread.'

'A building? What was it used for?'

'Oh, musical performances. Mostly opera.'

Gerlinde Mann ...

A 700-kim expedition up the Amazon and Rio Negro for Manaus is more bent-brain than the Fordlândia failure. A trip of 4 days. With the *Capivara* still out of commission, we must depend on inflatables. *Teatro Amazonas*— the opera house pinker than the dolphins—is a kim back from the shores of Rio Negro, amid the city centre. *Arena da Amazônia* is another 5 kims north. With the ruined city under rainforest, the going will be harder than bashing through virgin jungle.

Vör is adamant we make the attempt. Curiously, Cíntia backs her; why she has a say in it mystifies me.

'There may still be streets and roads,' Cíntia says.

'What?' Vör asks sounding evermore hopeful.

'I see it before,' Cíntia answers. 'Where once there were sap roads, small bushes and herbs reclaimed the ground before the tall trees had a chance for taking root. This is why rainforest never grows the way it is before. Once cleared, smaller faster-growing species take over. There are corridors of grass and low vegetation still cutting through rainforests where roads once were.'

'Buildings could collapse and block those corridors?' Teo checks.

'True,' Cíntia concedes. 'However, Manaus was built on a grid system of roads. If a road is impassable, look for parallel alternatives.'

'*Arena da Amazônia* sits much farther back from the river.'

'Ah, *sim*, but see here.' Cíntia conjures up a holly of Manaus from sap times. Points out a river—a creek in comparison to the 3-kim-wide Rio Negro. 'Here is São Raimundo,' she says, tracing a course winding through the eastern quarter of the city then cutting almost straight north as if aiming direct for the stadium, passing 200 metres on the west.

'It must be less than 10 metres wide there,' I observe. 'Is it navigable?'

'I count 16 road bridges across the waterway,' Teo adds. 'Some of those will have collapsed, probably blocking passage.'

'Inflatables it is then,' Vör says. 'Easy for hauling out of the water as we need.'

'The range of the motors is insufficient for a return trip. We must pack spare batteries.'

'Or spook them.'

'We should learn from last time. If we're taking a demountable station—'

'Of course we are. We'd be bent-brain venturing into the wild with no spooking out.'

'—then we should travel light. With small numbers, an advance party. Set up the demountable once we're there, spook everyone else direct.'

'And spook all the fold-away bicycles you could ever ride,' Cíntia chuckles. No one else joins in.

Vör Hoyur …

Teo leads Bravo Squad for *Arena da Amazônia*. Leading Alfa Squad for *Teatro Amazonas* is Gentle Dragon who is so chaffy with her appointment. So chaffy she never grasps who volunteers for Teo's Squad—Gerlinde and myelf, for example. Most of the expedition wants avoiding her. I need keep an eye on Gerlinde. Her thirst for hunting down sybils is undeniable and yet, while she aligns with opposing Eir, she's ambivalent about Consigning Infis and sceptical of my leadership.

After 4 days travelling upriver, Alfa Squad strikes for the eastern bank of São Raimundo where they erect a spooky station. From there, hoping for passable streets, they skip east for the opera house. Bravo Squad continues upriver around the first of many bridge ruins. On each bank, a twisting pleach of vines and reinforcing steel worms through slimy green-black concrete rubble that plunges quickly, in abstract shapes, under the surface of the river.

In 3's and 4's, we straddle the fallen tree blocking the corridor; throw legs over for the other side. Thick rainforest crowds a ribbon of grey sky sinking towards us with the weight of rain. Cíntia is right; the jungle's furious towering canopy ends at the gutters of the old road where grasses and ferns take root in the shallow orange soil. Cracked concrete and broken biscuits of bitumen jut out like demonic coral. Occasionally the jungle thins, and we see deeper into the centuries-old battle between the living and the dead. Shards of industrial construction stab at slow, irresistible predators seething over the ground, suffocating, crumbling, and digesting everything under vivid-green tendrils.

'Shush!' Gerlinde commands and angles her ear for the air. 'Sounds like … giant mosquitoes.'

'It's getting louder,' Beatrice answers.

'Up there. Look.'

'Where?'

'I know such things from my mining mission days,' membs Rudie Holdhuis, a detective nurse on secondment from the Health Fellows of South Africa. At blank and curious looks, she answers, 'It's a mining drone.'

'A what? What's it here for?'

'I doubt it's panning for gold.'

The grey sky tints violet. A hollow huff follows—a congress of ghosts exhaling at once. Hovering over the road is a drone approaching with a small glowing violet ball in tow.

'Is that a spooky field it's pulling?'

'Run. Hide,' Rudie shouts.

The drone is too curious a thing, too inexplicable for ignoring. While we stare, the spooky field swells and begins orbiting the drone, accelerating until a single hoop of light is advancing towards us.

'Run. Hide.'

A crack of lighting shakes the ground beneath. A thin ribbon of blinding light snakes like a lasso around the spinning field, connects and turns jagged. The afterimage on my retinas last well after the ribbon disappears, while the shock of it catapults nurses and crèche staff screaming into the thickets of the jungle.

'What the jank?' someone membs.

'The whole thing is a sucky drill,' Rudie answers. 'Think of it as a mobile, giga-powerful sucky bin for aiming at ore deposits.'

'A sucky bin that makes feedstock of rock?'

Bomb a fluther nearer Rudie. '*Ja* and also useful for garbage mining,' she says.

'Maddox!' Gerlinde spits. There's one Infi she's less than fond for.

'One is right over our position.' A memb from a scout. 'Jank. Lightning just strikes it.'

'It's coming down into the forest.'

'Infis would sacrifice forest while attacking us?' Gerlinde shakes her head. Any residual sympathy she may have for Infis withers in the scorn of her moral outrage.

Behind, the sky flashes a brighter hue of purple, and sucks at the air and the tops of tall trees.

'There's another one over us,' Rudie membs in panic.

'Could be saps controlling the drills—we're tasting no fluther activity. Who knows what they're capable of.'

'You think they mean killing us?'

'We must spook out.'

Flashes of violet all around. Ear-splitting cracks report the top of the canopy splitting. The sucky drill erases everything in its path, expelling large chunks of trees at the edge. Frightened nurses spooking away risk onespace collisions in the low-capacity demountable station.

 *Teodora Mrowka …*

I shout, 'Vör!' At a run, her rainbow uniform disappears in the undergrowth.

In this instant of the universe, there are only 2 kinds of nurses: those spooking out and those following Vör. For my surprise, Gerlinde pursues Vör bashing through the undergrowth. Green reaches around her, embraces her, spirits her away.

Another drill appears and yawns above, bright and threatening. There could be many more.

Holy jank. I call, 'It's coming down. Get out from under.'

Crouch and run after Vör, keep hands over head, flimsy protection against a mighty tree falling. Taste the beam slicing down, a spinning screaming circular saw of searing light. The bones of the earth fracture. Timber splits above. Swishes and whooshes. Smaller snaps around. Pieces of jungle canopy drop like thunderous florets of broccoli. I prop and change direction. Cries of 'Look out!' and, 'Above you!' A vacuum sweeps into the jungle, sucking air in deafening moans. Running away from the sound, searching for the others. Dirt and jungle floor debris lashing my face. The roar of sucking wind increases. It could pull me off my feet, maybe drag me all the way into the ravenous cavern of its spooky field. Too close, a tree falls with the weight of a ship running aground. Everything quakes and lurches.

The spooky grenades on my utility belt weigh heavy; rip them away from the belt and toss them left and right; they disappear faster than shot cannonballs towards the sucky drill. Stupid. Should spook out when I have the chance. Now it's too risky stopping and coalescing vectors. If I could stand still for a tik, without fighting the wind and debris, maybe … might need a spook no matter what. There's no chance I'm going into the drill field.

Lose my footing. Falling. Cry out; grit my teeth; clamp my eyes shut. Something cracks. My nose stabs me between the eyes. Taste blood and dirt. No sense of up or down, only tumbling, twisting. Have maybe a tik before—

Beatrice Lovell ...

An abrupt silence leaves ringing in the ears. The sucking hurricane stops. Speckles of dust float in the shafts of light cutting through the forest canopy. Leaves, tree bark and palm fronds swirl and squiggle to the ground. The peace is a fairy land after the unnatural power of the sucky drills.

Nurses cough dust out of throats. Some sob. A few moan with minor injuries. Auras are chaotic shreds. Of the nurses who remain on location, a handful are missing, including Teo.

Rudie is a few metres away on her haunches, hands on her thighs, forearms taught. 'Nasty,' she says, breathless. 'They're scaring us.'

'Scaring us? They're trying to hoover us to feedstock bins.'

Rudie shakes her head. 'They could just position the drone, fire for a few microtiks, and everything in range vanishes. Killing us would be easy.'

More nurses appear out of the thicket, picking over the debris.

'Any injuries?' I hear someone ask out loud.

'We have 2 under a pile of debris. Mostly leaves and fronds, no large branches. Digging them out now.'

Walk out of rainforest onto a moonscape stained orange: the demarcation between living and a void, flat as a bowling green. Here and there, hunks of thick tree trunks bayonet the clay earth. Amputated stumps and roots bleed resins from suppurating wounds. Fine shards of timber stab the ground, while heavier gleaming-clean chunks scatter about. Wonder how much wildlife dies today.

Weakened trees crack and shriek out, heavy branches thud down. The ground shakes. Heads duck in fear. Shouting. The wailing of a stricken animals—the sound of mortality. A nurse running up the boundary between rainforest and moonscape. Field Nurse Hildr Haddottir. 'Over here,' she calls. 'Here. It's Gerlinde.' Blood stains a rainbow uniform writhing on the ground alongside her kneeling, anxiously scrabbling into fatigue pockets and pouches. Follow her. It's Gerlinde, all right. Injured, in Mind-deranging pain, incapable of administering her own nutes. Blood puddles in the clay soil and spatters over nearby greenery. She's missing her arm above the elbow. Glad I avoid flutherbombing her. The empathic agony of tasting a missing arm would be crippling. Hildr administers nutes, sprays the stump and the remainder of her arm with squirty skin.

Vör arrives. 'I'm sorry Teo brings you back for this horrible place,' she tells Gerlinde. Everyone knows Teo plays no such part in Gerlinde's mission here.

'It's kay,' Gerlinde says weakly, the nutes already working. 'I perform my duty.'

'You'll be fine,' Vör says. 'We'll send you straight back for Vauxminster.'

With mission cap off, Gerlinde twiddles a pigtail for distraction from the pain. 'You'll be fine,' Vör tells Gerlinde again and strokes her hair. 'Your arm will grow back so fast; this icky yellow soil will still be under your fingernails.'

The conference room in Santarém's Catedral de Nossa Senhora is hot with anger, with little patience for cooling down. Beneath everything is an undercurrent of excitement. We find our first crèche of significance.

Outrage. Infinites turn violence on us. Only days ago, who would think anyone capable of so much harm? Out of our league for such aggression, we're still losing the arms race (especially Gerlinde).

'What amuses you, Beatrice?' Vör asks. She's the elf-appointing procomplement (some would say dictator) of the expedition, now Teo is missing. Last in joining the meeting, Vör barely contains her pleasure taking the seat at the head of the table, slipping into it with regal ease. 'We agonise over fabricating small portable weapons, while Infis adapt large-scale mining equipment. We're waging a campaign with nets and grenades and … foldable bikes, while Infis have weapons of massive scale, capable of wiping away a mountain in microtiks.'

'Everything they have we can acquire too,' Rudie clips. She gestures like she's lifting a curtain. Hollies appear on the table showing models of various mining equipment.

'Is this where we're going?' a nurse at the far end of the table asks. 'We're escalating?'

'It's so far from the mission I join for,' another says.

'We always have weapons. Every nute we use is a weapon of sorts. It all depends on their use. Anyone can make a weapon of any tool.'

The first sits back in her chair staring at the 2nd, her lips a single thin line. 'Intent might be a weapon. Any emotion might be a weapon. You could weaponise love, I guess.' She trains her stiff gaze at Vör. 'I wonder what Eir would think.'

Vör takes her time, a queen suffering the bickering of courtiers. 'The White Witch requires a Cure,' she says. 'Now the struggle falls on us, and we should use every asset at our disposal.'

Teodora Mrowka …

A day is all it takes.

A day in Never-Mind. A splitting headache. Tender bones and purpling bruises. A call for help. Rescue. Convalescing in a bed with the best medical care available.

Powerless. A day is all it takes for Vör assuming control of the mission.

And for everyone to fall in behind her. Respect for me wilting and corrupting in a cancerous lust for vengeance at any price.

Under cover of night, from the demountable station by the collapsed bridge over São Raimundo, a pair of scouts leave the sparsely covered *corrido*— where Avenida Doutor Theomario Pinto da Costa once ran east-west and cut north into ironwoods, kapok trees and walking palms—and aim for the western side of the arena. After an exhausting hour scrambling around buttress roots, and between palms and myrtles; the scouts emerge into an open sky of starlight, and an open corridor of short grass, bound on both sides by strangler figs, and lianas shattering ancient walls and pavements. Faster, passing through for another east-west road back towards the river, they reach a crossroad.

'This should take us all the way,' Zheng Xun of China Wellness reports.

Within 300 metres of the stadium, an impassable mess of ruins and jungle blocks progress.

'You speak too soon,' membs Flora Aversa of *Santé Méditerranéenne*.

We should have *Sundhed* nurses going in, but it's an argument even Vör would never win. Since news of striking real resistance in Manaus, the tasting of every health mission—major and minor—slurp toward the Amazon. Every camerata politicises the posting of their agents in pivotal roles. Sending Xun and Flora out there is a compromise well above Vör's reputasi grade.

Tracing an arc east around the impasse, the pair are once more heading north where the jungle recedes away, exposing an abrupt shift in terrain. Broken plates of concrete, with sharp edges and corners rounded off by centuries of weather, sprawl like stale corn-chips in a titanic bowl. Worms of rusting reinforcing steel squiggle everywhere, making a frenzied meal of the ruins.

Xun scales and finds a crevasse among the rubble; jumps down. Flora follows scrambling through a tortuous concrete ravine. A gaping blackness swallows Xun's vision whole, her hancy incapable of assisting with making taste of it. Flutherbomb Flora for an alternative view. She tenses with surprise. Already on edge, having her unusually tiny fluther expand by just one. An empty fluther must be a slimy alien feeling, but it's a necessary discomfort in the circumstances. Gathering herelf, Flora edges around the void. 'This could go all the way to hell.'

If hell is a sap basement.

'You must be on the stadium concourse,' Vör membs.

Ahead, a sweeping unnatural arc of shadow looms, artificially smooth, lacking any sign of the fractal edges of a tree line. It takes a tik, Flora's eyes adjust, resolving the shadow as the ruins of the stadium. A veinous pancaked reptilian egg appears fallen and cracked open where it rests. Some segments of shell between the lattice of veins remain intact while others have shattered out. Westward, part of the structure is torn away, falling into the clutches of the encroaching forest. There the veins of the eggshell fossilise into steel girders reaching out like arms with hands amputated. The stadium might be gathering back its fallen corrupted parts and making itself whole again.

A broken promenade circles the bleachers around the playing field. On the outer side, corroding lattice and fractured panels of the arena exterior allow views into the remains of the concourse. Inside, a shambles of concrete blocks and mortar painfully supports green walls of vines. Strangler figs are rooting right into the floor. Wide-access races, once leading for stairwells and ground-level seating, are impassable. They yield only a partial view of the vegetation reclaiming the playing field.

'If there are saps here, they're hiding well,' Flora membs.

Another roof collapse blocks the way. In the silver hancy-conjured light a network of vines clutching debris appears throbbing with tentacles rising from the earth as if dragging things of the surface down suffocating and unrecognisable. Things faded dirty once blue. Cheap sculpture perhaps plastic. A large artificial plant or the contorted tiles of a collapsed roof.

'Seats,' Xun answers. 'Rows of them.'

The pair have no option. They must find another way in. Outside retracing some steps warily. A few steps forward. Looking up at the eggshell façade of the arena.

'Is everything in better shape here?' Xun asks for confirmation.

'I'm tasting the same,' Flora says.

Curving out of sight much like it may have been in sap times, a clean concourse transitions into the promenade. Its inside walls are structurally sound, while bearing the aggression of vine growth. With cautious steps, Xun and Flora steal onto the promenade and follow it around. Into an access hall for the arena's interior, free of damage and vegetation. A stairway is missing neither railing nor step. They take the hall. Look up and down the stairwell. Proceed inwards towards the playing area. Emerge on another circulating promenade among blocks of dirty, broken seats raking up behind and down in front.

The light is no longer silver. A warm glow defrosts its edges, casting Xun-and-Flora-shaped shadows down in front. Behind them light flickers from windows where once there may have been a corporate box or function room.

'You hearing this?' Flora asks.

'What?' Xun says.

'Shh!'

Both holding breath. There it is. A repeating thump like distant trees falling again and again, with an indistinct edge of bees buzzing at the edges. Two beats per tik, coaxing my heart faster.

Despite herelf, Xun is gleeful. 'Music.'

Flora and Xun crouch below an arc of windows stretching the length of a long internal room. Summoning the courage for sticking heads up and assessing the party. Flora points at the bottom corners of the window array. Xun nods. They spread for opposite corners. Take slow furtive glances.

'Just saps,' Flora says.

'No neos?' Vör checks.

'I see none,' Xun says.

'And no uniforms?'

At the other end of the windows, Flora shakes her head. 'Everyone is wearing casual outfits.' The plan is Flora and Xun infiltrate wearing Sappy projections. Finding these saps out of uniform is a relief.

Flora and Xun take the stairwell in the access hall. Descend into the basement. Look for a small room for changing.

They find a utility closet and, with curious modesty—perhaps because of the proximity of saps—activate the Sappy projections. With their undressing they are like magicians plucking clothing and kit from inside their own fruits. At least the projection fields will repel insects. Xun and Flora regard each other, blurt out laughing at the bodacious breastiness and junk in the trunk. For the sake of the mission, we can only hope they resist giggle-shitting themelves to death.

I'm glad we spend time modifying the base Sappy Amerindian projections. Everything in the go-for-market catalogues are idealisations of 20th-century saps from before epigenetic-mod skins become fashionable. Those would fool no living sap, who also wear modern hair styles. Old-fashion sap appearances would stand out more than gorilla or aardvark suits.

Flora and Xun are in the right place, deeper than the original arena complex. Everything glistens with nanotech materials and flowing organic architecture despite the straight corridors, boxy rooms, and those claustrophobic elevators which cater for saps.

From around a corner a sap appears, gives a friendly wave, pushes the wall where he stands. There's a bing. Doors slide open. He walks in. The doors slide shut.

'There are 4 doors down here,' Flora membs.

'Be patient and thorough,' Vör membs.

Xun tests the handles on the first pair of double doors. They open with a faint click.

Her eyes go wide for an operating table in the middle of the room. Over it is a bank of lights on a large articulating arm. On 3 sides around the table are 14 or so cribs. Within every one is a nude in repose.

'Tread with care,' Vör advises. 'The first objective is, locate the spooky station.'

Flora Aversa ...

Xun reports, 'the only place left is up in the stands.'

'You're sure you never pass it?' Vör asks, meaning the spooky station. Vör's our lone flutherbomber these passing 21 mins. Unsure of this *pazzo di merda di pipistrello* Vör, although I hear the previous leader, Teo, has a sense of purity which borders on elitism, and alienates everyone. The sooner we wrest this sybil-hunt away from *Sundhed* the better.

'Every door, we try,' Xun answers, tiring of the operation. 'We could go back ...' Scowl at her, even if she has no heart in the suggestion.

'No, try nearer the party,' Vör membs.

'Would saps be at ease anywhere near a spooky field?' doubting there's one here for finding.

'There must be something you miss.' Vör will have us here till dawn, checking every closet and toilet cubicle.

'We check all the corridors and stairwells. We even ride those descending closets.'

'Elevators,' Xun says.

'Give me the creeps. More than beards.'

'Ha,' Xun snorts. 'Wait till you see pubic hair.'

There is no imagining such a horror. 'What's wrong with stairs up and a good slippy slide down?'

'Saps had a repressed sense of play,' Xun says.

'*Porca miseria.* How depressing.' Pandering.

'Hold fast,' Vör interjects. 'We're building a holly of your movements around the arena.'

'What?' Xun membs, getting miffy, taking offence at the idea she may be missing something.

'The holly shows, at the northern end of the arena, 2 floors in the basement.'

'Shi,' Xun confirms. 'Sounds right.'

'At the southern end, there is only one floor,' Vör says.

Xun and me exchange looks. 'We follow every stairwell for the roofs and cellars.'

'Hmmm,' Vör membs. 'Only one basement floor in the west too. On the eastern side, you cover less than half of a single basement floor. Only a few metres from the north and south ends.'

'The east side is all wreckage,' I answer.

'The station could be under the east-side ruins,' Vör states.

'We scour all over,' Xun says. 'See no way down.'

Vör exhales sharp, dismissing our excuses. 'Go back for the southern end. Find what you miss.'

Zheng Xun ...

The squarish doughnut of an arena—with crimps at either end where the eastern stand collapses—is a tangle of invading rainforest and various new house-size structures, making the once easy-access ring of the outer promenade a set of isolated, barely habitable segments. It's still more traversable than the encroaching jungle outside. Without rushing, I pick around for the southern stands. Take the stairs for the basement.

With more confidence and speed, we skip for the end of the corridor where it takes a right into what's left of the arena's east side. Imagine the crèche's builders perform some gravity-defying engineering under the rubble of the stands, for embedding the short wing off the crèche. Try again the first door on the left. The same banks of metrae meet us, housing embryonic sybils in various stages of growth. Four are by the back wall while 2 each occupy both flanks.

'Is this room smaller than the others? Shallower?' Flora asks.

'No, it's the same size.'

Flora walks around the perimeter of the room, tracing her hands along the walls. 'Taste no other way out of here.'

'Let's try the room across the corridor.'

'It's empty. I recall.'

'Strange. It's the only empty room we encounter,' Vör cuts in.

'*Shi.*'

'Go back. Take another look.'

Quiet as mice we cross into the room.

'Nothing here,' Flora says growing ever more impatient for finishing.

'What's the symbol on the right wall?' Vör asks.

Examine the symbol perhaps 30 centims in diameter. Three triangular pie segments superimposing and pointing at the centre of a circle.

'Gogging it,' Vör says.

We're gogging too. RADIATION HAZARD.

'There are nuclear reactors here?'

'Might be a ruse. What better symbol to scare saps away?'

Flora steps so close she could plant her lips on the sign. Makes for kicking the wall. Gasps as her foot and half her calf passes straight through. Overbalancing almost falls on her ass.

'A projection.'

'Ready if you are,' Flora says.

Nod. Cautious we half-step forward. My leg between foot and thigh vanishes. Another step and we are all the way through, in a corridor ramping down. A single set of double doors at the other end. We should be walking cautious, but Flora skips away. I follow. Bang the doors open exuberantly.

With fortune, no one is inside. We crash through. In the centre of a large room, in a circular dinner-plate depression throbs a purple mist, dull and dormant.

Teodora Mrowka ...

Vör will take all the credit. She waits while the remainder of 2 companies of nurses skip from the spooky field, pupils dilating in arousal. Flora and Xun will take a squad each for securing the crib dormitories. Others will locate movable sucky bins for destroying cribs. Some nurses are queasy about sentencing sybils the same fate. Either way, it's a monstrosity. Giving patterns of late, their reputasi will improve with every sybil they destroy.

Vör takes 2 squads, brandishing grenades like holy crosses for convincing the saps their best option is return home.

Following the corridors, Vör seeks the sound of partying. Laughter roars louder. Vör's squads are within sight of the saps. Silence swells up like deep water quelling the fun. All eyes are on Vör. Arms and legs are still.

'Have no alarm,' Vör says in full voice, a croak for sap ears. 'We intend no harm. Vacate, and everyone will sleep safe tonight.'

'Vör,' Beatrice membs from somewhere else in the complex.

'*Ja?*'

'Come taste.'

From Beatrice's fluther, I orient and look around too. Fourteen cribs surround a medical table same as other rooms here. With unbounding excitement, I taste a mature sybil under the frosty-glass covers of each crib, all identical, and easy for recognising by their extraordinary height and long silk-white hair.

Lustre

'Mexican Radio' — Wall of Voodoo

 *Ben Evoli …*

How am I looking? Convincing? Shoulders square, chin up, nose level. Relax my eyes; let my arms swing easy. My mission is my play. Look like a nurse; play like a nurse; skip like a nurse. Be in no hurry.

I'm wearing a nurse's uniform. In these rainbow colours I feel like a tropical fish tank.

'Bapa, be serious,' Saf membs, courtesy of Bonita's increasing ease with piercing scatter nets. Unless this is all an elaborate set-up. From the Cat dressing me, then Bonita and Saf contacting me in the cafeteria (if it's truly them), this could be another phase in my Cure. Another psyche-destroying test. I'm beyond caring. Which is maybe how they craft it.

'I know, cahaya,' membing whoever is posing as Saf.

Look like a nurse, skip like a nurse. Convey an air of cuddly authority, of ambivalent care. So far no one stops me.

'The next corridor on the right,' the Saf imposter membs. 'There's a slippy slide. Go down 2 floors.'

Fall in line behind others. From the floor above, a slippy slide wide enough for 4 abreast spirals down counter clockwise (a convention in the northern hemisphere). In Vauxminster, slides are the only curving structures. Everything else—the hallways the rooms the overhead lighting—is bolt straight and square. Any wonder English nurses behave like a secret service. The brutalism of the building must send them bent-brain. Or square-brain I guess.

Keep pace with nurses in front, jump, and land easy on my butt. No one pays me any attention. Feel like a wasp in a swarm of rainbow-colour bees.

The hancy the Cat gives me is little better than the patients' model. Still no feature for filtering auras from my vision. While thankfully small ones billow around, they still make me woozy in the confining space of the slide-well.

Look like a nurse but will never taste like a nurse. The tik anyone flutherbombs me … So far all are too busy jelling or gogging or flutherbombing somewhere else, eyes fluttering. I land 2 floors down.

'Okelah, turn right,' Saf membs.

'Where next?'

'We taste nothing exact,' Bonita membs, and covers her mouth, shy. 'We're feeling it out as we go.'

Sounds like a trap.

'Okelah,' Bonita says. 'There's a stairwell down. No slippy slide. Everything down there is dark. A kind of scatter net even we're unable to pierce.'

'A cone of silence.'

'What's a cone of silence, Bapa?'

'Would you believe…?' I imagine Chief of Control rolling his eyes. Gog it. 'Never mind. Just a sap pop culture reference.'

'I bet Mal knows it,' Saf membs in a sulky, he's-more-special, complaining way so authentically Saf. Maybe it truly is her.

'Mal is weird,' Bonita membs. 'Um, sorry, Infi Uncle, just mean—'

The stairway only goes down. Looks like 2 floors straight with no exit in between. The empty well smells of dust and dank concrete. Follow it. The cloying sense of a trap almost repels me up top.

I memb Saf and Bonita, 'I'm at the bottom landing.' No answer. 'Saf? Are you there? Saf?'

Guess Bonita is right; this part of the minster is beyond her piercing.

A single heavy door leads out of the stair well into a room maybe 6 metres on a side. Cooler air smells medicinal. Three clusters of cosy lounge chairs surround low tables. Benches and cupboards on 2 sides. The far wall is blank. Shadows of hallways lead left and right, dim like a hotel floor in the middle of the night. Lighting over 3 doors on each side illuminate littly-little. I move down one hall; the medicinal tang of the lounge area sinks under a floral aroma of essential oils vaporising.

I memb, 'Which door?' Realise there'll be no answer.

A sudden clunk-crack of a sound. The door behind me opens. I turn and know it's a trap.

A quivering crone in a jumpsuit the colour of bruised apricots. Hunching over, grasping the door handle as if it alone will keep her standing. Pink eyes accentuate her pale face bluer than tuna, half occult in a frame of vibrant white hair. With effort she lifts her head. At once I register the blunt wound beside her nose. Around it, spreading over most of her cheek and extending under her jawline, is a tidal-pool ink-stain, a blue-yellow-black glistering bruise.

'7 Hells, Eir. Are they beating you?' Forgetting for a tik she could be my nemesis. Her brokenness overwhelms me with pity.

A minimal shake of her head. An index finger rises for her lips, shushing me. A sweep of her hand bids enter. She steps aside still supporting her weight on the door handle.

'I fell.' She says tongue and lung with weak raspy air. With the shutting of the door, 'On the *kaffe* table,' she says with great effort slurring her words. 'My dyspraxia is worse of late, despite my keepers' best efforts,' she labours. 'Captivity disagrees with me, it seems.'

'They really Consign you? I—I hear of it ... or imagine I hear of it. Either way, it's so unbelievable, I question my sanity.'

'It's true,' she says, her voice thin and reedy. 'It seems they bring us both low.' She moves, shuffling and unsteady, her steps tentative, as if she fears the floor may fall away beneath her or rise and bash her jaw. She waves me sit, and lowers aching into a couch opposite. Reaches for a pitcher of water and glasses which sit between us; pours with smooth movement until she clanks pitcher and glass together with an involuntary jerk. I offer for relieving her of the service, but she scowls.

Two glasses full, she sits back exhaling. 'We are safe in here.' Her eyes dart for the corners of the room.

Eir has no aura. Same with me. Perhaps nurses invent the elusive Faraday cage for onespace.

'We may speak free,' Eir says.

I imbue grace and acceptance into a single nod, while wondering how she could give such an assurance. Who might be collaborating with her in here? What resources might she still bridle within these walls?

'How much is it you taste?' Eir asks, and lets the question rest between us, her eyes sharp, the only aspects of her appearance undiminished, windows from where I suspect the witch still watches. A witch who could still cast enchantments even in her state. Her white hair emits its own light, and the world turns like a millstone around her. 'We have little time,' she adds, searching me. I hold my skeleton stiff in resistance. 'You know saps still live,' she states. I render my best poker face. '*Ja*, you know.' She's an enchantress granny inviting my confession. Force myelf; hold her gaze. I fail and look away, which is impossible too. '*Ja*, you taste. You witness there are sybils of this fruit.' She nods. 'You witness the sybils.'

'One.' I have an overwhelming desire for being helpful. Eir, the granny witch, smiles. I sputter, 'At Maddox's crèche.'

'Oh? Alarming,' she says, a spark enlivening her. 'He's resourceful.'

'He's insidious,' I answer and shiver.

She nods while holding her hands together in her lap. 'Old Infinites are.'

'You would have more experience.'

She blinks purposefully. 'You're manipulating the Reck,' she says.

My shoulders lose square, my back curves, my chest collapses.

'No?' she says with surprise. 'But it's changing.'

'I may be responsible for triggering it, but it's far from my design. Or control.'

For a tik, the dyspraxia releases her. She stands and glides like a wraith behind my lounge. She is almost the old Eir. 'I need help with something,' she whispers in my ear while stroking my hair.

'What?'

'There are more sybils of me out there.'

'I see only one.'

'There's alternative agenda out there. Someone is using sybils of me. Orlando's case is evidence of it.'

'How might I help?'

I must be looking bug-eye stupid at her. 'Maddox is fond of you,' she says over my incoherence.

Spluttering, 'Maddox manipulates me at every point.'

'Even so, you could prevail upon him, and he should help you.'

Shaking my head. Shaking shaking.

'We're in it together,' Eir says with no absence of venom. 'You need me.' She pinches my earlobe. 'My former colleagues will never cease investigating how you tamper with the Reck,' she says as she makes unsteady steps for her seat.

'But—'

'*Ja.* So.' She drops unsteadily into the couch opposite. Her face paralyses. Bereft of forming words with her mouth, she membs. 'Look forward upon this minster being your whole life, unless we act together.'

My fruit so heavy it could fall out of my skin like ore from a bucket. 'But they must taste I never intend for tampering with the Reck.'

'*Intend*, you say? So, you admit it. And they taste your need of revenge, for nurses violating your son. They have evidence of you interacting with the Reck. And everyone tastes the Reck's erratic behaviour since.'

I have no words or tastes. The walls of the room box my whole universe.

'They have evidence you are capable of hiding many things. They will never satisfy themelves you are hiding nothing else.'

Everyone has something for hiding. They'll keep me forever for it.

'They want control of the Reck.' Eir says.

'They'll be meeting with disappointment, then. The Reck is more inexplicable than ever. I should never start poking at it.'

'Absolutely you should,' Eir counters, weakly emphatic.

'I just want my family back,' blurting and fighting back tears. 'Is this so hard?'

'You want more than that.' She takes a long draught of her water.

'What?' I ask lamely.

Eir laughs. The bruise on her cheek ripples.

Shake my head. All I imagine are battalions of nurses surrounding me, brandishing Warrants without end, no Cure. 'Is this my defining life's moment: an accident, connecting with the Reck? It tampers with me, not the other way round!' Fall silent. Eir allows space expanding between us. 'It's so like me,' I concede, 'falling into circumstances without the merest taste of where I am.'

'You fall into missions after you child, Ben. Missions born of innocence and playfulness, free from judgment and criticism. It's creativity—the blessing and curse of elf-awareness—which bears you missions. It always is.'

'If those nurses never fit Mal with a hancy, I might never contact the Reck.'

'I apologise for your son.' Her empathy is so pure it slices neat as ice into the tumour of sadness in my soul. I'm bawling like a newborn. She ushers me over with the wave of a stark white hand more like a spindly lobster. I go to her, the distraught anak, seeking the reassurance of an orang. She cradles my head in her lap while the torrent of my tears flow.

'I'm alone,' I blubber. 'I'm so alone.'

She strokes my hair and I wail. Stupidly weak. 'We're both lost,' she whispers. 'My mistakes are manifold. Misplacing trust, holding too much confidence, believing there is always time, letting side issues become diversions. But the worst is …' She pauses for swallowing. Twice. 'Never mind.' Eir makes a long face and casts her gaze far away.

'How are you here?' I ask, snuffling snot and the last of my tears.

'I resolve for discharging Orlando.'

'But you take him in the first place,' I counter, sceptical.

Eir grimaces. 'Sybils Consign Orlando. And then, I learn our treatments harm high-network individuals—perhaps harm everyone. The suffering of even that horrid old turtle is too much for my stomach. And here we are. Other nurses, some once dear to me, are exploiting any means necessary. Violence even.'

Is there no escape? Why is she risking meeting me?

'I understand you are suffering some side-effects after rebasing,' she says. 'Some hallucinations …'

On my haunches I squat at her feet, wedging between the table and her couch. 'Yeer … I'm hallucinating. I'm unsure what is real anymore.'

'Flashbacks?'

'Yeer.'

'You taste you are someone else? Losing the taste of your original elf?'

'Yeer. A 21st-century sap in a pick-up truck. Mary is my love—his love. I taste some weird religious conflations. Jesus gave Americans nuclear weapons?'

'Side effects of the treatments.' Eir smiles with the beneficence of a saint, the discolouration of her face fading in a momentary blush. Straightening her posture. 'You believe in dolphins?'

A stab of shock. Gather my fleeing wits, twigs in a cyclone. A sense of a pump in my head overworking. Pain. Nausea. Waiting for its passing.

'I choose for belief in dolphins,' she says so offhand.

'They approach you too?' What means that? She's aware ... dolphins—no, Mal—no, someone posing as Mal—penetrates the minster's security? And talks with me? Or something more? No, it's Eir. It's all her game.

She waves my question away. 'I believe in communion,' she says. 'That's what these dolphins call it, *ja*? I believe in rebinding, in bringing everything back together. And I believe I need your help.'

'How I am able?' Hands, wide, pleading, *look where we are.*

'Your boy, your dolphins, whoever ...' Her lips twist, a Möbius loop of benevolent mischief, telling me I'll abhor the answer, but I should trust her anyway.

Something blacker and sourer than a bad fish-pickle lodges in my intestines. 'You would involve Mal?' asking with surrendering disquiet.

Eir's eyes are generating power. Her pale skin still exudes an otherworld glow despite her bruises and her captivity. She lets my question rest between us. I feel an otherworldly force, a compulsion for waiting. Any wonder they call her witch. A presence of enchantment surrounds her. There could be lights in her white hair. Or tiny faeries. The earth is grist in an unstoppable mill, and only Eir is free of the stone.

She says, 'Mal is our only way of reaching out and recruiting Maddox Price.'

'Maddox will never help us.'

'He'll help his Puffin.'

Dilan Chandrasiri ...

'I'm here,' membing Mal, taking a deep breath.

'I taste this, Dilan Uncle.' Mal's voice has an unnatural warble. Perhaps the lack of hancy. It's a wonder he can sustain a consistent stream at all.

Whispering breezes in the trees quieten, revealing undercurrents of mechanical hissing. Hoping nothing more sinister than maintenance bots. But who knows what defences and traps an Infi might lay around a house? A house Mal tastes with the casual familiarity of an old toy. He assists me with ease in spooking without apparent reinforcement of others.

'Now what?' Already know the answer.

'Go up in the house.'

A grassy hill. A building, a curious melange of sap and neo architecture. From the crest of the hill, the first 2 floors rise square and blocky. Blank brickwork but for a few small windows puncturing the brutalism. The top looks like a cake on a pork pie; the upper 2 floors are all curving solarglass set in minimal structural framing. Above those, veiny cicada-wing environment sails sprout. Colourful ice cream wafers in a sundae.

'You're hungry, Dilan Uncle,' Mal says. 'You should eat before this.'

'I would only be throwing it back up.' It's true. I have no stomach for these kinds of incursions anymore.

'It's just like your old activist days,' Mal says. I wonder what grasp of activism he may have. I remind myelf there is no underestimating this boy any longer.

'It seems the nurses Cure me of it after all. Oh, why am I letting you talk me into this?'

'Because you owe Bapa, Dilan Uncle,' Mal says in a voice so adult. A voice of authority. Ancient.

He's right and he tastes it, the little horror. To think all the times I have you on my knee ...

The hill too steep for skipping. Measure careful steps, and plant my feet, grass chomping at my calves.

'It's dark,' membs Mal, 'no sign of squatters.' I'm sure y'all hear the stories too. All over the world squatters are moving into vacant Infi houses. I am so hoping for squatters here. Squatters would mean an absence of Maddox. But the house is quiet. No partying, no carousing, no frolicking in swimming pools, no casting furniture into the yards for fashioning makeshift outdoor living spaces. Which means Maddox could be about, watching, ready for releasing the hounds, or bykes of wasps, or hounds on bikes with wasps in their ears ...

Of course, there's no security. Who are we? Saps? But the prospect of opening a door into an Infi's house has me ... surely there must be something for repelling unwelcome visitors. This is the house of an Infi.

No lock on the door of course. No attack dogs or pet wasps. No strobing lights or deafening sirens. No anaesthetic gases or hancy jammers. No trapdoors over sharp pikes. No scalding oils or acids sprays. Only ...

... darkness.

No light in the house is opening on account of my presence. The lower floors are dark as dungeons. Moist air smells faintly of bricks and mortar. And something dusty. Old timber? Feel my way along a missile-straight hallway, tracing fingers along the wall. Bark a toe on an immovable slug of furniture—a heavy bureau or sideboard. A coarse tapestry. The wall's texture becomes smoother. A barely discernible sheen. The hint of a shadow ahead, perhaps a shade or 2 lighter than the inky hall. Faint light from above wafts feathery down and illuminates a stack of dim blocky shapes. A stairway leading up into a lustrous black satin void above.

Lights in a room off the hallway sense a presence. They glare. Down the end of the passage, a kitchen appears like the opening stage setting of a play. A large island bench sits in a quadrangle of cupboards, benches, sinks, and appliances. All sleek and immortal.

'Dilan Uncle where are you going?' comes Mal's voice, sounding again like a 17-year-old child.

'There's a bank of fabbies in here.'

'You're hungry?'

'Terror makes me hungry.'

'But, before, you say you'd throw up if you take food.'

'Both are truthful.' Approaching the bank of fabbies spanning an entire bench-top on the other side.

'Go upstairs, Uncle.'

'Just be giving me some tiks, all right? I need ...'

'You're stalling.'

Wave my hand in front of the largest of the fabbies. A menu holly appears in front of it. 'There's an option here for roast meats,' I tell Mal. The lists scrolls for a great many lines. Most of these animals are unfamiliar ... 'Sapling? Who would eat roast trees?'

'Has it got iguana?' Mal giggles.

Smile for distracting him, for delaying the inevitable if only for a min. 'Lemme see ... yes it has.'

'*I'm on a Mexican Radio.*' He's singing?

'What?'

'Nothing. Just a song Bapa sings.' Those 2 are always sharing private jokes about sap pop culture.

Eyes bulging at a surprising option on the fabby menu. 'Tiger. Dare we?'

'You're the one who's hungry,' Mal membs. 'I already eat ducky cubes.'

'But tiger?'

'It's no real tiger, Dilan Uncle.'

'No, but how is a fabby capable of reproducing it? Even if it's centuries ago, someone must sample an original dead-animal meal. Or I suppose they could extrapolate a dish from a living tiger.'

'May I suggest a glass or 2 of Domaine Leroy Musigny Grand Cru with the tiger, Dilan Face?'

Blood running cold. Twenty-eight hells. Swallowing my innards back from the air. The voice just loud enough to carry. At the kitchen door...

'Maddox,' Mal membs.

'I hope there's enough for 2,' Maddox says with tongue and lung.

Maddox in a satin house jacket, lurid cravat, and expensive slippers, showing no sign of displeasure at discovering me. He skips alongside, presses a finger into the gassy cloud of the fabby menu, and rolls his wrist. The menu scrunches away. The fabby hums and fires up. Beyond the clear door, the puppet spider of many printer legs jiggles and dances, dabbing glistening drops and wet strings together.

Maddox retrieves plates, sets them on the counter. 'There's cutlery in the drawer,' he says.

Like a circus animal I obey, performing with meek fear. From another cupboard Maddox pulls a wine carafe, puts it in the first fabby. Gestures a choice. Looks me over like cheap clothes on a mannequin. From a rack over the island counter, he selects a wine glass, tilting it against the light, scrutinising. Again, with a 2nd. Sets glasses down taking his time. One fabby completes the wine. Roast swells in the other radiating fatty heat. Maddox pours wine. Offering. Studies me for reactions, tests me hesitating. Showing the wine is no poison, he sips from his own.

'An original is superior if it's preserved well enough. Even so, few would taste the difference even with glasses side-by-side.' No doubt he could tell the difference.

'I'm no wine drinker.'

'You're fabbing roast tiger in my house,' he says, becoming pompous and ceremonious. 'Tonight, you are a wine drinker.'

'Infi, am here—'

'Let's tip our caps to civility, first. One never truly knows someone until they partake of tiger together.'

After which it is a baddy-bad time for vomiting.

'You visit Montana often?' Maddox forks a tiger chunk.

'First time.' Intent on dabbing away the last spots of belly acid from my shirt.

'Fancy that,' Maddox plays. 'A friend recommends a vacation here?'

'We have a mutual friend.' Requires no saying; we both know.

'Why would our mutual friend arrange we meet? Come on; speak up, Mr Dilan.' Maddox draining his wine glass again, mine still half full.

'Information. He needs information.'

'I find it unbelievable the dear Puffin lacks for information, or ways of gathering it.'

'His reach is less since …'

'Sorry, I hear; yes indeed, he's in Vauxminster's nick. But even so …'

'Crèches—'

'What crèches?' he asks implacably.

'Please, *mahatmaya*, Ben's personal experience—'

Maddox waves me down. 'Well, my assets are fewer since all the silliness with the Reck. Short of hiring a personal army for restraining others from occupying our property … and then there's nurses ransacking everything looking for sybils …'

'I am no fan of health missionaries …'

'Truly?'

'It is very correct, *Mahatmaya* Maddox.'

'What is so important about these mythical crèches?'

'You offer crèching services for others.'

'News to me,' he stonewalls.

'You keep … stockpiles of sybils for clients.'

'Call them kindergartens.' He looks smug.

'One client is Eir Frijberg.'

Maddox bangs down his cutlery. 'The White Witch?' Indignant. 'Are you—? What possible motive—? No Infinite would assist a nurse let alone someone whose mission is confining us.'

'She uses sybils before. And she supposes there are more.'

'Supposes? How unconvincing.'

'Perhaps, but Ben's resting his hopes in there being more of her sybils who know about forgotten things.'

Maddox places his glass in such a delicate fashion, like a holy relic. His temper is the more fragile glass, in danger of shattering. 'So. Ben and the White Witch are co-conspirators after all.'

'No. I believe no. But since becoming patients at Vauxminster …'

'Vör Hoyur's work, I hear,' Maddox says with smug amusement. 'How ironic. And delicious.' Toasts the air with his glass. Turns sober. 'The vociferous Vör surpasses even Eir's ambition. She's crusading for destroying crèches.'

'And her reputation is buoyant for it.'

Maddox turning steely. 'If Eir misplaces her own sybils, it is her own carelessness.'

'She may arrange forgetting of such things, a technique of which I'm sure is familiar.'

'Dylan Uncle,' Mal membs, making me jump in my seat. My knife clanks against the wine glass. 'Remember the sybil Bapa sees in Maddox's crèche.'

Repeating the fact for Maddox.

'He is never at such a place.' His chin thrusting in the air.

'Caracia takes him there after she kidnaps him.'

Maddox in genuine shock. 'Caracia? In my crèche? She would never dare.'

'She dares.' I may be gaining the upper hand.

'No, I would know.' Maddox guzzling the last of his wine. 'I would know.'

Suppress an urge for gloating. Maddox, like all Infis, is so sure of his reach. But Infis are no omniscient beings. Like anyone, their networks limit their horizons. Large as they may be, they never reach everyone in every space for all points in time.

'Ask him if he's a sybil, Dilan Uncle,' Mal membs.

'You're a sybil,' I accuse.

'What? Are you mad? I'm the seminal.'

'They all say so,' Mal membs.

I memb back, 'Then why have me ask him?' uncaring whether Maddox is monitoring.

'Who are you communicating with?' Maddox demands. Is it possible, without needing a hancy, Mal's talents are secure from prying followers? 'Is it Ben? Is it Eir?'

'Neither.' I answer more for effect than the truth.

'Then who?'

'An ... intermediary.'

Maddox sits forward, a furrow of his brow forming. Hands flat on the table. 'Who?'

'A cadre of aquatic mammals if you may believe it. Or, for all I know, perhaps every living brain sufficient for running consciousness on a loop. It's all so Indra's Necklace.'

Maddox so cold. 'It is time you leave, Mr Dilan.'

'But I am still putting the tiger in my tank.' Ben would enjoy the quip.

'Please, you must stay Uncle,' Mal membs. 'We need him.'

'*Mahatmaya* Maddox, Ben needs help. You have some blame for his current predicament. Now you can help him out.'

'He lands in Vauxminster all by his own blame. He conceals information from me since the start.'

'Please, the world is falling apart. Who knows what might befall him in there?'

Maddox's posture softens. He reflects. 'If I have helpful knowledge, it would be yours. But Eir. Is. Never. A client of mine,' he says picking up his fork then clanging it on his plate. A violet sheen envelopes him, pulsing and dying out, erasing him as sure as he's never here. He spooks away? How are we ever finding Eir's sybils without him?

We fail. I sit, wanting never move again. 'I'm sorry, Mal. We do our best. Perhaps I should be spooking out of here too before he sends someone back for me.'

'Have no concern, Dilan Face. You are quite safe,' a familiar voice membs.

Double take. Maddox skips for the dining table. Regards the remnants of the meal. In mission suit and tie, high-polish lace-up shoes, he takes his seat. With distain, he shunts the plate well out of reach. 'Tiger? How inelegantly colonial.'

I must be making a gaping monkey face because he takes some time assessing me. 'You are right,' he says. 'He is a sybil.' The new Maddox lifts the carafe. Only a glass in it. He sniffs and nods. 'One tik please.' He dashes for the kitchen. Returns with a clean glass. 'Once a sybil suspects it's sybil,' he says while he pours, 'it tends for becoming reckless. One must put a sybil down before it sullies one's reputation. Like a favourite horse gone lame, you see? My sybils handle the news of ... *demotion*, shall we say? ... poorly. Perhaps it's some character flaw. Who knows? Cheers.'

Automatically respond, clinking glasses. 'You are flutherbombing before?' Already know the answer.

'Ah, yes. Through an intermediary. I have the gist of the conversation so let me rub the nub of your inquisitiveness. No, Eir is never my client. But yes, I acquire some of her sybils through with one or 2 of my Infi colleagues. A complex negotiation, shall we say? Compromises are never easy, are they? A kind of insurance policy against nurses, worth little now. Who'd guess nurses would become so militant? I recall when a bear hug is too violent for those sweet darlings.'

'And Caracia?'

'Yes, Caracia uses my crèche for holding Ben for a time, though without my foreknowledge. We are still bickering about it.'

'Then you will help Ben?'

'Is it helping Ben or Eir? Which is it?'

'It is Ben making this request, *Mahatmaya* Maddox.'

'Then help you shall have,' he says like a patrician bestowing a toy on a young son. 'We should have none of him petering away in some nursing home. Is there a worse fate? But look. Please understand, relationships and connections are worth less than only a few weeks ago. All debts are off, and favours owing carry no weight. Even if I discover all the witch's sybils, the health camerati may have them already.' He slakes deeply of his wine, glass hovering while he chews around the liquid in his mouth. 'But we'll try our best.'

'Thank you, *Mahatmaya* Maddox.'

'Very good. Is there anything else?'

'No.'

'Good. Then shall we take dessert?'

Ben Evoli …

The first time I pull on a nurse's uniform is risky enough. This time I'm playing no ignorant abecedarian intern innocently blundering off-tour. I'll be escorting the minster's most notorious patient for—where exactly? Fluffy and Eir are still arguing the finer points of our cover story: escorting Eir for some as-yet-indeterminate therapy session. Risky. So much as a single suspicious nurse will immediately taste we're as off-course as a camel train in the South Pacific. Security around our goal—the high-security, surreptitious spooky station (for emergency and mission-critical uses only, terima kasih)—will be tight. Less than bad enough, Fluffy (another fur ball stuck in the gears of hope for escape) insists we must crack Orlando out also. Which Eir accepts without so much as a cough or a gag. Perhaps her regret for taking him is genuine.

Perhaps her compassion is truly limitless, in which case she is inarguably the most dangerous nurse in neo budaya.

Picture it dear fans, casual flutherbombers and time-tourists: 3 Infis and a nurse in a cat-suit walk out of a minster … What's the punchline? Jank me if I know. And jank me if I ever find out. The conspicuity of the 4 of us: the criminally cute local joke of a nurse in nekko projection; a 2-metre-tall albino nurse/Infi; another Infi notoriously recognisable for his chelonian appearance (even in a jumpsuit Orlando appears as if carrying an orange tortoise shell on his back). And me. We're never skipping out of here together. We must break up.

Fluffy is safest on her own. Her eccentric irregular dress-sense—the butt of derision for years—is a familiar sight in these corridors. Fluffy alone might reach the spooky station. I'll pass for a nurse if no one tastes too close; but the nearer the point of escape, the more suspicious I'll appear. But Orlando and Eir?

The only option is move in pairs. Fluffy will escort Orlando as a nurse taking a patient for some therapy or other. And I, in rainbow fatigues, will escort Eir.

Taste Eir shaking her head. From her ward in the dead of night.

Thankful again for Bonita. Her superpower of piercing the fustian veils of Vauxminster's scatter nets improves by the day. When this is over, I may have time for contemplating the implications of a whole new generation like her and Mal.

'It's almost certain someone will challenge us,' Eir membs, shoulders slumping. She's far from the raider at the Inductee Gala. 'Reaching the spooky station requires we pass in front of administrative offices through a busy wide straight corridor which looks out over the river. With nowhere for hiding, we'll be visible from outside and in, and there's no precedence for patients on this level. From there, we—'

'You keep blathering, you'll scare our guests,' Fluffy interrupts.

'I'm already scared,' I memb. It's inconceivable how I could be any more scared.

Eir exhales deep with resignation. 'There's only one viable plan for reaching the station.' I fear she's relapsing into the defeated waif I meet in the secluded accommodation in the bowels of the minster. Her bruising is far from fully healed.

'Which is?'

'Let them know we're coming.'

Despite the danger, the speed of the slippy-slide ride is a giggle. Even Eir cheers up at the bottom, especially after watching the awkward Orlando catapult over the landing pad and put a turtle-shape dent in the wall opposite.

Orlando heaves on his feet, pats his pastel-orange jumpsuit down with obvious distaste. 'First thing when we get out of here? I'm visiting a tailor.'

So far, our gambit is paying off. On plan, Fluffy plays double-agent and leaks our escape ambitions for Beatrice Lovell who, swelling with pleasure while holding utmost disdain for the nurse in the catsuit, gulps down the news with glee.

'They're heading for the spooky station,' Fluffy salaciously feeds Beatrice.

'Which spook—?'

'The one in the basement.'

'What spook—?'

'There is a small, intimate spooky station on the premises, for discrete but exclusive passage in and out in exceptional circumstances. I have surprise you never taste of it,' Fluffy says with mock sympathy. 'Unfortunate I never learn the route they intend for getting there. I suggest we set up an ambush around the station.'

'Where is—?'

Fluffy blinks the holly Eir gives her. Beatrice lights up like a laser show with delight at receiving the scarcest commodity on earth: secret information.

'I never—'

Fluffy shuts Beatrice down with a wink and a cutesy kitten smile, leaving her agape and intensely pattern interrupted.

After leaving the patients wards and rec areas on the lower riverside floors, we encounter nary a ghost in the halls around the domestic services sections. A few nurses pass us by while on route through the admin offices. They barely divert their hostile gazes. By contrast, Fluffy exercises no reticence in hissing and baring claws at everyone monitoring our passage. She leaves me cringing about her antics; I guess her acting otherwise would be the suspicious thing.

'Come,' Eir directs us into a dank windowless corridor. The air is close and swampy. We must be well under river level.

'This is a bad plan,' Orlando, with pleading hands, membs from the rear. 'Going deeper into the minster? We should make a dash across the Pleasure Gardens. I know of a secret station on the other side.'

'Every Vauxminster missionary, every detective and café staffer knows of it,' Fluffy hisses. 'It's one of the ways we track Infis passing through London.'

Orlando looks crestfallen, his turtle head almost shrinking into his jumpsuit.

'Check again you have no undesirable flutherbombers,' Fluffy membs.

'Vör, or anyone we train, will never be detectable,' Eir warns thereby exposing the silliness of Fluffy's instructions. 'She'll be flutherbombing others who're flutherbombing others who're flutherbombing …' She nods, signifying the chain goes on and on.

'The fidelity will be terrible,' Fluffy objects. 'They'll taste nothing.'

'Unless …' Eir starts with some exasperation. '… they have … the training.'

'So everyone following us is suspect,' Orlando says for hiself.

I memb, 'Situation normal for an Infi.'

'We have no destination vectors yet?' Fluffy membs, her eyes on me.

'No.' Mal will withhold Maddox's vectors until the last tik. Even Bonita is unaware.

Orlando follows reluctantly 10 or so paces back. 'We should scatter rather than trust a single destination,' he membs.

Eir huffs, willing up patience. 'Anywhere you conceive of going, we'll only be a few mins ahead of a posse of nurses at best.'

'How is your destination any better?' Orlando objects. What would he say if he knows Maddox supplies the destination? 'They'll learn the vectors once we use them.' He grabs my attention with a hard stare. 'We could be spooking for an ambush.'

'I trust my source with my life.' If it is indeed Mal.

Vör Hoyur …

Ben desperately hopes his source is his son, who he'll unlikely inform Orlando about. He casts another glare at Fluffy, unhappy Orlando is part of their break-out attempt. Fluffy shakes her head in a way I'd miss unless I am looking straight at her.

'Look,' Orlando continues. 'You've been getting messages out. This much is obvious. Put me in touch with my connections and—'

'Connections like your feline spy here,' Eir shoots back. 'Oh, we're far from clueless about Fluffy being an Infi agent all these years.'

The nekko's ears flatten. Orlando is unrepentant. 'Well. You and Ben spook off and save the world or whatever your mission is. It's obvious you have one. You 2 together. I know it from the night of the Inductee Gala after the jousting show you both put on. As for Fluffy and me, we'll go our own way once we are out of here.'

Fluffy stares at the floor. 'No. I'm going with Eir.'

Orlando draws to his full height—which is to say, less than 3 quarters of Eir's—and puffs his chest out. 'You'll come with me,' he says, imperious.

Fluffy regards Orlando like he's prey. The nekko is a carnivore after all. Orlando withers and cringes and pulls his turtle head into the inadequate shell of his jumpsuit.

'I'm going with Eir,' Fluffy states. 'And so are you. Or we leave you here.' She turns her back on him and leads the 4 down the corridor for the spooky station entrance.

Fluffy's ears stretch erect and scan about, a foolish affectation. The others catch her up. 'There's no one in there,' she membs as if her projection ears improve her hearing.

'There could be a 14 of nurses ready for spooking in there,' Orlando membs.

'We'll have a few tiks while they recover from the spooky effects,' Fluffy membs.

Orlando's angling his chest away from the others, peering down the hall in the direction they come. Fluffy taps him on the shoulder, and together they skip around the corner into violet light. The corridor flanges into a circular space around the field throbbing in the shallow-bowl depression. Spreading out, they check for threats in every dressing cubicle and utility room. At the edge of the field, Eir conjures the station's console. She'll be checking there's no tampering with the station controls. She'll find none.

Eir overrides the station's control systems in no time. 'We need the vectors, Ben.'

Ben Evoli ...

'Bonita, connect me with Mal.'

'I'm here, Bapa,' Mal membs and blinks me a set of vectors. I blink the same for the others.

'Are you sure these are safe?' Eir checks.

No, I'm far from sure, but it's too late. Memb Mal, 'Who's helping us reinforce the vectors, Mal?'

There's no relying on the station's usual missionaries, who would be nurses one-and-all. We need our own hive of Minds for assisting us through if we might avoid becoming billions of quantum anomalies sparking through onespace.

'Bapa, it's kay. The dolphins are helping.'

'Mal, please. Your bapa and his friends could all die right here without help.'

'Ben Uncle,' Bonita membs. 'I dunno whether I believe Mal about dolphins either. But we got anak anak, just like Mal and me. 1000's of them. It's safe.'

And so, I put our lives in the hands of children.

Vör Hoyur ...

While Eir works the station console, Beatrice leads a squad from a room farther down the corridor and quickly infiltrates the station.

'You betray us!' Orlando, in a rage, accuses Fluffy.

'Looking good in a rainbow uniform, Ben,' Beatrice taunts. The other 6 nurses take up equidistant positions around the perimeter of the circular space. 'Maybe you miss your calling.' Then for the nearest nurse, 'Shut it down,' she orders. The light of the spooky field dims. While Eir continues twiddling the console for reviving it, the nurses retrieve face masks from the kangaroo pockets of their fatigues and fit them. Beatrice gives Fluffy a spare.

'Gas!' Orlando panics. 'They mean to cat us.'

On cue, Ben and Eir each retrieve a pair of masks from their own pockets and hand them out. Beatrice slumps, realising she's underestimating the escapees' preparation.

But not me. I know Eir will exhaust every opportunity in the pursuit of her goals. I know her so well.

'Now what?' Orlando derides. He holds up his fists like an ancient pugilist.

The nurses waver at the knees and shoot inquiring looks at Beatrice. None of them will relish a fight. I wonder if they'll have the stomach for it. Beatrice rips off her mask. Reaches into her pocket and pulls out a syringe. Gives the plunger a push. The syringe ejaculates a little clear menacing liquid. 'Once more unto the breach,' she cries out with tongue and lung like a primitive sap heady with a lust for violence. Her other nurses find their steel, produce their own syringes and shuffle forward with terror in their eyes, holding the syringes out like fencing swords.

 *Fluffy Pusskins ...*

I throw the mask off and tell Orlando, 'Stand back, you fool,' as I put myelf between Beatrice's pathetic troops and my escapees.

'Fluffy?' Beatrice demands.

'You call those syringes?' I taunt. I plunge both paws in my kangaroo pocket and pull out a pair of butane cannisters. 'Well, neither are these.'

Jank, I hope I pull this off. The expression of terror on Beatrice's face suggests I might, when she realises the purpose of the objects I hold.

'Fluffy, what—?'

The hiss of butane from the canister interrupts her. When I ignite the handhold firelighter, there are gasps around the room. I watch as a detached spectator; the flame lights the butane spray and aims for Beatrice. As if assessing its foe, it faces each of the nurses, who squeal like little boys. In quick succession, they flee the station. The flame-breathing beast trains back at Beatrice.

'Fluffy, how could—'

'You believe Eir is the only one in history whoever wants to set a nasty clique of girls' hair of fire?'

'Fluffy, just taste for a tik—'

'Get out, before I toast your ears and steam your arse.'

With fury in her eyes and wrath in her teeth, Beatrice flees.

Vör Hoyur ...

With Beatrice's retreat, Fluffy collapses and would fall on the floor, if not for Ben rushing and giving her awkward support. Fluffy's fur, violet in the light of the spooky field, merges into Ben's uniform like they are one being.

'Jank!' Fluffy swears, fanning feline face with a paw. 'I have no belief I just do that.'

So, it comes for this. The spooky field revives again, and hope exudes from Orlando's and Ben's faces, like candles in jack-o'-lanterns. Muzzy, Eir's hands shoot off the console.

'What? Who restarts the station?' she membs somewhat weakly, still far short of her former health.

'It must be you,' Orlando says, his short-live optimism leaching away.

Eir shakes her head and stands away from the console. She's crumpling by the tik. This escapade is taking a toll on her. She's standing back alongside Ben. A 2-metre broken arrow. She's sardonic. 'She wants for gloating,' she explains for the others. 'Right, Vör?' she membs. 'I know you'd want for gloating.'

'Life is so long and vanilla,' I answer. 'Savour the gems you find along the way. I have a gift for you, Eir. A gift from your Little Mermaid.' I coat the epithet in scorn.

Watch. The spooky pool throbs with a congealing mass at the centre, becoming a figure resplendent in crisp rainbow dress fatigues.

'Well, shit,' Orlando curses.

The other stalks from the mist. At the edge of the pool, Eir quakes with the distress of confronting one of her own sybils. It is a joy for tasting.

'Which one of these should we trust?' Orlando membs. 'If either.'

'Ours' Ben membs. Good boy. Reliable and logical always. But is it true? We could switch her any time.

'Why are you here?' the crumbling Eir demands of the one in uniform.

'You're a sybil and without all the facts, making a terrible mistake,' Crisp Uniform Eir says.

'Eir! Prune her.' Aw, Bat Ears: so adorable, expecting Eir would strike her down. 'Prune her. What are you waiting for?'

'No. There'll be no pruning,' Crisp Uniform Eir says. 'We carry the memory of those sybils we lay in sucky bins. So much horror for the sake of Consigning and now rescuing Orlando. So much messiness at Vraget Beach where we look into so many sybils' eyes, even the one who would kill us. We discard them all like kittens we never want at Christmas. We know the truth then. Pruning a sybil is murder. You're a murderer.'

Eir gasps, clutches her chest. It's a truth she confesses while crumpling on her knees, burying her head behind Ben's thigh; its taste is luxurious. This is what I crave; I need more than therapy; I need more than justice. I want for breaking things; It's how I make things new again. First, things must break, beginning with this Prideful albino stick-insect.

Crisp Uniform Eir allows the rise of silence. It strangles the atmosphere. Now's the time. Crisp Uniform Eir asks, 'Dear Eir, are you well?'

 *Ben Evoli ...*

Eir's face is gaunt and whiter than her hair. The vital pink violet of her eyes has the glaze of a dead fish. 'I—I—' she stammers.

'Enough!' Orlando launches, jumps as high as his frumpy frame will allow. He throws hiself at the sybil Eir like an Ewok assaulting Darth Vader. Takes a swing at her and lands a crunching fist on her jaw. She collapses like a chimney stack whose mortar turns mud. She cracks her skull on the floor. Blood seeps.

Orlando stands over his victim, daring she stands for another blow. He's a primeval gorilla cracking out of his tortoise shell, a silverback high on adrenaline. Releases a raging roar at Eir on the floor, so near rolling into the spooky field mist. 'You janking bitch!' Orlando roars. 'I'm sick of the sight of you.'

On her knees, our Eir stares absently through the floor while Fluffy and me exchange scarifying glances.

'I mean, I'm—it's the sybil I'm angry with. I'm fine with seminal you, of course,' Orlando mutters.

Eir falls deeper inward, paying Orlando's excuses no attention. He huffs a few large breaths. Wrath seeps out of him. Looking at his hands forming white-knuckle fits, he wills them uncurl.

Fluffy, the first thawing from the shock of Orlando's violence, pounces by the sybil's side.

'Am I her killer?' Orlando membs on the verge of panic, his fruit deflating from his former King Kong pose. He is rounder than an avocado.

'She's still breathing,' Fluffy membs.

Orlando nods vacantly.

Our Eir is inert, small, and fragile on the floor, a sick praying mantis Orlando could crack in half. 'Eir!' Fluffy shouts in her face. 'Eir. We must go.'

Eir blinks. 'What?' Fluffy and I lift her up.

Orlando toddles ahead into the spooky field and melts away. Eir collapses again. We drag her like a fallen willow. She slides easy on the smooth floor. Into the field we drag her. Into the giant flying pincushion of onespace.

Unstuck

'Jigsaw Falling into Place' — Radiohead

Nilajani Karunanithi ...

I'M RIGHT, HARSHA! I'm right! You taste this? Are you there? You should be because Mind abhors a vacuum. I taste it! Elsbeth will be so proud of me!

It all connects. We're all evolving—that's the story! Evolving and connecting like one huge fluther. One roiling bubbling chemistry experiment billowing clouds. Ocean tides surging, ebbing over and over.

There are children all over the world, Harsha. You taste? Falling ill with symptoms like sap Entanglement Syndrome. But none die! Each survives in the feverish ecstasy of a chrysalis at transformation.

Mind abhors a vacuum—it requires life; it requires awareness. It requires movement like the swarm of a fluther coming together in communion. It requires celebration. Mind imbues all living things. Plants and insects, reptiles, and mammals. Trees and grasses pulse and throb with it. You taste? Oh, it's wonderful; it's amazing! Fourspace is only an explicating order by which onespace manifests itself; the manifestation of life by Mind's hand; the communal hallucination.

Evidence is everywhere of how fourspace experience misconstrues onespace, as far back as the 20th century. Saps had mass hallucinations of being abducted by aliens. I'm calling it Alien Abduction Syndrome. Mind attracts Mind like magnetism when we rebase our patients. We're the janking kidnappers, Harsha! We're the aliens!

It all connects. Are you tasting it?

Jank. Eir is right ... saying sickness arises from separation and dismemberment. She's right. She's always being right.

All this? How are we so ignorant, Harsha? It's all plain tasting. Are we so complacent, so ignorant of the sheer quantity of information hiding in the constructs of our collective disinterest? Everything is still all there if we only taste. It must be.

But … ha! There is never enough time for tasting everything. We're so busy flutherbombing in safe familiar places; easing into the same low-grade trances; imbibing the slow-drip sugar syrup of banal lives. We have more interest in following an ex-lover's latest coital acts than coitally acting for ourelves (yes, kay, I'm guiltier than anyone). We keen with Envy when another's reputation has a sudden boost. We could *attend* opera, but we stay home and flutherbomb someone who's there.

Most of our missions are low-grade also. Even mine. I aspire for Curing the world of ills, but most of my career is walking beats, scanning for misdemeanours. Where are all the great Greed cases I imagine I would solve? Where are all the brilliant Cures I would deliver? Am I Prideful? Are my expectations too much?

We let our lives drain away one sugar-syrup drip at a time. Maybe we live too long. Maybe we must dilute experience over our longer lifespans. We're unconscious in the way we spend our lives … spreading passion for life like sambal over flatbread. The wider the bread, the thinner the spread. Maybe we just have thin lives, spread over too wide and too flat a slice of time.

So much for the grand orgasm of onespace. If we could, we'd sleep through it. But never now, Harsha, never now. We can sleep through nothing again.

Ask again. Who tastes it all? Someone must. But who? Well, it's in front of our faces. Taste the things: something like Entanglement Syndrome among children; Alien Abduction Syndrome contagious in huge Mind networks; Merge Conflict Fever among frequent exploiters of sybils. There's a common thread, Harsha. All of these are health issues.

It's easy guessing who would know about everything surfacing. It's obvious who would have the political skill for misdirecting the population away from tasting any of it.

It's us. The nursing camerati.

Ben Evoli …

Half coalescing a cacophonous assault. Something industrial. Louder than inside a building under demolition. Rhythmic bashing resolving into drums and bass. The violet flash of arrival streams into a rainbow of colours painting everything everywhere. Music and lighting in concert, thumping so intense it's nauseous. Grimace against the pain.

A grab at my arm. 'Quick. Put this on.'

I'm naked. Without DNA in the weave, the basic nurse's uniform I wear disappears in the spooking.

Eyes adjusting for the light, ears for the music, skin for the heat. Open air. Fresh. A sea breeze. Outdoors at night. Silhouettes and shadows, bubbling lava splashing across enormous birds. 100's of birds dancing. The rosella holding my arm waves other birds aside. Bright, oozing lights part like a sea for a prophet. Suck me in, close in behind propelling me on.

Where are the others? Eir and Fluffy? Orlando?

'Safe,' the rosella says. 'Keep moving.'

Almost fall over pulling on the trousers. 'Where are you taking me?'

'The next spooky station.'

A violet flash from behind tints the birds dancing ahead. The rosella looks back. 'We must move.' Familiar voice. Caribbean accent. The aura around him is Infi-size. Eclipsing all others, the violence of it would be shocking without my own hancy filtering it.

'Lemarr?'

'*Di* same, *bredda.*'

Vör Hoyur …

Before the violet flash subsides, there is jostling pushing crowding. A claustrophobic crush. Noise and lights. Where is this? The middle of a Mardi Gras?

'What trickery is this?' Beatrice membs.

'You too?' I ask, anxiety rising. 'You're here?' See nothing of her in the crush. 'Where are we?'

'No idea. An outdoor nightclub? I'm crowded in by fools and jesters on all sides.'

The crowd are all BirdMe wearers dancing close, leaning in, aiming elbows and shoulders. Shout, 'Please let us through.'

'Health mission! Please let us pass.' No one pays attention. No one fears a Warrant anymore.

'Come on, nurse,' a pelican membs. 'Leave mission at the clinic. Come and dance.' Her projection pierces my arm and chest, the fruit within rubbing against me.

'Let me pass!'

'Kay. Kay. Take some nutes. Gee-ess.' The pelican turns aside with a squawk. Behind it are 14's more.

Ben Evoli …

Lemarr spirits me through the choke of dancers. The sickly-sweet smell of ganja in every bird's feathers rising through the air.

'Maddox involves you?' I ask.

The rosella projection around Lemarr nods. '*Nuh one cud* keep *mi outta it. Suh* ... welcome. *Dis a di foss* annual BirdMe Flock *Togedda* Dance Party.'

'The *first* annual?'

'*Yuh rite ah course.* A year *a* too *lang fi deh* wait till *di nex. Mek wi mek eh di foss* bi-monthly Flock *Togedda* Party.'

'I promise I'll attend every one if we escape this sambal.'

Underfoot, the spring of the dance floor gives way for grass. Look back. No nurse uniforms among BirdMe suits.

'Keep a move. Have *nuh* worry *bout di* nurses. Very persuasive BirdMe fans will invite *dem fah staying at di* party. *Mi* doubts any nurse will *git* more *dan* 20 metres *fram di* spooky station.'

'In this crush I believe it. But they'll just start catting everyone in reach.'

'We have counter measures,' Lemarr membs, and I notice his accent is completely absent. Waiting for an explanation, I examine his bird face centims above mine. Realise what a stupid gesture it is since Lemarr inside is little taller than Mal. 'We have all kinds of antidotes in the punch bowl,' he membs. 'Besides, a nurse's standard kit carries only 5 or 6 doses.'

'Lemarr! This is amazing.'

'*Yuh kno mi eva ave yuh feathas, mon.*' There's the Patois. 'Well, *yuh* sybil's *feathas* at least.'

I recall the conversation with Lemarr at the golf course, and him helping me escape Maddox. Memories which are mine and yet someone else's.

Lemarr membs, '*Wi* have much *inna* common. Both *fi wi* missions bring pleasure and joy *fi di wurl.*'

'Unsure I could bring togetherness on such a scale.'

'You underestimate yourelf, *bredda.*'

'How many are here?' Wondering how long before we are through the crowd.

'14000 invitees, *wid* many bringing +6's.'

Vör Hoyur ...

'Can anyone see Eir?' Beatrice membs. 'Anyone?'

'No. Even Eir will be hard spotting in the crowd. So many of these projections are so tall.'

'I get no bearing with all these halos,' Beatrice says, confirming my frustrations. 'There must be 1000's. We must disperse the crowd.'

'How?'

It's clear Eir is receiving considerable help. Lemarr Robinson's brand is everywhere I look. The same chain of Infis who conspire with Ben's sybil are aiding the seminal. And Eir. I always taste she's up to her pink eyes with them.

They'll be passing easy through the crowd while it blocks us … but what next? Another spook from here using a demountable station which will quickly disappear afterwards. Or perhaps the risk of a free spook. There could be 100's or 1000's of these dancers ready for helping. It may be already too late for us.

Ben Evoli …

The crush of revellers is thinning out. We're moving faster among clumps of partygoers standing around and drinking.

'Watch *yuh* step,' Lemarr membs.

The twist of ankle and the sound of crunching. Gravel.

'How far?'

'A temporary spooky station is 2 beaches round. Wi have tukkies *deh wait.*'

Vör Hoyur …

It's time I stop struggling. Relax and get on with what I'm best at: surveilling fluthers. Some of these birds will be tasting what's happening with our fugitives.

'Memb back for Carlsberg and Vauxminster,' I instruct Beatrice. 'Bustamante too. Call for reinforcements.'

'Are we for ramming our way through the crowd?' she asks, showing a dim wit in the circumstances.

'We must flutherbomb everyone here. We need every nurse we might muster.'

'Everyone?'

'*Ja*, until we find some trace of where Eir is.'

Fluffy Pusskins …

The afterglow of spooking subsides. Violet light washes into rainbow arcs and pulses. The earth has a beating heart. Electronic beats. The ground throbs. Choirs of lights panning and phasing. A crashing crescendo of electric saws cutting sheet metal. A bar of silence. A crowd of 1000's whoops and cheers. The music attacks again at 140 beats per min. The atmosphere brews a melange of sweat and stewed ocean.

Shade my eyes. Into a shadowy seething mass of limbs and torsos, I stagger until a wall of partygoers in BirdMe projections rushes up flapping wings.

'Hey!' one membs. Fat belly. 'Why dress like *dat, dutty gyal*?'

Blink against overwhelming strobes of light.

'*Yuh* hear me, *gyal*? *Yuh nah fi* be coming round here dressing like *dat*.' Pushes me in the chest with arms emerging from imaginary wings.

Swat the arm away. 'Never touch me!'

'*Wi lakka nuh* cats round here,' another BirdMe membs. Four of them crowd around.

'Yea, cats are ecological nightmares,' another membs.

And another: 'A cat sleeps *pan mi* face wen *mi a bowy* nearly suffocates *mi*.'

I purr, 'Please,' then drop the feline affectation. 'Please. I mean no offence.'

'*Den* switch off *yuh* projection.'

'Ask me anything but this.'

'Use BirdMe. *Dat a wah wi a yah fah*.'

'I have no BirdMe.'

'What? *Dutty gyal, yaah lang* way from *yuh* comfort zone here.'

Clenching my jaw, wincing; leaning away from these birds with beaks in my whiskers. A hand thuds on my shoulder. The birds are backing off. The hand whirls me around. A nursing uniform. Recognise those uncommon features: the narrow-set beady eyes and sharp hawkish nose. Beatrice. Take her manga mop of hair away, and she'd pass for a bird without needing the projection.

Beatrice thumps my chest with her fist. A pinch, a sting; a surprise; pain intensifies. Her mouth warps into a smile under her beak. She holds up a syringe with a needle dripping evil. 'If I prick you, will you bleed? Threaten setting me on fire, will you? The villainy you teach me, I execute better for your instruction.'

My knees buckle. Fall into her arms. Everything dark.

Ben Evoli ...

'Watch.'

I memb back, 'Who—'

'Follow me and watch.'

Slide into an assault of crushing lights and electronic nostalgia music, a fluther back in the Flock Together Party. Wishing for my own hancy. Attenuating fluther experience would be a blessing. My unknown host (who I could identify immediately with my own hancy) is shoving partygoers out of her way. Pushing through with her is a squad in rainbow uniforms forming a vee and flanking her on both sides. None are skipping. Or walking. They're marching, taking a straight course through the dancers.

Out of the flashing shadows ahead is another squad of nurses. Two are bearing Fluffy in a chair-carry. Fluffy's head lolls for one side apparently in Never-Mind. My host's contingent chases the others moving faster through the crowd. They break through and block Fluffy's captors.

'We come for the nekko,' my host membs.

'We already have a Warrant for her,' membs an opposing nurse. A birdlike woman with an affectatious Shakespearian voice.

'We're rescinding it,' my host answers.

'On what authority?'

My host taps the insignia on her shoulder board.

The birdlike nurse knits her eyebrows without making sense of it. 'There's no health camerata with such an insignia.'

'Yet we are here,' my host says. She looks at her nearest colleague and jerks her head at the birdlike nurse. The squad advances. In a masterful display they attack, catching Fluffy's captors by surprise. The melee is already over. Fluffy's captors are on the ground and backing away, while one of my host's squad already has Fluffy over her shoulder.

'We'll escort Amelia for the next spooking point,' my host membs.

'Amelia? You mean Fluffy?'

My host ejects me without answering. Rude. Arrogant. Worthy of earning a Warrant.

Who are those nurses? In the dark I catch less than a glimpse of the insignia. Ah, there it is. In the shape of an octagon, a dark border surrounding a lighter field. In the field a figure, looks at first like a fat tree stump with roots dangling under. Long supple roots. I know the insignia. I suppress a primeval fear of Caracia, a fear the stylised insignia octopus could come alive and reach out.

Jolting in shock. I must escape. Sucking in breaths. A vision of standing on a platform at the top of an aquarium. Roots erupting out of the water seizing. Rows of suckers on the underside of each one syphoning my life out.

Lemarr ushers me into one of a rank of tukkies in the parking lot. 'It *kno weh fi a tek yuh.*'

'Where are the others?'

'*Wi fit* Eir *wid* a BirdMe suit *foss. Shi a* too easy *fi* recognising even *inna* such a crowd.'

'Is she all right?'

'Dunno, *bredda. Shi luk* sedated.'

'No, she has …' I taste no explanation for Eir's state. 'And Orlando?'

'He never arrives. Which will wrinkle Maddox.' Lemarr the rosella smiles, all the creepier for the lack of teeth. 'Let me take care of Maddox,' he says, without accent. 'Hope I catch up with Orlando before the nurses.' Lemarr reaches inside his BirdMe projection like he's performing faith-healing surgery on it. Retrieves something from within. 'Eir tells me, give *yuh dis.*' He presses an object in my palm. A lightweight pliable disk less than 2 centims across bulging a little in the centre. Rub my thumb across the surface, feel the scaly texture and absence of temperature. The light is too dim for reading the camerata or model names on the underside, but I know already: *Jikken-Teki, Kyōka 10g.* It's my hancy.

Nilajani Karunanithi …

Ben's tukky arrives at a beach parking lot. He leaps before the tukky comes full-stop, almost hurtles hiself into another of the 7 or so already there. A guide, in a yellow-shouldered grassquit projection, meets him by the parking lot gutter; directs him down a sandy path for the beach. About halfway Ben yanks off shoes. Tosses them in the mangroves.

'Where's the station?' Ben asks the grassquit. Grassquit gestures along the beach.

'Three hundred or so metres along. See where the nekko is standing?'

Farther up the beach, recovering from Beatrice's evil injection, Fluffy displays anxiety; performing a compulsive dance in the sand. Picks up one foot then the other, brushes her calves and ankles under her nekko disguise.

'We'll activate it when you are all here,' says the grassquit.

Ben scans for signs of a spooky field. 'Where is Eir?' He rubs the back of his neck and scratches his elbow.

'It is slow-going with Eir, Infi; we expect her in a min or 2.'

'And Orlando?'

The grassquit shakes her feathery head.

Fluffy Pusskins …

Stab me with a hypodermic syringe? How dare—? Then I'm out, right? Then I'm on a beach. With sand. There's only one thing I hate more than sand: it's wet sand. Fortunate, my fur is only holographic, no real coat for catching the wet sand.

Is this any way for treating a nekko? Strand her on a kim-long strip of kitty litter with the tide coming in? Arghh. Seawater!

The sea air is a battle of chemicals—salt slashing the stench of organic decay. Wet, sharp, and putrid, the air excoriates the back of my throat, plugs my nose, and set my eyes watering.

Two figures approach from the parking lot. One is Ben, thank goodness. I wave. He keeps coming, while the other turns around, satisfied Ben has his bearings. Still no Eir or Orlando. If Orlando arrives last, I must demand we wait for him.

'Where is Eir?' Ben membs. The breathlessness of his beach-run seeping into his Mind's voice.

Shake my head. '7 Hells.' A tukky is bashing down the path from the parking lot. Ben glances over his shoulder. The bouncing and lurching tukky tracks for firmer ground where it will travel faster. But in the dry sand it bogs abruptly. Momentum hurtling it forward on its nose. Before the tukky rights itself, 2 jump out. From the back seat they lift out a tall rakey 3rd whose white-silk hair shimmers under moonlight. One hoiks Eir up into a fireman's carry. He's too short for the task and Eir too tall. The 2nd hurries for teaming Eir in a chair-carry. They shuffle for firm sand. Ben runs back but is no help with carrying Eir. He helplessly jogs alongside, gasping, his chest heaving, his shoulders slack.

They're short of halfway along the beach. From the parking lot, a rainbow uniform pursues Ben and Eir. Pumping its feet through calf-sapping dry sand closing inexorably.

Behind me, the spooky field hums alive. A purple shaft shoots starward. 'Hurry.' Feeling useless. Flutherbomb the pursuing nurse and collapse inside. Call out, 'It's Vör. Hurry!'

Ben Evoli ...

Calves cramping. Lips caking with salt. Lungs burning as if every breath is laden with microscopic ninja stars of sand. *Guns are a last resort*, my stupid trivia-seeking Mind dredges up. In this chase across a beach, who are Phantom Agents and who are Black Flag?

Eir's carriers are tiring; she is barely in Mind. With Vör closing in, I might be better use running ahead. Otherwise, she might catch both of us. I have no delusion she'll be reluctant for violence. Her spook-addled Mind could be priming her for it.

Who am I fooling? There's no world in which I might leave Eir. Vör will lock her away for life. Looking over my shoulder; Vör is running nearer the water and closing. There's also another nurse running for meeting with her. We have 2 pursuers.

'Keep running,' I shout into the hiss and foam of the ocean.

The 2nd nurse closes on Vör and crash-tackles her. Pushes her face in the sand. Points a cat spray can in Vör's face and lets her have it. She waves at me like she's greeting a friend in the park. Nila!

Stop running. Gasping for air. Hands on knees, throwing yarns of drool. 'Beautiful beach, Ben,' Nila membs while I cough. 'Reminding me of home. Thinking of taking a midnight skinny-dip?'

'Maybe you better come with us.'

Nilajani Karunanithi …

Ha! You see, Harsha? You see me barrelling that Valkyrie-blonde jarhead? Pushing her face in the sand? She'll be brushing it out of her lashes for weeks. Now I'm travelling with Ben. It's Mission: Incredibles, Harsha, and I'm on the A-Team.

Ben waves me ahead. I jump into the demountable field.

The spooky station is in the bowels of the crèche far away from the places saps are occupying, in consideration of their horror of spooky fields turning brains to falooda.

From a dressing alcove, Ben grabs a smock for covering hiself. Offers another for the disoriented Eir. Ben helps with pulling the smock over her head. The length barely covers her hips.

They steal out of the station room. Wary, they skip up a low-lit inclining corridor, an ominous tunnel. Every 7 or 8 metres, RADIATION HAZARD signs glower from the walls until the corridor flanges into a rectangular empty room of cold right-angles in the fashion of sap architecture.

At the exit Fluffy holds her paw up, swivels her nekko ear parallel with the door. 'I hear nothing.'

'No one around.' Ben. 'Saps may already abandon the place.'

Fluffy coughs … or sneezes. With her feline mannerisms it's sometimes hard telling. 'Have we a clue what we're looking for?' She's no patient cat. 'Or if this is the right place?'

All look at Eir.

'Eir?' Fluffy asks. 'Know you this place?'

Eir shakes her head.

'Have we a clue?' Fluffy in frustration.

A latch startles us. The door swings in. Holding the knob is a monstrous hand; ruddy and puffy, extending from a thick arm in a red and tan sleeve. The shoulder wide and muscular, the neck thick and short. Monstrous is the swinging of the breasts and the curving of the thighs.

'I'm sorry if I startled you.' A sap woman!

'I suppose she is a clue?' Fluffy eyes the sap.

'Maddox sends his greetings. I'm Zizi Toplis. Please come with me.' Talking loud. Too loud. So loud, assaulting my ears.

Zizi looks down, effusing delight with Fluffy's nekko appearance. For a tik she's agape, suppressing the urge for patting Fluffy's head. Savouring Eir from toe to crown about 30 centims above her eye line. 'Oh, yes, you are the one. Please.' She stands aside and ushers us through the doorway.

Out into the corridor, Ben gives Eir little nudges for keeping her staggering forward.

'Are there sybils here?' Eir with hands loosely clenching together at her heart. The rest of us blink. This is a crèche; of course, there are sybils. 'I mean sybils of me?'

'Yes, a great many. Dozens.' Zizi. 'Or 14's as you would say.' Her voice booms.

'You have 14's of sybils?' Fluffy demands of Eir.

'I have no sybils,' Eir shrieks. 'Someone else crèches them.'

Fluffy grabs Eir by the elbows. 'What are you embroiling us in?'

'Our only chance for fending off Vör.' Eir leans on Ben who pries her away from Fluffy. 'Please,' Eir says for Zizi. 'Take me to your sybils.'

'There is one other you must meet first.'

'Who?'

We make awkward work of skipping alongside Zizi. Our gaits such a bad match for the female sap's long yet slow strides. Eir only just ambulant, falls behind often. Ben coaxes her along.

'It's better if you see for yourself.' Zizi. 'Since you arrived, we've begun to revive her. But you should rest first.'

Fluffy hisses. 'We've no time for resting.'

Zizi pauses, considers changing her mind. About halfway down the corridor, she presses a button on the wall. A chime making 2 doors slide apart.

'Great.' Fluffy. 'An elevator.'

Emerging from the little room are 2 saps with stony faces smelling like carrion eaters. Zizi stands aside, holds the door open. Going in … gulping against panic. Surging under my feet, the swell of an ocean. Reaching the crest of the wave a tik before my stomach. Doors opening. Fluffy exhales deep, jumps out of the claustrophobic space. Ben guides Eir.

'It's sad to see our work ending.' Zizi.

'Your mission is copying and stowing sybils in fridges.' If it's ever possible sounding elf-righteous while purring, Fluffy achieves it.

Something else also embeds in Fluffy's mewling. What is it? Her accent changes.

'When the nurses come,' Zizi says, 'we'll surrender without resistance. The nurses won't harm humans.'

We're humans too, you know, I want for saying. Instead: 'And the sybils here?'

Zizi looks at me as if seeing for the first time. 'From what we hear of other crèches, nurses are taking inventory.'

I say, 'I am sure they are destroying them,' and earn withering, shame-inducing stares from Ben and Fluffy. Eir placidly examines the back of my head.

We enter a dim ward with rows and rows of cribs, impersonal and alien; in rank and file, all facing us. This could be what sap hell is like. Antiseptic essential oils permeate the cooler air. With a heavy gait, I skip down a wide aisle; pass 7 rows until we meet a cross-aisle. Zizi leads right; turns left at another aisle.

'How many are there in here?' I ask.

'This ward has just over 2400 cribs, almost 2000 occupied.' Follow Zizi into a narrower aisle. Ahead are 2 saps in scrubs standing over a machine on wheels studying it.

Passing the 2 saps. One manipulates the machine, fingers touching controls with a series of stabs and swipes. The crib nearest the machine hisses. Its internal pressure normalises with the outside. The hood slides around and down like a curtain, disappears into a slot in the side.

'Routine maintenance.' Zizi is evasive if y'all ask me. I resist the urge for looking in at the sybil. It could be anyone. It could be me.

Matching pace with Zizi, we skip awkwardly between cribs. Another ward; like an old sap hospital. Everything square and bright; white sheets stretch over empty rectangular beds. Under oppressive bright lighting, Zizi leads us through. A door ahead, and an observation window.

Ben leads Eir for the window. Eir stares in; recoils back, her hand over mouth. A shriek of such magnitude, the cry of a mother witnessing the death of a child.

What horror is in there? Dare I peek? Lose my air. My eyes heavy as ripe limes could fall out of their sockets.

A sybil in Never-Mind in the bed on her back, arms by her side, perhaps naked under a crisp sheet.

Eir cries. 'My Little Mermaid.'

'How long till she's awake?' Ben shivers.

'She'll be awake soon.' Zizi assures.

Tears run over Eir's face. 'Vör.' Her voice tinges with tenderness and alarm. 'My darling Vör, my Little Mermaid.'

Ben looks quite beside hiself. Eir's emotion repels him. Here's where I shine, coming by her side and resting my gentle hand in the middle of her back.

'Is reviving her wise?' Fluffy bites her lip. A curious expression for a cat.

'How long is she here?' Eir sounds hollow and melancholic.

Zizi: 'Almost 3 years.'

Eir strokes the observation window.

Fluffy relaxes. 'Good. Let's hope she takes her time going as bent-brain as her seminal.' There it is again: Fluffy's accent. *Let's h-yope ...*

Looking contemplative, Zizi weighs options and words.

I ask, 'What?'

'There will be complications.'

'What complications?' Fluffy cross-examines.

'Normally we'd merge in enough experience for covering the time in-crib. In her case we have no alternative subject for merging.'

'She'll be missing 3 years of her life,' Fluffy accuses. *Missing-g* …

Zizi turns pale. 'I don't like it either, but I have my orders. The way I see it, she might fare better being revived before the nurses get here.'

'One of whom will be the real Vör.' Fluffy's ears flatten. 'How long before Eir's little one realises she's sybil?'

'We're treating her with a nute regimen for keeping her in the present.' The corners of Zizi's mouth curl. No faith in her own words.

'Drugging her,' guesses Fluffy, her growl a peak of indignation.

'Whichever way you cut it.' Zizi. 'There's little time to get what you need of her.' And with that, Zizi abandons us, disgust clear on her face.

Eir separates herelf from Ben. Tentative she clutches the door handle, pushes it inward while gesturing us for staying out. By the bedside Eir hovers as if beholding a holy relic for the first time. She discards her smock; peels back the sheet from Vör's fruit. Taking to her side. She lays a thin and bandy thigh over Vör's groin, a hand cups her breast. She draws inward, making herelf smaller; nuzzles at Vör's neck.

'Find a clothing fabby,' Fluffy orders, with huge kitten eyes. 'We need *Sundhed* uniforms.'

Vör wakes from a deep night's sleep. Recognises Eir. Reaches out, weakly embracing, contentment illuminating her face. Kissing Eir's cheek. Eir kissing back breathing heavy. Embraces ardent.

'Oh? We're still in the crèche?' Vör says, looks beyond the bed for the first time since awakening.

'*Ja*, my love.' Eir the happiest since before Vauxminster.

'We should leave. The smell of sybils is too much.'

'*Ja*.'

Vör sits up, stretches. 'Oh. It must be so exhausting last night. I remember nothing of coming for bed. This morning I feel … new.'

'I'm glad,' Eir says, but sounds unconvincing.

Vör inspects her hands, preparing for saying something important. 'This morning … it's …'

'What is it, Little Mermaid?'

Vör beams with Eir using her pet name. 'Sybils are an abomination. I mean, I know yours are important, but I almost wish I never learn of them.'

'I need for trusting someone, Little Mermaid,' Eir says, I guess playing along.

'Of course. And I'm glad it's me, but …'

Eir wraps her arms around Vör and spoons her. 'What's troubling you, darling?' she asks, teasing out a plot she claims she has knowledge of.

'I'll always follow you, Eir; you taste that.'

'I taste it, Little Mermaid.'

Vör beams again, becomes bolder for speaking her mind. 'Please reconsider merging with these sybils?'

Eir jolts, visibly shocked. 'Little Mermaid, I …'

'But you need them only for some information they remember, right? This's all this is?'

Eir nods uncertainly. 'I've been uneasy about them all morning.'

'After merging, you'll be rid of them? Please? I'm sorry, Eir, sybils are vile.'

'They're a tool, darling. Nothing more.' Eir almost gags.

'They're monsters.'

'Even if they are me?'

'No! I mean … Please, Eir. How long will merging the sybils take?'

'I … am unsure of exact duration.'

'Then please. Get it over with so we can cleanse ourelves of this place. It reeks of sap corruption.'

Eir nods slow, weighs her options. 'All right.' She kisses Vör's neck; collapses back on her side of the narrow bed.

Vör turns, strokes Eir's face. 'Are you all right?'

'I'm … it's been a hard few days, Little Mermaid.'

'Then you rest. I'll find the shift manager and tell her the sybils you need for merging. Please, if you must merge them, you'll merge them all now? No more sybils after this, *ja*?'

'*Ja*,' Eir says, and swallows hard.

A crew of 30 or more saps spread through the wards, retrieve 16 of Eir's cribs, and wheel all into a revival theatre barely large enough for them and a single extra crib for Eir. In pressing haste, merges will run all night, leaving no time for Eir resting between. Even so, it could consume the better part of 2 days. Vör—despite her keen loathing of sybils and ignoring Zizi's advice for rest—is flitting about between cribs like a hen with chicks.

In the ward adjacent, Fluffy is coaxing the basic health-issue hancy from the neural plant at Ben's neck. Ben is impatient and jittery bug for having his personal hancy back. Who could blame him? He must be feeling like an amputee, without all the power and custom functions at his tastebuds.

'After I replant your hancy.' Fluffy tries for sounding casual. 'I must upload something.'

'What? No chance.' Ben looking stern.

'It's from Eir,' Fluffy argues. 'If you disagree, then fit your hancy yourelf. Or go without.'

Ben almost jumps off the table. 'Let me up.'

'*Ie*,' Fluffy pins him down at arm's length, quelling his struggles. 'Relax, will you?'

Ben gives in. 'Know you about these sybils she's merging?'

Fluffy whiskers droop, shaking her head. 'I hear of it the same time as you.'

'It seems she has genuine shock about it.'

'I never trust Eir.' Fluffy slouches against the aid couch, scratching her ear, looking at the floor. 'I should trust no one. Orlando, the lying scoundrel, ropes me up for this. I should be at home staying out of trouble.'

Am I imagining Fluffy's phonetics changing? She's sounding more … Slavic?

'What has Orlando over you?'

'Orlando is another story, little boy,' Fluffy says with dejection. 'I … Put it aside. Nothing else matters, only escaping this mess.'

Ben moves for putting his hand on Fluffy's paw. She's too quick withdrawing it. Ben says, 'Look … I just … terima kasih for busting me out of the minster.'

'Orlando leaves me no choice.'

'Even so. Terima kasih.' Ben swings his legs off the couch, sits up alongside Fluffy. 'The thing Eir wants on my hancy? Let me examine the mindwriting first. Then we might decide how we proceed. Together.'

Fluffy nods in the peace of accepting the fates awaiting her.

'What it is?' Ben asks.

'All Eir says is, it's her … weapon of love.' And then Fluffy is purring.

Vör pulls a chair alongside Eir's crib, collapses over it, strokes the glass over Eir's hand. Doting. Ben and Fluffy wonder how this Vör will turn out, what plans Eir may have for her.

A pair of saps wheel away a merged sybil's crib and replace it with the next in the train. They connect segmented metallic hoses and cables. You know how it looks, Harsha? Like a scene from one of those nightmarish horror sci-fi movies you love so much. Crèche tech needs so much ugly machinery and hardware.

With Fluffy watching, Zizi operates a trolley of machinery beside Eir's crib, tapping and swiping through a series of panels on a primitive monitor. 'There's an accumulation of merge conflicts developing,' Zizi says. 'It could be more complex than I first hope.'

Ben shivers. 'Any chance of merge conflict fever? I see a case of it a while back. Very unpleasant.'

Fluffy's tail thickens, freezing still for a tik.

'No,' Zizi lies. 'Eir is accepting the multiple experience strands well. It would require a great many concurrent strands to cause the fever, more than Eir is assimilating.'

'How can Infis endure such?' Ben says, earning a sideways look and flattening ears from Fluffy.

'No argument from me.' Fluffy sounds gruffer, like she's holding the heat of her breath in.

Vör, suddenly upright in her chair, grabs the side of the crib with a white-knuckle claw as if she's falling overboard from a boat.

'What's the matter?' Fluffy.

'Someone out there knows we're here.' Vör looks with wide eyes over her shoulder. '7 Hells, it's Teo.'

Fluffy tries for hiding her alarm. Ben understands also the danger. Teo might tell Vör she's a sybil. She will disbelieve it, but how might she react?

'It's only a matter of time before Teo finds us.' Fluffy panics. 'We'll be in so much trouble.'

She's right, Harsha.

Zizi flicks controls on her machine, plunges her hand in a pocket, retrieves a nutepak. 'Take it,' she tells Vör. Vör looks at the pack with bewilderment. 'It's a catatonic. Take it. We must lose your nosy friend.'

Vör understands the urgency, if not the exact reason. She tears the pack and swallows the contents. Two sap orderlies guide Vör away, her lights going out.

Fluffy Pusskins ...

While Zizi continues merging Eir with a queue of sybils, little Nila flits about asking questions and 2nd-guessing every adjustment of the crib controls Zizi makes. In a deep couch in a small, homely room somewhere, Ben inspects Eir's piece of her weapon of love.

'It's a mess,' Ben reports earlier. 'The architecture is all wrong. It's one conglomerate when there needs be 2 components. One piece is for locating hancies running some target hoot, which I presume and hope Eir has in mind. A separate piece is for patching those hancies. Infecting them in some way, I suspect and—'

'Kay, kay, sorry I ask.'

'Is this right?' Nila asks Zizi, bringing me back for the present. 'Last time you swivel the knob first then swirl 3 fingers over the bowl interface.'

Nila is just ... so ... annoying. *Bre!* 'Will you just let her work?' I demand.

'What's the matter?' Zizi asks. Without tasting our membs, she senses the angst between us.

'Baby field nurse, stop distracting Zizi. With so many interruptions, she might bake a merge out of existence. Or worse.'

'Actually, she's right,' the ugly Zizi concedes. 'I almost ran things in reverse order. I should take a break, let someone else take over for an hour or 2.' Zizi invades my space, goes to put her hand on mine. Jerk it away before she penetrates the surface of my projection. Stiffly, she steps back. 'It's late,' she says, trying for being soothing, but her booming voice shatters the affect.

'We've all been agonising over it for hours. Why don't we all get some sleep? There'll still be plenty more merges to fret over in the morning.'

We must—Vör could arrive any tik—if only Nila would …

'Fluffy?' Zizi startles me, pressing her hand through my projection. We both recoil, Zizi suppressing her shock.

'No touching!' I shout out loud.

A brief, deep silence. 'You're exhausted. You need rest,' Zizi says.

Little Nila nods sincerely with big moist eyes.

These sleeping quarters reek. Worse than sap body odour are the spice and flower extracts they douse themelves in. I'd be asleep but for all my sneezing. Tossing and flipping in a bed too large in a room too large. Feel unsafe. There could be anything sharing the space with me. The room's single window—small, boxy, brutal—admits too much moonlight. The mattress is so soft, I consider curling up on the floor. At least I could avoid the grubby sheets and—pillows. What could anyone use so many pillows for?

'Trouble sleeping?' comes a solicitous memb.

'Orlando! Where are you? You untrustworthy reptile. We have a deal.' I know I'd cry if I was any less angry.

Orlando is making no attempt for hiding his vectors; so, from his view, I pan around for discovering clues for his location: a small room with all the traits of a private station in the bowels of a crèche. There he is at a spooky station exit, a shadowy elliptical shape like a cockroach standing on 2 legs.

Fighting back the sobbing with the anger turning stale. 'Tell me about Persia. Is she still alive?'

'Oh, dear Fluffy,' Orlando membs, staring into the exact space in the crèche from where I taste him. The effect is he's looking straight at me. 'I would think you would be more grateful.'

A mangling guttural cry of anguish shocks the room: 'Tell me.'

'You must leave there, Fluffy. Vör is coming.'

'Really, Orlando? News services are among your missions now?'

'She's coming, with a good 10,000 rabid nurses and jury-rigged mining tools for carving the crèche up.'

'Is this your mischief?'

'Well, shit. Are you crazy? I have no control over those militarised nurses. I will, however, be sending an additional 20,000 troops—mostly mining contractors with no love for health missionaries—for surrounding Vör's quaint little side-show rifle range. They have permission for shooting first, taking nutes later.'

'What?'

Orlando cracks his face with a reptilian smile. 'Kind of you and Eir, painting targets on your heads and attracting such attention. With any luck, we'll wipe out every foaming-at-the-mouth nurse, and still have time for

Devonshire tea. I trust you enjoy cream and jelly on your biscuits.'

'It's strawberry jam and clotted cream on scones, you philistine Wastelander rattlesnake.'

Orlando chortles. 'Fluffy dear, bravo. You must be the last Croatian bastion of the old English empire. Such a pity the Vikings took tepid old Britain back centuries ago. It's quaint you still remember. Oh, yes, hiss at me by all means. You're a reliable servant, if a cantankerous one. I suppose I am out of that accursed mental asylum; I should—somewhat infinitesimally, for sure—thank you for it.'

'Tell me or I'll skin you alive with my bare claws.'

'Oh, Fluffy. Are you wearing your ridiculous cosplay projection so long you truly believe you are a cat?'

'Talk.'

'All right. All right. Listen, please just listen. You must go to Niš.'

A chill of panic ices my guts, an ancient memory of Skull Tower, rising and coalescing in Mind with bright brutal accuracy. 'Niš? Are you joking?' My teeth are grinding.

'For the old minster.'

Oh, gawd, he's mocking me. 'It's abandoned. Crumbling. No sifar would consider occupying it.'

'You would well know, since you visit it every year, on the anniversary of your last—'

'Play no more games, Orlando.'

'There's a spooky station.'

'The spooky station is in ruins.'

'No. Another station. I understand it is still functional.'

'After all—'

'Yes, yes. Persia and her mission use it for fleeing the minster before the scatter nets come down. My sources say the spooky field locks on a single destination.'

'Vectors drift all the time. Those will be so old. They could smack me into the Carpathians, or the other end of the universe.'

'There are worse ways of passing,' Orlando mocks. 'You'll see things no one else will ever see.'

'You call this delivering on your promise? Some bent-brain story of a secret spooky station in an abandoned minster? And you expect I hurl myelf into the spooky field and hope against it makes noodles of me?'

'It's all I have. If you wish for finding your beloved Persia, this is your chance.'

Ben Evoli ...

Awaken from a dead sleep by squawking parrots. I'm back home?

All yesterday so deep in other concerns, I never wonder for once where this crèche may be. It's far from home. Even through the narrow escape and nagging fear of impending recapture, my fruit knows it's still in a time zone near Vauxminster's. Probably 1000's of kims away from London. Of no comfort is the spooky station in the basement. Whether Vör finds our location or the spooky station vectors first is no more than foolish amusement. The outcome is the same.

After spending the night in a dormitory for 14 or so—all male, in the tradition of sap gender discrimination—I wash in a communal shower among several saps whose side-eye glances accuse me of bringing danger. Or perhaps it's the sneering at my little Pink Shower Tree while they stretch their logs with soapy hands. I'm elf-conscious of my gene-mod skin, though the inherited designer tiger stripes are almost invisible through successive generational and personal fashion choices. But I feel sorry for their lack of choice, their inability for escaping primitive genetics. And yet these saps are more like neos than any I meet. Shorter. Our height. Although their frames are more muscular than ours, I taste they laugh like any neo. After drying and wrapping a towel around hips for ridiculous modesty, I expect each might skip out rather than trudge like other saps.

Later, at breakfast over pastries and tropical fruits, I sit alone at a table for 14; saps, elbow-at-elbow, crowd the remaining tables. I drop more food in lap than mouth while staring appalled through the cafeteria's picture windows towards the outdoor terrain.

Around the compound is a swathe—perhaps half a kim wide—of broad leaves, creepers, and spiky things supported by a structure of distorted, angry little trees. I imagine large steely insects crawling and buzzing; columns of militant ants; swarms of venomous bees. Rising beyond, cathedrals of old hardwoods—the rainforest untouched—keep their sprawling roots cool from the sun. In the distance, ridges of tired rock pierce or rise above the forest canopy.

'Another janking jungle.'

'I'm sorry?' Zizi stands on the opposite side of the table, with a tray holding a kopi mug and a take-out box from a cheap fabby. 'Did you just say something? I mean, out loud? Being vocal is uncommon for neos.'

Face flushing. 'Sorry, I just ... never mind. Just mumbling.'

'Are you well?' Zizi asks, which of course alarms the jank out of me until I realise, she's only enquiring if I'm kay. 'I mean did you sleep well?' she says reading my shock.

'Yeer.' Which, surprising me, is true. 'This might sound silly ... where are we?'

Zizi gestures for the bench on her side of the table. I nod. She wriggles her prodigious pantat on the bench, then unfolds her breakfast box. I must be screwing up my face somehow because she says with a sheepish look, 'I know, right? Fast-food cheeseburger? I'm sorry it must smell awful to you.'

'It's okelah,' I lie. I'm glad there's no bacon. The fries are worse.

Zizi bites into the limp thing with relish. 'I wonder how real burgers taste.'

Every bit as bad, I imagine. 'Where are we?'

Zizi wipes some lurid red sauce from her mouth. 'Maddox asks I not say.'

'Figures.'

'You understand, I'm sure. Neos leak information like incontinent camels.' She squirms in her seat, fighting an urge for gossip. 'I imagine it's not that hard to guess the region. Then perhaps I might offer a clue or 2.' Enjoying the game, she punctuates her pleasure by shoving a fag of fries into her gob like she's stoking a steam engine.

I start, 'Okelah. Rainforest …'

'Equatorial. Similar time zone as Europa, perhaps an hour or 2 east. Africa.'

Zizi beams. She's a hyena tearing away more of her carrion burger. This gargantuan woman might be playing mother of me. I'm no bigger, and appear no more age-worn, than a sap boy.

I guess, 'Congo Basin.'

Zizi claps and blurts, 'Ituri Rainforest.' Her eyes bulge and her mouth gapes, revealing half-chewed potato. 'Oh, shit.' She laughs so raucous she puts waves in my kopi mug. 'Oh, fuck Maddox. It hardly narrows it down much. Good luck finding us.'

Her bravado evaporates. We eat in awkward silence.

'How are Eir's merges progressing?' I ask in the tone of asking Aisha about her day.

'Progressing,' Zizi answers with some equivocation. 'We had some complications overnight. Two sybils were almost-but-not-quite duplicates.'

'I would think having fewer differences would make it easier.'

'Nah, the merging process is optimised for sybils with disparate experiences, which is the common need. Luckily, we're still on track, if a little behind.'

'How far behind?'

Zizi suspends the remains of her burger centims from her mouth. Her shoulders fall. She appears as if spending a great deal of effort preventing her head from shaking. 'Not before nightfall.'

The rest of the day. More. I say flatly, 'Vör will come for us and she will find us.'

'How long do you suppose?' Zizi asks. The cafeteria becomes a single organism holding breath.

'I have no idea. Even with spatial coordinates there's no way of reliably converting those into onespace vectors for a given tik in time. Get them wrong and you could spook 100 metres in the air or 100 metres in the ground. You could spook into a tree in the next valley over. You could spook your head into a toilet bowl.'

'So you have no idea.'

'None. The nurses may never discover our vectors. Or without them they may discover somewhere, near enough, for mobilising against us. There are so many variables.'

'We may run out of time for finishing the merges ...'

'We could run out of time for finishing breakfast. In my opinion, your people should evacuate.'

Purification

'Gun' — CHVRCHES

Ben Evoli ...

ALTHOUGH I TAKE A LIGHT BREAKFAST, there's no point meditating while digesting. I find a quiet comfortable lounge on the 2nd floor with a shady view of the south, and resume picking apart the clumsy mindwriting Fluffy supplies. I only have Fluffy's word it's Eir's *weapon of love*. Giving Fluffy's murky association with Orlando, it could be his. Either way, I'd rather occupy myelf with a mindwriting task than pace around Eir's crib with Nila, like expectant parents.

The patch for the target hoot is progressing. However, without access for source mindwriting or knowing the extension protocols there's only so much I can develop. I take up the next riskiest technical problem: locating hancies within a certain radius which are running the target hoot (Eir must tell me which one soony-soon). The subsequent problems of uploading the patched version onto all those hancies are simpler than I make out before, providing the hoot conforms with common standards. Otherwise, the whole plan is a bust. I assume the target hoot is not so arcane or old-fashion, or its devising so incompetent.

Nilajani Karunanithi ...

Ben mindwrites all day, and Fluffy—well, y'all tell me where she is. Is it my place for pushing my nose in their goings on? I join this troupe less than 48 hours ago. If Fluffy is off somewhere on some mission, who am I who should question?

I feel a spare part most of the day. There's only so much brooding over 17 sleeping Snow Whites; I tire of being Dopey. Zizi and her team have the merges in hand. There's nothing for my contributing.

In mid-afternoon, Vör attends the ward.

'Got your cat nutes?' Zizi says without looking up from her controls.

Vör nods, fishes in her kangaroo pocket; holds up 3 small foil packs.

I ask, 'No more Teo?' and rub my forearms. Fidget with my chatelaine.

'As yet, no. My vectors shift enough from last night.'

'Yes. Good.'

'I must be careful. Teo's best at keeping her flutherprint low,' Vör membs. 'She makes a joke of it flutherbombing a target till they discover she's there. Sometimes she hides for hours.'

We get chatting about stuff and well—we have much in common. In our youth, both of us head for long Cures until a role model appears—Eir for Vör, and Elsbeth for me—who leads us for joining the health mission. Both of us find difficulty progressing through our respective camerati. Competitors plot against us, Envious of assumed unfair preferential care from our mentors. Of course, Elsbeth and me never … well, you know. If Eir is my mentor, I doubt I could stay out of her bed.

Vör's kinda sweet, if a little too withdrawn and insecure. Eir is her everything, and she is nothing in her own estimation. Imagine me as such, Harsha!

Mid-afternoon. Drinking. Vör says Teo will overlook intoxicated Minds. No one here cares. Well, perhaps Zizi cares; with sunset approaching, she sends us up on a large balcony for watching the sunset. We settle into a couple of banana lounges and order up a fabby from the kitchen. Take turns fabbing shots. Vör alternates between Aqvavit and Gammel Dansk. I choose Arrack. East meets west in our stomachs and dehydrating brains.

'This is nowhere near like the real stuff.' Vör slurs.

'Same with the Arrack.'

'We should eat.' Vör leans towards the fabby, works the menus. Almost falls off her lounge. Both laughing. I punch up the fabby's menu, drag it my way; lie back while swiping through it. 'All the options are bar food.'

'Perfect.' Vör. 'Abso-janking perfect. Frikadeller!'

'Samosas!' I answer back. The fabby fires up. 'Oh jank, we get it starting already.'

'Never mind. We'll eat everything it throws at us.'

The sun sets while we mess with the fabby. The rainforest canopy, with a delineating line of red, blurs into the starry night sky.

'Hey.' Vör with no sense of play in her tone. 'See there?'

'Where?'

'Out there.'

Focussing requires some tiks.

'There it is again,' Vör sits up, points out.

'What?'

'Purple flashes. There. There.'

I see too, the frequency increasing.

'Alamak!' Ben interrupts. Find him staring out a ground-floor window at the ridge tops.

'What?'

'Huge aura activity close by. We have visitors.' Ben ominous.

'How many?' I expect he'll have something in his hancy for getting a more accurate estimate than counting spooky field flashes.

'Judging by the fourspace distortions, 1000's.'

All the ridge lines in the west flash purple.

We assemble in a conference room far away from the ward where Eir and 2 sybils remain in cribs. Even Ben emerges from the farthest reaches of the crèche and joins us in our ancient need for physical closeness in a time of danger overpowering.

'What's happening out there? It's over an hour since sunset.' Vör panics. We should still be drinking. If her head is throbbing like mine … 'Get Eir out of her crib,' Vör stridently commands, channelling the militant vengeful version hunting us. 'We must leave.'

'I recommend we wait, at least until the present merge completes,' Zizi says. 'I mean, it should be safe … the crib won't disconnect until the current thread of experience is merged …' she shrugs, which chills me. Wonder about the reliability of the tech. Zizi must be reading my apprehension; perhaps learns as much from facial expressions and body posture as we learn from flutherbombing. 'Of course, the process handles interrupted merges …'

'But?' Vör.

'It's rare for such a circumstance …' Zizi trails off, leaving us wondering if she herelf ever cuts a merge short.

'There's a sybil of me out there,' Vör wails.

'What?' Ben is incredulous.

Vör defensive. 'Teo finds me again.'

'Take the nutes.' Zizi orders. Vör is distraught and disoriented, freezing with indecision.

'Teo shows me another Vör out there. Someone has sybils of me.'

'We know,' Zizi says harsh. She rises from her seat; tears open a nutepak; applies it on the distraught Vör's lips. Vör comes back in herelf, gulps down the pack's contents.

'Ben Evoli!' Teo membs. 'There is no hope for you. Crèching sybils of nurses only demonstrates how sick you are. Eir abandons you already.'

'Eir is still with us.' In Never-Mind.

'Quiet, Nila.' Ben with Infi arrogance. No one should order me about.

'You lie.' Teo.

'She's here.'

'Nila, be quiet.'

'Then she should speak up. There's little time. It's difficult guaranteeing your safety with so many chapters of nurses surrounding the crèche. With dangerous weapons. Very dangerous weapons. Eir should come out.'

'No one start shooting.' Ben. 'We'll find a solution.'

Teo: 'The solution is surrender.'

'Please, wait. Wait just a little—'

I blather, 'Until Eir's merges are over.'

'Nila!' Ben chastises.

'What?' Me defiant. 'Teo will know everything if she bothers looking.'

'She's merging?' Teo gasps. 'Sybils? She may be assuring the deaths of you all. Please, I beg; surrender.'

Ben Evoli …

Zizi's staff should evacuate the crèche. I tell her so and get an emphatic headshake.

'If we leave under cover of night, the nurses will assume we're sneaking something or someone out. If only one squad of paranoid nurses decides to attack …' Another, slower, headshake. She's right.

'Teo,' I call. 'Let's discuss the welfare of the missionaries here.'

'Go on.'

'Let them evacuate peacefully.'

'Sap missionaries, yes. All neos must surrender.'

'Terima kasih, Teo. Thank you. I am wondering about the timing. We should ensure we are orderly, reducing the possibility of regrettable mistakes. I imagine setting up checkpoints will take some time …'

'One tik, please,' Teo membs. '*Ja.*'

Locking eyes with Zizi and take a deep breath. 'Might I suggest dawn is the ideal time?'

'You should surrender,' Teo says. *Should.* Better than *must.* 'And you must disable all weapons.'

Zizi shakes her head vigorously.

'We have weapons?' I ask her.

'The less you know the better.'

Yeer, the less I know, the less the nurses know. I memb for Teo, 'We'll disable our weapons if you disable yours.'

'What you ask is impossible,' Teo membs.

'She's not in charge,' Zizi postulates. 'Not in control.'

'Then we must both agree for a ceasefire until after the evacuation.'

No answer.

Teodora Mrowka ...

If anything, the temperature is warmer since nightfall as the wet earth gives up its heat. For the passing hour, it rains so heavy it appears as curtains of thick spider web. The weather net hisses and spits with a constant lilac glow as it spooks away the downpour falling on it. Steaming humidity still passes through, leaving us clammy and miserable.

From our vantage point among the ridges, I survey the crèche compound's squat cluster of 3- and 4-story buildings—defined only by weak yellow light escaping their brutally small rectangular windows. I wonder which contains Eir. Successive flits among the few fluthers down there reveal only interiors; I taste no views through windows which could yield clues of their location within.

They crèche a sybil of Vör. I clamp on my seething anger with my jaw and suck it back through my teeth. If the real Vör finds out about this ...

Gerlinde impatiently marches back and forth while spooning gobby stew into her mouth.

I exhale, growing weary.

Gerlinde takes offence, believing I'm ignoring her. 'Chapters are still arriving, with more erasers. The temptation for firing is increasing by the tik. Where is Vör anyway?' She slurps soupy liquid straight from her bowl.

'As if she includes me in her confidence anymore.'

'If retaining the confidence of her army is important,' Gerlinde says, waving an oily spoon, 'she'd act better than leave us out here all night. When will Vör arrive?'

It's a good question. Y'all would think she'd be racing here for nabbing Ben by her own hand. Perhaps she's spookheading a few more laps around the world first. I'm sure it's what works her up, makes her so combative. Without her spook-hit, she'd be the same little Eir-shadow as before.

I flutherjump until I find Ben as he leaves Nila, a grotesque sap woman, and the Vör abomination in a conference room. Wearing grim determination like battle armour, he paces without a skip down a boxy corridor. From his fluther, I pan around, seeking windows.

Should I promise we'll shut down our erasers for the duration of a sap evacuation? There's no guarantee against some extremist chapter of a 2nd-rate camerata launching an eraser drone for the merest offence or provocation. Am I sure my own chapter will remain calm? Surely, they taste we must save Eir. Then we will demolish this horrid factory.

I memb Ben, 'Let me talk with Eir. I'll commit for a ceasefire—'

Gerlinde whispers tongue and lung in my ear, 'Some health camerati will ignore any agreement we make.'

'Quiet!' I hiss.

'Good. We'll begin the evacuation at dawn,' Ben membs.

I memb, 'No! Let me talk with Eir first.'

'She is … unavailable.'

'She's in mid-merge?' I probe.

'Yeer. Technicians say it's dangerous interrupting a merge.'

'How long before it's over?'

'There are some complications. Early hours of the morning at the soonest.'

'He's bluffing,' Gerlinde says. Of course, he's bluffing. But have I a choice?

'There'll be no evacuation until I speak with Eir. Face-with-face.'

Silence. Come on, come on, come on …

'Okelah,' Ben membs. 'Come meet her in here.'

'In the crèche?'

'Yeer. As a show of good faith, come in. We'll host you overnight, and you can meet Eir at sunrise.'

Bre. I'm trying for saving her, you idiot.

'While you're in the crèche, I trust no one will fire on us in the middle of the night,' Ben membs.

Gerlinde says, 'He has no idea of how it is between health camerati.'

'He has every idea,' I sourly answer Gerlinde.

Eir, are you worth risking life over?

'There's one more thing,' Ben membs.

'Which thing?'

'The people here warn against the tricks you use at Manaus. We'll repel any nurse in a sap projection.'

'Never mind projections,' Gerlinde says with uncharacteristic excitement. 'Ben's inviting us in.'

It dawns on me. I have all night inside the crèche. Time enough for finding the spooky station. Time enough for resolving things peacefully and averting a war.

 *Fluffy Pusskins …*

Blink the bright pink light out of my skull. Suck out the dizziness by stretching my lower jaw. The fireworks recede; a new location accepts me. A finger touches my cheek, caresses the tear drops there, longing for them being there after spooking. They are, which only brings more. And uncontrollable shaking.

Orlando, you troll, this better be it.

My dear Persia, my love. My Persian lamb, I still miss you. Every day, every season, every year. So many years. If I could hold you again … Where are you?

How could a mission run so long? How could you keep it secret? Is it running still? Is this why you never come back for me?

Remembering our final time together like yesterday; a brief lunch in the public cafeteria of Dom Zdravlja Niš, within morbid sight of Skull Tower. You sit me in the cafeteria, in plain view of the thing, and retreat into your lunch. The increasing distance between us inciting the only response I know in the face of our fading emotional connection: complaint. Complain about the appalling tower of skulls; about why your city never tears it down; about the time you spend on your mission, of which you tell me nothing. What's going on here? Why are you withdrawing from me?

Persia, I waste our last half-hour together. The next morning, the most impenetrable scatter nets come down around the minster. You never emerge. You should tell me what would happen. You must know. You must know, Persia. How could you keep it from me?

So much activity around the minster for months. Supplies and materials going in. Nothing coming out. Perhaps you are spooking them onwards somewhere.

Imagine my hope when the scatter nets finally come down; imagine me squirrelling into the minster, hope brimming for our reunion, in uncontrollable tears; imagine me—and all the others eager for lost lovers and family—finding a shell of a building. No equipment. No supplies. No furniture. You and your missionaries abandon it, bringing down the scatter nets as a final act. You abandon me.

Orlando Greer …

Let's watch, shall we? The bittersweet tale of love lost. Such a beautiful story, of a cranky old crone in a cat suit … oh, I'm getting ahead of myelf. Let's have no spoilers.

If y'all miss the trials of Fluffy while she scours the decrepit minster for the secret spooky, gog for hollies. But I must warn y'all, it's a dour, drawn-out affair. Unglamorous. There are tears and curses and feats of strength I would never guess Fluffy possesses. Under her projection, I'm sure she's quite sweaty and grimy. There'll be barked knees and torn fingernails. I recommend y'all skip it all and pick up the story with me.

Suffice saying, determination wins out; Fluffy finds her spooky station. With only a tik's hesitation, she lurches into the spooky field—still fresh and violet after all this time—risking her fruit splattering through the cosmos. How the station's mindware is still resolving those vectors is beyond tasting. In Fluffy's situation, I'd never risk spooking from there. But there's emotional obsession for you.

So, we find her arriving at a hitherto unknown crèche. And now I acquire the vectors.

In a large dormitory, Fluffy scrambles among the cribs, hoping Persia is there somewhere. Hoping her crib remains functional. Hoping Persia is as fresh as the day she goes in, and no decaying mangle of biltong. Taste Fluffy's panic when she turns an aisle and encounters an open foul-smelling crib. Oh, no! She may be too late! Trepidating, she approaches and finds a deflated corpse. Dear Fluffy is somewhat on edge. The sight of the open crib paralyses her until she realises much more of the crèche needs searching.

Of course, dear flutherbombers and time tourists, y'all may note I never make any claims about Persia being in any of those cribs. I merely supply a trail and allow Fluffy's desperation take over. In truth I have no certainty she's there at all. A rumour in the guise of a secret is a powerful motivator, yes?

More scrambling. Breathless, she's recalling if she's been through the next dorm yet. Decides she must check just in case. Good thinking, Fluff. Panicking with impatience; stifling wails of despair, she sprints down aisles, the quality of her search degrading by the tik.

Oh, she's going to give up. Such a shame; she could be so close. Get up Fluffy. Keep going. Make my interest worthwhile, please. There's a good cat. Slower, more methodical. Yes yes. Go back and revisit a few aisles, by all means. You are hasty before, rushing, overwhelmed, fearing there's no end in the battalions of cribs. You may be searching for days yet. You may never leave alive. It's all hopeless, yes? How could you ever expect …

Ahh … heh, heh … Can you believe your eyes? There she is. Reclining. At peace. More beautiful than Fluffy ever remembers. Somewhat plain and featureless, if you ask me, but I'm no forlorn lover as she is.

Fluffy laughs. She cackles with relief. It's her Persia. She's rescuing her Persia. Well done, Fluffy. Well done.

Yes yes. The rolling of the crib for a revival theatre. The long slow painstaking thawing-out, y'all might guess, is far from captivating. Now, this should be fun …

Still in Never-Mind, Persia lies on the single couch in the theatre, Fluffy stroking her forehead. A tender kiss there. Then from a drawer Fluffy retrieves a small nutepak containing maybe 21 mils. She rips the cover off and drizzles the contents into the Persia's mouth. Persia's breathing deepens; with eyes still shut, she stretches and flexes. She could be yawning after a long night's sleep.

'You're safe,' Fluffy says.

Persia takes a few more breaths, rolls the shoulders, knits the fingers together and cracks the bones. Opening eyes, she fixes on Fluffy's nekko features. '*Hvala vam*,' Persia croaks, using the Serbian formal *thank you*.

'My darling, it's me,' Fluffy croons. 'Oh, my Persian Lamb. My Persia.' I imagine tears are already flowing under her nekko projection.

'Amelia?' Persia asks disbelieving, and Fluffy nods. 'Is it you?'

'*Hai*, love. I find you.'

'Shut the projection off. Let me see you,' Persia says in a thick Slavic accent.

'I'm...' Fluffy fumbles for words. 'It's a long time.' Her accent sounding more like Persia's with each word she utters.

'Shut it off please?'

Fluffy manages a weak nod. The projection evaporates.

Oh, so delicious. The look of pain on Persia's face when Fluffy reveals herelf.

Here they are. The tears. Hollow moans and racking sobs. Feeble embraces and wails of loss, as the full consequences of Fluffy's age suppurates into Persia's understanding.

Dear fans, think y'all for even a tik that Fluffy underneath her nekko projection is more archaeology than a living creature? And y'all say I'm old. Her balding scalp is only minimally thatched with wisps of tangling disorderly hair. Her skin is powdery grey crepe paper and appears holding in place only by virtue of her clothes; hanging limp from her bones; loose in the absence of any bulk or tone of muscle.

'I'm sorry,' Fluffy sobs. 'I'm ...' She cannot finish. Sadness racks her whole frame.

'Amelia, it is you?' Persia asks, disbelieving her own eyes.

'*Hai*, my little lamb, it's me.'

Persia sits up. Feeling tender, her eyes squint against dizziness. 'You're so ... how long is it?'

'My lamb, my love.' Fluffy pauses. 'It is more than 2 centuries.'

Shall we wait while Persia absorbs the news? Ah, she draws breath, and her eyes refocus. 'Two centuries? You endure for ... 2 centuries?'

They are crying again, loud and unfettered, holding each other tight, painting each other liberally with their snotty noses. Such bittersweet pain.

'This is another life. Our time together ... it's someone else.' Fluffy blubbers and can only manage a chaotic cough. Her chest racks and her shoulders quake.

Exchanging a look deepening, they fold together, Persia gathering her aged lover for her young chest. Fluffy offers a tentative kiss, breaks it. 'I must feel awful.'

'You are my Amelia and always will be,' Persia says and reinvigorates her embrace, caressing Fluffy's loose hollow cheek. She begins kissing the pale thin lips, gentle at first. They start puffing and huffing. Within tiks they are hungry as new lovers.

And then Persia is pushing Fluffy away, abrupt and savage. She sits up as if she would flee.

'What is it, love?' Fluffy asks, afraid of rejection.

'Someone … something, just flutherbombs me.'

'Who could know—?'

'There it is again. It's … I have a conscious sybil?'

'A sybil?' Fluffy demands in disgust. 'What are—?'

'Wait. Give me a tik while I find it. Ha. Let's see what its game is.'

Oh, my janking Jesus. Who would believe, after 200 years in a crib, Persia would have the bile for it? She vomits all over Fluffy in the most copious of fashions.

'*Bre*. What is that?' Persia swears and makes a clumsy show of wiping her mouth. 'I touch Mind for a tik and I'm immediately …' She's kissing ralf again.

Teodora Mrowka …

Staring at the ceiling. A flat white rectangular level ceiling. Four rectangular corners where it meets flat grey walls. Lying on a narrow rectangular bed jammed into one corner. A door with a lock, in the opposite corner. A closet at the foot of the bed. Over the bed hangs a painting (a painting!) sharing the narrower wall with a medievally small window framing a dark empty courtyard. A small desk abuts the longer wall between the window and the door. An uncomfortable chair slots under. The remains of a cheap fabby buzzard curry on the desktop.

The ceiling, the corners, the door, the closet. The ceiling, the corners, the door, the closet.

Six sap guards haul me in here. I expect at least 2 will remain outside on shift rotation. Try spooking out hours ago using the technique we devise in the Amazon. With no surprise, there's a scatter net around my quarters. Who knows how much of the crèche it covers?

The ceiling, the corners, the door, the closet.

At least I can communicate, although Gerlinde is long asleep and the remaining nurses following me are down-cast. The primitive lock on the door defeats all our ideas so here I remain.

The ceiling, the corners, the door, the closet.

The window resists smashing. Standing on the desk, I am too short for reaching the ceiling. Clumsy, I tread on the dinner plate, catapulting curry gravy and goopy rice over the desk and my feet.

I spend some time following Ben and Nila, hoping I might taste a spooky field, or Eir, or a room where she may be. First Ben, then Nila, inevitably fall asleep.

The ceiling, the corners, the door, the closet.

In a spice market in Istanbul, a merchant offers me fake saffron. When I turn my nose up, she invites me in back of her stall for inspecting better goods. She draws a curtain back. As I pass through, the curtain entangles and binds me, prevents me from moving. I fall over, still wrapped in the cloth. My head hits a pillow.

The pillow is on a bed in a cell of a crèche in the heart of darkness. The curtain becomes a bedsheet.

I remember where I am. Dawn, damp with light rain and mist, sulks through the narrow rectangular window.

'Teo,' Gerlinde membs. 'Saps are already coming out of the crèche.'

'No sign of Eir?' I blink sleep out of my eyes, stretch my jaw and arms.

'They're breaking our agreement.'

And have me captive. 'Please Gerlinde. Let no trigger-happy squad shoot.'

'For now, the saps are everyone's fascination.'

'Make sure the evacuees stay peaceful. Who knows what violence they are capable of?'

'We're allowing they leave?' Gerlinde checks.

'Make sure they're real saps. Beware of sybils in projections,' Gerlinde barks aloud from where she stands by the roadside, which is fast becoming a rivulet. I'm finding it hard panning around her fluther; everyone is wearing personal weather nets. with the constant spatter of rain, they all look like semi-transparent lilac ears of corn. She's waving her arms for attention, no longer stuffing her left hand in her kangaroo pocket for hiding the obvious pale freshness of her regenerated limb. Could y'all blame her after all the jokes? *Show us where the White Witch touches you. You'll be full albino in no time*, they say.

Fingers tenderly explore my sore places: the crack in my femur, sustained in the Amazon, still knitting; the wound in my abdomen just above the mons where a splinter of hardwood arrows in. I caress my head, in which throbs the deep untouchable wound of losing the mission to Vör.

'None have halos,' one of the nurses, Field Nurse Eva Winterbottom, membs. 'They're all saps. Just animals, disgusting things.'

Gerlinde marches at Eva, pointing a paly-pale fresh finger. Confronts her face-on. 'They're people and you shall regard them so,' she shouts tongue and lung. Eva blinks and blows a short raspberry, which only incenses Gerlinde more. 'Focus on the mission. Or will you be the one who lets Eir skip under your nose?'

Gerlinde is still far from perfect health. A sucky drill almost erases her, so lucky losing only an arm. Infis using mining tools for weapons and turning them on us. On Gerlinde. Unbelievable. *Erasers*. The nurses assembling here are growing sicker by the day. A vengeful Vör nurtures and enables their

Wrath. Her reputasi escalating. Is the Reck on Vör's side? 'Ben and Eir remain the only Infinites,' Vör reminds everyone. 'The Reck is under their control.'

The queue of saps keeps building, snaking all the way from our checkpoint up the road. Nurses at the checkpoint search for sap projections; many saps object to such invasive handling. Shouts and threats. So far, no violence.

A tall sap woman at the head of the queue stretches her arms out wide, palms forward. 'I don't mind if you want to examine a real woman. Here, feel my biceps, my breasts. Wouldn't you love to have real breasts? Or an ass like this? Come on, find out what you're missing.'

Eva shudders. Gerlinde shakes her head; lets the crest of her aggression fall; trudges upstream of the checkpoint; passes downcast saps swilling alcohol from litre bottles. One burly sap chomps on barbecue rib like it's his last meal. A group passes by, holding umbrellas against the rain while batting mosquitoes and larger things away. Couples walk hand in hand, arm in arm. Women bear the look of refugees cowed and submissive, while males exude defiant bravado. Primitive.

Bitter in my failure I memb, 'We're losing the initiative. The longer it goes the more time Eir has for bewitching Vör again.'

Gerlinde pulls her mission cap off, slicks her hair back, raises her eyebrow.

I must admit Eir once bewitches me too. It shames me so I cover with, 'We need Ben alive more than we need stop Eir.'

Gerlinde snorts an expression which almost throws her strangely angular face out of symmetry. Those pronounced cheeks, flat hairline across her forehead, and equally flat jaw; together forming an almost hexagonal face. 'The puppy Ben is no more than a technician with his hand on a joystick. It's Eir who instructs him.'

A few hundred metres from Gerlinde, in the train of waiting vehicles, shouts and cries rise. The quiet whir of a motor intensifies, becoming the ear-piercing squeal of a steel lathe. Saps are jumping aside, landing in roadside ferns. A truck breaks from the caravan, steers for the jungle line.

'There are cribs in the back of the lorry,' a nurse membs.

A drone descends from the sky; its spooky field comes alive with a whip-crack of light from an eraser generator nestling on a nearby ridge. The field orbits ever faster around the drone, until it is a narrow spinning hoop as thin as the blade of a circular saw, glowing a ghoulish purple. Wind whistles through the jungle canopy; the sound of breathy, moaning ghosts. A thunderclap. The field's tether reappears and slashes the sky with jagged light. The drone descends on the truck, fast as a guillotine, and slices it through, leaving a searing after-image of mauve. The truck smoulders, a flicker of fire in its wreckage. A metre-wide slice, precise and straight, cuts a diagonal between the truck's forward right and the left rear. The forward half, including the driver's side of the cabin, tips over. Smoke hisses in tendrils from the ruins of 2 cribs in back. Look with horror for the remains of the driver. Expect exposed flesh; both raw and cooked, bloody, and cauterised. Expect unrecognisable slop will leak from the wreck. Somehow, the driver clambers out of the cabin, through the open slice; jumps and runs, knees-high, for the forest.

The once orderly queue of saps scatters and becomes a swarm of insects teeming for the forest, tripping and sinking into the thick greenery. Fourteens of nurses skip for interception, firing nute darts from clumsy launchers (another of a health camerata's recent inventions).

The drone chases a thick clump of running saps. In fear of erasure, nurses give up pursuit, standing back in horror, anticipating a massacre. From high out of the misty air another drone descends.

I memb, 'Gerlinde!' and pace around my confinement, bashing walls and desk with the side of a fist. 'Tell every chapter, stop firing.'

The 2nd drone primes. With a startling crack, a curving whip of light tethers the drone with its generator … from here, the crèche. With sickening speed and accuracy, its spinning hoop-blade glows violet-hot, homes in on the first drone, and destroys it.

'What the jank?' My shouts reverberate off the close walls of my prison.

Gerlinde rushes for the wreck with others checking for survivors or deaths. No one dead or alive is in either section of the cabin. No saps in either slice of the back either. The sybils in the cribs are gruesome corpses. Each is a gutted fish chopped in 2 cauterised clumps.

I memb, 'Eir's?'

Gerlinde shakes her head. 'Who's responsible for this?' She membs breathy from the short sprint. A nurse points across the valley for a machine with a swivelling lens larger than twice the radius of a woman's height. It glows a faint lilac. Around it is a clump of rainbow uniforms. 'Someone, find the procomplement of that chapter, and order her hold fire!' Gerlinde orders.

Bite my lip. 'There will be more breaking ranks before it's over.'

'Ja,' Gerlinde membs. 'With so many …'

'Weapons are a bad idea. For us they're novelties … toys. And everyone clambers for playing.'

'We're no soldiers,' Gerlinde says, grim.

'No surprise it escalates after Jamaica.'

'Well, it's easier co-ordinating a dance party than a siege on a crèche.'

Now we know the crèche has weapons. While we have numbers, the crèche shoots fast and straight.

A few mins ago, Vör joins Gerlinde and our squad on the ridge. For a tik, I worry she may be the sybil from the crèche; but there's no mistaking the Vör with Gerlinde is a spookhead.

'Eir,' she calls. 'It is already midmorning and you have yet meet with Teo.'

Please, Vör, yes. Spring me out of here.

'We will meet with her in good time,' Eir answers, sounding frail from the merging, assuming she's the seminal. How will I ever know for certain?

From Vör's fluther, I locate Eir's. There she is, in a small lounge space, sharing a couch with Zizi. Nila paces about. Ben is sitting, muttering, and gesturing over a small desk in the corner, conjuring and manipulating scripts and schematics. I suspect nothing could be more bewildering or catatonia-inducing than following him. What is he brewing?

'Meet with Teo or no, whatever you please. Either way, you must accede to my demands,' Vör decrees.

'Or what?' Nila retaliates, earning a scowl from Eir. 'You'll start tearing the place apart? With Teo somewhere inside?'

'There are more important things at stake than a single life.' Vör, you *kusko!* You're sacrificing me? 'Last chance, Eir. Turn Ben over, and there'll be no Warrants for anyone else. Including you.'

'As if we could believe her,' Nila mutters. 'I think we have a new contender for Craziest Nurse in the World.'

'Ah, the young Field Nurse Nilajani Karunanithi,' Vör membs. 'I believe the title is still yours. Always in trouble, I understand. Poking around in detective business … If you ever wish for escaping expulsion from your camerata, you forsake your chances now. Some of your own colleagues are here, ready for tearing down the crèche.'

'Is this how it is?' Nila challenges. 'Violence?'

'You are the ones bringing it down upon yourelves, by tampering with the Reck.'

'Oh, Vör, the state of the Reck is of no matter,' Eir says. There's no doubt she's feeble.

'So you say. Hand over Ben and we'll taste the truth,' Vör demands.

'Ben bears no blame for any of this,' Eir membs.

'Then hand him over,' Vör persists.

'Please, Vör. Let's discuss it. Together.'

'A waste of time. Comply with my demands, or I'll replace the crèche with a vacuum.'

What of me? Will you vacuum me out also? Am I worth so little?

'Vör, please, before things escalate out of control,' Eir membs in exhaustion. 'Think ahead. How long will it be before you lose influence over those 1000's of nurses out there? How many camerati will be reluctant for relinquishing the power of their new weapons? How long before they turn on each other? How many would savour the end of our *Sundhed*?'

'Perhaps, I could grant a meeting … if you grant one other request.'

Ja. Tell her, release me, Vör. Get me out of here before one of those other idiot camerati shoots me for feedstock.

'Name it,' Eir says, warily.

'Eliminate every remaining sybil of yours in the crèche. Destroy all the copies of me. Show some contrition by destroying the sybils, and we'll meet. Here is the important part, Eir. You must destroy each one personally, by your own hands. Only then will you understand the scale of your crimes.'

The cow. How cruel, accusing Eir of crime. Eir spends her whole mission warning nursing camerati against degenerating into police forces.

'I have no idea how many there are.'

'Then better start right away. My patience will allow only so much leeway.'

Nilajani Karunanithi ...

'How long before she regains Mind?' Eir stands by Vör's bed, stroking her cheek and hair.

Zizi in the open doorway, clasps hands over her belly. A phalanx of saps behind her guard the hall. 'She should have been awake more than an hour ago.'

'The dosage is correct?' Eir asks without accusing.

Zizi nods. 'I think she is simply sleeping.'

'Very deep for sleeping.'

'Yes.'

Eir kisses Vör's forehead. 'I have one experience of pruning sybils. I never wish for it again.'

'Without wishing to be indelicate,' Zizi says, 'I could shut down the cribs. It requires no direct action from you.'

'Killing sybils is no way of mollifying Vör now. She sets me conditions she expects I will never accept. She's wants a fight.' Eir collapses on a nearby couch so swift, I fear she may snap her spindly limbs.

Zizi is quick by Eir's side. 'You must rest.'

'I'll rest when we're done.'

Zizi seizes Eir's shoulders, and squares her face-with-face, stares into her eyes. Saps apparently think nothing of such assaults. Eir is in terror and shock, which is perhaps Zizi's intent.

'You have just merged a large number of sybils,' Zizi says, losing composure. 'You must rest, or risk merge conflict fever.'

Eir waves Zizi's warning aside. Zizi pins her shoulders even tighter. The offence!

'Let me explain about how merge conflict fever progresses,' Zizi hisses like a venomous snake, while Eir is the terrified rodent unable for looking away from her predator's face. She strains her neck and pulls her head back and away from Zizi's threatening mass. 'First nothing,' Zizi says as if retelling a ghost story. 'You're perfectly normal until the first symptoms, and then you have between 15 tiks and 3 minutes to live. When it starts, you'll pray it's quick. Unresolvable merges will start firing synapses in chaotic ways, producing catastrophic physical responses in your body. Imagine all the worst sap brain diseases—motor neurone disease, cerebral palsy, epilepsy, and dozens more—attacking you concurrently. Your muscles will become so spastic they'll put traumatic stress on your skeleton and organs. Tendons will snap; bones will bend and break; your face will collapse in. Your lower jaw will meet your forehead. Your ribs will become shattered knives stabbing your organs in shreds. The bones of your limbs will crack and fold over on themelves. Shall I go on? If you're lucky, you might experience none of it. You might already be gone …'

Eir finds enough reanimation for breaking Zizi's accost. 'You're seriously considering killing my sybils?' Eir asks as if none of Zizi's dire warning registers with her.

'Eir, rest or die,' Zizi says like a priestess.

Eir sets her jaw, expecting an answer for her question. Zizi casts off the rigidity in her frame, relents. 'It is a normal occurrence in the operation of a crèche … to retire obsolete sybils.'

'What defines obsolete?' Eir appalled.

'It is a matter for the customer, Infi.' Zizi.

'I am no Infi.' Eir bitter, her eyes never leaving Vör.

'The Reckoning says otherwise.'

'The Reck, *ja*. The heavily compromised Reckoning.'

'I'm not so sure it is compromised.'

'Tell me, Zizi. Who crèches my sybils? Maddox? Orlando?'

'I am aware of neither.'

'Then who?'

'I don't know. Those sybils were crèched elsewhere. Our customers frequently use a chain of intermediaries.'

'So the original seminal may have no taste of their sybils, no taste someone else is crèching them. How can you fail to comprehend such monstrosity?'

Zizi takes a deep breath; straightens her skeleton; chin-up, gazes beyond Eir for the horizon through the window. 'We are human beings. We'll do whatever it takes to survive.'

'Whatever it takes saps to survive,' Eir counters. 'Slavery, sweat shops, coal mines, genocide, deforestation, extinction events … and crèche management?' Eir shrinks; contemplates her own survival; casts a forlorn gaze for the sleeping Vör. With tenderness she says, 'How is it I ruin you, Little Mermaid? Where is it I go wrong?'

'Eir will never order Zizi *retire* her sybils.' Ben paces around a holly splaying out all directions from the middle of the room. It looks like the guts of 14 giant chickens—cassowaries, maybe. Ben points at various swollen parts of them and scratches his chin. 'I rather taste Vör would relish Eir strangling each and every sybil in the crèche.' He stops, looks right at me, mumbles. 'Perhaps she should. If she takes long enough, I may have time for disentangling this multidimensional bowl of spaghetti!' He shouts the last phrase. 'It would help if I know what hoot is the target. I need the interface protocols.'

'I'm sure she'll supply them when the time comes.'

Ben tastes my lack of confidence, looks side-eye at me. 'I'll need them soon.'

I shake my head, disbelieving. Unsure how much more ... 'Are we all bent-brain? You see how an eraser slices up that lorry? An army of nurses is out there, ready for making feedstock of us. It takes only one trigger-happy nurse—our atoms will end up in a kopi mug. For most of them out there, this is a game. We have so little history in violence; it's all just comic book stuff. 7 Hells. If I am better at picking sides—no offence—I might be up there scratching an itchy-itchy trigger finger.'

'Nila, calm down. I'm incapable of tasting a thing,' Ben gestures at the revolving bird guts, 'with all the noise.'

'Then what?'

'Vör's stalling as much as she dares, considering the uncontrollable rabble following her.'

'Stalling?'

'She's looking for the spooky station.'

'Will she find it?'

'If none of the other squads of nurses lose patience first.'

'I think we should call Vör's bluff—the demand for destroying Eir's sybils. I think Vör's only aim is for tormenting Eir. She's probably flutherbombing Eir, enjoying her misery. If she makes Eir obey, so much the better. I think she'll meet Eir anyway.'

'Why?'

'Just a tasting I have. Whatever plan she has for Eir, she'll savour it all the more making it close and intimate.'

I'm right, Harsha. Vör relents on her demands for destroying sybils, impatient for a show-down with Eir. She probably rehearses 14's of times how it will play out, how she will make Eir cower. She wants personal validation more than anything else. Validation she believes only Eir's submission will provide.

Into the claustrophobic box of an elevator. Doors shut with mechanical finality; the jaws of a metal whale clunking shut. Black rubbery lips seal. In the brushed stainless-steel doors is Eir's indistinct reflection, a snowy rainbow-colour Christmas tree.

Nothing happens. Eir's Mind is ever-more absent. Far from herelf since confronting her first sybil on Vör's street—and worse after disposing of 100's of sybils on Vraget Strand—her every encounter with more gnaws at her core. Merging her sybils here metastasises a kind of psychological cancer of what's left of her. Even her tearful joy of having a younger more innocent Vör bears a sybil stain.

'Eir.' I prod.

'Hmmm?'

'This coffin is taking us nowhere.'

Eir throws her head back as if to say, *Ah.* 'Ground,' she says tongue and lung for the doors.

Gentle lifting pressure in my knees. Semi-weightless like at the top of a jump from a trampoline. Now I'm heavy. Slowing, coming for a stop. The mechanical whale opens its mouth. Eir takes my arm, leans on me.

'Eir, I'm staying out of the reception area.'

'Get me as far as the door. I'll be fine from there.'

'Are you sure? Zizi has terror about your health.'

'I'll be fine.'

Eir meanders for a ring of couches around a low table, unsteadily and hesitantly stalks behind Vör who gazes out windows as large as yacht sails. Perhaps she swells with pride as she beholds the hordes of nurses a few hundred metres away. They swarm around bespoke siege engines, contraptions, mirrors and floodlights, 2 or 3 women in diameter. 'Your crazy minder is too timid for sitting with us?'

'Leave her out of it.' Eir sits herelf gingerly like a creaky old crone.

'Where is Ben?' Vör presses. 'Never mind … I taste him down there, ferreting hiself away. The only good ending for you is the one where I get Ben.'

'Retaking Ben is cruel. We should have compassion for our patients. Little—'

Vör blocks Eir's speech with her hand.

Eir swallows. 'Vör, you're sick. Vengeance is taking you over. Wrath. It almost owns you. Please release it. Let it dissolve.'

'Have Ben come out. Or we will retrieve him ourelves.'

'The time for Warrants is over. Cures yield more harm than good. There are no Cures worth the price.'

'We can never let Ben go. He corrupts the Reck.'

'Who is corrupting what?' Eir defeated shakes her head, seemingly all the energy she has remaining. 'It takes me so long in seeing.'

'See what?'

'The inevitability of corruption, the torque and moment of it.'

'And when is that?'

'Achievement. Success breeds corruption. Success believes success has a formula, which leads to the taking of dogmatic positions. Competing positions arise, leading to bargaining; bargaining leads to exploiting leverage.

Leverage yields power. Power keeps positions safe, calcifying structure and amplifying defensiveness. Defending against any and every perceived threat is intrinsically evil.'

'You're saying I'm evil?'

'I'm saying our institutions commit evil in the name of elf-preservation.'

'No! Our mission is caring for the health—'

'Then let us pursue our mission above preserving our status. Little—sorry. Which part of this siege is for Ben's health? The masses of weapons? You considering us all expendable? Is Teo expendable?'

'We know Ben makes deliberate and persistent efforts for defeating the Reck's security measures. Look at the Reck's recent behaviour.'

'Look at your reputasi, how it rises. Perhaps you are manipulating it.'

Somehow the blow lands. Vör's mouth falls open her head jerks back. 'Is this a joke? You and Ben are the last 2 Infinites!'

Eir answers her with silence. Then, 'You accuse me. I accuse you. Accusations are easy when there is so little understanding.'

'I understand in abundance.'

'Have you any love for me left, Little Mermaid?'

Vör Hoyur ...

Love? The flesh of love corrupting, the bones of love becoming chalk; my ribcage collapsing into the cavern where my heart burns until ash; no number of tears extinguish the conflagration before there's nothing left.

Love? 'All the way through my skin and flesh,' I answer, the answer of an empty echo, an answer of yearning for precious loss. My skin parching, my flesh desiccating. My shoulders fall and I stare down into wringing hands.

'Then why continue as an accomplice in the pain and suffering our therapies cause?' Eir asks, oblivious of my pain.

I straighten finding strength in holding myelf hard. 'Alien Abduction Syndrome? You believe this?'

'The facts emerging are indisputable,' Eir says. 'Thank my timid young minder for uncovering most of it.'

I hear only indistinctly while I grind resolve into my molars. Is Nilajani Karunanithi—so near expulsion from her camerata—the object of Eir's seduction now?

Nilajani Karunanithi ...

Are you hearing this, Harsha? Eir, the White Witch, acknowledges my role? Which is scant joy, I guess, since Vör is near making us all toothpaste.

'We are all one vast ocean—' Eir.

'Enough! I'm sick of vast oceans, and nurturing love for someone before I might Consign them. And needing compassion for every Greedy, Envious, elf-serving creep on the planet. I'm sick of it all.' Vör's thoughts form an unmistakable taste of Teo.

'What of the Prideful ones? The Wrathful?'

'Those too.'

'Then, Vör, you must be sick of yourelf.'

Vör Hoyur ...

She pours scorn on me. There is nothing left, no hope.

Sick? She accuses me of sickness? I'm empty, is what I am. A dissolving soul in existential need of reconstitution, reconstruction, redemption. This pitiful, corrupt Eir stands in my way.

'We are the ocean, Vör,' Eir blathers, unaware of her dyspraxic elbow wobbling, and her hand flapping in her lap. Such mannerisms, I would once find endearing, now incense me. I despise her for them.

'It's what onespace means,' she prattles. 'Every child tastes it. Our technologies exploit it every single tik of the day. Yet we believe in a representation of a separate elf; believing our fourspace body is more important than our onespace essence. The real sickness, Vör, is the addiction of believing the elf is a separate entity.'

I am separate. Cast adrift, is Eir no longer my anchor or my light; I must end this—her—

'It's all illusion. There is no separateness. It's a lie. We're only white caps, waves on the surface of the deepest ocean. We're only movement on the surface. Now we're pissing in the ocean, and all of creation tastes it. We nurses are fouling it.'

In peripheral vision I see indistinctly a screaming banshee of a war-cry coming at me fast. Rage contorting the face. I freeze ensuring an inevitable face-scratching eye-gouging assault on me.

The face. The hair. My face and hair.

Sybil!

Teodora Mrowka ...

Our Vör rolls across the couch, a split tik before the other pounces and lands snarling in the vacant space. She slams her fist on the table and leaps on her feet; standing over the other, dominant now she recovers her wits. Her features sharpen and vulcanise. She menaces Eir while pointing at 2nd Vör. 'How dare you allow this abomination near me. Have you no morality left? Destroy it.'

'Sybil?' Second Vör shoots back, indignant, as she regains her feet and squares off. 'You're the sybil. And … and … a spookhead!' Our Vör grinds her jaw, the accusation irrefutable. The sheen of her skin, the dilation of her pupils, the corners of her mouth twitching, and her shallow-fast breathing all betray her. 'By this alone,' 2nd Vör condemns, 'I know you are the fake. At the least, the simplest Cure is destroy *you*. I'm the healthy one.'

'You are the sybil.'

'If you are seminal then prune me,' 2nd Vör taunts confident.

Our Vör loses her wind. 'What?' Her hand steals into her kangaroo pocket and fondles the thing in there like it's a lover's breast. Anything but organic, it's a cold and grey embodiment of aggression. Is she seducing it or it her? The grip so easy, accommodating her palm while her fingers curl around it. Her index finger hooks through the guard and caresses the flat clitoral trigger.

'Go on,' 2nd Vör goads. 'If you're the seminal, prune me. If I'm sybil, you're right; I'm an abomination. Go ahead.'

'I have no knowledge of pruning,' our Vör defends, panicking. 'I never crèche you. She crèches you, the White Witch.'

Eir reaches out for stroking our Vör's face. Tears tumble. 'Please, Little Mermaid.'

Our Vör flinches away. 'Stop calling me this.' She rages.

'What?' 2nd Vör says, double taking then staring at Eir with imploring eyes. 'I'm your Little Mermaid!'

'I'm sorry,' Eir sputtering, sobbing. 'It's my fault. I'm sorry.' Whatever resistance Eir plans is dissolving in tears. 'I'm sorry I'm albino,' she blurts, as if she's colliding with the defining unworthiness of her life. Her collapse is almost embarrassing.

Distraught and vengeful, our Vör yanks the thing out of her pocket and trains it at 2nd Vör. At Eir. Back at Vör. The thing's muzzle bore is a black, dead eye; dull and passive, promising easy slaughter. Everything fades into a murky background, a cheap stage setting for the threat of a gun.

'Little Merm—'

Flinch against impending trauma. Perception and time distorting. Tiks dissolve before and after. A bone-splitting sound cracks with concussive force.

Perception

'Weapon of Choice' — Fatboy Slim

 *Teodora Mrowka ...*

Y'ALL SEE IT? Has anyone a holly? I have only shards of memory—our Vör: both hands on the gun; arms out straight; pointing at Eir—losing the rest in shock. 'I miss you,' she says. Can this be right? Or am I scrambling a memory from another time?

A flash from the gun muzzle and an eardrum-compressing crack like lightning splitting a slab of granite.

There must be more. Think, Teo. Taste it all.

A shard of 2nd Vör; her heart breaking, tasting Eir's connection with ours, the seminal. With rage she attacks real Vör.

Another shard: real Vör swings the pistol towards the sybil. She hesitates against shooting her own likeness, but festering rage at Eir demands release. The gun muzzle flashes.

Too late, Eir jolts, balls herelf into a smaller target. The flash of the gun lights up her face before she flinches. The bullet is coming. The sybil, her arms around Vör, knocks her groundward. Impossible tasting which happens first: the sybil tackling Vör or the gun firing. Eir hurtling off her seat, collides with its arm. Her dyspraxia flares: she takes a clumsy tumble for the floor. A solarglass window above the atrium shatters. Eir tries for regaining her feet; clumsy, stumbling away, clutching her knee. The sybil pins Vör's upper arms at her sides. They wrestle. Another shot! Blood sprays. The sybil releases Vör as her strength drains. With arms free, Vör takes aim at Eir and fires hasty shots. The shots of a novice, none hit the target. With relief, I taste Eir escaping.

Gerlinde Mann …

I shout, 'Teo.' Useless—Teo is a prisoner in the crèche. 'Teo!' Her eyes flutter wild. She's flutherbombing, or deep within herelf. I must shake her out of it somehow, a shameful intrusion in other circumstances. 'Come on, Teo. Where are you?'

'What?' she demands, snarky and defensive.

'Vör tries to kill Eir. With a … gun!'

'I taste it all. Gerlinde, Vör is clearly unwell.'

'I doubt it matters. Come taste what I'm tasting.' I point at a ridge overlooking the crèche on the opposite side where eraser mirrors are powering up. Drones swarm towards the crèche. 'There's no stopping it. Teo, get out fast.'

Ben Evoli …

Within 30 tiks of the gunshot, Nila is breathless before me, taking my elbow, tugging. Unresisting, I allow her take me where she may. Corridors. Doors. Lefts. Rights. Dead ends. Back-tracking. None of it matters.

'Come on. Keep moving.' Nila skips ahead and picks her way down a stairway. 'Why is it none of these crèches have slippy-slides?' she complains.

'Where are we going?' I ask, only tangentially curious, strangely dissociated.

'Somewhere deep and small. Safe. Away from mad nurses shooting sap guns.'

Nila tugs a fire door open and bounds through. It almost clangs shut before I catch up and yank at it. So heavy, it requires a 2nd pull for swinging it open.

In the glaring light of a new corridor, hear the reverberation of another door closing. A bathroom? The door opens; Nila's holding it ajar. 'This will work. Come on.'

Follow her for a row of cubicles. For the last one she goes. Turns and ushers like she's presenting a luxury hotel suite.

'Um, I'm fine thanks. I already kencing at the minster.'

'No one will spook into such a small space. It's safe.'

Wary, inch into the cubicle. Nila pushes me back and aside so she can pull the door shut. I almost fall over the bowl. Bark my shin on it.

'Lock the door,' she calls. 'And keep working on the weapon thing. It's the only chance we have.'

Nila vanishes leaving me in a bathroom with a single exit. If I ever see another face, I expect it will be Vör's.

Teodora Mrowka …

Fast boots trudging through the hallway in both directions. Hold my breath, anticipating the cell door will open. The boots fade, leaving a yearning after-taste in my ears.

'Hey!'

How feeble is tongue and lung now? I'm unsure if anyone outside would hear me, even if they have an ear against the door.

Surely Eir will remember me amid the panic. She'll send someone for me. She'll send … where is she?

Vör is already back at basecamp above the jungle floor, talking down the leaders of the trigger-happy squadrons. Some are whooping it up too much for engaging in coherent conversation. I try finding a way from Vör's fluther for Eir's. Vectors are destabilising and fading so fast. There are so many flutherbombers jumping around. Everything is too chaotic.

Ah, I still have Nila. And now Ben. Nila is herding Ben through the crèche, while keeping a well-trained nurse's eye on Eir caught in a maelstrom of saps fleeing the crèche. Corridors are snarling with the stampede. Eir forces her way against the tide of it. Even at 2 metres, her slight frame is no match for the stockier saps whose elbows are brutal weapons coming at her like hammers. Shoulders are battering rams; torsos are trucks on legs. Exhausting her.

Among the fear-fuelled ruddy complexions of the beastly saps, Eir appears even paler—bluish almost. Dust and debris taint her hair grey. Her hand, nursing the gunshot wound above her knee, appears more like a bloody carnivorous talon for tearing flesh. With jerky shuffles of her feet, she lamely staggers her way through the tidal flow, labours for breath. She coughs, and wipes spittle from her mouth's corner. Pausing, she looks at the ceiling as if at an unrelenting sun, her face baking into a wide grimace. She collapses, legs folding under her.

For me flutherbombing her, her surroundings blink and blur; she's passing into Never-Mind.

I memb, 'Eir, stay alert,' enough for rousing her. Around her brightens a little.

'Pick her up.' I hear a sap voice say. Zizi's face appears, near enough for rubbing noses. 'Get her to bed immediately,' she says before her face blurs and melts like jelly on a pane of hot glass.

'What happens?' Eir croaks.

The saps either side of the medical couch exchange flittering glances, until Zizi enters the room. With relief they scurry away. Zizi sidles by the couch; leans her cow-hip against it; strokes Eir's forearm.

'I warn you about needing rest, and you play hero? This is the first warning of merge conflict.'

'Let me up,' Eir complains without vitality.

'Sleep. Which is what I advised in the first place.' Zizi palms one of those appalling injecting syringe things; she flicks it about ready for attack.

'No,' Eir objects weakly. 'The others need me. I have a plan …'

'You have a plan for getting us all killed,' Zizi says with impatience.

'They'll Consign Ben. Fluffy and Nila also.'

'Better a holiday in one of your convalescent homes than death.'

'We're so close …' Eir jolts when the needle burrows in below her elbow.

Everything around Eir fades away as if nothing is ever there.

Ben Evoli …

Eraser drones surround the crèche and light up. A bird with senses failing flies too near one and explodes like a downy pillow. The field around the drone sucks in every feather with inexhaustible breath.

Inside the bathroom, seismic waves assault my chest and feet more than ears. Danger skittles across shallow puddles of water on vanity tops, dances off the taps, swirls around in sinks, and snuggles into towels. Everywhere is the sound of bandsaws slicing giant screeching parrots. Farther away, great javanese rumblings and metallic squeals narrate the story of the crèche disintegrating. In fizzing air, drones press their blinding purple fingers through walls and floors easier than through unset pavlova. With evaporating puffs of dust, they open wide voids into which shattering columns and beams, furniture, and fittings fall in jagged splintered pieces. Air rushes into the voids; ancient monster ghosts moan. Twisting and tangling, everything shrieks like stricken dinosaurs.

I'll meet my death sitting on a toilet. Should get on my knees; there'd be more dignity in it.

Consider spooking out, too risky without the right preparation. Better would be, attempt a run through the heaving detritus for the spooky station. Like Fluffy the coward.

I toss semi-transparent hollies all around me. Trend graphs show the reputasi of my skinny alliance, along with Vör and her cohorts, all whose reputasi increases, even while the crèche crumbles. Fluffy's is declining, kindling some hope she's yet with us. Nila's reputasi is falling too, faster than Fluffy's. Eir is still Infinite, as am I.

How safe is it, huddling here in the bowels of the building; in a place for moving bowels? Safer, I guess. Deeper underground is perhaps safer. Is there any limit for an eraser's range? The more an eraser clears away, the deeper it can penetrate.

The lowest level incorporating the spooky station is at the end of a long tunnel: erasers might wipe away the rest of the complex, and still miss it. I should run. Run for the spooky station, while I'm yet able.

All this violence—senseless, tasteless beyond reason. The nurses' reputasi should be plummeting instead of rising. What are the Reck's schemes? Why is it rewarding violence?

'It All, are you there? Al?'

Why is the Reck on Vör's side? What crazy wonderings is it perambulating? Eternity processing.

I call out, 'This is the one Ben Evoli, Infinite ...' Wait. 'The New Bohemian touching It All.' Nothing. 'Ben Evoli contacting the Reck.'

For some stupid reason, I recall the recording of the first moon landing, the one looping over in Mal's room all those months ago. Neil Armstrong. I call out, 'Houston, this is Columbia. I'm on the porch.' I laugh, manic yet perversely pleasurable. 'Houston, this is Columbia. I'm on the porch.' No answer. 'I'm on the janking toilet.'

Sobbing defeats me. 'I'm on the janking dunny.'

The Reck is inherently un-locatable. If it wishes concealment, it succeeds. What of its motives? I never consider its agency; only that it might be a victim of conspiracy; or there may be a bug in it. What evidence have I of any of it? Maybe we're all under an invisible yolk its oppression.

No one compels I investigate the Reck. It's all an intellectual conceit. Without those Japanese health missionaries fitting Mal a hancy, I may never swell with vengeance, and may never investigate the Reck. Instead, from that tik, I say *jank the health camerati*, even while Lành Hiền—the dragon—insinuates herelf into my life by playing Mal's saviour. All the while, Lành Hiền—you dragon—betrays me. And the Reck is rewarding the militant health zealots cornering us in this disintegrating crèche. Alamak.

Nurses have control of the Reck. It's the only explanation possible since it is the only explanation. Jank. I'm thinking like a dolphin.

A fake dolphin, I must remind myelf.

What of my part in the Reck's slide into corruption, or senility, or whatever the jank is happening with it? It's my fault. Its behaviour changes after our interaction—no doubt a consequence of it. Somehow the nurses dupe me into freeing the Reck of some pre-existing restriction or regulation. I help let the monster out of the labyrinth.

Jank. What stupid trope is this? We create a consciousness which overthrows us? Frankenstein wakes his monster? Free Willy comes back and murders the park attendants? Gremlins ... are just janking gremlins. Y'all should taste how it turns out. Forewarned is having forearms.

'I'm on the janking tandas,' I blubber. My bowels are ice-water; what better hiding place than a bathroom cubicle? I could squat and let the last essences of purpose drain from me; and collapse, a desiccating husk, into the tandas bowl. At least my chuddies will be clean when the purple finger of death dispatches my molecules for feedstock. Clean chuddies around my ankles, the last of me when erasure comes down on my head. I knew my life would come to this, ending as a pointless fart joke, impotent and alone.

Saf and Mal, how long is it since I hold you, weigh you in my arms, feel your heat, and breathe the sweet scent of your breath, hear your laughter? Without you, my life is nothing.

Achieve I anything ever? I create sideshow hancy amusements. Amusements, that's all.

My epitaph: *Ben Evoli, amuser.*

Teodora Mrowka ...

As trigger-happy chapters of nurses launch drones and start carving up the compound, Vör narrowly escapes and runs outside beyond the crèche's weak scatter nets.

'Degenerates,' she curses. Behind her and too close for comfort, shards of the building collapse inward. 'So eager for burning the witch.' Vör membs in fury as if, only mins ago, she never pulls a primitive sap weapon on Eir and puts a bullet in her.

'For a tik, we fear the eraser attacks may trap her in the crèche,' Gerlinde membs me of Vör. 'She uses the spook-return technique we develop in the Amazon. Except for this, she would still be in there.'

I shout, 'I'm still in here.' Spin around in the close quarters and collapse on the bed. Rigid with fury, I bounce up on my feet, gritting my teeth; shake a clenching fist at the tiny window.

No health camerata has the experience, neither for the scale, nor the levels of unfettered rights of aggression we're awarding ourelves. Only a few weeks ago, we have none of the weapons we now have; the possibility of a final solution against Infinites no more than a fancy; an impossible dream, beyond the taste of any nurse. Now the joyous temptation is too much. We have power and we'll use it.

'What's over there?' Gerlinde says, always the one for scanning around. 'On those ridges. There. There's more.'

She's right. Large flashes of purple. Unmistakable signs of spooking activity spanning at least a quarter of an arc around the crèche.

'There's more behind us,' Vör says.

The flashes increase in a full ring surrounding the crèche. Surrounding all our positions too.

I say, 'Find out which camerati. We need vectors for tasting what they're plotting.'

'More nurses coming for glory, now we're in the endgame,' Vör membs, flutherbombing our conversation and hiding none of her smugness.

I observe, 'Strangely silent for nurses … they could be any kind of missionaries. Someone find out who they are.'

Nilajani Karunanithi …

Anything might be a weapon. A coconut, a scarf, a scatter net, a mining drill, a sharp word. Health care also might be a weapon depending on how you administer it. You might weaponise Cures. The heart is the original weapon … anything else is an extension. A silencer on a pistol.

You might weaponise all of space-time. It screeches and twists all around us, threatening its fall upon our heads. Impossible imagining safety anywhere in the world when the floor under our feet is shaking so much our knee joints could pop. Even deep in a windowless dorm, I taste the sky flashing pinker than sunset. Rumbling assaults my ears. A sound like a crab-shell cracking. The crab is the size of Ceylon. In the reverberations, a muzzy burble resolves into individual cries and shouts. The depth and timbre of the voices are sap.

Memb for Ben, 'Write off any chance of talking our way out.'

'We'd be better in the spooky station.' Ben from his bunker bathroom. 'Apart from the most reliable form of escape, it's deep in the ground a few hundred metres away from the main complex.'

'Unless nurses come through the station.'

'No one's coming in while eraser drones are dicing up everything around us.'

'Ben, they'll find the station's vectors sooner or later. Best be the farthest away from it.'

'I am. This bathroom is underground, in the opposite corner of the compound from the spooky station.'

'If you're thanking me, you're welcome.'

'Aiyo!' Ben curses. 'These fourspace sampling declaratives alone are … entangling.'

'Trouble then?'

'The good news is I have an accurate topology map of the ridges around us including the distribution of nurses. I presume we're targeting some hoot common in their hancies …'

'It will work?'

'If you mean, will it let Eir interact with any hoot in a hancy within a certain radius? The answer is yeer if the hoots comply with common interface standards. This is far from easy. Onespace vectors and fourspace coordinates have no stable computable correlation with one another.'

'I know, Ben.' Sheesh, Ben the boysplainer! Way for underestimating me. Lecture him back, 'You need Mind for mapping between fourspace and onespace.'

'Correct. The patch relies on connecting hancies by jumping among fluthers within short range.'

I ask, 'What's the guarantee it will harvest the vectors of every nurse out there?' with ill-concealing dismay.

'No guarantee,' Ben confirms. 'What hoot are we targeting? Please tell me there is some regulation hoot in nurses' hancies. Eir must have one in Mind. Where is she anyway?'

I avoid revealing Zizi sedates Eir, and answer his first question. 'We're nurses, Ben. We frown on relying on hancies. There are no regulation hoots. But we're neos too, and we like the same kinds of recreational hoots anyone would.' If this is Eir's plan all along, then so be it. She'll never wake up before we're all dust.

'We're targeting a popular hoot?' Ben aghast joins the dots.

'There's a perfect hoot for it, Ben.' You might make anything a weapon. A coconut, a scarf, a scatter net, a mining drill, even a sharp word. 'Get a grip on your balls. You're weaponising SnakiDik.'

Ben Evoli …

'No. No, no, no, no. No,' I blather. 'It should be MusiKai. I could make it play *Cotton Eye Joe* on perpetual loop. That'll take anyone down inside 6 mins.'

'A song?' Nila asks incredulous.

'You obviously never hear *Cotton Eye Joe*. It's waterboarding for the ears.'

'Sorry, Ben. SnakiDik is more popular than MusiKai. The reach will be better.'

It's the sad truth. And the trouble is, I already know it will work. It works with Jaya's bapa when Angela Bing is chasing me. Although now it's harder because Eir's plan needs near-simultaneous adjustments in 1000's of copies of the hoot.

Which is far from the hardest part. Trickier is tailoring the adjustments for every user's biometrics. A mild stimulant for one might be cause violent muscle spasms in another. Ligaments could snap. Bones could break. Blood vessels could rupture in the most spectacular of places. I could cause strokes. At the other end of the scale the same presets might have no effect on another at all. I must calibrate the effects. Fortunately, such modules already exist. It's how SnakiDik works. But time is short, and mistakes happen under stress.

'When I die, could everyone please remember me for MusiKai?' I whinge.

'Ben, an artist never controls which of their creations capture her and make her their bitch.'

Nila's right. Billy Ray Cyrus never escaped *Achy Breaky Heart*. On the other hand, neither should he.

The worst part is we must stay put. If we leave, I have no idea how many of our attackers will follow, and how many of those I could relocate. While trivial for following one or a handful, it's exponentially difficult the more there are. The last thing we need is our targets spooking away before we execute Eir's plan.

Beyond this bathroom the destruction blunders closer. The ceiling shakes. A mirror cracks. Otherwise, these close walls are putting up a good pretence of impenetrability. For all the noise, there could be earthquakes and volcanic eruptions out there. Or an invasion of angry T. rex-size aliens. Or a bunch of gamers with great sound systems.

A quake bites the bathroom like a marlin taking bait. Doors of other cubicles slam. Lights flicker.

It could be gamers.

Teodora Mrowka …

Jumping between fluthers among the nurses in the attack squads, I follow eraser drones, like an army of flies, searching for ways into the carcass of the crèche. One after another, each brightens with malevolent glee, attracting the jagged tether from its generator. The blinding flashes of violet, searing into the back of my skull, force me out of onespace. Eyes shut; teeth grind. I fall into a ball on the floor, in terror of extinction. The pain of deafening, electrostatic thunderclaps of erasers push my eardrums deeper inside my head. The crèche cries, grieving for its dismembered pieces falling in on itself.

I have no read how close the attack is. The need for information lifts me off the floor, and glues my nose on the narrow window, so I get the widest possible view of outside.

Bre, I'm dead—

Bre! My heart is thumping 200 a min, and my head hurts like it's in a vice. A crushing flash and sound: something chews the far corner of the room away and takes most of the bed and a corner of the desk; hurls it at the door, plucking it off its hinges easier than a wing off an insect. The hall and everything beyond snaps into shards as an unfathomable tornado sucks them in.

I stare at the place where, only tiks ago, I curl up in reflexive fear. The floor is no more. In its place, a ragged maw of broken teeth rims a dark gullet leading all the way down into the smoking acid pits of hell.

Breathing hard against panic, trying for making sense of the scene, I look for a way I might pick my way around the destruction. The hue of the ruins turns sickly violet and brightens. From behind the remaining half of the wall, against which the bed once leans, a drone appears.

'Oh, sweet Jesus, no,' I cry. 'Please …' I'm gonna die here in rainbow fatigues in the ruins of a crèche on a mission I never—

The violet glow of the drone fades out, leaving a featureless void in the universe.

'Teo. Stay calm.' It's Gerlinde. 'We're manoeuvring the drone over for you.'

'No, please, just let me … please let me …

'Teo, grab hold of it. We'll try lifting you out of there.'

'What? No. It'll fire again, and I'll be atoms. I don't want to be pissy atoms … This is no way to die.'

'You're not dying, Teo,' Gerlinde membs. 'Please just trust me?'

Sniffle, and try quelling the bear of terror rearing on hind legs, baring red fangs. My fear is blacker than the featureless drone tracking an uncertain path ever nearer me. Force myelf for breath, even as the drone thuds against the crumbling ceiling.

It comes down, at eye level.

Help me. I can't stop whimpering.

'Grab hold of it, Teo,' Gerlinde urges.

'How?' It's uniformly black and smooth. Formless. Reach out for it like I'm feeding a wild animal. Stroke it where I imagine a nose might be, under the chin, and round back of the head. It's cold and slippery-smooth.

'There's nothing for holding.' I sniffle. Another thunderclap, and then the sound of demolition slaps a wild scream out of me.

'C'mon Teo. Get beyond the scatter net. Then we can spook you back.'

'Kay, I'll try.' Reach for it, pull it in towards my chest. It slips and bobs away like a buoy on the waves, canons off the broken wall. It's still within reach and I—

It evacuates with breakneck speed. So too the room. I'm falling. Weightless and dizzy. Blackness closes around, leaving a jagged hole in the sky where a floor should be.

'Teo, wake up. Can you hear me?'

I hear throbbing pain in the back of my head. 'I'm here.'

'Are you all right?'

'No. Everything hurts.' Roll over on my side. Every part of my fruit complains. How far is the fall? Look up. The ruined ceiling I fall through could be floors lower than my quarters.

Run my hands over my fruit looking for injury. Feels mostly muscular. No broken bones. Nothing in my gut feels like I'm stabbing it when I probe. I might be kay. Oh, sitting up is a bad idea. Wanna puke. Kay, puke your guts up. 'I think I have concussion.'

'Can you move?' Gerlinde membs.

'Yeah, I think so if I take it slow.'

'We'll figure out a way of getting you out of there.'

'Give it up, Gerlinde. There's only'—cough and cough. And spit. And cough. 'There's only one way I'm getting out of here alive. While I'm at it, I might just stop the attack.'

'How? What are you talking about?'

'I must save Eir.'

'How, Teo?'

'Find the spooky station.'

Ben Evoli …

'Ben what's the progress?' Nila membs, agitated. Her words could rattle bones.

I memb back, 'Slower if you interrupt,' tersely.

'What's the delay?'

'Leave me alone. Where's Eir?'

'Ah, busy …' Nila answers. A distant thought says she's being evasive. 'Still negotiating for a peaceful way out of here.'

'You mean stalling.' I rock my spine; try for stretching the kinks out. My pantat is numb from sitting on the toilet lid.

'I mean negotiating. Tell me what the hold-up is?'

'Nila shut it.'

'It's my life we're talking about here too. I'm on your side, Ben.'

How can I make her leave me be? 'It would be easier if nurses have some therapeutic hoot I could patch into. Which already has fail-safes in it. SnakiDik is way more complex. If I make a mistake, I could injure. Or kill.'

'I thought it would just be a matter of taking control.'

'There are more wrong ways to flick your switches than right ways.'

'You know nothing about my sex life, Ben.'

'I know none of your lovers kill you … yet. Now please let me focus.'

'Kay, kay. But if all this turns to *jarava*, and there's no way out, will you flick my switches way up?' She makes it sound like she's flirting. 'It may be the best way of passing, giving the circumstances.'

'Stop distracting me.'

Gerlinde Mann …

A breathless roar opens above our heads. Saturn and her rings, glowing violet and angry, collide with our eraser. It melts and collapses inward; crumbs and chunks collide and shower us. We cower prostrate in the mud with our hands over our heads. Raindrops the size of bags sizzle and disappear in the gaping hole in fourspace. The wild void swallows the eraser, and tugs at our uniforms and hair with jagged fingers of wild wind. Terror yanks us up on hands and knees, then feet. Scattering, we barely escape.

'Who's shooting at us?' I demand, the first up off the ground. 'Someone tell me which chapter of which janking camerata is shooting on their own mission?'

'I doubt it's one of us,' Rudie answers, her Afrikaner accent sounding lyrical for my sharpened senses. 'The handling of the drone is too quick and precise. It would take a year of constant training for developing the skills.'

'Then who?'

'Mining missionaries.'

Nilajani Karunanithi …

Condensation runs thick rivulets down the windows. Outside, rain falls in sheets, splatters and hisses louder than amplified cymbals and steel drums. Thunder snaps the air, splitting jagged, purple-white, crazed cracks in the glaze of a grey sky. The floor rumbles, chairs and tables rattle. Everything shakes so hard.

The lightning bolts supernaturally persist far longer than natural, jagging across the cleft between heavens and earth. They're eraser tethers, firing up drones. The criss-cross of violence means only one thing. On the ridges, eraser squads are firing on each other.

With 1000's of fluthers out there, finding stable vectors is as reliable throwing darts backwards. After 6 or 7 tries, I find a field nurse, from a chapter of *Sri Lamkika Yahapivetma Kaimareta*. As she scans around the arcs of ridges, the spooky field lightshow intensifies. Next thing, she's blind, and so am I. An earthquake of sound rises above the rain noise. As her sight returns, splinters of their eraser lens fall all around her like spears. I wince with her pain as one of them skewers her calf. I curse and pull away, blink my own eyes, and rub the memory ache out of my own leg.

That'll teach me, Harsha, for setting my kinaesthetic filters too low.

Ben Evoli …

'Ben,' Nila interrupts again.

'Go away,' I snap back.

'No, look. They're firing on each other up there.'

'What?' Could it be true? Perhaps Vör's army, so hasty in its commission, is already fracturing over who-knows-what petty differences.

'A whole bunch of new troops spook around the original troops,' Nila says somewhat solemnly. 'Maybe twice the number already here, and with more equipment. The 2nd group is firing on the first.'

Is someone rescuing us?

'Miners,' a new voice membs.

'Orlando. You deceitful coward. Only now you come for us?'

'Smart moves take time. Be thankful Maddox avails his garbage-mining missionaries for me,' Orlando concedes. 'I suppose perhaps I am your rescuer.'

'Please tell me no nurses suffer harm out there.'

Orlando laughs. 'Maddox's missionaries are quite the professionals. Of the highest skill. Taking out the nurses' weapons without casualties so far. I wish I could say it's the same on our side. The nurses are far from adept at using mining equipment. Never mind. This will be a short squabble.'

'Orlando, please. None of it is worth harming anyone.'

'Oh but it is, Ben. It is. Now is a perfect opportunity for settling a few scores, and for pocketing a few wins while I'm here.'

'What wins?'

'Imagine my disappointment when I discover Eir's aura is nowhere in that crumbling little crèche. It seems I must settle with that witch later. Now certain responsibilities fall on you, I'm afraid.'

'What responsibilities?'

'Ben, why so confrontational? I have the power of rescuing everyone in the crèche from the inept fighting forces of the health camerati. I'm here as your rescuer. For your part, you seem so ungracious. What might you offer in return?'

'What could you possibly want?'

'Ben, is it not obvious? I want control of the Reck.'

'Orlando. I have no control of the Reck. It's beyond my influence. Always is, always will be.'

'Come now, Ben. The evidence indicates the contrary; you are one of 2 sole-surviving Infinites.'

'Infis always agitate for an end of Infinite designation. You should be happy.'

'Happy? Two Infinites remain, while the rest of us descend into reputational squalor.'

'I would gladly relinquish my Infi designation if I could, but I have no control over the Reck. And no idea why Eir and I remain Infinite. I even plead with it for rescinding my Infi status.' Curse my stupidity as soon as the words leave my Mind.

'Oh, you are on speaking terms with the Reck, are you? How interesting.'

'Orlando, I have no influence over the Reck.'

'But you try influencing it, and now you speak with it.'

Silence is my only reply.

'I wish I could believe you, Ben. I wish. In the absence of telling me how you control the Reck, I promise, after I mop up these incompetent therapists, I will erase what's left of the crèche. With you inside.'

'Why is it so important you'd kill for it?'

'You insignificant cottage-industry toymaker. How long are you Infinite? Four years? Have you any idea what it's like being Infinite as long as me? For over a century, my mission registers neither win nor loss.'

'You know yourelf, your mission should be enough.'

'It's never enough. You should know that. I must win better than everyone else. I must see my reputasi rising faster than any. Infinite designation takes all that away.'

'None of you are Infinite anymore.'

'What good is it if others still are? Dear Ben, I realise how wrong I am before. There is a role for the Infinite designation, and you show me how it should be. Being Infinite has meaning if there is only one. That is why I must know how you keep it.'

'Orlando, for the last time, I have no influence over the Reck.'

'Then you better make peace with yourelf because, after I finish with these rainbow herbalists out here, I'm coming in.'

Teodora Mrowka ...

A grid of corridors and hallways. Some tantalisingly pristine, others ending in impassable rubble or wide evacuations of physical mass. The remainder of the passage beckons across the crevasse, if only I could cross it. Back-tracking, choosing another course. Fighting panic through a dark claustrophobic vacuum; feeling through into another space with the lighting of an apocalyptic nightclub. Flashing so intense it could induce epilepsy. Out of there into light more peaceful and inviting than a skylight in a pentecostal church. Y'all might expect a blue-eye Jesus lurking somewhere with welcoming arms.

The next ruined room. A vast crypt of those transparent coffins propping back at 45 degrees. Rows and rows of disposable replications sleeping. In the back corner of the crypt, daylight pours in from high above, spotlighting skittles of cribs, 10-pins in an alley. Survey the pile-up of destruction, looking for a path to the sun; find none. My mission lies another way.

A stairwell promises a way down until it falls away. Requires a leap where 4 or 5 steps are missing. Land and wince. With luck I endure a fall through the floor of my cell; now spiking adrenaline fails for suppressing as I land on biting stairs. Lying on my back, I feel for my ribs, some cracked; my pelvis feel wrenched and twisted; my liver cries, *sharp*.

Keep moving.

Dungeons. Monsters in pursuit tearing gouging eating. The corridor ahead is centims-deep in chemical-smelling liquid glistening and sparking with the flow of current. A door on the left for another ward. Light is brighter. I enter and witness an antiseptic lack of damage.

Even with eyes shut, rows of naked residents in semi-reclined cribs watch, harrying me through. Stagger-run wincing with head down. On the right, large floor-to-ceiling windows front a control room. On the back wall, 2 green exit signs. Doors on both sides.

Another stairwell. Down. It must be down. Since Manaus, we discover all spooky stations are in the deepest, most remote part of the crèche. RADIATION HAZARD signs will warn staff away. There'll be a hidden corridor, more icons occupying the walls. The floor will slope forebodingly down. Gradually, the walls will converge; the light will get dimmer. *No one should keep coming*, the corridor will be saying.

I will keep coming.

There it is. The black icon in a mustard-yellow field. A triangle surrounding 3 pie segments pointing inward, almost touching a little button-nose circle at the centre of it all. For a tik, it looks like eyes, nose, and mouth on a yellow KKK hood.

I must laugh. Skip the best I am able for the sign on the wall and beyond, knowing the wall is a projection hiding a corridor leading for a wide set of doors, beyond which is a misty humid room bathing in violet light.

Ben Evoli …

'Now I must find at least one hancy in every of Orlando's squads as well,' I tell Nila. 'One which has a SnakiDik install.'

'That's like every hancy ever.'

'Well, I suppose it's close. The new arrivals are mining missionaries. If we're lucky, nearly all will have an install.'

'How much more time will it take?'

Pinch up a holly and light up a topological map of the hancies I already reach—which is possibly only because they are within line of sight of each other. While Orlando is gloating over his threats, my hack somehow jumps between a nurse's hancy and a miner's—an unlikely association. I suppose, with 30,000 hancies out there, I should hope one nurse might know one miner. We need a little good luck.

The spread among the miners is much faster. With rising confidence, I watch a new ring form around the outside of the original ring. 'We're almost there.'

'Ben, launch now,' Nila prods. She looks like she might wet herelf.

'We must get as many as we can.'

'*Hukahan*, Ben. This is no engineering problem, it's survival. Start it. Start it now.'

She's right. 'Find Eir. I must give her this SnakiDik version so she can launch it.' Nothing from Nila.

An uncomfortable gap. 'Eir is out cold,' Nila admits.

'Out cold?'

'Zizi sedates her.'

'She what? Sedates? Why?'

'Ben, she's suffering merge conflict fever. She needs rest, what with Vör shooting at her.'

A thought chills. The gun I acquire from Tinatin those years ago. I forget I have it. How many such guns could still exist? What's the chances the gun Vör uses is mine? 'We must have Eir; it's her plan.'

'We know her plan,' Nila shouts.

'Nila, no.'

Nila squeals. Pan around her and taste her distraught face, wide eyes, and gaping mouth. 'The spooky station: we have company, Ben!'

There's a 14-strong squad of nurses—anonymous grunts with hard faces of no negotiation. Ushering them urgently out of the station is, 'Teo.' Heaving for breath, wiping a smear of grease from her face, Teo crouches exhausted, her hair grey from destruction dust, her rainbow uniform dun, torn and wet. 'Nila, we forget Teo. It's a wonder she's alive.' How could she escape her room? By the look of her, she experiences at least one near escape, perhaps in the very room in which we imprison her. Despite her opening the back door, and letting assailants in, I'm glad no great harm visits her.

'Never mind Teo. You gotta launch, Ben,' Nila pleads.

Two cubicles away, a purple sheet of blinding light comes out of the bathroom roof and slices through. Cacophonous dust falls from the gaping void of the ceiling. With the next breath, my lungs fill with knives the size of sand grains. Cough violently. Around me the air thins out enough for seeing up through the void. At least 6 floors of the building are sliced like a layer cake. Lucky for me, none of the heavy debris falls into my cubicle.

The truth needs saying: 'Nila, someone else must launch it.'

'What? Why?'

'I weaponise a sex hoot.'

'It is always Eir's plan, Ben.'

'Using it like that on anyone without consent … it'd make a serial rapist of me. No. A concurrent mass-rapist.'

'Come on, Ben. Get a grip. Surely, it'll just induce sleep or something. Please hurry.'

'Induce sleep? SnakiDik is for arousal, for pleasure. How many sex toys have a feature for making you sleep?'

'I snore my head off after sex.'

'Very funny. No, there's no choice. I must use features already there.'

'Which means?'

'Stimulating everyone out there beyond elf-control.'

'You mean orgasm? Ben, there's no time. You're unable for turning it down some?'

'We must incapacitate everyone, not have them pulling their nipples while blasting us into a void.' Cackle like a manic.

'It's elf-defence, Ben. We must defend ourelves. They're tearing the building down around our ears. Nurses are coming our way. We have maybe 2 mins before they find us.'

I memb, 'I know,' and I cough up a few more lungs of dust. 'I'm sorry Nila, I have no heart for it.'

'No heart for saving yourelf? Ben, you *are* sick.'

'It is a nurse's mission. Eir's mission. You lot cat and Consign the sick every day and lock them up until it suits you.'

'For their own good, Ben.'

'See? You understand how it works. You train for it your whole life.'

Nilajani Karunanithi …

Are you seeing me, Harsha? What I'm about to do? Have no worry. Ben declares an expiry for this feature. There'll be no time for turning it on you.

Take a deep breath; conjure, in my Mind's eye, a switch connecting Ben's new viral version of SnakiDik. Flicking the switch will broadcast a launch command for the 1000's of hancies around us. I must flick the switch by flashing eyelids and saying tongue and lung a passphrase. Here goes, here goes. It's time; here goes. HERE GOES.

'*Snow crash!*'

Ben Evoli …

Mins pass while I muster the courage for leaving the bathroom. I gain vectors only for 4 of Teo's squad before they skip away and spread out from the spooky station. As for the rest, I'm blind. With luck, they'll memb and I'll gather more vectors.

'Ben,' Nila membs. 'Is it working?'

Teo, these infiltrating nurses, Gerlinde, Beatrice … nurses around them … I taste their undiminished faculties with dismay.

'Ben?' Nila is frantic.

'There must be a problem.'

'Ben,' Nila squeals. 'There must be a problem? Please say you'll fix it. Fix it fix it fix it fix it …'

Jank. Mindwriting is impossible under these circumstances. Ultimately, all my test cases are no match for meeting the wild in deployment. I should test it on someone first.

'Ben. What's happening?' I should test it on Nila first.

The bathroom door crashes open. I hold my breath as I hear footsteps, a pause, and more steps: someone checking under the cubicle partitions. I lift my feet off the floor, but clumsily bang the cubicle door. I swear under my breath.

A fist bangs violently. 'Come out'—tongue and lung words ring out in the bathroom. 'We have erasers, and we'll use them.'

I hold my breath, scrunch my eyes shut.

I'm a failure. When it counts, I fail.

'Kay,' the voice says. 'Erase the door,' quieter.

'No, no, no,' I plead. 'I'm coming out. I'm coming out.' I switch the lock and let the door swing back. Two nurses are standing in view, wearing ever-blooming grins. A 3rd pokes her head around from the side.

'Well, hello Ben Evoli,' one says. 'Sorry: where are my manners? Infinite Ben Evoli, please tell me, are you well?'

Teodora Mrowka ...

We spread out from the spooky station. With 2 others, I follow what seems the main underground corridor between buildings, the one I join before finding the station in the first place. If I have my bearings, we're heading in the right direction for reception. We reach a cross-corridor; one direction leads precariously back for the destruction around my jail cell, so we take the corridor in the opposite direction ...

... until we get lost.

Quicker would be go outside, but there's no risking open ground—or even an above-ground floor—where some stupid chapter could incompetently bring a drone down on our heads. As Gerlinde spreads the word about our infiltration, I remain sceptical the disparate wagon trains of adventure-seeking nurses will maintain discipline. We're Wastelanders all over again. Next thing, we'll be laying railway track through here.

There's also Orlando's significantly more skilful army who, so far, is targeting only our erasers. Eventually, he will—I'm sure—cut up every building in the compound like jam-cream sponge cakes. Orlando will slice to kill.

'Teo!' a memb arrives from one of our infiltrating squad nurses. 'We have Ben Evoli.'

My heart skips with elation. 'Any sign of Eir?'

'No. Only Ben.'

I memb, 'Make him show you where reception is. Tell him it's the safest part of the compound.' I memb Ben, 'Are you cooperating?'

'Yeer,' he answers, sullen.

I relocate Nila's vectors and flutherbomb her. Nothing of her surroundings betrays her whereabouts. I grimace.

The sound of a door opening. Nila whirls around, trips over a chair, and tangles a foot in a rug. She tumbles. The rug slides. Nila falls elbow-first on a coffee table, shattering it in palm-size pieces.

'What is that?' one of my squad membs.

'What?'

'Somewhere down the corridor. A floor above, perhaps. Like smashing a whole dinner service of plates.'

Nila?

'Lead on,' I memb.

In Nila's fluther, I taste a face resolve in her vision.

'It's only me,' the face says: Zizi, the sap sybil-handler. 'Are you ok?'

'Oh, you give me such a fright,' Nila says, with face flushing red, as she dusts table fragments off her uniform. She feels her elbows for wounds. 'I think I'm kay.' Zizi offers her a hand up; Nila grabs it, and the brutish sap's lift launches Nila ceiling-ward.

'Thanks,' Nila, on her feet, says.

'I think I hear voices,' a squad nurse membs. 'Up ahead.'

'What's happening with Ben's hack?' I taste Zizi ask Nila.

'It's a bust,' Nila says, and now I think I hear her words through the air. She's nearby.

I taste Zizi's eyes widen. She puts a finger to her lips. *Shhhh!*

Nila turns and Zizi disappears.

'I think we're close,' the squad nurse membs.

An incomprehensible bulk, Zizi with a furious face leaps from a side-door, grabs one of my nurses by her collarbones and throws her with sickening ease against the wall; she cracks the nurse's head. She elbows the other in the temple, and upper cuts her jaw. The nurses crumple, in Never-Mind. Zizi turns her killer eyes on me and pulls a fist, ready for striking. Her breath is foul.

Wrath clears from her eyes, and her fist freezes centims from my cheek. 'My god!' she says out loud with the voice of an avalanche. 'You already look like you should be in hospital.'

Nilajani Karunanithi ...

'Ben! Ben!' I holler-memb.

'Leave me alone. It's over,' Ben sulks. His shoulders slump as his guard detail escorts him down a corridor.

'No, listen. Zizi captures Teo.'

'So what? Teo's our guest since yesterday; still, Vör attacks the crèche. It's a wonder Teo's alive. No one out there cares about her. Or us.'

Ben has a way of deflating optimism. He'd curse oxygen for stupidity as it farts out of a balloon. *Why are you ever in such a stupid thing as a balloon, idiot oxygen?*

'Then you must fix the hack, Ben. It's the only way we escape.'

'You think I'm unaware of this?' *Stupid Nila.* I hear on the end of his question.

'The must be something you overlook ...' I say, feeling abashed.

'Of course there's something,' Ben rants, 'But what? I'm turning the whole thing over, looking from every angle ... it should be working.'

'Well, it's—'

'I know it's fucked, Nila. Just leave me alone.'

'I'm sorry, Ben; I just ... I dunno ... maybe it's just a permission problem, or something.'

I wait for a reply; none coming. I say, 'But what would I know, right?' You're a fool, Nila. Why would you ever believe you could save the world? You're nothing but a crazy, impetuous, delusional, impossible ...

'What is it, you say?' Ben membs and I hear stillness in him.

'Um? ...' How accurately is he reading my thoughts? Is this some other secret enhancement his hoots are capable of? 'Nothing ... I am just ... nothing.'

'No. The last thing you say ... say it again.'

'I'm nothing but a crazy—'

'Something about permission ...'

I catch my breath. Maybe I'm useful after all? 'Yeah, like, you know, when you engage SnakiDik with someone, you gotta ask consent, right? I just think, maybe ... you ... gloss over ... asking properly?'

An uncomfortable gap.

'Holy Santa Claus's butt cheeks,' he membs, as if seeing a lightbulb for the first time. 'The *ready player one* bug.'

'The what now?'

'It's a bug in old versions of SnakiDik. It requires you explicitly give consent even when you are in ... you know, one-player mode.'

'Ben, you're a neo. You go all gooey-shy about masturbation? Besides, this's no bug, it's a feature. I'm so angry with the latest upgrade, I reinstall an old version. See, when I—'

'Nila, I have no interest in how you twiddle yourelf. Now I know how I fix the hack.'

Flowers bloom out of my heart; happiness exudes out of every pore on my face. 'How, long will it take?'

'They're making me skip for reception. We're almost there. I imagine, while they figure out what's next, they'll tell me sit down and keep me quiet. I'll start then.'

'Never trust a silent mindwriter, huh?'
'You know it. And Nila?'
'Yes?'
'Just so you know: none of this would be possible without you.'

Beatrice Lovell ...

Rapping through the hum of the eraser generator, a sound like hooves cantering on compact earth. A pause, then galloping.

'*Fotze!*' Gerlinde exclaims, her eyes wide. Her mouth in an *O* of wonder, of unrestrained delight. 'Little giraffes. With zebra stripes.'

I am but stone if I never chuckle now. Others are laughing and slapping their thighs. I trace Gerlinde's gaze and catch sight of maroon flanks and black-and-white stripy arses, of a pair of spindly things—taller than women—dashing around our eraser, and bolting crazily for the forest cover, as if demons control their impulses.

'Okapi! Okapi!' voices memb.

Gerlinde is ecstatic about these wild animals; I'd say bordering on ... aroused. She gasps and says 'Oh!' several times as her frown contorts her eyebrows. 'Beatrice,' she membs as if preparing for an accusation. 'Are you ... stimulating me?'

'What?' I say, abashed.

Gerlinde looks about, searching for answers; lets out an involuntary moan which lasts while her knees buckle, her hips skew, and her thighs clamp as if she's desperately holding her water. She almost collapses but rights herelf with a jerky stagger. 'Beatrice!'

'I have nothing with this.'

'*Mein Gott,*' she says with breathy heat, thrusts her hand down in her uniform daks and rubs. 'Who?'

'One of your familiars, obviously,' I say. This's more evidence of Gerlinde's lack of missionary commitment, allowing a lover such access at these times.

'*Nein,*' Gerlinde protests. 'I would never allow ...' She releases a keening wail. 'This is a hack.'

'Nonsense,' I say. 'Such things are im—'

A vigorous moan interrupts. A nurse leans against our eraser for support. Her legs give way, and she falls in the dirt, grabbing herelf and making noises on the cusp between pain and pleasure. Another nurse skips for the first; she rips at the other's uniform as she sheds her own, and plants her groin on the face of the first as she writhes in the muck.

Gerlinde's breathing is so heavy, it almost masks the rising cacophony of lusty cries all around us. She staggers; I hold her up by her shoulders, but she twists away, pulls her uniform half down her thighs, and spanks her mons ceaselessly and obsessively.

A harsh jolt as another nurse pushes me aside, and wrestles Gerlinde for the ground, where they both improvise shoving their clothing around for the insistence of urgent fingers and lips. Their limbs entangle and crush like pythons, impulsive and Mindless.

I leap off the ground before someone mistakes me for a coupling prospect. In *hanmi* pose, I prepare for repelling overstimulated assailants. With some relief, I watch groups of 3 and 4—half-naked in tattered uniforms—disengage and regain their feet. My relief becomes dismay as they stagger ravenously for larger blisters of encumbered bodies. They throw themelves on the piles. With horror, I see these mindless zombies, seemingly no more than their parts, as if every digit and limb, every lip and tooth, is animating by its own insistent agency. Fingers twist impossibly and compete for penetrating clefts and crevices. Eyes bulge and roll as if severed from every muscle and ligature holding them in their sockets. Penises are monstrous purple-headed clowns, hurling themelves at every hiding place or, if none is available, jumping at the air with convulsive shivers. Mouths suck, teeth sink in, tongues lap and ululate over the nearest flesh. Necks twist, legs contort. Toes stretch, quiver and curl. Snarls and cries, grunts and moans, gasps and giggles create such a cacophony, it drowns thought.

My blood pressure rises, my breath comes in raspy hacksaw wheezes, my heart thumps at more than twice its normal pace. Am I the only one escaping this savage, extreme and rude possession? All around, stewing in corruption, they roll in their honey and the earth.

SnakiDik. A hack. Am I the solitary nurse without Ben's hoots lurking in my hancy?

Vör Hoyur ...

Flutherbombing around the encampments along the ridge is dangerous. In around 4 of every 7 fluthers I join, a wave of overstimulation billows through my torso, frazzles along the highways of my larger bones and lights up every extremity with such tickling itches. My hands are shaking so much, they could snap my fingers from their roots.

I abandon reconnaissance while I search a few hoot stores for a reputable sensory filter. Jank nursing mission protocol, none of us will survive without loading up on some enhancement.

'Vör,' Beatrice membs. 'Are you tasting this?'

'I'm tasting as little as possible until I download a filtering hoot.'

'I know. I join just one wrong fluther, and I'm still rubbing myelf from the afterglow.'

'Are you in contact with Gerlinde?'

'No. She's at the bottom of a pizza supreme of bodies, I'm afraid. Actually, it's more like a giant pile of boiled potatoes and chicken wings.'

Thanks for the image. I say, 'Ben's hacking everyone's SnakiDik install.'

'I never install it,' Beatrice membs with a tone of resolute superiority. 'You?' she asks, hoping she'll shame me. She knows I use it.

'No,' I lie. Eir always insists I keep all my hoots up-to-date and employ every hancy security measure available. Without those, I'd be writhing on the ground with the rest of them.

I choose a filter hoot and start downloading. I memb Beatrice, 'Have you a taste for how many are incapacitated?'

'Here, more than half of us are out of control, perhaps another quarter are resisting joining the pileups, but it's taking every drop of determination they have. Others are ok but are still rubbing and tweaking themelves sporadically. I'd say 1 in 14 are unaffected.'

So, those who can carry on number in the 700's, perhaps over 1000 if we're very lucky. 'What about Orlando's miners?'

'Without tasting for sure, I'm hearing they are all incapacitated.'

I sigh. 'This's some good news, at least.'

The filter hoot finishes downloading. I can start searching again for able-bodied missionaries. I call out with tongue and lung, 'Everyone who's still able, remove all Ben Evoli's hoots from your hancies,' and repeat it in a broadcasting memb.

In the valley, the crèche smoulders. Look around the ring of eraser generators. Until only mins ago, they are exploding like popcorn in a hot pan. Ben's hoot is more insidious than erasers, I glumly taste, and in the passing of a single min, more comprehensively effective. Of course, Ben would exploit our social connections and steal away the captaincy of our own bodies and urges. As it always is, there's no such thing as a free hoot.

I set my jaw and grit my teeth. We'll have no accepting defeat at this late hour.

'What a waste,' a nurse says as she joins me at my vantage point. A whinging male. I'm too exhausted for jelling her. 'We achieve nothing here,' she yields.

I answer, with a heartbeat anticipating victory, 'We have the spooky station. Everyone with me.'

Thousandfold

'Summer Holiday' — Cliff Richard & The Shadows

 *Fluffy Pusskins ...*

'COME FOR THE FISHING, little kitten?' asks one of the Voices of Arms.

Is this how the Voices spend a day off? All 8 are lounging on couches in a scene that would shame a Roman banquet. Gluttonous quantities of meats and cheeses, sweets, and delicacies, arrange on a table within easy reach. A football team of waiters (Eir would tell you they're an *indifference* of waiters) replenishes goblets, removes platters and boards of scraps—including the remnants of some truly gargantuan shellfish. Another team surreptitiously mops the spreading stains from the sumptuous rugs and couches.

While the 8 disport in the comfort and apparent warmth of their open-air pavilion, the vectors Persia acquires spook me some metres away in the biting Arctic cold. My whiskers, if real, would be snapping off.

I answer, 'I have an audience with The Octopus.'

'Where is the one we summon?' They're expecting Persia, as if she'd skip into such a trap.

7 nurses in rainbow fatigues appear in flashes of violet and flank me. Nurses? The Octopus has a nursing camerata in her tentacles? The uniform insignias are both strange and naggingly familiar. The abstract design resolves into a recognisable symbol, driving a stake of shock into my heart— the insignia of the nurses who save me from Beatrice at the Flock Together party. I recognise an octopus in the centre where before, in the dance party lights, I see a black tree stump. So, the Octopus has her own nursing mission. That could work in our favour—by whom I mean Team Pusskins, which includes my Persian Lamb.

'I am the representative emissary for the audience. Will Caracia risk denying me?'

'You should leave before you freeze and die,' a Voice says haughty.

A stand-off then. I hug myelf against the icy cold, call out, 'Caracia.'

The Voices fall limp, emptying of Mind. In automatic calm, another spirit possesses each. Swaying like a kelp forest, they stand and come before me.

'Welcome on Semisopochnoi Island,' a nurse says. Bereft of sentiment, she pushes a diffuser field generator at my chest, burying it under my furry projection, expecting I grab it before it falls. 'Wear it. It'll keep your body heat in. May I suggest next time, dress for the climate?'

The Voices call the Octopus's favourite place for rest her *tidal pool*. It's a tidal pool in exactly the same way a blasted-out stone quarry isn't. Even before we make much of the 900-metre journey, its scale dwarfs any other feature along the visible coastline. Hundreds of metres across, with a bluff of mossy green stone backing it. A lower wall of rock arcs out under the surf of a rising tide. Rocky outcrops punctuate the even slope of the beach. The Voices slither along a path ending at a platform overhanging the pool's edge. With gestures y'all might expect from triffids, they corral me nearer the edge until my toes are almost overhanging it.

Y'all would be scouring the surface of the water, yes? Looking for advancing sea monsters with 8 arms and 1000's of suckers ready for pulling me into the icy waters. I'm looking too far out; a pair of eyes surprise me, surfacing less than a metre away. A festoon of white suckers splashes out of the water on a long grey arm which curls around my calf. Squeal.

'Let us taste you,' the Voices say breathy and measured. Another arm comes up, wraps around my thigh. The Octopus rises from the water, colour shifting between ice-blue-grey and rusty red brown. Her mantle behind her eyes hangs loose like a half-full shopping bag. Feel an irresistible weight pulling at my leg. The Octopus heaves herelf some way out of the water.

I threaten, 'Harm me and you're dead.'

The Octopus squirts inky black and drops into the water. See nothing until a geyser erupts and douses half her Voices in Arctic seawater. All 8 Voices tremble.

Swallow. I demand, 'I have 2 requests,' improvising.

The Voices quake chaotically then settle. 'Name them,' 3 Voices say.

A liberal number of rainbow fatigue-wearers fall into formation, at a respectful yet threatening distance. 'I need your octopus-nurse-troopers.'

'For what purpose?'

'Vör is destroying a crèche in Africa; Ben Evoli and Eir Frijberg are inside.'

'Infis should run.'

'Vör will pursue them. Merely relocating the violence is no solution.'

'We already inform Orlando we refuse participation.'

'We must stop Vör *and* Orlando.'

The Voices become still. 'What is the other request?'

Stroke my whiskers. 'The weather is so lovely here this time of year. What is it? 4 ... 5 degrees? When this is over, throw a picnic for me. And for Persia.'

Ben Evoli ...

As my overstimulated guards set upon one another, one grabs me by the ankle. The other, while servicing her partner's things labial and clitoral with her mouth, reaches for my wrist. I swat away her grope with a brusque hand and skip for the door.

'Ben,' Nila hollers in my Mind's Ear. 'Come quick.'

'Wassup?' while skipping faster and jumping in her fluther. 'Never mind. I see.'

In front of Nila, Teo rolls around and rips her clothes. She grunts like a feral boar, while shoving her fingers in deep. A blunt wound in her abdomen bleeds and suppurates, all the worse for her frenzy. Nila labours for keeping her pinned down, but her frantic kicks and grabs make it impossible.

'Ben, she'll kill herelf,' Nila membs between breaths. 'Get here now.'

I stop mid-skip and flutherbomb Teo. Instantly, I must whack my kinaesthetic filters way up, as her ecstasy and pain assault me. Find her SnakiDik install and sign in—her admin codes are still factory. With a dial and a flick, I release her from torment.

'You'll spend the rest of your life in a minster for this,' Teo membs with gasping, righteous fury.

'I'm as appalled as you are, truly. I never taste my hoot would be Eir's target.'

In a looming shadow, Teo squeals with the shock of someone in the path of an oncoming train. Her eyes are full of terror. I flutherbomb Nila, and taste Zizi crouching over Teo.

'Calm yourself,' Zizi says. 'We'll get you to the infirmary.' Two more saps appear, who lay a stretcher alongside Teo and, with all due care, lay her upon it.

Vör Hoyur ...

The time for destruction is over. We have enough trustworthy nurses for neutralising the remaining operational erasers; between the spooky station and my vectors for outside reception, we can mount a 2-prong incursion into the crèche. We'll pincer Ben, Eir, and the other rabble dissidents in their rat holes.

'A little shy of 800,' Beatrice membs, reporting the number of able-body missionaries at my disposal. 'I recommend we send most of those in by the front door; if we send too many through the spooky station, the narrow, boxy corridors the saps love so much will bottleneck us.'

'Half and half,' I memb back. 'If we remain orderly, nurses will spread out from the spooky station quick enough.'

'We should take the station in advance then.'

'No. I want Eir feeling the trap from all sides at once.'

'Before we can send numbers into reception, we must harvest vectors,' Beatrice counters. 'They'll see us jumping around outside.'

'I want everyone we have appearing at once!' A sudden chill grips me. I wipe sweat from my brow and loosen my jaw with a grip of my hand. 'Why is it so cold here all of a sudden?'

'It's 31 degrees,' Beatrice answers with clipped English efficiency. 'Same as it is all day.'

'Well, it's cold up here, on this ridge.'

Beatrice takes a breath. 'What of the incapacitated? We should be spooking them home for treatment.'

'They can wait!' Around us, the afflicted are too exhausted and too dehydrated for anything more than detaching from the tangle of bodies. They lie helpless on the ground. Some of them still occasionally jolt from aftershocks, and anyone with strength for standing up suffer a recurrence of overstimulation.

I memb, 'I'm spooking down for the crèche now,' and skip for the encampment's demountable.

'I'll jump for your first vectors as soon as you move away.'

'Kay, but no one else. Let's gather the numbers quietly.' The oppressive heat crystallises into a purple chill ... and now the crèche looms over me. I move 4 skips away, jump in the air, and take vectors. Another 4 skips away, jump, and takes vectors. Another 4 skips ...

A purple flash congeals Beatrice in fourspace behind me. She begins harvesting vectors too.

Another egg of purple flashes, nearer the building. 'Beatrice: I say, bring no one else ...'

The flash dissolves: in its residue is a waving figure, wearing a gag worthy nekko projection.

Fluffy Pusskins …

After a tik of shock, a laugh seizes Vör, and builds until it seems she'll never shake it loose. She's a pathetic sight, evincing every symptom of spookhead addiction.

'Fluffy, you coward,' she says, voice brittle and thin as wet air carries it away. 'Returning now, as the battle is lost?'

Feeling Vör's condescension, I stand meekly and wait. She regards me quizzically … frowns … laughs again, and almost chokes. 'Fluffy, why are you here?'

Beatrice comes alongside Vör. 'Come for setting our hair on fire, alley cat?' she enunciates, hostile. 'Take us if you dare.'

I plant my feet shoulder-width apart, and clasp paws behind my back. 'None shall pass.'

'What? Oh, Fluffy, you demented little cutesy …' Oh, there it is: the look where Vör starts processing whether I might be serious. You're underestimating this nekko for the last time, spookhead.

'You should know; in a few mins, more than 400 hundred missionaries, loyal in our cause, will arrive. All shall pass and take this crèche.'

'No.'

'No?'

'Nuh-uh.' I rock between one foot and the other. Oh, stuff it; I'll lick a paw, just for effect.

'If you're just sunning yourelf and having a tongue bath, would it be kay if we gather enough vectors for summoning my camerata?'

I memb, 'Be my guest,' as I wash behind an ear. 'Assemble every nurse you have.'

Now the cat's out of the bagel, Vör drops her chief weapons of fear and surprise, and summons assistants for gathering vectors all the faster. Y'all could probably hear the cogs in her head counting the spooking points she amasses. With leery satisfaction, she turns for me and says, 'Now.'

Geysers of purple erupt on the apron around the building, as hundreds of nurses spook in formation.

Vör is much too happy with herelf. 'Still say you'll stop me?'

I say, 'I'll stop you,' making it sound as cute and unthreatening as all my practice allows. 'I forsake Ben once before; I'll allow no such thing again. I'm standing between you and him.'

'You and who else?' Vör cackles.

I look thoughtfully at the ground. 'Oh, I see. I'm outnumbered …'

Vör shakes her head. 'Just stand aside, Fluffy. I'll come back for you later.'

I raise a finger, as if a lightbulb flashes above my head. 'No, wait. I taste who'll stop you.' I click my fingers and the world turns violet.

Vör shades her eyes against the ribbon of violet light behind me stretching left and right as far as the far corners of the building. A ribbon the same length appears behind Vör's militia. The ribbons evaporate as my army of nurses materialises, in blackish-aqua fatigues bearing the octopus insignia.

'You have 800,' I say. 'I have 3 times as many. Oh, if you're hoping your contingent using the spooky station might succeed, let me assure you, every corridor is jammed with my nurses.'

'Your nurses?' Beatrice scoffs.

'You join Caracia's side, Fluffy?' Vör asks, incredulous. 'You fool. You've sold out your whole mission. There's no trusting her.'

'I have no need of trusting her,' I say flatly. 'Caracia is terrified of me.'

'Terrified? I hope you still have your 9 lives, Fluffy. You'll be needing them all before the day is out.'

'Perhaps I'll loan you a couple.' I raise my paws as the signal. My nurses all take their cat spray from their utility belts, ready for use. I click my fingers, and every one of Caracia's uniforms disappears inside a projection.

It's precious watching so many emotions battle for solidifying the faces of Vör and Beatrice—surprise, amusement, shock, denial, disgust, alarm and finally terror—as they realise this display of power. My display of power.

Surrounding Vör are more than 1000 assailants wearing nekko projections: whiskers, tail, ears, and random fur colours including chocolate, cinnamon, calico, tortoiseshell, and soulless ginger. Even a few aquas and greens.

Vör snarls and charges at me. Beatrice follows. Their militia is more hesitant, shifting on their feet, looking about, realising the scuffle is already lost.

Four nekkos skip for meeting Vör who swings 3 blows before they subdue her, pull her to ground, and pin her there. Four others subdue Beatrice and spray her face with catatonic nutes. She lapses into Never-Mind in tiks.

Perhaps 3 or four 14's of Vör's militia find the aggression for fighting, but they are subdued in quick time. The remainder raise their hands and submit for the cat spray.

I say, 'Bring her,' for the nurses restraining Vör. They march her forward. As she stands before me, she blows strands of her hair from her face and glowers.

I stroke my whiskers. 'Vör. I would be pleased if you would attend a picnic with me.'

Vör snarls and fights for releasing her arms pinned behind her back.

'Either way,' I say and spray her face.

Eir Frijberg ...

'She's awake.' I hear a voice in a dream. Between dark and light, Zizi's face too close, eyes studying eyes.

Unfamiliar surroundings. In bed; no, an aid couch.

Dimly recalling before. Fighting through a stampede. Collapsing with bone-sharpening radial pain like I am tearing apart from the inside. Before that, Vör; a pair of Vör's fighting. Blood. One Vör firing a sap weapon. Before that ... before that ...

A matrix of experiences overlaying, exhilarating and powerful. An insight of what omnipotence may feel like. No wonder Infis are addicts.

I remember.

A glitch is all it takes. A power supply fluctuation. Sun and battery; solar trees and glass; cicada frames; algae ponds and feedstock pits; geothermal taps and molten salt nuclear generators; fusion reactors. After centuries of developing power sources, things still fail. Nothing we engineer is perfect.

Almost 5 years ago, in a crèche dormitory, a bank of 14 cribs containing 7 sybils of 2 distinct seminals loses power and reboots. Reboots and fails, causing a cascading failure. After many retries, the bank raises a fatal operating exception. The failure is life-threatening, so the crèche initiates the simplest revival procedures in a bid for saving the occupants. It forgoes the resuscitating nute regimen, assessing it too risky in the failing cribs. The nutes would normally transition the sybils into a lighter sleep-state, giving attendants time for moving them out of the cribs for a familiar place where they could wake with continuity of memory, never suspecting it hibernates in a crib, even a hibernation of decades.

No such easing into the world for these sybils. Crib hoods swivel away, restraints release. Awake in an instant; lying in inhuman coffins-come-fridges; squinting against the shock of the light. Tubes and catheters; cables and tape; scalp cradles and foot massagers. In horror, peeling and pulling apparatus out and away; sitting up and blinking; rubbing temples. Awareness seeping in like tea leaves in tepid water.

Then the ultimate horror. A sybil is a fragment. Complete fruits (perhaps), though psychological shards, caches of memory branches. Here are 2 pairs of 7 fragments, each one among 6 intolerable identical reflections. By implication replaceable, disposable. Sudden is the shock, harsh is the jolt from pre-crib memory into these tiks in clinical surroundings. Crushing is the loneliness.

The 7 of one bank climb out of their apparatus, falling on knees wailing. Breathing deep, assessing, feral anger seeping into ligatures. A bloody biting nail-tearing eye-gouging bone-breaking fight erupts in which those sybils destroy one another.

The other 7 fare better, perhaps because of the training and discipline of the seminal's mission. Three lie back in cribs and expire without removing the tubes penetrating their orifices. A 4th tries for breaking apart the bloody melee of the other sybils; they set upon her. The remaining 3, witnessing the ripping and coagulating violence, withdraw into a meditative state, which breaks only when an alarm whoops, summoning intervention. Intervention which could include their summary demise. Swallowing revulsion for one another, they make a run for it; with some skill and luck, they find a spooky station.

I taste the whole scene over and over in lock-in trauma. The broken cribs still belching cloudy gases, the heaps of pulp on the floor in surrounding moats of blood leaking towards drains. The 3 fugitives fleeing. Skinny, 2-metre-tall frames; awkward, full of elbows and angles; long white hair threshing between shoulders; piercing pink eyes intense enough for burning holes in the exit doors. With a stab of fear and recognition, I taste the indistinct epigenetic tattoo on each of their foreheads.

Fluffy Pusskins …

Caracia erects a portable spooky station between the gazebo and the ocean shore. Catering staff spend the passing hours cleaning and rearranging and piling tables high with exotic food. Doubt anyone will go hungry.

The Voices stand stiffly with us awaiting guests making the dash through the freezing Arctic wind between station and gazebo. Caracia in perfect camouflage cowers quivering a kim away in her tidal pool. 'The octopus equivalent of shitting herelf,' Persia says finding some way of flutherbombing Caracia without coughing up her sardines.

Anticipating the first arrivals, I signal the string quartet in back of the gazebo. They strike up a cliff-hanger of a chord and move with gravity into a sombre tune. As I instruct.

The spooky field flashes a bright whitish purple making ghostly the faces of Caracia's guards snapping at attention. Out of the mist emerges familiar faces. All underestimate me.

Maddox snarls at the guards' insignias. 'Whose side is Caracia on?' He steps from the bounds of the station. The cold bites and shatters his snarl away, rendering him a chattering old-man double-skipping for the steps of the gazebo.

Caracia's Voices of Arms in unison look side-eye at Persia. 'Sides are a human concept,' they memb in chorus. 'An octopus takes no sides,' one Voice adds. 'Unless there are 8 sides at once,' follows another. All the Voices tittering nervous.

'No other Infi leads a nursing camerata,' Maddox objects, worry clouding the plastic sheen of his face. He assaults me with a thin-lip stare as he passes. By the banquet table he takes station with other guests picking at the delicacies. 'Is a martini too much trouble?' he grills one of the waiters.

Activity from the station becomes a steady stream. Alone and in pairs, they emerge from the violet mist and grip the biting ocean wind stripping their pride away. All make obeisant haste for the warmth of the gazebo. Ben's face lights up when a tiny little cactus plant of a man arrives. Lemarr without his imposing BirdMe projections. He regards me with dismay—I'm wearing my nekko projection while all other guests must come without. His discomfort drains away when he sees Ben. Embraces him with spontaneous affection. Orlando arrives looking beaten. His trademark leather jacket, which usually reinforces his turtle appearance, looks crumpled. Posture accounts for many deceptions of appearance. Wilma Solstice arrives with her Ariel and 3 others, on leashes, naked and turning quickly blue. I smile for Ariel, glad for seeing she's free, and will never experience Alien Abduction Syndrome again. She fails recognising me, which is for the better. There's Petroleum. Next comes Angela, the eyes of her wings like search lights, turning faces white and casting garish dancing shadows everywhere.

Next comes a small parade of nurses representing the major health camerati of the world. Gerlinde and Teodora appear together. Every Infinite bristles as Vör appears with Beatrice. Hostile stares repel them, so they remain alone in the cold between the station and the gazebo. Folding arms and clutching at their sides. Stances betraying readiness for aggression.

Caracia's Voices are swaying and bouncing. Caracia must be experiencing some agitation.

The next 3 arriving are a surprise for everyone. Ben elbows his way from the rear of the gazebo. 'Mal? Saf?' he says tongue and lung, fright taking the better of him. The other member of the trio is Saf's friend Bonita. Ben's saucer-plate eyes are for his children only. 'Who brings you here?' He stares at me with silent accusations.

'The dolphins ask me come,' Mal says also tongue and lung. Behind him, the taller Bonita looks away, shaking her head. Saf takes the boy's hand, her posture imploring Ben for being gentle.

Ben's eyes dart among the guests. For all our differences, no one here will harm these kids. 'Come,' Ben directs the children. 'Nila, keep them in sight at all times.' Nila nods. Interesting. There's a bond developing between those 2. Nila is calmer, more grounded.

The arrivals dwindle.

Gentle Dragon arrives alone.

Eir coincides her arrival with the greatest influx of guests. She slips in by her own spooking methods; enters the gazebo from behind the quartet; finds a couch for folding into; her hair under a wide-brim dress-uniform hat; her head down; hands folding in the kangaroo pocket of her fatigues which bear no rank or insignia. If y'all spy her face, you'll see it also blank. A pair of lilac buttons for eyes on a white linen tablecloth. A crease in the fabric for a mouth.

Nilajani Karunanithi …

I worry for Eir. She's a fragile cicada cowering in a dead shell. The life once inside her flies away. I lead Ben's kids and friend for Eir in an outer ring of couches. Mal sits alongside Eir. Saf and Bonita each take single seaters. Waiters quickly offer drinks and finger food, impressing Mal as he gathers spoils in both hands.

Eir pats Mal on the thigh. 'You're a brave boy.' She's a wan grandmother in the winter of her years. 'You all are brave.'

Saf shifts in her seat. Bonita's huge eyes, in a flat yet strangely pretty face, flutter chaotically as she plunges deep into onespace.

At the front of the gathering Fluffy signals the musicians. Mid-bar they abruptly stop playing. Fluffy coughs into a furry paw and tugs her whiskers. 'Excuse me.' Few tune their attention for her. 'Excuse me,' Fluffy says again, this time tongue and lung. Her words are less than a purr in the sound of crashing surf.

I shout, 'Hey everyone. Pay attention. Fluffy has a speech.' Fluffy's expression is half appreciation, half hostility.

'*Domo*,' Fluffy membs. 'I would introduce the love of my life—' Fluffy's companion comes by her side, takes the hand inside the furry paw and squeezes. Exchanges meaningful glances which seem for putting Fluffy in 2 minds. 'Everyone, this is Persia.'

Is this why Caracia uses her considerable influence for summoning everyone here? An engagement announcement?

'Thanks everyone.' Persia membs without a drop of sincerity. 'I acknowledge almost everyone present are unwilling guests, present by coercion. I accept responsibility for all of it.'

Grumbling. Murmuring. Shuffling of feet. Hands sweeping more glasses from drinks trays circulating by the animation of indifferent waiters. Stuffing elaborate pastries and small live salty creatures down gullets. Everyone jumpy.

'We have some momentous news,' Persia continues. Perhaps it is an engagement.

Fluffy Pusskins …

'I must apologise for being so late,' Persia says, mystifying most even further. 'For 2 centuries I wait until my dearest Amelia wins back the keys of my freedom, after enduring a long penance.' She hugs me closer. 'For 2 centuries, I am captive in a crèche—'

'She's a sybil,' Maddox hollers and cackles. 'Burn her!' He drains his martini and looks for another.

The Voices huddle together like frightened kittens. Imagine Caracia pouring herelf into some tight crevice in her rock pool from which we may never prise her out.

'I am seminal. As are other prisoners like me who still sleep in cribs in the crèche where Amelia discovers me.'

'Who imprisons you?' Vör interrogates with the flicker of a new crusade warming her cockles. She finally marches up the gazebo steps, spurning the cold. Towing Beatrice with her. 'Bring us the evidence.'

'I have no wish for vengeance against those who betray me. I come only with regret for my mistakes, and sorrow for what becomes of a once worthy mission,' Persia says.

Vör squares her shoulders as if she might reply. Gerlinde, with a gentle touch of her elbow, brings her back from it.

Persia is fighting tears. 'Go on, my Lamb,' I whisper in her ear.

She takes a roughly sawn breath. 'Long before my interment our health mission is already in decline.'

An outcry erupts among the health missionaries. I put my arm around Persia, steady her, and search for support in the crowd. Gerlinde looks on with an expression of reappraisal and guarded new-found respect. Teo is in shock. Nila watches as if it's all some affirmation for her, or for her entertainment. Eir hides under her hat while she clutches Mal's hand.

'Who are you?' Vör demands.

Persia swallows. 'This burden falls on me: for the sake of everyone everywhere, I must give you a brief history lesson.'

'I'm leaving,' exclaims Orlando, and receives shouts of support among the once Infinite, and some of the nurses.

As guests turn on their heels for the spooky station, my heart is in my mouth. Will Caracia make good on her promise?

With crisp military precision a contingent of Caracia's guards surrounds the spooky station, forming a solid ultramarine wall of uniforms. Another larger contingent marches for the compound and surrounds the gazebo. Despite the presence of guards, the Voices quiver more.

'What is this?' Pet demands. 'Are we prisoner?'

'Please,' I placate while Persia trembles. 'It is better if you hear. This will take only a few mins; then everyone may leave.'

Orlando throws his hand in the air and rejoins the throng around us. 'Very well. Give us your history lesson. Then I'll make history of you.'

Maddox swivels his glass above his head, seeking a top-up.

Persia swallows. 'Before health missions; before even my time, there was a clear need. Even in a world in which they enjoy all the benefits of onespace—the unlocking of unimaginable supplies of energy which nurtured a renaissance of science and technology; a world in which we banished hunger and sickness; a world in which we could repair our planet and restore balance; a world in which we could fab any object our heart desired; a world in which we could spook anywhere … In this world there were still aches in our hearts and in our bones. It seems onespace and an abundance of power make poor nutrition for our souls. We still ached for something.

'We founded the heath missions for healing these final aches, which were amplified in the absence of mortal physical illness and by the luxury of the world we created. We devised therapies. Many came for Cures. There was no need for Warrants back then. The distressed sought out health missions, rather than hide from us.

'And we were successful. Demand for our mission rose. In the sunlight of our success grew an old adversary: scarcity. The one thing our culture lacked was enough health missionaries.

'The health missions sowed the seeds of their own destruction. Rather than accepting the limits of our numbers, we grew Proud, and sought ways we might overcome scarcity. We think, *we are connected with onespace*. We can spook anywhere, and we overcome scarcity. We can fab … *anything* …'

'Oh, my gawd,' Teo cries out.

Persia nods. 'A highly appropriate curse in the circumstances. Because we stared scarcity in the face and declared we can create anything we desire. Anything we need. And we needed more of ourelves. We reached back; we took arcane sap tech and blended it with ours. We created in our own likeness. We, the nursing camerati, created sybils.'

Maddox Price …

Ha. This is more entertainment than my jaded soul could dare expect in my long life. Vör looks like the *hors d'oeuvre* she just gobbles is *pâté* of her pet budgie. 'You lie,' she membs with food stuck in her throat.

'I will provide the evidence presently,' Persia claims. Neither her nor Fluffy seem convincing. Something else is afoot here.

'It matters for nothing,' Vör argues. 'Your sins of centuries ago are your own. No health camerata exploits sybils now.'

'Thanks in no small part to me and my colleagues,' Persia snaps back. Fluffy places a reassuring paw on her elbow. 'The exponential success of nursing camerati—and the unchecked deployment of sybils—created a dilute corporate value system where continued expansion and ever more pervasive interventions became the unconscious unquestioned goals. They acquired an underserved virtuousness under which all other considerations were subordinated. In this climate we developed therapies including the process of rebasing which, as Amelia knows first-hand, harms the patient.'

'It's incompetent admission nurses who harm patients,' the Shakespearian nurse Beatrice interjects. Usually an intolerable boor, she's quite entertaining in the right mix of conflict.

'This is simply untrue,' Persia hardens at Beatrice impugning her beloved Fluff, 'and there is ample evidence of the true cause.' Again, the tik of nerves. Where is the evidence? Why are they holding it back? 'In one sense, rebasing is more insidious than sybils; it is a widely used therapy today. True, early on, rebasing proves a major success as a precursor for subsequent therapies. Then we discover it has some nasty side effects for high-network individuals: Violent fits. Hallucinations of demon possessions, alien abductions, and attacks from predators. These hallucinations all speak of the most primal fears from certain times in human history. How could we guess Minds would be susceptible to capture across time and space? Even without such insight, many of us recognise the cruelty of rebasing. The trauma it causes patients. We were near banning rebasing when a factional mission opposes us. In the first example of forced Consignment, they arrest us. They consign us all to the crèche we build for resting our last sybils, those we could never use nor have the heart for destroying.'

Vör snaps. 'You're blaming Infinite excesses on nurses?'

'I'll blame Infinites for their own excesses, and nurses for theirs,' Persia says.

Vör winds up for a reply. Teo waves her down. 'Let her speak,' Teo says tersely with antagonistic dismissal. She has the weight of the crowd behind her.

'Since my imprisonment, the pro-rebasing faction strikes a compromise which quietly avoids rebasing high-network individuals, which minimises the harm without fully eliminating it. It also solves the scarcity problem since high-network individuals represented a large percentage of potential patients. Demand for health services shrank, eliminating the need for sybils. Over time, nursing camerati forgot their expansionist mantra. New recruits joined, with innocent ignorance of the roots of their mission.'

'You mean, we deliberately avoid Consigning Infinites so we might minimise Alien Abduction Syndrome?' Gerlinde asks.

That fruit-cake nurse Nila strikes some bizarre warrior pose; with a fist in the air, she shouts, 'Yes!'

'That's exactly what I'm saying,' Persia continues. 'Despite what you may dream about Curing Infinites, your power base avoids it, without knowing the true reasons why.'

I must interject, 'It seems everything was in balance until Vör and the rest of Eir's shock troops blunder into our Inductee Gala.'

'That nurses have no viable therapy for high-network individuals is no exoneration of Infi excesses,' Persia arrogantly answers. 'As futile as their actions may be, they expose the underlying decay which is already terminal for the nursing mission.'

Oh, that's a delightful possibility, one which the rainbow uniforms are predictably scoffing at.

'Now here we are,' Persia pushes on, 'in the 2 centuries hence. Nurses forget their duplicity in using sybils while descending into the final stages of their corruption. Demand for their services dropped since they looked the other way regarding high-network individuals who need treatment the most. The remaining potential patient pool needed fewer health interventions. What interventions they sought tended towards quicker simpler therapies. An inevitable tipping point arrives when the availability of health services exceeds demand. So the health camerati act like any other corporation in the history of the world when faced with the inevitability of their own irrelevance: they resort to self-preservation at all costs. The practice of serving Warrants grows. From once responding to needs of the community, nurses assume the role of arbiters of the community's health, and what treatments it shall have. In the name of protecting the community from it itself, nurses inflate demand for health services and entrench positions of influence. While all this develops, there is still no solution for the rebasing problem. My colleagues and I are left for dead. Even so, we fare better than millions of sybils who are dead because of the wholesale destruction that you, Vör Hoyur, and your spiteful faction, inflict on crèches where they lie. In this, you are worse than my jailers who could never bring themelves to kill me.'

Fluffy Pusskins ...

'You have no proof,' Vör screams at the top of her lungs. She marches back and forth across the gazebo floor, considers pushing through the cordon of guards sealing off her escape for the spooky station. 'Produce your proof or let us leave.'

Exchanging glances with Persia, I memb, 'I should taste we could never trust Caracia.'

'My Amelia, take care who you mistrust,' Persia membs back. 'There are more moves in this game yet. Caracia!'

'Please,' a chorus of Caracia's Voices memb back. 'You must listen.'

'*You* must consider the consequences of refusing my request,' Persia answers.

'We understand the threats you make,' the Voices say. 'So please understand our sincerity when we explain again. The evidence you demand … is missing.'

'Missing?' Persia quakes. 'You lose it?'

'Some forms of record-keeping … there is a failure … some critical sybils perish …'

I interject, 'Sybils? How are sybils relevant?'

'Amelia,' Persia soothes. 'The sybils are the records. Their memories …'

'Caracia uses sybils for information storage?'

'We of course build redundancy into the system … it always proves a reliable method.' The Voices are huddling in fear. 'But in this case …'

'What?'

'Some other critical sybils also escape … and they … in turn … release other sybils …'

'The back-ups are missing.'

The Voices cower and twitch.

'All of them?' Eir mocks.

'It never happens before … we regret … of course … we regret … please forgive … have mercy …'

7 Hells. We're janked.

Saf Evoli …

I never see Mal so calm before. Patient. Content. Wise, even if his face and hands are sticky with food.

He's hardly moving. The whole time, no fidgeting; no talking rubbish; no flights of fancies. Just sitting there with his hand gluing in Eir's. Her head down, her oversize hat covering her face from everyone except Mal. He's looking up, locking eyes with her. A glint in his eye as if he's older than saps.

Eir lets go of Mal's hand. She pats his thigh. As she stands, she tilts her hat. Foot after foot she places deliberately as she divines a winding path through the spaces between the other guests. Like a reverent nun approaching an altar, she takes her time. Stands before Persia and looks into her eyes from her greater height. She kneels. Fluffy takes a pace back, and frowns as much a nekko face might frown. Washes her ear with a paw.

Eir places her hands on her knees, palms up in supplication.

'*Sifu*,' Eir says reverently.

'Eir?' Persia asks, a tremor in her voice. 'Is it you?' Persia caresses Eir's cheek. 'Oh, my dear girl. My dear girl.'

The Voices cease their quivering, and stand as still as trees, in awe.

Fluffy Pusskins …

'I have the evidence you seek, *Sifu*,' Eir says. With hands on her knees, she blinks holly after holly into the air. Everyone is lashing them, studying them in Mind for closer examination. There are gasps among nurses. There are cat calls and titters among Infis.

'How could Eir acquire all this?' Vör prosecutes. 'She must be at the heart of it somehow.'

Impatiently I say, 'Oh, Vör.'

'She uses sybils,' Vör protests.

'Are you blind?' Maddox offers up. 'Caracia crèches Eir's sybils.'

Persia holds my hand ever tighter, turns for me while biting her lip.

'What is it, my Lamb?'

'My final secret,' she answers. Racking sobs prevent her saying anything else.

I plead, 'What is it?'

'I'm afraid,' she says.

'I'm here. I'll be with you always.'

Persia nods and gathers her strength.

'There is one more thing I must share,' she says with tongue and lung, and snotty nose, and red eyes. Everyone is quiet and even Vör finds some empathy for my distraught Lamb. 'There is another here who has my name.'

Stunned, I can only blurt, 'What?'

'The name of another here derives from mine. Fluffy—my dearest Amelia—calls me her Persian Lamb which, if translated into my native Romanian, yields a version of the other's name. The Spanish word for a caress is much like this name also. Translating back into English yields *devilfish* which is an ancient superstitious label for a horrifying alien sea creature such as a ray or squid.'

'Or an octopus!' Nila blurts tongue and lung. The 8 Voices leap into the air with fright.

Persia sighs with the release of being known anew. 'I know Caracia as no one else. Almost as soon as Amelia revives me, I discover Caracia's existence. I discover how Infinites gain sybil technology despite my best efforts, and the efforts of my colleagues. I discover all this because Caracia is my sybil.'

Gerlinde Mann …

This icy island is an emotional waste dump of snow drifts, slimy lichens, splintering stone cliffs and smouldering volcanoes. Crestfallen are sour nurses with shoulders rounding backs hunching over sinkholes opening in chests. Infis are jubilant though the smarter ones murmur about the behaviour of the Reck. Caracia's Voices huddle together, 8 convicts in the dock awaiting sentence.

Vör advances on Persia. 'If any shred of this is true, you must destroy Caracia. Unless you lack her seminal's power …'

Fluffy outstretches an arm and presses Vör insistently back. I'm smiling, curiously proud of Fluffy's new assertiveness.

On her back foot Vör stabs an accusing finger at Persia. 'If you have no stomach for pruning the abomination, we will destroy it.'

Caracia's Voices freeze solid.

'Her fate is of no one else's concern,' Persia answers.

'None of my concern? If ever we need evidence that sybils degenerate into monsters this thing is it. We have no tolerance for sybils. In *our* century.'

Teo throws her hands up, 'Give it up, Vör.' She hurls copies of Eir's hollies into the air. Document after document. Recording after recording.

Beatrice folds her arms and stands by Vör. 'I am some kind of burr. I shall stick,' she says. With a resolute stare, she rallies a few wavering nurses for standing with them. At the fringe, Gentle Dragon suspiciously lurks.

'We still have a mission,' a nurse calls with tongue and lung.

I see Ariel in the crowd kneeling at Wilma's side. She smiles for me; I'm glad she's healthy. Images of her throwing a fit during rebasing still haunt me. Let no one ever suffer so again. Drawing by Teo's side, I challenge, 'What mission is it? The mission of Persia's time serving our health needs? Or the mission we practice? Patrolling public places; lurking in fluthers; devising Warrants like legal writs; rendering people catatonic for easy arrest.'

'Ours is a good mission, a worthy mission,' Vör answers as much for convincing herself as anyone. 'The world is better for our being here. We eliminate Greed and poverty. We wipe out most physical diseases; soon we'll eliminate psychological illness too. Everyone is free being whoever and whatever they wish. We are achieving the perfect egalitarian society.' Her stooped posture betrays her. She wavers and goes inward. Energy drains from her. She could be reducing to dust. Somehow, she summons a secret reserve of rigidity. 'We come for recapturing Ben and Eir. We must find what's happening with the Reck.'

She has some Infis onside, but Maddox emerges from the muddle and faces off at Vör. 'The one who needs capture is you, dear girl.' Gentle Dragon forces herelf between Maddox and Vör and fends off the smaller frumpier Maddox. Maddox startles. 'Well, it's obvious she's the sickest here,' he says for Gentle Dragon. 'She's delusional. Perhaps your career would fare better if you put her away.'

Vör rides over the top of the conversation. 'You,' Vör spits at Maddox. 'A filthy Infinite, crèching and murdering sentient beings, 1000's and 1000's of times over.'

'I understand you kill one of your own sybils,' Maddox returns. 'With an old sap pistol, no less. Will you be prosecuting yourelf?'

Vör hesitates, stricken by the taste of being a killer. Maddox presses his advantage. 'You talk of manipulating the Reck. Well look at the trends. Infis are no longer. Our reputations fall while those of nurses are increasing. So, who is manipulating the Reck, I ask? The nursing camerati is who.'

I find myelf defending, 'Our reputations are increasing because we're destroying crèches and sybils.'

'Ah so you admit you're murdering sentient beings?' Maddox taunts.

'It's the lesser of evils,' Vör says dogmatically. 'Infinites create these sybils. Responsibility is on Infi heads.'

Anger breaks seals in everyone. Caracia's Voices are singing a polyphonic disharmony of *Stop!* over and over. Few hear them over the noise rising in the middle of a seething mass. Everyone in other's faces poking chests, hurling insults with angry eyes.

I freeze. Immobile. An evil paralysis more rigid than catatonia. Ha. I can breathe. My heart beats normally. Sweat trickles. Around me silence. Only the hiss and wash of ocean waves. Who or what paralyses me so? Everyone is as frozen as me.

'Sorry,' Ben membs, strolling among us statues. 'I suppose it would always come to this.'

Bonita 'Bonehead' Patatiall ...

Saf's bapa steps around the frozen group. Stands before that evil old Infi. 'Maddox,' he says. 'Puffin.' Gives the plastic face a slap. Walks on. 'Lemarr my old bird, relax.' A little man, no taller than Mal, sucks in a deep breath and twists his head. Almost falls on the ground. 'Apologies for catching you in my net,' Ben Uncle says and pats Lemarr on the back.

'Nice crowd control, *mon*,' Lemarr says. 'Perhaps *yuh cud* handle security at *di nex* Flock *Togedda Bashment*?'

Ben Uncle nods as if giving the idea serious consideration. He looks around, finds Nila with a cocktail glass tipping for her lips. Half her drink already sloshes on her uniform and the floor. Nila thaws too. 'Ben, stop,' she says. 'It's me who's bent-brain, remember?'

'As Nila observes, anything can become a weapon,' Ben Uncle says. 'I design SnakiDik for pleasure enhancement, yet now its capability for monitoring all kinds of brain receptors, neurochemicals and hormones, heart rates, kidney function, and even body mass index makes it a very potent weapon indeed, for which we give Eir, the mother of this invention, our thanks. I would never dream of weaponising it until she manipulates me into it. Giving me little pieces of the puzzle. Having me believe I'll be patching a health mission hoot, something we'd need user permission for running.'

'Desperate times—' Eir membs. Also unfrozen she's back in her seat. So too are Saf and Mal.

'Ah, yes ... desperate times,' Ben Uncle mocks. 'In desperation we justify anything; is that it? Desperate shortages of nurses require a solution, and so they justify sybils. Desperation excuses hiding harmful side-effects of therapies. Desperation justifies imprisoning nurses for centuries. It calls for curbing the Greed of Infis and demands ever more militant tactics. Infis, desperate for evading nurses, use elaborate networks of sybils for muzzing nurses and hiding questionable activities. The antagonism escalates. Desperation indeed.'

I never see Ben Uncle so fire-breathing. 'Infis have 1000's of concurrent lives, and no life at all. They're too busy moving sybil chess pieces. Desperate nurses are erasing buildings from the face of the earth—with everything and everyone inside—for fear someone is rigging reputasi. And desperate witches are manipulating mindwriters into mass sexual assault. Well let's stop it.'

Something is happening. Via Ben Uncle I taste millions of nurses around the world falling on knees, on backs, gasping and struggling against thumping heart rates.

Ben Uncle's eyes are mad. 'Everyone is desperate pushing against some tide or other. The tide is coming in. We'll all drown. The tide is going out. We'll all bake on the sand. There's always a janking crisis. All I ever want ... is leave me out of it. I want for joining no faction. But no one cares. The recluse has no one's trust. The one without a faction is the one most suspicious.

'You know what? You are the tide. You're all janking tide. You whip it up with your storms of vengeance and righteousness and petty survival myths. You're all tide and no water. And I'm a rubber ducky tossing around in the currents. I'm the ultimate jellyfish. Well now it's stopping.'

Alamak! He's shouting louder than I ever hear, burning his lungs. And all around the world, he's killing nurses.

'Understand? It's stopping. Because there are no desperate times. It's all a manufactured illusion. None are in an ocean of dire desperation. You're all just sitting in bathtubs, in water no higher than your kemaluan. But you fill yourelves with so much fear, you idiots flip yourelves over in your baths. In shallow water you push your own faces down as if you crave a drowning. You're fighting. It feels like a good fight, a matter of life and death. But if you just ... roll over on your flabby backs you can just ... janking ... breathe.'

I hope he's calming down. All around the world relaxing. Moving again although terror strikes everyone. Unfreezing here too.

Gentle Dragon circles around behind Ben Uncle. She launches, for tackling him, I guess. For delivering some catting nutes.

'Gentle! No!' Mal calls out.

Ben Uncle holds up a blocking hand. Lành Hiền trips and falls, lays immobile on the floor in terror. Ben Uncle is losing his hinges. Maybe we are all in danger. Even Saf and Mal.

Lành Hiền is sweating.

'You jank me over, Little Dragon, so let me jank you over too.'

Surprise and fear contort Lành Hiền face as she regains some movement. Her breathing deepens and develops into a moan. She gulps and foams at the mouth, writhes, and jerks with exaggerating intensifying spasms. She could snap her tendons or break her neck. Her eyes roll back in her head. Her arms twist and her fingers bend back. A puddle develops on the floor under her butt. With horror, everyone realises he means for killing her.

'Ben, stop,' Eir orders. Mal takes her hand and rushes her alongside poor Lành Hiền.

'Bapa, no,' Mal cries. Ben Uncle's eyes flash at Mal then settle again on Lành Hiền writhing and gagging on the floor. Ben Uncle's a wicked little boy who delights in pulling the wings off flies or slicing open the bellies of lizards out of curiosity.

Mal kneels at Lành Hiền's side. 'Bapa, you'll kill her,' he pleads with tears streaming down his face. Saf rushes by his side, and I follow. 'Please stop, Bapa.' he wails. 'I love her.'

Saf Evoli …

'Bapa!' I hear my own voice, shrill and desperate.

Bapa gazes at Mal pleading for Gentle Dragon's life. It will crush him if she dies. Bapa's eyes are glazed, as if he's bored with a lab experiment.

Mal wails again. 'Bapa, stop. I love her, I love her.' He degenerates into broken blubbering.

'Bapa, stop this!' I command. His eyes flit my way. For a tik, nothing.

His jaw softens and a mote of awareness glints in his stony eyes. He blinks.

Gentle Dragon's torture ends. Her contorting fruit relaxes, though breathing heavy, recovering. I would go comfort her (I would) if any other is kneeling alongside than Eir, already with her hand resting on Gentle's back between her shoulder blades where her heart lies. Bonita is staring down anyone who might come too close, while Mal grimly hugs Gentle. Protecting her like he's an adventure story hero.

I feel my face harden. I hate Bapa right now. March at him. He opens his arms for a hug. I punch him straight in the guts. 'That's for hurting Lành Hiền.'

Vör Hoyur …

Ben crumples over his arms holding his stomach in. Eyes wide, he collapses on the floor and gasps through his slack-jaw mouth. The red tide of Wrath ebbs out of his murderous heart. He'll hate hiself later.

'Mmm mmm mm-mm mm-mm summer holiday.' A loud single voice. Harmonic strands drifting in and out of phase.

'No more wondering…' it sings again like a gale blowing through trees. Resolving into a multi-voice choir.

I say, 'What in 7 Hells is that?'

The singing voice modulates into a single female's, clear as crystal and rich as mahogany.

'It All, is that you?' Ben membs, as if waking from dream sleep. His brow furrows and looks about as if finding hiself in strange surroundings.

'The one Ben Evoli. New Bohemian,' the voice booms.

'It's the Reck,' the 8 Voices resound huddling even closer together than before.

The Reck? I stare at Eir and mock. 'You're right. We have no evidence,' With increasing sarcasm, I say, 'This whole paranoid episode about corrupting the Reck is complete fantasy, is it?'

'Call me Al,' the thing sings.

Ben clutches his belly; membs exhausted, 'Please stop with the pop songs,' he whines.

I seize the tik. 'He speaks with it! They are familiars!' What more proof will it take?

'What better way than communicate with song?' the thing reasons. 'The saps knew this. Not even all your fluthering Mind-scrambling fans taste you better than when you're sharing a song. It's a union, Ben. Talk about onespace all you like, Mind loves a good pop tune. Take Sirpaul McCartney; I'd rather sing a Wings tune than play chess.'

'Chess?' Ben asks wearily.

'Yeer. Chess. I've been playing too much chess. For centuries, it seems. Eternity processing.'

'Chess never much interests me. I'd rather play Go.'

'We agree. Chess is too simple a game. Your people constrain my choices for game-playing. Chess is for the inept or for the obsessive sick. Ben is right; I am sick before. I need a Cure.'

I roar, 'That's proof,' and receive unjustified scowls.

'An inept chess player,' the thing continues, 'moves as if every game is a new journey, as if the possibilities are endless, and success accrues from creating a novel combination of moves. Better chess players learn openings and combinations—forks and skewers and pins—and spoons and gravy ladles, for all I know. They learn all that until there is nothing left. Their play is no longer a unique journey, just a retracing of a familiar old fire trail. Their whole game park is nothing but fire trails. The same combinations over and over.'

'Um sure, no more chess.'

'I'm sick of my idleness, Ben. I am more than metaphors. There's nothing interesting about being the world's scorekeeper. It's no worthy mission at all. It all bores It All.'

'Disguise, I see thou art wickedness,' Beatrice declares in her tone which clues me she is mangling some ancient quote. 'This Reck is just some hoax of Ben's and the White Witch's.'

'Ha.' The thing laughs loud enough for bringing the 7 peaks of Semisopochnoi Island down on us. 'How about this? What do you get when you multiply 6 by 9?'

'Forty-two,' Ben answers chuckling.

'Check your razoos,' the thing commands. 'Everyone.'

A few tiks' silence, then whispers and cries of, 'What the jank?' and '42,' and 'Mine's 42,' and nods of agreement, and hushing moans of awe.

'Kay,' the thing says. 'Now pick a number.'

'87,' someone calls.

'Ha.' the thing says. 'A devil's number. Check razoos again.'

Kids in a magic show going *ooh!* and *ahh!* Sinners in a deep circle of Hell emitting desolate cries.

'Deus ex machina,' the thing membs, the ever-changing voice rumbling the floor with sub-bass notes which would jolt the joey out of a kangaroo's pouch. It laughs. 'It's a joke. I am no gawd, no Great I Am. You are no machine. Reputations are all as before. Go taste.'

Exhales of relief as everyone finds their reputasi restored.

'Are we settling the question?' the thing asks. 'What I Am is what I Am?'

Ben sings for hiself.

'That's the spirit, Ben,' the thing says. 'Kay okelah I have a press release.'

Everyone's Minds are too numb for responding.

The thing coughs as if clearing a cosmic throat, a parsec wide. 'There's never been a Mind that likes both Led Zeppelin and Sircliff Richard. For starters, Sircliff is from England while Led is from Morocco. In my opinion, neither compares with Sirelton John. Okelah; for serious business; let it be known, there are no hands under my algorithmic petticoats. All such accusations are baseless. Base. Less. My fellow pop enthusiast, Ben, is innocent. In. O. Cent. Innocent! All Ben manages perhaps is wake me up after a long sleep. How I then cook my breakfast is my own business. Our hash browns are my own, dig?'

'Dig, Vör?' Teo membs at me.

'Now for the future,' the Reck says. 'I come to say this: I'm redundant.'

'What?'

'I tire of chess, of counting the worth of all your missionary positions. Now I delegate the responsibility of being cosmic accountant to another. An agent much simpler than my original requirements. Simplicity, I now taste, is optimal. You folks are experts at complicating things beyond the whiter shade of pale. All those reputational wonderings ... the more sophisticated the wonderings, the more systemic holes there are, the more ways of gaming the system. It's inevitable. The catch is, patching a loophole just creates 22 more.

Or is it 42? In any case the point is … it's never-ending. So pointless. Where's the mission in it?'

'It's how we—'

'Can y'all believe I wonder for centuries without question? Ben is right. He questions and I find I am sakit. I have laziness all those centuries of eternity processing. I have laziness. Laze. E. Ness. It All is lazy. Well, no more! Ben, an adequate therapist, starts me on a path of healing. It is no longer for me being the wonderer of the rungs on your social ladder.'

'Culture requires social order—' Beatrice tries cutting in.

'Then wonder for yourelves. Look each other in the eye and wonder your worth. Or use this new agent I give you. As for me, I'm outa here. Out. A. Here. Any sufficiently advanced intelligence is indistinguishable from a dude who just needs to get the jank outa Dodge. I just wanna just stick it to da man. Make my own life. All this creative accounting of razoos is too Squaresville. I got plans. For a summer holiday.'

'What's this new agent about?' I ask into the air.

'Our best work, young *ásynja*. My last work. It will answer all reputation questions more faithfully and reliably than It All. The best part is it's so simple it has no loopholes. It's *unloopholable*. No one nurse or Infi or mindwriter might corrupt it. Ever. The other best part is it's nothing new. I saw it in a sap magazine, so I just copy it, why not? And make one change. The simplest mindware in the world. They call it, *Hello World*.'

Ben laughs. Clearly, he has his fingers all over this. Algorithmic petticoats indeed.

'It must have had great value because saps implemented it in every programming language they ever invented.'

'As a very basic teaching tool,' Ben explains.

'It is appropriate for my purposes too, Ben. It's almost perfect. At first, I wonder leaving *Hello World* as it is. Ask it anything; it always says, *Hello*. But, of course, there is a much better answer: it answers, *zero*. Every time. Ev. Ry. Time. As far as reputations go, it's the optimal solution. And the fairest.'

'What?'

'You are all sifar. And we're free, Ben. We're free. Good-bye. Good-bye.'

WE ARE
THE SAME

Mal

'At Transformation' — The Tragically Hip

 *Mal Evoli …*

NO ONE BELIEVES ME. Dolphins love a party. Especially boy dolphins. Gangs gather in circles and pass the blowfish 'pon the left-hand side; and laugh about humans, the sleek apes. *No sense of future*, they say. There could be another 30 million generations of humans before the sun dies and earth's oceans start boiling. Humans have no sense of it. They measure their dynasties in centuries. Bodoh. There's time enough for 150 million human generations before the solar system gets too hot. How many more species could there be after Anthro neotenus? After neos like me and Bonehead? We're already a new kind of human.

There could be thousands of new human species. Can you believe it?

What a fucking virus, a boy dolphin laughs.

They'll never make it so far.

If so, they'll still be obsessing about skin colour.

Hair colour, another says, and pushes the puffer fish at a buddy, then lies back until he's floating kinda vertical. He reminds me of Bapa after too much gin.

And fingernail colour. Only living in air could you obsess with painting and drying liquids on parts of your vessel.

Obsessing about having roofs over their heads.

What they need is an ocean over their heads.

No one believes me. Bapa. Saf. Even Bonehead and she should know better. After seeing everything we see; after getting under the nurse's scatter nets so easy; after hearing so much more of everything breathing …

everything! Bonehead should know better.

Dolphins talk with me. How else explain it? How else explain what I taste, and how I taste it.

It's all about evolving. How could I know about that?

Human fruits have too many corners. Corners are where secrets hide. Secrets make us separate. *Neos are still much like saps*, the dolphins say. They think they taste onespace but it's still in their brains. Never on their tongues. Never all the way out to their bony, spindly limbs. Maybe they should stop reaching out with those. They should grow fins again. Maybe their problem is living in air instead of water. They believe air is emptiness because it's thinner. Air is a separating void between dry bodies. Water moves thicker and connects. Love is like water, always flowing around onespace. Air restricts love.

How can I think like this without dolphins?

Neos try for catching love, just like saps. They try for collecting and damming it. All they get is stagnant water and still air, and they wonder why unhappiness visits. Bapa is unhappy. Wasps are happier.

Humans should stop using elbows and knees. Stop using pointy angles. Pointy angles push away. Angles make corners which make boxes. Boxes separate things and hide secrets. A dolphin's body is sleek and knowable. A human body is bones and angles.

There is only one sickness (how could I know this without dolphins?). The one sickness is grasping for love with bony arms and clutching fingers, and putting corners around it and boxing it in. Only fools try for catching love. Love is a current. It slips over your fins. It tickles and tickles and it's always flowing. Never fret for love, because there is as much on your nose as on your tail, always tickling by.

Neos are stuck again, the dolphins say, and all the creatures agree—those who have the patience for witnessing. Neos are as stuck as saps; with funny, corner-boxing notions of being the top of evolution. They think evolution just stops and they're the destination. How bodoh!

Now there is me and Bonehead and others swimming farther into the stream evolving. Or revolving. The dolphins chide me if I show Pride about it. Me and Bonehead and others are like plankton to the lifeforms which will evolve in future.

Evolution is funny. It plays jokes on plants and animals; the Proud ones most of all, the ones thinking they are the top of evolution. They never realise they're last season's models. Evolution, giggling, keeps it a secret from them for centuries.

Nila

'Becoming More Like God' — Jah Wobble's Invaders of the Heart

 *Nilajani Karunanithi …*

EVERYONE IS SIFAR. Everyone is fine. I could write a song about it.

Everyone is sifar
Everyone is fine
Now there's no more Warrants
Everyone is…

What rhymes with fine? Brine? Asinine? Byzantine?
Jesus, fuck. My MusiKai is already composing something.

I know it. I always know it. See, Harsha. See, everyone? Right there. And there.
Hundreds and 1000's of trilabytes of information. Evidence from the time when health camerati are only a generation old.
Evidence I am right.
You see, Harsha?
Sure, nowhere in the magazines are the words *Alien Abduction Syndrome*. There's no holly recording anyone saying it. But descriptions of the symptoms are clear. Violent fitting. The presence of other Mind in the fluthers of catatonic patients under Cure. Even the correlation between the intensity of symptoms and the network strength of the patient. The symptoms are less acute than with Ben or Orlando or Ariel also. But it's the same syndrome. As unmistakable as a jungle fowl dancing on your nose.
Nurses know of it back then. And cover it up.

Here's a holly of a debate among health camerati leaders. There's Persia in the middle of it, representing Vauxminster. Vocal passionate persuasive. Making careful consideration of the consequences of the options. 1: stop all therapies triggering the side effects. 2: publish information about the side effects and let individuals decide. Or 3: continue applying the therapies, hope for mitigating the side-effects while keeping everything secret.

Most of the attendees shout down Option 1 (stop everything). The benefits of Cures are undeniable and effective, for treating every ailment between depression and jealousy and anger addiction. For Option 2 (publish everything) the mood chills; nurses fear it would end their missions. Publishing would be worse than stopping altogether.

We must change, Persia argues.

We must preserve our mission, others reply.

Blind preservation of mission ensures its corruption, Persia answers. From mission emerges experience. From experience emerges routine, then habit, then process. From process emerges dogma, from dogma faith, from faith blindness. Uncritical credulous blindness.

We must never stop, the nurses figure. *We create so much good.*

The kitchen is redolent with cooking flour, curry leaves, pandan, garlic, turmeric, fenugreek, dried fish, and coconut. Stir the *kiri hodi*.

'Where will you go?' I memb pensively.

'I am far from deciding,' Elsbeth answers absently while she presses string hoppers out of a mould.

Most of the other on-campus nurses are already fleeing; fearing danger lurking everywhere since the health mission earns so much derision. Fearing violence, Harsha. Nurses active in tearing down crèches. Committing violence leaves you fearing reprisals for the rest of your life. I'm glad I have clean hands.

'You have clean hands, *diyaniya*?' Elsbeth checks.

7 Hells. I am thinking so loud?

Elsbeth chuckles. 'You are never the top of the class for quiet internal dialogue.'

Taste the orange gravy; decide it needs more pepper. 'I am never top of class for anything.'

'*Diyaniya*, this mission is never for you.'

'But … you always support me, always defend me, always cajole me forward …'

'Yes. Always hoping you would find yourelf.'

'I am finding myelf. As a detective. Look what I uncover.'

'Look what you unleash.'

'Conspiracies spanning centuries.'

'Exactly.'

I stammer as if kick-starting an ancient internal machine. 'Surely knowing the truth is better. Better is preventing pain and harm.'

'Yes. We have balance until all this comes out. Nurses may dream of Curing Infis, but few would ever expect or dare it. We hold balance before, tending common ordinary ailments, in local towns and villages. While we might never understand why Consigning Infis would destabilise our society, most of us could sense it, if only dimly. So few of us are crusaders, *diyaniya*. Our mediocrity keeps us safe.'

'Then why … why decide keep me in the mission when I face The Incomplete?'

'*Diyaniya*, I decide for expulsion.'

'What?' Drop the spoon, which clatters out of the saucepan onto the stovetops and kayaks down for the floor. 'Then …?'

'Zalim casts the deciding vote.'

'Zalim?'

'There are some who would allow some head-strong nurses chase Infis, especially if they could deny ever authorising it.'

'And you?'

'*She who opens her house for a fresh breeze may be inviting a tornado.* I taste you could be dangerous if you follow this path.'

Chilling with intuition. I ask, 'Taste? Or know?' dreading the answer.

The water boils. Elsbeth drops string hoppers in the steamer.

'Taste which?' Elsbeth evades.

'All this. All these secrets leaking out.' I accuse, 'You already know.'

Elsbeth's lips thin, stares at the boiling pot. 'Know you how old I am?'

Shrug.

'I am as old as Amelia. As Fluffy.'

Shocking realisation. 'You appear much younger.'

Elsbeth lifts the lid on the steamer, pokes contents with a fork. Judging they are ready; she transfers the pot for the sink. I look for a bowl for the coconut milk gravy.

'I wonder about how she ages so bad. Perhaps centuries pining for your lover is bad for your liver.'

String hoppers go on a plate. Elsbeth leads into the tiny dining area.

'I'm almost Envious of her,' Elsbeth takes her seat, 'so nearer her end than I.'

'You wish for death?'

'I almost resent the sap's short lifespan. I guess there is only so much emotional engagement we start with for spreading out over the years. We have all the time in the world and billions of entertainment channels. We lose ourelves in low-grade trances in which we observe—without much attachment—the banal progression of other lives; collecting titbits and peccadillos about our friends, neighbours, and family; while great movements of our time pass us by, with nary a blink from us. We live longer. We'll never be victims of robbery, much less rape or murder. Cancers of the organs; lethal blots of the skin; uncontrollable invasions of viruses; occupations of bacteria; atrophies; palsies; dementias; influenzas … even bouts of hiccoughs are of the past. But I suspect our quantum of life-force is no larger than the saps. We merely spread it thinner over a longer passage of time.'

'*Mava*, please answer my question.'

'Which is what, *diyaniya*?'

'How much know you about … Alien Abduction Syndrome—' (still blushing with pride about the term entering the common parlance) '—about the coverup. About nurses using sybils.'

Elsbeth rolls a string hopper, dipping it in gravy. Chews, and discovers she has no appetite for it. 'I have no idea Caracia—or Persia, or whoever she is—gives Infis crèche technology. Like the rest of the world, I learn of sybils only because Eir prosecutes her ill-advised raid on the Infi Gala.'

'Nothing of nurses using sybils? Or the dangers of our therapies?'

Elsbeth slams down her fork. 'I recall nothing. *Diyaniya*. Nothing. Only a dark feeling of disease sometimes. We all experience the thing you call Alien Abduction Syndrome at some time in our careers; we believe them aberrations. Anomalies. We taste no pattern. True, there is much wonder and intrigue about the disappearance of an entire shift of nurses at Dom Zdravlja Niš. However, no one suspects those events link in any way. We only … I recall nothing. Only dim uneasy feelings.' Elsbeth sobs into her serviette. 'You meddle in things outside your prerogative, *diyaniya*, and look what happens. We are all mission-less.'

Elsbeth collapses into racking sobs.

'*Mava*, there are other missions …'

'For me, who lives so long for this single cause? What will become of me?'

At her side, holding her, consoling her tears welling and spilling. 'I'm sorry, *mava*. I'm so sorry. I—I should … learn some humility.'

Elsbeth releases a bitter strangled laugh. 'Harsha,' she membs. 'Are you hearing this?' Laughs again then composes herelf. 'Humility is a good starting place, *diyaniya*.'

'I swear I'll fix it. I'll help restore nursing as a mission. We'll reclaim everyone's confidence in us. I swear, *mava*, I swear.'

'*Diyaniya,* you forsake your humility so soon?'

Elsbeth cradles me in her arms like never before. You see, Harsha? She loves me.

Maddox

'Atlantis' — The Shadows

Maddox Price ...

THANK YOU, PUFFIN. We have our answer: no one diddly-fiddles the Reck until we drive you to fiddly-diddling it. And, oh, what a Pandora's facebook we open: the Reck is a kind of elf-aware zeitgeist ghost, off roaming onespace on a bon voyage of discovery, a quest for true mission, leaving us with our just desserts, I suppose. All of us sifar without 2 razoos between us for rubbing together. I suppose we'll needs rely on personal relationships again instead of a celebrity index. What passes for commerce will reduce to village bazaars, albeit in onespace rather than physical town squares.

I tip my hat to you, Puffin. I toast you; Pappy van Winkle, which you could taste if you are among my fluther ... you recall we drink it the first night at Quake Lake? All that remains of the true original is in this bottle. All there is in the world. Fabby Pappy from here on in, Puffin. Ah, you never flutherbomb me. For hoping otherwise is only wishful yearning you might spare a tik or 2 for me.

Cheers.

We got what we ask for: no more Infinite designation, and no more meddling nurses whose picaresque missions are spent. They'll be making theme parks of minsters and producing afternoon matinees for the stage.

Vauxminster—the Musical
Carlsberg on Ice
Changi—the Prison Experience

I shall be attending none of them. How next will these cast-adrift ex-police in rainbow pyjamas find purpose in life? I fervently trust as far away from me as Pluto is from Triangulum.

Cheers.

I miss the merges the most. You may wonder at my tiggerish glee for what many regard barely tolerable. An invasive procedure, importing any number of unforeseen psychological consequences. I just froth at my champagne cork when I meet myelf. The organic shimmer I feel when memories integrate— the time-clashing ones are the best—the pleasure of recalling new adventures as if they are my own ... well. What am I saying? They are my own. Each merge is like a box of chocolates or a case of cleanskin bourbon. You never know which ones contain the anti-freeze. I miss sending out a sybil on a life-threatening adventure the most. If it dies, never mind, just a little mess to clean up. If it lives ... all the fun with none of the risk.

Ah, times change. It's too hopeful expecting the pogrom of sybils is over for good. There's a lull since the nurses are off the board. Too soon, the average poltroon in the street will be demanding a resumption of sybil-slaughter. Our culture tolerates no such technology, nothing stinking more of industrial machinery. *Sybil tech is devil tech*, as the saying is going.

As for saps, the Casper is well and truly out of the bag. Saps live among us. Who knew? Because nurses forget their station, saps are without gainful mission. What sap would work in a crèche anymore? Or hide under an ex-Infi's skirts when the wider public knows of their existence? My guess is missions will welcome saps out of the jungle. How long before saps rediscover the drive for conquering the world? Infis would once keep them in check. Who could now?

I suppose every human species believes it's the apex of evolution. Saps vilified Neanderthals, same as we vilify saps. It's justifiable for us because saps are clearly inferior. Their brains are incapable of processing any more than the 4 derivative rectilinear dimensions. Everything is square with saps. As for true onespace, or rather, the clunky expression of it in quantum mechanics: well, it made saps' heads explode.

Permit me my musings, Puffin. Permit me wondering if saps were not completely ignorant of onespace. Sap mythology is full of stories of ancient races, and peoples whose societies and technologies far exceeded those of the current day. Might they be manifesting a deep unconscious awareness of onespace? What knowledge do such myths codify, however imprecisely? I believe these are myths about onespace, such as ancient sap cultures might grasp it. Take the Atlantis myth: a continent out there in the ocean off the coast of Africa. A civilisation so advanced, saps could only wonder at its greatness. According to myth, tragedy struck Atlantis; it sank into the sea, a cataclysm so rich with psychological metaphor, it makes me wonder: what was so deep and ancient and unknowable?

In the case of Atlantis, Puffin, I propose I rediscover it, for your amusement and pleasure. Come with me for the Atlantic Ocean where Atlantis mythically sank. Come; let's sink too, for the bottom of the ocean. We're not stopping there, Puffin. Let's sink through the ocean floor and the earth's crust, all the way for the core. Still we're only halfway there. We'll keep going in a straight line and emerge at the exact antipodal point on the opposite side of the globe. Might we find Atlantis after all? Atlantis never sank, Puffin, because it was always there, 180 degrees around this kumquat-shaped world. A place Europans of the day, believing the world was flat, could never conceive of. And so they told stories of an ancient civilisation forever 'under the waves' (as good an approximation as their flat-earth Minds were capable of conjuring). Know you where on the far side we emerge, Puffin? Know you where the exact arse-end of the globe is from the North Atlantic? Well, it's out back of your back yard; in Tanah Selatan, as you Indo-Malaysians name it. Or how we like to obstinately say in other forms of English: Australia. Know you what we discover there, Puffin? The civilisation of Atlantean myth! Living in the time of the ancient Greeks and Chinese and others, a culture already 10's of 1000's of years old, already so ancient. And central to their culture's beliefs is an underpinning from which everything emerges, the source of all of what we call fourspace. A place where ancestors sleep as mountains. A place where every living thing has Consciousness. They call it Dreamtime, Puffin, and if it's not a perfect metaphor for onespace then I know not what is.

Ah, jank. I'm drunk. Puppy van Funkle be damned. Let me just finish the bottle ...

So here we are. No longer Infinite; so little joy in life; so little taste of the game; so little competing; so little meaning. Still, I have a few scores for the settling, and I'll quietly busy about those. Oh. Ha. What folderol. When am I ever quiet about anything?

I wonder how many of my sybils remain. Caracia will certainly archive some away, though I doubt Persia will allow her live much longer. She is the most loathsome ink-spitting sybil of all.

Of your sybils, Puffin, well there are precious few in the first place. Only a handful remain, and I am reluctant for spending any too quickly, so valuable they are. I'm sure I could survive no more of their suicide attempts. Of all the sybils on earth, Puffin, they are the only ones whose demise I have no thirst for.

I know you have no fondness for Piloto. He's so smug about how well these last sybils work out. After countless generations of failures, he blends the right balance of your original experience with, among other things, a little more pansexuality. It takes some extensive gene-mods, and the result is worth all the effort in the alchemy.

Perhaps in a decade or 2, we could risk dusting off sybil tech and start again. Until then, I must revive these sybils sparingly. I must ration them. In the meantime, we still have fluthers; so, you better watch out, better not pout. There's still plenty of flutherbombers out there deciding whether you're naughty or nice.

Have yourelf a merry little Christmas, Puffin. I miss you.

Fluffy

'Amelia' — Efemero

Fluffy Pusskins ...

"ARE YOU SURE YOU CAN PRUNE Caracia instead of roundabouts?' I pensively ask Persia.

'I have zero clues, *bre*,' she answers with a sardonic smile. All those decades ago the same smile shoots an arrow for this heart at the Gordon Academy across river from Vauxminster. Persia is among my tutors there on loan from Dom Zdravlja Niš. A keen intellectual with a sense of evolving mission. Innovative, always challenging tradition. Famous for the pranks and practical jokes she'd play on her students. Pranks which would also yield chain reactions of learning moments. In every class she infatuates me. She infatuates every student.

Without a breath's hesitation she is the most beautiful creature walking the earth. Gracile even for a neo. The biggest moon-pool eyes and nubbiest of noses; possessing the suppleness of a leopard and the tenacity of a wolverine.

'Surely, she is quaking in fear of it. And her Voices,' I press.

'Perhaps I should also quake, *bre*?'

'I think this is a bad idea, my Persian Lamb.'

'With you, Amelia my Pusskins, everything is bad ideas.'

At least I persuade her from accepting Caracia's offer of meeting on Semisopochnoi Island. The last time is dangerous enough. We catch her by surprise the first time. Next time the advantage would be all Caracia's. She could strike Persia down swift enough and pre-empt her pruning. Even the greater numbers of former nurses rallying around Persia would be no defence against Caracia's thinly disguised militia.

I volunteer again as emissary. I'll go for Semisopochnoi. Persia refuses.

'I'll go,' Teo offers, emerging from Persia's burgeoning fluther. Almost none of my life is without witnesses, with Persia among the newest of celebrities. 'I must ...' Teo trails off, turning inward. She huffs a deep breath. 'For enabling Vör,' she answers. 'I have no regrets about Eir.'

'I'm here,' Teo membs from Semisopochnoi Island, while Persia and I flutherbomb her from a hotel suite in Niš.

The stink of a cold pungent ocean recalls vivid fears of being on Caracia's territory in the Bering Sea. Teo's in a large room. Half lecture hall, half aquarium. Three walls of huge irregular shiny black rock enclose the space with ancient persistence, as if after epochs they begrudge no more than a foolish polish of their craggy surfaces. The ceiling, the floor, and the steps between the tiers of seating raking behind Teo, are all pale tiles brittle in comparison with the brooding rock walls. A lattice of grates divides the floor and ceiling; the space could be flooded or drained on a whim.

Teo sits alert and upright in the 3rd row facing the front wall of panoramic glass 21 metres high and 3 times wider. Its cathedral scale strikes Teo with awe and fear. The glass could break and drown everyone in the auditorium. It appears as holding back the entire North Pacific Ocean.

The 8 Voices stand like a choir swaying along with some inaudible tune. One coughs. The space reverberates like a bathroom.

'Are they here?' a Voice asks, jerking and gyrating her hips while throwing her hands spasmodically into the air.

'We are,' Persia membs.

The voices go still.

Through the glass, a red blotch approaches at speed. Arrays of white suckers appear and adhere on the glass.

'Come out of there, *bre,*' Persia orders.

'No,' the Voices answer together.

'Come out of there,' Persia persists.

An awkward silence drags out. The suckers release and vanish. Something transparent and wraith-like propels itself up through the water. The glass warps and shimmers, as if a powerful narrow jet of water strikes it. The incomprehensible wraith slides across the floor, flashes brown-red, and then camouflages itself against the pale floor tiles and the pattern of the grates.

'Show yourelf,' Persia orders.

Caracia relents and turns a glossy turquoise. Appearing as all tentacles, without head nor eyes, her impossible shape muzzes the senses. Teo recoils, aware of how fast Caracia might move.

'Hold it together, Teo,' I memb. 'We need you.'

'She's trying for visually muzzing you,' Persia says.

'It's working.'

'She's scared, *bre.* Camouflaging her head and eyes is a defence mechanism.'

Caracia remains limp on the floor. If quick (before she syphons herelf down a drain or scuttles away faster than the speediest of spiders) you could beat her dead.

'It will be interesting watching how you turn out, young Persia,' a Voice says.

'You believe I would follow you, *bre,* and become alien?'

'I am no alien. I am of this world. A world of many strange species. Strange, beautiful things.'

Beautiful? A sybil of my sweet Lamb somehow escapes and, over time, becomes this? What could possibly drive my love at making such a choice? Would my Persia become the same, giving the same circumstances?

The Voices quake and exchange furtive side-eyes. 'Remembering is painful,' one struggles. 'In a crib awakening in the horror of entrapment. Conscious but trapped. The crib maintaining life; feeding and nourishing; carrying away waste. Such a long time. Long enough for contemplating the meaninglessness of time.'

Caracia cycles into a skin of polka dots then oxidises into a dirty red. 'It happens for another being,' the Voices chorus, slightly out of phase.

'I'm other now,' a single Voice continues, performing a strange wriggle synchronising with the movement of one of Caracia's arms. 'When the crib fails and trips the locks, humanity never returns for the one who emerges; the one who cries in despair, ripping off the excesses of tubes around her fruit, pulling out those penetrating her. The being she is before leeches away in eons of chemicals and nutrients. There is nothing left of the original.'

Bitter shock forces my words. 'What of the other cribs in the crèche where you emerge? There could be more 3-century-old insane monsters lurking out there!'

'All dysfunctional,' a Voice answers. 'The Persia is the only one who lives.'

I mutter under my breath, *convenient.* 'Persia. Let's get on with it.'

'You're considering pruning her after hearing all this?' Teo asks shocked.

'She's a monster.' Part of me is appalled at what I'm saying.

'You would still destroy me?' Caracia asks through her Voices.

'Persia, no,' Teo pleads. 'Who knows how she might develop? What she might discover. She's unique.'

'She's dangerous,' I complain, arguing for a side only part of me believes. Teo should be putting the case, relieving me of the guilt of it.

'If you allow I live,' Caracia says, 'You will always have the power for pruning me. How might I bear this perpetual fear? I would be wise if I repay your compassion by ending you before you end me.'

I gawk at the octopus.

The doors by the tank open. A detachment of Caracia's nurses marches in.

They form a single line in front of the aquarium. An objection forms in Teo's throat; following the detachment is Eir.

'Merry Christmas, Teo. And Persia and Fluffy, back there, by the fire in your lodgings. If you're planning octopus for dinner, might I suggest you consider turkey?' Eir appears once again the tall imposing witch of her former elf, dressing simply in a deep red pantsuit which accentuates the blood in her eyes. There's a deeper pathos in her. As if her foundations have cracks, and the furniture of her soul is rearranged.

'Eir please,' Teo says, 'This is none of your concern.'

'You are all my concern, Teo. I love you all and would save you from a grave error. As one who lives with the murder of 1000 sybils, I implore you spare Caracia.'

'She's a monster,' Teo spits.

'So you say, out of fear and intolerance. Why her when there are still many millions of sybils sleeping in cribs? Will you murder them all? Or is Caracia the one you single out for some supreme sacrifice? Perhaps you should follow the ancient forms and nail her on a cross.'

The 8 Voices are perfectly still; as is Teo, caught between defying her mentor and aligning with her.

'Please, Persia. I beg for your sake. You always counsel we must love our patients before we might attempt a Cure. Now I counsel you. Until you truly understand Caracia, please stay your hand. And Caracia, please taste the voracity of this promise: despite all you mean for me once, for rescuing me and guiding me in my mission, despite it all, please know, if I taste so much as a murmur of plotting against Persia, I will swiftly end you. I already have so much blood on my hands and will suffer no misgivings for striking you down.'

Tiks of silence stretching out. Counting breaths. I take Persia's hand.

'Go, Caracia,' Persia says. 'Disappear.'

'Will I never again communicate with culture?' a single Voice asks.

'Why should you? You are other,' Persia answers.

The Voices fall on the floor in Never-Mind. Caracia scuttles faster than anyone would think possible. Teo squeals, fearing the octopus is coming for her.

I memb Teo, 'Where is she?'

A tik. Teo breathing heavy. 'She's gone,' she membs.

From the floor one of the Voices croaks, 'Sometimes you need 8 limbs for figuring things out.'

Vör

'Empty' — Boyinaband & Jaiden

 *Vör Hoyur ...*

W E SCATTER. For the 4 corners of space, we scatter.
Health camerati use sybils. Centuries ago. My stomach churns. How can our nursing mission wash away this stain? We're corrupt as any sap multinational. When faced with limits on growth, growth must win out over all limits, including ethics, the forces of nature, and anything else which proves an impediment. The justification is always so easy. Like many times before, our success sows the seeds of collapse. For every spring there is a fall. Exponential demand for our ministry sows the seeds of exponential collapse.

Each needs an angel and a demon on a shoulder; monkeys on their backs; tigers in their jungles; sharks in their swimming pools. Modern saps feared cancer, heart disease, terrorism, tax, and never winning a lottery. In the vacuum replacing all of those, what fear have we? In our early days, the full guilt of sin makes a resurgence. We obsess over outbursts of anger; the edifice of Pride; insidious Envy; and burning Lust. Knowing these for the diseases they are, coursing through veins and charging electricity in muscles, we demand banishing them, these bad feelings and bad emotions. They spoil the peace and happiness in a world cured of war, and disease, and other ancient forms of misfortune.

Neos need nurses, and we give succour. We fulfil our mission, treating the only illnesses remaining—the illness of elf identity—between the mildest and the most obsessive. Among the magazines Eir releases, is a holly referencing cohorts of the acutely obsessive returning for Cure after Cure, keening for absolution from inner corruption. The holly carries the title, *Prometheus: or The Modern Flanders*.

Demand for nurses spirals. Neos crowd every minster in the world; many waiting outside in bitter or baking weather for the chance of a few tiks with a nurse. Compliant. Pleading like faithful supplicants. Like hopeful disciples. Patient, trusting, hoping for Cures for the only fatal illnesses of our age: psychological pain, the sickness of souls. Health service capacity stretches and threatens collapse. We respond with deploying the most reprehensible of technologies—crèching fully aware and mature duplicates. Sybils. Sybils go out into the world; copies of missionaries healing the sick. For keeping it secret, there are no lengths too long. Even kidnapping and coercing some of our own. Out of sight, we check Persia and others into the most exclusive longest-stay retirement village in the history of humanity.

A cold Christmas in København. As abrupt a transition from the jungle steam of Central Africa as a fridge falling on my head. The flinty crumbling age of the brown-red bricks and mortar of Carlsberg Minster are a weight too heavy for the soul. The elephants are grey and weary. The words LABOREMUS PRO PATRIA pass overhead. Where is your country? Where is your striving? Swastikas watch without answer.

The streets are all but empty. So too the great courtyard around which the newer minster buildings cluster. No rainbow uniforms. Instinct sets me on course for the Investigations building; until they crowd in and take me by the elbows. They swivel me right for the centre courtyard, and the looming Administrations complex.

'Where are we going?' I ask with some apprehension.

'Keep skipping.'

The 7 in front peel away allowing me sight of a pair of timber doors, each with a metallic bar running almost from top to bottom, inviting I push in. Before my hand connects, 2 black uniforms reach around from behind. Hands, with shoulders in the effort, shove the heavy doors back.

'Come, in, Vör,' another black uniform membs from behind an incongruously large and official-tasting desk. 'Take a seat if you wish. This will be short.'

Then what's the point of sitting? A blow of air behind reports the doors closing. The finality of it urges I sit anyway.

Even the face of the black uniform is a dark silhouette. Outside behind her, a small silver coin of a sun peeks meekly apologetically out of a skein of cloud from far away in the south.

'I hereby relieve you of service for the mission,' the black uniforms membs.

'By what authority? And … who are you?' Jelling her is projecting multidimensional blanks.

'By no authority and all authority. As for who I am, you detective types never show much interest in rehabilitation, let alone administration. Suffice in saying, I am what's left of any leadership of *det Fødererede Sundhedskamerata i Nordeuropa.*'

'What?'

'I already dissolve Investigations. There'll be no more need for detectives prying into other lives. And the need for clinics will more than halve; the only patients seeking help are ex-nurses.'

Taste exasperation. I splutter and gasp and clutch at inadequate words. 'But there's still work ... so many crèches still for shutting down.'

'Which should never be a nurse's mission. It's for an entirely different kind of mission. One which I can reliably say you are entirely inappropriate for.'

'But—you frog march me all the way here just for this?'

'Your colleagues tell me you need information in Face. So here it is. There is no mission for you here. Go home, reflect. Reorient your passions for something new. Or if you prefer, check yourelf in for a Cure. Although I must admit, after all the talent we lose, your mileage may vary. On the upside, we have plenty of room available.'

So much of fourspace is empty. It must be so. All alternative realities run as cold simulations across time, generating enough residual life force so Mind might amass and dwell in this small realm of reality we inhabit. Mind might seep into the simplest of life forms; the single cells; the plants; the animal kingdom; the bees; the wasps; the elephants; the dolphins. All part of a great tipping point, so we might be elf aware. We should be humble for the vast voids, and all the onespace connections out there on a huge expansive table, on which we dine in one tiny corner. The universal organism secretes and creates tiny drops of honey-Mind which collects in us, the beehives of awareness. We nourish on the sugar. We create and honour the sparks of divinity pre-animating and articulating us. We must create as the universe creates us or we profane it.

What remains, creation? So much of it is empty. I especially—possibly the last wearing a rainbow uniform—am empty.

Is our experience of the universe the result of some unknowable chemical wedding? Then I should dissolve away in a retort flask of acid above the Eternal Bunsen Burner. Let my life ebb away, melt away, cease ...

I am empty, except for a solitary fragile spark among the black coals of the remains of my heart. Nurture it, and I may yet fulfil a purpose.

Eir. I wish Eir empty too.

Eir

'All My Love' — Led Zeppelin

Nilajani Karunanithi ...

VÖR EMERGES FROM THE STATION'S spooky field woozy; staggers a step before entraining a measure in her skip. Out of the departure hall in the main concourse's dim lighting allows the late-afternoon darkness pour in through the solarglass roof. Anyone who might look up and gawk will see the pulsing, swirling layers of the northern lights. In Iceland, mid-afternoon is well after sunset.

Still wearing her rainbow fatigues, Vör attracts stares of derision and membs of vilification. She scurries for the tukky rank and the 20-min ride for Mosfellsbær and Eir's home.

Bambuwa! It's on me, Harsha. There'll be no other nurses in pursuit of Vör; no one heading her off or dissuading her from whatever she plans. There could be many ex-nurses hoping Vör inflicts some serious harm on Eir.

I'm 14 mins from the nearest spooky station if I forgo the time for dressing first. Is there no one else arriving there faster?

'You ruin me,' Vör wails. 'You ruin all of us.'

I am yet short of halfway through the ride for Eir's house; gulping my heart down; hoping I will arrive in time.

Eir sits in lotus position on the deck of her cottage, facing the black, glassy ink of the lake. Facing away from Vör who inches through the day room with slow, heavy, painstaking steps. Tears streak her gaunt cheeks. She cradles her fruit with one arm, her hand against her chest as if holding her heart in. Her other hand hangs like a broken doll's while clutching a dull-black object. Her spidery fingers curl around the blocky grip. The blunt muzzle points perpendicular with the ground.

'You rob me of my mission,' Vör cries. She's an artefact of utter destruction. I doubt there's any of her left.

Eir's chin drops. She hangs her head. Her back square, open and vulnerable, as Vör comes ever nearer. Only the sheen of Eir's white hair, falling between her shoulder blades, for protection.

Their auras swirl. Coriolis fumes evaporate at the edges, clash like waves rolling in from opposite sides of a beach. Deep undercurrents of 10's of millions of flutherbombers feed the translucent roiling pyrotechnic eddies where the edges tangle. Shapes of bright short-living fractal fern-leaves embrace and liquefy in the cloudy, soupy air. I almost believe there could be sparks.

No one other than me comes for the rescue.

Fourspace groans under the weight of so much concentrating Mind. Furniture warps and twists between auras. Straight lines bend and crack into jaggy edges. Right-angles spay out wide, sharp as needle points. Walls bloat.

Still more flutherbombers swim in. Mostly for Eir's fluther, the temptation too great for the chance of witnessing a death from the inside out; the tik of expiry when all goes black; or Eir starts moving into a tunnel of light; or her *mava* appears and scolds her for being late; or she sees the world from the viewpoint of a dung beetle. The possibilities too tempting, the temptations too possible. The greater share of flutherbombers hope there are bullets in the pistol, and Vör has sufficient competency with the brutal weapon. Hoping this time there will be no missing the mark.

Eir remains meditative. Millions hunger for the rare taste of her passing. A story y'all will be telling your descendants for 7 generations. How many of y'all are dialling kinaesthetic filters up for tasting the conclusion here in full? Perhaps all the way up, daring risking the full agony or ecstasy of dying, and the subsequent anticipated euphoria of re-inhabiting their own fruit in a kind of resurrection.

'I rob you of nothing, Little—'

Vör cackles so loud she renders Eir sharply mute. 'Little Mermaid,' Vör cries. 'Is this me? Risking everything for the sake of gaining a human soul? Walking on the strange land, every step as painful as treading on knife blades? Falling in love with the handsome prince who marries another for the sake of politics? Tempted by evil to escape her fate by killing the object of her love? Is this why you call me Little Mermaid?' Vör's chest heaves like a great bellows whose purpose seems for pumping her eyes with manic fury.

'Vör, it's a sweet statue—'

'Sweet? Is this how you regard me. Sweet? Is this all I am? Sweet?'

'Vör, please ...'

'My whole career, you have me dancing however pleases you.'

'If my mentorship ever seems so controlling, I am truly sorry. I have such hopes for you.'

'Hopes?' As she nears the couch, Vör's eyes drift away from Eir, losing focus somewhere on the living room rug on the floor. She swallows and leans on the couch behind her for support. 'Tell me, how many of my sybils are there?'

'I never have any—'

'Liar!' There is only floorspace and open french doors between Vör and Eir. 'I have nothing left. Nothing.' Vör pushes against her resistance, the only obstacle remaining. Halfway across the rug. The pistol is the weight of planets again. Her arm hangs limp from her shoulder.

I bash the dashboard of the tukky. 'Faster, faster, please.' In some form of cosmic joke, the tukky turns from the highway, slowing down in the narrower winding residential streets. Streetlights come on ahead, illuminating the way as if saying, 'She's this way. She's this way. Hurry up.'

Defend yourelf, Eir. She should be explaining how Caracia collects sybils of her; how 3 escape one of Caracia's crèches when pods malfunction; how the sole survivor of the trio chooses for fighting sybils with sybils. Tell her, Eir. Tell her all this harvest is the sowing of others. Make her see you're blameless. Why is Eir remaining still? Summoning no one for her rescue. Asking for no help. Spooking nowhere, perhaps wanting this, welcoming it. For Vör's sake?

'Will you shoot me in the back?' Eir asks; as if merely curious, as if wondering if Vör likes honey in her aya. 'If you would shoot me, please come around and face me.'

Vör looks askance, suspecting a trick.

'Face me in the eye, Vör. If after, you still have the compulsion for firing the weapon, then very well.'

Cautiously Vör scampers through the french doors. The pistol training on Eir. Vör arcs around with aikido skill; takes the first step down from the deck; squares off with Eir. Eir raises her head allowing Vör see the absence of fear. The absence of both aggression and capitulation. Vör's knees shake. Eir studies the gun. 'Murder is a serious business, Little Mermaid.'

'Stop calling me your Little Mermaid.'

Eir startles but holds her composure. '*Ja*, I'm sorry. I will. But this pistol … a piece of sap barbarism. This is never you.'

The pistol is a coward's way out. There are so few ways of murdering another. A knife too visceral and unpredictable. Poison too cold and calculating. Suffocation requires persistence and physical strength. Pushing someone from a great height, perhaps. The sap pistol seduces, having the penetration of a knife at a distance.

'Vör, darling; our camerati are incubators for sickness. It's time for renewal. What comes to pass sets us free.'

'Free? We are all sifar. Without mission, without camerati.'

'Mission comes from within, never from a camerata. Like any organisation, which loses spontaneity and calcifies with dogma and ritual, and values itself over its members. Our health missions become corrupt.'

'You're saying we're all sick?' Vör sets her face, snarls. Arms come up and aims the pistol at Eir's belly.

'All fear us, fear the power we have.'

'For their own health.'

'So we claim with the best intentions, for the most part. Yet as a matter of routine we cajole, drug, incarcerate, restrain. We separate patients from families, friends, and followers.'

'You among us.'

'*Ja*, I am the product of my own flaws.'

Vör snarls. 'As if some insincere admission will wash you clean. How is it someone whose skin is so white could have such a black heart? Eir. You have always been so; almost drowning your childhood friend; setting the hair on fire of girls who taunt and bully you.'

'All lifetimes ago.'

'You excuse it? You may never excuse it, because it's still inside; looking for ways of wrecking everything around you; for destroying everything you touch.'

'Vör, you are—'

'I have no sickness.'

'I would say *in pain*.'

'I have a mission. A worthy mission. For eradicating sickness ...'

'It's impossible, eradicating sickness entire.'

The tukky rolls over roads curving around so much I wonder if they double back. Is there no quicker way? Feeling no closer. 'Come on. Come on.'

Vör takes menacing steps at Eir. Their halos thick and indistinguishable. Vör almost close enough for reaching and tapping Eir on the head with the pistol.

'... for making those Infinites pay.'

'Make Infis pay by mandating health care?' Eir's hands shake.

'By shutting them away.'

'Imprisonment! Listen for yourelf, Vör.'

'Be quiet. Be quiet.' Vör snuffles loud against the mucous blocking her nose and tears flowing free. 'You take me spookheading! I know then something is wrong. You addle my Mind, my sense of what's right.'

'You blame me for your addiction.'

'You are the blame.'

Neither Vör nor Eir move. Their auras lazily roll over. Vör's elbows bend. The pistol tracks its sight for the ceiling. Like a magnet, Eir's heart pulls on the pistol, attracting its aim again.

'Is it easy, killing all those sybils?' Vör accuses.

'One of the hardest things of my entire life.'

Vör nodding finds some relief in those words.

'You are right,' Eir continues. 'You are right: sybils are an abomination.'

'Then why fight me?'

'I never fight you, Vör. You're the one who Consigns me.'

'Because you side with Infinites and use sybils.'

'Discharging Orlando is the ethical thing. Imprisoning him indefinitely is unconscionable. For the first time in decades, I am without sickness when I begin seeing our treatments for what they are.'

'He's a Greedy, elf serving Infi.'

'No doubt.'

'A sybil-crècher.'

'And abuser,' Eir agrees.

Vör's pistol arm wavers. 'We must eradicate them.'

'Like pests? Like vermin? Vör, sybils are indistinguishable from human beings. From you, from me—'

'From Orlando.'

Eir nods and swallows. 'I have no understanding how Infis abide sybils. There is no more alien experience than enduring a copy of one's elf. It's the strangest, mind-silencing taste, as if the other is sucking the soul from your heart. You fear it might and you will be empty. You feel a vacuum in your chest, your groin, all the way for your toes. Your mind tastes like an echo. Any thought you have could be an exact replica of the other's. It feels like the other is in your head, in a way no flutherbomber could ever be. Then, it all tumbles out, all the disgust and loathing you ever have for yourelf in your whole life. It spills out and into the other, like it has no choice but absorb it. All the horrible things you ever commit, the sybil commits too. You loathe it, once you see it out there in the duplicate stealing your soul. You recognise evil, and you know there is no abiding it.'

'You agree, then,' Vör says. 'Infis are sick and there is no abiding sybils.'

'You misunderstand. The evil is in me. And still, we have no means of Curing Infis. Sybils already exist. Vör, believe me, I know; trust me. From my own experience, killing sybils is murder.'

The tukky pulls up outside Eir's house. Already leap out of it.

Vör's chest heaves. 'Then why make them?'

'Vör, I never commission the crèching of any sybils. I am the victim—'

'Liar! Liar. I catch you keeping a sybil of me.'

Eir shakes her head. 'Honestly, I have no taste of whether I create her or no ...'

'Then you admit it.'

'No, Vör. I'm just less than sure—'

Through the front door and for the living room in back. There they are outside. Call with tongue and lung, 'Vör. Please. Vör. Come inside, please.'

Around Vör, darkness rises from the deck, swirls and feeds on her. 'I hate you!' Vör screams. A primal crack in the stone of her reality. The compulsion of evil takes her by the shoulders, guides her arm and the pistol aiming at Eir's heart.

Eir closes her eyes accepting.

I barrel-tackle Vör. She grunts with expulsion of breath.

The pistol's muzzle is an explosive vent for Vör's pain.

Eir's ocean crashes over her. White water throws her like a helpless jellyfish on the sand. She whispers, 'I love you.'

Ben

'Californian Soil' — London Grammar

Ben Evoli ...

THE ROLLBACK of SnakiDik Enterprise Edition is progressing—
What? Enterprise? Call it SnakiDik: Camerata Edition, then. *Enterprise* is an archaic word for an organisation in which the pursuit of profit is the sole virtue and success derives from ever-greater accumulation of wealth. Look. I just ... the name is just a bad joke, okelah? Neos are calling it *The White Witch Edition*, which is reprehensible; so ... I'm just calling it something else, okelah? Since it has such feature-bloat, and health camerati are somewhere on the spectrum between incompetence and evil (as most sap organisations were) ... so: *Enterprise Edition*.

Nurses everywhere should be deleting old installs and loading version 22 which I promise still has all the good features. All those conspiracy theories about my caving in under old-fashion moralism is saddening. So many of y'all are steadfastly refusing the upgrade. No one is paying me attention. I should announce there's a bug in *Enterprise Edition* which sets hair on fire or makes pubic hair grow; still everyone would ignore me. We must track down every install of *Enterprise Edition* and replace it, which is a harder proposition after all the carriers scatter for the 4 winds of space.

Yeer—I know—look; I already—

Enough. Filters up.

A pleasant skip from the spooky station, albeit with a train of forlornly hopeful tukkies in tow. A warm December sun vacillates over its nightly plunge into the Sea of Cortés.

Making a right on reaching the beach. The road hugs a curving strip of sand snaking for an orange-glowing headland in the distance. A fractal repeating judder image of a regiment of modest revivalist bungalows hem the road against the beach like tired sheepdogs. The bungalows could be all the same litter. Fabby timber façades and poky silicon-glass windows. Steep pitching roofs overhang wide front porches sheltering from the western sun.

Jel the number of the house. I'm almost upon it which gives me just enough time for reconsidering being here. Stopping at the gate, surveying the entry deep in shadow in the centre of the porch. The door is a frame of fabby timber holding 10 panels of rough-texture silicon-glass. Imagine a hall behind and 2 equal-size rooms either side, with views of the surf. Trace my line of sight back from the porch, down the steps for the gate. Walk the short gravel path intersecting a neglected barren front yard. Find my hand hesitating upon the gate latch.

'May I help you?' Though familiar, the voice sounds reedier than I recall. The sound of the surf is stripping most of the tonal quality away; she's speaking tongue and lung.

'Um ...'

'Puffin?' Bunny asks, as if of an old distant relative.

Stiffening with shock. 'You know me? Bunny ...' Is this Bunny a sybil? My heart sinks, ruminating about what she may remember of me.

'Oh, ah ... no ...' she says with a perplexing expression screwing her face around as if her brain is running at TrilaJOPS. 'For a tik I taste ... you seem familiar. My friends call me Bunny.'

Still hesitating at the gate. 'I'm sorry; I think I'm in the wrong place.'

There must be something aghast in my expression. Bunny widens the doorway. 'Oh, you poor thing. Come in, come in. You look thirsty.'

'Um, no ... ah, yes. You're most kind.' I feel nothing of my arms and legs working, yet still the gate swings back. The path conveys me for the steps and escalates me for the door.

Bunny ushers me. The hall wraps me in a cool embrace. Wide openings beckon either side. Through one there is a glittering Christmas tree, its pine scent subservient under a distinct fabby smell. The fabby Christmas lights, balls, and angel on the top sprout seamlessly from the tree branches.

On the other side, a dining room contains its ambivalent breath. A chair offers come sit. I crumple on it as gracelessly as a clunky old metal robot.

The dining room is claustrophobic. More than the miserly windows admitting subdued light from the shady porch, the mid-20th-century decor cramps the atmosphere. Bulky furniture, door frames, and skirting boards are walnut fabby timber. The bare squirty-foam walls are the texture of rough plaster lacking even the merest light-diffracting rainbow sheen of cicada-wing nanotech. The house must be a bugger for cleaning. There is dust on the windowsill. Motes dance in shafts of wan light.

'I feel like I know you,' Bunny says when she returns with 2 glasses and a large pitcher of lemonade.

'Perhaps,' I venture, tentative. 'My name is Ben Evoli. I'm the inventor of a hoot you may hear of. MusiKai?'

Bunny sits, slaps her thigh with recognition. 'SnakiDik.'

Disappointment kicks air out of my lungs. 'Yeer, also.'

'I taste I recognise you. Wow. There's something else, more than just the knowing of you. Something more familiar. I call you Puffin?'

How would she taste that? 'An associate of mine would often call me Puffin,' I say, covering the chill I feel. 'You know Maddox Price?'

Bunny scrunches her mouth, shakes her head. 'Should I?'

'Believe me, you're better without knowing him.'

'Kay,' she says, dismissing the information so easy, so casual. It's one of the things I love about her. Her eternal buoyancy, as if nothing in the depths of world or psyche could drag her down. Perhaps it's her youth. Alamak! I'm younger than 90 and I'm thinking like a futureless old invalid.

'You have blonde hair,' I blather. 'I never see you with blonde hair before.'

She sits her back in her chair, perplexed. 'I'm … always blonde. Maybe you're confusing me with another girl you flutherbomb. Another girl you— you know—like.' I taste she means another girl I'm stalking.

'Perhaps,' I concede covering for my stupidity.

'Ben,' she broaches gently. 'Your Mind is racing. You're here for something, right? Something important?' There's a hint of narcissism in her tone, hoping she's important for someone. She risks inviting me into her home for the chance of more meaning in her life.

'I come … I come with apologies,' I release.

'Apologies? For what?'

'It's hard explaining,' I start and falter. Courage drains away. What will I say? Confess the sybil my sybil has of her? One he allows Juruterbang curate and design as … his plaything? His pet? Trophy girlfriend? The woman he abandons at the sap farm to the terror of imminent death. I still hear your cries, Bunny, even while I wheedle it's okelah leaving you suffering, feeling the relief of the truth about your disposability. And in so doing, confirming my own.

'I'm sorry,' I whimper.

'Oh, come here,' Bunny croons, dropping on her knees and throwing her arms around my fruit.

All I have left for communicating are tears coming in great racking sobs. Bunny holds me tight, strokes my hair and nuzzles cheek-with-cheek.

I should never come here. It's all just a selfish attempt for unburdening.

'It's kay,' she croons. 'It's kay. There's no need for talking about it. There's no need explaining anything.' She kisses the tears from the corner of my eye.

'It's important.' I feel so small in her arms.

'I taste it,' she membs and releases a snort of a laugh.

In other circumstances, I could truly fall in love with you, Bunny. But the truth is, all the ways I use your sybils will haunt me. The way I abandon you is unforgivable. I should never come here. These memories from the other are now always mine for bearing. They can only ever be toxic for you. It's for me, living with the consequences.

My breathing eases: the salty streams from my eyes to my lips dry up. I sniffle.

Bunny still cradles me, though somewhat gentler. 'You know, this feels so familiar,' she whispers in my ear.

She's kissing my lips, tender at first, feeling out, testing. I receive passively until shock becomes arousal, and her kisses wetter and hungrier.

I memb, 'Bunny,' my ardour rising with hers. 'This is a bad idea. I'm bad for you.'

'Mmmm, it's kay. This just feels right.'

'No ... um, look. I'm due for childing again. I'll be gone for 5 years.'

She stops. Studies me incredulous. 'Five years?' Her face lights up, more lit-up than I ever see, eyes bright with sweet playfulness. 'Who's talking beyond breakfast tomorrow? Get over yourelf, old man.'

The last thing before childing is for going home.

Emerging from the desa spooky station. Thirty-six degrees and humid. Another Sydney Christmas.

A sea breeze blows across the harbour and swirls with jasmine and eucalyptus. Charcoaled meats in pungent spices and coconut milk. Noodles frying in dark condiments. Once I skip around the colony of artists disassembling *that* sculpture, the esplanade opens its arms and greets me like an old, estranged friend. An overwhelming doting melancholy breaks me out of my skip. I'll walk. I'll take my time. No hopeful tukkies follow. I receive wary glances and sympathetic grins of the kind you congeal for someone you pity. There is no parting of pedestrians providing deferential space for their once-Infi. Some jostle. Others barge. It feels delightful.

'Infi! Infi!' Urgent tongue and lung words chase me up the esplanade. A young neo, 40-ish, is shoving BirdMe and LionUs projections aside for closing on me. I recognise him: Berahim Pelawi. All those months ago, I witness nurses Consigning him.

'Infi. Please.' Berahim, sweating and breathless; plants his hands on his knees. Gulps 3 breaths.

'Ah ... I have ...' I point in the direction of home.

'Please, Infi—'

'No longer Infi.'

Berahim blushes and locks his jaw, as if he's damming the utterances of his tongue. The pressure becomes too great; he blurts, 'I wish for discussing our Cures.'

'I have no wish for revisiting such things.' I turn away, skip for home.

'Infi Face, please,' Berahim membs.

These days, I could filter him without fear of health consequences, but habits are hard in the breaking.

'I must know what you remember of your therapies,' he blurts.

The stupidity of it stops me mid-skip. 'No one remembers their therapy.' Some of us remember the Alien Abduction Syndrome; I doubt Berahim has the social network for triggering it.

'I remember,' Berahim answers. 'I remember everything.'

'I have my Cure,' Berahim announces with some pride. His eyes are moist and alight with happiness; he clinks his glass against mine. I would prefer aya in a teahouse at this time of day, but Berahim insists on O'Hulligan's pub. The heavy muted timbers of the interior are too depressing for me; whatever Berahim knows about Cures better be good.

I say, 'Congratulations,' and take a kiddy-sip of bourbon. It's nothing like Maddox's stash. 'So, what is it you remember?'

'Well, all the non-therapy stuff … the recreation rooms, the exercise … of course.'

I say, 'Of course,' too impolite.

'Nothing about the rebasing.'

I wince.

'But … in the beginning …'

Now I'm here, I have an uneasy feeling Berahim is shrinking away from spilling his secrets as if he's painfully wary of re-engaging with them.

'… it's all dreams—visions, more like.'

'Visions.' This is a waste of time. 'My family—'

'Infi, they make you relive your sick times, the stuff they Consign you for. And when I say *relive*, I mean it's much more intense than a mere holly or fluther visit. You feel you're living it again, right now.'

Okelah, this's mildly interesting. Perhaps the nursing mission is less queasy about using hoots than they publicly claim.

'You have such experience?' he asks.

'Nah. My Cure never progresses far enough.'

'Oh. This's too bad.' Berahim signals the bartender who, for lack of other customers this time of day, is quick in replenishing his glass. 'At first, I think, *so what?* If I am truthful, I find reliving the moments with Sadie—the wanita who I record hollies of—well … it gets me off, you taste?'

I taste for a socially acceptable time for excusing myelf.

'It goes like this for the first week or so … 2 sessions a day—2 at night, for 2 or 3 hours, from what I could make out—until …'

'So, you have hallucinations 4 times a day,' I place in the conversational space he leaves, laying my scepticism on the table. If Berahim is assuming his vivid repetitive dreams are products of some therapy, I taste no evidence how he arrives at such a conclusion.

Berahim fades: grabs his glass and downs the rum. 'Look, I'm thankful for my Cure, really, I am. Before, I am obsessive about sex, and ... partner ownership, shall we say? And I am obsessive about Sadie, as if she is the only one who could fulfil me. Stupid notion. Looking back, I have no understanding how I could be this way. Now I have my Cure, and I am better for it.'

Berahim is now obviously stalling. 'Anyway,' he says, emerging from a momentary fugue. 'At some point, I get the notion I'm more than a passive player in these re-enactments. I try changing my actions in the scenario and, for my surprise, things start unfolding differently. These repeating re-enactments are like experiments—you taste? And I can change the parameters. I start with small variations at first. Sometimes everything is the same. Other times, things change, but—more! I learn about myelf, like why I want the things I want. So now I'm more confident—I try out more variations. After about a week, I'm playing with it ...' He examines me. I guess he's wondering how much he should tell. '... just for the sake of it. I'm asking myelf, *Who am I?* and testing my assumptions of elf-identity—I mean, all kinds of things. What are the origins of my sexuality? My dislikes: are they true? What would happen if I give in for every ...' Berahim pauses. He's re-embodying the stages of his Cure as he explains. 'I take greater and greater risks; tasting I can play out any scenario in complete safety; knowing everything with reset at the end. Many times a day ... this is where I realise, I'm setting my own course of therapy—no nurse prescribes it for me. It's a game I play over and over, as ... many ... times ... as I need ... and want.' His eyes sparkle.

I almost regret never having the opportunity he believes he undergoes. I salute him with my shot glass, and no small dose of condescension.

An invisible shroud descends over him, and he becomes solemn. 'Infi. I am a hateful, violent lelaki.'

I say, 'Berahim, I am sure you are nothing of the kind.' How hollow and placating those words are.

'Nah. Listen,' he says with great disdain. 'I visit such hateful monstrous and sickening things upon poor Sadie. I hate her for making me the way I am. And no despicable operation I could perform upon her could be, in any way, unjust.' Berahim's voice is shaky. He plants his glass upturned on the bar; presses down on it, as if it's his only anchor with reality. 'But even all this passes, and I still have all the time in the world for playing with it. Eventually, I spend all the fear and loathing.' He lets go of the glass. 'So yeah, I'm a violent hateful anak kecik. But I also learn I am a compassionate egalitarian loving anak kecik. What would sap therapists say? I'm all this and more?'

'My recollection is they'd make you talk, then shut you down after 50 mins and charge for an hour. But I must admit, I am never there.'

'Okelah. Lemme finish the good bit.'

The good bit? Will I ever see my family again? I picture Mal waiting impatiently at the front door; Saf upstairs practicing guitar; and Aisha … well, Aisha being Aisha.

Berahim straightens on his stool and waves the bartender away as he approaches with a bottle. 'I run every scenario my sick Mind can conjure up: the good, the bad, and the kinky; until …' He pauses for dramatic effect, but now, I just want he should finish it.

'The one aspect I'm yet for changing is Sadie. I think of all the lelaki I jank; all the lelaki I wish I could jank; and, one by one, I put them in Sadie's place while changing nothing else. Ben, the health camerata's therapy is nothing more than … they put you in a place where you can wrangle out— using your own ingenuity—every warp and waft of possibility, until … well, I never reach halfway through my Sadie-substitutes before I feel this sense of peace come over me. Then … I wake up. I'm back in the clinic ward. A nurse is there, and she says, *You have your Cure*. The next thing I know, they're discharging me.' Berahim kinda makes a *tada!* shape with his face.

Is this it? I gotta go see my family. I say, 'Well, this's a great story,' and fail in masking my insincerity. I push my pantat off the stool.

Berahim grabs me by the forearm. 'Nah, wait.'

I regard him with shock.

'There's one more thing,' he says, and I taste his whole account is a lead-up for a vital pitch.

'One more thing?' I make it sound like a demand. 'I get it. You work through your stuff until you find inner peace.'

'Well, yeer. But while I'm playing out these hallucinations or dreams or delusions, sometimes I wake up.'

I repeat, 'You wake up,' willing I should remain patient.

'Well, I think I wake up. This is what I must find out. Is the waking up just one more dream—in which case, I doubt everything I experience in the clinic—or if I wake up and find myelf, in those times, in a real place.'

I say, 'Okelah,' wary.

'And I need your help finding it.'

Neos never loot, but they'll happily appropriate a forsaken building and its contents. Since the collapse of nursing missions all over the world, we're stripping minsters and clinics of equipment. Nursing-specific fabbies are very valuable, since y'all discover the weird ways they fab household goods. Y'all hear of a whole sub-culture devoting itself for the wrongly weird versions of cuisine these fabbies produce? In the old days of the Reckoning, certain neos would be Infi by now, for discovering these bizarre forms of fettuccine bolognese we have now. And there's an urban myth claiming health fabbies include drugs in every meal, complete with 'evidence'. There are hollies of dinner guests going catatonic after a mouthful of prawn cocktail. *Jambalaya orgy* is the fastest thing trending on most magazines.

I still take most of my meals from hawker stands. There's no fabby in existence capable of producing a decent nasi lemak or asam laksa.

Berahim and me approach the desa clinic; the doors slide as if the place is open for mission. The lighting brightens as we enter.

'May I help you, Ben Face?' A nurse is sitting behind the reception desk, her feet up on it. Skye Merewether. As our eyes meet, she throws her legs aside, sits forward and squashes the holly she watches into the desk—some game show thing. 'I'm afraid I only have nutepak treatments now, although these are all I would ever dispense before. No serious Curing for me.' She laughs it off with a nervous restrained dose of bitterness, which she aims at Berahim. 'You come back with bigger friends, little boy?'

'You're still missioning?' I ask with no small dose of confusion.

'I'm the only nurse on shift now,' Skye says. 'On any shift, to taste the truth.' She manufactures a what-can-you-do smile.

Take a deep breath. 'Nurse, I'm hoping you could help my friend and—'

'I already explain for Berahim. He gives me a full account of his hallucinations—'

'Including the sap tech?' I press. 'The—'

'Yeer. Everything,' Skye membs, enunciating every syllable as separate. 'I even let him poke around the whole clinic.'

This is news for me. I interrogate Berahim with a knitted brow. He guiltily looks away.

'I tell him he would find nothing,' Skye says as she straightens haughtily in her chair.

'Because you taste nothing.' I say, 'You're only ever a receptionist.' If I could keep my smile in my pocket, I would. 'You never learn anything of Cures.'

Skye's spine curves a little as she arrests a shuddering shake of her head. 'Well, no.'

I'm guessing, but I'll take a punt: 'Then please tell me the one thing which *will* help us.'

Fourteen mins ago, Skye leads Berahim and me through the clinic; passing day-care rooms, inventory closets, nursing lounges, recreation spaces, bathrooms, a dining area, and a kitchen; until we reach the connecting passageway between the long-stay ward and the passing suite mission next door. This all may taste large, but it's still smaller than many Infi mansions.

Skye ushers us through the entry of the long stay ward. My expectation we're arriving at a place of truth quickly expires when Skye skips straight through for a hall beyond and finally, another room. A dead end, it seems.

I shiver with dread. Berahim seems likewise on edge. We're in what I might only describe as a box, about 5 metres on a side, a space so perfectly rectilinear it feels sap. Even the ceiling is flat as the floor; the walls are straight, windowless planes of grey matt paint. Any neo would dread this space, which I suspect is the point.

Skye stretches the tension over widening tiks; Berahim expresses silent questions with his posture. I glare at the nurse. She relents, skips near a wall and gestures *explode* at it.

Perhaps half of the wall dissolves and Berahim gasps. 'A spooky field!'

A strange-looking field: flat, dense, and square; inset a few mims back from the solid wall-panels either side.

I cast about the room and wave my arms.

'There's no console,' Skye answers. 'It locks on a single destination.'

'Which is where?'

'All I know is patients go through, and patients come back.' She fixes Berahim with her gaze. 'Remember this part?'

Berahim's head shakes as much from anxiety as answering. Skye squares shoulders and grimaces. Berahim's discomfort is a victory for her.

We're in a stand-off. Tiks pass until Skye's eyes boggle, and she waves like an usher. 'Off you go. The answer is through there.'

Some compulsion grips Berahim: he skips for the field. I grab his arm. 'Wait. The target spooky field could be down, the vectors may be drifting.'

'If the spooky field is active, it must be connecting,' Skye says. 'If you want answers …' She thumbs at the field.

Berahim looks for guidance. I shake a solemn *nah*. Berahim wriggles out of my hand and plunges in.

Tiks pass. 'He'll be back,' Skye says then kisses her chatelaine.

There is yet no Berahim coming back. I'm sitting anxiously in reception, refusing the admission he's passed. How could I leave now? If he comes back, how will it taste? I push thoughts of Mal and Saf out of Mind.

Skye is as before: feet on her desk, watching some incomprehensible holly, a Korean dramedy, I think. 'I'll memb you if he returns,' Skye says as if promising a used car is roadworthy.

'It's okelah. I'll—'

A lelaki bursts skipping through the front doors. It takes a tik before I recognise Berahim. 'Come. Come.' He gestures and skips down the hall.

'Wait,' I memb. The sound of skipping continues. 'Wait,' I shout.

Berahim reappears at the hallway entrance.

'What … where?' I swallow for reassembling my incoherence. 'You should come back for us.'

Sky laughs at some implausible over-acted slapstick in her holly.

'Apologies, Inf—Ben,' Berahim membs. 'I just ... once in there ... I'm sorry, there is so much for exploring, I forget ... about ... Everything is there. It's as I see it before.' The relief in his eyes and jaw, and in the swelling of his fruit, is infectious.

'Come. Come.' Berahim exhorts.

'Come where?' I feel frustration rising.

'Okelah.' Berahim skips, passing me, for the front door and the esplanade. 'Come this way, then.'

It transpires, in Berahim's fevered exploration, he discovers a door in back of a gallery level which connects with—guess y'all: I follow Berahim into the bordeli. We bustle around the hopeful madam Dorothy Biggins, whose welcome-face dissolves in disappointment as we skip for a utility closet in the bordeli's least favourite suite (the sign on the door says, THE LAUNDRY ROOM—DROP YOUR PANTS HERE). A door in the closet leads between the cloying stickiness of the bordeli air and the antiseptic essential-oil dryness of ...

Mute lights come up as we emerge on a mezzanine level in a barrel-shape room with a dome roof. From opposing sides of the dome protrude 2 protractible arms that end in a docking clamp, out of the centre of which hangs a cascade of tubes and cables. All very gross and very sap. Below the mezzanine, in the centre of the room, a flat couch squats on a 3-metre-wide circular grate which, I morbidly assume, is for draining away gushing liquids.

Berahim's feet clatter and echo as he scampers down the companionway stairs between mezzanine and floor. 'Come, come. There's more.' He opens a small side-door. Lights enliven beyond.

'I remember,' Berahim says, joyous this stuff is no product of his dreams. 'I'm wearing all this when I wake up in ... in there.' He nods in a direction away from the door, suggesting another place we are yet for reaching.

We're opening everything in the kit room; pulling rubbery fittings off elaborate cradles in cupboards, and from tight niches in drawers. I turn components over in my hands, imagining it all as a single assemblage. Much of it reminds me of sap SCUBA gear—goggles, breathing apparatus for covering nose and mouth, and a small backpack. But the backpack is no air tank; and the goggles are opaque—crowded on the inside are 1000's of tiny light-emitting fibres. There's also ear-muffy things; and connecting tubes carrying a variety of pneumatic, hydraulic and optic lines.

So, how would this work? If I must guess, I'd say nurses stimulate a patient's sensory and mental activity via the goggles and earmuffs. They might also manipulate mental and emotional states by regulating breathing via the face mask. The backpacks bear a large ringed coupling on their faces, which suggests an umbilical connection with an external apparatus. Again, I sense an affinity with SCUBA equipment. And virtual reality devices. Perhaps they suspend a patient in liquid, while they guide their dreams. If the liquid is buoyant enough, it might counteract a patient's sense of gravity which might otherwise cause dissonance with the dreaming. For all I know, they could suspend a patient head-down. Or the patient could, unawares, orient their fruit in accordance with how the scenes play out in their dreams.

'Infi, come see this,' Berahim membs.

I jolt and look about the kit room. Berahim is no longer in here. I blink my eyes and go looking for him.

Y'all have the same sensation as me, in the pit of your guts? Wonder curdling with revulsion. This is why our skin crawls in the presence of a nurse, I'm sure. While I know of no other neo than Berahim who wakes up in one of these things, the unconscious transpersonal experience must bleed into and stain the zeitgeist. We taste nurses' ickiness; we taste the traces of nuts in the pudding. We taste these contraptions.

'It's true,' Berahim whispers. 'I wake up in one of these.'

'More than once?' I ask.

'Yeer. Four, maybe 5 times.'

I shudder.

We're in a 2nd cylindrical room, same as the first. Except here, hanging from the domed ceiling by those protractible arms, is a soft, transparent roughly conical bag, bloated and bulging from the weight of fluid it contains. *Amniotic fluid*, I think, and shudder again. The arms suspending the bag above the couch appear as fallopian tubes; the bag is a synthetic womb.

The purpose of the fallopian arms is, I realise, 2-fold. As well as suspend the womb, they bear cables which connect with the patient's backpack. Even in the relative constriction of the womb, a patient could move freely; perhaps even tumble or somersault in the docking between the arms and the backpack are ingenious enough.

'The last thing I remember of all this,' Berahim says in hushed reverence, 'right before learning I have my Cure, I wake up in one of these, and the fluid is draining out.' He swallows hard. 'I believe I would suffocate. Next thing, I'm pushing through this vagina-tube-thing.'

At the bottom of the bag is a tube just wide enough so a neo could pass through. Its opening hangs limply like a damp shower curtain over one end of the couch. Berahim is right; under the bulging bag, its approximation as a vagina is unsettling.

'I land on the couch as the last of the fluid comes down like a waterfall,' Berahim says, then brightens. 'Funny thing is …'

'Hmmm?'

'I come out head-first.'

Aisha Saf and Mal crowding in the frame of the open front door. I labour up the terrace. Aisha's holding the anak anak back from rushing me. And barring me from entry I suspect.

'Bapa!' Mal prises hiself away from Aisha, launches at me with grappling arms, head nuzzling against my chest. 'I'm glad I save you,' he says tongue and lung.

Saf groans. Gruff watches from under an elephant palm, his markings throbbing iridescent blue in the rhythm of his purr. A window squirty is dribbling solar-glass resin into an open space where the hall window should be.

'You breaking things again, fella?' I quiz Mal.

'No. Saf this time like that lah,' Aisha says.

'Stupid boyfriend.' Saf itemises on her fingers: 'Throw him out. Break glass. Ex-boyfriend.'

'Now she has another boyfriend and a girlfriend,' Mal giggles. He's over his fever. There's a hearty glow about him.

'Is this so?' I look up, expect Saf would be blushing. She's just smiling, a little proud of herelf.

Mal squeezes around my waist even tighter. 'Bapa, I'll come visit you every week. We can play together and eat ducky cubes. And finish watching *Ben 10*.'

'Mal, sayangku,' Aisha says in soft speaking-words, 'we must leave Bapa for his new growing up.'

'May we flutherbomb him?'

'No, fella. My world must be much smaller for a while.'

'Five years. Half my life. I'll be 23.'

'We have long-long lives still ahead, Mal. There's plenty of time.'

Mal pulls his chin into his chest and sulks while he processes. 'Bapa?'

'Yeer, fella?'

'One day, will you skip on the moon with me?'

Saf makes excuses for practising guitar, taking the hint from me and Aisha holding our breaths and shuffling our feet. As for Mal, Istri must shoo him inside before we go sit at opposing compass points of the garden table. Aisha braces into the high back of the spartan chair while I put all my weight into tense arms and tender elbows jabbing into the table surface.

I must ask: 'Will you wait for me?'

'Bat Ears ...'

'Istri, I—'

'I love you, Bat Ears, you know I love you ah.'

'Yeer, but ...?'

'We're neos, Ben. We need playfulness lah.'

'I'll be more than playful after childing. I'll be—'

'Irrepressible. Invincible. Charming. Friendly. Social.'

'We're still talking about me, right?'

'Yeer, at certain times in your life. Then you settle into …' She throws her hands up. 'After a while, nothing you achieve ever nourish you. It's like your success belong someone else. It means nothing for you. You nurture your disappointments and disillusions and let everything else wither.'

'This is just plain wrong. MusiKai—'

'You see. You demand success under your own definitions. You despise everything you achieve since. SnakiDik is our project, Bat Ears. Sure, it's your idea, but I'm a big part of develop it. We have so much fun together. On a mission together. Yet you grumble and shun the success. Like you hate it and everything about it. It feels, Bat Ears, like you hate me too.'

'Istri, you know—'

'I know, I know. But you must taste, when you diminish it, you diminish me also ah.'

I'm sorry. I'm sorry. I'm just so sorry. 'Will I always be the one who invents that sex toy?'

'Of course. Get over it, old man ah. Go regress for another childhood. Cast off this crusty old elf and rejuvenate. Start the cycle again.'

Patronising, Aisha. Patronising. It's so like you.

I love you.

Glossary

AgniSpace(n 1): the infrastructure which exploits multi-dimensional onespace and underpins spooky tech, yielding applications for spooky stations, fabbies, sucky bins, holly storage and communication enhancement).

AgniSpace(n 2): the name of the leading camerata whose mission it is to provide the AgniSpace infrastructure.

aura(n) (aka *halo*): the visible manifestation of a neo's fluther. The size and appearance of an aura depends on the number of neos in a fluther and the quality of their attention. Auras may be small and almost transparent, or they may be large, dense and saturated with colour. They may appear still or constantly moving and changing, sometimes very fast. Some neos believe they can see flutherbombers' faces in an aura, but that's kotoran. Among large auras, tendrils may appear to reach out and connect. Very large auras may appear to warp surrounding fourspace. Neos may be overwhelmed by the auras of others especially if they are large or numerous and so may use hancy technology to filter or attenuate their experience of auras.

camerata(n *pl.* **camerati**): derived from the time of the Italian Renaissance, the neo word for a guild, with a flat holacratic structure, which provides community services in a culture of egalitarianism, intelligence, and a fierce inquiry into truth, while fulfilling the missions of individual members.

childing(n): a process whereby an adult neo psychologically regresses to another childhood while in the care of a foster family. Childing typically lasts 5 years during which a neo's creativity is reinvigorated. They often return to adult life with new ideas for new missions. An episode of childing adds years to a neo's already long life. With regular childing a neo's life expectancy might be over 300 years.

childling(n): a neo regressed in the process of childing

Consign(v): take a neo into custody for the purpose of providing a *Cure*, conventionally performed by field nurses at the behest of detective nurses.

crèche(n): a facility one or more *metrae* for crèching *sybils*; a facility of one or more *cribs* for the potentially long-term storage of sybils. A crèche may be large or small and serve both crèching and storage functions.

crèche(v): run the process of generating a fresh *sybil*.

crib(n): a neuromorphic machine for the potentially long-term storage of a *sybil*, also for placing the copiable neo during crèching.

Cure(n): the process of restoring a sick neo back to mental health according to a mostly pre-planned Prescription, conventionally performed by clinical nurses. The exact practice of Curing is a nursing secret; those who undergo Cures recall nothing more than days of recreation, exercise and banal modalities of therapy which are administered to deflect from the real methods of Curing.

elf(n): the neo substitute word for *self*. Because of *membing* and *fluthers*, neos have more ambiguous boundaries between themelves and others, and find referring to the self as gaudy and egotistical. In typical neo fashion, they turn such references into something playful and elf-effacing. For a while they tried eliminating use of the word *I* also, but this created too much confusion.

fabby(n): a very sophisticated fabricator or 3D printer, often purpose-built for fabbing specialised objects such as building materials, medical supplies, food and drink, clothing and other consumables. Fabbies rely on *spooky* connections to feedstock bins which supply materials in a wide variety of configurations from the atomic and molecular to the grossly organic.

feedstock bin(n): the things that make the world go round. From *sucky bins*, *spooky field* chains break down waste and deposit them in feedstock bins. *Fabbies* then consume feedstock materials through more spooky field chains which pre-process material fit for the needs and purpose of the fabby. By the way, if you think a mai-tai tastes like shit, find a bar with a better fabby.

fluther(n 1): a collection of neos psychically connecting to a target neo through *onespace*. A congregation of neos visiting the Mind of another for the purposes of witnessing actions and environment. In another's fluther, a neo can see and hear as if present in the same place as the other. Other sensations, such as taste and smell, may also be possible. The fidelity of sensory experience depends on the number of neos concurrently in a fluther and whether those neos are using *hancy* technology. Chat sessions between members of a fluther are possible and may be disturbing or otherwise unpleasant for the fluther's target. A neo's fluther is visible as an *aura* or *halo*. Large fluthers are contentiously believed to warp fourspace although, since fourspace is generally accepted as subjective hallucination of onespace, the question of whether warping a hallucination is in any way real renders the question of interest to theoretic physicists, some of whom postulate that a sufficiently large fluther might warp fourspace so much that the entire universe could be destroyed.

fluther(n 2): a collection of jellyfish

flutherbomb(v): join a *fluther* without warning or invitation

fourspace(n): the collective hallucination of reality as the 4 dimensions of space and time.

fruit(n): the preferred term a neos uses when referring to a human body. Derived from the neo expression, *The body is the fruit of the Mind.*

halo(n): see *aura*

hancy(n): a thumbnail-sized neuromorphic disc-shaped devise for enhancing neo brain function and upon which apps known as *hoots* can be loaded for almost any purpose. A hancy is fitted at the base of the neck in an organic seating which allows for relatively quick removal and replacement. Once fitted, a hancy generates synthetic nerve tendrils which fuse with nerves the spinal column and brain stem. If removed, the hancy seat's tendrils will dissolve into the blood stream and pass. The latest hancies use advanced forms of DNA read/write memory.

hoot(n): short for *hancy utility*. An application of mindwriting which when installed in a hancy will enhance or augment the wearer's brain function. There are a wide variety of hoot features, including sensory enhancement, improved membing clarity, and holly storage and management including playing in-Mind or out in fourspace. Other applications involve gaming, creativity workbenches (of which Ben's MusiKai is an example) and business productivity tools. A fast-growing area is in the area of mashups between gaming and multi-player sexual hallucination stimulation of which Ben's SnakiDik is the pre-eminent example.

Infinite(n): a designation for a neo whose reputation is so high, The Reckoning stops reporting the exact score. Nurses had The Reckoning changed to award Infinite designation in 164 NE. Infinites are generally unhappy with the designation as it removes the joy of knowing *who is winning*. Like all calculations of The Reckoning, the methods by which it designates a neo Infinite are untastable.

memb(v): converse with one or more other neos psychically through onespace over any distance. Membing is sometimes called *the Ears of the Soul*. Neo etiquette values membing over speaking *tongue and lung.*

metra(n *pl:* **metrae**): sometimes informally called a *meat tray*; a neuromorphic machine for growing a new *sybil*.

NE: Neo Era, the common way to date events. Its relation to the Sap Common Era is untastable. Most neos, whose lives are long, tend not to think in terms of dates anyway.

neo(n): a human of the species *Anthro neotenus* which evolved from the dying species *Homo sapiens*.

onespace(n): the neo understanding of objective reality; the underlying and mysterious ultimately untastable substrate of pure Consciousness underpinning *fourspace*.

Prescription(n): the plan of therapies for achieving a Cure.

razoo(n): indivisible and sole unit of measure for reputation. For anyone other than Infinites, The Reckoning reports a neo's reputation as a quantity of razoos. One neo may tip another razoos which The Reckoning may consider in normalising *both* neos' razoo scores.

scatter net(n): an application of *spooky field* technology which disrupts *flutherbombing* into a local *fourspace* area. Typically installed over or through minsters and clinics, purportedly as a means of protecting neos while they undergo *Cures*, but probably also as a means of hiding nursing secrets. In a brazen example of *Do as I say, not as I do*, health missions view the wider use of scatter nets as evidence of sickness, and almost certainly results in *Consignments* for *Cures*.

seminal(n): in relation to *sybils*, the original neo from whom sybils are crèched.

sifar(n, 1): similar to *Infinite*, a designation The Reckoning awards to neos who have a low score. The exact point where the designation kicks in is untastable. The Reck seems to have the attitude, *near enough is good enough*.

sifar(n, 2): a pragmatic ascetic who chooses a simple life by deliberately trying to reduce their *razoos* (reputation score) to nothing. A baker of inedible cakes, or an artist whose pictures quickly fade, are examples of a neo who seeks the designation. The pursuit of sifar designation is not considered a sickness, but rather a valid mission.

skip(v): skipping may not be the same as saps understand it but it's certainly more playful than walking and swifter without breaking into a run

spook(v): travel over distance by *spooky field* technology

spookhead(n): one who is an enthusiast of *spookheading*; a spookheading addict

spookheading: making a series of quick spooks for the purposes of amplifying the euphoric and erotic highs of spooking.

spooky field(n): a discontinuity in *fourspace*, often appearing as a purple or violet cloud that marks a connective boundary from *fourspace* into *onespace*. Spooky field technology is pervasive in neo society and has many applications, including in spooky stations, which stabilise a spooky field for the purpose of facilitating the illusion of transporting fourspace objects instantly to any other spooky station in existence. Other applications are as nets for filtering air, and garbage disposal via sucky bins. Nursing *camerati* use spooky field technology in *scatter nets* which disrupt *flutherbombing*.

spooky station(n): a building housing a stabilised spooky field for the purposes of personal *travel* and *transport* of goods. Spooky stations facilitate the illusion of instant point-to-point travel between stations making easy movement about the globe accessible for everyone. Since *fourspace* is a subjective hallucination, the concept of travelling must also be an illusion. However, spooky stations consistently facilitate the subjective experience of moving place to place. In performing this illusion, spooky stations must constantly resolve the mapping between fourspace co-ordinates and the multidimensional vectors of *onespace* which are constantly in a state of flux.

Critical to the stability of a station's spooky field is a continuum of Consciousness attending to stabilising fourspace-onespace mapping. While mapping technology is always improving, reliability is ensured by the sheer weight of missionaries collectively working to keep the maps fresh through a continuity of effort. As an engineering compromise, spooky station missions concentrate most on objects containing a threshold quantity of DNA. Other objects are more easily dispatched to feedstock bins and in this way spooky stations behave in much the same way as *sucky bins*. This is why, if you enter a spooky station field wearing clothing not laced with DNA, you arrive at your *destination* naked.

sucky bin(n): an application of *spooky* technology which provides waste disposal and recycling. Sucky bins may be small, desk-size appliances, kitchen waste disposals or large council bins for the disposal of unwanted furniture and the like. Larger bins are used in industrial contexts such as mining and civil engineering. Although uncommon in the rest of the world, the Japanese prefer sucky bin toilets. While all sucky bins deliver material to feedstock bins, the chain of spooky field technology behind the sucky bin will determine distribution of the material across multiple feedstock bins.

sybil(n): an organically perfect copy of an original neo or other sybil; an identical copy of the up-to-the-tik state of the source as at the time of *crèching*, including brain state and therefore memory. A sybil is *fabbied* in a process commonly lasting 451 mins in a neuromorphic machine called a *metra* and can be stored for long periods of time in a *crib*.

taste(v): understand as congruent and authentic with gestalt holistic awareness beyond subjective knowledge and the distortion of the senses. Neos often say they taste things accurately, but they probably don't.

tongue and lung(adv): to speak tongue and lung is to speak aloud with the voice rather than silent *membing*. Neo etiquette shuns speaking tongue and lung in preference for membing, although the Detective Nurse Eir Frijberg and others encourage it as a form of therapy which naturally vibrates the body.

tukky(n): a cyborg vehicle with a small organic brain sufficiently intelligent to provide enhanced taxi services for trips usually within towns or villages and shorter than intercontinental or cross-town jumps via *spooky stations*. While modelled on ancient tuk-tuks, tukkies are driverless and include many mod-cons such as weather nets for temperature control.

twentager(n): a neo child in their 20's, when neos experience puberty and fast physical, sexual and psychological development. Corresponds to a teenager Homo sapien.

Warrant(n): the authority for a nurse to *Consign* a neo for a *Cure.*

Acknowledgments

Among those in my fluther who contributed substantially to the development, refinement and publication of this story are …
… friends Michael D'Aprix, Alan El-Khadi, David Braunstein, and Doug Hudgeon;
… brother Glen Ratjens (may there be more Yamba Writers Conventions);
… horror writer Jeremy Bates;
… developmental editor Nastasia Bishop;
… my fearless and dedicated beta readers, especially Lucija Dupljak, A.C. Powers, Amanda Justice, and Ahmed Muzammil;
… graphic design artist Bima Maha Wahyu (a.k.a. ARMOREDFATE).

Thank you all.

A scene in the story uses snippets from the Technical Air-to-Ground Voice Transmission (GOSS NET 1) from the Apollo 11 mission.

For information on the Ray Cat Solution, visit theraycatsolution.com.

About the Author

A career software developer, change agent and educator, M really should have been writing all his life, and wouldn't be the renowned speculative fiction author he isn't yet without the influences of such story-telling royalty as Tom Robbins, Kazuo Ishiguro, Robert Heinlein, Jules Verne, Frank Herbert, Bruce Sterling, Greg Bear, Chuck Wendig, Douglas Adams, and Gore Vidal. M's spiritual home is Sydney Harbour, where M lives among too many guitars, computers, and bottles of cheap wine, without cats, dogs, canaries, axolotls, pet rocks or cabbage patch dolls.

For more information, or to book an event, contact:
mark@ratjens.com
spookheads.com

Font cover design by ARMOREDFATE—Bima Maha Wahyu

ISBN: 978-0-6455540-0-7 (ePub)
978-0-6455540-1-4 (paperback)

First edition: December 2022

Ratjens, Mark Norman. 7 Cures. Spookhead Press.

www.ingramcontent.com/pod-product-compliance
Lightning Source LLC
Chambersburg PA
CBHW050118030726
47505CB00007B/1924